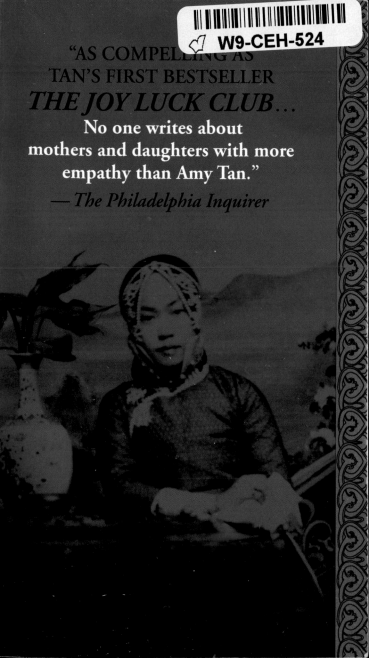

"AS COMPELLING AS
TAN'S FIRST BESTSELLER
THE JOY LUCK CLUB...
No one writes about
mothers and daughters with more
empathy than Amy Tan."
— *The Philadelphia Inquirer*

"[A] SPLENDID NEW NOVEL . . . SUPERB STORYTELLING."
—*The New York Times Book Review*

"Compelling . . . Readers who loved Amy Tan's best-selling novels about the complex ties between mothers and daughters, *The Joy Luck Club* and *The Kitchen God's Wife,* will also be captivated by *The Bonesetter's Daughter.*"

—*The Orlando Sentinel*

"A woman's struggle to find her voice has long been a favorite theme of Amy Tan. Nowhere has she explored it with more compassion or charm than in this touching new novel."

—*The Richmond Times-Dispatch*

"An enchanting story of a mother and daughter, the secrets they have kept from one another, and the common ground they finally come to occupy. . . . A powerful, luminously written saga in which past and present are bound together into the tangled skein of a human life."

—*The Anniston Star*

"A riveting, multi-layered tale . . . Tan's storytelling skills are strong, and her plot line appeals to the rebellious daughter in all of us."

—*Toronto Globe and Mail*

Please turn the page for more reviews. . . .

"A BOOK TO READ, TO CHERISH, TO REMEMBER."
—*The Providence Sunday Journal*

"*The Bonesetter's Daughter* is a moving examination of the very core of what it means to be human. . . . It is concerned with the true power of myth, with the meaning of the past as it interacts with the present, with the voids that separate and bind cultures. . . . The prose is deeply textured, the flow of dialogue and action hypnotic. . . . Reading this book is a journey that will alter your future. The last 50 or so pages strike directly to the heart. Be prepared."
> —*Statesman Journal* (Salem, OR)

"LuLing Young, the central character in Amy Tan's new novel, is so full of energy she just about jumps off the page."
> —*The Oregonian*

"This is a novel about many things—how the past shapes the present, how family and cultural history influence the direction of our future. It is about the importance of language and memory, the relationship of words and perception and experience. But it is, most of all, about mothers and daughters."
> —*St. Louis Post Dispatch*

"Who but Amy Tan could conjure up such a many-layered tale? . . . *The Bonesetter's Daughter* is another triumph, a worthy successor to her first novel, National Book Award winner *The Joy Luck Club*."
> —*Charleston Sunday Gazette* (WV)

THE BONESETTER'S DAUGHTER

Amy Tan

BALLANTINE BOOKS • NEW YORK

A Ballantine Book
Published by The Ballantine Publishing Group
Copyright © 2001 by Amy Tan

All rights reserved under International and Pan-American Copyright Conventions. Published in the United States by The Ballantine Publishing Group, a division of Random House, Inc., New York, and distributed in Canada by Random House of Canada Limited, Toronto.

Ballantine is a registered trademark and the Ballantine colophon is a trademark of Random House, Inc.

www.ballantinebooks.com

ISBN 0-345-45571-1

This edition published by arrangement with G. P. Putnam's Sons, a division of the Putnam Berkley Publishing Group, Inc.

Manufactured in the United States of America

First Ballantine Books International Edition: August 2001
First Ballantine Books Domestic Edition: February 2002

10 9 8 7 6 5 4 3 2 1

I give endless thanks to my dear friend and editor, the late, great Faith Sale. To my astonishment, she could always sense the difference between what I was trying to write and what I wanted to write. She promised she would see me through this book, and though she died before I finished, I believe she kept her promise.

My writing teacher and longtime mentor, Molly Giles, took over as editor and resurrected this book during those days when I was scared to turn the pages. Thank you, Molly, for your keen eye and ear, as well as for suggestions that were always true to my intentions. I also much appreciated the heavy doses of optimism during times we can now acknowledge as dire.

I am blessed to have had the help, kindness, and protection of Lou and Greg, the guidance of Sandra Dijkstra, Anna Jardine, and Aimee Taub, and the spiritual sustenance of the late-night posters on AOL's Caregivers' Support for the Elderly.

As luck and fate would have it, two ghostwriters came to my assistance during the last draft. The heart of this story belongs to my grandmother, its voice to my mother. I give them credit for anything good, and have already promised them I will try harder the next time.

On the last day that my mother spent on earth,
I learned her real name, as well as that of my grandmother.
This book is dedicated to them.

TRUTH

These are the things I know are true:

My name is LuLing Liu Young. The names of my husbands were Pan Kai Jing and Edwin Young, both of them dead and our secrets gone with them. My daughter is Ruth Luyi Young. She was born in a Water Dragon Year and I in a Fire Dragon Year. So we are the same but for opposite reasons.

I know all this, yet there is one name I cannot remember. It is there in the oldest layer of my memory, and I cannot dig it out. A hundred times I have gone over that morning when Precious Auntie wrote it down. I was only six then, but very smart. I could count. I could read. I had a memory for everything, and here is my memory of that winter morning.

I was sleepy, still lying on the brick k'ang bed I shared with Precious Auntie. The flue to our little room was furthest from the stove in the common room, and the bricks beneath me had long turned cold. I felt my shoulder being shaken. When I opened my eyes, Precious Auntie began to write on a scrap of paper, then showed me what she had written. "I can't see," I complained. "It's too dark."

She huffed, set the paper on the low cupboard, and motioned that I should get up. She lighted the teapot brazier,

1

and tied a scarf over her nose and mouth when it started
to smoke. She poured face-washing water into the teapot's chamber, and when it was cooked, she started our
day. She scrubbed my face and ears. She parted my hair
and combed my bangs. She wet down any strands that
stuck out like spider legs. Then she gathered the long part
of my hair into two bundles and braided them. She banded
the top with red ribbon, the bottom with green. I wagged
my head so that my braids swung like the happy ears of
palace dogs. And Precious Auntie sniffed the air as if she,
too, were a dog wondering, What's that good smell? That
sniff was how she said my nickname, Doggie. That was
how she talked.

She had no voice, just gasps and wheezes, the snorts of
a ragged wind. She told me things with grimaces and
groans, dancing eyebrows and darting eyes. She wrote
about the world on my carry-around chalkboard. She also
made pictures with her blackened hands. Hand-talk, face-
talk, and chalk-talk were the languages I grew up with,
soundless and strong.

As she wound her hair tight against her skull, I played
with her box of treasures. I took out a pretty comb, ivory
with a rooster carved at each end. Precious Auntie was
born a Rooster. "You wear this," I demanded, holding it
up. "Pretty." I was still young enough to believe that
beauty came from things, and I wanted Mother to favor
her more. But Precious Auntie shook her head. She pulled
off her scarf and pointed to her face and bunched her
brows. *What use do I have for prettiness?* she was saying.

Her bangs fell to her eyebrows like mine. The rest of her
hair was bound into a knot and stabbed together with a
silver prong. She had a sweet-peach forehead, wide-set

eyes, full cheeks tapering to a small plump nose. That was the top of her face. Then there was the bottom.

She wiggled her blackened fingertips like hungry flames. *See what the fire did.*

I didn't think she was ugly, not in the way others in our family did. "Ai-ya, seeing her, even a demon would leap out of his skin," I once heard Mother remark. When I was small, I liked to trace my fingers around Precious Auntie's mouth. It was a puzzle. Half was bumpy, half was smooth and melted closed. The inside of her right cheek was stiff as leather, the left was moist and soft. Where the gums had burned, the teeth had fallen out. And her tongue was like a parched root. She could not taste the pleasures of life: salty and bitter, sour and sharp, spicy, sweet, and fat.

No one else understood Precious Auntie's kind of talk, so I had to say aloud what she meant. Not everything, though, not our secret stories. She often told me about her father, the Famous Bonesetter from the Mouth of the Mountain, about the cave where they found the dragon bones, how the bones were divine and could cure any pain, except a grieving heart. "Tell me again," I said that morning, wishing for a story about how she burned her face and became my nursemaid.

I was a fire-eater, she said with her hands and eyes. *Hundreds of people came to see me in the market square. Into the burning pot of my mouth I dropped raw pork, added chilis and bean paste, stirred this up, then offered the morsels to people to taste. If they said, "Delicious!" I opened my mouth as a purse to catch their copper coins. One day, however, I ate the fire, and the fire came back, and it ate me. After that, I decided not to be a cook-pot anymore, so I became your nursemaid instead.*

I laughed and clapped my hands, liking this made-up

story best. The day before, she told me she had stared at an unlucky star falling out of the sky and then it dropped into her open mouth and burned her face. The day before that, she said she had eaten what she thought was a spicy Hunan dish only to find that it was the coals used for cooking.

No more stories, Precious Auntie now told me, her hands talking fast. *It's almost time for breakfast, and we must pray while we're still hungry.* She retrieved the scrap of paper from the cupboard, folded it in half, and tucked it into the lining of her shoe. We put on our padded winter clothes and walked into the cold corridor. The air smelled of coal fires in other wings of the compound. I saw Old Cook pumping his arm to turn the crank over the well. I heard a tenant yelling at her lazy daughter-in-law. I passed the room that my sister, GaoLing, shared with Mother, the two of them still asleep. We hurried to the south-facing small room, to our ancestral hall. At the threshold, Precious Auntie gave me a warning look. *Act humble. Take off your shoes.* In my stockings, I stepped onto cold gray tiles. Instantly, my feet were stabbed with an iciness that ran up my legs, through my body, and dripped out my nose. I began to shake.

The wall facing me was lined with overlapping scrolls of couplets, gifts to our family from scholars who had used our ink over the last two hundred years. I had learned to read one, a poem-painting: "Fish shadows dart downstream," meaning our ink was dark, beautiful, and smooth-flowing. On the long altar table were two statues, the God of Longevity with his white-waterfall beard, and the Goddess of Mercy, her face smooth, free of worry. Her black eyes looked into mine. Only she listened to the woes and wishes of women, Precious Auntie said. Perched around the statues were spirit tablets of the Liu ancestors, their wooden faces carved with their names. Not all my ancestors were there, Precious Auntie told me, just the ones my family considered most important. The in-between ones and those belonging to women were stuck in trunks or forgotten.

Precious Auntie lighted several joss sticks. She blew on them until they began to smolder. Soon more smoke rose—a jumble of our breath, our offerings, and hazy clouds that I thought were ghosts who would try to yank me down to wander with them in the World of Yin. Precious Auntie once told me that a body grows cold when it is dead. And since I was chilled to the bone that morning, I was afraid.

"I'm cold," I whimpered, and tears leaked out.

Precious Auntie sat on a stool and drew me to her lap. *Stop that, Doggie,* she gently scolded, *or the tears will freeze into icicles and poke out your eyes*. She kneaded my feet fast, as if they were dumpling dough. *Better? How about now, better?*

After I stopped crying, Precious Auntie lighted more joss sticks. She went back to the threshold and picked up one of her shoes. I can still see it—the dusty blue cloth, the black piping, the tiny embroidery of an extra leaf where she had repaired the hole. I thought she was going to burn her shoe as a send-away gift to the dead. Instead, from the shoe's lining, she took out the scrap of paper with the writing she had showed me earlier. She nodded toward me and said with her hands: *My family name, the name of all the bonesetters*. She put the paper name in front of my face again and said, *Never forget this name,* then placed it carefully on the altar. We bowed and rose, bowed and rose. Each time my head bobbed up, I looked at that name. And the name was—

Why can't I see it now? I've pushed a hundred family names through my mouth, and none comes back with the belch of memory. Was the name uncommon? Did I lose it because I kept it a secret too long? Maybe I lost it the same way I lost all my favorite things—the jacket GaoLing gave me when I left for the orphan school, the dress my second husband said made me look like a movie star, the first baby dress that Luyi outgrew. Each time I loved something with a special ache, I put it in my trunk of best things. I hid those things for so long I almost forgot I had them.

This morning I remembered the trunk. I went to put away the birthday present that Luyi gave me. Gray pearls from Hawaii, beautiful beyond belief. When I opened the lid, out rose a cloud of moths, a stream of silverfish. Inside I found a web of knitted holes, one after the other. The embroidered flowers, the bright colors, now gone. Almost all that mattered in my life has disappeared, and the worst is losing Precious Auntie's name.

Precious Auntie, what is our name? I always meant to claim it as my own. Come help me remember. I'm not a little girl anymore. I'm not afraid of ghosts. Are you still mad at me? Don't you recognize me? I am LuLing, your daughter.

PART ONE

ONE

For the past eight years, always starting on August twelfth, Ruth Young lost her voice.

The first time it happened was when she moved into Art's flat in San Francisco. For several days, Ruth could only hiss like an untended teakettle. She figured it was a virus, or perhaps allergies to a particular mold in the building.

When she lost her voice again, it was on their first anniversary of living together, and Art joked that her laryngitis must be psychosomatic. Ruth wondered whether it was. When she was a child, she lost her voice after breaking her arm. Why was that? On their second anniversary, she and Art were stargazing in the Grand Tetons. According to a park pamphlet, "During the peak of the Perseids, around August 12th, hundreds of 'shooting' or 'falling' stars streak the sky every hour. They are actually fragments of meteors penetrating the earth's atmosphere, burning up in their descent." Against the velvet blackness, Ruth silently admired the light show with Art. She did not actually believe that her laryngitis was star-crossed, or that the meteor shower had anything to do with her inability to speak. Her mother, though, had often told Ruth throughout her childhood that shooting stars were really "melting ghost bodies" and it was bad luck to see them. If you did, that meant a ghost was trying to talk to you. To her mother, just about anything was a sign of ghosts: broken bowls, barking dogs, phone calls with only silence or heavy breathing at the other end.

The following August, rather than just wait for muteness to strike, Ruth explained to her clients and friends that she was taking a planned weeklong retreat into verbal silence. "It's a yearly ritual," she said, "to sharpen my consciousness about words and their necessity." One of her book clients, a New Age psychotherapist, saw voluntary silence as a "wonderful process," and decided he would engage in the same so they could include their findings in a chapter on either dysfunctional family dynamics or stillness as therapy.

From then on, Ruth's malady was elevated to an annual sanctioned event. She stopped talking two days before her voice faded of its own accord. She politely declined Art's offer that they both try speaking in sign language. She made her voiceless state a decision, a matter of will, and not a disease or a mystery. In fact, she came to enjoy her respite from talk; for a whole week she did not need to console clients, remind Art about social schedules, warn his daughters to be careful, or feel guilty for not calling her mother.

This was the ninth year. Ruth, Art, and the girls had driven the two hundred miles to Lake Tahoe for the Days of No Talk, as they called them. Ruth had envisioned the four of them holding hands and walking down to the Truckee River to watch the nightly meteor showers in quiet awe. But the mosquitoes were working overtime, and Dory whimpered that she saw a bat, to which Fia teased, "Who cares about rabies when the forest is full of ax murderers?" After they fled back to the cabin, the girls said they were bored. "There's no cable television?" they complained. So Art drove them to Tahoe City and rented videos, mainly horror flicks. He and the girls slept through most of them, and though Ruth hated the movies, she could not stop watching. She dreamed of deranged baby-sitters and oozing aliens.

On Sunday, when they returned home to San Francisco, cranky and sweaty, they discovered they had no hot water. The tank had leaked, and the heating element apparently had fried to death. They were forced to make do with kettle-warmed baths; Art didn't want to be gouged by emergency plumbing rates. Without a voice, Ruth couldn't argue, and she was glad. To argue would mean she was offering to foot the bill, something she had done so often over their years of living together that it had become expected of her. But because she did not offer, she felt petty, then irked that Art said nothing further about the matter. At bedtime he nuzzled her neck and bumped gently into her backside. When she tensed, he said, "Suit yourself," and rolled over, and this left her feeling rebuffed. She wanted to explain what was wrong—but she realized she did not know. There was nothing specific beyond her bad mood. Soon Art's sonorous breathing rumbled out of sync with her frustration, and she lay wide-eyed in the dark.

It was now nearly midnight, and in another few hours, Ruth would be able to talk. She stood in the Cubbyhole, a former pantry that served as her home office. She stepped onto a footstool and pushed open a tiny window. There it was, a sliver of a million-dollar view: the red towers of the Golden Gate Bridge that bifurcated the waters, marking bay from ocean. The air was moist and antiseptically cold against her face. She scanned the sky, but it was too light and misty to see any "ghost bodies" burning up. Foghorns started to blare. And after another minute, Ruth saw the billows, like an ethereal down comforter covering the ocean and edging toward the bridge. Her mother used to tell her that the fog was really the steam from fighting dragons, one water, the other fire. "Water and fire, come together make steam," LuLing would say in the strangely British-accented English she had acquired in Hong Kong. "You know this. Just like teapot. You touch, burn you finger off."

The fog was sweeping over the ramparts of the bridge, devouring the headlamps of cars. Nine out of ten drivers were drunk at this hour—Ruth had read that somewhere. Or maybe she had written that for a client. She stepped down, but left the window open.

The foghorns continued to wail. They sounded like tubas in a Shostakovich opera, comedically tragic. But was tragedy ever funny? Or was it only the audience who laughed knowingly as the victims walked into trapdoors and trick mirrors?

Still wide awake, Ruth turned to her desk. Just then she felt a tug of worry, something she was not supposed to forget. Did it have to do with money, a client, or a promise she had made to the girls? She set to straightening her desk, aligning her research books, sorting faxes and drafts, color-coding them according to client and book. Tomorrow she had to return to routine and deadlines, and a clean desk gave her the sense of a fresh start, an uncluttered mind. Everything had its place. If an item was of questionable priority or value, she dumped it in the bottom right-hand drawer of her desk. But now the drawer was full with un-answered letters, abandoned drafts, sheets of jotted-down ideas that might be usable in the future. She pulled out a clipped stack of paper from the bottom of the drawer, guessing she could toss out whatever had lain there the longest by neglect.

They were pages written in Chinese, her mother's writing. LuLing had given them to her five or six years before. "Just some old things about my family," she had said, with the kind of awkward nonchalance that meant the pages were important. "My story, begin little-girl time. I write for myself, but maybe you read, then you see how I grow up, come to this country." Ruth had heard bits of her mother's life over the years, but she was touched by her shyness in asking Ruth to read what she had obviously labored over. The pages contained precise vertical rows, without crossouts, leaving Ruth to surmise that her mother had copied over her earlier attempts.

Ruth had tried to decipher the pages. Her mother had once drilled Chinese calligraphy into her reluctant brain, and she still recognized some of the characters: "thing," "I," "truth." But unraveling the rest required her to match LuLing's squiggly radicals to uniform ones in a Chinese-English dictionary. "These are the things I know are true," the first sentence read. That had taken Ruth an hour to translate. She set a goal to decipher a sentence a day. And in keeping with her plan, she translated another sentence the next evening: "My name is LuLing Liu Young." That was easy, a mere five minutes. Then came the names of LuLing's husbands, one of whom was Ruth's father. Husbands? Ruth was startled to read that there had been another. And what did her mother mean by "our secrets gone with them"? Ruth wanted to know right away, but she could not ask her mother. She knew from experience what happened whenever she asked her mother to render Chinese characters into English. First LuLing scolded her for not studying Chinese hard enough when she was little. And then, to untangle each character, her mother took side routes to her past, going into excruciating detail over the infinite meanings of Chinese words: "Secret not just mean cannot say. Can be hurt-you kinda secret, or curse-you kind, maybe do you damage forever, never can change after that. . . ." And then came rambling about who told the secret, without saying what the secret itself was, followed by more rambling about how the person had died horribly, why this had happened, how it could have been avoided, if only such and such had not occurred a thousand years before. If Ruth showed impatience in listening to any of this, LuLing became outraged, before sputtering an oath that none of this mattered because soon she too would die anyway, by accident, because of bad-luck wishes, or on purpose. And then the silent treatment began, a punishment that lasted for days or weeks, until Ruth broke down first and said she was sorry.

So Ruth did not ask her mother. She decided instead to set aside several days when she could concentrate on the translation. She told her mother this, and LuLing warned, "Don't wait too long." After that, whenever her mother asked whether she had finished her story, Ruth answered, "I was just about to, but something came up with a client." Other crises also intervened, having to do with Art, the girls, or the house, as did vacation.

"Too busy for mother," LuLing complained. "Never too busy go see movie, go away, go see friend."

The past year, her mother had stopped asking, and Ruth wondered, Did she give up? Couldn't be. She must have forgotten. By then the pages had settled to the bottom of the desk drawer.

Now that they had resurfaced, Ruth felt pangs of guilt.

Perhaps she should hire someone fluent in Chinese. Art might know of someone—a linguistics student, a retired professor old enough to be versed in the traditional characters and not just the simplified ones. As soon as she had time, she would ask. She placed the pages at the top of the heap, then closed the drawer, feeling less guilty already.

When she woke in the morning, Art was up, doing his yoga stretches in the next room. "Hello," she said to herself. "Is anyone there?" Her voice was back, though squeaky from disuse.

As she brushed her teeth in the bathroom, she could hear Dory screeching: "I want to watch that. Put it back! It's my TV too." Fia hooted: "That show's for babies, and that's what you are, wnnh-wnnh-wnnh."

Since Art's divorce, the girls had been dividing their time between their mom and stepdad's home in Sausalito and Art's Edwardian flat on Vallejo Street. Every other week, the four of them—Art, Ruth, Sofia, and Dory—found themselves crammed into five miniature rooms, one of them barely big enough to squeeze in a bunk bed. There was only one bathroom, which Ruth hated for its antiquated inconvenience. The claw-footed iron tub was as soothing as a sarcophagus, and the pedestal sink with its separate spigots dispensed water that was either scalding hot or icy cold. As Ruth reached for the dental floss, she knocked over other items on the windowsill: potions for wrinkles, remedies for pimples, nose-hair clippers, and a plastic mug jammed with nine toothbrushes whose ownership and vintage were always in question. While she was picking up the mess, desperate pounding rattled the door.

"You'll have to wait," she called in a husky voice. The pounding continued. She looked at the bathroom schedule for August, which was posted on both sides of the door. There it said, clear as could be, whose turn it was at each quarter-hour. She had assigned herself to be last, and because everyone else ran late, she suffered the cumulative consequences. Below the schedule, the girls had added rules and amendments, and a list of violations and fines for infractions concerning the use of the sink, toilet, and shower, as well as a proclamation on what constituted the right to privacy versus a TRUE EMERGENCY (underlined three times).

The pounding came again. "Ru-uuth! I said it's the phone!" Dory opened the door a crack and shoved in a cordless handset. Who was calling at seven-twenty in the morning? Her mother, no doubt. LuLing seemed to have a crisis whenever Ruth had not called in several days.

"Ruthie, is your voice back? Can you talk?" It was Wendy, her best friend. They spoke nearly every day. She heard Wendy blow her nose. Was she actually crying?

"What happened?" Ruth whispered. Don't tell me, don't tell me, she mouthed in rhythm to her racing heart. Wendy was about to tell her she had cancer, Ruth was sure of it. Last night's uneasy feeling started to trickle through her veins.

"I'm still in shock," Wendy went on. "I'm about to . . . Hold on. I just got another call."

It must not be cancer, Ruth thought. Maybe she was mugged, or thieves had broken into the house, and now the police were calling to take a report. Whatever it was, it must have been serious, otherwise Wendy would not be crying. What should she say to her? Ruth crooked the phone in her neck and dragged her fingers through her close-cropped hair. She noticed that some of the mirror's silver had flaked off. Or were those white roots in her hair?

She would soon turn forty-six. When had the baby fat in her face started to recede? To think she used to resent having the face and skin of a perpetual teenager. Now she had creases pulling down the corners of her mouth. They made her look displeased, like her mother. Ruth brightened her mouth with lipstick. Of course, she wasn't like her mother in other respects, thank God. Her mother was permanently unhappy with everything and everybody. Lu-Ling had immersed her in a climate of unsolvable despair throughout Ruth's childhood. That was why Ruth hated it whenever she and Art argued. She tried hard not to get angry. But sometimes she reached a breaking point and erupted, only to wonder later how she had lost control.

Wendy came back on the line. "You still there? Sorry. We're casting victims for that earthquake movie, and a million people are calling all at once." Wendy ran her own agency that hunted extras as San Francisco local color— cops with handlebar mustaches, six-foot-six drag queens, socialites who were unknowing caricatures of themselves. "On top of everything, I feel like shit," Wendy said, and stopped to sneeze and blow her nose. So she wasn't crying, Ruth realized, before the phone clicked twice. "Damn," Wendy said. "Hang on. Let me get rid of this call."

Ruth disliked being put on hold. What was so dire that Wendy had to tell her first thing in the morning? Had Wendy's husband had an affair? Joe? Not good old Joe. What, then?

Art ducked his head through the doorway and tapped his watch. Seven twenty-five, he mouthed. Ruth was about to tell him it was Wendy with an emergency, but he was already striding down the narrow hallway. "Dory! Fia! Let's hustle! Ruth is taking you to the ice rink in five minutes.

Get a move on." The girls squealed, and Ruth felt like a horse at the starting gate.

"I'll be there in a sec!" she called out. "And girls, if you didn't eat breakfast, I want you to drink milk, a full glass, so you won't fall over dead from hypoglycemic shock."

"Don't say 'dead.' " Dory griped. "I hate it when you say that."

"My God. What's going on there?" Wendy was back on the line.

"The usual start of the week," Ruth said. "Chaos is the penance for leisure."

"Yeah, who said that?"

"I did. So anyway, you were saying . . . ?"

"Promise me first you won't tell anyone," Wendy sneezed again.

"Of course."

"Not even Art, and especially not Miss Giddy."

"Gideon? Gee, I don't know if I can promise about *him*."

"So last night," Wendy began, "my mother called in a state of euphoria." As Wendy went on, Ruth dashed to the bedroom to finish getting dressed. When she was not in a hurry, she enjoyed listening to her friend's ramblings. Wendy was a divining rod for strange disturbances in the earth's atmosphere. She was witness to bizarre sights: three homeless albinos living in Golden Gate Park, a BMW suddenly swallowed up by an ancient septic tank in Woodside, a loose buffalo strolling down Taraval Street. She was the maven of parties that led people to make scenes, start affairs, and commit other self-renewing scandals. Ruth believed Wendy made her life more sparkly, but today was not a good time for sparkles.

"Ruth!" Art said in a warning tone. "The girls are going to be late."

"I'm really sorry, Wendy. I have to take the girls to ice-skating school—"

Wendy interrupted. "Mommy married her personal trainer! That's what she called to tell me. He's thirty-eight, she's sixty-four. Can you believe it?"

"Oh . . . Wow." Ruth was stunned. She pictured Mrs. Scott with a groom in a bow tie and gym shorts, the two of them reciting vows on a treadmill. Was Wendy upset? She wanted to say the right thing. What, though? About five years before, her own mother had had a boyfriend of sorts, but he had been eighty. Ruth had hoped T.C. would marry LuLing and keep her occupied. Instead T.C. had died of a heart attack.

"Listen, Wendy, I know this is important, so can I call you back after I drop off the girls?"

Once she had hung up, Ruth reminded herself of the tasks she needed to do today. Ten things, and she tapped first her thumb. One, take the girls to skating school. Two, pick up Art's suits at the dry cleaner's. Three, buy groceries for dinner. Four, pick up the girls from the rink and drop them off at their friend's house on Jackson Street. Five and Six, phone calls to that arrogant client, Ted, then Agapi Agnos, whom she actually liked. Seven, finish the outline for a chapter of Agapi Agnos's book. Eight, call her agent, Gideon, whom Wendy disliked. And Nine—what the hell was Nine? She knew what Ten was, the last task of the day. She had to call Miriam, Art's ex-wife, to ask if she would let them have the girls the weekend of the Full Moon Festival dinner, the annual reunion of the Youngs, which she was hosting this year.

So what was Nine? She always organized her day by the

number of digits on her hands. Each day was either a five or a ten. She wasn't rigid about it: add-ons were accommodated on the toes of her feet, room for ten unexpected tasks. Nine, Nine . . . She could make calling Wendy number One and bump everything back. But she knew that call should be a toe, an extra, an Eleven. What was Nine? Nine was usually something important, a significant number, what her mother termed the number of fullness, a number that also stood for *Do not forget, or risk losing all*. Did Nine have something to do with her mother? There was always *something* to worry about with her mother. That was not anything she had to remember in particular. It was a state of mind.

LuLing was the one who had taught her to count fingers as a memory device. With this method, LuLing never forgot a thing, especially lies, betrayals, and all the bad deeds Ruth had done since she was born. Ruth could still picture her mother counting in the Chinese style, pointing first to her baby finger and bending each finger down toward her palm, a motion that Ruth took to mean that all other possibilities and escape routes were closed. Ruth kept her own fingers open and splayed, American style. What was Nine? She put on a pair of sturdy sandals.

Art appeared at the doorway. "Sweetie? Don't forget to call the plumber about the hot-water tank."

The plumber was *not* going to be number Nine, Ruth told herself, absolutely not. "Sorry, honey, but could you call? I've got a pretty full day."

"I have meetings, and three appeals coming up." Art worked as a linguistics consultant, this year on cases involving deaf prisoners who had been arrested and tried without access to interpreters.

It's your house, Ruth was tempted to say. But she forced

herself to sound reasonable, unassailable, like Art. "Can't you call from your office in between meetings?"

"Then I have to phone you and figure out when you'll be here for the plumber."

"I don't know *exactly* when I'll be home. And you know those guys. They say they're coming at one, they show up at five. Just because I work at home doesn't mean I don't have a real job. I've got a really crazy day. For one thing, I have to . . ." And she started to list her tasks.

Art slumped his shoulders and sighed. "Why do you have to make everything so *difficult*? I just thought *if* it were possible, *if* you had time—Aw, forget it." He turned away.

"Okay, okay, I'll take care of it. But if you get out of your meetings early, can you come home?"

"Sure thing." Art gave her a kiss on the forehead. "Hey, thanks. I wouldn't have asked if I weren't completely swamped." He kissed her again. "Love you."

She didn't answer, and after he left, she grabbed her coat and keys, then saw the girls standing at the end of the hallway, staring critically at her. She wiggled her big toe. Twelve, hot water.

Ruth started the car and pumped the brakes to make sure they worked. As she drove Fia and Dory to the skating rink, she was still mulling over what Nine might be. She ran through the alphabet, in case any of those letters might trigger a memory. Nothing. What had she dreamed the night before, when she finally fell asleep? A bedroom window, a dark shape in the bay. The curtains, she now recalled, had turned out to be sheer and she was naked. She had looked up and saw the neighbors in nearby apartments grinning. They had been watching her most private moments, her most private *parts*. Then a radio began to blare.

Whonk! Whonk! Whonk! "This has been a test of the American Broadcasting System's early-warning signal for disaster preparedness." And another voice came on, her mother's: "No, no, this is not test! This real!" And the dark shape in the bay rose and became a tidal wave.

Maybe number Nine was related to the plumber after all: tidal wave, broken water heater. The puzzle was solved. But what about the sheer curtains? What did that mean? The worry billowed up again.

"You know that new girl Darien likes?" she heard Fia say to her sister. "She has the best hair. I could just kill her."

"Don't say 'kill'!" Dory intoned. "Remember what they told us in assembly last year? Use that word, go to jail."

Both girls were in the backseat. Ruth had suggested that one of them sit up front with her, so she wouldn't feel like a chauffeur. But Dory had replied, "It's easier to open just one door." Ruth had said nothing in response. She often suspected the girls were testing her, to see if they could get a rise out of her. When they were younger, they had loved her, Ruth was sure of it. She had felt that with a ticklish pleasure in her heart. They used to argue over who could hold her hand or sit next to her. They had cuddled against her when scared, as they had often pretended to be, squeaking like helpless kittens. Now they seemed to be in a contest over who could irritate her more, and she sometimes had to remind herself that teenagers had souls.

Dory was thirteen and chunky, larger than her fifteen-year-old sister. They wore their long chestnut hair alike, pulled into ponytails high on their heads so that they cascaded like fountain spray. All their friends wore their hair in an identical style, Ruth had noticed. When she was their age, she had wanted to grow her hair long the way the other girls did, but her mother made her cut it short. "Long hair look like suicide maiden," LuLing had said. And Ruth knew she was referring to the nursemaid who had killed herself when her mother was a girl. Ruth had had nightmares about that, the ghost with long hair, dripping blood, crying for revenge.

Ruth pulled up to the unloading zone at the rink. The girls scrambled out of the car and swung their satchels onto their backs. "See ya!" they shouted.

Suddenly Ruth noticed what Fia was wearing—low-slung jeans and a cropped shirt that bared a good six inches of belly. She must have had her jacket zipped up when they had left home. Ruth lowered the car window and called out: "Fia, sweetie, come here a second. . . . Am I wrong, or did your shirt shrink drastically in the last ten minutes?"

Fia turned around slowly and rolled her eyes upward.

Dory grinned. "I told you she would."

Ruth stared at Fia's navel. "Does your mother *know* you're wearing that?"

Fia dropped her mouth in mock shock, her reaction to most things. "Uh, she *bought* it for me, okay?"

"Well, I don't think your dad would approve. I want you to keep your jacket on, even when you're skating. And Dory, you tell me if she doesn't."

"I'm not telling on nobody!"

Fia turned and walked away.

"Fia? Fia! Come back here. You promise me now, or I'm going to take you home to change clothes."

Fia stopped but didn't turn around. "All right," she grumbled. As she yanked up the jacket zipper, she said to Dory, loud enough for Ruth to hear: "Dad's right. She loves to make everything *sooo difficult*."

The remark both humiliated and rankled her. Why had Art said that, and especially in front of the girls? He knew how much that would hurt her. A former boyfriend had once told her she made life more complicated than it was, and after they broke up, she was so horrified that his accusations might be true that she made it a point to be reasonable, to present facts, not complaints. Art knew that and had even assured her the boyfriend was a jerk. Yet he still sometimes teased that she was like a dog that circles and bites its own tail, not recognizing she was only making herself miserable.

Ruth thought of a book she had helped write a few years before, *The Physics of Human Nature*. The author had recast the principles of physics into basic homilies to remind people of self-defeating behavioral patterns. "The Law of Relative Gravity": Lighten up. A problem is only as heavy as you let it be. "The Doppler Effect of Communication": There is always distortion between what a speaker says and what a listener wants it to mean. "The Centrifugal Force of Arguments": The farther you move from the core of the problem, the faster the situation spins out of control.

At the time, Ruth thought the analogies and advice were simplistic. You couldn't reduce real life into one-liners. People were more complex than that. She certainly was, wasn't she? Or was she too *complicated*? Complex, complicated, what was the difference? Art, on the other hand, was the soul of understanding. Her friends often said as much: "You are *so* lucky." She had been proud when she first heard that, believing she had chosen well in love. Lately she had considered whether they might have meant he was to be admired for putting up with *her*. But then Wendy reminded her, "You were the one who called Art a fucking saint." Ruth wouldn't have put it that way, but she knew the sentiment must have been true. She remembered that before she ever loved Art, she had admired him—his calm, the stability of his emotions. Did she still? Had he changed, or was it she? She drove toward the dry cleaner's, mulling over these questions.

She had met Art nearly ten years before, at an evening yoga class she had attended with Wendy. The class was her first attempt in years to exercise. Ruth was naturally thin and didn't have an incentive at first to join a health club. "A thousand bucks a year," she had marveled, "to jump on a machine that makes you run like a hamster in a wheel?" Her preferred form of exercise, she told Wendy, was stress. "Clench muscles, hold for twelve hours, release for a count of five, then clench again." Wendy, on the other hand, had put on thirty-five pounds since her days as a high school gymnast and was eager to get back into shape. "Let's at least take the free fitness test," she said. "No obligation to join."

Ruth secretly gloated when she scored better than Wendy in sit-ups. Wendy cheered aloud at besting Ruth in push-ups. Ruth's body-fat ratio was a healthy twenty-four percent. Wendy's was thirty-seven. "It's the enduring genetics of my Chinese peasant stock," Ruth kindly offered. But then Ruth scored in the "very poor" range for flexibility. "Wow," Wendy remarked. "According to this chart, that's about one point above rigor mortis."

"Look here, they have yoga," Wendy later said as they perused the schedule of classes at the club. "I hear yoga can change your life. Plus they have night classes." She nudged Ruth. "It might help you get over Paul."

In the locker room that first night, they overheard two women talking. "The guy next to me asked if I'd like to go with him to that midnight class, Togaless Yoga. You know, he says, the *nude* one."

"*Nude?* What a scumbag! . . . Was he at least good-looking?"

"Not bad. But can you imagine facing the naked butts of twenty people doing Downward-Facing Dog?" The two women walked out of the locker room. Ruth turned to Wendy. "Who the hell would do nude yoga?"

"Me," Wendy said. "And don't look at me like that, Miss Shock-and-Dismay. At least it wouldn't be boring."

"Nude, with total strangers?"

"No, with my CPA, my dentist, my boss. Who do you think?"

In the crowded workout room, thirty disciples, most of them women, were staking out their turf, then adjusting mats as stragglers came in. When a man rolled out his mat next to Ruth's, she avoided looking at him, in case he was the scumbag. She glanced around. Most of the women had pedicured nails, precision-applied nail polish. Ruth's feet were broad, and her naked toes looked like the piggies from the children's rhyme. Even the man next to her had better-looking feet, smooth skin, perfectly tapered toes. And then she caught herself—she shouldn't have nice thoughts about the feet of a potential pervert.

The class started with what sounded like a cult incantation, followed by poses that seemed to be saluting a heathen god. *"Urdhva Muka Svanasana! Adho Muka Svanasana!"* Everyone except Ruth and Wendy knew the routines. Ruth followed along as if she were playing Simon Says. Every now and then the yoga teacher, a ropy-muscled woman, walked by and casually bent, tilted, or lifted a part of Ruth's body. I probably look like a torture victim, Ruth thought, or one of those freaks my mother saw in China, boneless beggar boys who twisted themselves up for the amusement of others. By this time she was perspiring heavily and had observed enough about the man next to her to be able to describe him to the police, if necessary. "The nude yoga rapist was five-eleven, maybe a hundred and sixty pounds. He had dark hair, large brown eyes and thick eyebrows, a neatly cropped beard and mustache. His fingernails were clean, perfectly trimmed."

He was also incredibly limber. He could wrap his ankles around his neck, balance like Baryshnikov. She, in comparison, looked like a woman getting a gynecological exam. A *poor* woman. She was wearing an old T-shirt and faded leggings with a hole in one knee. At least it was obvious she wasn't on the prowl, not like those who were wearing designer sports outfits and full makeup.

And then she noticed the man's ring, a thick band of hammered gold on his right hand, no ring on his left. Not all married men wore rings, of course, but a wedding band on the right hand was a dead giveaway, at least in San Francisco, that he was gay. Now that she thought about it, the signs were obvious: the neat beard, the trim torso, the graceful way he moved. She could relax. She watched the bearded man bend forward, grab the bottoms of his feet, and press his forehead to his knees. No straight man could do that. Ruth flopped over and dangled her hands to midcalf.

Toward the end of the class came the headstands. The novices moved to the wall, the competitive types rose immediately like sunflowers toward the noon sun. There was no more room at the wall, so Ruth simply sat on her mat. A moment later, she heard the bearded man speak: "Need some help? I can hold on to your ankles until you get balanced."

"Thanks, but I'll pass. I'm afraid I'd get a cerebral hemorrhage."

He smiled. "Do you always live in such a dangerous world?"

"Always. Life's more exciting that way."

"Well, the headstand is one of the most important postures you can do. Being upside down can turn your life around. It can make you happy."

"Really?"

"See? You're already laughing."

"You win," she said, placing the crown of her head on a folded blanket. "Hoist away."

Within the first week, Wendy was off yoga and onto a home gizmo that looked like a rickshaw with oars. Ruth continued with yoga three times a week. She had found a form of exercise that relaxed her. She especially liked the practice of staying focused, of eliminating everything from her mind except breath. And she liked Art, the bearded man. He was friendly and funny. They started going to a coffee shop around the corner after class.

Over decaf cappuccinos one evening, she learned that Art had grown up in New York, and had a doctorate in linguistics from UC Berkeley. "So what languages do you speak?" she asked.

"I'm not a true polyglot," he said. "Most linguists I know aren't. My actual language specialty at Berkeley was American Sign Language, ASL. I now work at the Center on Deafness at UCSF."

"You became an expert on silence?" she joked.

"I'm not an expert on anything. But I love language in all forms—sounds and words, facial expressions, hand gestures, body posture and its rhythms, what people mean but don't necessarily say with words. I've always loved words, the power of them."

"So what's your favorite word?"

"Hm, that's an *excellent* question." He fell quiet, stroking his beard in thought.

Ruth was thrilled. He was probably groping for a word that was arcane and multisyllabic, one of those crossword items that could be confirmed only in the *Oxford English Dictionary*.

"Vapors," he said at last.

"Vapors?" Ruth thought of chills and cold, mists and suicide ghosts. That was not a word she would have chosen.

"It appeals to all the senses," he explained. "It can be opaque but never solid. You can feel it, but it has no permanent shape. It might be hot or cold. Some vapors smell terrible, others quite wonderful. Some are dangerous, others are harmless. Some are brighter than others when burned, mercury versus sodium, for instance. Vapors can go up your nose with a sniff and permeate your lungs. And the sound of the word, how it forms on your lips, teeth, and tongue—*vaporzzzzzz*—it lilts up, then lingers and fades. It's perfectly matched to its meanings."

"It is," Ruth agreed. "Vaporzzzz," she echoed, savoring the buzz on her tongue.

"And then there's vapor pressure," Art continued, "and reaching that balance point between two states, one hundred degrees Celsius." Ruth nodded and gave him what she hoped was a look of intelligent concentration. She felt dull and badly educated. "One moment you have water," Art said, his hands forming undulating motions. "But under pressure from heat, it turns into steam." His fingers flittered upward.

Ruth nodded vigorously. Water to steam, that she understood, sort of. Her mother used to talk about fire and water combining to make steam, and steam looked harmless but could peel your skin right off. "Like yin and yang?" she ventured.

"Duality of nature. Exactly."

Ruth shrugged. She felt like a fraud.

"What about you?" he said. "What's your favorite word?"

She put on her idiot face. "Gosh oh golly, there are so many! Let's see. 'Vacation.' 'Jackpot.' Then there's 'free.' 'Sale.' 'Bargain.' You know, the usual."

He had laughed throughout, and she felt pleased. "Seriously," he said. "What?"

Seriously? She plucked at what surfaced in her mind, but they sounded trite: *peace, love, happiness.* And what would those words say about her? That she lacked those qualities? That she had no imagination? She considered saying *onomatopoeia*, a word that had enabled her to win a spelling bee in the fifth grade. But *onomatopoeia* was a jumble of syllables, not at all like the simple sounds it was supposed to represent. Crash, boom, bang.

"I don't have a favorite yet," she finally answered. "I guess I've been living off words for so long it's hard to think about them beyond what's utilitarian."

"What do you do?"

"I used to be in corporate communications. Then I started freelance editing, and a few years ago I took on more full-scale book collaboration, mostly inspirational and self-improvement books, better health, better sex, better soul, that kind of thing."

"You're a book doctor."

Ruth liked that he said that. Book doctor. She had never

called herself that, nor had anyone else. Most people called her a ghostwriter—she hated the term. Her mother thought it meant that she could actually write to ghosts. "Yes," she told Art. "I suppose you could say that, book doctor. But I tend to think of myself as more of a translator, helping people transfer what's in their brain onto the blank page. Some books need more help than others."

"Have you ever wanted to write your own book?"

She hesitated. Of course she had. She wanted to write a novel in the style of Jane Austen, a book of manners about the upper class, a book that had nothing to do with her own life. Years before, she had dreamed of writing stories as a way to escape. She could revise her life and become someone else. She could be somewhere else. In her imagination she could change everything, herself, her mother, her past. But the idea of revising her life also frightened her, as if by imagination alone she were condemning what she did not like about herself or others. Writing what you wished was the most dangerous form of wishful thinking.

"I suppose most people want to write their own book," she answered. "But I think I'm better at translating what others want to say."

"And you enjoy that? It's satisfying?"

"Yes. Absolutely. There's still a lot of freedom to do what I want."

"You're lucky."

"I am," she conceded. "I certainly am."

It pleased her to discuss such matters with him. With Wendy she tended to talk about peeves more than passions. They commiserated on rampant misogyny, bad manners, and depressed mothers, whereas Art and she talked to discover new things about themselves and each other. He wanted to know what inspired her, what the difference was between her hopes and her goals, her beliefs and her motivations.

"Difference?" she asked.

"Some things you do for yourself," he answered. "Some things you do for others. Maybe they're the same."

Through such conversations, she realized for instance that she was lucky to be a freelance editor, a book doctor. The discoveries were refreshing.

One evening, about three weeks after she met him, their conversation became more personal. "Frankly, I like living alone," she heard herself saying. She had convinced herself this was true.

"And what if you met the ideal partner?"

"He can stay ideal in his place, and I'll stay ideal in mine. Then we won't get into all that shit about whose pubic hair is clogging up the drain."

Art chuckled. "God! Did you actually live with someone who complained about *that*?"

Ruth forced a laugh, staring into her coffee cup. She was the one who had complained. "We were opposites about cleanliness," she answered. "Thank God we didn't marry." As she said this, she sensed the words were at last true and not a cover-up for pain.

"So you were going to marry."

She had never been able to confide fully to anyone, not even Wendy, about what had happened with her and Paul Shinn. She had told Wendy of the many ways Paul irked her, that she was tempted to break up with him. When she announced to Wendy that they had split up, Wendy exclaimed, "*Finally* you did it. Good for you." With Art, the past seemed easier to talk about, because he had not been part of it. He was her yoga buddy, on the periphery of her life. He did not know what her earlier hopes and fears had been. With him, she could dissect the past with emotional detachment and frank intelligence.

"We thought about marriage," she said. "How can you not when you live together for four years? But you know what? Over time, passion wanes, differences don't. One day he told me he'd put in for a transfer to New York and it had come through." Ruth recalled to herself how surprised she had been, and how she complained to Paul about his not telling her sooner. "Of course, I can work almost any-where," she had told him, annoyed yet excited at the prospect of moving to Manhattan, "but it's a jolt to uproot, not to mention leave my mother behind, and relocate in a city where I don't have any contacts. Why'd you tell me at the last minute?" She had meant that rhetorically. Then came Paul's awkward silence.

"I didn't ask to go, he didn't ask me to come," she told Art simply. She avoided eye contact. "It was a civil way to break up. We both agreed it was time to move on, only separately. He was decent enough to try to put the blame on himself. Said he was immature, whereas I was more *re-sponsible*." She gave Art a goofy grin, as if this were the most ironic thing anyone could have said about her. "The worst part was, he was so *nice* about it—like he was em-barrassed to have to do this to me. And naturally, I spent the last year trying to analyze what it was about us, about *me*, that didn't work. I went over just about every argument that we'd had. I had said he was careless, he said I made simple problems have difficult solutions. I said he never planned, he said I obsessed to the point of killing all spon-taneity. I thought he was selfish, he said I worried over him to the point of suffocation, then pitied myself when he didn't fall all over himself saying thank you. And maybe we were both right and that was why we were wrong for each other."

Art touched her hand. "Well, I think he lost a terrific woman."

She was flooded with self-consciousness and gratitude.

"You are. You're terrific. You're honest and funny. Smart, interested."

"Don't forget responsible."

"What's wrong with being responsible? I wish more people were. And you know what else? You're willing to be vulnerable. I think that's endearing."

"Aw, shucks."

"Seriously."

"Well, that's sweet of you to say. I'll buy you coffee next time." She laughed and put her hand over his. "How about you? Tell me about your love life and all your past disasters. Who's your current partner?"

"I don't have one right now. Half the time I live alone, the other half I'm picking up toys and making jelly sandwiches for my two daughters."

This was a surprise. "You adopted them?"

He looked puzzled. "They're mine. And my ex-wife's, of course."

Ex-wife? That made three gay men she knew who had once been married. "So how long were you married before you came out?"

"Came out?" He made a screwy face. "Wait a minute. Do you think I'm *gay*?"

In an instant, she knew her mistake. "Of course not!" she scrambled to say. "I meant when you came out from New York."

He was laughing convulsively. "This whole time you thought I was *gay*?"

Ruth flushed. What had she said! "It was the ring," she admitted, and pointed to his gold band. "Most of the gay couples I know wear rings on that hand."

He slipped off the ring and rotated it in the light. "My best friend made it for my wedding," Art said solemnly. "Ernesto, a rare spirit. He was a poet and a goldsmith by avocation, made his living as a limo driver. See these indentations? He told me they were to remind me that there are a lot of bumps in life and that I should remember what lies between them. Love, friendship, hope. I stopped wearing it when Miriam and I split up. Then Ernesto died, brain cancer. I decided to wear the ring to remind me of him, what he said. He was a good friend—but *not* a lover."

He slid the ring over to Ruth so she could see the details. She picked it up. It was heavier than she had thought. She held it to her eye and looked through its center at Art. He was so gentle. He was not judgmental. She felt a squeezing in her heart that both hurt her and made her want to giggle and shout. How could she not love him?

As she gathered up Art's clothes at the dry cleaner's, Ruth flexed her big toe and remembered she was supposed to call Wendy. Mrs. Scott and a boy toy, what a shock. She decided to wait until she was in the parking lot by the grocery store, rather than risk a head-on collision during a juicy cell-phone conversation.

She and Wendy were the same age. They had known each other since the sixth grade, but had gone through periods when they did not see each other for years. Their friendship had grown via accidental reunions and persistence on Wendy's part. While Wendy was not the person Ruth would have chosen for her closest friend, Ruth was glad it had turned out to be so. She needed Wendy's boisterousness as balance to her own caution, Wendy's bluntness as antidote to her reserve. "Stop being such a worrywort," Wendy often ordered. Or "You don't always have to act so fucking polite," she might say. "You're making me look like shit."

Wendy answered on the first ring. "Can you believe it?" she said, as though she had not stopped repeating this since their last conversation. "And I thought she was over the top when she had the facelift. Last night she told me that she and Patrick were getting it on twice a night. She's telling me this—*me,* the daughter she once sent to confession for asking how babies were made."

Ruth imagined Mrs. Scott taking off her Chanel suit, her trifocals, her diamond-encrusted designer crucifix, then embracing her beach boy.

"She's getting more sex than I am," Wendy exclaimed. "I can't remember the last time I even wanted to do anything in bed with Joe except sleep."

Wendy had often joked about her dwindling sex drive. But Ruth didn't think she meant it was absent. Would this happen to her as well? She and Art were not exactly the red-hot lovers they'd been in earlier years. They prepared less for romance and accepted more readily excuses of fatigue. She wiggled a toe: Get estrogen levels checked. That might be the reason she felt a sense of unease, fluctuating hormones. She had no other reason to feel anxious. Not that her life was perfect, but whatever problems she had, they were small. And she should keep them that way. She vowed to be more affectionate with Art.

"I can see why you're upset," Ruth consoled her.

"Actually, I'm more worried than upset," Wendy said. "It's just weird. It's like the older she gets, the younger she acts. And part of me says, Good for her, you go, girl. And the other part is like, Whoa. Is she crazy or what? Do I have to watch over her now, act like her mother and make sure she doesn't get herself in trouble? You know what I mean?"

"I've been that way with my mother all my life," Ruth said. Suddenly she remembered what had been eluding her. Her mother was supposed to see the doctor at four this afternoon. Over the past year, Ruth had been vaguely worried about her mother's health. Nothing was terribly wrong; it was just that LuLing seemed slightly off, hazy. For a while, Ruth had reasoned that her mother was tired, that her hearing might be going, or that her English was getting worse. As a precaution, Ruth had also gnawed over the worst possibilities—brain tumor, Alzheimer's, stroke—believing this would ensure that it was not these things. History had always proven that she worried for nothing. But a few weeks before, when her mother mentioned she had an appointment for a checkup, Ruth said she would drive her.

After she and Wendy finished their conversation, Ruth stepped out of the car and walked toward the grocery store, still thinking. Nine, Mom's doctor. And she started to count on her fingers the questions she should ask the doctor. Thank God she could speak once again.

TWO

In the vegetable aisle, Ruth headed toward a bin of beauti-fully shaped turnips. They were each the size of apples, symmetrical and scrubbed, with striations of purple. Most people did not appreciate the aesthetics of turnips, Ruth thought as she chose five good ones, whereas she loved them, their crunchiness, the way they absorbed the flavor of whatever they were immersed in, gravy or pickling juice. She loved cooperative vegetables. And she loved turnips best when they were sliced into wedges and pre-served in vinegar and chilies, sugar and salt.

Every year, before their family reunion dinner in Sep-tember, her mother started two new fermenting jars of spicy turnips, one of which she gave to Ruth. When Ruth was a little girl, she called them *la-la*, hot-hot. She would suck and munch on them until her tongue and lips felt in-flamed and swollen. She still gorged on them from time to time. Was it a craving for salt, or for pain? When the supply grew low, Ruth would toss in more chopped-up turnips and a pinch of salt, and let them pickle for a few days. Art thought the taste was okay in small doses. But the girls said they smelled like "something farted in the fridge." At times Ruth secretly ate the spicy turnips in the morning, her way of seizing the day. Even her mother considered that strange.

Her mother—and Ruth tapped her ring finger to remind herself again of the doctor's appointment. Four o'clock. She had to squeeze a lot of work into the shortened day. She hurried, grabbing Fuji apples for Fia, Granny Smiths for Dory, Braeburns for Art.

At the meat counter, she evaluated the options. Dory would not eat anything with eyes, and ever since seeing that pig movie *Babe*, Fia had been trying to be a vegetarian. Both girls made an exception for fish, because seafood was "not cute." When they announced that, Ruth said to them, "Just because something isn't cute, is its life worth less? If a girl wins a beauty contest, is she better than a girl who doesn't?" And Fia scrunched up her face and replied: "What are you talking about? Fish don't enter beauty contests."

Ruth now pushed her cart toward the fish counter. She longed for prawns in the shell, always her first choice. Art wouldn't eat them, however. He claimed that the predominant taste of any crustacean or mollusk was that of its alimentary tract. She settled on Chilean sea bass. "That one," she told the man at the counter. Then she reconsidered: "Actually, give me the bigger one." She might as well ask her mother to dinner, since they were already going to the doctor's together. LuLing was always complaining she didn't like to cook for just herself.

At the checkout counter, Ruth saw a woman in front of her scoop up bunches of ivory- and peach-colored tulips, at least fifty dollars' worth. Ruth was amazed at how some people casually bought flowers as household staples, as if they were as necessary as toilet paper. And tulips, of all choices! They wilted and dropped their petals after a few days. Was the woman having an important dinner party on a weeknight? When Ruth bought flowers, she had to assess their value in several ways to justify what she bought. Daisies were cheerful and cheap, but they had an unpleasant smell. Baby's breath was even cheaper, but as Gideon pointed out, it was *the* lowest of floral low taste, what old queens used, along with lace doilies they inherited from their grandmothers. Tuberoses smelled wonderful and gave an architectural touch, but they were expensive at this store, nearly four dollars a stalk. At the flower mart, they were only a dollar. She liked hydrangeas in a pot. They were making a comeback, and while they cost a lot, they lasted a month or two, *if* you remembered to water them. The trick was to cut them before they died, then let them dry in a pottery pitcher, so you could keep them as a permanent floral arrangement, that is, until someone like Art threw them out, citing that they were already dead.

Ruth had not grown up with flowers in the house. She could not remember LuLing ever buying them. She had not thought this a deprivation until the day she went grocery shopping with Auntie Gal and her cousins. At the supermarket in Saratoga, ten-year-old Ruth had watched as they dumped into the cart whatever struck their fancy at the moment, all kinds of good things Ruth was never allowed to eat: chocolate milk, doughnuts, TV dinners, ice-cream sandwiches, Hostess Twinkies. Later they stopped at a little stand where Auntie Gal bought cut flowers, pink baby roses, even though nobody had died or was having a birthday.

Remembering this, Ruth decided to splurge and buy a small orchid plant with ivory blooms. Orchids looked delicate but thrived on neglect. You didn't have to water

them but once every ten days. And while they were somewhat pricey, they bloomed for six months or more, then
went dormant before surprising you with new blooms all
over again. They never died—you could count on them to
reincarnate themselves forever. A lasting value.

Back at the flat, Ruth put the groceries away, set the orchid
on the dining room table, and went into the Cubbyhole.
She liked to think that limited space inspired limitless
imagination. The walls were painted red with flecks of
metallic gold, Wendy's idea. The overhead light was softened by a desk lamp with an amber mica shade. On the
lacquer-black shelves were reference books instead of jars
of jam. A pull-out cutting board held her laptop, a flour bin
had been removed for knee space.

   She turned on her computer and felt drained before she
even started. What was she doing ten years ago? The same
thing. What would she be doing ten years from now? The
same thing. Even the subjects of the books she helped
write were not that different, only the buzzwords had
changed. She took a deep breath and phoned the new
client, Ted. His book, *Internet Spirituality,* was about the
ethics created by cosmic computer connections, a topic
he felt sure was hot right now but would lose its cachet if
the publisher didn't get it to market as soon as possible. He
had said so in several urgent phone messages he had left
over the weekend when Ruth was in Tahoe.

   "I have nothing to do with arranging publishing dates,"
Ruth now tried to explain.

   "Stop thinking in terms of constraints," he told her. "If
you write this book with me, you have to believe in its
principles. Anything is possible, as long as it's for the good
of the world. Make the exception. Live exceptionally. And

if you can't do that, maybe we should consider whether you're right for this project. Think about it, then let's talk tomorrow."

Ruth hung up. She thought about it. The good of the world, she muttered to herself, was her agent's job. She would warn Gideon that the client was pushy and might try to change the publication date. She would stand firm this time. To do what the client wanted while meeting her other commitments would require her to work 'round the clock. Fifteen years earlier she could have done that—in the days when she also smoked cigarettes and equated busyness with feeling wanted. Not now. Untense the muscles, she reminded herself. She took another deep breath and exhaled as she stared at the shelves of books she had helped edit and write.

The Cult of Personal Freedom. The Cult of Compassion. The Cult of Envy.

The Biology of Sexual Attraction. The Physics of Human Nature. The Geography of the Soul.

The Yin and Yang of Being Single. The Yin and Yang of Being Married. The Yin and Yang of Being Divorced.

The most popular books were *Defeat Depression with Dogs, Procrastinate to Your Advantage,* and *To Hell with Guilt.* The last book had become a controversial bestseller. It had even been translated into German *and* Hebrew.

In the coauthoring trade, "Ruth Young" was the small-type name that followed "with," that is, if it appeared at all. After fifteen years, she had nearly thirty-five books to her credit. Most of her early work had come from corporate communications clients. Her expertise had woven its way into communication in general, then communication problems, behavioral patterns, emotional problems, mind-body connections, and spiritual awakening. She had been in the business long enough to see the terms evolve from "chakras" to "ch'i," "prana," "vital energy," "life force," "biomagnetic force," "bioenergy fields," and finally back to "chakras." In bookstores, most of her clients' words of wisdom were placed in the light or popular sections— Self-Help, Wellness, Inspirational, New Age. She wished she were working on books that would be categorized as Philosophy, Science, Medicine.

By and large, the books she helped write were interesting, she often reminded herself, and if not, it was her job to *make* them interesting. And though she might pooh-pooh her own work just to be modest, it irked her when others did not take her seriously. Even Art did not seem to recognize how difficult her job was. But that was partly her fault. She preferred to make it look easy. She would rather that others discern for themselves what an incredible job she did in spinning gold out of dross. They never did, of course. They didn't know how hard it was to be diplomatic, to excavate lively prose from incoherent musings. She had to assure clients that her straightforward recasting of their words still made them sound articulate, intelligent, and important. She had to be sensitive to the fact the authors saw their books as symbolic forms of immortality, believing that their words on the printed page would last far longer than their physical bodies. And when the books were published, Ruth had to sit back quietly at parties while the clients took the credit for being brilliant. She often claimed she did not need to be acknowledged to feel satisfied, but that was not exactly true. She wanted *some* recognition, and not like the kind she had received two weeks before, at the party for her mother's seventy-seventh birthday.

Auntie Gal and Uncle Edmund had brought along a

friend from Portland, an older woman with thick glasses, who asked Ruth what she did for a living. "I'm a book collaborator," she answered.

"Why you say that?" LuLing scolded. "Sound bad, like you traitor and spy."

Auntie Gal then said with great authority, "She's a ghostwriter, one of the best there is. You know those books that say 'as told to' on the cover? That's what Ruth does—people tell her stories and she writes them down, word for word, exactly as told." Ruth had no time to correct her.

"Like court stenographers," the woman said. "I hear they have to be very fast and accurate. Did you go through special training?"

Before Ruth could answer, Auntie Gal chirped: "Ruthie, you should tell my story! Very exciting, plus all true. But I don't know if you can keep up. I'm a pretty fast talker!"

Now LuLing jumped in: "Not just type, *lots* work!" And Ruth was grateful for this unexpected defense, until her mother added, "She correct spelling too!"

Ruth looked up from her notes on her phone conference with the *Internet Spirituality* author and reminded herself of all the ways she was lucky. She worked at home, was paid decent money, and at least the publishers appreciated her, as did the publicists, who called her for talking points when booking radio interviews for the authors. She was always busy, unlike some freelance writers who fretted over the trickle of jobs in the pipeline.

"So busy, so success," her mother had said recently when Ruth told her she didn't have any free time to see her. "Not free," LuLing added, "because every minute must charge money. What I should pay you, five dollar, ten dollar, then you come see me?" The truth was, Ruth did not have much free time, not in her opinion. Free time was the most precious time, when you should be doing what you loved, or at least slowing down enough to remember what made your life worthwhile and happy. Her free time was usually usurped by what seemed at the time urgent and later unnecessary. Wendy said the same thing: "Free time doesn't exist anymore. It has to be scheduled with a dollar amount attached to it. You're under this constant pressure to get your money's worth out of rest, relaxation, and restaurants that are hard to get into." After hearing that, Ruth didn't agonize as much over time constraints. It wasn't her fault she didn't have enough time to do what was necessary. The problem was universal. But try explaining that to her mother.

She pulled out her notes for chapter seven of Agapi Agnos's latest book, *Righting the Wronged Child,* and punched Agapi's number. Ruth was one of the few people who knew that Agapi's real name was Doris DeMatteo, that she had chosen her pseudonym because *agapi* meant "love" and *agnos* referred to ignorance, which she redefined as a form of innocence. That was how she signed her books, "Love & Innocence, Agapi Agnos." Ruth enjoyed working with her. Though Agapi was a psychiatrist, she didn't come across as intimidating. She knew that much of her appeal was her Zsa Zsa Gabor shtick, her accent, the flirtatious yet intelligent personality she exuded when she answered questions in TV and radio interviews.

During their phone meeting, Ruth reviewed the chapter that presented the Five Don'ts and Ten Do's of becoming a more engaged parent.

"Darling," Agapi said, "why does it always have to be a list of five and ten? I can't always limit myself to such regular numbers."

"It's just easier for people to remember in series of fives and tens," Ruth answered. "I read a study somewhere about that." Hadn't she? "It probably has to do with counting on our fingers."

"That makes perfect sense, my dear! I knew there was a reason."

After they hung up, Ruth began work on a chapter titled "No Child Is an Island." She replayed a tape of Agapi and herself talking:

". . . A parent, intentionally or not, imposes a cosmology on the little child—" Agapi paused. "You want to say something?" What cue had she given that let Agapi know she wanted to add a thought? Ruth seldom interrupted people.

"We should define 'cosmology' here," she heard herself say, "perhaps in a sidebar. We don't want people to think we're talking about cosmetics or astrology."

"Yes, yes, excellent point, my dear. Cosmology, let's see . . . what we *believe*, subconsciously, implicitly, or both, how the universe works—you want to add something?"

"Readers will think we mean planets or the Big Bang theory."

"You are such a cynic! All right, you write the definition, but just include something about how each of us fits into our families, society, the communities we come into contact with. Talk about those various roles, as well as how we believe we got them—whether it's destiny, fate, luck, chance, self-determination, et cetera, et cetera. Oh, and Ruth, darling, make it sound sexy and easy to grasp."

"No problem."

"All right, so we assume everyone understands cosmology. We go on to say that parents pass along this cosmology to children through their behaviors, their reactions to daily events, often mundane—You look puzzled."

"Examples of mundane."

"Mealtime, for instance. Perhaps dinner always happens at six and Mom is an elaborate planner, dinner is a ritual, but nothing happens, no talk, unless it's argument. Or meals are eaten catch-as-catch-can. With just these contrasts, the child might grow up thinking either that day and night are predictable, though not always pleasant, or that the world is chaotic, frantic, or freely evolving. Some children do beautifully, no matter what the early influences. Whereas others grow up into great big adults who require a lifetime of very, *very* expensive psychotherapy."

Ruth listened to their laughter on the tape. She had never gone into therapy, as Wendy had. She worked with too many therapists, saw that they were human, full of foibles, in need of help themselves. And while Wendy thought it worthwhile to know that a professional was dedicated to her and her alone for two one-hour sessions a week, Ruth could not justify spending a hundred fifty dollars an hour to listen to herself talk. Wendy often said Ruth should see a shrink about her compulsion with number counting. To Ruth, however, the counting was practical, not compulsive; it had to do with remembering things, not warding off some superstitious nonsense.

"Ruth, darling," Agapi's taped voice continued, "can you look at the folder marked 'Fascinating Case Studies' and pick out suitable ones for this chapter?"

"Okay. And I was thinking, how about including a section on the cosmology imparted by television as artificial caregiver? Just a suggestion, since it would probably also work as an angle for television shows and radio interviews."

"Yes, yes, wonderful! What shows do you think we should do?"

"Well, starting with the fifties, you know, *Howdy Doody*, *The Mickey Mouse Club*, all the way to *The Simpsons* and *South Park*—"

"No, dear, I mean what shows *I* might be on. *Sixty Minutes*, *Today*, *Charlie Rose*—oh, I would love to be on *that* show, that man is *so* sexy. . . ."

Ruth took notes and started an outline. No doubt Agapi would call her that night to discuss what she had written. Ruth suspected she was the only writer in the business who believed a deadline was an actual date.

Her watch sounded at eleven. She tapped her finger, Eight, call Gideon. When she reached him, she began with the demands of the *Internet Spirituality* author. "Ted wants me to push everything else aside and make his project top priority under rush deadlines. I was very firm about saying I couldn't do that, and he hinted pretty strongly that he might replace me with another writer. Frankly, I'd be relieved if he fired me," Ruth said. She was preparing herself for rejection.

"He never will," Gideon replied. "You'll cave in, you always do. You'll probably be calling HarperSanFrancisco by the end of the week, persuading them to change the schedule."

"What makes you say that?"

"Face it, sweetheart, you're accommodating. Willing to bend over backward. And you have this knack for making even the dickheads believe they're the best at what they do."

"Watch it," Ruth said. "That's a hooker you're describing."

"It's true. You're a dream when it comes to collaboration," Gideon went on. "You listen as the clients blather on, egos unchecked. They walk all over you, and you just take it. You're easy."

Why wasn't Art hearing this? Ruth wanted to gloat: See, *others* don't think I'm difficult. Then she realized Gideon was saying she was a pushover. She wasn't really, she reasoned. She knew her limits, but she wasn't the type to get into a conflict over things that were ultimately not that important. She didn't understand people who thrived on argument and being right all the time. Her mother was that way, and what did that get her? Nothing but unhappiness, dissatisfaction, and anger. According to her mother's cosmology, the world was against her and no one could change this, because this was a curse.

But the way Ruth saw it, LuLing got into fights mainly because of her poor English. She didn't understand others, or they didn't understand her. Ruth used to feel she was the one who suffered because of that. The irony was, her mother was actually *proud* she had taught herself English, the choppy talk she had acquired in China and Hong Kong. And since immigrating to the United States fifty years before, she had not improved either her pronunciation or her vocabulary. Yet her sister, GaoLing, had come to the States around the same time, and her English was nearly perfect. She could talk about the difference between crinoline and organza, name the specific trees she liked: oak, maple, gingko, pine. To LuLing, cloth was classified as "cost too much," "too slippery," "scratchy skin," and "last long time." And there were only two kinds of trees: "shady" and "drop leaf all the time." Her mother couldn't even say Ruth's name right. It used to mortify Ruth when she shouted for her up and down the block.

"Lootie! Lootie!" Why had her mother chosen a name with sounds she couldn't pronounce?

But this was the worst part: Being the only child of a widow, Ruth had always been forced to serve as LuLing's mouthpiece. By the time she was ten, Ruth was the English-speaking "Mrs. LuLing Young" on the telephone, the one who made appointments for the doctor, who wrote letters to the bank. Once she even had to compose a humiliating letter to the minister.

"Lootie give me so much trouble," LuLing dictated, as if Ruth were invisible, "maybe I send her go Taiwan, school for bad children. What you think?"

Ruth revised that to: "Perhaps Ruth might attend a finishing school in Taiwan where she can learn the manners and customs of a young lady. What is your opinion?"

In an odd way, she now thought, her mother was the one who had taught her to become a book doctor. Ruth had to make life better by revising it.

At three-ten, Ruth finished paying the plumber. Art had never come home, nor had he called. A whole new water heater was needed, not just a replacement part. And because of the leak, the plumber had had to shut off the electricity to the entire flat until he had suctioned out the standing water and removed the old tank. Ruth had been unable to work.

She was running late. She faxed the outline to Agapi, then raced around the house, gathering notes, her cell phone, her address book. Once in the car, she drove to the Presidio Gate and then through the eucalyptus forest to California Street. Her mother lived fifty blocks west, in a part of San Francisco known as the Sunset district, close to Land's End.

The doctor's appointment was ostensibly a routine visit. Her mother had overlooked having an annual checkup for the last few years, though it was included free in her HMO plan. LuLing was never sick. Ruth could not remember the last time she had had the flu or even a cold. At seventy-seven, her mother had none of the common geriatric problems, arthritis, high cholesterol, or osteoporosis. Her worst ailment—the one she frequently complained about to Ruth, in excruciating detail—was constipation.

Recently, though, Ruth had some concerns that her mother was becoming not forgetful, exactly, but careless. She would say "ribbon" when she meant "wrapping paper," "envelope" when she meant "stamp." Ruth had made a mental list of examples to tell the doctor. The accident last March, she should mention that as well. LuLing had bashed her car into the back of a truck. Luckily, she had only bumped her head on the steering wheel, and no one else was hurt. Her car was totaled.

"Scare me to pieces," LuLing had reported. "My skin almost fall off." She blamed a pigeon that had flown up in front of her windshield. Maybe, Ruth now considered, it was not a flutter of wings, but one in her brain, a stroke, and the bump on her head was more serious, a concussion, a skull fracture. Whatever was wrong, the police report and insurance company said it was LuLing's fault, not the pigeon's. LuLing was so outraged that she canceled her car insurance, then complained when the company refused to reinstate her policy.

Ruth had related the incident to Agapi Agnos, who said inattention and anger could be related to depression in the elderly.

"My mother's been depressed and angry all her life,"

Ruth told Agapi. She did not bring up the threats of suicide, which she had heard so often she tried not to react to them.

"I know of some excellent therapists who've worked with Chinese patients," Agapi said. "Quite good with cultural differences—magical thinking, old societal pressures, the flow of ch'i."

"Believe me, Agapi, my mother is *not* like other Chinese people." Ruth used to wish her mother were more like Auntie Gal. She didn't talk about ghosts or bad luck or ways she might die.

"In any case, my dear, you should have a doctor give her a thorough, thorough checkup. And you put your arms around her and give that mother of yours a great big healing hug from me." It was a nice thought, but Ruth rarely exchanged embraces with LuLing. When she tried, her mother's shoulders turned rigid, as if she were being attacked.

Driving toward LuLing's building, Ruth entered the typical fog of summer. Then came block after block of bungalows built in the twenties, cottages that sprang up in the thirties, and characterless apartments from the sixties. The ocean view skyline was marred by electrical wires strewn from pole to house and house to pole. Many of the picture windows had sea-misty smears. The drainpipes and gutters were rusted, as were the bumpers of old cars. She turned up a street lined with more upscale homes, architectural attempts at Bauhaus sleekness, their small lawns decorated with shrubs cut in odd shapes, like the cotton-candy legs of show poodles.

She pulled up to LuLing's place, a two-unit Mediterranean-style with an apricot-colored curved front and a fake bay window balcony with wrought-iron grating. LuLing had once proudly tended her yard. She used to water and cut the hedge herself, neaten the border of white stones that flanked the short walkway. When Ruth lived at home, she had had to mow the seven-by-seven foot squares of lawn. LuLing always criticized any edges that touched the sidewalk. She also complained about the yellow urine spots, made by the dog from across the street. "Lootie, you tell that man don't let dog do that." Ruth reluctantly went across the street, knocked on the door, asked the neighbor if he had seen a black-and-white cat, then walked back and told her mother that the man said he would try. When she went away to college and came home to visit, her mother still asked her to complain to the man across the street almost as soon as she walked in the door. The missing-cat routine was getting old, and it was hard to think of new excuses for knocking on the man's door. Ruth usually procrastinated, and LuLing nagged about more and more yellow spots, as well as Ruth's laziness, her forgetfulness, her lack of concern for family, on and on. Ruth tried to ignore her by reading or watching TV.

One day Ruth worked up the courage to tell LuLing she should hire a lawyer to sue the man or a gardener to fix the lawn. Her college roommate had suggested she say this, telling Ruth she was crazy to let her mother push her around as if she were still six years old.

"Is she *paying* you to be a punching bag?" her roommate had said, building the case.

"Well, she does give me money for college expenses," Ruth admitted.

"Yeah, but every parent does that. They're supposed to. But that doesn't give them the right to make you their slave."

Thus bolstered, Ruth confronted her mother: "If it bothers you so much, you take care of it."

LuLing stared at her, silent for five full minutes. Then she burst like a geyser: "You wish I dead? You wish no mother tell you what to do? Okay, maybe I die soon!" And just like that, Ruth had been upended, flung about, was unable to keep her balance. LuLing's threats to die were like earthquakes. Ruth knew that the potential was there, that beneath the surface, the temblors could occur at any time. And despite this knowledge, when they erupted she panicked and wanted to run away before the world fell down.

Strangely, after that incident, LuLing never mentioned anything about the dog peeing on the lawn. Instead, whenever Ruth came home, LuLing made it a point to take out a spade, get on her hands and knees, and painfully dig out the yellow spots and reseed them, two square inches at a time. Ruth knew it was her mother's version of emotional torture, but still it made her stomach hurt as she pretended not to be affected. LuLing finally did hire someone to take care of the yellow spots, a cement contractor, who constructed a frame and a mold, then poured a patio of red and white concrete diamonds. The walkway was red as well. Over the years, the red diamonds faded. The white ones turned grimy. Some areas looked as though they had experienced the upheavals of Lilliputian volcanos. Spiny weeds and strawlike tufts grew in the cracks. I should call someone to spruce up the place, Ruth thought as she approached the house. She was sad that her mother no longer cared as much about appearances. She also felt guilty that she had not helped out more around the house. Perhaps she could call her own handyman to do cleanup and repairs.

As Ruth neared the steps to the upper unit, the downstairs tenant stepped out of her doorway, signaling that she wanted to speak to her. Francine was an anorexically thin woman in her thirties, who seemed to be wearing a size-eight skin over a size-two body. She often griped to Ruth about repairs needed for the building: The electricity kept shorting out. The smoke detectors were old and should be replaced. The back steps were uneven and could cause an accident—and a lawsuit.

"Never satisfy!" LuLing told Ruth.

Ruth knew not to take sides with the tenant. But she worried that there might really be a problem like a fire one day, and she dreaded the headlines "Slum Landlady Jailed, Ignored Deadly Hazards." So Ruth surreptitiously handled some of the more resolvable problems. When she bought Francine a new smoke detector, LuLing found out and became apoplectic. "You think she right, I wrong?" As had happened throughout Ruth's childhood, LuLing's fury escalated until she could barely speak, except to sputter the old threat: "Maybe I die soon!"

"You need to talk to your mom," Francine was now saying in a whiny voice. "She's been accusing me of not paying the rent. I *always* pay on time, the first of the month. I don't know what she's talking about, but she goes on and on, like a broken record."

Ruth had a sinking feeling. She did not want to hear this.

"I even showed her the canceled check. And she said, 'See, you still have the check!' It was weird, like she wasn't making any sense."

"I'll take care of it," Ruth said quietly.

"It's just that she's harassing me like a hundred times a day. It's making me nuts."

"I'll get it straightened out."

"I hope so, because I was just about to call the police to get a restraining order!"

Restraining order? Who's the nut here? "I'm sorry this happened," Ruth said, and remembered a book she helped write on mirroring a child's feelings. "You must be frustrated when it's clear you've done nothing wrong."

It worked. "Okay, then," Francine said, and backed into her doorway like a cuckoo in a Swiss clock.

Ruth used her own key to let herself into her mother's apartment. She heard LuLing call to her: "Why so late?"

Seated in her brown vinyl easy chair, LuLing looked like a petulant child on a throne. Ruth gave her a once-over to see if she could detect anything wrong, a twitch in her eye, a slight paralysis, perhaps, on one side of her face. Nothing, the same old mom. LuLing was wearing a purple cardigan with gold-tone buttons, her favorite, black slacks, and size-four black pumps with low heels. Her hair was smoothed back and gathered like Fia's and Dory's, only she had the ponytail wound into a netted bun, thickened with a hairpiece. Her hair was jet-black, except for the roots at the back, where she could not see that she had failed to apply enough dye. From a distance, she looked like a much younger woman, sixty instead of seventy-seven. Her skin was even-toned and smooth, no need for foundation or powder. You had to stand a foot away before you could see the fine etching of wrinkles on her cheeks. The deepest lines were at the corners of her mouth, which were often turned down, as they were now.

LuLing groused. "You say doctor visit one o'clock."

"I said the appointment was at four."

"No! One o'clock! You say be ready. So I get ready, you don't come!"

Ruth could feel the blood draining out of her head. She tried another tack. "Well, let me call the doctor and see if we can still get in at four." She went to the back, where her mother did her calligraphy and painting, to the room that had been her own long before. On her mother's drawing table lay a large sheet of watercolor paper. Her mother had started a poem-painting, then stopped in mid-character. The brush lay on the paper, its tip dried and stiff. LuLing was not careless. She treated her brushes with fanatical routine, washing them in spring water, not tap, so that chlorine would not damage them. Perhaps she had been in the middle of painting and heard the teakettle crying and bolted. Maybe the phone rang after that, one thing after another. But then Ruth looked closer. Her mother had tried to write the same character over and over again, each time stopping at the same stroke. What character? And why had she stopped in mid-flight?

When Ruth was growing up, her mother supplemented her income as a teacher's aide with side businesses, one of which was bilingual calligraphy, Chinese and English. She produced price signs for supermarkets and jewelry stores in Oakland and San Francisco, good-luck couplets for restaurant openings, banners for funeral wreaths, and announcements for births and weddings. Over the years, people had told Ruth that her mother's calligraphy was at an artist's level, first-rate classical. This was the piecework that earned her a reliable reputation, and Ruth had had a role in that success: she checked the spelling of the English words.

"It's 'grapefruit,' " eight-year-old Ruth once said, exasperated, "not 'grapefoot.' It's a fruit not a foot."

That night, LuLing started teaching her the mechanics of writing Chinese. Ruth knew this was punishment for what she had said earlier.

"Watch," LuLing ordered her in Chinese. She ground an inkstick onto an inkstone and used a medicine dropper to add salt water in doses the size of tears. "Watch," she said, and selected a brush from the dozens hanging with their tips down. Ruth's sleepy eyes tried to follow her mother's hand as she swabbed the brush with ink, then held it nearly perpendicular to the page, her wrist and elbow in midair. Finally she began, flicking her wrist slightly so that her hand waved and dipped like a moth over the gleam of white paper. Soon the spidery images formed: "Half Off!" "Amazing Discounts!" "Going Out of Business!"

"Writing Chinese characters," her mother told her, "is entirely different from writing English words. You think differently. You feel differently." And it was true: LuLing was different when she was writing and painting. She was calm, organized, and decisive.

"Bao Bomu taught me how to write," LuLing said one evening. "She taught me how to think. When you write, she said, you must gather the free-flowing of your heart." To demonstrate, LuLing wrote the character for "heart." "See? Each stroke has its own rhythm, its balance, its proper place. Bao Bomu said everything in life should be the same way."

"Who's Bao Bomu again?" Ruth asked.

"She took care of me when I was a girl. She loved me very much, just like a mother. *Bao,* well, this means 'precious,' and together with *bomu*, this means 'Precious Auntie.' " Oh, *that* Bao Bomu, the crazy ghost. LuLing started to write a simple horizontal line. But the movements were not simple. She rested the tip of the brush on the paper, so it was like a dancer *sur les pointes*. The tip bent slightly downward, curtsied, and then, as if blown by capricious winds, swept to the right, paused, turned a half-step to the left and rose. Ruth blew out a sigh. Why even try? Her mother would just get upset that she could not do it right.

Some nights LuLing found ways to help Ruth remember the characters. "Each radical comes from an old picture from a long time ago." She made a horizontal stroke and asked Ruth if she could see what the picture was. Ruth squinted and shook her head. LuLing made the identical stroke. Then again and again, asking each time if Ruth knew what it was. Finally, her mother let out a snort, the compressed form of her disappointment and disgust.

"This line is like a beam of light. Look, can you see it or not?"

To Ruth, the line looked like a sparerib picked clean of meat.

LuLing went on: "Each character is a thought, a feeling, meanings, history, all mixed into one." She drew more lines—dots and dashes, downstrokes and upstrokes, bends and hooks. "Do you see this?" she said over and over, *tink-tink-tink*. "This line, and this and this—the shape of a heavenly temple." And when Ruth shrugged in response, LuLing added, "In the *old* style of temples," as if this word *old* would bump the Chinese gears of her daughter's mind into action. *Ping-ping!* Oh, I see.

Later LuLing had Ruth try her hand at the same character, the whole time stuffing Chinese logic into her resistant brain. "Hold your wrist this way, firm but still loose, like a young willow branch—ai-ya, not collapsed like a beggar lying on the road. . . . Draw the stroke with grace, like a bird landing on a branch, not an executioner chopping off a devil's head. The way you drew it—well, look, the whole thing is falling down. Do it like this . . . light first, then temple. See? Together, it means 'news from the gods.' See how this knowledge always comes from above? See how Chinese words make sense?"

With Chinese words, her mother did make sense, Ruth now reasoned to herself. Or did she?

She called the doctor and got the nurse. "This is Ruth Young, LuLing Young's daughter. We're coming to see Dr. Huey for a checkup at four, but I just wanted to mention a few things. . . ." She felt like a collaborator, a traitor and a spy.

When Ruth returned to the living room, she found her mother searching for her purse.

"We don't need any money," Ruth said. "And if we do, I can pay."

"No, no pay! Nobody pay!" LuLing cried. "Inside purse put my health card. I don't show card, doctor charge me extra. Everything suppose be free."

"I'm sure they have your records there. They won't need to see the card."

LuLing kept searching. Abruptly she straightened herself and said, "I know. Leave my purse at GaoLing house. Must be she forget tell me."

"What day did you go?"

"Three days go. Monday."

"Today's Monday."

"How can be Monday? I go three days go, not today!"

"You took BART?" Since the car accident, LuLing had been taking public transportation when Ruth wasn't able to act as chauffeur.

"Yes, and GaoLing late pick me up! I wait two hour. Fin'y she come. And then she accuse me, say, Why you come early, you suppose come here eleven. I tell her, No, I never say come eleven. Why I say coming eleven when I already know I coming nine o'clock? She pretend I crazy, make me so mad."

"Do you think you might have left it on the BART train?"

"Left what?"

"Your purse."

"Why you always take her side?"

"I'm not taking sides. . . ."

"Maybe she keep my purse, don't tell me. She always want my things. Jealous of me. Little-girl time, she want my *chipao* dress, want my melon fruit, want everybody attention."

The dramas her mother and Auntie had gone through over the years resembled those off-Broadway plays in which two characters perform all the roles: best friends and worst enemies, archrivals and gleeful conspirators. They were only a year apart, seventy-seven and seventy-six, and that closeness seemed to have made them competitive with each other.

The two sisters came to America separately, and married a pair of brothers, sons of a grocer and his wife. LuLing's husband, Edwin Young, was in medical school, and as the elder, he was "destined" as LuLing put it, to be smarter and more successful. Most of the family's attention and privileges had been showered on him. GaoLing's husband, Edmund, the little brother, was in dental school. He was known as the lazy one, the careless boy who would always need a big brother to watch over him. But then big brother Edwin was killed in a hit-and-run car accident while leaving the UCSF library one night. Ruth had been two years old at the time. Her uncle Edmund went on to become the leader of the family, a well-respected dentist, and an even more savvy real estate investor in low-income rental units.

When the grocer and then his wife died, in the 1960s, most of the inheritance—money, the house, the store, gold and jade, family photos—went to Edmund, with only a small cash gift given to LuLing in consideration of her brief marriage to Edwin. "Only give me *this much*," LuLing often described, pinching her fingers as if holding a flea. "Just because you not a boy."

With the death money, along with her years of savings, LuLing bought a two-unit building on Cabrillo and Forty-seventh, where she and Ruth lived in the top flat. GaoLing and Edmund moved to Saratoga, a town of vast-lawned ranch-style homes and kidney-shaped pools. Occasionally they would offer LuLing furniture they were going to re-place with something better. "Why I should take?" she would fume. "So they can pity for me? Feel so good for themself, give me things they don't want?"

Throughout the years, LuLing lamented in Chinese, "Ai-ya, if only your father had lived, he would be even more successful than your uncle. And still we wouldn't spend so carelessly like them!" She also noted what *should* have been Ruth's rightful property: Grandmother Young's jade ring, money for a college fund. It shouldn't have mattered that Ruth was a girl or that Edwin had died. That was old Chinese thinking! LuLing said this so often Ruth could not help fantasizing what her life might have been like had her father lived. She could have bought patent-leather shoes, rhinestone-covered barrettes, and baby roses. Sometimes she stared at a photo of her father and felt angry he was dead. Then she felt guilty and scared. She tried to convince herself that she deeply loved this fa-ther she could not even remember. She picked the flower-like weeds that grew in the cracks of sidewalks and put them in front of his framed picture.

Ruth now watched as LuLing searched in the closet for her purse. She was still pointing out GaoLing's transgressions. "Later grown-up time, want my things too. Want your daddy marry her. Yes, you don't know this. Edwin not Edmund, because he oldest, more success. Every day smile for him, show off her teeth, like monkey." LuLing turned around and demonstrated. "But he not interest in her, only me. She so mad. Later she marry Edmund, and when you daddy die, she say, Ooooh, so lucky I not marry Edwin! So stupid she saying that. To my face! Don't consider me, only concerning herself. I say nothing. I never complaining. Do I ever complaining?"

Ruth joined in the search, sticking her hands under seat cushions.

LuLing straightened herself to all four feet, eleven inches of indignity. "And now you see! Why GaoLing *still* want my money? She crazy, you know. She always think I got more, hiding somewhere. That's why I think she take my purse."

The dining room table, which LuLing never used, was a raft of junk mail. Ruth pushed aside the Chinese-language newspapers and magazines. Her mother had always been sanitary, but never neat. She hated grease but didn't mind chaos. She kept junk mail and coupons, as if they were personal greeting cards.

"Here it is!" Ruth cried. What a relief. She pulled out a green pocketbook from underneath a mound of magazines. As LuLing checked that her money and credit cards were still inside, Ruth noticed what had obscured the purse in the first place: new issues of *Woodworking Today*,

Seventeen, Home Audio and Video, Runner's World, Cosmopolitan, Dog Fancy, Ski, Country Living—magazines her mother would never read in a million years.

"Why do you have all these?"

LuLing smiled shyly. "First I thinking, Get money, then tell you. Now you ask, so now I show you." She went to the kitchen drawer where she kept years of expired coupons and pulled out an oversized envelope.

"News from the gods," LuLing murmured. "I won ten million dollar! Open and see."

Sure enough, inside were a sweepstakes promotion coupon that resembled a check, and a sheet of peel-off miniature magazine covers. Half the covers were missing. LuLing must have ordered three dozen magazines. Ruth could picture the mail carrier dragging over a sackful of them every day, spilling them onto the driveway, her mother's hopes and logic jumbled into the same pile.

"You surprise?" LuLing wore a look of absolute joy.

"You should tell the doctor your good news."

LuLing beamed, then added, "I win all for you."

Ruth felt a twinge in her chest. It quickly grew into an ache. She wanted to embrace her mother, shield her, and at the same time wanted her mother to cradle her, to assure her that she was okay, that she had not had a stroke or worse. That was how her mother had always been, difficult, oppressive, and odd. And in exactly that way, LuLing had loved her. Ruth knew that, felt it. No one could have loved her more. Better perhaps, but not more.

"Thanks, Ma. It's wonderful. We'll talk about it later, what to do with the money. But now we have to go. The doctor said we could still come at four, and we shouldn't be late."

LuLing turned crabby again. "You fault we late."

Ruth had to remind her to take her newly found purse, then her coat, finally her keys. She felt ten years old again, translating for her mother how the world worked, explaining the rules, the restrictions, the time limits on money-back guarantees. Back then she had been resentful. Now she was terrified.

THREE

In the hospital waiting room, Ruth saw that all the patients, except one pale balding man, were Asian. She read the blackboard listing of doctors' names: Fong, Wong, Wang, Tang, Chin, Pon, Kwak, Koo. The receptionist looked Chinese; so did the nurses.

In the sixties, mused Ruth, people railed against race-differentiated services as ghettoization. Now they demanded them as culturally sensitive. Then again, San Francisco was about a third Asian, so Chinese-targeted medicine could also be a marketing strategy. The balding man was glancing about, as if seeking an escape route. Did he have a last name like Young that had been mistakenly identified as Chinese by a race-blind computer? Did he also get calls from Chinese-speaking telemarketers trying to sign him up for long-distance calling plans for Hong Kong and Taiwan? Ruth knew what it meant to feel like an outsider, because she had often been one as a child. Moving to a new home eight times made her aware of how she didn't fit in.

"Fia start six grade?" LuLing was now asking.

"You're thinking of Dory," Ruth answered. Dory had been held back a year because of attention deficit disorder. She now received special tutoring.

"How can be Dory?"

66

"Fia's the older one, she's going into tenth. Dory's thirteen. She'll be in seventh."

"I know who who!" LuLing grumbled. She counted, flipping her fingers down as she listed: "Dory, Fia, oldest one Fu-Fu, seventeen." Ruth used to joke that Fu-Fu, her feral cat, born with a nasty disposition, was the grandchild LuLing never had. "How Fu-Fu do?" LuLing asked.

Hadn't she told her mother Fu-Fu had died? She must have. Or Art had. Everyone knew that Ruth had been depressed for weeks after it happened.

"Fu-Fu's dead," she reminded her mother.

"Ai-ya!" LuLing's face twisted with agony. "How this can be! What happen?"

"I told you—"

"No, you never!"

"Oh . . . Well, a few months ago, she went over the fence. A dog chased her. She couldn't climb back up fast enough."

"Why you have dog?"

"It was a neighbor's dog."

"Then why you let neighbor's dog come your backyard? Now see what happen! Ai-ya, die no reason!"

Her mother was speaking far too loudly. People were looking up from their knitting and reading, even the balding man. Ruth was pained. That cat had been her baby. She had held her the day she was born, a tiny wild ball of fur, found in Wendy's garage on a rainy day. Ruth had also held her as the vet gave the lethal shot to end her misery. Thinking about this nearly put Ruth over the edge, and she did not want to burst into tears in a waiting room full of strangers.

At that moment, luckily, the receptionist called out, "LuLing Young!" As Ruth helped her mother gather her purse and coat, she saw the balding man leap up and walk quickly toward an elderly Chinese woman. "Hey, Mom," Ruth heard him say. "How'd everything check out? Ready to go home?" The woman gruffly handed him a prescription note. He must be her son-in-law, Ruth surmised. Would Art ever take her mother to the doctor's? She doubted it. How about in the case of an emergency, a heart attack, a stroke?

The nurse spoke to LuLing in Cantonese and she answered in Mandarin. They settled on accented English as their common ground. LuLing quietly submitted to the preliminaries. Step on the scale. Eighty-five pounds. Blood pressure. One hundred over seventy. Roll up your sleeve and make a fist. LuLing did not flinch. She had taught Ruth to do the same, to look straight at the needle and not cry out. In the examination room, Ruth turned away as her mother slipped out of her cotton camisole and stood in her waist-high flowered panties.

LuLing put on a paper gown, climbed onto the examining table, and dangled her feet. She looked childlike and breakable. Ruth sank into a nearby chair. When the doctor arrived, they both sat up straight. LuLing had always had great respect for doctors.

"Mrs. Young!" the doctor greeted her jovially. "I'm Dr. Huey." He glanced at Ruth.

"I'm her daughter. I called your office earlier."

He nodded knowingly. Dr. Huey was a pleasant-looking man, younger than Ruth. He started asking LuLing questions in Cantonese, and her mother pretended to understand, until Ruth explained, "She speaks Mandarin, not Cantonese."

The doctor looked at her mother. *"Guoyu?"*

LuLing nodded, and Dr. Huey shrugged apologetically. "My Mandarin is pretty terrible. How's your English?"

"Good. No problem."

At the end of the examination, Dr. Huey smiled and announced, "Well, you are one very strong lady. Heart and lungs are great. Blood pressure excellent. Especially for someone your age. Let's see, what year were you born?" He scanned the chart, then looked up at LuLing. "Can you tell me?"

"Year?" LuLing's eyes darted upward as if the answer were on the ceiling. "This not so easy say."

"I want the truth, now," the doctor joked. "Not what you tell your friends."

"Truth is 1916," LuLing said.

Ruth interrupted. "What she means is—" and she was about to say 1921, but the doctor put up his hand to stop her from speaking. He glanced at the medical chart again, then said to LuLing, "So that makes you . . . how old?"

"Eighty-two this month!" she said.

Ruth bit her lip and looked at the doctor.

"Eighty-two." He wrote this down. "So tell me, were you born in China? Yes? What city?"

"Ah, this also not so easy say," LuLing began shyly. "Not really city, more like little place we call so many different name. Forty-six kilometer from bridge to Peking."

"Ah, Beijing," the doctor said. "I went there on a tour a couple of years ago. My wife and I saw the Forbidden City."

LuLing warmed up. "In those day, so many thing forbidden, can't see. Now everyone pay money see forbidden thing. You say this forbidden that forbidden, charge extra."

Ruth was about to burst. Her mother must sound garbled to Dr. Huey. She had had concerns about her, but she didn't want her concerns to be fully justified. Her worries were supposed to preclude any real problem. They always had.

"Did you go to school there as well?" Dr. Huey asked.

LuLing nodded. "Also my nursemaid teach me many things. Painting, reading, writing—"

"Very good. I was wondering if you could do a little math for me. I want you to count down from a hundred, subtracting seven each time."

LuLing went blank.

"Start at a hundred."

"Hundred!" LuLing said confidently, then nothing more.

Dr. Huey waited, and finally said, "Now count down by seven."

LuLing hesitated. "Ninety-two, ah, ninety-three. Ninety-three!"

This is not fair, Ruth wanted to shout. She has to convert the numbers into Chinese to do the calculations, then remember that, and put the answer back into English. Ruth's mind raced ahead. She wished she could lay out the answers for her mother telepathically. Eighty-six! Seventy-nine!

"Eighty . . . Eighty . . ." LuLing was stuck.

"Take your time, Mrs. Young."

"Eighty," she said at last. "After that, eighty-seven."

"Fine," Dr. Huey declared, with no change of expression. "Now I want you to name the last five presidents in reverse order."

Ruth wanted to protest: Even I can't do that!

LuLing's eyebrows bunched in thought. "Clinton," she said after a pause. "Last five year still Clinton." Her mother had not even understood the question! Of course she hadn't. She had always depended on Ruth to tell her what people meant, to give her what they said from another angle. "Reverse order" means "go backward," she would have told LuLing. If Dr. Huey could ask that same question in fluent Mandarin, it would be no problem for LuLing to give the right answer. "This president, that president," her mother would have said without hesitation, "no difference, all liar. No tax before election, more tax after. No crime before, more crime after. And always don't cut welfare. I come this country, I don't get welfare. What so fair? No fair. Only make people lazy to work!"

More ridiculous questions followed.

"Do you know today's date?"

"Monday." Date and day always sound the same to her.

"What was the date five months ago?"

"Still Monday." When you stop to think about it, she's right.

"How many grandchildren do you have?"

"Don't now. She not married yet." He doesn't see that she's joking!

LuLing was like the losing contestant on *Jeopardy!* Total for LuLing Young: minus five hundred points. And now for our final *Jeopardy!* round . . .

"How old is your daughter?"

LuLing hesitated. "Forty, maybe forty-one." To her mother, she was always younger than she really was.

"What year was she born?"

"Same as me. Dragon year." She looked at Ruth for confirmation. Her mother was a Rooster.

"What month?" Dr. Huey asked.

"What month?" LuLing asked Ruth. Ruth shrugged helplessly. "She don't know."

"What year is it now?"

"Nineteen ninety-eight!" She looked at the doctor as if

he were an idiot not to know that. Ruth was relieved that her mother had answered one question right.

"Mrs. Young, could you wait here while your daughter and I go outside to schedule another appointment?"

"Sure-sure. I not go anywhere."

As Dr. Huey turned for the door, he stopped. "And thank you for answering all the questions. I'm sure you must have felt like you were on the witness stand."

"Like O.J."

Dr. Huey laughed. "I guess everyone watched that trial on TV."

LuLing shook her head. "Oh no, not just watch TV, I there when it happen. He kill wife and that friend, bring her glasses. Everything I see."

Ruth's heart started to thump. "You saw a documentary," she said for Dr. Huey's benefit, "a reenactment of what might have happened, and it was *like* watching the real thing. Is that what you're saying?"

LuLing waved to dismiss this simple answer. "Maybe *you* see document. *I* see real thing." She demonstrated with motions. "He grab her like this, cut neck here—very deep, so much blood. Awful."

"So you were in Los Angeles that day?" Dr. Huey asked.

LuLing nodded.

Ruth was flailing for logic. "I don't remember you *ever* going to L.A."

"How I go, don't know. But I there. This true! I follow that man, oh he sneaky. O.J. hide in bush. Later, I go his house too. Watch him take glove, stick in garden, go back inside change clothes—" LuLing caught herself, embarrassed. "Well, he change clothes, course I don't look, turn my eyes. Later he run to airport, almost late, jump on plane. I see whole thing."

"You saw this and didn't tell anyone?"

"I scared!"

"The murder must have been an awful thing for you to see," Dr. Huey said.

LuLing nodded bravely.

"Thank you for sharing that. Now, if you'll just wait here a few minutes, your daughter and I are going to step into another room and schedule your next appointment."

"No hurry."

Ruth followed the doctor into another room. "How long have you noticed this kind of confusion?" Dr. Huey asked right away.

Ruth sighed. "It's been a little worse in the last six months, maybe longer than that. But today she seems worse than usual. Except for the last thing she said, she hasn't been that weird or forgetful. It's more like mix-ups, and most of it is due to her not speaking English that well, as you may have noticed. The story about O.J. Simpson— you know, that may be another language problem. She's never been good at expressing herself—"

"It sounded pretty clear to me that she thought she was there," Dr. Huey said gently.

Ruth looked away.

"You mentioned to the nurse that she had a car accident. Was there a head injury?"

"She did bump her head on the steering wheel." Ruth was suddenly hopeful that this was the missing piece to the puzzle.

"Does her personality seem to be changing? Is she depressed, more argumentative?"

Ruth tried to guess what an affirmative response might

indicate. "My mother's always gotten into arguments, all her life. She has a terrible temper. And as long as I've known her, she's been depressed. Her husband, my father, was killed forty-four years ago. Hit-and-run. She never got over it. Maybe the depression is becoming worse, but I'm so used to it I'd be the last one to notice. As for her confusion, I was wondering if it was a concussion from the car accident or if she might have had a mini-stroke." Ruth tried to remember the correct medical term. "You know, a TIA."

"So far I don't see any evidence of that. Her motor movements are good, reflexes are fine. Blood pressure is excellent. But we'll want to run a few more tests, also make sure she's not diabetic or anemic, for instance."

"Those could cause problems like this?"

"They could, as could Alzheimer's and other forms of dementia."

Ruth felt her stomach had been punched. Her mother wasn't *that* bad off. He was talking about a horrible terminal illness. Thank God she had not told the doctor about the other things she had tabulated: the argument her mother had had with Francine over the rent; the ten-million-dollar check from the magazine sweepstakes; her forgetting that Fu-Fu had died. "So it could be depression," Ruth said.

"We haven't ruled out anything yet."

"Well, if it is, you'll have to tell her the antidepressants are ginseng or *po chai* pills."

Dr. Huey laughed. "Resistance to Western medication is common among our elderly patients here. And as soon as they feel better, they stop taking it to save money." He handed her a form. "Give this to Lorraine at the computer station around the corner. Let's schedule your mother to see the folks in Psychiatry and Neurology, then have her come back to see me again in a month."

"Around the Full Moon Festival."

Dr. Huey looked up. "Is that when it is? I can never keep track."

"I only know because I'm hosting this year's family reunion dinner."

That evening, as Ruth steamed the sea bass, she told Art in an offhanded way, "I took my mom to see the doctor. She may have depression."

And Art said, "So what else is new?"

At dinner, LuLing sat next to Ruth. "Too salty," she remarked in Chinese, poking at her portion of fish. And then she added: "Tell those girls to finish their fish. Don't let them waste food."

"Fia, Dory, why aren't you eating?" Ruth said.

"I'm full," Dory answered. "We stopped at Burger King in the Presidio and ate a bunch of fries before we came home."

"You shouldn't let them eat those things!" LuLing scolded, continuing in Mandarin. "Tell them you don't allow this anymore."

"Girls, I wish you wouldn't ruin your appetites with junk food."

"And I wish you two would stop talking like spies in Chinese," Fia said. "It's like really rude."

LuLing glared at Ruth, and Ruth glanced at Art, but he was looking down at his plate. "Waipo speaks Chinese," Ruth said, "because that's the language she's used to." Ruth had told them to call LuLing "Waipo," the Chinese honorific for "Grandmother," and at least they did that, but then again, they thought it was just a nickname.

"She can speak English too," Dory said.

"Tst!" LuLing grumbled to Ruth. "Why doesn't their father scold them? He should tell them to listen to you. Why doesn't he have more concern for you? No wonder he never married you. No respect for you. Say something to him. Why don't you tell him to be nicer to you? . . ."

Ruth wished she could go back to being mute. She wanted to shout for her mother to stop complaining about things she could not change. Yet she also wanted to defend her to the girls, especially now that something was wrong with her. LuLing acted eternally strong, but she was also fragile. Why couldn't Fia and Dory understand that and act a little kinder?

Ruth remembered how she felt when she was their age. She too had resented LuLing's speaking Chinese in front of others, knowing they couldn't understand her covert remarks. "Look how fat that lady is," LuLing might say. Or, "Luyi, go ask that man to give us a better price." If Ruth obeyed, she was mortified. And if she didn't, as she now recalled, even more dire consequences followed.

By using Chinese words, LuLing could put all kinds of wisdom in Ruth's mind. She could warn her away from danger, disease, and death.

"Don't play with her, too many germs," LuLing told six-year-old Ruth one day, nodding toward the girl from across the street. The girl's name was Teresa, and she had two front teeth missing, a scab on one knee, and a dress smeared with handprints. "I saw her pick up old candy off the sidewalk and eat it. And look at her nose, sickness pouring out all over the place."

Ruth liked Teresa. She laughed a lot and always kept in her pockets things she had found: balls of foil, broken marbles, flower heads. Ruth had just started at another new school, and Teresa was the only girl who played with her. Neither of them was very popular.

"Did you hear me?" LuLing said.

"Yes," Ruth answered.

The next day, Ruth was playing in the schoolyard. Her mother was on the other side of the yard, monitoring other kids. Ruth climbed up the slide, eager to tumble down the silver curl into cool, dark sand. She had done this with Teresa a dozen times without her mother's seeing.

But then a familiar voice, loud and shrill, rang across the playground: "No! Luyi, stop! What are you doing? You want to break your body in half?"

Ruth stood at the top of the slide, frozen with shame. Her mother was the busybody watcher of kindergartners, whereas Ruth was in the first grade! Some of the other first-graders were laughing down below. "Is that your mother?" they shouted. "What's that gobbledy-gook-gook she's saying?"

"She's not my mother!" Ruth shouted back. "I don't know who she is!" Her mother's eyes locked on hers. Although she was clear across the playground, she heard everything, saw everything. She had magic eyes on the back of her head.

You can't stop me, Ruth thought fiercely. She threw herself down the slide, head first, arms straight out—the position that only the bravest and wildest boys would take—fast, fast, fast into the sand. And then she crashed face first, with such force that she bit her lip, bumped her nose, bent her glasses, and broke her arm. She lay still. The world was burning, shot full of red lightning.

"Ruthie's dead!" a boy yelled. Girls began screaming.

I'm not dead, Ruth tried to cry out, but it was like speaking in a dream. Nothing came from her lips the way she wanted. Or was she truly dead? Was that how it felt, this oozing from her nose, the pain in her head and arm, the way she moved, as slowly and heavily as an elephant in water? Soon she felt familiar hands brushing over her head and neck. Her mother was lifting her, murmuring tenderly, "Ai-ya, how could you be so foolish? Look at you."

Blood ran from Ruth's nose and dripped onto the front of her white blouse, staining the broad lace-trimmed collar. She lay limply in her mother's lap, looking up at Teresa and the faces of the other children. She saw their fright, but also their awe. If she could have moved, she would have smiled. At last they were paying attention to her, the new girl at school. She then saw her mother's face, the tears streaming down her cheeks, falling on her own face like wet kisses. Her mother wasn't angry, she was worried, full of love. And in her amazement, Ruth forgot her pain.

Later she lay on a cot in the nurse's office. Her nose-bleed was stanched with gauze, her punctured lip was cleansed. A cold washcloth covered her forehead, and her arm was elevated on a bag of ice.

"She may have fractured her arm," the nurse told LuLing. "And her nerves might be torn. There's a great deal of swelling, but she's not complaining of too much pain."

"She good, never complain."

"You need to take her to the doctor. Do you understand? Go see a doctor."

"Okay, okay, go see doctor."

As LuLing led her out, a teacher said, "Look how brave she is! She's not even crying." Two popular girls gave Ruth big smiles of admiration. They waved. Teresa was also there, and Ruth gave her a quick, secret smile.

In the car on the way to the doctor's office, Ruth noticed that her mother was strangely quiet. She kept looking at Ruth, who expected harsh words to start any moment: I told you that big slide was dangerous. Why didn't you listen to me? You could have cracked open your brain like a watermelon! Now I have to work overtime to pay for this. Ruth waited, but her mother only asked every now and then if she was hurting. Each time Ruth shook her head.

As the doctor examined Ruth's arm, LuLing sucked air between her teeth in agony and moaned: "*Ai-ya!* Careful, careful, careful. She hurt real bad." When the cast was put on, LuLing said proudly, "Teacher, children, all very impress. Lootie no cry, no complain, nothing, just quiet."

By the time they arrived home, the excitement had worn off, and Ruth felt a throbbing pain in her arm and head. She tried not to cry. LuLing put her in her vinyl La-Z-Boy and made her as comfortable as possible. "You want me to cook you rice porridge? Eat. That will help you get well. How about spicy turnips? You want some now, while I cook dinner?"

The less Ruth said, the more her mother tried to guess what she might want. As she lay in the recliner, she heard LuLing talking to Auntie Gal on the phone.

"She was almost killed! Scared me to death. Really! I'm not exaggerating. She was nearly yanked from this life and on her way to the yellow springs. . . . I just about cracked my own teeth to see how much pain she was in. . . . No, no tears, she must have inherited the strength of her grandmother. Well, she's eating a little bit now. She can't talk, and I thought at first she bit off her tongue, but I think it's only the fright. Come over to visit? Fine, fine, but tell your kids to be careful. I don't want her arm to fall off."

They came bearing gifts. Auntie Gal brought a bottle of

eau de toilette. Uncle Edmund gave Ruth a new tooth-brush and matching plastic cup. Her cousins handed her coloring books, crayons, and a stuffed dog. LuLing had pushed the television set close to the La-Z-Boy, since Ruth had a hard time seeing without her glasses.

"Does it hurt?" her younger cousin, Sally, asked.

Ruth shrugged, though her arm was now aching.

"Man oh man, I wish I had a cast," Billy said. He was the same age as Ruth. "Daddy, can I have one too?"

"Don't say such bad-luck things!" Auntie Gal warned.

When Billy tried to change the television channel, Uncle Edmund sternly ordered him to put it back to the program Ruth had been watching. She had never heard her uncle be strict with her cousins. Billy was a spoiled brat.

"Why aren't you talking?" Sally asked. "Did you break your mouth too?"

"Yeah," Billy said. "Did the fall make you stupid or something?"

"Billy, stop teasing," Auntie Gal said. "She's resting. She has too much pain to talk."

Ruth wondered whether this was true. She thought about making a little sound so small no one would even hear. But if she did, then all the good things that were happening might disappear. They would decide she was fine, and everything would go back to normal. Her mother would start scolding her for being careless and disobedient.

For two days after the fall, Ruth was helpless; her mother had to feed, dress, and bathe her. LuLing would tell her what to do: "Open your mouth. Eat a little more. Put your arm in here. Try to keep your head still while I brush your hair." It was comforting to be a baby again, well loved, blameless.

When she returned to school, Ruth found a big streamer

of butcher paper hanging at the front of the classroom. "Welcome Back, Ruth!" it said. Miss Sondegard, the teacher, announced that every single boy and girl had helped make it. She led the classroom in clapping for Ruth's bravery. Ruth smiled shyly. Her heart was about to burst. She had never been as proud and happy. She wished she had broken her arm a long time before.

During lunch, girls vied with one another to present her with imaginary trinkets and serve as her maiden-in-waiting. She was invited to step into the "secret castle," a rock-bordered area near a tree at the edge of the sandbox. Only the most popular girls could be princesses. The princesses now took turns drawing on Ruth's cast. One of them gingerly asked, "Is it still broken?" Ruth nodded, and another girl whispered loudly: "Let's bring her magic potions." The princesses scampered off in search of bottle caps, broken glass, and fairy-sized clover.

At the end of the day, Ruth's mother went to her classroom to pick her up. Miss Sondegard took LuLing aside, and Ruth had to act as though she were not listening.

"I think she's a bit tired, which is natural for the first day back. But I'm a little concerned that she's so quiet. She didn't say a word all day, not even ouch."

"She never complain," LuLing agreed.

"It may not be a problem, but we'll need to watch if this continues."

"No problem," LuLing assured her. "She no problem."

"You must encourage her to talk, Mrs. Young. I don't want this to turn into a problem."

"No problem!" her mother reiterated.

"Make her say 'hamburger' before letting her eat a hamburger. Make her say 'cookie' before she gets a cookie."

That night LuLing took the teacher's advice literally:

she served hamburger, which she had never done. LuLing did not cook or eat beef of any kind. It disgusted her, reminded her of scarred flesh. Yet now, for her daughter's sake, she put an unadorned patty in front of Ruth, who was thrilled to see her mother had actually made American food for once.

"Hambugga? You say 'hambugga,' then eat."

Ruth was tempted to speak, but she was afraid to break the spell. One word and all the good things in her life would vanish. She shook her head. LuLing encouraged her until the hamburger's rivulets of fat had congealed into ugly white pools. She put the patty in the fridge, then served Ruth a bowl of steaming rice porridge, which she said was better for her health anyway.

After dinner, LuLing cleared the dining table and started to work. She laid out ink, brushes, and a roll of paper. With quick and perfect strokes, she wrote large Chinese characters: "Going Out of Business. Last few days! No offer refused!" She set the banner aside to dry, then cut a new length of paper.

Ruth, who was watching television, noticed after a while that her mother was staring at her. "Why you not do study?" LuLing asked. She had made Ruth practice reading and writing since kindergarten, to help her be "one jump ahead."

Ruth held up her broken right arm in its cast.

"Come sit here," her mother said in Chinese.

Ruth slowly stood up. Uh-oh. Her mother was back to her old ways.

"Now hold this." LuLing placed a brush in Ruth's left hand. "Write your name." Her first attempts were clumsy, the R almost unrecognizable, the hump of the h veering off the paper like an out-of-control bicycle. She giggled.

"Hold the brush straight up," her mother instructed, "not at a slant. Use a light touch, like this."

The next results were better, but they had taken up a whole length of paper.

"Now try to write smaller." But the letters looked like blotches made by an ink-soaked fly twirling on its back. When it was finally time for bed, the practice session had consumed nearly twenty sheets of paper, both front and back. This was a sign of success as well as extravagance. LuLing never wasted anything. She gathered the used sheets, stacked them, and set them in a corner of the room. Ruth knew she would use them later, as practice sheets for her own calligraphy, as blotters for spills, as bundled-up hot pads for pans.

The following evening, after dinner, LuLing presented Ruth with a large tea tray filled with smooth wet sand gathered from the playground at school. "Here," she said, "you practice, use this." She held a chopstick in her left hand, then scratched the word "study" on the miniature beach. When she finished, she swept the sand clean and smooth with the long end of the chopstick. Ruth followed suit and found that it was easier to write this way, also fun. The sand-and-chopstick method did not require the delicate, light-handed technique of the brush. She could apply a force that steadied her. She wrote her name. Neat! It was like playing with the Etch-A-Sketch that her cousin Billy received last Christmas.

LuLing went to the refrigerator and brought out the cold beef patty. "Tomorrow what you want eat?"

And Ruth scratched back: B-U-R-G-R.

LuLing laughed. "Hah! So now you can talk back this way!"

The next day, LuLing brought the tea tray to school and

filled it with sand from the same part of the schoolyard where Ruth had broken her arm. Miss Sondegard agreed to let Ruth answer questions this way. And when Ruth raised her hand during an arithmetic drill and scrawled "7," all the other kids jumped out of their chairs to look. Soon they were clamoring that they too wanted to do sand-writing. At recess, Ruth was very popular. She heard them fussing over her. "Let me try!" "Me, me! She said I could!" "You gotta use your left hand, or it's cheating!" "Ruth, you show Tommy how to do it. He's so dumb."

They returned the chopstick to Ruth. And Ruth wrote quickly and easily the answers to their questions: Does your arm hurt? *A little.* Can I touch your cast? *Yes.* Does Ricky love Betsy? *Yes.* Will I get a new bike for my birthday? *Yes.*

They treated her as though she were Helen Keller, a genius who didn't let injury keep her from showing how smart she was. Like Helen Keller, she simply had to work harder, and perhaps this was what made her smarter, the effort and others' admiring that. Even at home, her mother would ask her, "What you think?" as if Ruth would know, just because she had to write the answers to her questions in sand.

"How does the bean curd dish taste?" LuLing asked one night.

And Ruth etched: *Salty.* She had never said anything bad about her mother's cooking before, but that was what her mother always said to criticize her own food.

"I thought so too," her mother answered.

This was amazing! Soon her mother was asking her opinion on all kinds of matters.

"We go shop dinner now or go later?" *Later.*

"What about stock market? I invest, you think I get lucky?" *Lucky.*

"You like this dress?" *No, ugly.* Ruth had never experienced such power with words.

Her mother frowned, then murmured in Mandarin. "Your father loved this old dress, and now I can never throw it away." She became misty-eyed. She sighed, then said in English: "You think you daddy miss me?"

Ruth wrote *Yes* right away. Her mother beamed. And then Ruth had an idea. She had always wanted a little dog. Now was the time to ask for one. She scratched in the sand: *Doggie.*

Her mother gasped. She stared at the words and shook her head in disbelief. Oh well, Ruth thought, that was one wish she was not going to get. But then her mother began to whimper, "Doggie, doggie," in Chinese. She jumped up and her chest heaved. "Precious Auntie," LuLing cried, "you've come back. This is your Doggie. Do you forgive me?"

Ruth put down the chopstick.

LuLing was now sobbing. "Precious Auntie, oh Precious Auntie! I wish you never died! It was all my fault. If I could change fate, I would rather kill myself than suffer without you. . . ."

Oh, no. Ruth knew what this was. Her mother sometimes talked about this Precious Auntie ghost who lived in the air, a lady who had not behaved and who wound up living at the End of the World. That was where all bad people went: a bottomless pit where no one would ever find them, and there they would be stuck, wandering with their hair hanging to their toes, wet and bloody.

"Please let me know you are not mad at me," her mother went on. "Give me a sign. I have tried to tell you how sorry

I am, but I don't know if you've heard. Can you hear me? When did you come to America?"

Ruth sat still, unable to move. She wanted to go back to talking about food and clothes.

Her mother put the chopstick in Ruth's hand. "Here, do this. Close your eyes, turn your face to heaven, and speak to her. Wait for her answer, then write it down. Hurry, close your eyes."

Ruth squeezed her eyes shut. She saw the lady with hair to her toes.

She heard her mother speak again in polite Chinese: "Precious Auntie, I did not mean what I said before you died. And after you died, I tried to find your body."

Ruth's eyes flew open. In her imagination, the long-haired ghost was walking in circles.

"I went down into the ravine. I looked and looked. Oh, I was crazy with grief. If only I had found you, I would have taken your bones to the cave and given you a proper burial."

Ruth felt something touch her shoulder, and she jumped. "Ask her if she understood everything I just said," LuLing ordered. "Ask her if my luck has changed. Is the curse over? Are we safe? Write down her answer."

What curse? Ruth now stared at the sand, half believing the dead woman's face would appear in a pool of blood. What answer did her mother want? Did *Yes* mean the curse was gone? Or that it was still there? She put the chopstick in the sand, and not knowing what to write, she drew a line and another below that. She drew two more lines and made a square.

"Mouth!" her mother cried, tracing over the square. "That's the character for 'mouth'!" She stared at Ruth. "You wrote that and you don't even know how to write

Chinese! Did you feel Precious Auntie guiding your hand? What did it feel like? Tell me."

Ruth shook her head. What was happening? She wanted to cry but didn't dare. She wasn't supposed to be able to make a sound.

"Precious Auntie, thank you for helping my daughter. Forgive me that she speaks only English. It must be hard for you to communicate through her this way. But now I know that you can hear me. And you know what I'm saying, that I wish I could take your bones to the Mouth of the Mountain, to the Monkey's Jaw. I've never forgotten. As soon as I can go to China, I will finish my duty. Thank you for reminding me."

Ruth wondered what she had written. How could a square mean all that? Was there really a ghost in the room? What was in her hand and the chopstick? Why was her hand shaking?

"Since I may not be able to go back to China for a long time," LuLing continued, "I hope you will still forgive me. Please know that my life has been miserable ever since you left me. That is why I ask you to take my life, but to spare my daughter if the curse cannot be changed. I know her recent accident was a warning."

Ruth dropped the chopstick. The lady with bloody hair was trying to kill her! So it was true, that day at the playground, she almost died. She had thought so, and it was true.

LuLing retrieved the chopstick and tried to put it in Ruth's hand. But Ruth balled her fist. She pushed the sand tray away. Her mother pushed it back and kept babbling nonsense: "I'm so happy you've finally found me. I've been waiting for so many years. Now we can talk to each other. Every day you can guide me. Every day you can tell me how to conduct my life in the way I should."

LuLing turned to Ruth. "Ask her to come every day." Ruth shook her head. She tried to slide off her chair. "Ask," LuLing insisted, and tapped the table in front of the tray. And then Ruth finally found her voice.

"No," she said out loud. "I can't."

"Wah! Now you can talk again." Her mother had switched to English. "Precious Auntie cure you?"

Ruth nodded.

"That mean curse gone?"

"Yes, but she says she has to go back now. And she said I need to rest."

"She forgive me? She—"

"She said everything will be all right. *Everything*. All right? You're not supposed to worry anymore."

Her mother sobbed with relief.

As Ruth drove her mother home after dinner, she marveled at the worries she had had at such an early age. But that was nothing compared with what most children had to go through these days. An unhappy mother? That was a piece of cake next to guns and gangs and sexually transmitted diseases, not to mention the things parents had to be concerned about: pedophiles on the Web, designer drugs like ecstasy, school shootings, anorexia, bulimia, self-mutilation, the ozone layer, superbacteria. Ruth counted these automatically on her hand, and this reminded her she had one more task to do before the end of the day: call Miriam about letting the girls come to the reunion dinner.

She glanced at her watch. It was almost nine, an iffy time to telephone people who were not close friends. True, she and Miriam were bound by the closest of reasons, the girls and their father. But they treated each other with the politeness of strangers. She often ran into Miriam at drop-off and pick-up points for the girls, at school athletic events, and once she'd seen her in the emergency room, where Ruth had taken Dory when she broke her ankle. She and Miriam made small talk about recent illnesses, bad weather, and traffic jams. If it weren't for the circumstances, they might have enjoyed each other's company. Miriam was clever, funny, and opinionated, and Ruth liked these qualities. But it bothered Ruth when Miriam made passing remarks about intimacies she had shared with Art when they were married: the funny time they had on a trip to Italy, a mole on his back that had to be checked for melanoma, his love of massage. For Art's birthday the year before, Miriam had given him a certificate for two sessions with her favorite massage therapist, a gift Ruth thought inappropriately personal. "Do you still get that mole checked every year?" Miriam asked Art on another occasion, and Ruth pretended not to hear, all the while imagining what they had been like together when they were younger and in love, and she still cared deeply enough to notice the slightest change in the size of a mole. She pictured them lazing about in a Tuscan villa with a bedroom window that overlooked rolling hills of orchards, giggling and naming moles on each other's naked backs as if they were constellations. She could see it: the two of them massaging olive oil into their thighs with long-reaching strokes. Art once tried that on her, and Ruth figured he must have learned the maneuver from *someone*. Whenever he tried to massage her thighs, though, it made her tense. With massage, she just couldn't relax. She felt she was being tickled, pushed out of control, then felt claustrophobic, panicky enough to want to leap up and run.

She never told Art about the panic; she said only that with her, massage was a waste of time and money. And although she was curious about Art's sex life with Miriam and other women, she never asked what he had done in bed with his former lovers. And he did not ask about hers. It shocked her that Wendy badgered Joe to give her explicit details about his past escapades in beds and on beaches, as well as tell her his precise feelings when he first slept with her. "And he tells you whatever you ask?" Ruth said.

"He states his name, birthdate, and Social Security number. And then I beat him up until he tells me."

"Then you're happy?"

"I'm pissed!"

"So why do you ask?"

"It's like part of me thinks everything about him is mine, his feelings, his fantasies. I know that's not right, but emotionally that's how I feel. His past is my past, it belongs to me. Shit, if I could find his childhood toy box I'd want to look inside that and say, 'Mine.' I'd want to see what girlie magazines he hid under the mattress and pulled out to masturbate to."

Ruth laughed out loud when Wendy said that, but inside she was uncomfortable. Did most women ask men those kinds of questions? Had Miriam asked Art things like these? Did more of Art's past belong to Miriam than it did to her?

Her mother's voice startled her. "So how Fu-Fu do?"

Not again. Ruth took a deep breath. "Fu-Fu's fine," she said this time.

"Really?" LuLing said. "That cat old. You lucky she not dead yet."

Ruth was so surprised she snorted in laughter. This was like the torment of being tickled. She couldn't stand it, but she could not stop her reflex to laugh out loud. Tears stung her eyes and she was glad for the darkness of the car.

"Why you laugh?" LuLing scolded. "I not kidding. And don't let dog in backyard. I know someone do this. Now cat dead!"

"You're right," Ruth answered, trying to keep her mind on the road ahead. "I'll be more careful."

FOUR

On the night of the Full Moon Festival, the Fountain Court restaurant was jammed with a line flowing out the door like a dragon's tail. Art and Ruth squeezed through the crowd. "Excuse us. We have reservations."

Inside, the dining room roared with the conversations of a hundred happy people. Children used chopsticks to play percussion on teacups and water glasses. The waiter who led Ruth and Art to their tables had to shout above the clatter of plates being delivered and taken away. As Ruth followed, she inhaled the mingled fragrances of dozens of entrées. At least the food would be good tonight.

Ruth had picked Fountain Court because it was one of the few restaurants where her mother had *not* questioned the preparation of the dishes, the attitude of the waiters, or the cleanliness of the bowls. Originally Ruth had made reservations for two tables, seating for her side of the family and friends, as well as the two girls and Art's parents, who were visiting from New Jersey. Those she had not counted on were Art's ex-wife Miriam, her husband Stephen, and their two little boys, Andy and Beauregard. Miriam had called Art the week before with a request.

When Ruth learned what the request was, she balked.

"There isn't room for four more people."

"You know Miriam," Art said. "She doesn't accept no as an answer to anything. Besides, it's the only chance my folks will have to see her before they leave for Carmel."

"So where are they going to sit? At another table?"

"We can always squeeze in more chairs," Art countered. "It's just a dinner."

To Ruth, this particular gathering was not "just a dinner." It was their Chinese thanksgiving, the reunion that she was hosting for the first time. She had given much thought to setting it up, what it should mean, what family meant, not just blood relatives but also those who were united by the past and would remain together over the years, people she was grateful to have in her life. She wanted to thank all the celebrants for their contribution to her feeling of family. Miriam would be a reminder that the past was not always good and the future was uncertain. But to say all this would sound petty to Art, and Fia and Dory would think she was being mean.

Without more disagreement, Ruth made the last-minute changes: Called the restaurant to change the head count. Revised the seating plan. Ordered more dishes for two adults and two children who didn't like Chinese food all that much. She suspected that Fia's and Dory's fussiness over unfamiliar food came from their mother.

Art's parents were the first to arrive at the restaurant. "Arlene, Marty," Ruth greeted them. They exchanged polite two-cheek kisses. Arlene hugged her son, and Marty gave a light two-punch to his shoulder and then his jaw. "You knock me out," Art said, supplying their traditional father-son refrain.

The Kamens were impeccable in their classy outfits and stood out amid the crowd of casually attired customers. Ruth wore an Indonesian batik-print top and crinkled

skirt. It occurred to her that Miriam dressed like the Kamens, in designer-style clothing that had to be profession-
ally pressed and dry-cleaned. Miriam loved Art's parents,
and they adored her, whereas, Ruth felt, the Kamens had
never warmed to her. Even though she had met Art after
the divorce was nearly final, Marty and Arlene probably
saw her as the interloper, the reason Miriam and Art did
not reconcile. Ruth had sensed that the Kamens hoped she
was only a brief interlude in Art's life. They never knew
how to introduce her. "This is Art's, uh, Ruth," they'd say.
They were nice to her, certainly. They had given her lovely
birthday presents, a silk velvet scarf, Chanel No. 5, a lacquered tea tray, but nothing she might share with Art or
pass on to his girls—or any future children, for that matter,
since she was beyond the possibility of giving the Kamens
additional grandchildren. Miriam, on the other hand, was
now and forever the mother of the Kamens' granddaugh-
ters, the keeper of heirlooms for Fia and Dory. Marty and
Arlene already had given her the family sterling, china,
and the mezuzah kissed by five generations of Kamens
since the days they lived in the Ukraine.

"Miriam! Stephen!" Ruth exclaimed with enthusiastic
effort. She shook hands, and Miriam gave her a quick hug
and waved to Art across the table. "Glad you could join
us," Ruth said awkwardly, then turned to the boys. "Andy,
Beauregard, how you doing?"

The younger one, who was four, piped up: "I'm called
Boomer now."

"It's awfully nice of you to include us," Miriam gushed
to Ruth. "I hope it wasn't any trouble."

"Not at all."

Miriam opened wide her arms toward Marty and Arlene, and rushed to give them effusive hugs. She was

wearing a maroon-and-olive outfit with a huge circular pleated collar. Her copper-colored hair was cut in a severe page boy. Ruth was reminded why the hairstyle was called that. Miriam looked like one of those pages in Renaissance paintings.

Ruth's cousin Billy—now called Bill by others—showed up, trailed by his second wife, Dawn, and their combined four children, ages nine through seventeen. Ruth and Billy rocked in embrace. He thumped her back, as guys did with their buddies. He had been a skinny brat and a bully to Ruth in childhood, but those qualities had turned out to be leadership skills. Today he ran a biotech company and had grown chubby with success. "God, it's good to see you," he said. Ruth immediately felt better about the dinner.

Sally, always the social one, made a loud entrance, shouting names and squealing as her husband and two boys followed. She was an aeronautical engineer, who traveled widely as an expert witness for law firms, plaintiff attorneys only. She inspected records and sites of airplane disasters, mostly small craft. Always a talker, she was perky and outgoing, not intimidated by anyone or any new adventure. Her husband, George, was a violinist with the San Francisco Symphony, quiet but happy to take the lead whenever Sally fed him a line. "George, tell them about the dog that ran onstage at Stern Grove and peed on the microphone and shorted out the entire sound system." Then George would repeat exactly what Sally had just said.

Ruth looked up and saw Wendy and Joe, gazing about the crowd. Behind them was Gideon, nattily dressed and perfectly groomed as usual, holding an expensive bouquet of tropical flowers. When Wendy turned and saw him, she smiled in mock delight, and he pretended to be just as enthusiastic. She had once called him "a star-fucker who practically gives himself neck strain looking past your shoulder for more important people to talk to." Gideon, in turn, had said that Wendy was "a vulgarian, who lacks the nuance to know why it's not good manners to grace every-body with lurid details of one's menstrual problems at the dinner table." Ruth had thought about inviting one and not the other, but in a stupid moment of resolve, she decided they would just have to work it out between them, even if it gave her heartburn to watch.

Wendy waved both hands when she spotted Ruth, and then she and Joe eased their way through the restaurant. Gideon trailed a comfortable distance behind. "We found a parking space right in front!" Wendy boasted. She held up her lucky charm, a plastic angel with the face of a parking meter. "I tell you, works every time!" She had given one to Ruth, who had placed it on the dashboard but only received parking tickets. "Hi, sweetie," Gideon said in his usual low-key manner. "You're looking radiant. Or is that sweat and nervousness?" Ruth, who had told him on the phone about Miriam's crashing the party, kissed him on both cheeks and whispered where Art's ex was. He had already suggested he act as spy and report everything appalling that she said.

Art came up to Ruth. "How's it going?"

"Where are Fia and Dory?"

"They went to check out a CD at Green Apple Annex."

"You let them go by themselves?"

"It's just up the street, and they said they'd be back in ten minutes."

"So where are they?"

"Probably abducted."

"That's *not* funny." Her mother used to say it was bad luck even to speak words like that. On cue, LuLing entered, her petite frame contrasting with GaoLing's sturdier one. A few seconds later, Uncle Edmund came in. Ruth sometimes wondered whether this was how her father would have looked—tall, stoop-shouldered, with a crown of thick white hair and a large, relaxed swing to his arms and legs. Uncle Edmund was given to telling jokes badly, consoling scared children, and dispensing stock market tips. LuLing often said the two brothers weren't similar at all, that Ruth's father had been much more handsome, smarter, and very honest. His only fault was that he was too trusting, also maybe absentminded when he was concentrating too hard, just like Ruth. LuLing often recounted the circumstances in which he died as a warning to Ruth when she was not paying attention to her mother. "You daddy see green light, he trust that car stop. Poom! Run over, drag him one block, two block, never stop." She said he died because of a curse, the same one that made Ruth break her arm. And because the subject of the curse often came up when LuLing was displeased with Ruth, as a child Ruth thought the curse and her father's death were related to her. She had recurrent nightmares of mutilating people in a brakeless car. She always tested and retested her brakes before heading out in the car.

Even from across the big room, Ruth could see that LuLing was beaming at her with motherly adoration. This gave Ruth heart pangs, made her both happy and sad to see her mother on this special day. Why wasn't their relationship always like this? How many more gatherings like this would they have?

"Happy Full Moon," Ruth said when her mother reached the table. She motioned for LuLing to sit next to her. Auntie Gal took the other chair next to Ruth, and then the rest of the family sat down. Ruth saw that Art was with

Miriam at the other table, what was fast becoming the non-Chinese section.

"Hey, are we in the white ghetto or what?" Wendy called out. She was sitting with her back to Ruth.

When Fia and Dory finally showed up, Ruth did not feel she could chastise them in front of their mother or Arlene and Marty. They did a mass wave, "Hi, everybody," then gurgled, "Hi, Bubbie and Poppy," and threw their arms around their grandparents' necks. The girls never voluntarily hugged LuLing.

The dinner began with a flurry of appetizers set on the lazy Susan, what LuLing called the "go-round." The adults oohed and aahed, the children cried, "I'm starved!" The waiters set down what Ruth had ordered by phone: sweetly glazed phoenix-tail fish, vegetarian chicken made out of wrinkly tissues of tofu, and jellyfish, her mother's favorite, seasoned with sesame oil and sprinkled with diced green onions. "Tell me," Miriam said, "is that animal, vegetable, or mineral?"

"Here, Ma," Ruth said, holding the jellyfish platter, "you start since you're the oldest girl."

"No-no!" LuLing said automatically. "You help youself."

Ruth ignored this rite of first refusal and placed a heap of noodle-like strands of jellyfish on her mother's plate. LuLing immediately started to eat.

"What's that?" Ruth heard Boomer ask at the other table. He scowled at the jiggling mound of jellyfish as it swung by on the lazy Susan.

"Worms!" Dory teased. "Try some."

"Ewww! Take it away! Take it away!" Boomer screamed. Dory was hysterical with laughter. Art passed along the entire table's worth of jellyfish to Ruth, and Ruth felt her stomach begin to ache.

More dishes arrived, each one stranger than the last, to judge by the expressions on the non-Chinese faces. Tofu with pickled greens. Sea cucumbers, Auntie Gal's favorite. And glutinous rice cakes. Ruth had thought the kids would like those. She had thought wrong.

Halfway through the dinner, Nicky, Sally's six-year-old, spun the go-round, perhaps thinking he could launch it like a Frisbee, and the spout of a teapot knocked over a water glass. LuLing yelped and jumped up. Water dripped from her lap. "*Ai-ya!* Why you do this?"

Nicky crossed his arms, and tears started to well up in his eyes.

"It's okay, honey," Sally told him. "Say you're sorry, and next time spin it more slowly."

"She was mean to me." He aimed a pout in the direction of LuLing, who was now busy dabbing at her lap with a napkin.

"Sweetie, Grand-Auntie was just surprised, that's all. It's only that you're so strong—like a baseball player."

Ruth hoped her mother would not continue to berate Nicky. She remembered when her mother would enumerate all the times she had spilled food or milk, asking aloud to unseen forces why Ruth could not learn to behave. Ruth looked at Nicky and imagined what she would have been like if she had had children. Perhaps she too would have reacted like her mother, unable to restrain the impulse to scold until the child acted beaten and contrite.

More drinks were ordered. Ruth noticed Art was on his second glass of wine. He also seemed to be having an animated conversation with Miriam. Another round of dishes arrived, just in time to dissipate the tension. Eggplant sautéed with fresh basil leaves, a tender sable fish coated in a mantle of garlic chips, a Chinese version of polenta

smothered in a spicy meat sauce, plump black mushrooms, a Lion's Head clay pot of meatballs and rice vermi-
celli. Even the "foreigners," LuLing reported, enjoyed the
food. Above the noise, Auntie Gal leaned toward Ruth and
said: "Your mother and I, we ate excellent dishes at Sun
Hong Kong last week. But then we almost went to jail!"
Auntie Gal liked to throw out zingers and wait for listeners
to take the bait.

Ruth obliged. "Jail?"

"Oh, yes! Your mother got into a big fight with the
waiter, said she already paid the bill." Auntie Gal shook
her head. "The waiter was right, it was not yet paid." She
patted Ruth's hand. "Don't worry! Later, when your mother
was not looking, I paid. So you see, no jail, and here we
are!" GaoLing took a few more bites of food, smacked her
lips, then leaned toward Ruth again and whispered, "I gave
your mother a big bag of ginseng root. This is good to cure
confusion." She nodded, and Ruth nodded in turn. "Sometimes your mother calls me at the train station to say she's
here, and I don't even know she's coming! Course, this is
fine, I always welcome her. But at six in the morning? I'm
not an early birdie!" She chuckled, and Ruth, her mind
awhirl, gave out a hollow laugh.

What was wrong with her mother? Could depression
cause confusion like this? The next week, when they had
the follow-up visit with Dr. Huey, she would discuss it
with him. If he ordered her mother to take antidepressants,
maybe she would obey. Ruth knew she should visit her
mother more often. LuLing often complained of loneli-
ness, and she was obviously trying to fill a void by going to
see GaoLing at odd hours.

During the lull before dessert, Ruth stood up and gave a
brief speech. "As the years go on, I see how much family

means. It reminds us of what's important. That connection to the past. The same jokes about being Young yet getting old. The traditions. The fact that we can't get rid of each other no matter how much we try. We're stuck through the ages, with the bonds cemented by sticky rice and tapioca pudding. Thank you all for being who you are." She left out individual tributes since she had nothing to say about Miriam and her party.

Ruth then passed out wrapped boxes of moon cakes and chocolate rabbits to the children. "Thank you!" they cried. "This is neat!" At last Ruth was somewhat becalmed. It was a good idea to host this dinner after all. In spite of the uneasy moments, reunions were important, a ritual to preserve what was left of the family. She did not want her cousins and her to drift apart, but she feared that once the older generation was gone, that would be the end of the family ties. They had to make the effort.

"More presents," Ruth called out, and handed out packages. She had found a wonderful old photo of LuLing and Auntie Gal as girls, flanking their mother. She had a negative made of the original, then ordered eight-by-tens and had those framed. She wanted this to be a meaningful tribute to her family, a gift that would last forever. And indeed, the recipients gave appreciative sighs.

"This is amazing," Billy said. "Hey, kids, guess who those two cute girls are?"

"Look at us, so young," Auntie Gal sighed wistfully.

"Hey, Auntie Lu," Sally teased. "You look kind of bummed-out in this picture."

LuLing answered: "This because my mother just die."

Ruth thought her mother had misheard Sally. "Bummed out" was not in LuLing's vocabulary. LuLing and GaoLing's mother had died in 1972. Ruth pointed to the photo. "See? Your mother is right there. And that's you."

LuLing shook her head. "That not my real mother."

Ruth's mind turned in loops, trying to translate what her mother meant. Auntie Gal gave Ruth a peculiar look, tightening her chin so as not to say anything. Others had quiet frowns of concern.

"That's Waipo, isn't it?" Ruth said to Auntie Gal, struggling to stay nonchalant. When GaoLing nodded, Ruth said happily to her mother, "Well, if that's your sister's mother, she must be yours as well."

LuLing snorted. "GaoLing *not* my sister!"

Ruth could hear her pulse pounding in her brain. Billy cleared his throat in an obvious bid to change the subject.

Her mother went on: "She my sister-in-*law*."

Everyone now guffawed. LuLing had delivered the punch line to a joke! Of course, they were indeed sisters-in-law, married to a pair of brothers. What a relief! Her mother not only made sense, she was clever.

Auntie Gal turned to LuLing and huffed with pretend annoyance. "Hey, why do you treat me so bad, hah?"

LuLing was fishing for something in her wallet. She pulled out a tiny photo, then handed it to Ruth. "There," she said in Chinese. "This one right here, she's my mother." A chill ran over Ruth's scalp. It was a photograph of her mother's nursemaid, Bao Bomu, Precious Auntie.

She wore a high-collared jacket and a strange headdress that looked as if it were made of ivory. Her beauty was ethereal. She had wide tilted eyes, with a direct and immodest stare. Her arched eyebrows suggested a questioning mind, her full lips a sensuality that was indecent for the times. The picture obviously had been taken before the accident that burned her face and twisted it into a constant expression of horror. As Ruth peered more closely at the photo, the woman's expression seemed even more oddly disturbing, as if she could see into the future and knew it was cursed. This was the crazy woman who had cared for her mother since birth, who had smothered LuLing with fears and superstitious notions. LuLing had told her that when she was fourteen, this nursemaid killed herself in a gruesome way that was "too bad to say." Whatever means the nursemaid used, she also made LuLing believe it was her fault. Precious Auntie was the reason her mother was convinced she could never be happy, why she always had to expect the worst, fretting until she found it.

Ruth quietly tried to steer her mother back to coherence. "That was your nursemaid," she coaxed. "I guess you're saying she was *like* a mother to you."

"No, *this* really my mother," LuLing insisted. "That one GaoLing mother." She held up the framed photo. In a daze, Ruth heard Sally asking Billy how the skiing was in Argentina the month before. Uncle Edmund was encouraging his grandson to try a black mushroom. Ruth kept asking herself, What's happening? What's happening?

She felt her mother tapping her arm. "I have present for you too. Early birthday, give you now." She reached into her purse and pulled out a plain white box, tied with ribbon.

"What's this?"

"Open, don't ask."

The box was light. Ruth slipped off the ribbon, lifted the lid, and saw a gleam of gray. It was a necklace of irregularly shaped black pearls, each as large as a gumball. Was this a test? Or had her mother really forgotten that Ruth had given her this as a gift years before? LuLing grinned knowingly—Oh yes, daughter cannot believe her luck!

"Best things take now," LuLing went on. "No need wait to I dead." She turned away before Ruth could either refuse or thank her. "Anyway, this not worth much." She was patting the back of her bun, trying to stuff pride back into her head. It was a gesture Ruth had seen many times. "If someone show-off give big," her mother would say, "this not really giving big." A lot of her admonitions had to do with *not* showing what you really meant about all sorts of things: hope, disappointment, and especially love. The less you showed, the more you meant.

"This necklace been in my family long time," Ruth heard her mother say. Ruth stared at the beads, remembered when she first saw the necklace in a shop on Kauai. "Tahiti-style black pearls," the tag said, a twenty-dollar bit of glassy junk to wear against sweaty skin on a tropically bright day. She had gone to the island with Art, the two of them newly in love. Later, when she returned home, she realized she had forgotten her mother's birthday, had not even thought to telephone while she was sipping mai-tais on a sandy beach. She had boxed the twice-worn trinket, and by giving her mother something that had crossed the ocean, she hoped she would also give the impression she had been thinking of her. Her downfall lay in being honest when she insisted the necklace was "nothing much," because LuLing mistook this modesty to mean the gift was quite expensive and thus the bona fide article, proof of a daughter's love. She wore it everywhere, and Ruth would feel the slap of guilt whenever she overheard her mother boast to her friends, "Look what my daughter Lootie buy me."

"Oh, very pretty!" GaoLing murmured, glancing at what Ruth held in her hand. "Let me see," and before Ruth could think, GaoLing snatched the box. Her lips grew

tight. "Mmm," she said, examining the bauble. Had Auntie
Gal seen this before? How many times had LuLing worn it
to her house, bragging about its worth? And had GaoLing
known all along that the necklace was fake, that Ruth, the
good daughter, was also a fake?

"Let me see," Sally said.

"Careful," LuLing warned when Sally's son reached for
the pearls, "don't touch. Cost too much."

Soon the pearls were making the rounds at the other
table as well. Art's mother gave the necklace an especially
critical eye, weighing it in her hand. "Just *lovely*," she said
to LuLing, a bit too emphatically. Miriam simply observed, "Those beads are certainly large." Art gave the
pearls a once-over and cleared his throat.

"Eh, what wrong?"

Ruth turned and saw her mother scrutinizing her face.

"Nothing," Ruth mumbled. "I'm just a little tired, I
guess."

"Nonsense!" her mother said in Chinese. "I can see
something is blocked inside and can't come out."

"Watch it! Spy talk!" Dory called from the other table.

"Something is wrong," LuLing persisted. Ruth was
amazed that her mother was so perceptive. Maybe there
was nothing the matter with her after all.

"It's that wife of Art's," Ruth finally whispered in her
American-accented Mandarin. "I wish Art had not let her
come."

"Ah! You see, I was right! I knew something was wrong.
Mother always knows."

Ruth bit hard on the inside of her cheek.

"Now, now, don't worry anymore," her mother soothed.
"Tomorrow you talk to Artie. Make him buy you a gift. He
should pay a lot to show that he values you. He should buy

you something like this." LuLing touched the necklace, which had been returned to Ruth's hands.

Ruth's eyes smarted with held-back tears.

"You like?" LuLing said proudly, switching back to the public language of English. "This real things, you know."

Ruth held up the necklace. She saw how the dark pearls glistened, this gift that had risen from the bottom of the sea.

FIVE

Ruth held LuLing's arm as they walked to the hospital parking garage. Her slack-skinned limb felt like the bony wing of a baby bird.

LuLing acted alternately cheerful and cranky, unchanged by what had just transpired in the doctor's office. Ruth, however, sensed that her mother was growing hollow, that soon she would be as light as driftwood. *Dementia.* Ruth puzzled over the diagnosis: How could such a beautiful-sounding word apply to such a destructive disease? It was a name befitting a goddess: Dementia, who caused her sister Demeter to forget to turn winter into spring. Ruth now imagined icy plaques forming on her mother's brain, drawing out moisture. Dr. Huey had said the MRI showed shrinkage in certain parts of the brain that were consistent with Alzheimer's. He also said the disease had probably started "years ago." Ruth had been too stunned to ask any questions at the time, but she now wondered what the doctor meant by "years ago." Twenty? Thirty? Forty? Maybe there was a reason her mother had been so difficult when Ruth was growing up, why she had talked about curses and ghosts and threats to kill herself. Dementia was her mother's redemption, and God would forgive them both for having hurt each other all these years.

"Lootie, what doctor say?" LuLing's question startled Ruth. They were standing in front of the car. "He say I die soon?" she asked humorously.

"No." And for emphasis, Ruth laughed. "Of course not."

Her mother studied Ruth's face, then concluded: "I die, doesn't matter. I not afraid. You know this."

"Dr. Huey said your heart is fine," Ruth added. She tried to figure a way to translate the diagnosis into a condition her mother would accept. "But he said you may be having another kind of problem—with a balance of elements in your body. And this can give you troubles . . . with your memory." She helped LuLing into the front seat and snapped her seat belt in place.

LuLing sniffed. "Hnh! Nothing wrong my memory! I 'member lots things, more than you. Where I live little-girl time, place we call Immortal Heart, look like heart, two river, one stream, both dry-out. . . ." She continued talking as Ruth went to the other side of the car, got in, and started the engine. "What he know? That doctor don't even use telescope listen my heart. Nobody listen my heart! You don't listen. GaoLing don't listen. You know my heart always hurting. I just don't complain. Am I complain?"

"No—"

"See!"

"But the doctor said sometimes you forget things because you're depressed."

"Depress 'cause can *not* forgot! Look my sad life!"

Ruth pumped the brakes to make sure they would hold, then steered the car down the falling turns of the parking garage. Her mother's voice droned in rhythm with the engine: "Of course depress. When Precious Auntie die, all happiness leave my body. . . ."

Since the diagnosis three months before, LuLing had come to Art and Ruth's for dinner almost every night. Tonight Ruth watched her mother take a bite of salmon. LuLing chewed slowly, then choked. "Too salty," she gasped, as if she had been given deer lick for the main course.

"Waipo," Dory interjected, "Ruth didn't add any salt. I watched. *None.*"

Fia kicked Dory. She made an X with her index fingers, the symbolic cross that keeps movie Draculas at bay. Dory kicked her back.

Now that Ruth could no longer blame her mother's problems on the eccentricities of her personality, she saw the signs of dementia everywhere. They were so obvious. How could she not have noticed before? The time-shares and "free vacations" her mother ordered via junk mail. The accusations that Auntie Gal had stolen money from her. The way LuLing obsessed for days about a bus driver who accused her of not paying the fare. And there were new problems that caused Ruth to worry into the night. Her mother often forgot to lock the front door. She left food to defrost on the counter until it became rancid. She turned on the cold water and left it running for days, waiting for it to become hot. Some changes actually made life easier. For one thing, LuLing no longer said anything when Art poured himself another glass of wine, as he was doing tonight. "Why drink so much?" she used to ask. And Ruth had secretly wondered the same. She once mentioned to him that he might want to cut back before it became a habit. "You should take up juicing again." And he had calmly pointed out that she was acting like her mother. "A couple of glasses of wine at dinner is not a problem. It's a personal choice."

"Dad?" Fia asked. "Can we get a kitten?"

"Yeah," Dory jumped in. "Alice has the cutest Himalayan. That's what we want."

"Maybe," Art replied.

Ruth stared at her plate. Had he forgotten? She had told him she was not ready for another cat. She would feel disloyal to Fu-Fu. And when the time was right for another pet, an animal she inevitably would wind up feeding and cleaning, she preferred that it be a different species, a little dog.

"I once drive to Himalaya, long ways by myself," LuLing bragged. "Himalaya very high up, close to moon."

Art and the girls exchanged baffled looks. LuLing often issued what they considered non sequiturs, as free-floating as dust motes. But Ruth believed LuLing's delusions were always rooted in a deeper reason. Clearly this instance had to do with word association: Himalayan kitten, Himalayan mountains. But why did LuLing believe she had driven there by car? It was Ruth's job to untangle such puzzles. If she could find the source, she could help LuLing unclog the pathways in her brain and prevent more destructive debris from accumulating. With diligence, she could keep her from driving off a cliff in the Himalayas. And then it occurred to her: "My mother and I saw this really interesting documentary on Tibet last week," Ruth said. "They showed the road that leads to—"

But Dory interrupted her to say to LuLing, "You can't *drive* to the Himalayas from here."

LuLing frowned. "Why you say this?"

Dory, who like LuLing often acted on impulse, blurted, "You just can't. I mean, you're crazy if you think—"

"Okay I crazy!" LuLing sputtered. "Why you should believe me?" Her anger escalated like water in a teakettle— Ruth saw it, the rolling bubbles, the steam—and then LuLing erupted with the ultimate threat: "Maybe I die soon! Then everybody happy!"

Fia and Dory shrugged and gave each other knowing looks: Oh, this again. LuLing's outbursts were becoming more frequent, more abrupt. Fortunately, they quickly abated, and the girls were not that affected by them. Nor did they become more sensitive to the problem, it seemed to Ruth. She had tried to explain several times to them that they shouldn't contradict anything LuLing said: "Waipo sounds illogical because she is. We can't change that. This is the disease talking, not her." But it was hard for them to remember, just as it was hard for Ruth not to react to her mother's threats to die. No matter how often she had heard them, they never ceased to grab her by the throat. And now the threat seemed very real—her mother was dying, first her brain, then her body.

The girls picked up their plates. "I have homework," Fia said. "Night, Waipo."

"Me, too," Dory said. "Bye, Waipo."

LuLing waved from across the table. Ruth had once asked the girls to give LuLing kisses. But she had stiffened in response to their pecks.

Art stood up. "I have some documents to look over for tomorrow. Better get started. Good night, LuLing."

When LuLing toddled off to the bathroom, Ruth went to the living room to speak to Art. "She's getting worse."

"I noticed." Art was shuffling papers.

"I'm afraid to leave her alone when we go to Hawaii."

"What are you going to do?"

She noted with dismay that he had asked what *she* would do, had not said "we." Since the Full Moon Festival dinner, she had become more aware of the ways she and Art failed to be a family. She had tried to push this out of her mind, but it crept back, confirming to her that it was not an unnecessary worry. Why did she feel she didn't belong to anyone? Did she unconsciously choose to love people who kept their distance? Was she like her mother, destined to be unhappy?

She couldn't fault Art. He had always been honest about their relationship. From the beginning, he said he didn't want to marry again. "I don't want us to operate by assumptions," he had told her, cradling her in bed soon after they started to live together. "I want us to look at each other every morning and ask, 'Who is this amazing person I'm so lucky to love?' " At the time, she felt adored like a goddess. After the second year, he had spontaneously offered to give her a percentage ownership in the flat. Ruth had been touched by his generosity, his concern for her security. He knew how much she worried over the future. And the fact that they had not yet changed the deed? Well, that was more her fault than his. She was supposed to decide on the percentage interest she should have, then call the lawyer and set up the paperwork. But how could you express love as a percentage? She felt as she had when a college history professor of hers had told the students in the class to grade themselves. Ruth had given herself a B — and everyone else had taken an A.

"You could hire someone to check on your mother a few times a week," Art suggested. "Like a housekeeper."

"That's true."

"And call that service, Meals on Wheels. They might be able to deliver food while we're gone."

"That's an idea."

"In fact, why don't you start now, so she gets used to the food? Not that she isn't welcome to dinner here whenever she wants. . . . Listen, I really have to get some work done now. Are you going to take her home soon?"

"I guess."

"When you get back, we'll have some rum raisin ice cream." He named her favorite flavor. "It'll make you feel better."

LuLing had objected to the idea of having anyone come to her house to help clean. Ruth had anticipated she would. Her mother hated spending money on anything she believed she could do herself, from hair coloring to roof repairs.

"It's for an immigrant training program," Ruth lied, "so they won't have to go on welfare. And we don't have to pay anything. They're doing it free so they can put work experience on their résumé." LuLing readily accepted this reasoning. Ruth felt like a bad child. She would be caught. Or maybe she wouldn't, and that would be worse. Another reminder that the disease had impaired her mother's ability to know and see everything.

A few days after the first housekeeper started, LuLing called to complain: "She think come to America everything so easy. She want take break, then tell me, Lady, I don't do move furniture, I don't do window, I don't do iron. I ask her, You think you don't lift finger become millionaire? No, America not this way!"

LuLing continued to give the immigrant good advice until she quit. Ruth started interviewing new prospects, and until someone was hired, she decided she should go to LuLing's a few times a week to make sure the gas burners weren't on and water wasn't flooding the apartment. "I was in the neighborhood to drop off some work for a client," she explained one day.

"Ah, always for client. Work first, mother second."

Ruth went to the kitchen, carrying a bag of oranges, toilet paper, and other grocery essentials. While there, she checked for disasters and danger. The last time she'd been there, she found that LuLing had tried to fry eggs with the shells still on. Ruth did a quick sweep of the dining room table and picked up more junk mail offers LuLing had filled out. "I'll mail these for you, Mom," she said. She then went into the bathroom to make sure the faucets weren't running. Where were the towels? There was no shampoo, only a thin slice of cracked soap. How long had it been since her mother had bathed? She looked in the hamper. Nothing there. Was her mother wearing the same clothes every day?

The second housekeeper lasted less than a week. On the days she didn't visit, Ruth felt uneasy, distracted. She was not sleeping well and had broken a molar grinding her teeth at night. She was too tired to cook and ordered pizza several times a week, giving up her resolve to set a low-fat example for Dory, and then having to endure LuLing's remarks that the pepperoni was too salty. Recently Ruth had developed spasms across her shoulders that made it hard to sit at her desk and work at her computer. She didn't have enough fingers and toes to keep track of everything. When she found a Filipina who specialized in elder care, she felt a huge burden removed. "I love old people," the woman assured her. "They're not difficult if you take time to get to know them."

But now it was night, and Ruth lay awake listening to the foghorns warning ships to stay clear of the shallows. The day before, when she picked up her mother for dinner, Ruth learned that the Filipina had quit.

"Gone," LuLing said, looking satisfied.

"When?"

"Never work!"

"But she was at your house until what? Two days ago? Three days ago?"

After more questioning, Ruth deduced that the woman had not been coming since the day after she started. Ruth would never be able to find another person before she left for Hawaii. That was only two days from now. A vacation across the ocean was out of the question.

"You go," Ruth told Art in the morning. They had already paid for the rental, and there was a no-refund policy.

"If you don't go, what fun would that be? What would I do?"

"Not work. Not get up. Not return phone calls."

"It won't be the same."

"You'll miss me dreadfully and tell me you were miserable."

Eventually, much to Ruth's chagrin, he agreed with her logic.

The next morning, Art left for Hawaii. The girls were at Miriam's for the week, and though Ruth was accustomed to working alone during the day, she felt empty and anxious. Soon after she settled in at her desk, Gideon called to say that the *Internet Spirituality* author had fired her— *fired,* a first in her career. Although she had finished his book earlier than scheduled, he had not liked what she had written. "I'm as pissed as you are," Gideon said. And Ruth knew she should be outraged, maybe even humiliated, but in fact, she was relieved. One less thing to think about. "I'll try to do damage control with the contract and HarperSan Francisco," Gideon went on, "but I may also need for you to document your time spent and outline why his complaints were not in keeping with reality. . . . Hello? Ruth, are you still there?"

"Sorry. I was a little preoccupied. . . ."

"Hon, I've been meaning to talk to you about that. Not to imply that you're somehow at fault for what happened. But I am concerned that you haven't been your usual self. You seem—"

"I know, I know. I'm not going to Hawaii, so I can catch up."

"I think that's a good idea. By the way, I think we're going to hear about that other book project today, but frankly I don't think you'll get it. You should have told them you had an emergency appendectomy or something." Ruth had failed to show up at an interview because her mother had called in a panic, thinking her alarm clock was the smoke detector going off.

At four, Agapi called to discuss final edits for *Righting the Wronged Child*. An hour later, they were still talking. Agapi was eager to start a new book, which she wanted to call either *Past-Perfect Tension* or *The Embedded Self*. Ruth kept staring at the clock. She was supposed to pick up her mother at six for dinner at Fountain Court. "Habit, neuro-musculature, and the limbic system, that's the basis . . ." Agapi was saying. "From babyhood and our first sense of insecurity, we clench, grasp, flail. We *embed* the response but forget the cause, the past that was imperfect. . . . Ruth, my dear, you seem to be somewhere else. Should you ring me later when you feel more refreshed?"

At five-fifteen, Ruth called her mother to remind her she

was coming. No answer. She was probably in the bathroom. Ruth waited five minutes, then called again. Still no answer. Did she have constipation? Had she fallen asleep? Ruth tidied her desk, put the phone on speaker, and hit automatic redial. After fifteen minutes of unanswered ringing, she had run through all the possibilities, until they culminated in the inevitable worst possible thing. Flames leaping from a pot left on the stove. LuLing dousing the flames with oil. Her sleeve catching fire. As Ruth drove to her mother's, she braced herself to see a crackling blaze eating the roof, her mother lying twisted in a blackened heap.

Just as she feared, when Ruth arrived she saw lights flickering in the upper level, shadows dancing. She rushed in. The front door was unlocked. "Mom? Mommy! Where are you?" The television was on, blasting *Amor sin Límite* at high volume. LuLing had never figured out how to use the remote control, even though Ruth had taped over all but the Power, Channel Up, and Channel Down buttons. She turned off the TV, and the sudden silence frightened her.

She ran to the back rooms, flung open closets, looked out the windows. Her throat tightened. "Mommy, where are you?" she whimpered. "Answer me." She ran down the front steps and knocked on the tenant's door.

She tried to sound casual. "By any chance, have you seen my mother?"

Francine rolled her eyes and nodded knowingly. "She went charging down the sidewalk about two or three hours ago. I noticed because she was wearing slippers and pajamas, and I said to myself, 'Wow, she looks really flipped out.' . . . Like it's none of my business, but you should take her to the doctor and get her medicated or something. I mean that in the good sense."

Ruth raced back upstairs. With shaky fingers, she called a former client who was a captain in the police department. Minutes later, a Latino officer stood at the doorway. He was bulging with weapons and paraphernalia and his face was serious. Ruth's panic notched up. She stepped outside.

"She has Alzheimer's," Ruth jabbered. "She's seventy-seven but has the mind of a child."

"Description."

"Four-eleven, eighty-five pounds, black hair pulled into a bun, probably wearing pink or lilac pajamas and slippers . . ." Ruth was picturing LuLing as she said this: the puzzled look on her mother's face, her inert body lying in the street. Ruth's voice started to wobble. "Oh God, she's so tiny and helpless. . . ."

"Does she look anything like that lady there?"

Ruth looked up to see LuLing standing stock still at the end of the walkway. She was wearing a sweater over her pajamas.

"*Ai-ya!* What happen?" LuLing cried. "Robber?"

Ruth ran toward her. "Where were you?" She appraised her mother for signs of damage.

The officer walked up to the two of them. "Happy ending," he said, then turned toward his patrol car.

"Stay there," Ruth ordered her mother. "I'll be right back." She went to the patrol car and the officer rolled down his window. "I'm sorry for all the trouble," she said. "She's never done this before." And then she considered that maybe she had, but she just didn't know it. Maybe she did this every day, every night. Maybe she roamed the neighborhood in her underwear!

"Hey, no problem," the policeman said. "My mother-in-law did the same thing. Sundowning. The sun went down, she went wandering. We had to put alarm triggers on all the doors. That was one tough year, until we put her in a nursing home. My wife couldn't do it anymore—keeping an eye on her day and night."

Day and night? And Ruth thought she was being diligent by having her mother over for dinner and trying to hire a part-time housekeeper. "Well, thanks anyway," she said.

When she returned to her mother, LuLing complained right away: "Grocery store 'round the corner? I walk 'round and 'round, gone! Turn into bank. You don't believe, go see youself!"

Ruth wound up staying the night at her mother's, sleeping in her old bedroom. The foghorns were louder in this section of the city. She remembered listening to them at night when she was a teenager. She would lie in bed, counting the blasts, matching them to the number of years it would be before she could move out. Five years, then four, then three. Now she was back.

In the morning, Ruth opened the cupboards to look for cereal. She found dirty paper napkins folded and stacked. Hundreds. She opened the fridge. It was packed with plastic bags of black and greenish mush, cartons of half-eaten food, orange peels, cantaloupe rinds, frozen goods long defrosted. In the freezer were a carton of eggs, a pair of shoes, the alarm clock, and what appeared to have been bean sprouts. Ruth felt sick. This had happened in just one week?

She called Art in Kauai. There was no answer. She pictured him lying serenely on the beach, oblivious to all problems in the world. But how could he be on the beach? It was six in the morning there. Where was he? Hula dancing in someone's bed? Another thing to worry about. She could call Wendy, but Wendy would simply commiserate by saying her own mother was doing far crazier things. How about Gideon? He was more concerned about clients and contracts. Ruth decided to call Auntie Gal.

"Worse? How can she be worse?" GaoLing said. "I gave her ginseng, and she said she was taking it every day."

"The doctor said none of those things will help—"

"Doctor!" GaoLing snorted. "I don't believe this diagnosis, Alzheimer's. Your uncle said the same thing, and he's a dentist. Everybody gets old, everybody forgets. When you're old, there's too much to remember. I ask you, Why didn't anyone have this disease twenty, thirty years ago? The problem is, today kids have no time anymore to see parents. Your mommy's lonely, that's all. She has no one to talk to in Chinese. Of course her mind is a little rusted. If you stop speaking, no oil for the squeaky wheel!"

"Well, that's why I need your help. Can she come visit you, maybe for the week? It's just that I have a lot of work this week and can't spend as much time—"

"No need to ask. I'm already offering. I'll come get her in one hour. I need to do some shopping there anyway."

Ruth wanted to weep with relief.

After Auntie Gal left with her mother, Ruth walked a few blocks to the beach, to Land's End. She needed to hear the pummeling waves, their constancy and loudness drowning out her own pounding heart.

SIX

As Ruth walked along the beach, the surf circled her ankles and tugged. Go seaward, it suggested, where it is vast and free.

When Ruth was a teenager, her mother had once run off in the middle of an argument, declaring she was going to drown herself in the ocean. She had waded in to her thighs before her daughter's screams and pleas had brought her back. And now Ruth wondered: If she had not begged her mother to return, would LuLing have let the ocean decide her fate?

Since childhood, Ruth had thought about death every day, sometimes many times a day. She thought everyone must secretly do the same, but no one talked openly about it except her mother. She had pondered in her young mind what death entailed. Did people disappear? Become invisible? Why did dead people become stronger, meaner, sadder? That's what her mother seemed to think. When Ruth was older, she tried to imagine the precise moment when she could no longer breathe or talk or see, when she would have no feelings, not even fear that she was dead. Or perhaps she would have plenty of fear, as well as worry, anger, and regrets, just like the ghosts her mother talked to. Death was not necessarily a portal to the blank bliss of absolute nothingness. It was a deep dive into the unknown. And that contained all sorts of bad possibilities. It was that unknown which made her decide that no matter how terrible and unsolvable her life seemed, she would never willingly kill herself.

Although she remembered a time when she had tried.

It happened the year she turned eleven. Ruth and her mother had moved from Oakland to the flatlands of Berkeley, to a dark-shingled bungalow behind a butter-yellow cottage owned by a young couple in their twenties, Lance and Dottie Rogers. The bungalow had been a potting shed and garage that Lance's parents remodeled into an illegal in-law unit during World War Two and rented to a series of brides whose husbands had departed for battle in the Pacific via the Alameda Naval Station.

The ceilings were low, the electricity often shorted out, and the back wall and one side abutted a fence on which alley cats howled at night. There was no ventilation, not even a fan over the two-burner gas stove, so that when LuLing cooked at night, they had to open the windows to let out what she called the "greasy smell." But the rent was cheap, and the place was in a neighborhood with a good intermediate school attended by the smart and competitive sons and daughters of university professors. That was why LuLing had moved there in the first place, she liked to remind Ruth, for her education.

With its small-paned windows and yellow shutters, the bungalow resembled a dollhouse. But Ruth's initial delight soon turned into peevishness. The new home was so small she had no privacy. She and her mother shared a cramped, sunless bedroom that allowed for nothing more than twin beds and a dresser. The combined living room, eating area, and efficiency kitchen afforded no place to hide. Ruth's only refuge was the bathroom, and perhaps for this reason she developed numerous stomach ailments that year. Her mother was usually in the same room as she was, doing her calligraphy, cooking, or knitting, activities that kept her hands busy but left her tongue all too free to interrupt Ruth when she was watching TV. "You hair getting too long. Hair cover your glasses like curtain, can't see. You think this good-looking, I telling you *not* good-looking! You tune off TV, I cut hair for you. . . . Eh, you hear me. Tune off TV. . . ."

Her mother took Ruth's television-watching as a sign that she had nothing better to do. And sometimes she would see this as a good opportunity for a talk. She would take down the sand tray from the top of the refrigerator and set it on the kitchen table. Ruth's throat would grow tight. *Not this again.* But she knew that the more she resisted, the more her mother would want to know why.

"Precious Auntie mad-it me?" her mother would say when Ruth had sat for several minutes without writing anything in the sand.

"It's not that."

"You feel something else matter? . . . Another ghost here?"

"It's not another ghost."

"Oh. Oh, I know. . . . I die soon. . . . I right? You can say, I not afraid."

The only time her mother didn't bother her was when she was doing her homework or studying for a test. Her mother respected her studies. If she interrupted her, all Ruth had to do was say, "Shh! I'm reading." And almost always, her mother fell quiet. Ruth read a lot.

On good-weather days, Ruth would take her book to the

dwarf-sized porch of the bungalow, and there she'd sit with tucked legs on a bouncy patio chair with a clam-shaped back. Lance and Dottie would be in the yard, smoking cigarettes, pulling weeds out of the brick walkway or pruning the bougainvillea that covered one wall of their cottage like a bright quilt. Ruth would watch them surreptitiously, peering over the top of her book.

She had a crush on Lance. She thought he was handsome, like a movie star with his neatly cropped hair, square jaw, and lanky, athletic body. And he was so easygoing, so friendly to her, which made her even more shy. She had to pretend to be fascinated by her book or the snails that slimed the elephant plants, until finally he noticed her and said, "Hey there, squirt, you can go blind reading too much." His father owned a couple of liquor stores, and Lance helped with the family business. He often left for work in the late morning and returned at three-thirty or four, then took off again at nine and came back late, long after Ruth had given up listening for the sound of his car.

Ruth wondered how Dottie had been lucky enough to marry Lance. She wasn't even that pretty, though Ruth's new friend at school, Wendy, said that Dottie was cute in a beach-bunny way. How could she say that? Dottie was tall and bony, and about as huggable as a fork. Plus, as her mother had pointed out, Dottie had big teeth. Her mother had demonstrated to Ruth by pulling her own lips back with her fingers so that her gums showed on the top and bottom. "Big teeth, show too much inside out, like monkey." Later Ruth stared in the bathroom mirror and admired her own small teeth.

There was another reason Ruth thought Dottie did not deserve Lance: She was bossy and talked too loud and fast. Sometimes her voice was milky, as if she needed to clear her throat. And when she yelled, it sounded like rusty metal. On warm evenings, when their back windows were open, Ruth listened as Lance's and Dottie's garbled voices drifted across the yard and into the bungalow. On quite a few occasions, when they argued, she could hear clearly what they were saying.

"Damn it, Lance," she heard Dottie yell one night, "I'm going to throw out your dinner if you don't come right now!"

"Hey, gimme a break. I'm on the can!" he answered.

After that, whenever Ruth was in the bathroom, she imagined Lance doing the same, the two of them trying to avoid the people who nagged them without end.

Another night, as Ruth and her mother sat at the kitchen table with the sand tray between them, Dottie's husky voice rang out:

"I know what you did! Don't you play Mr. Innocent with me!"

"Don't tell me what the fuck I did, 'cause you don't know!"

This was followed by two door slams and the revving of the red Pontiac before it roared off. Ruth's heart was racing along with it. Her mother shook her head and clucked her tongue, then muttered in Chinese, "Those foreigners are crazy."

Ruth felt both thrilled and guilty over what she had heard. Dottie had sounded just like her mother, accusing and unreasonable. And Lance suffered as she did. The only difference was, he could talk back. He said exactly what Ruth wished she could tell her mother: Don't tell me what I think, 'cause you don't know!

* * *

In October, her mother asked her to give the rent check to the Rogerses. When Dottie opened the door, Ruth saw that she and Lance were busy unloading a huge box. Inside was a brand-new color television set, brought home in time to watch *The Wizard of Oz*, Dottie explained, which was going to air at seven o'clock that night. Ruth had never seen a color TV before, except in a store window.

"You know that part in the movie where everything is supposed to go from black-and-white to color?" Dottie said. "Well, on this set, it really does turn to color!"

"Hey, squirt," Lance said, "why'ncha come over and watch with us?"

Ruth blushed. "I don't know. . . ."

"Sure, tell your mom to come over too," said Dottie.

"I don't know. Maybe." Then Ruth rushed home.

Her mother did not think she should go. "They just polite, don't really mean."

"Yes, they do. They asked me twice." Ruth had left out the part about their inviting LuLing as well.

"Last year, report card, you get one Satisfactory, not even Good. Should be everything Excellent. Tonight better study more."

"But that was in PE!" Ruth wailed.

"Anyway, you already see this Ozzie show."

"It's *The Wizard of Oz*, not *Ozzie and Harriet*. And this one's a movie, it's *famous*!"

"Famous! Hnh! Everybody don't watch then no longer famous! Ozzie, Oz, Zorro, same thing."

"Well, Precious Auntie thinks I should watch it."

"What you mean?"

Ruth didn't know why she had said that. The words just popped out of her mouth. "Last night, remember?" She searched for an answer. "She had me write something that looked like a letter Z, and we didn't know what it meant?"

LuLing frowned, trying to recall.

"I think she wanted me to write O-Z. We can ask her now, if you don't believe me." Ruth went to the refrigerator, climbed the step stool, and brought down the sand tray.

"Precious Auntie," LuLing was already calling in Chinese, "are you there? What are you trying to say?"

Ruth sat with the chopstick poised for action. For a long time nothing happened. But that was because she was nervous she was about to trick her mother. What if there really was a ghost named Precious Auntie? Most of the time she thought the sand-writing was just a boring chore, that it was her duty to guess what her mother wanted to hear, then move quickly to end the session. Yet Ruth had also gone through times when she believed that a ghost was guiding her arm, telling her what to say. Sometimes she wrote things that turned out to be true, like tips for the stock market, which her mother started investing in to stretch the money she had saved over the years. Her mother would ask Precious Auntie to choose between two stocks, say IBM and U.S. Steel, and Ruth chose the shorter one to spell. No matter what she picked, LuLing profusely thanked Precious Auntie. One time, her mother asked where Precious Auntie's body was lying so she could find it and bury it. That question had given Ruth the creeps, and she tried to steer the conversation to a close. *The End,* she wrote, and this made her mother jump out of her chair and cry, "It's true, then! GaoLing was telling the truth. You're at the End of the World." Ruth had felt a cold breath blow down her neck.

Now she steadied her hand and mind, conjuring the wisdom Precious Auntie might impart like the Wizard. O-Z, she wrote, and then started to write *good* slowly and in large letters: G-O-O. And before she could finish, LuLing exclaimed, "Goo! *Goo* means 'bone' in Chinese. What about bone? This concern bone-doctor family?"

And so by luck all fell into place. *The Wizard of Oz,* Precious Auntie was apparently saying, was also about a bone doctor, and she would be happy for Ruth to see this.

At two minutes to seven, Ruth knocked on Lance and Dottie's door. "Who is it?" Lance yelled.

"It's me. Ruth."

"Who?" And then she heard him mutter, "God damn it."

Ruth was humiliated. Maybe he really had asked her only out of politeness. She bolted down the steps of the front porch. Now she'd have to hide in the backyard for two hours so her mother would not know about her mistake or her lie.

The door swung open. "Hey there, squirt," he said warmly, "come on in. We almost gave up on you. Hey, Dottie! Ruth's here! While you're in the kitchen, get her a soda, will you. Here, Ruth, sit yourself down here on the sofa."

During the movie, Ruth had a hard time paying attention to the television screen. She had to pretend to be comfortable. The three of them were sitting on a turquoise-and-yellow sofa that had the woven texture of twine and tinsel. It scratched the backs of Ruth's bare legs. Besides that, Ruth kept noticing things that shocked her, like how Dottie and Lance put their feet up on the coffee table— without removing their shoes. If her mother saw that, she'd have more to talk about than Dottie's big teeth! What's more, Lance and Dottie were both drinking a golden-colored booze and they weren't even in a cocktail lounge. But what most bothered Ruth was the stupid way Dottie was acting, babyish, stroking her husband's left knee and thigh, while crooning things like, "Lancey-pants, could you turn up the volume a teensy-weensy smidge?"

During a commercial, Dottie untangled herself, stood up, and wobbled about tipsily like the scarecrow in the movie. "How about some pop-pop-pop popcorn, every-body?" And then with arms swinging widely, she took one step backward and loped out of the room, singing, "Ohhhh, we're off to see the kitchen. . . ."

Now Ruth found herself on the sofa alone with Lance. She stared ahead at the television, her heart thumping. She heard Dottie humming, the sound of cabinets being opened and shut.

"So what do you think?" Lance said, nodding toward the television.

"It's really neat," Ruth answered in a small, serious voice, her eyes trained on the screen.

She could smell the oil heating in the kitchen, hear the machine-gun spill of popcorn kernels into the pot. Lance swished the ice cubes in his glass and talked about the pro-grams that he hoped were broadcasting in color: football, *Mister Ed*, *The Beverly Hillbillies*. Ruth felt like she was on a date. She turned slightly toward him. *Listen with a fascinated expression.* Wendy had told her this was what a girl should do to make a boy feel manly and important. But what came after that? Lance was so close to her. All at once, he patted her knee, stood up, and announced, "I guess I better use the can before the show comes back on." What he said was embarrassingly intimate. She was still blushing when he came back a minute later. This time he sat down even closer than before. He could have scooted over to where Dottie had been, so why hadn't he? Was it on purpose? The movie resumed. Was Dottie coming back soon? Ruth hoped not. She imagined telling Wendy how nervous she felt: "I thought I was going to pee in my pants!" That was just an expression, but now that she had thought it, she really did have to pee. This was terrible. How could she ask Lance if she could use the bathroom? She couldn't just get up and wander the house. Should she be casual like him and just say she had to use the can? She gripped her muscles, trying to hold on. Finally, when Dottie came in with the bowl of popcorn, Ruth blurted, "I have to wash my hands first."

"Through the back, past the bedroom," Dottie said.

Ruth tried to act casual, walking speedily while clenching the tops of her thighs together. As she flew past the bedroom, she smelled stale cigarettes, saw an unmade bed, pillows, towels, and Jean Naté bath oil at the foot of the bed. Once in the bathroom, she pulled down her pants and sat, groaning with relief. Here's where Lance had just been, she thought, and she giggled. And then she saw the bathroom was a mess. She was embarrassed for Lance. The grout between the pink tiles on the floor was grungy gray. A bra and panties lay mashed on top of the hamper. And car magazines were sloppily shoved into a built-in wall rack across from the toilet. If her mother could see this!

Ruth stood, and that's when she noticed the dampness on her bottom. The toilet seat had been wet! Her mother had always warned her not to sit on other people's toilets, even those at her friends' homes. Men were supposed to lift the seat, but they never did. "Every man forget," her mother had said, "they don't care. Leave germ there, put on you."

Ruth thought about rubbing off the pee with toilet paper. But then she decided it was a sign, like a pledge of love. It was Lance's pee, his germs, and leaving it on made her feel brave and romantic.

A few days later, Ruth saw a movie in gym class that showed how eggs floated in a female body, traveling along primordial paths, before falling out in a stream of blood. The movie was old and had been spliced in many places. A lady who looked like a nurse talked about the beginning of spring, and in the middle of describing the emergence of beautiful buds she disappeared with a *clack*, then reappeared in another room describing buds moving inside a branch. While she was explaining about the womb as a nest, her voice turned into a flapping-bird sound and she disappeared into the cloud-white screen. When the lights came on, all the girls squinted in embarrassment, for now they were thinking about eggs moving inside them. The teacher had to call in a slouching, slack-mouthed boy from the audiovisual department; this made Wendy and several other girls squeal that they wanted to curl up and die. After the boy spliced the reel back together, the movie took up again, to show a tadpole called a sperm traveling through a heart-shaped womb while a bus driver voice called out the destinations: "vagina," "cervix," "uterus." The girls shrieked and covered their eyes, until the boy swaggered out of the room, acting proud, as if he had seen them all naked.

The movie continued and Ruth watched the tadpole find the egg, which gobbled it up. A big-eyed frog began to grow. At the end of the movie, a nurse with a starched white cap handed a googly baby to a beautiful woman in a pink satin jacket, as her manly husband declared, "It's a miracle, the miracle of life."

When the lights came on, Wendy raised her hand and asked the teacher how the miracle got started in the first place, and the girls who knew the answer snorted and giggled. Ruth laughed as well. The teacher gave them a scolding look and said, "You have to get married first."

Ruth knew that wasn't entirely true. She had seen a Rock Hudson and Doris Day movie. All it took was the right chemistry, which included love, and sometimes the wrong chemistry, which included booze and falling asleep. Ruth was not quite sure how everything occurred, but she was pretty certain those were the main things that activated a scientific change: it was similar to how Alka-Seltzer turned plain water into bubbly. Plop, plop. Fizz, fizz. That wrong chemistry was why some women had babies born out of wedlock, babies that were illegitimate, one of the b-words.

Before the class ended, the teacher passed out white elastic belts with clips, and boxes containing thick white pads. She explained that the girls were due to have their first periods soon, and they should not be surprised or frightened if they saw a red stain on their panties. The stain was a sign that they had become women, and it was also an assurance that they were "good girls." A lot of the girls tittered. Ruth thought the teacher was saying her period was due in the same way as homework, meaning it was due tomorrow, the day after, or next week.

While she and Ruth walked home from school, Wendy explained what the teacher had left out. Wendy knew things, because she hung out with her brother's pals and their girlfriends, the hard girls who wore makeup and stockings with nail polish dabbed over the runs. Wendy had a big blond bubble hairdo that she teased and sprayed during recess, while chewing gum she saved between classes in a wad of tinfoil. She was the first girl to wear white go-go boots, and before and after school she rolled up her skirt so that it was two inches above her knees. She had been in detention three times, once for coming to school late and twice for saying the other *b*-words, "bitch" and "boner," to the gym teacher. On the way home, she bragged to Ruth that she had let a boy kiss her during a basement make-out party. "He had just eaten a neopolitan ice cream sandwich and his breath tasted like barf, so I told him to kiss my neck but not to go below. Below the neck and you're a goner." She peeled open her collar and Ruth gasped, seeing what looked like a huge bruise.

"What's that?"

"A hickey, you dummy. Course they didn't show that in that crummy movie. Hickeys, hard-ons, home runs, *it*. Speaking of *it*, there was an older girl at this party puking her guts out in the bathroom. A tenth-grader. She thought she was preggers from this boy who's in juvenile hall."

"Does she love him?"

"She called him a creep."

"Then she doesn't have to worry," Ruth said knowingly.

"What are you talking about?"

"It's the chemistry that gets you pregnant. Love is one of the ingredients," Ruth declared as scientifically as possible.

Wendy stopped walking. Her mouth hung open. Then she whispered: "Don't you know *anything*?" And she explained what Ruth's mother, the lady in the movie, and the teacher had not talked about: that the ingredient came from a boy's penis. And to ensure everything was now perfectly clear to Ruth, Wendy spelled it out: "The boy *pees* inside the girl."

"That's not true!" Ruth hated Wendy for telling her this, for laughing hysterically. She was relieved when they reached the block where she and Wendy went in opposite directions.

The last two blocks home, the truth of Wendy's words bounced in Ruth's head like pinballs. It made terrible sense, the part about the pee. That was why boys and girls had separate bathrooms. That's why boys were supposed to lift the seat, but they didn't, just to be bad. And that was why her mother always told her never to sit on the toilet seat in someone else's bathroom. What her mother had said about *germs* was really a warning about *sperms*. Why couldn't her mother learn to speak English right?

And then panic grabbed her. For now she remembered that three nights before she had sat on pee from the man she loved.

Ruth checked her underwear a dozen times a day. By the fourth day after the movie, her period had not come. Now look what's happened, she cried to herself. She walked around the bungalow, staring blankly. She had ruined herself and there was no changing this. Love, pee, booze, she counted the ingredients on her fingers over and over. She remembered how brave she had felt, falling asleep without wiping off the pee.

"Why you act so crazy?" her mother often asked. Of course, she could not tell her mother she was pregnant. Experience had taught her that her mother worried too much even when she had no reason to worry. If there was something *really* wrong, her mother would scream and pound her chest like a gorilla. She would do this in front of Lance and Dottie. She would dig out her eyes and yell for the ghosts to come take her away. And then she would really kill herself. This time for sure. She would make Ruth watch, to punish her even more.

Now whenever Ruth saw Lance, she breathed so hard and fast her lungs seized up and she nearly fainted from lack of air. She had a constant stomachache. Sometimes her stomach went into spasm and she stood over the toilet heaving, but nothing came out. When she ate, she imagined the food falling into the baby frog's mouth, and then her stomach felt like a gunky swamp and she had to run to the bathroom and make herself retch, hoping the frog would leap into the toilet and her troubles could be flushed away.

I want to die, she moaned to herself. Die, die, die. First she cried a lot in the bathroom, then sliced her wrist with a dinner knife. It left a row of plowed-up skin, no blood, and it hurt too much to cut any deeper. Later, in the backyard, she found a rusty tack in the dirt, poked her fingertip, and waited for blood poisoning to rise up her arm like liquid in a thermometer. That evening, still alive and miserable, she filled the tub and sat in it. As she sank under and was about to open her mouth wide, she remembered the water was now dirty with nasty stuff from her feet, her bottom, and the place between her legs. Still determined, she got out of the tub, dried off, and filled the sink, then lowered her face until it touched the water. She opened her mouth. How easy it was, drowning. It didn't hurt at all. It was like drinking water, which, after a while, she realized was what she was doing. So she pushed her face lower into the water and opened her mouth again. She took a deep breath, welcoming death at last. Her whole body backfired in stinging protest. She began coughing in such a loud and hacking way that her mother rushed in without knocking and pounded her back, put her hand on her forehead, and murmured in Chinese that she was sick and should go to bed right away. Having her mother comfort her so lovingly only made Ruth feel worse.

The first person Ruth finally confessed her secret to was Wendy. She knew things, she always knew what to do. Ruth had to wait until she saw her at school, because there was no way she could talk about this on the party-line phone without having her mother or someone else overhear.

"You have to tell Lance," Wendy said, then reached over and squeezed Ruth's hand.

That made Ruth cry even harder. She shook her head. The cruel world and its impossibility swam in front of her. Lance didn't love her. If she told him, he would hate her, Dottie would hate her. They would kick her mother and her out of the bungalow. The school would send Ruth to juvenile hall. And her life would be over.

"Well, if you don't tell Lance, I will," Wendy said.

"Don't," Ruth managed to choke out. "You can't. I won't let you."

"If I don't tell him, how else will he realize that he loves you?"

"He doesn't love me."

"Sure he does. Or he will. Lots of times it happens that way. The guy finds out a baby is coming, and them boom— love, marriage, baby carriage."

Ruth tried to imagine it. "Yep, it's yours," Wendy would say to Lance. She pictured Lance looking like Rock Hudson when he learned Doris Day was going to have his baby. He would look stunned, but slowly he would begin to smile, then grin like a fool and race into the street, un- mindful of traffic or people he bumped into, people who shouted back that he was nuts. And he would yell, "I *am* nuts, nuts about her!" Soon he was by her side, on his knees, telling her he loved her, had always loved her, and now wanted to marry her. As for Dottie, well, she would soon fall in love with the postman or someone. Everything would work out. Ruth sighed. It was possible.

That afternoon, Wendy went home with Ruth. LuLing worked the afternoon shift at a nursery school and would not be home for another two hours. At four, while they were outside, they saw Lance stride to his car, whistling and jingling his keys. Wendy broke away from Ruth, and Ruth ran to the other side of the bungalow, where she could both hide and watch. She could hardly breathe. Wendy was walking toward Lance. "Hello?" she called to him.

"Hey there, girlie," he said. "What's up?"

And then Wendy turned around and fled. Ruth started to cry and when Wendy came back, she consoled Ruth, telling her she had a better plan. "Don't worry," she said. "I'll take care of it. I'll think of something." And she did. "Wait here," she said, smiling, and ran up to the back porch of the cottage. Ruth dashed into the bungalow. Five minutes later, the back door to the cottage flew open and Dottie raced down the porch steps. Through the window, Ruth saw Wendy wave to her before walking away quickly. Then came pounding on the door to the bungalow, and when Ruth answered, Dottie was there, grabbing her by both hands. She stared into her eyes with a stricken face and whispered hoarsely in her milk-and-metal voice, "Are you really—?"

Ruth started bawling, and Dottie put her arm around her shoulders, soothing her, then squeezing her so hard Ruth thought her bones would pop out of their sockets. It hurt but also felt good. "That bastard, that dirty, filthy bastard," Dottie kept saying through gritted teeth. Ruth was shocked to hear the *b*-word, but even more so to realize that Dottie was angry—not with her, but with Lance!

"Does your mommy know?" Dottie asked.

Ruth shook her head.

"All right. For now, we don't need to tell her, not yet. First, let me think how we're going to take care of this. Okay? It won't be easy, but I'll figure out what to do, don't worry. Five years ago, the same thing happened to me."

So that was why Lance had married her. But where was the baby?

"I know how you feel," Dottie went on. "I really do."

And Ruth cried even harder, bursting with more feelings than she ever thought a heart could hold. Someone was angry for her. Someone knew what to do.

That night, as her mother cooked with the windows cracked open, loud voices punctured the air above the sound of spitting oil. Ruth pretended to read *Jane Eyre*. Her ears were straining to hear the words from outside, but the only thing she could make out was Dottie's high-pitched shriek: "You filthy bastard!" Lance's voice was a low rumble, like the revving of his Pontiac.

Ruth went into the kitchen and reached under the sink. "I'm going to take out the garbage." Her mother gave her a raised eyebrow but kept cooking. As Ruth approached the cans by the side of the cottage, she slowed down to listen.

"You think you're so hot! How many others have you screwed? . . . You're nothing but a thirty-second wonder—yeah, wham, bam, thank you, ma'am!"

"What makes you the goddamn expert, I'd like to know!"

"I do know! I know what a *real* man is! . . . Danny . . . yeah, him, and he was good, Danny is a *real man*. But you! You gotta stick it up little girls who don't know any better."

Lance's voice rose and broke like a crying boy's: "You goddamn fucking whore!"

When Ruth went back into the house, she was still shaking. She had not expected everything to be so crazy and ugly. Being careless could cause terrible trouble. You could be bad without even meaning to be.

"Those people *huli-hudu*," her mother muttered. She set the steaming food on the table. "Crazy, argue over nothing." And then she closed the windows.

Hours later, as Ruth lay wide awake in bed, the muffled shouts and screams suddenly stopped. She listened for them to begin again, but all she detected were her mother's snores. She arose in the pitch dark and went into the bathroom. She climbed on the toilet seat and looked out the window across the yard. The cottage lights were burning. What was going on? And then she saw Lance walk out with a duffel bag and hurl it into the trunk of his car. A moment later, he spun the tires on the gravel and took off with a roar. What did that mean? Had he told Dottie he was going to marry Ruth?

The next morning, Saturday, Ruth barely touched the rice porridge her mother had heated up. She waited anxiously for the Pontiac to return, but everything remained quiet. She slumped onto the sofa with her book. Her mother was putting dirty clothes, towels, and sheets into a bag draped over a cart. She counted out the quarters and dimes needed for the laundromat, then said to Ruth, "Let's go. Wash-clothes time."

"I don't feel so good."

"Ai-ya, sick?"

"I think I'm going to throw up."

Her mother fussed over her, taking her temperature, asking her what she had eaten, what her stools looked like. She made Ruth lie down on the sofa and placed a bucket nearby, in case she really did get sick. At last her mother departed for the laundromat; she would be gone for at least three hours. She always pushed the cart to a place twenty minutes away, because the washers there were a nickel cheaper than those at the closer places and the dryers didn't burn the clothes.

Ruth put on a jacket and strayed outside. She slid into the chair on the porch, opened her book, and waited. Ten minutes later, Dottie opened the back door of the cottage, climbed down the four steps, and strode across the yard. Her eyes were puffy like a toad's, and when she smiled at Ruth, the upper half of her face looked tragic.

"How ya doin', kiddo?"

"Okay, I guess."

Dottie sighed, sat down on the porch, and dropped her chin onto her knees. "He's gone," she said. "But he's going to pay, don't you worry."

"I don't want any money," Ruth protested.

Dottie laughed once, then sniffed. "I mean he's going to jail."

Ruth was frightened. "Why?"

"Because of what he did to you, of course."

"But he didn't mean to. He just forgot—"

"Forgot you were only eleven? Jeez!"

"It was my fault too. I should have been more careful."

"Honey, no, no, no! You don't have to protect him. Really. It's not your fault or the baby's. . . . Now listen, you're going to have to talk to the police—"

"No! No! I don't want to!"

"I know you're scared, but what he did was wrong. It's called statutory rape, and he has to be punished for it. . . . Anyway, the police will probably ask you a lot of questions, and you just tell them the truth, what he did, where it happened. . . . Was it in the bedroom?"

"The bathroom."

"Jeez!" Dottie nodded bitterly. "Yeah, he always did like it in there. . . . So he took you to the bathroom—"

"I went by myself."

"All right, and then he followed you, and then what? Did he have his clothes on?"

Ruth was aghast. "He stayed in the living room, watching TV," she said in a tiny voice. "I was in the bathroom by myself."

"Then when did he do it?"

"Before me. He peed first, then I did."

"Wait a second. . . . He *what*?"

"He peed."

"On you?"

"On the toilet seat. Then I went in and sat on it."

Dottie stood up, her face twisted with horror. "Oh no, oh my God!" She grabbed Ruth by the shoulders and shook her. "That's *not* how babies are made. Pee on the toilet seat. How could you be so *stupid*? He has to stick his cock in you. He squirts sperm, not piss. Do you realize what you've done? You accused an innocent man of raping you."

"I didn't—" Ruth whispered.

"Yes, you did, and I believed you." Dottie stomped off, cursing.

"I'm sorry," Ruth cried after her. "I said I'm sorry." She was still not certain what she had done.

Dottie turned around and sneered. "You have no idea what sorry really is." Then she went inside and banged the door shut.

Though she was no longer pregnant, Ruth felt no relief. Everything was still awful, maybe even worse. When her mother returned from the laundromat, Ruth was lying under the covers in bed, pretending to be asleep. She felt stupid and scared. Would she go to jail? And though she knew now that she was not pregnant, she wanted to die more than ever. But how? She pictured herself lying under the wheels of the Pontiac, Lance starting the car and taking off, crushing her without even knowing it. If she died like her father, he would meet her in heaven. Or would he too think she was bad?

"Ah, good girl," her mother murmured. "You sleep, feel better soon."

Later that afternoon, Ruth heard the sounds of the Pontiac pulling into the driveway. She peeked out the window. Lance, grim-faced, carried out some boxes, two suitcases, and a cat from the cottage. Then Dottie came out, dabbing her nose with a tissue. She and Lance never looked at each other. And then they were gone. An hour later, the Pontiac returned, but only Lance got out. What had Dottie told Lance? Why did Dottie have to move out? Would Lance now march up to their door and tell her mother what Ruth had done and demand that they move out that same day as well? Lance hated her, Ruth was sure of that. She had thought being pregnant was the worst thing that could have happened to her. But this was far worse.

She stayed home from school on Monday. LuLing became increasingly fearful that a ghost was trying to take her daughter away. Why else was Ruth still sick? LuLing rambled about bony teeth from a monkey's jaw. Precious Auntie would know, she kept saying. She knew about the curse. This was punishment for something the family had done a long time ago. She put the sand tray on a chair by Ruth's twin bed, waiting. "Both us die," she asked, "or only me?"

No, Ruth wrote, *all O.K.*

"What okay-okay? Then why she sick, no reason?"

On Tuesday, Ruth could not stand her mother's fussing over her any longer. She said she was well enough to go to school. Before opening the door, she looked out the window, then down the driveway. Oh no, the Pontiac was still there. She was trembling so hard she feared her bones might break. After taking a deep breath, she darted out the door, scooted down the side of the driveway farther from the cottage, then edged past the Pontiac. She turned left, even though school was to the right.

"Hey, squirt! I've been waiting for you." Lance was on the porch, smoking a cigarette. "We need to talk." Ruth stood rooted to the sidewalk, unable to move. "I *said* we need to talk. Don't you think you owe me that? . . . Come here." He threw the burning cigarette onto the lawn.

Ruth's legs moved shakily forward. The top half of her was still running away. When she reached the top of the porch, she was numb. She looked up. "I'm sorry," she squeaked. The quiver in her chin shook open her mouth, and sobs burbled out.

"Hey, hey," Lance said. He looked nervously down the street. "Come on, you don't have to do that. I wanted to talk so we could have an understanding. I just don't want this to ever happen again. Okay?"

Ruth sniffed and nodded.

"All right, then. So settle down. Don't get all spooky on me."

Ruth wiped at her teary face with her sweater sleeve. The worst was over. She started to go down the stairs.

"Hey, where you going?"

Ruth froze.

"We still have to talk. Turn around." His voice was not quite so gentle. Ruth saw he had opened the door. She stopped breathing. "Inside," he ordered. She bit her lip and slowly climbed back up, then glided past him. She heard the door close and saw the room go dim.

The living room smelled like booze and cigarettes. The curtains were closed and there were empty TV-dinner trays on the coffee table.

"Sit down." Lance gestured toward the scratchy couch. "Want a soda?" She shook her head. The only light came from the TV, which was tuned to an old movie. Ruth was glad for the noise. And then she saw a commercial, a man selling cars. In his hand was a fake saber. "We've slashed our prices—so come on down to Rudy's Chevrolet and ask to see the slasher!"

Lance sat on the sofa, not as close as he had been that night. He took her books from her arms and she felt unprotected. Tears blurred her eyes, and she tried hard not to make any sounds as she cried.

"She left me, you know."

A sob burst out of Ruth's chest. She tried to say she was sorry, but she could make only mouselike sniffles.

Lance laughed. "Actually, I kicked her out. Yeah, in a way, you did me a favor. If it weren't for you, I wouldn't have found out she was screwing around. Oh sure, I kind of suspected it for a while. But I told myself, Man, you got to have trust. And you know what, she didn't trust me. Can you believe it? Me? Let me tell you something, you can't have a marriage if you don't have trust. You know what I mean?" He looked at her.

Ruth desperately nodded.

"Nah, you won't know for another ten years." He lit another cigarette. "You know, in ten years, you'll look back and say, 'Boy, I sure was dumb about how babies are made!' " He snorted, then cocked his head to get her reaction. "Aren't you going to laugh? I think it's kind of funny myself. Don't you?" He started to pat her arm and she flinched without intending to. "Hey, what's the matter? Uh-oh, don't tell me. . . . *You* don't trust me. What are you, like her? After what *you* did and what I certainly did *not* do, do you think I now *deserve* this kind of treatment from you?"

Ruth was quiet for a long time, trying to make her lips move right. Finally she said, in a cracked voice, "I trust you."

"Yeah?" He patted her arm again, and this time she didn't jerk stupidly. He continued talking in a weary but reassuring voice. "Listen, I'm not going to yell at you or nothing, okay? So just relax. Okay? Hey, I said *'Okay?'* "

"Okay."

"Give me my smile."

She forced her lips to pull upward.

"There it is! Oops. Gone again!" He stubbed out his cigarette. "All right, are we friends again?" He stuck out his hand for her to shake. "Good. It'd be terrible if we couldn't be friends, since we live next to each other."

She smiled at him and this time it came naturally. She tried to breathe through her clogged nose.

"And being neighbors, we gotta help each other, not go around accusing someone innocent of doing wrong. . . ."

Ruth nodded and realized she was still gripping her toes. She relaxed. Soon this would be over. She saw that he had dark circles under his eyes, lines running from his nose to his jaw. Funny. He looked much older than she remembered, no longer as handsome. And then she realized it was because she was no longer in love with him. How strange. She had believed it was love, and it never was. Love was forever.

"So now you know the real way babies are made, don'cha?"

Ruth stopped breathing. She ducked her head.

"Well, do you or don't you?"

She nodded quickly.

"How? Tell me."

She squirmed, her mind turning around and around. She saw terrible pictures. A brown hot dog squirting yellow mustard. She knew the words: penis, sperm, vagina. But how could she say them? Then the nasty picture would be there in front of both of them. "You know," she whimpered.

He looked at her sternly. It was as if he had X-ray eyes. "Yeah," he finally said. "I know." He was silent for a few seconds, and then added in a friendlier voice. "Boy, were you dumb. Babies and toilet seats, Jeez." Ruth kept her head down, but her eyes glanced up at him. He was smiling. "I hope you one day do a better job teaching your kids about the facts of life. Toilet seat! Pee? Pee-*you*!"

Ruth giggled.

"Ha! I knew you could laugh." He poked his finger under her armpit and tickled her. She squealed politely. He tickled her again, lower along her ribs, and she spasmed as a reflex. Then suddenly, his other hand reached for her other armpit and she groaned with laughter, helpless, too scared to tell him to stop. He twirled his fingers around her back, along her stomach. She balled herself up like a sow bug and fell to the rug below with terrible gasping giggles.

"You think a lot of things are funny, don't you?" He twiddled his fingers up and down her ribs as if they were harp strings. "Yeah, I can see that now. Did you tell all your little girlfriends? Ha! Ha! I almost put that guy in jail."

She tried to cry no, stop, don't, but she was laughing too hard, unable to take a breath on her own, unable to control her arms or legs. Her skirt was tangled, but she couldn't pull it down. Her hands were like that of a marionette, twitching toward wherever he touched as she tried to keep his fingers away from her stomach, her breasts, her bottom. Tears poured out. He was pinching her nipples.

"You're just a little girl," he panted. "You don't even have any titties yet. Why would I want to mess around with you? Shit, I bet you don't even have any tushy hairs—" And when both of his hands shot down to pull off her flowered panties, her voice broke free and blasted out as screeches. Over and over, she made a fierce, sharp sound that came from an unknown place. It was as though another person had burst out of her.

"Whoa! Whoa!" he said, holding up his hands like someone being robbed. "What are you doing? Get a hold of yourself. . . . Would you just calm down, for chrissake!"

She continued the sirenlike wail, scuttling on her bottom away from him, pulling up her panties, pushing down her dress.

"I'm not hurting you. I am *not* hurting you." He repeated this until she settled into whimpers and wheezes. And then there came just fast breathing in the space between them.

He shook his head in disbelief. "Am I imagining things, or weren't you just laughing a moment ago? One second we're having fun, the next second you're acting like— well, I don't know, you tell me." He squinted hard at her. "You know, maybe you have a big problem. You start to get this funny idea in your head that people are doing something wrong to you, and before you can see what's true, you accuse them and go crazy and wreck everything. Is that what you're doing?"

Ruth got up. Her legs were shaky. "I'm going to go," she whispered. She could hardly walk to the door.

"You're not going anywhere until you promise you're not going to spread any more of your goddamn lies. You got that straight!" He walked toward her. "You better not say I did something to you when I didn't. 'Cause if you do, I'm going to get really mad and do something that'll make you sorrier than hell, you hear?"

She nodded dumbly.

He blew air out of his nose, disgusted. "Get out of here. Scram."

That night, Ruth tried to tell her mother what had happened. "Ma? I'm scared."

"Why scare?" LuLing was ironing. The room had the smell of fried water.

"That man Lance, he was mean to me—"

Her mother scowled, then said in Chinese: "This is because you're always bothering him. You think he wants to play with you—he doesn't! Why do you always make trouble? . . ."

Ruth felt sick to her stomach. Her mother saw danger where there wasn't. And now that something was truly really awful, she was blind. If Ruth told her the actual truth, she would probably go crazy. She'd say she didn't want to live anymore. So what difference did it make? She was alone. No one could save her.

An hour later, while LuLing was knitting and watching television, Ruth took down the sand tray by herself. "Precious Auntie wants to tell you something," she told her mother.

"Ah?" LuLing said. She immediately stood up and turned off the TV, and eagerly sat down at the kitchen table. Ruth smoothed the sand with the chopstick. She closed her eyes, then opened them, and began.

You must move, Ruth wrote. *Now.*

"Move?" her mother cried. "Ai-ya! Where we should move?"

Ruth had not considered this. *Far away,* she finally decided.

"Where far?"

Ruth imagined a distance as big as an ocean. She pictured the bay, the bridge, the long bus rides she had taken with her mother that made her fall asleep. *San Francisco,* she wrote at last.

Her mother still looked worried. "What part? Where good?"

Ruth hesitated. She did not know San Francisco that well, except for Chinatown and a few other places, Golden Gate Park, the Fun House at Land's End. And that was how it came to her, an inspiration that moved quickly into her hand: *Land's End.*

Ruth recalled the first day she had walked by herself along this stretch of beach. It had been nearly empty, and the sand in front of her had been clean, untrampled. She had escaped and reached this place. She had felt the waves, cold and shocking, grab at her ankles, wanting to pull her in. She remembered how she had cried with relief as the waves roared around her.

Now, thirty-five years later, she was that eleven-year-old child again. She had chosen to live. Why? As she now kept walking, she felt comforted by the water, its constancy, its predictability. Each time it withdrew, it carried with it whatever had marked the shore. She recalled that when her younger self stood on this same beach for the first time, she had thought the sand looked like a gigantic writing surface. The slate was clean, inviting, open to possibilities. And at that moment of her life, she had a new determination, a fierce hope. She didn't have to make up the answers anymore. She could ask.

Just as she had so long before, Ruth now stooped and picked up a broken shell. She scratched in the sand: *Help*. And she watched as the waves carried her plea to another world.

SEVEN

When Ruth returned to LuLing's apartment, she began to throw away what her mother had saved: dirty napkins and plastic bags, restaurant packets of soy sauce and mustard and disposable chopsticks, used straws and expired coupons, wads of cotton from medicine bottles and the empty bottles themselves. She emptied the cupboards of cartons and jars with their labels still attached. There was enough rotten food from the fridge and freezer to fill four large garbage sacks.

Cleaning helped her feel that she was removing the clutter from her mother's mind. She opened more closets. She saw hand towels with holly motifs, a Christmas present that LuLing never used. She put them in a bag destined for Goodwill. There were also scratchy towels and bargain-sale sheets she remembered using as a child. The newer linens were still in the department-store gift boxes they had come in.

But as Ruth reached for the old towels, she found she could not get rid of them any more than her mother could. These were objects suffused with a life and a past. They had a history, a personality, a connection to other memories. This towel in her hands now, for instance, with its fuchsia flowers, she once thought it was beautiful. She

151

used to wrap it around her wet hair and pretend she was a queen wearing a turban. She took it to the beach one day and her mother scolded her for using "best things" instead of the green towel with frayed ends. By upbringing, Ruth could never be like Gideon, who bought thousands of dollars' worth of Italian linens each year and tossed out last year's collection as readily as last month's *Architectural Digest*. Perhaps she was not as frugal as her mother, but she was aware of the possibility that she might regret the loss of something.

Ruth went into LuLing's bedroom. On the dresser were bottles of toilet water, about two dozen, still in their cellophane-bound boxes. "Stinky water," her mother called it. Ruth had tried to explain to her that toilet water was not the same as water from a toilet. But LuLing said that how something sounded was what counted, and she believed these gifts from GaoLing and her family were meant to insult her.

"Well, if you don't like it," Ruth once said, "why do you always tell them it's just what you wanted?"

"How I cannot show polite?"

"Then be polite, but throw it away later if it bothers you so much."

"Throw away? How I can throw away? This waste money!"

"Then *give* it away."

"Who want such thing? *Toilet* water!—*peh!*—like I big insult them."

So there they sat, two dozen bottles, two dozen insults, some from GaoLing, some from GaoLing's daughter, who were unmindful that LuLing rose each morning, saw these gifts, and began the day feeling the world was against her. Out of curiosity, Ruth opened a box and twisted the cap of the bottle inside. Stinky! Her mother was right. Then again, what was the shelf life of scented water? It was not as though toilet water aged like wine. Ruth started to put the boxes into the Goodwill bag, then caught herself. Resolute but still feeling wasteful, she put them into the bag destined for the dump. And what about this face powder? She opened a compact case of a gold-tone metal with fleur-de-lys markings. It had to be at least thirty years old. The powder inside was an oxidized orange, the cheek accent of ventriloquists' dummies. Whatever it was looked like it could cause cancer—or Alzheimer's. Everything in the world, no matter how apparently benign, was potentially dangerous, bulging with toxins that could escape and infect you when you least expected it. Her mother had taught her that.

She plucked out the powder puff. Its edges were still nubby, but the center was worn smooth from its once-daily skimming over the curves of LuLing's face. She threw the compact and powder puff in the trash bag. A moment later, she panicked, retrieved the compact and nearly cried. This was part of her mother's life! So what if she was being sentimental? She opened the compact again and saw her pained face in its mirror, then noticed the orange powder again. No, this wasn't being sentimental. It was morbid and disgusting. She stuffed the compact once more into the trash bag.

By nightfall, one corner of the living room was jammed with items Ruth had decided her mother would not miss: a rotary Princess phone, sewing patterns, piles of old utility bills, five frosted iced-tea glasses, a bunch of mismatched coffee mugs bearing slogans, a three-pod lamp missing one pod, the old rusted clam-shaped patio chair, a toaster with a frayed cord and curves like an old Buick fender, a kitchen clock with knife, fork, and spoon as hour, minute, and second hands, a knitting bag with its contents of half-finished purple, turquoise, and green slippers, medicines that had expired, and a spidery thatch of old hangers.

It was late, but Ruth felt even more energized, full of purpose. Glancing about the apartment, she counted on her fingers what repairs were needed to prevent accidents. The wall sockets needed to be brought up to code. The smoke detectors should be replaced. Get the water heater turned down so that her mother could not be scalded. Was the brown stain on the ceiling the result of a leak? She followed where the water might be dripping, and her discerning eye skidded to a stop on the floor near the couch. She rushed over and peeled back the rug, and stared at the floorboard. This was one of her mother's hiding places, where she hoarded valuables that might be needed in time of war or, as LuLing said, "disaster you cannot even imagine, they so bad." Ruth pressed on one end of the board, and lo and behold, like a seesaw, the other end lifted. Aha! The gold serpentine bracelet! She plucked it out and laughed giddily as if she had just picked the right door on a game show. Her mother had dragged her into Royal Jade House on Jackson Street and bought the bracelet for a hundred twenty dollars, telling Ruth it was twenty-four-carat gold and could be weighed on a scale and traded for full value in an emergency.

And what about LuLing's other hiding spots? At the never used fireplace, Ruth lifted a basket containing photo albums. She pried at a loose brick, pulled it out, and—sure enough—it was still there, a twenty-dollar bill wrapped around four singles. Unbelievable! She felt giddy at finding this small treasure, a memento from her adolescent past. When they moved into this place, LuLing had put five twenty-dollar bills under the brick. Ruth would check every now and then, always noting that the bills lay in the same perfectly aligned wad. One day she put a piece of her hair on top of the money; she had seen this trick in a movie about a boy detective. Every time she looked after that, the hair was still there. When Ruth was fifteen, she began to borrow from the stash during times of her own emergencies—when she needed a dollar here and there for forbidden things: mascara, a movie ticket, and later, Marlboro cigarettes. At first she was always anxious until she could replace the bill. And when she did, she felt relieved and elated that she had not been caught. She rationalized that she *deserved* the money—for mowing the lawn, washing the dishes, being yelled at for no good reason. She replaced the missing twenties with tens, then fives, and eventually, just the singles wrapped with the one remaining twenty.

And now, thirty-one years afterward, in seeing the reminder of her small larceny, she was both the girl she once was and the observer of that younger version of herself. She remembered the unhappy girl who lived in her body, who was full of passion, rage, and sudden impulses. She used to wonder: Should she believe in God or be a nihilist? Be Buddhist or a beatnik? And whichever it should be, what was the lesson in her mother's being miserable all the time? Were there really ghosts? If not, did that mean her mother was really crazy? Was there really such a thing as luck? If not, why did Ruth's cousins live in Saratoga? At times, she became resolute in wanting to be exactly the opposite of her mother. Rather than complain about the world, she wanted to do something constructive. She would join the Peace Corps and go into remote jungles. Another day, she chose to become a veterinarian and help injured animals. Still later, she thought about becoming a teacher to kids who were retarded. She wouldn't point out what was wrong, as her mother did with her, exclaiming that half her brain must be missing. She would treat them as living souls equal to everyone else.

She gave vent to these feelings by writing them down in a diary that Auntie Gal had given her for Christmas. She had just finished reading *The Diary of Anne Frank* in sophomore English class, and like all the other girls, she was imbued with a sense that she too was different, an innocent on a path to tragedy that would make her posthumously admired. The diary would be proof of her existence, that she mattered, and more important, that someone somewhere would one day understand her, even if it was not in her lifetime. There was a tremendous comfort in believing her miseries weren't for naught. In her diary, she could be as truthful as she wanted to be. The truth, of course, had to be supported by facts. So her first entry included a list of the top ten songs on the radio hit list, as well as a note that a boy named Michael Papp had a boner when he was dancing with Wendy. That was what Wendy had said, and at the time Ruth thought *boner* referred to a puffed-up ego.

She knew her mother was sneaking looks at what she had written, because one day she asked Ruth, "Why you like this song 'Turn, Turn, Turn'? Just 'cause someone else like?" Another time her mother sniffed and said, "Why smell like cigarette?" Ruth had just written about going to Haight-Ashbury with friends and meeting some hippies in the park who offered them a smoke. Ruth took some glee in her mother's thinking it was cigarettes they were smoking and not hashish. After that interrogation, she hid the diary in the bottom of her closet, between her mattresses, behind her dresser. But her mother always managed to find it, at least that was what Ruth figured, on the basis of what she was next forbidden to do: "No more go beach after school." "No more see this Lisa girl." "Why you so boy-crazy?" If she accused her mother of reading her diary, LuLing would become evasive, never admitting that she had done so, while also saying, "A daughter should have no secrets from a mother." Ruth did not want to censor her writing, so she started recording it in a combination of pig Latin, Spanish, and multisyllabic words that she knew her mother would not understand. "Aquatic amusements of the silica particulate variety," was her reference to the beach at Land's End.

Didn't Mom ever realize, Ruth now mused, how her demands for no secrets drove me to hide even more from her? Yet maybe her mother did sense that. Maybe it made her hide certain truths from Ruth about herself. *Things too bad to say.* They could not trust each other. That was how dishonesty and betrayal started, not in big lies but in small secrets.

Ruth now remembered the last place where she had hidden her diary. She had forgotten about it all these years. She went to the kitchen, hoisted herself onto the counter with less ease than she had at sixteen. Patting along the top of the cabinet, she soon found it: the heart-patterned diary, some of the hearts coated with pink nail polish to obliterate the names of various boys she had immortalized as crushes of the moment. She climbed down with the dusty relic, leaned against the counter, and rubbed the red-and-gold cover.

She felt her limbs drain, felt unsure of herself, as if the diary contained an unalterable prediction of what would happen the rest of her life. Once again she was sixteen years old. She undid the clasp and read the words on the inside of the jacket, scrawled in two-inch block letters: STOP!!! PRIVATE!!! IF YOU ARE READING THIS YOU ARE GUILTY OF TRESPASSING!!! YES! I DO MEAN *YOU*!

But her mother had read it, had read and committed to heart what Ruth had written on the second-to-last page, the words that nearly killed them both.

The week before Ruth wrote those fateful words, she and LuLing had been escalating in their torment of each other. They were two people caught in a sandstorm, blasted by pain and each blaming the other as the origin of the wind. The day before the fight culminated, Ruth had been smoking in her bedroom, leaning out the window. The door was closed, and as soon as she heard her mother's footsteps coming toward her room, she dropped the cigarette outside, flopped onto her bed, and pretended to read a book. As usual, LuLing opened the door without knocking. And when Ruth looked up with an innocent expression, LuLing shouted, "You smoking!"

"No I wasn't!"

"Still smoking." LuLing pointed toward the window and marched over. The cigarette had landed on the ledge below the window, announcing its whereabouts with a plume of smoke.

"I'm an American," Ruth shouted. "I have a right to privacy, to pursue my own happiness, not yours!"

"No right! All wrong!"

"Leave me alone!"

"Why I have daughter like you? Why I live? Why I don't die long time 'go?" LuLing was huffing and snorting. Ruth thought she looked like a mad dog. "You want I die?"

Ruth was shaking but shrugged as nonchalantly as she could. "I really don't care."

Her mother panted a few more times, then left the room. Ruth got up and slammed the door shut.

Later, over sobs of righteous indignation, she began to write in her diary, knowing full well her mother would read the words: "I hate her! She's the worst mother a person could have. She doesn't love me. She doesn't listen to me. She doesn't understand anything about me. All she does is pick on me, get mad, and make me feel worse."

She knew that what she was writing was risky. It felt like pure evil. And the descending mantle of guilt made her toss it off with even more bravado. What she wrote next was even worse, such terrible words, which later—too late—she had crossed out. Ruth now looked at them, the blacked-out lines, and she knew what they said, what her mother had read:

"You talk about killing yourself, so why don't you ever do it? I wish you would. Just do it, do it, do it! Go ahead, kill yourself! Precious Auntie wants you to, and so do I!"

At the time, she was shocked that she could write such horrible feelings. She was shocked now to remember them. She had cried while writing the words, full of anger, fear, and a strange freedom of finally admitting so openly that she wanted to hurt her mother as much as her mother hurt her. And then she had hidden the diary in the back of her underwear drawer, an easy enough place to look. She had arranged the book just so, spine facing in, a pair of pink-flowered panties on top. That way Ruth would know for sure that her mother had been snooping in there.

The next day, Ruth had dawdled before coming home from school. She walked along the beach. She stopped at a drugstore and looked at makeup. She called Wendy from a phone booth. By the time she returned home, her mother would have read the words. She expected a huge fight, no dinner, just shouting, more threats, more rants about how Ruth wanted her dead so she could live with Auntie Gal. LuLing would wait for Ruth to admit that she wrote those hateful words.

Then Ruth imagined it another way. Her mother reading the words, pounding her chest with one fist to shove her suffering back into the private area of her heart, biting her lips to keep from crying. Later, when Ruth came home, her mother would pretend not to see her. She would fix dinner, sit down, and chew silently. Ruth would not give in and ask if she could have some dinner too. She would eat cereal from the box at every meal, if that's what it took. They would act like this for days, her mother torturing Ruth with her silence, her absolute rejection. Ruth would stay strong by not feeling any pain, until nothing mattered anymore, unless, of course, it went the way it usually did, and Ruth broke down, cried, and said she was sorry.

And then Ruth had no more time to imagine any other versions of what might happen. She was home. She steeled herself. Thinking about it was just as bad as going through with it. Just get it over with, she told herself. She walked up the stairs to the door, and as soon as she opened it, her mother ran to her and said in a voice choked with worry, "Finally you're home!"

Only she realized in the next moment that this was not her mother but Auntie Gal. "Your mother is hurt," she said, and grabbed Ruth by the arm to steer her back out the door. "Hurry, hurry, we're going to the hospital now."

"Hurt?" Ruth could not move. Her body felt airless, hollow and heavy at the same time. "What do you mean? How did she get hurt?"

"She fell out the window. Why she was leaning out, I don't know. But she hit the cement. The downstairs lady called the ambulance. Her body is broken, and something is wrong with her head—I don't know what—but it's very bad, the doctors say. I just hope there's no brain damage."

Ruth burst into sobs. She doubled over and began crying hysterically. She had wished for this, caused this to happen. She cried until she had dry heaves and was faint from hyperventilating. By the time they arrived at the hospital, Auntie Gal had to take Ruth to Emergency too. A nurse tried to make her breathe into a paper bag, which Ruth slapped away, and after that someone gave her a shot. She became weightless, all worries lifted from her limbs and mind. A dark, warm blanket was placed over her body, then pulled over her head. In this nothingness, she could hear her mother's voice pronouncing to the doctors that her daughter was quiet at last because they were both dead.

Her mother, as it turned out, had suffered a broken shoulder, a cracked rib, and a concussion. When she was released from the hospital, Auntie Gal stayed a few more days to help cook and set up the house so LuLing could learn to bathe and dress herself easily. Ruth was always standing off to the side. "Can I help?" she periodically asked in a weak voice. And Auntie Gal had her make rice or wash the tub or put fresh sheets on her mother's bed.

Over the following days, Ruth anguished over whether her mother had told Auntie Gal what she had read in Ruth's diary, why she had jumped out the window. She searched Auntie Gal's face for signs that she knew. She analyzed every word she said. But Ruth could not detect any anger or disappointment or false pity in how Auntie Gal spoke. Her mother was just as puzzling. She acted not angry but sad and defeated. There was *less* of something— but what was that? Love? Worry? There was a dullness in her mother's eyes, as if she did not care what was in front of her. All was equal, all was unimportant. What did that mean? Why didn't she want to fight anymore? LuLing accepted the bowls of rice porridge Ruth brought her. She drank her tea. They spoke, but the words were about meaningless facts, nothing that could lead to disputes or misunderstanding.

"I'm going to school now," Ruth would say.

"You have lunch money?"

"Yeah. You need more tea?"

"No more."

And each day, several times a day, Ruth wanted to tell her mother that she was sorry, that she was an evil girl, that everything was her fault. But to do so would be to acknowledge what her mother obviously wanted to pretend never existed, those words Ruth had written. For weeks, they walked on tiptoe, careful not to step on the broken pieces.

On her sixteenth birthday, Ruth came home from school and found her mother had bought some of her favorite foods: the sticky rice wrapped in lotus leaves, both kinds, one with meat filling, one with sweet red-bean paste, as well as a Chinese sponge cake stuffed with strawberries and whipped cream. "Cannot cook you better things," LuLing said. Her right side was still supported in a sling, and she could not lift anything with that arm. It was hard enough for her to haul bags of groceries from the market with her left hand. Ruth saw these offerings as a gesture of forgiveness.

"I like this stuff," Ruth said politely. "It's great."

"No time buy gift," her mother mumbled. "But I find some things, maybe you still like." She pointed to the coffee table. Ruth slowly walked over and picked up a lumpy package that was clumsily wrapped in tissue paper and tape, no ribbon. Inside she found a black book and a tiny purse of red silk, fastened with a miniature frog clasp. And within the purse was a ring Ruth had always coveted, with a thin gold band and two oval pieces of apple-green jade. It had been a gift from Ruth's father, who had received it from his mother to give to his future bride. Her mother never wore it. GaoLing had once hinted that the ring should belong to her, so it could be passed along to her son, who was also the only grandson. Forever after, LuLing brought up the ring in the context of that greedy remark of her sister's.

"Wow, wow, wow." Ruth stared at the ring in her palm.

"This is very good jade, don't loose," her mother warned.

"I won't lose it." Ruth slid the ring onto her middle finger. Too small for that one, but it did fit her ring finger.

Finally Ruth looked at the other gift. It was a pocket-sized book with black leather covers, a red ribbon for a place marker.

"You holding backward," her mother said, and flipped it so the back was the front but facing the wrong way. She turned the pages for Ruth, left to right. Everything was in Chinese. "Chinese Bible," her mother said. She opened it to a page with another place marker, a sepia-toned photograph of a young Chinese woman.

"This my mother." LuLing's voice sounded strangled. "See? I make copy for you." She pulled out a wax-paper sleeve with a duplicate of the photograph.

Ruth nodded, sensing this was important, that her mother was giving her a message about mothers. She tried to pay attention and not look at the ring on her finger. But she could not help imagining what the kids at school would say, how envious they would be.

"When I little-girl time, hold this Bible here." LuLing patted her chest. "Sleep time, think about my mother."

Ruth nodded. "She was pretty then." Ruth had seen other photos of LuLing and GaoLing's mother—Waipo is what Ruth called her. In those, Waipo had a doughy face with wrinkles as deep as cracks and a mouth as severe, straight, and lipless as a sword slash. LuLing slipped the pretty picture into the Bible, then held one hand, palm up. "Now give back."

"What?"

"Ring. Give back."

Ruth didn't understand. Reluctantly she put the ring in LuLing's hand and watched as she returned it to the silk purse.

"Some things too good use right now. Save for later, 'preciate more."

Ruth wanted to cry out, "No! You can't do that! It's *my* birthday present."

But she said nothing, of course. She stood by, her throat tightening, as LuLing went to her vinyl easy chair. She pulled up the bottom cushion. Underneath was a cutting board, and beneath that a flap, which she lifted. Into this shallow cavern, her mother placed the Bible and the ring in its purse. So that's where she also hid things!

"Someday I give you forever."

Someday? Ruth's throat ached. She wanted to cry. "When's forever?" But she knew what her mother meant—forever as in, "When I forever dead, then you don't need listen me anymore." Ruth was a mix of emotions, happy that her mother had given her such nice presents, because this meant she still loved her, yet filled with a new despair that the ring had been taken away so soon.

The next day, Ruth went to the easy chair, pulled back

the cushion and cutting board, then reached her hand into the hollow to feel for the silk purse. She extracted the ring and looked at it, now a forbidden object. She felt as if she had swallowed it and it was caught in her throat. Maybe her mother had shown her the ring just to torture her. That was probably it. Her mother knew exactly how to make her miserable! Well, Ruth would not let her have the satisfaction. She would pretend she didn't care. She would force herself never to look at the ring again, to act as though it did not exist.

A few days after that, LuLing came into Ruth's room, accusing her of having gone to the beach. When Ruth lied and said she had not, LuLing showed Ruth the sneakers she had left by the front door. She banged them together and a storm of sand rained down.

"That's from the sidewalk!" Ruth protested.

And so the fights continued, and felt to Ruth both strange and familiar. They argued with increasing vigor and assurance, crossing the temporary boundaries of the last month, defending the old terrain. They flung out more pain, knowing already they had survived the worst.

Later, Ruth debated over throwing away her diary. She retrieved the dreaded book, still in the back of her underwear drawer. She turned the pages, reading here and there, weeping for herself. There was truth in what she had written, she believed, some of it, at least. There was a part of her in these pages that she did not want to forget. But when she arrived at the final entry, she was stricken with a sense that God, her mother, and Precious Auntie knew that she had committed near-murder. She carefully crossed out the last sentences, running her ballpoint pen over and over the words until everything was a blur of black ink. On the next page, the last page, she wrote: "I'm sorry. Sometimes I just wish you would say you're sorry too."

Though she could never show her mother those words, it felt good to write them. She was being truthful and neither good nor bad. She then tried to think of a place where her mother would never find her diary. She climbed onto the kitchen counter and stretched her arm way up and tossed the diary on top of the cabinet, so far out of reach that she too forgot about it over time.

Ruth now reflected that in all the years gone by, she and her mother had never talked about what had happened. She put down the diary. Forever did not mean what it once had. Forever was what changed inevitably over time. She felt a curious sympathy for her younger self, as well as an embarrassed hindsight in how foolish and egocentric she had been. If she had had a child, it would have been a daughter who grew up to make her just as miserable as she had made her mother. That daughter would have been fifteen or sixteen right about now, shouting that she hated Ruth. She wondered whether her mother had ever told her own mother that she hated her.

At that moment, she thought of the photos they had looked at during the Moon Festival dinner. Her mother had been around fifteen in the photo with Auntie Gal and Waipo. And there was another photo, the one of Precious Auntie, whom LuLing had mistakenly identified as her mother. A thought ran through her mind: The photo her mother kept in the Bible. She had also said that was her mother. Who was in that picture?

Ruth went to the vinyl chair, removed the cushion and the cutting board. Everything was still there: the small black Bible, the silk pouch, the apple-green-jade ring. She opened the Bible, and there it was, the wax-paper sleeve with the same photo her mother had shown her at the family reunion dinner. Precious Auntie, wearing the peculiar headdress and high-collared winter clothes. What did this mean? Was her mother demented thirty years before? Or was Precious Auntie really who her mother said she was? And if she was, did that mean her mother was *not* demented? Ruth stared at the photo again, searching the features of the woman. She couldn't tell.

What else was in the bottom of the chair? Ruth reached in and pulled out a package wrapped in a brown grocery bag and tied with red Christmas ribbon. Inside was a stack of paper, all written on in Chinese. At the top of certain sheets was a large character done in stylish brushed-drawn calligraphy. She had seen this before. But where? When?

And then it came to her. The other pages, the ones buried in her bottom right-hand desk drawer. "Truth," she recalled the top of that first page read. "These are the things I know are true." What did the next sentences say? The names of the dead, the secrets they took with them. What secrets? She sensed her mother's life was at stake and the answer was in her hands, had been there all along.

She looked at the top page of this new stack in her hands, the large calligraphed character. She could hear her mother scolding her, "Should study harder." Yes, she should have. The large character was familiar, a curved bottom, three marks over it—*heart!* And the first sentence, it was like the beginning of the page she had at home. "These are the things I—" And then it was different. The next word was *ying-gai*, "should." Her mother used that a lot. The next, that was *bu*, another word her mother often said. And the one after that . . . she didn't know. "These are the things I should not—" Ruth guessed what the next word might be: "These are the things I should not *tell*." "These are the things I should not *write*." "These are the things I should not *speak*." She went into her bedroom, to a shelf where her mother kept an English-Chinese dictionary. She looked up the characters for "tell," "write," "speak," but they did not match her mother's writing. She feverishly looked up more words, and ten minutes later, there it was:

"These are the things I should not forget."

Her mother had given her those other pages—what?— five or six years before. Had she written these at the same time? Did she know then that she was losing her memory? When did her mother intend to give her these pages, if ever? When she eventually gave her the ring to keep? When it was clear that Ruth was ready to pay attention? Ruth scanned the next few characters. But nothing except the one for "I" looked familiar, and there were ten thousand words that could follow "I." Now what?

Ruth lay down on the bed, the pages next to her. She looked at the photo of Precious Auntie and put that on her chest. Tomorrow she would call Art in Hawaii and see if he could recommend someone who could translate. That was One. She would retrieve the other pages from home. That was Two. She would call Auntie Gal and see what she knew. That was Three. And she would ask her mother to tell her about her life. For once, she would ask. She would listen. She would sit down and not be in a hurry or have anything else to do. She would even move in with her mother, spend more time getting to know her. Art would not be too happy about that. He might take her moving out as a sign of problems. But someone had to take care of her mother. And she wanted to. She wanted to be here, as her mother told her about her life, taking her through all the detours of the past, explaining the multiple meanings of Chinese words, how to translate her heart. Her hands would always be full, and finally, she and her mother could both stop counting.

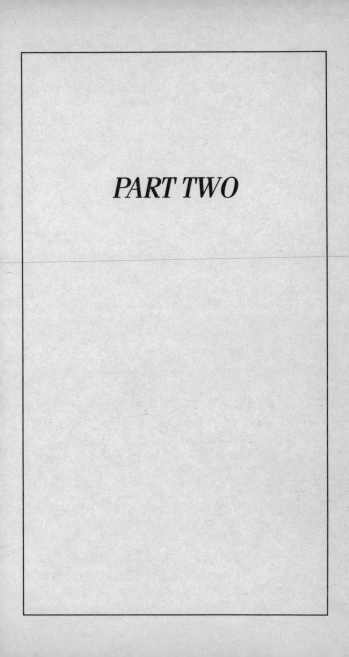

PART TWO

HEART

These are the things I must not forget.

I was raised with the Liu clan in the rocky Western Hills south of Peking. The oldest recorded name of our village was Immortal Heart. Precious Auntie taught me how to write this down on my chalkboard. *Watch now, Doggie,* she ordered, and drew the character for "heart": *See this curving stroke? That's the bottom of the heart, where blood gathers and flows. And the dots, those are the two veins and the artery that carry the blood in and out.* As I traced over the character, she asked: *Whose dead heart gave shape to this word? How did it begin, Doggie? Did it belong to a woman? Was it drawn in sadness?*

I once saw the heart of a fresh-killed pig. It was red and glistening. And I had already seen plenty of chicken hearts in a bowl, waiting to be cooked. They looked like tiny lips and were the same color as Precious Auntie's scars. But what did a woman heart look like? "Why do we have to know whose heart it was?" I asked as I wrote the character.

And Precious Auntie flapped her hands fast: *A person should consider how things begin. A particular beginning results in a particular end.*

I remember her often talking about this, how things begin. Since then I have wondered about the beginning

173

and end of many things. Like Immortal Heart village. And the people who lived there, myself included. By the time I was born, Immortal Heart was no longer lucky. The village lay between hills in a valley that dropped into a deep limestone ravine. The ravine was shaped like the curved chamber of a heart, and the heart's artery and veins were the three streams that once fed and drained the ravine. But they had gone dry. So had the divine springs. Nothing was left of the waterways but cracked gullies and the stench of a fart.

Yet the village began as a sacred place. According to legend, a visiting emperor himself had planted a pine tree in the middle of the valley. The tree was to honor his dead mother, and his respect for his mother was so great he vowed that the tree would live forever. When Precious Auntie first saw the tree, it was already more than three thousand years old.

Rich and poor alike made a pilgrimage to Immortal Heart. They hoped that the tree's vital energy would rub off on them. They stroked the trunk, patted the leaves, then prayed for baby sons or big fortunes, a cure for dying, an end to curses. Before leaving, they chipped off some bark, snapped off some twigs. They took them away as souvenirs. Precious Auntie said this was what killed the tree, too much admiration. When the tree died, the souvenirs lost their strength. And because the dead tree was no longer immortal, it was no longer famous, nor was our village. That tree was not even ancient, people said afterward, maybe only two or three hundred years old. As for the story about the emperor honoring his mother? That was a fake feudal legend to make us think the corrupt were sincere. Those complaints came out the same year that the old Ching Dynasty fell down and the new Republic sprang up.

The nickname of our village is easy for me to remember: Forty-six Kilometers from Reed Moat Bridge. Reed Moat Bridge is the same as Marco Polo Bridge, what people now call the turnoff point to and from Peking. GaoLing's probably forgotten the old name, but I have not. During my girlhood, the directions to get to Immortal Heart went like this: "First find the Reed Moat Bridge, then walk backward forty-six kilometers."

That joke made it sound as if we lived in a pitiful little hamlet of twenty or thirty people. Not so. When I was growing up, nearly two thousand people lived there. It was crowded, packed from one edge of the valley to the other. We had a brick maker, a sack weaver, and a dye mill. We had twenty-four market days, six temple fairs, and a primary school that GaoLing and I went to when we were not helping our family at home. We had all kinds of peddlers who went from house to house, selling fresh bean curd and steamed buns, twisted dough and colorful candies. And we had lots of people to buy those goods. A few coppers, that was all you needed to make your stomach as happy as a rich man's.

The Liu clan had lived in Immortal Heart for six centuries. For that amount of time, the sons had been inkstick makers who sold their goods to travelers. They had lived in the same courtyard house that had added rooms, and later wings, when one mother four hundred years ago gave birth to eight sons, one a year. The family home grew from a simple three-pillar house to a compound with wings stretching five pillars each. In later generations, the number of sons was less, and the extra rooms became run-down and were rented to squabbling tenants. Whether those people laughed at coarse jokes or screamed in pain, it did not matter, the sounds were the same, ugly to hear.

All in all, our family was successful but not so much that we caused great envy. We ate meat or bean curd at almost every meal. We had new padded jackets every winter, no holes. We had money to give for the temple, the opera, the fair. But the men of our family also had ambitions. They were always looking for more. They said that in Peking, more people wrote important documents. Those important documents required more good ink. Peking was where more of the big money was. Around 1920, Father, my uncles, and their sons went there to sell the ink. From then on, that was where they lived most of the time, in the back room of a shop in the old Pottery-Glazing District.

In our family, the women made the ink. We stayed home. We all worked—me, GaoLing, my aunts and girl cousins, everybody. Even the babies and Great-Granny had a job of picking out stones from the dried millet we boiled for breakfast. We gathered each day in the ink-making studio. According to Great-Granny, the studio began as a grain shed that sat along the front wall of the courtyard house. Over the years, one generation of sons added brick walls and a tile roof. Another strengthened the beams and lengthened it by two pillars. The next tiled the floors and dug pits for storing the ingredients. Then other descendants made a cellar for keeping the inksticks away from the heat and cold. "And now look," Great-Granny often bragged. "Our studio is an ink palace."

Because our ink was the best quality, we had to keep the tables and the floors clean year-round. With the dusty yellow winds from the Gobi, this was not easy to do. The window openings had to be covered with both glass and thick paper. In the summer, we hung netting over the doorways to keep out the insects. In the winter, it was sheep hides to keep out the snow.

Summer was the worst season for ink-making. Heat upon heat. The fumes burned our eyes and nostrils and lungs. From watching Precious Auntie tie her scarf over her marred face, we got the idea of putting a wet cloth over our mouths. I can still smell the ingredients of our ink. There were several kinds of fragrant soot: pine, cassia, camphor, and the wood of the chopped-down Immortal Tree. Father hauled home several big logs of it after lightning cracked the dead tree right down the middle, exposing its heart, which was nearly hollow because of beetles eating it inside out. There was also a glue of sticky paste mixed with many oils—serpentine, camphor, turpentine, and tung wood. Then we added a sweet poisonous flower that helped resist insects and rats. That was how special our ink was, all those lasting smells.

We made the ink a little at a time. If a fire broke out, as it had a couple of hundred years before, all the supplies and stock would not be lost at once. And if a batch was too sticky or too wet, too soft or not black enough, it was easier to find out who was to blame. Each of us had at least one part in a long list of things to do. First there was burning and grinding, measuring and pouring. Then came stirring and molding, drying and carving. And finally, wrapping and counting, storing and stacking. One season I had to wrap, only that. My mind could wander but my fingers still moved like small machines. Another season I had to use very fine tweezers to pluck bugs that had fallen onto the sticks. Whenever GaoLing did this, she left too many dents. Precious Auntie's job was to sit at a long table and press the sooty mixture into the stone molds. As a result, the tips of her fingers were always black. When the ink was dry, she used a long, sharp tool to carve the good-luck words and drawings into the sticks. Her calligraphy was even better than Father's.

It was boring work, but we were proud of our secret family recipe. It yielded just the right color and hardness. An inkstick of ours could last ten years or more. It did not dry out and crumble, or grow soggy with moisture. And if the sticks were stored in the coolness of a root cellar, as ours were, they could last from one great period of history to another. Those who used our ink said the same. It didn't matter how much heat or moisture or dirt from fingers soaked into the page, their words lasted, black and strong.

Mother claimed the ink was why our hair remained the blackest black. It was better for the hair than drinking black-sesame-seed soup. "Work hard all day making ink, look young at night while you sleep." That was our joke, and Great-Granny often boasted: "My hair is as black as the burnt shell of a horse chestnut and my face as wrinkly white as the meat inside." Great-Granny had a clever tongue. One time she added, "Better than having white hair and a burnt face," and everyone laughed, even though Precious Auntie was in the room.

In later years, however, Great-Granny's tongue was not so sharp or fast. Often she said with a worried brow, "Have you seen Hu Sen?" You could say yes, you could say no, and a moment later, she chirped like a bird, "Hu Sen? Hu Sen?" always requesting her dead grandson, very sad to hear.

Toward the end of her life, Great-Granny had thoughts that were like crumbling walls, stones without mortar. A doctor said her inner wind was cold and her pulse was slow, a shallow stream about to freeze. He advised foods with more heat. But Great-Granny only grew worse. Precious Auntie suspected that a tiny flea had crawled into her ear and was feasting on her brain. Confusion Itch was the name of the malady, Precious Auntie said. It is the reason people often scratch their heads when they cannot remember. Her father had been a doctor, and she had seen other patients with the same problem. Yesterday, when I could not remember Precious Auntie's name, I wondered if a flea had run in my ear! But now that I am writing down so many things, I know I don't have Great-Granny's disease. I can recall the smallest details even though they were long ago and far away.

The compound where we lived and worked—that comes back to me as if I were now standing before the gate. It was on Pig's Head Lane. The road started at the east, near the market square where pigs' heads were sold. From the square, it hooked to the north and ran past the former location of the once famous Immortal Tree. Then it tightened into the little crooked alley where one compound bumped into another. The end of Pig's Head Lane was a narrow perch of earth above the deepest part of the ravine. Precious Auntie told me that the perch was originally made by a warlord thousands of years before. He dreamed that the insides of the mountain were made of jade. So he ordered everyone to dig, dig, don't stop. Men, women, and children dredged for his dream. By the time the warlord died, the children were old, with crooked backs, and half the mountain lay on its side.

Behind our compound, the perch became a cliff. And way down, if you fell head over toes, was the bottom of the ravine. The Liu family had once owned twenty *mu* of land behind the compound. But over the centuries, with each heavy rainfall, the walls of the ravine had collapsed and widened, rumbled and deepened. Each decade, those twenty *mu* of land grew smaller and smaller and the cliff crept closer to the back of our house.

The moving cliff gave us the feeling we had to look behind us to know what lay ahead. We called it the End of the World. Sometimes the men of our family argued among themselves whether we still owned the land that had crashed down into the ravine. One uncle said, "What you own is the spit that travels from your own mouth to the bottom of that wasteland." And his wife said, "Don't talk about this anymore. You're only inviting disaster." For what lay beyond and below was too unlucky to say out loud: unwanted babies, suicide maidens, and beggar ghosts. Everyone knew this.

I went to the cliff many times with my brothers and GaoLing when we were younger. We liked to roll spoiled melons and rotten cabbages over the edge. We watched them fall and splat, hitting skulls and bones. At least that was what we thought they had hit. But one time we climbed down, sliding on our bottoms, grabbing onto roots, descending into the underworld. And when we heard rustling sounds in the brush, we screamed so loud our ears hurt. The ghost turned out to be a scavenger dog. And the skulls and bones, they were just boulders and broken branches. But though we saw no bodies, all around were bright pieces of clothing: a sleeve, a collar, a shoe, and we were sure they belonged to the dead. And then we smelled it: the stink of ghosts. A person needs to smell that only once to know what it is. It rose from the earth. It wafted toward us on the wings of a thousand flies. The flies chased us like a storm cloud, and as we scrambled back up, First Brother kicked loose a stone that gouged out a piece of Second Brother's scalp. We could not hide this wound from Mother, and when she saw it, she beat us all, then told us that if we ever went down to the End of the World again, we might as well stand outside the walls of the compound forever and not bother to come in.

The walls of the Liu home were made of rocks exposed from the washed-down earth. The rocks were stacked and held together with a mud, mortar, and millet paste, then plastered over with lime. They were sweaty damp in summer, moldy damp in winter. And in the many rooms of that house, here and there was always another roof leak or drafty hole in the wall. And yet when I remember that house, I have a strange homesickness for it. Only there do I have a memory of secret places, warm or cool, of darkness where I hid and pretended I could escape to somewhere else.

Within those walls, many families of different positions and generations lived together at the same time, from landlord to tenants, Great-Granny to smallest niece. I guess we were thirty or more people, half of which was the Liu clan. Liu Jin Sen was the eldest of four sons. He was the one I called Father. My uncles and their wives called him Eldest Brother. My cousins called him Eldest Uncle. And by position my uncles were Big Uncle and Little Uncle, and their wives were Big Aunt and Little Aunt. When I was very small, I used to think Father and Mother were called Eldest because they were much taller than my uncles and aunts. First Brother and Second Brother were also large-boned, as was GaoLing, and for a long time I did not know why I was so short.

Baby Uncle was the fourth son, the youngest, the favorite. His name was Liu Hu Sen. He was my real father, and he would have married Precious Auntie, if only he had not died on their wedding day.

* * *

Precious Auntie was born in a bigger town down in the foothills, a place called Zhou's Mouth of the Mountain, named in honor of Emperor Zhou of the Shang Dynasty, whom everyone now remembers as a tyrant.

Our family sometimes went to the Mouth of the Mountain for temple fairs and operas. If we traveled by road, it was only about ten kilometers from Immortal Heart. If we walked through the End of the World, it was half that distance but a more dangerous way to go, especially in the summertime. That was when the big rains came. The dry ravine filled, and before you could run to the cliffs, climb up, and cry out, "Goddess of Mercy," the gullies ran by like thieves, grabbing you and whatever else was not deeply rooted in the soil. Once the rain stopped, the floodwaters drained fast and the mouths of the caves swallowed the dirt and the trees, the bodies and the bones. They went down the mountain's throat, into its stomach, intestines, and finally the bowels, where everything got stuck. *Constipated,* Precious Auntie once explained to me. *Now you see why there are so many bones and hills: Chicken Bone Hill, Old Cow Hill, Dragon Bone Hill. Of course, it's not just dragon bones in Dragon Bone Hill. Some are from ordinary creatures, bear, elephant, hippopotamus.* Precious Auntie drew a picture of each of these animals on my chalkboard, because we had never talked about them before.

I have a bone, probably from a turtle, she told me. She fished it from a tuck in her sleeve. It looked like a dried turnip with pockmarks. *My father almost ground this up for medicine. Then he saw there was writing on it.* She turned the bone over, and I saw strange characters running up and down. *Until recently, these kinds of bones weren't so valuable, because of the scratches. Bone diggers used to smooth them with a file before selling them to medicine* shops. *Now the scholars call these oracle bones, and they sell for twice as much. And the words on here? They're questions to the gods.*

"What does it say?" I asked.

Who knows? The words were different then. But it must be something that should have been remembered. Otherwise, why did the gods say it, why did a person write it down?

"Where are the answers?"

Those are the cracks. The diviner put a hot nail to the bone, and it cracked like a tree hit by lightning. Then he interpreted what the cracks meant.

She took back the divining bone. *Someday, when you know how to remember, I'll give this to you to keep. But for now you'll only forget where you put it. Later we can go looking for more dragon bones, and if you find one with writing on it, you can keep it for yourself.*

In the Mouth of the Mountain, every poor man collected dragon bones when he had a chance. So did the women, but if they found one, they had to say a man found it instead, because otherwise the bone was not worth as much. Later, middlemen went around the village buying the dragon bones, and then they took them to Peking and sold them to medicine shops for high prices, and the shops sold them to sick people for higher prices yet. The bones were well known for curing anything, from wasting diseases to stupidity. Plenty of doctors sold them. And so did Precious Auntie's father. He used bones to heal bones.

For nine hundred years, Precious Auntie's family had been bonesetters. That was the tradition. Her father's customers were mostly men and boys who were crushed in the coal mines and limestone quarries. He treated other maladies when necessary, but bonesetting was his specialty.

He did not have to go to a special school to be a bone doctor. He learned from watching his father, and his father learned from his father before him. That was their inheritance. They also passed along the secret location for finding the best dragon bones, a place called the Monkey's Jaw. An ancestor from the time of the Sung Dynasty had found the cave in the deepest ravines of the dry riverbed. Each generation dug deeper and deeper, with one soft crack in the cave leading to another farther in. And the secret of the exact location was also a family heirloom, passed from generation to generation, father to son, and in Precious Auntie's time, father to daughter to me.

I still remember the directions to our cave. It was between the Mouth of the Mountain and Immortal Heart, far from the other caves in the foothills, where everyone else went to dig up dragon bones. Precious Auntie took me there several times, always in the spring or the autumn, never summer or winter. To get there, we went down into the End of the World and walked along the middle of the ravine, away from the walls, where the grown-ups said there were things that were too bad to see. Sometimes we passed by a skein of weeds, shards of a bowl, a quagmire of twigs. In my childish mind, those sights became parched flesh, a baby's skullcap, a soup of maiden bones. And maybe they were, because sometimes Precious Auntie put her hands over my eyes.

Of the three dry streambeds, we took the one that was the artery of the heart. And then we stood in front of the cave itself, a split in the mountain only as tall as a broom. Precious Auntie pulled aside the dead bushes that hid the cave. And the two of us took big breaths and went in. In words, it is hard to say how we made our way in, like trying to describe how to get inside an ear. I had to twist my body in an unnatural way far to the left, then rest a foot on a little ledge that I could reach only by crooking my leg close to my chest. By then I was crying and Precious Auntie was grunting to me, because I could not see her black fingers to know what she was saying. I had to follow her huffs and handclaps, crawling like a dog so I would not hit my head or fall down. When we finally reached the larger part of the cave, Precious Auntie lighted the candle lamp and hung it on a long pole with footrests, which had been left by one of her clan from long ago.

On the floor of the cave were digging tools, iron wedges of different sizes, hammers and claws, as well as sacks for dragging out the dirt. The walls of the cave were many layers, like an eight-treasure rice pudding cut in half, with lighter, crumbly things on top, then a thicker muddy part like bean paste below, and growing heavier toward the bottom. The highest layer was easiest to chip. The lowest was like rock. But that was where the best bones were found. And after centuries of people's digging through the bottom there was now an overhang waiting to crash down. The inside of the cave looked like the molars of a monkey that could bite you in two, which was why it was called the Monkey's Jaw.

While we rested, Precious Auntie talked with her inky hands. *Stay away from that side of the monkey's teeth. Once they chomped down on an ancestor, and he was ground up and gobbled with stone. My father found his skull over there. We put it back right away. Bad luck to separate a man's head from his body.*

Hours later, we would climb back out of the Monkey's Jaw with a sack of dirt and, if we had been lucky, one or two dragon bones. Precious Auntie held them up to the sky and bowed, thanking the gods. She believed the bones from this cave were the reason her family had become famous as bonesetters.

When I was a girl, she said once as we walked home, *I remember lots of desperate people coming to see my father. He was their last chance. If a man could not walk, he could not work. And if he could not work, his family could not eat. Then he would die, and that would be the end of his family line and all that his ancestors had worked for.*

For those desperate customers, Precious Auntie's father had remedies of three kinds: modern, try-anything, and traditional. The modern was the Western medicine of missionaries. The try-anything was the spells and chants of rogue monks. As for the traditional, that included the dragon bones, as well as seahorses and seaweed, insect shells and rare seeds, tree bark and bat dung, all of the highest quality. Precious Auntie's father was so talented that patients from the five surrounding mountain villages traveled to the Famous Bonesetter from the Mouth of the Mountain (whose name I will write down, once I remember it).

Skilled and famous though he was, he could not prevent all tragedies. When Precious Auntie was four, her mother and older brothers died of an intestine-draining disease. So did most of the other relatives from both sides of the family, dead just three days after they attended a red-egg ceremony and drank from a well infected with the body of a suicide maiden. The bonesetter was so ashamed he could not save his own family members that he spent his entire fortune and went into a lifetime of debt to hold their funerals.

Because of grief, Precious Auntie said with her hands, *he spoiled me, let me do whatever a son might do. I learned to read and write, to ask questions, to play riddles,*

to write eight-legged poems, to walk alone and admire na-
ture. The old biddies used to warn him that it was dan-
gerous that I was so boldly happy, instead of shy and
cowering around strangers. And why didn't he bind my
feet, they asked. My father was used to seeing pain of the
worst kinds. But with me, he was helpless. He couldn't
bear to see me cry.

So Precious Auntie freely followed her father around in
his study and shop. She soaked the splints and plucked the
moss. She polished the scales and tallied the accounts. A
customer could point to any jar in the shop and she could
read the name of its contents, even the scientific words for
animal organs. As she grew older, she learned to bleed
a wound with a square nail, to use her own saliva for
cleansing sores, to apply a layer of maggots for eating pus,
and to wrap torn flaps with woven paper. By the time she
passed from childhood to maidenhood, she had heard
every kind of scream and curse. She had touched so many
bodies, living, dying, and dead, that few families considered her for a bride. And while she had never been possessed by romantic love, she recognized the throes of
death. *When the ears grow soft and flatten against the*
head, she once told me, *then it's too late. A few seconds*
later, the last breath hisses out. The body turns cold. She
taught me many facts like that.

For the most difficult cases, she helped her father put
the injured man on a light latticework pallet of rattan. Her
father lifted and lowered this by pulleys and rope, and she
guided the pallet into a tub filled with salt water. There the
man's crushed bones floated and were fitted into place.
Afterward, Precious Auntie brought her father rattan strips
that had been soaked soft. He bent them into a splint so the
limb could breathe but remain still. Toward the end of the

visit, the bonesetter opened his jar of dragon bones and used a narrow chisel to chip off a sliver tiny as a fingernail clipping. Precious Auntie ground this into a powder with a silver ball. The powder went into a paste for rubbing or a potion for drinking. Then the lucky patient went home. Soon he was back in the quarries all day long.

One day, at dinnertime, Precious Auntie told me a story with her hands that only I could understand. *A rich lady came to my father and told him to unbind her feet and mold them into more modern ones. She said she wanted to wear high-heeled shoes. "But don't make the new feet too big," she said, "not like a slave girl's or a foreigner's. Make them naturally small like hers." And she pointed to my feet.*

I forgot that Mother and my other aunts were at the dinner table, and I said aloud, "Do bound feet look like the white lilies that the romantic books describe?" Mother and my aunts, who still had bound feet, gave me a frowning look. How could I talk so openly about a woman's most private parts? So Precious Auntie pretended to scold me with her hands for asking such a question, but what she really said was this: *They're usually crimped like flower-twist bread. But if they're dirty and knotty with calluses, they look like rotten ginger roots and smell like pig snouts three days dead.*

In this way, Precious Auntie taught me to be naughty, just like her. She taught me to be curious, just like her. She taught me to be spoiled. And because I was all these things, she could not teach me to be a better daughter, though in the end, she tried to change my faults.

I remember how she tried. It was the last week we were together. She did not speak to me for days. Instead she wrote and wrote and wrote. Finally she handed me a bundle of pages laced together with cord. *This is my true story,* she told me, *and yours as well.* Out of spite, I did not read most of those pages. But when I did, this is what I learned.

One late-autumn day, when Precious Auntie was nineteen by her Chinese age, the bonesetter had two new patients. The first was a screaming baby from a family who lived in Immortal Heart. The second was Baby Uncle. They would both cause Precious Auntie everlasting sorrow, but in two entirely different ways.

The bawling baby was the youngest son of a big-chested man named Chang, a coffinmaker who had grown rich in times of plagues. The carvings on the outside of his coffins were of camphor wood. But the insides were cheap pine, painted and lacquered to look and smell like the better golden wood.

Some of that same golden wood had fallen from a stack and knocked the baby's shoulder out of its socket. That's why the baby was howling, Chang's wife reported with a frightened face. Precious Auntie recognized this nervous woman. Two years before, she had sat in the bonesetter's shop because her eye and jaw had been broken by a stone that must have fallen out of the open sky. Now she was back with her husband, who was slapping the baby's leg, telling him to stop his racket. Precious Auntie shouted at Chang: "First the shoulder, now you want to break his leg as well." Chang scowled at her. Precious Auntie picked up the baby. She rubbed a little bit of medicine inside his cheeks. Soon the baby quieted, yawned once, and fell asleep. Then the bonesetter snapped the small shoulder into place.

"What's the medicine?" the coffinmaker asked Precious Auntie. She didn't answer.

"Traditional things," the bonesetter said. "A little opium, a little herbs, and a special kind of dragon bone we dig out from a secret place only our family knows."

"Special dragon bone, eh?" Chang dipped his finger in the medicine bowl, then dabbed inside his cheek. He offered some to Precious Auntie, who sniffed in disgust, and then he laughed and gave Precious Auntie a bold look, as if he already owned her and could do whatever he pleased.

Right after the Changs and their baby left, Baby Uncle limped in.

He had been injured by his nervous horse, he explained to the bonesetter. He had been traveling from Peking to Immortal Heart, and during a rest, the horse startled a rabbit, then the rabbit startled the horse, and the horse stepped on Baby Uncle's foot. Three broken toes resulted, and Baby Uncle rode his bad horse to the Mouth of the Mountain, straight to the Famous Bonesetter's shop.

Baby Uncle sat in the blackwood examination chair. Precious Auntie was in the back room and could see him through the parted curtain. He was a thin young man of twenty-two. His face was refined but he did not act pompous or overly formal, and while his gown was not that of a rich gentleman, he was well groomed. She heard him joke about his accident: "My mare was so crazy with fright I thought she was going to gallop straight to the underworld with me stuck astride." When Precious Auntie stepped into the room, she said, "But fate brought you here instead." Baby Uncle fell quiet. When she smiled, he forgot his pain. When she put a dragon bone poultice on his naked foot, he decided to marry her. That was Precious Auntie's version of how they fell in love.

I have never seen a picture of my real father, but Precious Auntie told me that he was very handsome and smart, yet also shy enough to make a girl feel tender. He looked like a poor scholar who could rise above his circumstances, and surely he would have qualified for the imperial examinations if they had not been canceled several years before by the new Republic.

The next morning, Baby Uncle came back with three stemfuls of lychees for Precious Auntie as a gift of appreciation. He peeled off the shell of one, and she ate the white-fleshed fruit in front of him. The morning was warm for late autumn, they both remarked. He asked if he could recite a poem he had written that morning: "You speak," he said, "the language of shooting stars, more surprising than sunrise, more brilliant than the sun, as brief as sunset. I want to follow its trail to eternity."

In the afternoon, the coffinmaker Chang brought a watermelon to the bonesetter. "To show my highest appreciation," he said. "My baby son is already well, able to pick up bowls and smash them with the strength of three boys."

Later that week, unbeknownst one to the other, each man went to a different fortune-teller. The two men wanted to know if their combination of birthdates with Precious Auntie's was lucky. They asked if there were any bad omens for a marriage.

The coffinmaker went to a fortune-teller in Immortal Heart, a man who walked about the village with a divining stick. The marriage signs were excellent, the fortune-teller said. See here, Precious Auntie was born in a Rooster year, and because Chang was a Snake, that was nearly the best match possible. The old man said that Precious Auntie also had a lucky number of strokes in her name (I will write the number down here when I remember her name). And as a bonus, she had a mole in position eleven, near the fatty part of her cheek, indicating that only sweet words fell from her obedient mouth. The coffinmaker was so happy to hear this that he gave the fortune-teller a big tip.

Baby Uncle went to a fortune-teller in the Mouth of the Mountain, an old lady with a face more wrinkled than her palm. She saw nothing but calamity. The first sign was the mole on Precious Auntie's face. It was in position twelve, she told Baby Uncle, and it dragged down her mouth, meaning that her life would always bring her sadness. Their combination of birth years was also inharmonious, she a fire Rooster and he a wood Horse. The girl would ride his back and peck him apart piece by piece. She would consume him with her insatiable demands. And here was the worst part. The girl's father and mother had reported the date of her birth was the sixteenth day of the seventh moon. But the fortune-teller had a sister-in-law who lived near the bonesetter, and she knew better. She had heard the newborn's wails, not on the sixteenth day, but on the fifteenth, the only day when unhappy ghosts are allowed to roam the earth. The sister-in-law said the baby sounded like this: *"Wu-wu, wu-wu,"* not like a human but like a haunted one. The fortune-teller confided to Baby Uncle that she knew the girl quite well. She often saw her on market days, walking by herself. That strange girl did fast calculations in her head and argued with merchants. She was arrogant and headstrong. She was also educated, taught by her father to know the mysteries of the body. The girl was too curious, too questioning, too determined to follow her own mind. Maybe she was possessed. Better find another marriage match, the fortune-teller said. This one would lead to disaster.

Baby Uncle gave the fortune-teller more money, not as a tip, but to make her think harder. The fortune-teller kept shaking her head. But after Baby Uncle had given a total of a thousand coppers, the old lady finally had another thought. When the girl smiled, which was often, her mole was in a luckier position, number eleven. The fortune-teller consulted an almanac, matched it to the hour of the girl's birth. Good news. The Hour of the Rabbit was peace-loving. Her inflexibility was just a bluff. And any leftover righteousness could be beaten down with a strong stick. It was further revealed that the fortune-teller's sister-in-law was a gossip known for exaggeration. But just to make sure the marriage went well, the fortune-teller sold Baby Uncle a Hundred Different Things charm that covered bad dates, bad spirits, bad luck, and hair loss. "But even with this, don't marry in the Dragon Year. Bad year for a Horse."

The first marriage proposal came from Chang's match-maker, who went to the bonesetter and related the good omens. She boasted of the coffinmaker's respect, as an ar-tisan descended from noted artisans. She described his house, his rock gardens, his fish ponds, the furniture in his many rooms, how the wood was of the best color, purple like a fresh bruise. As to the matter of a dowry, the coffin-maker was willing to be more than generous. Since the girl was to be a second wife and not a first, couldn't her dowry be a jar of opium and a jar of dragon bones? This was not much, yet it was priceless, and therefore not insulting to the girl's worth.

The bonesetter considered the offer. He was growing

old. Where would his daughter go when he died? And what other man would want her in his household? She was too spirited, too set in her ways. She had no mother to teach her the manners of a wife. True, the coffinmaker would not have been his first choice of son-in-law, if he had had another, but he did not want to stand in the way of his daughter's future happiness. He told Precious Auntie about the generous offer from the coffinmaker.

To this, Precious Auntie huffed. "The man's a brute," she said. "I'd rather eat worms than be his wife."

The bonesetter had to give Chang's matchmaker an awkward answer: "I'm sorry," he said, "but my daughter cried herself sick, unable to bear the thought of leaving her worthless father." The lie would have been swallowed without disgrace, if only the offer from Baby Uncle's matchmaker had not been accepted the following week.

A few days after the future marriage was announced, the coffinmaker went back to the Mouth of the Mountain and surprised Precious Auntie as she was returning from the well. "You think you can insult me, then walk away laughing?"

"Who insulted whom? You asked me to be your concubine, a servant to your wife. I'm not interested in being a slave in a feudal marriage."

As she tried to leave, Chang pinched her neck, saying he should break it, then shook her as if he truly might snap off her head like a winter twig. But instead he threw her to the ground, cursing her and her dead mother's private parts.

When Precious Auntie recovered her breath, she sneered, "Big words, big fists. You think you can scare a person into being sorry?"

And he said these words, which she never forgot: "You'll soon be sorry every day of your miserable life."

Precious Auntie did not tell her father or Hu Sen what had happened. No sense in worrying them. And why lead her future husband to wonder if Chang had a reason to feel insulted? Too many people had already said she was too strong, accustomed to having her own way. And perhaps this was true. She had no fear of punishment or disgrace. She was afraid of almost nothing.

A month before the wedding, Baby Uncle came to her room late at night. "I want to hear your voice in the dark," he whispered. "I want to hear the language of shooting stars." She let him into her *k'ang* and he eagerly began the nuptials. But as Baby Uncle caressed her, a wind blew over her skin and she began to tremble and shake. For the first time, she was afraid, she realized, frightened by unknown joy.

The wedding was supposed to take place in Immortal Heart village, right after the start of the new Dragon Year. It was a bare spring day. Slippery pockets of ice lay on the ground. In the morning, a traveling photographer came to the bonesetter's shop in the Mouth of the Mountain. He had broken his arm the month before, and his payment was a photograph of Precious Auntie on her wedding day. She wore her best winter jacket, one with a high fur-lined collar, and an embroidered cap. She had to stare a long time into the camera, and as she did so, she thought of how her life would soon change forever. Though she was happy, she was also worried. She sensed danger, but she could not name what it was. She tried to look far into the future, but she could see nothing.

For the journey to the wedding, she changed her clothes to her bridal costume, a red jacket and skirt, the fancy headdress with a scarf that she had to drape over her head once she left her father's home. The bonesetter had borrowed money to rent two mule carts, one to carry gifts for the groom's family, the other for the bride's trunks of blankets and clothes. There was an enclosed sedan chair for the bride herself, and the bonesetter also had to hire four sedan carriers, two carters, a flute player, and two bodyguards to watch out for bandits. For his daughter, he had procured only the best: the fanciest sedan chair, the cleanest carts, the strongest guards with real pistols and gunpowder. In one of the carts was the dowry, the jar of opium and the jar of dragon bones, the last of his supply. He assured his daughter many times not to worry about the cost. After her wedding, he could go to the Monkey's Jaw and gather more bones.

Halfway between the villages, two bandits wearing hoods sprang out of the bushes. "I'm the famous Mongol Bandit!" the larger one bellowed. Right away, Precious Auntie recognized the voice of Chang the coffinmaker. What kind of ridiculous joke was this? But before she could say anything, the guards threw down their pistols, the carriers dropped their poles, and Precious Auntie was thrown to the floor of the sedan and knocked out.

When she came to, she saw Baby Uncle's face in a haze. He had lifted her out of the sedan. She looked around and saw that the wedding trunks had been ransacked and the guards and carriers had fled. And then she noticed her father lying in a ditch, his head and neck at an odd angle, the life gone from his face. Was she in a dream? "My father," she moaned. "I want to go to him." As she bent over the body, unable to make sense of what had happened, Baby Uncle picked up a pistol that one of the guards had dropped.

"I swear I'll find the demons who caused my bride so much grief," he shouted, and then he fired the pistol toward heaven, startling his horse.

Precious Auntie did not see the kick that killed Baby Uncle, but she heard it, a terrible crack, like the opening of the earth when it was born. For the rest of her life she was to hear it in the breaking of twigs, the crackling of fire, whenever a melon was cleaved in the summer.

That was how Precious Auntie became a widow and an orphan in the same day. "This is a curse," she murmured, as she stared down at the bodies of the men she loved. For three sleepless days after their deaths, Precious Auntie apologized to the corpses of her father and Baby Uncle. She talked to their still faces. She touched their mouths, though this was forbidden and caused the women of the house to fear that the wronged ghosts might either possess her or decide to stay.

On the third day, Chang arrived with two coffins. "He killed them!" Precious Auntie cried. She picked up a fire poker and tried to strike him. She beat at the coffins. Baby Uncle's brothers had to wrestle her away. They apologized to Chang for the girl's lunacy, and Chang replied that grief of this magnitude was admirable. Because Precious Auntie continued to be wild with admirable grief, the women of the house had to bind her from elbows to knees with strips of cloth. Then they laid her on Baby Uncle's *k'ang*, where she wiggled and twisted like a butterfly stuck in its cocoon until Great-Granny forced her to drink a bowl of medicine that made her body grow limp. For two days and nights, she dreamed she was with Baby Uncle, lying on the *k'ang* as his bride.

When she revived, she was alone in the dark. Her arms

and legs had been unbound, but they were weak. The house was quiet. She went searching for her father and Baby Uncle. When she reached the main hall, the bodies were gone, already buried in Chang's wooden handiwork. Weeping, she wandered about the house and vowed to join them in the yellow earth. In the ink-making studio, she went looking for a length of rope, a sharp knife, matches she could swallow, anything to cause pain greater than she felt. And then she saw a pot of black resin. She lowered a dipper into the liquid and put it in the maw of the stove. The oily ink became a soup of blue flames. She tipped the ladle and swallowed.

Great-Granny was the first to hear the thump-bumping sounds in the studio. Soon the other women of the household were there as well. They found Precious Auntie thrashing on the floor, hissing air out of a mouth blackened with blood and ink. "Like eels are swimming in the bowl of her mouth," Mother said. "Better if she dies."

But Great-Granny did not let this happen. Baby Uncle's ghost had come to her in a dream and warned that if Precious Auntie died, he and his ghost bride would roam the house and seek revenge on those who had not pitied her. Everyone knew there was nothing worse than a vengeful ghost. They caused rooms to stink like corpses. They turned bean curd rancid in a moment's breath. They let wild creatures climb over the walls and gates. With a ghost in the house, you could never get a good night's sleep.

Day in and day out, Great-Granny dipped cloths into ointments and laid these over Precious Auntie's wounds. She bought dragon bones, crushed them, and sprinkled them into her swollen mouth. And then she noticed that another part of Precious Auntie had become swollen: her womb.

Over the next few months, Precious Auntie's wounds

changed from pus to scars, and her womb grew like a gourd. She had once been a fine-looking girl. Now all except blind beggars shuddered at the sight of her. One day, when it was clear she was going to survive, Great-Granny said to her speechless patient: "Now that I've saved your life, where will you and your baby go? What will you do?"

That night, the ghost of Baby Uncle came once again to Great-Granny, and the next morning, Great-Granny told Precious Auntie: "You are to stay and be nursemaid to this baby. First Sister will claim it as hers and raise it as a Liu. To those you meet, we'll say you're a distant relation from Peking, a cousin who lived in a nunnery until it burned down and nearly took you with it. With that face, no one will recognize you."

And that's what happened. Precious Auntie stayed. I was the reason she stayed, her only reason to live. Five months after my birth in 1916, GaoLing was born to Mother, who had been forced by Great-Granny to claim me as her own. How could Mother say she had two babies five months apart? That was impossible. So Mother decided to wait. Exactly nine months after my birth, and on a very lucky date in 1917, GaoLing was born for sure.

The grown-ups knew the truth of our births. The children knew only what they were supposed to pretend. And though I was smart I was stupid. I did not ever question the truth. I did not wonder why Precious Auntie had no name. To others she was Nursemaid. To me, she was Precious Auntie. And I did not know who she really was until I read what she wrote.

"I am your mother," the words said.

I read that only after she died. Yet I have a memory of her telling me with her hands, I can see her saying this with her eyes. When it is dark, she says this to me in a clear voice I have never heard. She speaks in the language of shooting stars.

CHANGE

In the year 1929, my fourteenth year, I became an evil person.

That was also the year the scientists, both Chinese and foreign, came to Dragon Bone Hill at the Mouth of the Mountain. They wore sun hats and Wellington boots. They brought shovels and poking sticks, sorting pans and fizzing liquids. They dug in the quarries, they burrowed in the caves. They went from medicine shop to medicine shop, buying up all the old bones. We heard rumors that the foreigners wanted to start their own dragon bone factories, and a dozen villagers went to the quarries with axes to chase them away.

But then some of the Chinese workers who dug for the scientists passed along the rumor that two of the dragon bones might have been teeth from a human head. And everyone thought they meant a recently dead one. From whose grave? Whose grandfather? Whose grandmother? Some people stopped buying dragon bones. Big signs in the medicine shops declared: "None of our remedies contains human parts."

At the time, Precious Auntie still had four or five dragon bones left from our visits to the family cave, not counting the oracle bone her father had given her long ago. The others she had used as medicine for me over the years, and those, she assured me, were not human. Soon after she said this, her father, the Famous Bonesetter, came to her in a dream. "The bones you have are not from dragons," he said. "They are from our own clan, the ancestor who was crushed in the Monkey's Jaw. And because we stole them, he's cursed us. That's why nearly everyone in our family has died, your mother, your brother, myself, your future husband—because of this curse. And it doesn't stop with death. Ever since I arrived in the World of Yin, his shadow has been jumping on me from every turn. If I were not already dead, I would have died of fright a thousand times."

"What should we do?" Precious Auntie asked in her dream.

"Return the bones. Until they're reunited with the rest of his body, he'll continue to plague us. You'll be next, and any future generations of our family will be cursed, too. Believe me, daughter, there is nothing worse than having your own relative out for revenge."

The next morning, Precious Auntie rose early, and she was gone almost the entire day. When she returned, she seemed more at ease. But then the workmen from Dragon Bone Hill passed along this news: "The teeth," they said, "are not only human but belong to a piece of skullcap from our oldest ancestors, one million years old!" "Peking Man" was what the scientists decided to call the skullcap. They just needed to find more pieces to make a whole skullcap, and a few more after that to connect his skull to his jaw, his jaw to his neck, his neck to his shoulders, and so on, until he was a complete man. That meant a lot of pieces had to be found, and that was why the scientists were asking the villagers to bring all the dragon bones they had lying around their houses and medicine shops. If the dragon bones proved to be from ancient humans, the owner would receive a reward.

One million years! Everyone kept saying this. One day they had no need to say this number, the next day they could not say it enough. Little Uncle guessed that a person might earn a million coppers for a single piece of dragon bone. And Father said, "Coppers are worth nothing these days. A million silver taels are more likely." By guesses and arguments, the amount grew to be a million gold ingots. The whole town was talking about this. "Old bones grow new fat," became the saying people had on their lips. And because dragon bones were now worth so much, at least in people's wild imaginations, no one could buy them for medicine anymore. Those folks with life-draining ailments could no longer be cured. But what did that matter? They were the descendants of Peking Man. And he was famous.

Naturally, I thought about the dragon bones that Precious Auntie had put back in the cave. They were human, too—her father had said so in her dream. "We could sell them for a million ingots," I told her. I reasoned I was not just thinking selfishly. If Precious Auntie made us rich, my family might respect her more.

A million or ten million, she scolded with her moving hands, *if we sell them, the curse will return. A ghost will then come and take us and our miserable bones with it. Then we'll have to wear the weight of those million ingots around our dead necks to bribe our way through hell.* She poked my forehead. *I tell you, the ghosts won't rest until all of our family is dead. The entire family, gone.* She knocked her fist against her chest. *Sometimes I wish I were already dead. I wanted to die, really I did, but I came back for you.*

"Well, I'm not afraid," I answered. "And since the curse is on you and not me, I can go get the bones."

Suddenly Precious Auntie slapped the side of my head. *Stop this talk!* Her hands sliced the air. *You want to add to my curse? Never go back. Never touch them. Say you won't, say it now!* She grabbed my shoulders and rattled me until a promise fell out of my clacking mouth.

Later I daydreamed of sneaking to the cave. How could I sit by while everyone in the Mouth of the Mountain and the surrounding villages went looking for immortal relics? I knew where the human bones were, and yet I could say nothing. I had to watch as others gouged where their sheep chewed grass, gutted where their pigs wallowed in the mud. Even First Brother and Second Brother, along with their wives, dredged the remaining land between our compound and the cliff. From the muck they yanked out roots and worms. They guessed that these might be ancient men's fingers and toes, or even the fossilized tongue that spoke the first words of our ancestors. The streets filled with people trying to sell all kinds of dried-up relics, from chicken beaks to pig turds. In a short while, our village looked worse than a burial ground dug up by grave robbers.

Day and night the family talked of Peking Man and almost nothing else. "Million years?" Mother wondered aloud. "How can anyone know the age of someone who has been dead that long? Hnh, when my grandfather died, no one knew if he was sixty-eight or sixty-nine. Eighty was how long he should have lived, if only he had had better luck. So eighty was what our family decided he was—luckier, yes, but still dead."

I, too, had something to say on the new discovery: "Why are they calling him Peking Man? The teeth came from the Mouth of the Mountain. And now the scientists are saying that skullcap was a woman's. So it should be called Woman from the Mouth of the Mountain." My aunts and uncles looked at me, and one of them said: "Wisdom from a child's lips, simple yet true." I was embarrassed to hear such high words. Then GaoLing added, "I think he should be called Immortal Heart Man. Then our town would be famous and so would we." Mother praised her suggestion to the skies, and the others did as well. To my mind, however, her idea made no sense, but I could not say this.

I was often jealous when GaoLing received more attention from the mother we shared. I still believed I was the eldest daughter. I was smarter. I had done better in school. Yet GaoLing always had the honor of sitting next to Mother, of sleeping in her *k'ang*, while I had Precious Auntie.

When I was younger, that did not bother me. I felt I was lucky to have her by my side. I thought the words "Precious Auntie" were the same as what others meant by "Ma." I could not bear to be separated from my nursemaid for even one moment. I had admired her and was proud that she could write the names of every flower, seed, and bush, as well as say their medicinal uses. But the bigger I grew, the more she shrank in importance. The smarter I thought I had become, the more I was able to reason that Precious Auntie was only a servant, a woman who held no great position in our household, a person no one liked. She could have made our family rich, if only she did not have crazy thoughts about curses.

I began to increase my respect for Mother. I sought her favor. I believed favor was the same as love. Favor made me feel more important, more content. After all, Mother was the number-one-ranking lady of the house. She decided what we ate, what colors we should wear, how much pocket money we received for those times she allowed us to go to the market. Everyone both feared her and wanted to please her, all except Great-Granny, who was now so feeble-minded she could not tell ink from mud.

But in Mother's eyes, I had no charms. To her ears, my words had no music. It did not matter how obedient I was, how humble or clean. Nothing I did satisfied her. I became confused as to what I must do to please her. I was like a turtle lying on its back, struggling to know why the world was upside down.

Often I complained to Precious Auntie that Mother did not love me. *Stop your nonsense,* Precious Auntie would answer. *Didn't you hear her today? She said your sewing stitches were sloppy. And she mentioned your skin was getting too dark. If she didn't love you, why did she bother to criticize you for your own good?* And then Precious Auntie went on to say how selfish I was, always thinking about myself. She said my face looked ugly when I pouted. She criticized me so much I did not consider until now that she was saying she loved me even more.

One day—I remember this was sometime before Spring Festival—Old Cook came back from the market and said big news was flying through Immortal Heart. Chang the coffinmaker had become famous and was soon to be very rich. Those dragon bones he had given to the scientists? The results had come back: They were human. How old was not certain yet, but everyone guessed they were at least a million years, maybe even two.

We were in the ink-making studio, all the women, girls, and babies, except for Precious Auntie, who was in the root cellar, counting the inksticks she had already carved. I was glad she wasn't in the studio, because whenever anyone mentioned Chang's name, she spat. So when he delivered wood, she was sent to her room, where she cursed him by banging on a pail so long and loud that even the tenants yelled back.

"What a peculiar coincidence," Big Aunt now said. "The same Mr. Chang who sells us wood. His luck could have been ours just as easily."

"The association goes back even farther than that," Mother boasted. "He was the man who stopped his cart to help after Baby Brother was killed by the Mongol bandits. A man of good deeds, that Mr. Chang."

It seemed there was no end to the many ways we were connected to the now famous Mr. Chang. Since Mr. Chang would soon be even richer than before, Mother thought he would surely reduce the price of his leftover wood. "He should share his luck," Mother agreed with herself. "The gods expect him to do no less."

Precious Auntie came back to the ink studio, and in a short while she realized who it was everyone was talking about. She stamped her feet and punched the air with her fists. *Chang is evil,* she said, her arms flailing. *He killed my father. He is the reason Hu Sen is dead.* She made a rasping sound as if the whole of her throat would slough off.

That was not true, I thought. Her father had fallen off a wagon when he was drunk, and Baby Uncle had been kicked by his own horse. Mother and my aunts had told me so.

Precious Auntie grabbed my arm. She looked into my eyes, then talked fast with her hands, *Tell them, Doggie, tell them what I'm saying is true. And the dragon bones Chang has,* and she poured imaginary ones into her palm, *I realize now that they probably are the ones that belonged to my father, my family. Chang stole them from us on my wedding day. They were my dowry. They are bones from the Monkey's Jaw. We need to get them back from Chang, return them to the cave or the curse will go on and on. Hurry, tell them.*

Before I could, Mother warned: "I don't want to hear any more of her crazy stories. Do you hear me, Daughter?"

Everyone stared at me, including Precious Auntie. *Tell them,* she signaled. But I turned to Mother, nodded, and said, "I heard." Precious Auntie ran out of the ink studio with a choking sound that twisted my heart and made me feel evil.

For a while, it was very quiet in the studio. Then Great-Granny went up to Mother and said with a worried face: "Eh, have you seen Hu Sen?"

"He's in the courtyard," Mother answered. And Great-Granny shuffled out.

My uncles' wives began to cluck their tongues. "Still crazy from what happened," Little Aunt muttered, "and that was almost fifteen years ago." For a moment, I did not know if they were talking about Great-Granny or Precious Auntie.

Big Aunt added, "Good thing she can't talk. It would be a terrible embarrassment to our family if anyone knew what she was trying to say."

"You should turn her out of the house," Little Aunt said to Mother. And then Mother nodded toward Great-Granny, who was now wandering about, scratching at a bloody spot on the back of her ear. "It's because of old Granny," she said, "that the lunatic nursemaid has stayed all these years." And I knew then what Mother really meant but could not say. When Great-Granny died, she could finally tell Precious Auntie to go. All at once, I felt tender toward my nursemaid. I wanted to protest that Mother must not do this. But how could I argue against something that had not yet been said?

A month later, Great-Granny fell and hit her head on the brick edge of her *k'ang*. Before the Hour of the Rooster she was dead. Father, Big Uncle, and Little Uncle returned home from Peking, though the roads had become dangerous. A lot of shooting among warlords was going on between Peking and the Mouth of the Mountain. Lucky for us, the only fighting we saw was among the tenants. We had to ask them several times not to scream and shout while we were paying respects to Great-Granny as she lay in the common hall.

When Mr. Chang delivered the coffin, Precious Auntie stayed in her room and cursed him with her banging pail. I was sitting on a bench in the front courtyard, watching as Father and Mr. Chang unloaded the cart.

I thought to myself, Precious Auntie is wrong. Mr. Chang didn't look like a thief. He was a large man with friendly manners and an open face. Father was eagerly discussing with him his "important contribution to science, history, and all of China." To this, Mr. Chang acted both modest and pleased. Then Father left to get Mr. Chang's money for the coffin.

Though it was a cold day, Mr. Chang was sweating. He wiped his brow with his sleeve. After a while, he noticed I was staring at him. "You've certainly grown big," he called to me. I blushed. A famous man was talking to me.

"My sister is bigger," I thought to say. "And she's a year younger."

"Ah, that's good," he said.

I had not intended for him to praise GaoLing. "I heard that you had pieces of Peking Man," I then said. "What parts?"

"Oh, only the most important."

And I, too, wanted to seem important, so I blurted without thinking, "I once had some bones myself," before I slapped my hand over my mouth.

Mr. Chang smiled, waiting for me to continue. "Where are they?" he said after a while.

I could not be impolite. "We took them back to the cave," I answered.

"Where's that?"

"I can't say where. My nursemaid made me promise. It's a secret."

"Ah, your nursemaid. She's the one with the ugly face." Mr. Chang stiffened his fingers like a crab and held them over his mouth.

I nodded.

"The crazy person." He looked toward the sounds of the banging pail. I said nothing.

"And she found bones from this place you can't talk about?"

"We found them together, she took them back," I answered quickly. "But I can't say where."

"Of course. You shouldn't tell a stranger."

"Oh, you're not a stranger! Our family knows you very well. We all say so."

"Still, you shouldn't tell me. But surely you've told your own father and mother."

I shook my head. "No one. If I did, they would want to dig them out. Precious Auntie said so. She said the bones have to stay in the cave or she would suffer the consequences."

"What consequences?"

"A curse. She'll die if I say."

"But she is already quite old, is she not?"

"I don't know. I don't think so."

"Often women die at all sorts of ages and it's not because of a curse. Illness or accident, that's often the cause. My first wife died ten years ago. She was always clumsy and one day she fell off a roof. Now I have a new wife and she's even better than the last. If your nursemaid dies, you can get a new one, too."

"I'm too old for another," I said. I did not like our conversation anymore. Soon Father returned with Mr. Chang's money. They chatted a few more minutes in a friendly manner, and then Mr. Chang called to me, "Next time I see you, we'll talk again," and he left with his empty cart. Father seemed pleased that Mr. Chang, who was now such a well-known man in our town, had found me worthy of attention.

A few days later, we had a proper funeral for Great-Granny. Everyone wailed loudly, but Mother was the loudest, as was the custom, she being the number-one-ranking lady of the house. She did a very good job sounding sad beyond hope. And I, too, cried, sad but also afraid. And when the funeral was over, I became nervous of what would happen next: Mother would make Precious Auntie leave.

But she did not, and this was why.

Mother believed Great-Granny was still around, haunting the outhouse and making sure everyone still followed her rules. Every time Mother squatted over the hole, she heard a voice asking, "Have you seen Hu Sen?" When she told us this, Third Aunt said, "The sight of your bare bottom should have scared away any ghost." And we all laughed, but Mother became angry and announced she was cutting off everyone's allowance for the next month. "To teach you to have more respect for Great-Granny," she said. For the ghost in the outhouse, Mother went to the village temple every day and gave special offerings. She went to Great-Granny's grave and burned silver paper, so Great-Granny could buy her way to a better level. After ninety days of constipation, Mother went back to the funerary ship and bought a paper automobile large as life, complete with chauffeur. Great-Granny had seen a real one once at a temple fair in the Mouth of the Mountain. It was in the parking lot where carts and donkeys were kept, and when the automobile roared away, she said, it was loud enough to scare the devil and fast enough to fly to heaven.

So the paper auto went up in flames, and Great-Granny's ghost traveled from the latrine to the World of Yin. And then our household went back to its normal, noisy ways. For the rest of the family, the concerns were on little daily matters: mold in the millet, a crack in the glass, nothing at all of lasting importance.

And only I worried about what would happen to Precious Auntie.

I remember the day Mother received a surprise letter from Peking. It was the period of Great Heat, when mosquitoes were their happiest and fruit left outside rotted in less than an hour under the sun. Great-Granny had been dead for more than ninety days. We sat in the shade of the big tree in the courtyard, waiting to hear the news.

We all knew the letter writer, Old Widow Lau. She was a cousin, within eight degrees of kinship on Father's side and five degrees on Mother's side, close enough to follow the mourning rituals of family. She had come to Great-Granny's funeral and had wailed as loudly as the rest of us.

Since Mother could not read, she asked GaoLing, and I had to hide my disappointment that she had been chosen for this important task. GaoLing smoothed her hair, cleared her throat, licked her lips, then read: " 'Dear Cousin, I send greetings from all those who have asked after you with deep feeling.' " GaoLing then stumbled through a long list of names, from those of brand-new babies to people Mother was sure were already dead. On the next page, our old cousin wrote something like this: "I know you are still in mourning and barely able to eat because of grief. So it is not a good time to invite everyone to come visit in Peking. But I have been thinking about what you and I discussed when we last saw each other at the funeral."

GaoLing broke off reading and turned to Mother. "What did you discuss?" I, too, was wondering this.

Mother slapped GaoLing's hand. "Don't be nosy. You just read, and I'll tell you what you should know."

The letter continued: " 'I wish to humbly suggest that your number-one daughter' "—she was speaking of me, and my heart swelled—" " 'come to Peking and acciden-tally meet a distant relation of mine.' " GaoLing threw me a scowl, and I was pleased she was jealous. " 'This rela-tion,' " GaoLing went on reading in a less enthusiastic voice, " 'has four sons, who are seventh cousins of mine, three times removed, with a different surname. They live in your same village, but are barely related to you, if at all.' "

When I heard the words "barely related," I knew this accidental meeting meant she wanted to see whether I might be a marriage match for a certain family. I was fourteen (this was by my Chinese age), and most of the girls my age were already married. As to which family, Old Widow Lau did not want to say, unless she knew for certain that our family believed such an accident could be beneficial. "To be honest," she wrote, "I would not have thought of this family on my own. But the father came to me and asked about LuLing. They have apparently seen the girl and are impressed with her beauty and sweet nature."

My face flushed. At last Mother knew what others were saying about me. Perhaps she might see these good qualities in me as well.

"I want to go to Peking, too," GaoLing said like a complaining cat.

Mother scolded her: "Did anyone invite you? No? Well, then, you only look stupid for saying you want to go." When she whined again, Mother yanked her braid and said, "Shut your mouth," before handing me the letter to finish reading.

I sat up straight, facing Mother, and read with much expression: " 'The family suggests a meeting at your family's ink shop in Peking.' " I stopped a moment and smiled at GaoLing. I had never seen the shop, nor had she. " 'In this way,' " I continued, " 'if there is any disharmony of interest, there will be no public embarrassment to either family. If both families are in agreement about the match, then this will be a blessing from the gods for which I can take no credit.' "

"No credit," Mother said with a snort, "just a lot of gifts."

The next part of the letter went like this: "A good daughter-in-law is hard to find, I'm sure you will agree. Perhaps you remember my second daughter-in-law? I am ashamed to admit that she has turned out to be cold-hearted. Today she suggested that your daughter's nurse-maid should not accompany her to Peking. She said that if a person were to see the two together, he would re-member only the shocking ugliness of the nursemaid and not the emerging beauty of the maiden. I told her that was nonsense. But as I write this letter, I realize now that it would be inconvenient to accommodate another ser-vant, since mine already complain that there is not enough room for them to sleep in one bed. So perhaps it would be better if the nursemaid does not come after all. I apolo-gize that nothing can be done about the poverty of our household. . . ."

Only when I was done reading did I look up at Precious Auntie, embarrassed. *Never mind,* she signed to me qui-etly. *I'll tell her later that I can sleep on the floor.* I turned to Mother, waiting to hear what more she had to say.

"Write a letter back. Tell Old Widow Lau that I will have you go in a week. I'd take you myself, but it's the ink season and we have too much to do. I'll ask Mr. Wei to take you in his cart. He always makes a medical delivery to Peking on the first and won't mind an extra passenger in exchange for a little cash."

Precious Auntie flapped her hands for my attention. *Now is the time to tell her you can't go alone. Who will make sure it's a good marriage? What if that busybody idiot cousin tries to barter you off as a second wife to a poor family? Ask her to consider that.*

I shook my head. I was afraid to anger Mother with a lot of unnecessary questions and ruin my chances to visit Peking. Precious Auntie tugged my sleeve. I ignored her. Lately I had done this a few times, and it infuriated Precious Auntie. Since she could not speak and Mother could not read, when I refused to talk for her, she was left wordless, powerless.

Back in our room, Precious Auntie beseeched me. *You are too young to go to Peking by yourself. This is more dangerous than you can imagine. You could be killed by bandits, your head chopped off and put on a stake.* . . . I did not answer her, I did not argue, I gave her no ground on which to keep her footing. On and on she went that day, the next, and the day after that. At times, she expressed anger at what Old Widow Lau had written. *That woman does not care about what's best for you. She sticks her nose in other people's business for money. Soon she'll stink like the bottoms she's been smelling.*

Later Precious Auntie handed me a letter, which I was supposed to give to GaoLing so she could read it to Mother. I nodded, and as soon as I was out of the room and around the corner, I read it: "Besides all the shooting and unrest, the summer air there is full of diseases. And in Peking, there are strange ailments we have never even experienced here, maladies that could make the tips of LuLing's nose and fingers fall off. Luckily, I know the remedies to treat such problems so that LuLing does not return home bringing with her an epidemic. . . ."

When Precious Auntie asked me if I had given Mother the letter, I made my face and heart a stone wall. "Yes," I lied. Precious Auntie sighed, relieved. This was the first time she had believed a lie of mine. I wondered what had changed within her that she could no longer sense if I was telling the truth. Or was it I who had changed?

The night before I was to leave, Precious Auntie stood before me with the letter, which I had wadded into a little ball and stuffed in a pocket of my trousers. *What is the meaning of this?* She grabbed my arm.

"Leave me alone," I protested. "You can't tell me what to do anymore."

You think you're so smart? You're still a silly baby.

"I'm not. I don't need you anymore."

If you had a brain then you wouldn't need me.

"You want to keep me here only so you won't lose your position as nursemaid."

Her face turned dark, as if she were choking. *Position? You think I am here only for a lowly position as your nurse-maid? Ai-ya! Why am I still alive to hear this child say such things?*

Our chests were heaving. And I shouted back what I had often heard Mother and my aunts say: "You're alive because our family was good and took pity on you and saved your life. We didn't have to. And Baby Uncle never should have tried to marry you. It was bad luck that he tried. That's why he was killed by his own horse. Everyone knows it."

Her whole body slumped, and I thought she was ac-knowledging that I was right. At that moment, I pitied her in the same way I pitied beggars I could not look in the eye. I felt I had grown up at last and she had lost her power over me. It was as if the old me was looking at the new me, ad-miring how much I had changed.

The next morning, Precious Auntie did not help me with my bundle of clothes. She did not prepare a lunch I could take along. Instead, she sat on the edge of the *k'ang*, refusing to look at me. The sun was not up yet, but I could see that her eyes were red and puffy. My heart wobbled, but my mind was firm.

Two hours before daybreak, Mr. Wei came by with his donkey loaded with cages of snakes for medicine shops. I tied on a scarf to keep the sun off my face. As I climbed into the cart next to him, everyone except Precious Auntie was standing at the gate to see me off. Even GaoLing was there with her unwashed face. "Bring me back a doll," she shouted. At thirteen, she was still such a baby.

The day was a long ride of never-ending dust. Whenever the donkey stopped to drink water, Mr. Wei dipped a large rag into the stream and wrapped it around his head to keep himself cool. Soon I was doing the same with my scarf. At lunchtime, Mr. Wei pulled out a tin with dumplings inside. I had nothing. I had not wanted to ask Old Cook to fix me a tin, for fear he would tell Mother that it was too much of a nuisance to send me to Peking. Of course, Mr. Wei offered me some of his food. And naturally, I pretended that I was not hungry. And then he offered only twice more; the last offer never came. So I had to ride the rest of the way with an empty stomach and eight cages of ugly snakes.

In the late afternoon, we approached Peking. I instantly revived from the listlessness of the heat and my hunger. When we entered the inspection station, I worried that we would be refused permission to go on. A policeman with a cap poked through my small bundle and looked inside the cages with Mr. Wei's snakes.

"What is your reason for being in Peking?" the policeman asked.

"Delivery of medicine." Mr. Wei nodded to the snake cages.

"Marriage," I answered truthfully, and the policeman turned to another and called out my answer and they both laughed. After that, they let us go in. Soon I saw a tall memorial archway in the distance, its gold letters glinting like the sun. We passed through this and entered a roadway as wide as the greatest of rivers. Rickshaws raced by, more in one glance than I had seen in a lifetime. And over there, an automobile, like the paper one Mother had burned for Great-Granny. I began to measure all the sights in comparison with my life before. The markets were larger and louder. The streets were filled with busier crowds. I saw men in loose-weave long jackets, others in Western suits. Those men looked more impatient, more important. And there were many girls in floating dresses, wearing hairstyles exactly like those of famous actresses, the fringe in front crimped like dried noodles. I thought they were prettier than any of the girls in Immortal Heart. We passed walkways lined with peddlers selling every kind of bird, insect, and lizard on a stick, and they were ten times more expensive than the best snack we could buy in our own town. Farther on, I saw persimmons that were more golden, peanuts that were fatter, and sugar-coated haws that were a shinier red. I heard a crisp crack, saw the freshly opened gut of a more delicious-looking melon. And those who could not resist a slice looked more satisfied than any other melon-eaters I had ever seen.

"If you gawk any more, your head will twist right off," Mr. Wei said. I kept tallying the sights in my head so I could tell everyone all that I had seen. I was imagining their awe, Mother's admiration, GaoLing's envy. I could also see the disappointment in Precious Auntie's face. She would not want me to have a good time. So I pushed her out of my mind.

Mr. Wei stopped several times to ask for directions to a certain shop near Lantern Market Street, then went looking for a particular alleyway, and finally we stood in front of the gate that led into the cramped courtyard of Old Widow Lau's house. Two dogs ran toward me, barking.

"Ai! Are you a girl or a yellow mud statue!" Old Widow Lau said in greeting. Dirt ringed my neck, my hands, every place where my body had a crease or a bend. I stood in a four-walled courtyard compound that was so chaotic my arrival raised almost no notice. Right away, Old Widow Lau told me dinner was almost ready so I'd better hurry and wash up. She handed me a beaten bucket and told me where the well pump was. As I filled the bucket, I recalled that Mother had said Peking water was sweet. I took a sip, but it was brackish, terrible-tasting. No wonder Precious Auntie had told me that Peking was once the wasteland of the bitter sea. Just then, I realized this was the first time she was not there to help me with my bath. Where was the tub? Where was the stove for warming the water? I was too scared to touch anything. I squatted behind a mat shed and poured cold water over my neck, angry with Precious Auntie for turning me into such a stupid girl, one now afraid to show everyone how stupid I really was.

After I finished, I realized I had not thought to bring a comb for my hair or wooden sticks for cleaning under my nails. Precious Auntie always remembered those things for me. *She* was the reason I forgot! At least I had brought a clean shirt-jacket and trousers. But of course, these were wrinkled and dusty when I pulled them out from my bundle.

During the evening meal, another thought came to me. This was the first time I did not have Precious Auntie telling me which things I should and should not eat. For that I was glad. "Not too many greasy-spicy things," she would have warned, "or you'll break out in boils and other dampness diseases." So I ate several helpings of spicy pork. But later I had a queasy feeling and worried that my stomach was blistering inside out.

After dinner, I sat in the courtyard with Old Widow Lau and her daughters-in-law, listening to the buzz of mosquitoes and gossiping voices. I slapped the insects away, recalling the big fan Precious Auntie used to chase the heat and the bugs from both of us. When my eyes kept falling down, Old Widow Lau told me to go find my bed. So I went to the sad little shed that held my bundle and a rope-cot. As I fingered the holes of the cot's rattan weave, I realized yet another thing: This was the first time I had to sleep by myself. I lay down and closed my eyes. As I tumbled into thoughtlessness, I heard rats scratching along the wall. I leaned over to see if cups of turpentine had been placed under the legs of the cot. They had not. And again, rather than be grateful that Precious Auntie had always done all these things for me, I blamed her for keeping me so stupid.

When I awoke, I found I had no one to fix my hair or inspect my ears and nails. Having no comb, I used my fingers to undo the tangles. The shirt-jacket and trousers I had worn to bed were sweaty, and no fresh clothes lay in their place. They were not suitable to wear for my accidental meeting that day. And the costume that I had chosen to wear now did not look quite right, but that was all I had thought to bring. I was a grown girl, and there I was, helpless and stupid beyond belief. That was how well Precious Auntie had raised me.

When I appeared before Old Widow Lau, she exclaimed, "Is your head just an empty eggshell? Why are you wearing a padded jacket and winter trousers? And what's the matter with your hair?"

How could I answer? That Precious Auntie had refused to advise me? The truth was, when I had chosen these clothes, I was thinking only that I should bring my best things with the nicest embroidery. And my best had not seemed too uncomfortable when I had put them in my bundle during the cooler hours of the morning the day before.

"What a disaster!" Old Widow Lau muttered as she flung about all the clothing I had brought. "Pity the family that takes in this stupid girl for a daughter-in-law." She hurried to her trunks to search among the slim dresses of her youth. At last she settled on a dress borrowed from one of her daughters-in-law, a lightweight *chipao* that was not too old-fashioned. It had a high collar, short sleeves, and was woven in the colors of summer foliage, lilac for the body and leafy green for the trim and frog clasps. Old Widow Lau then undid my messy braids and dragged a wet comb through my hair.

At noon she announced we were leaving for the ink shop. She informed her servant we would not eat our lunch at home. She was certain her cousin the inkmaker was preparing a special meal at his place. "If the other family is also there," she warned me, "eat a little of each dish to show you are not picky, but don't be greedy. Let others be served first and act like you are the least important."

Lantern Market Street was not far from the Pottery-Glazing District, perhaps a thirty-minute rickshaw ride. But Old Widow Lau was afraid we might accidentally miss our accidental meeting if we did not allow for a few extra minutes to ensure that we arrived on time. "After all," she fretted aloud, "what if the rickshaw driver is old and lame? What if it begins to rain?"

Sometime after the noon hour, I found myself standing before our family's ink shop, anxious to see Father. Old Widow Lau was paying the rickshaw driver—or rather, arguing with him that he should not charge us so much for an extra passenger since I was still a small child. "Small child?" the driver said with a huff. "Where are your eyes, old woman?" I stared at the lap of the lilac dress I had borrowed, patted the neatly knotted bun at the back of my head. I was embarrassed but also proud that the driver thought I was a grown-up woman.

Almost every door on the street led to a shop, and flanking each door were red banners with good-luck couplets. The couplet by our family's shop was particularly fine. It had been written in a cursive style, the one Precious Auntie was teaching me to copy. The manner was more like a painting than writing, very expressive, running down like cloud-swept branches. You could tell that whoever had written this was an artist, cultured and deserving of respect. Reluctantly, I admitted to myself that this calligraphy must have been Precious Auntie's.

At last, Old Widow Lau was done haggling with the driver and we stepped inside Father's shop. It was north-facing, quite dim inside, and perhaps this was why Father did not see us at first. He was busy with a customer, a man who was distinguished-looking, like the scholars of two decades before. The two men were bent over a glass case, discussing the different qualities of inksticks. Big Uncle welcomed us and invited us to be seated. From his formal tone, I knew he did not recognize who we were. So I called his name in a shy voice. And he squinted at me, then laughed and announced our arrival to Little Uncle, who apologized many times for not rushing over sooner to greet us. They rushed us to be seated at one of two tea tables for customers. Old Widow Lau refused their invitation three times, exclaiming that my father and uncles must be too busy for visitors. She made weak efforts to leave. On the fourth insistence, we finally sat. Then Little Uncle brought us hot tea and sweet oranges, as well as bamboo latticework fans with which to cool ourselves.

I tried to notice everything so I could later tell GaoLing what I had seen, and tease out her envy. The floors of the shop were of dark wood, polished and clean, no dirty footprints, even though this was during the dustiest part of the summer. And along the walls were display cases made of wood and glass. The glass was very shiny and not one pane was broken. Within those glass cases were our silk-wrapped boxes, all our hard work. They looked so much nicer than they had in the ink-making studio at Immortal Heart village.

I saw that Father had opened several of the boxes. He set sticks and cakes and other shapes on a silk cloth covering a glass case that served as a table on which he and the customer leaned. First he pointed to a stick with a top shaped like a fairy boat and said with graceful importance, "Your writing will flow as smoothly as a keel cutting through a glassy lake." He picked up a bird shape: "Your mind will soar into the clouds of higher thought." He waved toward a row of ink cakes embellished with designs of peonies and bamboo: "Your ledgers will blossom into abundance while bamboo surrounds your quiet mind."

As he said this, Precious Auntie came back into my mind. I was remembering how she taught me that everything, even ink, had a purpose and a meaning: Good ink cannot be the quick kind, ready to pour out of a bottle. You can never be an artist if your work comes without effort. That is the problem with modern ink from a bottle. You do not have to think. You simply write what is swimming on the top of your brain. And the top is nothing but pond scum, dead leaves, and mosquito spawn. But when you push an inkstick along an inkstone, you take the first step to cleansing your mind and your heart. You push and you ask yourself, What are my intentions? What is in my heart that matches my mind?

I remembered this, and yet that day in the ink shop, I listened to what Father was saying, and his words became far more important than anything Precious Auntie had thought. "Look here," Father said to his customer, and I looked. He held up an inkstick and rotated it in the light. "See? It's the right hue, purple-black, not brown or gray like the cheap brands you might find down the street. And listen to this." And I heard a sound as clean and pure as a small silver bell. "The high-pitched tone tells you that the soot is very fine, as smooth as the sliding banks of old rivers. And the scent—can you smell the balance of strength and delicacy, the musical notes of the ink's perfume? Expensive, and everyone who sees you using it will know that it was well worth the high price."

I was very proud to hear Father speak of our family's ink this way. I sniffed the hot air. The smell of spices and camphor was very strong.

"This soot," Father continued, "is far better than Anhui pine. We make it from a kind of tree so rare that it's now forbidden to chop it down. Luckily, we have a supply felled by lightning, blessed by the gods." Father asked the customer if he had heard about the ancient human skullcap recently unearthed from the quarry at Dragon Bone Hill. The old scholar nodded. "Well, we're from the village one hill over," Father explained. "And the trees in our village are said to be *more* than a million years old! How do we know? Think about it. When those million-year-old folks roamed the earth around Dragon Bone Hill, didn't they need trees to sit under? Trees for shade? Trees to make fires? Trees to build stools and tables and beds? Aha, am I right? Well then, we, the people from the village next to Dragon Bone Hill, supplied that need. And now we're the ones who own the remains of those ancestral trees. We call them Immortal Heart wood."

Father motioned to the shelves. "Now, look here, on this shelf there's only a pinch per stick, so the cost is less. In this row, two pinches. And in this case, it is almost entirely the soot of Immortal Tree wood. The ink draws easily into the brush, like nectar into a butterfly's nostril."

In the end, the customer bought several of the most expensive sticks and left the shop. I wanted to clap, as if I had just seen a play for the gods. And then Father was coming toward us, toward me. I rose from the chair with a leaping heart. I had not seen him since Great-Granny's funeral more than three months before. I wondered if he would say anything about my more grown-up appearance.

"What! Is it already five o'clock in the evening?" he asked.

This caused Old Widow Lau to jump up and cry, "We're too early! We should leave and come back later!"

That was how I learned what time we were supposed to come, five o'clock, not one. Old Widow Lau was so upset by this open announcement of her mistake that my father had to insist five times that she be seated again. And then my uncles brought more tea and more oranges, but still everything was awkward.

After a while, Father expressed his care and his concern for me. "You look too thin," he said. Or perhaps he said I was looking quite plump. Next he asked after the health of my mother, then that of GaoLing and my younger brothers, then that of the various aunts and in-laws. Good, well, fine, I chattered like a duck. Wearing those new clothes, it was hard for me to answer in a natural way. Finally he asked if I had eaten yet. And although I was hungry enough to faint, I had no chance to answer, for Old Widow Lau was crying: "We've eaten, we're full enough to burst! Please don't let us be any more trouble. Go on with your work."

"We're not busy at all," Father answered out of politeness, "not too busy for family."

And Old Widow Lau answered even more politely, "Really, we must go . . . but before we leave, have you heard what happened to . . . ?" And she started talking nervously of some distant relations. After Old Widow Lau had mentioned at least five or six more relatives, my father set down his teacup and stood up.

"Cousin Lau, where are my manners? I shouldn't force you to entertain me any longer. I know you came early so you and my daughter could wander the city streets and become lost in marvelous sights." He handed me a few coins for sweets and dumplings, warning me I should treat Elder Aunt well and not wear her out. "Take your time," he told her. "No need to rush back for our sake."

Old Widow Lau was embarrassed to be dismissed in this clever way. I was overjoyed. And soon we were outside in the festering heat.

Down the lane we found a dumpling stall where we could sit on outdoor benches. As I gobbled down my dumplings, Old Widow Lau complained that the hot dampness was swelling her feet: "Soon they'll be as soft and useless as rotted bananas." She was too frugal to take a rickshaw home to Lantern Market Street, only to have to turn around and come back. But she worried aloud that when we returned to the shop at five o'clock, we would have our accidental meeting with someone important, and there we would be, mouths open, tongues out, panting like worm-infested gutter dogs. "Don't sweat," she warned me.

We started walking, searching for shade. I listened to Old Widow Lau's complaints with one ear as I watched people pass us on the streets: Young men who appeared to be students or apprentices. Old Manchu women with heavy bundles. Girls with short modern hairstyles and Western clothes. Everyone walked with purpose, a quick step that was not the style of people back home. Now and then, Old Widow Lau pushed my shoulder and snapped, "Eh! Don't gawk like you're an old greasy-hat from the countryside."

And so we continued our ramble, two streets east, then two streets north, then two streets east again. That was the method my old cousin took to avoid our getting lost. Soon we found ourselves in a park with weeping willows and walkways over a pond covered with floating flowers and twitching larva. Old Widow Lau sat down on a bench under the shade of a tree and began to fan herself vigorously, complaining that she was going to explode like an overbaked yam. In a short while, her jaw dropped onto her chest and she was asleep.

Close by was an open-air pavilion made of dark wood lattice screens and rows of column posts supporting its heavy tiled roof. I went to a corner of the pavilion and squeezed against a post, trying to make myself still and unseen like a lizard. From there, I watched a man mastering his mind over his sword. I saw an old man blowing musical notes out of a metal comb, while the old woman beside him peeled an orange and tried to catch a butterfly that dipped and swooped toward the rind. Down a flight of stairs, a young couple sat by a small pond, pretending to admire ducks while the tips of their fingers secretly touched. There was also a foreigner, although I did not recognize him as such at first, for he was dressed in the clothes of a scholar, a long summer gown and trousers. His eyes were gray like muddy water. Around another pillar, a nursemaid was cooing to a baby, trying to get him to look at her, but the baby was screaming, trying to look back at the foreigner. And then another man, very elegant in his dress and manners, walked to a tree and parted the curtains of a cage I had not even noticed before. Birds immediately began to sing. I felt that I had entered a world a thousand years old and that I had always been there, but only just now had opened my eyes to see it.

I stayed until the pavilion was nearly empty. And then I heard Old Widow Lau bellowing my name. "You scared my body right out of my skin," she scolded, and pinched my arm hard.

As we walked back to my father's shop, I was a different girl. My head was a sandstorm, ideas and hopes whirling about freely. I was wondering all the while what those people at the pavilion would remember the next day and the day after that. Because I knew I would never forget a moment of that day, the day I was to begin my new life.

Just as Old Widow Lau had planned, my prospective mother-in-law accidentally passed by the shop promptly at five o'clock. The woman was younger than Mother. She had a stern countenance and was critical-looking. On her wrists she wore much gold and jade, to show how valuable she was. When Old Widow Lau called to her, she acted puzzled at first, then delighted.

"What luck that we should run into you here," Old Widow Lau cried in a high voice. "When did you arrive in Peking? . . . Oh, visiting a cousin? How are things back in Immortal Heart?" After we had recovered from our fake surprise, Old Widow Lau introduced the woman to Father and my uncles. I was concentrating so hard on not showing any expression whatsoever that I did not hear the woman's name.

"This is my cousin's Eldest Daughter, Liu LuLing," Old Widow Lau said. "She is fifteen."

"I'm fourteen," I corrected, and Old Widow Lau gave me a scolding glance before adding, "Almost fifteen. She is visiting Peking this week. The family lives in Immortal Heart village as well but they sell their ink in Peking. And as you can see," she said, sweeping her hand out to indicate the shop, "their business is doing not too bad."

"In part, we have your husband to thank," Father then said. "We buy much of our excellent wood from him."

"Really?" Old Widow Lau and the woman said at once. My ears turned toward him, curious now that our family knew this family.

"That's correct. We get the camphor wood from Mr. Chang," Father continued. "And he has also supplied us with coffins on less fortunate occasions, and always of the best quality."

Chang the coffinmaker. As exclamations of more surprise and pleasure rang out, I could imagine Precious Auntie pounding the air with her fists. She would never allow me to marry into this family. And then I reminded myself that this was not her decision to make.

"We, too, are thinking of starting a business in Peking," Mrs. Chang said.

"Is that so? Perhaps we can help you in some way," Father said politely.

"We wouldn't want to trouble you," Mrs. Chang said.

"No trouble at all," Father countered.

"You should get together and discuss the possibility," Old Widow Lau suggested, at just the right moment.

As Mrs. Chang paused to think of the excellence of this idea, Father added: "In any case, I've been eager to talk to your husband more about the dragon bones he contributed to the great scientific discovery of Peking Man."

Mrs. Chang nodded. "We were astonished that those ugly little bones were so valuable. Lucky we didn't eat them up as medicine."

I was thinking what it would mean if I married into this rich and famous family. GaoLing would be spitting with envy. Mother would treat me with special fondness. Of course, the Changs probably would not allow Precious Auntie to come as nursemaid to their future grandchildren, especially if she kept spitting and thrashing whenever their name was mentioned.

At the end, it was decided that Old Widow Lau, my father, and I should visit a house in Peking belonging to Chang's cousin, where we could see some unusual rocks in the garden. This was good news to Old Widow Lau, for it meant that the signs were good that the Changs considered me a prospect. And I was glad, for this meant I could stay longer in Peking.

Two evenings later, we went to the cousin's house for a Viewing the Moon party. I wore another borrowed dress. I sat quietly and did not eat too much and talked even less.

Mr. Chang had come up from Immortal Heart, and he and Father discussed Peking Man.

"All the pieces of the skull must stay in China," Father said. "That is not only proper, it's the agreement with the foreigners."

"Those foreigners," Chang said, "you can't trust them to keep their word. They'll find a way to sneak out some pieces. They'll find excuses, make new treaties, put up pressure."

"No treaty can change that Peking Man is a Chinese man and should stay where he lived and died."

Suddenly Mr. Chang saw me sitting on a garden stool. "Maybe one day you and I can collect more Peking Man together. How would you like that?"

I nodded eagerly.

The next day, I was a contented girl as I rode home. I had never felt such importance. I had not shamed Old Widow Lau or my family. In fact, I had been a great success. My father had criticized me in small ways about unimportant matters. So I knew he was proud of me. Old Widow Lau had bragged to her daughters-in-law that I had looks and manners to warrant ten marriage proposals. She was certain I would receive a marriage offer from the Changs within the week.

Though I had yet to meet the Changs' fourth son, who was back in Dragon Bone Hill, I knew he was two years older than I was. Like the other sons, he was an apprentice in his father's coffin-making business. What's more, there had been talk that he, the youngest son, might expand the coffin-making business to Peking, just as our family had done with the ink business. That meant I would live in Peking.

During all these discussions, I did not ask if my future

husband was smart, if he was educated, if he was kind. I did not think about romantic love. I knew nothing of that. But I did know that marriage had to do with whether I improved my station in life or made it worse. And to judge by the Changs' manners and the jewelry the Chang wife wore, I, too, was about to become a more important person. What could be wrong with that?

Mr. Wei had come before dawn to take me back. The sky was dark and the air was still clear of summer's rotting smells. In the cart, I began to dream of all the ways I had to change my life. Of course, I needed new clothes right away. And I should be more careful to keep my face out of the sun. I did not want to look like a dark little peasant girl. After all, we were artisans and merchants from an old clan, very respected.

By the time the stars faded and the sun rose, Peking had disappeared from the horizon, and the landscape before me returned to the same dusty dull.

Hours later, the cart climbed the last hill that hid Immortal Heart. I could hear the crowing of cocks, the yowling of dogs, all the familiar sounds of our village.

Mr. Wei started bellowing a peasant love song loud enough to burst his lungs. As we turned the bend, we came upon Sheepherder Wu gathering his flock. The late-afternoon sun sliced through the trees and fell on the backs of the sheep. Wu lifted his stick and called a greeting to Mr. Wei and me. Just then his herd turned in one motion, one direction, like a cloud bringing a storm, and I sensed a great danger. I recalled that Mother had once spoken quietly of this sheepherder's being a widower, who needed a new wife to help him run the looms for his wool. I could practically feel the graininess of yellow Gobi dust as my fingers picked through the wool. I could smell the lamb stink seeping into my fingers, my bones. And now that I stared at the sheepherder with his grin and his upraised stick, I was even more determined that I should marry the son of the Changs. Perhaps that son would turn out to be a one-eyed idiot. So be it. I would still be daughter-in-law to a famous family who ran a business in Peking.

As quickly as it takes to snap a twig—that's how fast the mind can turn against what is familiar and dear. There I was, about to arrive at my old home, and I was not filled with sentimental fondness for all I had grown up with. Instead I noticed the ripe stench of a pig pasture, the pock-marked land dug up by dragon-bone dream-seekers, the holes in the walls, the mud by the wells, the dustiness of the unpaved roads. I saw how all the women we passed, young and old, had the same bland face, sleepy eyes that were mirrors of their sleepy minds. Each person's life was the same as the next person's. Each family was as important as the next, which was to say, not very important. They were country people, both naive and practical, slow to change but quick to think that a disturbance of ants on the ground was a sign of bad luck from the gods high above. Even Precious Auntie had become this way in my mind, a sleepy-headed greasy-hat from the country.

I remembered a funny saying about life in a slow village: When you have nothing else to do, you can always busy yourself picking maggots out of rice. Once I had laughed at that saying. Now I saw that it was true.

Mr. Wei was still singing his loud folk songs as we rode into the town square. And then we came to Pig's Head Lane. I passed all the familiar faces and listened to their harsh, dust-choked greetings. As we came closer to the bend of the neck where our house stood, my heart began to drum in my ears. I saw the family gateway, the arch with its peeling timber, the fading red couplet banners that hung on the pillars.

But just as I pushed open the gate, my heart flew back into my chest, and I was filled with a longing to see Precious Auntie. She would be glad to see me. She had cried when I left. I dashed into the front courtyard: "I'm home! I'm home already!" I went into the ink studio, where I saw Mother and GaoLing. "Ah, back so soon?" Mother said, not bothering to stop her work. "Cousin Lau sent me a note that the meeting went well, and the Changs will probably take you."

I was bursting to tell them about my adventures, the pleasures I had enjoyed. But Mother stopped me: "Hurry and clean up, so you can help your little sister and me grind this up." And GaoLing wrinkled her nose and said, "*Cho!* You smell like the hind end of a donkey."

I went to the room I shared with Precious Auntie. Everything was in its usual place, the quilt folded just so at the bottom of the *k'ang*. But she was not there. I wandered from room to room, from little courtyard to little courtyard. With each passing moment, I felt more anxious to see her.

And then I heard a pot banging. She was in the root cellar, eager that I should know she was there. I peered down the steep ladder and into the tunnel. She waved, and as she climbed up from the shadows, I saw that she still had the figure of a girl. In the brief moment of seeing only half of her face lit by the sun, she was again as beautiful as she had seemed to me when I was a small child. When she emerged from the hole, she put the pot down and stroked my face, then said with her hands, *Have you really come back to me, my Doggie?* She pulled my tangled braid and snorted. *Didn't take your comb? No one to remind you? Now you know why you need me. You have no brains!* She jabbed the side of my head, and this made me irritable. With spit on her finger, she rubbed dirt from my cheek, then felt my forehead. *Are you sick? You seem feverish.*

"I'm not sick," I said. "I'm hot." She went back to unraveling the mats of my hair. I glanced at her ropy scars, her twisted mouth.

I pulled away. "I can clean myself," I said.

She began to make hissing sounds. *Gone one week and now you're so grown-up?*

I snapped back: "Of course. After all, I'm about to be a married woman."

I heard. And not as a concubine but as a wife. That's good. I raised you well, and everyone can see that.

I knew then that Mother had not told her the name of the family. She had to hear it sooner or later. "The family is the Changs," I said, watching the words cut her in two. "That's right, Chang the coffinmaker."

She sounded as if she were drowning. She rocked her head like a clanging bell. And then she told me with slashing hands, *You cannot. I forbid you.*

"It's not for you to decide!" I shouted back.

She slapped me, then pushed me against the wall. Again and again, she beat me on my shoulders, around my head, and at first I whimpered and cowered, trying to protect myself. But then I became angry. I pushed her back and stood tall. I drained all expression out of my face and this surprised her. We stared at each other, breathing hard and fast, until we no longer recognized each other. She dropped onto her knees, pounding her chest over and over, her sign for *useless*.

"I need to go help Mother and GaoLing," I said, then turned from her and walked away.

鬼

GHOST

Just as expected, the Changs asked our family if I could join theirs as a daughter-in-law. If I went there right away, Old Widow Lau added, my family would receive a money gift and I would immediately be known as a daughter-in-law during all the family and town ceremonies, including the special one that would happen during the Moon Festival, honoring Mr. Chang for his scientific achievements.

"She should go now," Big Aunt and Little Aunt advised Mother. "Otherwise, they might later change their minds. What if they discover something wrong with her background and want to end the marriage contract?" I thought they were talking about my poor sewing skills or some naughtiness I had forgotten but they had not. But of course, they were talking about my birth. They knew whose daughter I really was. The Changs and I did not.

Mother decided I would join the Chang family in a few weeks, before the town ceremony at the Moon Festival. She assured me that would give her and my aunts enough time to sew together quilts and clothes suitable for my new life. After Mother announced this news, she cried for joy. "I've done well by you," she said proudly. "No one can complain." GaoLing cried as well. And though I shed some tears, not all of them were for joy. I would leave my

238

family, my familiar house. I would change from a girl to a wife, a daughter to a daughter-in-law. And no matter how happy I was sure to be, I would still be sad to say good-bye to my old self.

Precious Auntie and I continued to share the same room, the same bed. But she no longer drew my bath or brought me sweet water from the well. She did not help me with my hair or worry over my daily health and the cleanliness of my fingernails. She gave no warnings, no advice. She did not talk to me with her hands.

We slept at the farthest ends of the *k'ang* away from each other. And if I found myself huddled next to her familiar form, I quietly moved away before she awoke. Every morning she had red eyes, so I knew she had been crying. Sometimes my eyes were red, too.

When Precious Auntie was not working in the ink-making studio, she was writing, sheet after sheet after sheet. She sat at her table, grinding the inkstick into the inkstone, thinking what, I could not guess. She dipped her brush and wrote, paused and dipped again. The words flowed without blots or cross-outs or backward steps.

A few days before I was supposed to leave to join the Changs, I awoke to find Precious Auntie sitting up, staring at me. She raised her hands and began to talk. *Now I will show you the truth.* She went to the small wooden cupboard and removed a package wrapped in blue cloth. She put this in my lap. Inside was a thick wad of pages, threaded together with string. She stared at me with an odd expression, then left the room.

I looked at the first page. "I was born the daughter of the Famous Bonesetter from the Mouth of the Mountain," it began. I glanced through the next few pages. They concerned the tradition of her family, the loss of her mother, the grief of her father, all the things she had already told me. And then I saw where it said: "Now I will tell how bad this man Chang really is." Right away, I threw those pages down. I did not want Precious Auntie poisoning my mind anymore. So I did not read to the end where she said she was my mother.

During our evening meal, Precious Auntie acted as if I were once again helpless. She pinched pieces of food with her chopsticks and added these to my bowl. *Eat more,* she ordered. *Why aren't you eating? Are you ill? You seem warm. You forehead is hot. Why are you so pale?*

After dinner, we all drifted to the courtyard as usual. Mother and my aunts were embroidering my bridal clothes. Precious Auntie was repairing a hole in my old trousers. She put down the needle and tugged my sleeve. *Did you already read what I wrote?*

I nodded, not wishing to argue in front of the others. My cousins, GaoLing, and I were playing weaving games with strings looped around our fingers. I was making lots of mistakes, which caused GaoLing to howl with glee that the Changs were getting a clumsy daughter-in-law. Upon hearing this, Precious Auntie threw me stern looks.

The evening wore on. The sun went down, the sounds of darkness came, the chirp, creak, and flap of unseen creatures. All too soon it was time for bed. I waited for Precious Auntie to go first. After a long while, when I thought she might already be asleep, I went into the dark room.

Immediately Precious Auntie sat up and was talking to me with her hands.

"I can't see what you're saying," I said. And when she went to light the kerosene lamp, I protested, "Don't bother, I'm sleepy. I don't want to talk right now." She lit the lamp anyway. I went to the *k'ang* and lay down. She followed me and set the lamp on the ledge, crouched, and stared at me with a glowing face. *Now that you have read my story, what do you feel toward me? Be honest.*

I grunted. And that little grunt was enough for her to clasp her hands, then bow and praise the Goddess of Mercy for saving me from the Changs. Before she could give too many thanks, I added: "I'm still going."

For a long time, she did not move. Then she began to cry and beat her chest. Her hands moved fast: *Don't you have feelings for who I am?*

And I remember exactly what I said to her: "Even if the whole Chang family were murderers and thieves, I would join them just to get away from you."

She slapped her palms against the wall. And then she finally blew out the lamp and left the room.

In the morning, she was gone. But I was not worried. A few times in the past, when she had become angry with me, she left but always came back. She was not at the table for breakfast, either. So I knew her anger was greater than in the past. Let her be angry, then, I said to myself. She doesn't care about my future happiness. Only Mother does. That is the difference between a nursemaid and a mother.

These were my very thoughts as my aunts, GaoLing, and I followed Mother to the ink-making studio to begin our work. As we entered the dim room, we all saw the mess. Stains on the walls. Stains on the bench. Long spills along the floor. Had a wild animal broken in? And what was that rotten sweet smell? Then Mother began to wail, "She's dead! She's dead!"

Who was dead? In the next moment, I saw Precious Auntie, the top half of her face limestone white, her wild eyes staring at me. She was sitting crooked against the far wall. "Who's dead?" I called to Precious Auntie. "What happened?" I walked toward her. Her hair was unbound and matted, and then I saw that her neck was clotted with flies. She kept her eyes on me, but her hands were still. One held a knife used to carve the inkstones. Before I could reach her, a tenant pushed me aside so she could better gawk.

Of that day, that was all I remembered. I didn't know how I came to be in my room, lying on the *k'ang*. When I awoke in the dark, I thought it was still the morning before. I sat up and shuddered, shaking off my nightmare.

Precious Auntie was not in the *k'ang*. Then I remembered she was angry with me and had left to sleep elsewhere. I tried to fall back asleep, but now I could not lie still. I got up and stepped outside. The sky was thick with stars, no lamp burned in any room, and even the old rooster did not rustle in alarm. It was not morning but still night, and I wondered if I was dreamwalking. I made my way across the courtyard, toward the ink-making studio, thinking that Precious Auntie might be sleeping on a bench. And then I remembered more of the bad dream: black flies feasting on her neck, crawling along her shoulders like moving hair. I was scared to see what was inside the studio, but my shaking hands were already lighting the lamp.

The walls were clean. So was the floor. Precious Auntie was not there. I was relieved, and returned to bed.

When I woke up the next time, it was morning and GaoLing was on the edge of the *k'ang*. "No matter what," she said with a tearful face, "I promise to always treat you like a sister." Then she told me what had happened, and I listened as if I were still in a bad dream.

The day before, Mrs. Chang had come over with a letter from Precious Auntie clutched in her hand. It had arrived in the middle of the night. "What is the meaning of this?" the Chang woman wanted to know. The letter said that if I joined the Chang household, Precious Auntie would come to stay as a live-in ghost, haunting them forever. "Where is the woman who sent this?" Mrs. Chang demanded, slapping the letter. And when Mother told her that the nursemaid had just killed herself, the Chang wife left, scared out of her wits.

After that, Mother rushed over to the body, GaoLing said. Precious Auntie was still leaning on the wall in the studio. "This is how you repay me?" Mother cried. "I treated you like a sister. I treated your daughter like my own." And she kicked the body, again and again, for not saying thank you, sorry, I beg your pardon a thousand times. "Mother was crazy with anger," GaoLing said. "She told Precious Auntie's body, 'If you haunt us, I'll sell LuLing as a whore.' " After that, Mother ordered Old Cook to put the body in a pushcart and throw it over the cliff. "She's down there," GaoLing said, "your Precious Auntie is lying in the End of the World."

When GaoLing left, I still did not understand everything she had said, and yet I knew. I found the pages Precious Auntie had written for me. I finished reading them. At last, I read her words. *Your mother, your mother, I am your mother.*

That day I went to the End of the World to look for her. As I slid down, branches and thorns tore at my skin. When I reached the bottom, I was feverish to find her. I heard the drumming of cicadas, the beating of vulture wings. I walked toward the thick brush, to where trees grew sideways just as they had fallen with the crumbling cliff. I saw moss, or was that her hair? I saw a nest high in the branches, or was that her body stuck on a limb? I came upon branches, or were those her bones, already scattered by wolves?

I turned and went the other direction, following the turns of the cliff's wall. I glimpsed tatters of cloth—her clothes? I saw crows carrying shreds—pieces of her flesh? I came to a wasteland with rocky mounds, ten thousand pieces of her skull and bones. Everywhere I looked, it was as if I were seeing her, torn and smashed. I had done this. I was remembering the curse of her family, *my* family, the dragon bones that had not been returned to their burial place. Chang, that terrible man, he wanted me to marry his son only so I would tell him where to find more of those bones. How could I be so stupid not to have realized this before?

I searched for her until dusk. By then, my eyes were swollen with dust and tears. I never found her. And as I climbed back up, I was a girl who had lost part of herself in the End of the World.

For five days I could not move. I could not eat. I could not even cry. I lay in the lonely *k'ang* and felt only the air leaving my chest. When I thought I had nothing left, my body still continued to be sucked of breath. At times I could not believe what had happened. I refused to believe it. I thought hard to make Precious Auntie appear, to hear her footsteps, see her face. And when I did see her face, it was in dreams and she was angry. She said that a curse now followed me and I would never find peace. I was doomed to be unhappy. On the sixth day, I began to cry and did not stop from morning until night. When I had no more feeling left, I rose from my bed and went back to my life.

No more mention was ever made of my going to live

with the Changs. The marriage contract had been canceled, and Mother no longer pretended I was her daughter. I did not know where I belonged in that family anymore, and sometimes when Mother was displeased with me, she threatened to sell me as a slave girl to the tubercular old sheepherder. No one spoke of Precious Auntie, either once living or now dead. And though my aunts had always known I was her bastard daughter, they did not pity me as her grieving child. When I could not stop myself from crying, they turned their faces, suddenly busy with their eyes and hands.

Only GaoLing talked to me, shyly. "Are you hungry yet? If you don't want that dumpling, I'll eat it." And I remember this: Often, when I lay on my *k'ang*, she came to me and called me Big Sister. She stroked my hand.

Two weeks after Precious Auntie killed herself, a figure ran through our gate, looking like a beggar chased by the devil. It was Little Uncle from Peking. His clothes and the hollows of his eyes were full of soot. When he opened his mouth, choking cries came out. "What's wrong? What's wrong?" I heard Mother shout as I climbed out of the root cellar. The others stumbled out of the ink-making studio. Some of the tenants rushed over as well, trailed by crawling babies and noisy dogs.

"Gone," Little Uncle said. His teeth chattered as if he were cold. "Everything's burnt up. We're finished."

"Burnt?" Mother cried. "What are you saying?"

Little Uncle collapsed onto a bench, his face bunched into knots. "The shop on the lane, the sleeping quarters in back, everything gone to cinders." GaoLing clasped my arm.

Bit by bit, Mother and the aunts pulled the story out of

him. Last night, he said, Precious Auntie came to Father. Her hair was unbound, dripping tears and black blood, and Father instantly knew she was a ghost and not an ordinary dream.

"Liu Jin Sen," Precious Auntie had called. "Did you value camphor wood more than my life? Then let the wood burn as I do now."

Father swung out his arm to chase her away and knocked over the oil lamp, which was not in his dream but on a table next to his cot. When Big Uncle heard the crash, he sat up and lit a match to see what had spilled onto the floor. Just then, Little Uncle said, Precious Auntie knocked the match out of his fingertips. Up burst a fountain of flames. Big Uncle shouted to Little Uncle to help him douse the fire. By Precious Auntie's trickery, Little Uncle said, he poured out a jar of *pai gar* wine instead of the pot of cold tea. The fire jumped higher. Father and the two uncles rousted their sons from the next room; then all the men of our family stood in the courtyard, where they watched the flames eat up the bedding, the banners, the walls. The more the fire ate, the hungrier it became. It crept to the ink shop to hunt for more food. It devoured the scrolls of famous scholars who had used our ink. It licked the silk-wrapped boxes holding the most expensive ink-sticks. And when the resin of those sticks leaked out, it roared with joy, its appetite increased. Within the hour, our family's fortunes wafted up to the gods as incense, ashes, and poisonous smoke.

Mother, Big Aunt, and Little Aunt clapped their hands over their ears, as if this was the only way to keep their senses from dribbling out. "The fates have turned against us!" Mother cried. "Could there be anything worse?" Little Uncle then cried and laughed and said indeed there was.

The buildings next to our family's ink shop also began to burn, he said. The one on the east sold old scholar books, the one on the west was filled to the rafters with the works of master painters. In the middle of the orange-colored night, the shopkeepers dumped their goods into the ashy lane. Then the fire brigade arrived. Everyone joined in and tossed so many buckets of water into the air it looked like it was raining. And then it really did rain, shattering down hard, ruining the saved goods, but saving the rest of the district from being burned.

By the time Little Uncle finished telling us this, Mother, my aunts, and GaoLing had stopped wailing. They looked as though their bones and blood had drained out of the bottoms of their feet. I think they felt as I did when I finally understood that Precious Auntie was dead.

Mother was the first to regain her senses. "Take the silver ingots out of the root cellar," she told us. "And whatever good jewelry you have, gather it up."

"Why?" GaoLing wanted to know.

"Don't be stupid. The other shopkeepers will make our family pay for the damages." And then Mother pushed her. "Get up. Hurry." She pulled a bracelet off GaoLing's wrist. "Sew jewelry into the sleeves of your worst-looking jackets. Hollow out the hardest crab apples and put the gold inside those. Pile them in the cart and put more apples on top, rotten ones. Old Cook, see if the tenants have any wheelbarrows they can sell us, and don't bargain too hard. Everyone put a bundle together, but don't bother with trifles. . . ." I was amazed at how Mother's mind flowed, as if she were accustomed to running two paces ahead of a flood.

The next day Father, Big Uncle, and their sons came home. They already looked like paupers with their unwashed faces, their smoky clothes. Big Aunt and Little Aunt went to them, jabbering:

"Will we lose the house?"

"Will we starve?"

"Do we really have to run away?"

The smaller children began to cry. Father was like a deaf mute. He sat in his elmwood chair, rubbing its arm, declaring it the finest thing he had ever owned and lost. That night, nobody ate. We did not gather in the courtyard for the evening breezes. GaoLing and I spent the night together, talking and crying, swearing loyalty to die together as sisters. We exchanged hairpins to seal our pledge. If she felt that Precious Auntie was to blame for our disasters, she did not say so as the others had continued to do. She did not blame my birth for bringing Precious Auntie into their lives. Instead, GaoLing told me that I should feel lucky that Precious Auntie had already died and would therefore not suffer the slow death of starvation and shame that awaited the rest of us. I agreed yet wished she were with me. But she was at the End of the World. Or was she really wandering the earth, seeking revenge?

The next day, a man came to our gate and handed Father a letter with seals. A complaint had been made about the fire and our family's responsibility for the damages. The official said that as soon as the owners of the affected shops had tallied their losses, the figure would be given to the magistrate, and the magistrate would tell us how the debt should be settled. In the meantime, he said, our family should present the deed for our house and land. He warned us that he was posting a notice in the village about this matter, and thus people would know to report us if we tried to run away.

After the official left, we waited to hear from Father

what we should do. He sagged into his elmwood chair. Then Mother announced, "We're finished. There's no changing fate. Today we'll go to the market and tomorrow we'll feast."

Mother gave all of us more pocket money than we had held in our entire lives. She said we should each buy good things to eat, fruits and sweets, delicacies and fatty meats, whatever we had always denied ourselves but longed for. The Moon Festival was coming up, and so it was not unusual that we would be shopping like the rest of the crowd for the harvest meal.

Because of the holiday, it was a bigger market day, with a temple fair, jugglers and acrobats, vendors of lanterns and toys, and more than the usual numbers of tricksters and hucksters. As we pushed through the hordes, GaoLing and I clung to each other's hands. We saw crying lost children and rough-looking men who stared at us openly. Precious Auntie had constantly warned me of hooligans from the big cities who stole stupid country girls and sold them as slaves. We stopped at a stall selling mooncakes. They were stale. We turned up our noses at pork that was gray. We looked into jars of fresh bean curd, but the squares were gooey and stunk. We had money, we had permission to buy what we wanted, yet nothing looked good, everything seemed spoiled. We wandered about in the thick crowd, pressed one to the other like bricks.

And then we found ourselves in Beggars Lane, a place I had never been. There we saw one pitiful sight after another: A shaved head and a limbless body that rocked on its back like a tortoise on its shell. A boneless boy whose legs were wrapped around his neck. A dwarf with long needles poked through his cheeks, belly, and thighs. The beggars had the same laments: "Please, little miss, I beg you, big brother, have pity on us. Give us money, and in your next life you won't have to suffer like us."

Some passing boys laughed, most other people turned away their eyes, and a few old grannies, soon bound for the next world, threw down coins. GaoLing clawed at my arm and whispered: "Is that what we're destined to become?" As we turned to leave, we bumped into a wretch. She was a girl, no older than we were, dressed in shredded rags, strips tied onto strips, so that she looked as if she were wearing an ancient warrior's costume. Where the orbs of her eyes should have been, there were two sunken puckers. She began to chant: "My eyes saw too much, so I plucked them out. Now that I can't see, the unseen come to me."

She shook an empty bowl in front of us. "A ghost is now waiting to speak to you."

"What ghost?" I asked right away.

"Someone who was like a mother to you," the girl answered just as fast.

GaoLing gasped. "How did she know Precious Auntie was your mother?" she whispered to me. And then she said to the girl, "Tell us what she says."

The blind girl held up her empty bowl again and shook it. GaoLing threw in a coin. The girl tipped the bowl and said, "Your generosity does not weigh much."

"Show us what you can do first," GaoLing said.

The girl crouched on the ground. From one tattered sleeve she pulled out a sack, then untied it and poured its contents on the ground. It was limestone silt. From her other sleeve she removed a long, slender stick. With the flat length of the stick, she smoothed the silt until its surface was as flat as a mirror. She pointed the stick's sharp end to the ground, and with her sightless eyes aimed toward heaven, she began to write. We crouched next to her. How did a beggar girl learn to do this? This was no ordinary trick. Her hand was steady, the writing was smooth, just like a skilled calligrapher's. I read the first line.

A dog howls, the moon rises, it said. "Doggie! That was her nickname for me," I told the girl. She smoothed the silt and wrote more: *In darkness, the stars pierce forever.* Shooting stars, that was in the poem Baby Uncle wrote for her. Another sweep, another line: *A rooster crows, the sun rises.* Precious Auntie had been a Rooster. And then the girl write the last line: *In daylight, it's as if the stars never existed.* I felt sad, but did not know why.

The girl smoothed the dirt once more and said, "The ghost has no more to say to you."

"That's it?" GaoLing complained. "Those words make no sense."

But I thanked the girl and put all the coins from my pocket into her bowl. As we walked home, GaoLing asked me why I had given the money for nonsense about a dog and a rooster. At first I could not answer her. I kept repeating the lines in my head so I would not forget them. Each time I did, I grew to understand what the message was and I became more miserable. "Precious Auntie said I was the dog who betrayed her," I told GaoLing at last. "The moon was the night I said I would leave her for the Changs. The stars piercing forever, that is her saying this is a lasting wound she can never forgive. By time the rooster crowed, she was gone. And until she was dead, I never knew she was my mother, as if she had never existed."

GaoLing said, "That is one meaning. There are others."

"What, then?" I asked. But she could not think of anything else to say.

* * *

When we returned home, Mother and Father, as well as our aunts and uncles, were bunched in the courtyard, talking in excited voices. Father was relating how he had met an old Taoist priest at the market, a remarkable and strange man. As he passed by, the priest had called out to him: "Sir, you look as if a ghost is plaguing your house."

"Why do you say that?" Father asked.

"It's true, isn't it?" the old man insisted. "I feel you've had a lot of bad luck and there's no other reason for it. Am I right?"

"We had a suicide," Father admitted, "a nursemaid whose daughter was about to be married."

"And bad luck followed."

"A few calamities," Father answered.

The young man standing next to the priest then asked Father if he had heard of the Famous Catcher of Ghosts. "No? Well, this is he, the wandering priest right before you. He's newly arrived in your town, so he's not yet as well known as he is in places far to the north and south. Do you have relatives in Harbin? No? Well, then! If you had, you'd know who he is." The young man, who claimed to be the priest's acolyte, added, "In that city alone, he is celebrated for having already caught one hundred ghosts in disturbed households. When he was done, the gods told him to start wandering again."

When Father finished telling us how he had met these two men, he added, "This afternoon, the Famous Catcher of Ghosts is coming to our house."

A few hours later, the Catcher of Ghosts and his assistant stood in our courtyard.

The priest had a white beard, and his long hair was piled like a messy bird's nest. In one hand he carried a walking stick with a carved end that looked like a flayed dog stretched over a gateway. In the other, he held a short beating stick. Slung over his shoulders was a rope shawl from which hung a large wooden bell. His robe was not the sand-colored cotton of most wandering monks I had seen. His was a rich-looking blue silk, but the sleeves were grease-stained, as if he had often reached across the table for more to eat.

I watched hungrily as Mother offered him special cold dishes. It was late afternoon, and we were sitting on low stools in the courtyard. The monk helped himself to everything—glass noodles with spinach, bamboo shoots with pickled mustard, tofu seasoned with sesame seed oil and coriander. Mother kept apologizing about the quality of the food, saying she was both ashamed and honored to have him in our shabby home. Father was drinking tea. "Tell us how it's done," he said to the priest, "this catching of ghosts. Do you seize them in your fists? Is the struggle fierce or dangerous?"

The priest said he would soon show us. "But first I need proof of your sincerity." Father gave his word that we were indeed sincere. "Words are not proof," the priest said.

"How do you prove sincerity?" Father asked.

"In some cases, a family might walk from here to the top of Mount Tai and back, barefoot and carrying a load of rocks." Everyone, especially my aunts, looked doubtful that any of us could do that.

"In other cases," the monk continued, "a small offering of pure silver can be enough and will cover the sincerity of all members of the immediate family."

"How much might be enough?" Father asked.

The priest frowned. "Only *you* know if your sincerity is little or great, fake or genuine."

The monk continued eating. Father and Mother went to

another room to discuss the amount of their sincerity. When they returned, Father opened a pouch and pulled out a silver ingot and placed this in front of the Famous Catcher of Ghosts.

"This is good," the priest said. "A little sincerity is better than none at all."

Mother then drew an ingot from the sleeve of her jacket. She slid this next to the first so that the two made a clinking sound. The monk nodded and put down his bowl. He clapped his hands, and the assistant took from his bundle an empty vinegar jar and wad of string.

"Where's the girl that the ghost loved best?" asked the priest.

"There," Mother said, and pointed to me. "The ghost was her nursemaid."

"Her mother," Father corrected. "The girl's her bastard."

I had never heard this word said aloud, and I felt as if blood was going to pour out of my ears.

The priest gave a small grunt. "Don't worry. I've had other cases just as bad." Then he said to me: "Fetch me the comb she used for your hair."

My feet were locked to the ground until Mother gave me a little knock on the head to hurry. So I went to the room Precious Auntie and I had shared not so long before. I picked up the comb she used to run through my hair. It was the ivory comb she never wore, its ends carved with roosters, its teeth long and straight. I remembered how Precious Auntie used to scold me for my tangles, worrying over every hair on my head.

When I returned, I saw the assistant had placed the vinegar jar in the middle of the courtyard. "Run the comb through your hair nine times," he said. So I did.

"Place it in the jar." I dropped the comb inside, smelling

the escape of cheap vinegar fumes. "Now stand there perfectly still." The Catcher of Ghosts beat his stick on the wooden bell. It made a deep *kwak, kwak* sound. He and the acolyte walked in rhythm, circling me, chanting, and drawing closer. Without warning, the Catcher of Ghosts gave a shout and leapt toward me. I thought he was going to squeeze me into the jar, so I closed my eyes and screamed, as did GaoLing.

When I opened my eyes, I saw the acolyte was pounding a tight-fitting wooden lid onto the jar. He wove rope from top to bottom, bottom to top, then all around the jar, until it resembled a hornet's nest. When this was done, the Catcher of Ghosts tapped the jar with his beating stick and said, "It's over. She's caught. Go ahead. Try to open it, you try. Can't be done."

Everyone looked, but no one would touch. Father asked, "Can she escape?"

"Not possible," said the Catcher of Ghosts. "This jar is guaranteed to last more than several lifetimes."

"It should be more," Mother grumbled. "Stuck in a jar forever wouldn't be too long, considering what she's done. Burned down our shop. Nearly killed our family. Put us in debt." I was crying, unable to speak on Precious Auntie's behalf. I was her traitor.

The next day, our family held its banquet, the best dishes, food we would never again enjoy in this lifetime. But no one except the youngest children had any appetite. Mother had also hired a man to take photographs, so we could remember the days when we had plenty. In one, she wanted a picture of just her and GaoLing. At the last moment, GaoLing insisted I come and stand near Mother as well, and Mother was not pleased but did not say anything. The following day, Father and my two uncles went to

Peking to hear what the damages would be against our family.

While they were gone, we learned to eat watery rice porridge flavored with just a few bites of cold dishes. Want less, regret less, that was Mother's motto. About a week later, Father stood in the courtyard, bellowing like a madman.

"Make another banquet," he shouted.

Then our uncles followed: "Our bad luck has ended! No damages! That was the magistrate's decision—no damages at all!"

We rushed toward them, children, aunts, tenants, and dogs.

How could this be? And we listened as Father explained. When the other shop owners brought in their damaged goods for inspection, the magistrate discovered that one had rare books that had been stolen from the Hanlin Academy thirty years before. Another, who claimed he had works of master calligraphers and painters, was actually selling forgeries. The judges then decided the fire was fitting punishment to those two thieves.

"The Catcher of Ghosts was right," Father concluded. "The ghost is gone."

That evening everyone ate well, except me. The others laughed and chatted, all worries gone. They seemed to forget that our inksticks had returned to charcoal, that the ink shop was just floating ash. They were saying their luck had changed because Precious Auntie was now knocking her head on the inside of a stinky vinegar jar.

The next morning, GaoLing told me Mother needed to talk to me right away. I had noticed that since Precious Auntie had died, Mother no longer called me Daughter. She did not criticize me. She almost seemed afraid I, too, would turn into a ghost. As I walked toward her room, I wondered if she had ever felt warmly toward me. And then I was standing in front of her. She seemed embarrassed to see me.

"In times of family misfortune," she began in a sharp voice, "personal sadness is selfish. Still, I am sad to tell you we are sending you to an orphanage." I was stunned, but I did not cry. I said nothing.

"At least we are not selling you as a slave girl," she added.

Without feeling, I said, "Thank you."

Mother went on: "If you remain in the house, who can tell, the ghost might return. I know the Catcher of Ghosts guaranteed this would not happen, but that's like saying drought is never followed by drought, or flood by flood. Everyone knows that isn't true."

I did not protest. But still she became angry. "What is that look on your face? Are you trying to shame me? Just remember, all these years I treated you like a daughter. Would any other family in this town have done the same? Maybe your going to the orphanage will teach you to appreciate us more. And now you'd better get ready. Mr. Wei is already waiting to take you in his cart."

I thanked her again and left the room. As I packed my bundle, GaoLing ran into the room with tears streaming down her cheeks. "I'll come find you," she promised, and gave me her favorite jacket.

"Mother will punish you if I take it," I said.

"I don't care."

She followed me to Mr. Wei's cart. As I left the courtyard and the house for the last time, she and the tenants were the only ones to see me off.

When the cart turned down Pig's Head Lane, Mr. Wei

began to sing a cheerful tune about the harvest moon. And I thought about what Precious Auntie had told the beggar girl to write:

A dog howls, the moon rises.
In darkness, the stars pierce forever.
A rooster crows, the sun rises.
In daylight, it's as if the stars never existed.

I looked at the sky, so clear, so bright, and in my heart I was howling.

DESTINY

The orphanage was an abandoned monastery near Dragon Bone Hill, a hard climb up a zigzag road from the railway station. To spare the donkey, Mr. Wei made me walk the last kilometer. When he let me off and said good-bye, that was the start of my new life.

It was autumn, and the leafless trees looked like an army of skeletons guarding the hill and the compound at the top. When I walked through the gate, nobody greeted me. Before me was a temple of dried-out wood and peeling lacquer, and in the bare open yard stood rows of girls in white jackets and blue trousers, lined up like soldiers. They bent at the waist—forward, side, back, side—as if obedient to the wind. There was another strange sight: two men, one foreign, one Chinese. It was only the second time I had seen a foreigner so close. They walked across this same courtyard, carrying maps, followed by a troop of men with long sticks. I was afraid I had stumbled upon a secret army for the Communists.

As I stepped over the threshold, I nearly jumped out of my skin. Dead bodies in shrouds, twenty or thirty. They stood in the middle of the hall, along the sides, some tall, some short. Immediately, I thought they were the Returning Dead. Precious Auntie had once told me that in her childhood some families would hire a priest to put a dead body under a spell and make it walk back to its ancestral home. The priest led them only at night, she said, so the dead wouldn't meet any living people they could possess. By day, they rested in temples. She didn't believe the story herself until she heard a priest banging a wooden bell late at night. And rather than run away like the other villagers, she hid behind a wall to watch. *Kwak, kwak,* and then she saw them, six of them, like giant maggots, leaping forward ten feet into the air. *What I saw I can't say for certain,* Precious Auntie told me. *All I know is that for a long time afterward, I was not the same girl.*

I was about to run out the door when I saw the glint of golden feet. I looked more carefully. They were statues of gods, not dead people. I walked toward one and pulled off the cloth. It was the God of Literature with his horned head, a writing brush in one hand, a valedictorian's cap in the other. "Why did you do that?" a voice called out, and I turned around and saw a little girl.

"Why is he covered?"

"Teacher said he is not a good influence. We should not believe in the old gods, only Christian ones."

"Where is your teacher?"

"Who have you come to see?"

"Whoever arranged to take Liu LuLing as an orphan." The girl ran off. A moment later, two lady foreigners were standing before me.

The American missionaries had not been expecting me, and I had not expected them to be Americans. And because I had never talked to a foreigner, I could not speak, only stare. They both had short hair, one white, the other curly red, and they also wore glasses, which made me think they were equally old.

"Sorry to say, no arrangements have been made," the white-haired lady told me in Chinese.

"Sorry to say," the other added, "most orphans are much younger."

When they asked my name, I was still unable to talk, so I used my finger to paint the characters in the air. They talked to each other in English voices.

"Can you read that, can you?" one of them asked me, pointing to a sign in Chinese.

" 'Eat until full, but do not hoard,' " I read.

One of the ladies gave me a pencil and a sheet of paper. "Can you write those same words down?" I did, and they both exclaimed: "She didn't even look back at the sign." More questions flew at me: Could I also use a brush? What books had I read? Afterward, they again spoke to each other in foreign talk, and when they were done, they announced that I could stay.

Later I learned I had been welcomed so that I could be both student and tutor. There were only four teachers, former students of the school, who now lived in one of the thirty-six rooms and buildings in the compound. Teacher Pan taught the older girls. I was his helper. When he had been a student fifty years before, the school was for boys only. Teacher Wang taught the younger girls, and her widowed sister—we called her Mother Wang—took care of the babies in the nursery, as did older girls she assigned as helpers. Then there was Sister Yu, a tiny woman with a bony hunched back, a hard hand, and a sharp voice. She was in charge of Cleanliness, Neatness, and Proper Behavior. Besides scheduling our baths and our tasks for the week, she liked to boss around the cook and his wife.

The missionary ladies, I found out, were not equally old. Miss Grutoff, the curly-haired one, was thirty-two, half the age of the other. She was the nurse and head-mistress of the school. Miss Towler was the director of the orphanage, and she begged donations from people who should have pity on us. She also led our Sunday chapel, conducted dramas of Christian history, and played the piano while teaching us to sing "like the angels." At the time, of course, I did not know what an angel was. I also could not sing.

As for the foreign men, they were not Communists but scientists who worked the quarry where the bones of Peking Man had been found. Two foreign and ten Chinese scientists lived in the north end of the monastery compound, and they ate their morning and evening meals in the temple hall with us. The quarry was nearby, about a twenty-minute walk down and up and down a winding path.

Altogether, there were seventy or so children: thirty big girls, thirty little girls, and ten babies, more or less, depending on how many grew up and how many died. Most of the girls were like me, the love children of suicides, singsong girls, and unmarried maidens. Some were like the entertainers GaoLing and I had seen on Beggars Lane—girls without legs or arms, a cyclops, a dwarf. And there were also half-breed girls, all of them fathered by foreigners, one English, one German, one American. I thought they were strangely beautiful, but Sister Yu was always mocking them. She said they had inherited haughtiness in the Western part of their blood and this had to be diluted with humility. "You can have pride in what you do each day," said Sister Yu, "but not arrogance in what you were born with." She also often reminded us that self-pity was not allowed. That was an indulgence.

If a girl wore a long face, Sister Yu would say, "Look at Little Ding over there. No legs, and still she smiles all day long." And Little Ding's fat cheeks rose and nearly swallowed her eyes, she was that glad to have buds instead of limbs. According to Sister Yu, we could find immediate happiness by thinking of someone else whose situation was much worse than our own.

I acted as big sister to this same Little Ding without legs, and Little Ding was big sister to a younger girl named Little Jung who had only one hand. Everyone had a relationship like that, being responsible to someone else, just like in a family. The big and small girls shared the same living quarters, three rooms of twenty girls each, three rows of beds in each room. The first row was for the youngest girls, the second row was for the in-between girls, and the third row was for the oldest girls. In this way, Little Ding's bed was below mine, and Little Jung's was below Little Ding's, everyone positioned by her level of responsibility and respect.

To the missionaries, we were Girls of New Destiny. Each classroom had a big red banner embroidered with gold characters that proclaimed this. And every afternoon, during exercise, we sang our destiny in a song that Miss Towler had written, in both English and Chinese:

We can study, we can learn,
We can marry whom we choose.
We can work, we can earn,
And bad fate is all we lose.

Whenever special visitors came by the school, Miss Grutoff had us perform a skit and Miss Towler played piano music, very dramatic to hear, like the kind in silent movies. One group of girls held up signs that were connected to Old Fate: opium, slaves, the buying of charms.

They stumbled around on bound feet and fell down help-less. Then the New Destiny girls arrived as doctors. They cured the opium smokers. They unbound the feet of the fated ones and picked up brooms to sweep away the use-less charms. In the end, they thanked God and bowed to the special guests, the foreign visitors to China, thanking them as well for helping so many girls overcome bad fate and move forward with their New Destiny. In this way, we raised a lot of money, especially if we could make the guests cry.

During chapel, Miss Towler always told us that we had a choice to become Christians or not. No one would ever force us to believe in Jesus, she said. Our belief had to be genuine and sincere. But Sister Yu, who had come to the orphanage when she was seven, often reminded us of her old fate. She had been forced to beg as a child, and if she did not collect enough coins, she was given nothing but curses to eat. One day when she protested she was hungry, her sister's husband threw her away like a piece of gar-bage. In this school, she said, we could eat as much as we wanted. We never had to worry that someone would kick us out. We could choose what we wanted to believe. How-ever, she added, any student who did not choose to believe in Jesus was a corpse-eating maggot, and when this un-believer died, she would tumble into the underworld, where her body would be pierced by a bayonet, roasted like a duck, and forced to suffer all kinds of tortures that were worse than what was happening in Manchuria.

Sometimes I wondered about the girls who could not choose. Where would they go when they died? I remember seeing a baby even the missionaries did not think had a New Destiny, a baby that had been fathered by her own grandfather. I saw her in the nursery, where I worked every morning. No one gave her a name, and Mother Wang told me not to pick her up, even if she cried, because something was wrong with her neck and head. She never made a sound. She had a face as flat and round as a large platter, two big eyes, and a tiny nose and mouth stuck in the middle. Her skin was as pale as rice paste, and her body, which was too small for her head, was as still as a wax flower. Only her eyes moved, back and forth, as if watching a mosquito drift across the ceiling. And then one day, the crib where she once lay was empty. Miss Grutoff said the baby was now a child of God, so I knew she had died. Over the years that I lived at the orphanage, I saw six other babies that looked the same, always fathered by a grandfather, born with the same "universal face," as Mother Wang called it. It was as though the same person had come back into the same body for someone else's mistake. Each time, I welcomed that baby back like an old friend. Each time, I cried when she left the world again.

Because I came from a family of inkmakers, I was the best calligraphy student the school had ever had. Teacher Pan said so. He often recounted to us the days of the Ching, how everything had become corrupt, even the examination system. Yet he also spoke of those old times with a sentimental fondness. He said to me, "LuLing, if you had been born a boy back then, you could have been a scholar." Those were his exact words. He also said I was a better calligrapher than his own son, Kai Jing, whom he taught himself.

Kai Jing, who was a geologist, was actually a very good calligrapher, especially for someone whose right side had been weakened by polio when he was a child. Lucky for him, when he fell ill, the family spent a great deal of money, their entire savings, to hire the best Western and

Chinese doctors. As a result, Kai Jing recovered with only a small limp and a drooped shoulder. The missionaries later helped him get a scholarship at the famous university in Peking where he studied to become a geologist. After his mother died, he returned home to take care of his father and work with the scientists in the quarry.

Every day he rode his bicycle from the orphanage to the quarry and back, pedaling right to the door of his father's classroom. Teacher Pan would perch sideways on the back of the bicycle, and as his son pedaled off to their rooms at the other end of the compound, we students and teachers called out, "Be careful! Don't fall off!"

Sister Yu admired Kai Jing a great deal. She once pointed him out to the children and said, "See? You, too, can set a goal to help others rather than remain a useless burden." Another time I heard her say, "What a tragedy that a boy so handsome has to be lame." Perhaps this was supposed to comfort the students as well. But to my mind she was saying Kai Jing's tragedy was greater than that of others simply because he had been born more pleasing to the eye. How could Sister Yu, of all people, think such a thing? If a rich man loses his house, is that worse than if a poor man loses his?

I asked an older girl about this, and she said, "What a stupid question. Of course! The handsome and the rich have more to lose." Yet this did not seem right to me.

I thought of Precious Auntie. Like Kai Jing, she had been born with a natural beauty, and then her face was ruined. I heard people say all the time, "How terrible to have a face like that. It would have been better if she had died." Would I have felt the same if I had not loved her? I thought of the blind beggar girl. Who would miss her?

Suddenly I wanted to find that beggar girl. She could

talk to Precious Auntie for me. She could tell me where she was. Was she wandering in the End of the World or was she stuck in the vinegar jar? And what about the curse? Would it find me soon? If I died this moment, who would miss me in this world? Who would welcome me in the next?

When the weather was good, Teacher Pan took us older girls to the quarry at Dragon Bone Hill. He was proud to do so, because his son was one of the geologists. The quarry had started as a cave like the one that belonged to Precious Auntie's family, but when I saw it, it was a giant pit about one hundred fifty feet deep. From top to bottom and side to side, the walls and floor had been painted with white lines, so that it looked like a giant's fishnet had been placed inside. "If a digger finds a piece of an animal, a person, or a hunting tool," Kai Jing explained to us, "he can write down that it came from this square of the quarry and not that one. We can calculate the age of the piece by where it was found, the eighth layer being the oldest. And then the scientists can go back to that spot and dig some more."

We girls always brought thermoses of tea and small cakes for the scientists, and when they saw us arrive, they quickly climbed up from the bottom, refreshed themselves, and said with grateful sighs, "Thank you, thank you. I was so thirsty I thought I would turn into another one of these dried-up bones." Every now and then, a rickshaw made its way up the steep road, and a pipe-smoking foreigner with thick glasses stepped out and asked if anything new had been found. Usually the scientists pointed this way and that, and the man with glasses nodded but seemed disappointed. But sometimes he became very excited, and sucked on his pipe faster and faster as he talked. Then he got back in the rickshaw and went down the hill, where a shiny black car would be waiting to take him back to Peking. If we ran to a lookout point on the hill, we could see to the far end of the flat basin, and there was the black car, running along the narrow road, sending up streams of dust.

When winter came, the scientists had to hurry before the ground grew too hard and the season of digging came to an end. They let some of us girls climb down and help put the dug-up dirt in boxes, or repaint the white lines on the quarry floor, or carefully sift what had already been sifted ten times. We were not allowed in any of the places where there were ropes—that was where human bones had been found. To an inexperienced eye, it was easy to mistake the bones for rocks or bits of pottery, but I knew the difference from all those times I had collected bones with Precious Auntie. I also knew that Peking Man was the bones not just from one person, but from many—men, women, children, babies. The pieces were small, not enough to make even one whole person. I did not say these things to the other girls. I did not want to show off. So like them, I helped only where the scientists said we could be, where there were mostly animal bones, deer horns, and turtle shells.

I remember the day Teacher Pan's son gave me special praise. "You are a careful worker," Kai Jing said. After that, sifting dirt carefully was my favorite job. But then the weather turned icy cold and we could no longer feel our fingers or cheeks. So that was the end of that kind of work and praise.

My next-favorite job was tutoring the other students. Sometimes I taught painting. I showed the younger students how to use the brush to make cat ears, tails, and whiskers. I painted horses and cranes, monkeys, and even a hippopotamus. I also helped the students improve their calligraphy and their minds. I recalled for them what Precious Auntie had taught me about writing characters, how a person must think about her intentions, how her *ch'i* flowed from her body into her arm, through the brush, and into the stroke. Every stroke had meaning, and since every word had many strokes, it also had many meanings.

My least favorite job was whatever Sister Yu assigned me to do for the week: sweeping the floors, cleaning the basins, or lining up the benches for chapel and putting them back at the tables for lunch. These jobs would not have been so bad if Sister Yu had not always picked apart what I had done wrong. One week, for a change, she put me in charge of crawling insects. She complained that the monks had never killed them, thinking they might have been former mortals and holy ones. "Former landlords is what these bugs likely were," Sister Yu grumbled, then told me: "Step on them, kill them, do whatever you must to keep them from coming in." The doors to most of the rooms, except those belonging to the foreigners, were never closed except in the winter, so the ants and cockroaches marched right over the thresholds. They also came in through any crack or hole in the wall, as well as through the large wooden latticed panels that allowed breezes and light to come in. But I knew what to do. Precious Auntie had taught me. I glued paper over the lattices. And then I took a stick of chalk from the schoolroom and drew a line in front of all the thresholds and around the cracks. The ants would sniff that chalk line and get confused, then turn around and leave. The cockroaches were braver. They walked right through the chalk, and the dust went into their joints and under their shells, and the next day they lay upside down, with their legs in the air, choked to death.

That week Sister Yu did not criticize me. Instead I received an award for Remarkable Sanitation, two hours free to do anything I wanted, as long as it was not evil. In that crowded place, there was no room to be alone. So that was what I chose to do with my prize. For a long time, I had not reread the pages Precious Auntie had written to me before she died. I had resisted because I knew I would cry if I saw those pages again, and then Sister Yu would scold me for allowing self-pity in front of Little Ding and the other younger girls. On a Sunday afternoon, I found an abandoned storeroom, smelling of must and filled with small statues. I sat on the floor against one wall near a window. I unfolded the blue cloth that held the pages. And for the first time I saw that Precious Auntie had sewn a little pocket into the cloth.

In that pocket were two wondrous things. The first one was the oracle bone she had shown me when I was a girl, telling me I could have it when I had learned to remember. She had once held this, just as her father had once held this. I clutched that bone to my heart. And then I pulled out the second thing. It was a small photograph of a young woman wearing an embroidered headwrap and a padded winter jacket with a collar that reached up to her cheeks. I held the picture up to the light. Was it . . . ? I saw that it was indeed Precious Auntie before she had burned her face. She had dreamy eyes, daring eyebrows that tilted upward, and her mouth—such plump pouting lips, such smooth skin. She was beautiful, but she did not look the way I remembered her, and I was sorry it was not her burnt face in the photo. The more I looked, however, the more she became familiar. And then I realized: Her face, her hope, her knowledge, her sadness—they were mine. Then I cried and cried, glutting my heart with joy and self-pity.

Once a week, Miss Grutoff and the cook's wife went to the railway station to pick up packages and mail. Sometimes there were letters from their friends at other missionary schools in China or from the scientists at Peking Union Medical College. Other times there would be letters with pledges of money. These came from far away: San Francisco in California, Milwaukee in Wisconsin, Elyria in Ohio. Miss Grutoff would read the letters aloud at Sunday chapel. She would show us on a globe, "Here we are, there they are. And they are sending you love and lots of money." Then she would spin the globe so we could become dizzy with this idea.

I used to wonder, Why would a stranger love another stranger? Mother and Father were like strangers to me now. They did not love me. To them, I no longer existed. And what about GaoLing's promises to find me? Had she tried? I did not think so.

One afternoon, after I had been at the orphanage for two years, Miss Grutoff handed me a letter. I recognized the handwriting immediately. It was noontime, and in that noisy main hall, I became deaf. The girls nearest me clamored to know what the letter said and who had written it. I ran away from them, guarding my treasure like a starved dog. I still have it, and this is what I read:

"My dearest sister, I apologize for not writing sooner. Not one day has passed that I don't think of you. But I could not write. Mr. Wei would not tell me where he had taken you. Neither would Mother. I finally heard in the market last week that the quarries at Dragon Blue Hill were becoming busy again, and that the American and

Chinese scientists were living in the old monastery, along with the students of the orphanage. The next time I saw First Brother's Wife, I said, 'I wonder if LuLing has met the scientists, since she lives so close to them.' And she answered, 'I was wondering the same.' So then I knew.

"Mother is well, but she complains that she is so busy her fingertips are always black. They are still working hard to replenish the inksticks lost in the fire. And Father and our uncles had to rebuild the shop in Peking. They borrowed the money and lumber from Chang the coffinmaker, who now owns most of the business. They received part of the business when I married Chang Fu Nan, the fourth son, the boy you were supposed to marry.

"Mother said we were lucky the Changs wanted any of the girls in our family at all. But I don't think I'm lucky. I think you are lucky that you did not become a daughter-in-law to this family. Every day, with each bite I eat, I am reminded of the Changs' position over our family. We are in debt to them for the wood, and the debt keeps growing. In a hundred years, the Liu clan will still be working for them. The inksticks no longer sell as well or for as much money. To be honest, the quality is no longer as good, now that the ingredients are inferior and Precious Auntie is no longer here to do the carvings. As reminder of our family's debt, I receive no spending money of my own. To buy a stamp for this letter, I had to barter away a hairpin.

"You should also know that the Chang family is not as rich as we believed when we were children. Much of their fortune has been drained away by opium. One of the other son's wives told me that the problem began when Fu Nan was a baby and tore his shoulder out of the socket. His mother began feeding him opium. Later, the mother died, beaten to death, some say, although Chang claims she fell off the roof by accident. Then Chang took another wife, who used to be the girlfriend of a warlord who had been trading opium for coffins. The second wife had the habit, too. The warlord told Chang that if he ever harmed her, he would turn him into a eunuch. And Chang knew this could happen, because he had seen other men who were missing parts of their body for failing to pay their opium debts.

"This household is a misery of shouting and madness, a constant search for money for more opium. If Fu Nan could sell pieces of me for his smoke, he would do so. He's convinced I know where to find more dragon bones. He jabbers that I should tell him, so we will all be rich. If only I did know, I would sell them to leave this family. I would even sell myself. But where would I go?

"Sister, I am sorry for any suffering or worry this letter causes you. I write this only so you know why I have not come to see you and why you are lucky to be where you are. Please do not write back to me. This would only cause me trouble. Now that I know where you are, I will try to write again. In the meantime, I hope your health is good and you are content. Your sister, Liu GaoLing."

When I finished, the letter was still shaking in my hands. I remembered that I had once been jealous of GaoLing. Now her fate was worse than mine. Sister Yu had said we could find happiness in our own situation when we thought of people whose lives were much worse. But I was not happy.

Yet in time, I did become less unhappy. I accepted my life. Maybe it was the weakness of memory that made me feel less pain. Perhaps it was my life force growing stronger. All I knew was, I had become a different girl from the one who had arrived at the orphanage.

Of course, by then even the gods in the monastery had

changed their minds. Over the years, Miss Towler had been removing the coverings from the statues, one by one, as cloth was needed for making clothes or quilts. Eventually, all the statues revealed themselves, mocking Miss Towler, so she said, with their red faces, three eyes, and bare bellies. And there were many, many statues, both Buddhist and Taoist, because the monastery had been occupied by both kinds of monks in different centuries, depending on which warlord was in charge of the land. One day, before Christmas, when it was too cold to go anywhere, Miss Grutoff decided that we should convert the Chinese gods into Christians. We would baptize them with paint. The girls who had grown up in the orphanage since they were babies thought this would be a lot of fun. But some of the students who had come later did not want to deface the gods and tempt their wrath. They were so scared that when they were dragged to the statues they screamed and foamed at the mouth, then fell to the ground as if possessed. I was not afraid. I believed that if I was respectful to both the Chinese gods and the Christian one, neither would harm me. I reasoned that Chinese people were polite and also practical about life. The Chinese gods understood that we were living in a Western household run by Americans. If the gods could speak, they, too, would insist that the Christian deities have the better position. Chinese people, unlike foreigners, did not try to push their ideas on others. Let the foreigners follow their own ways, no matter how strange they were, that was their thinking. As my brush ran over their gold-and-red faces, I said, "Pardon me, Jade Ruler, forgive me, Chief of the Eight Immortals, I am only making a disguise for you, in case the Communists or the Japanese come and recruit statues for a bonfire." I was a good artist. With some of the gods, I glued on sheep's hair for beards, noodles for long hair, feathers for wings. In this way, Buddha became fat Jesus, the Goddess of Mercy was Mary of the Manger, the Three Pure Ones, boss gods of the Taoists, turned into the Three Wise Men, and the Eighteen Lohan of Buddha were converted to the Twelve Apostles with six sons. Any small figures in hell were promoted to angels. The following year, Miss Grutoff decided we should also paint the little Buddha carvings throughout the compound. There were hundreds of those.

The year after that, Miss Grutoff found the musty storeroom where I had gone to reread Precious Auntie's pages. The statues there, Sister Yu said, were for a Taoist diorama that showed what would happen if a person went to the underworld. There were dozens of figures, very realistic and scary to see. One was a kneeling man with horned animals feeding on his entrails. Three figures dangled from a pole like pigs on a spit. Four people sat in a vat of boiling oil. And there were giant devils, red-faced with pointed skulls, ordering the dead to go into battle. When we finished painting those, we had a complete nativity scene, Baby Jesus, Mother Mary, Father Joseph, everybody including Santa Claus. Even so, the mouths on the statues were still wide open in screaming fright. No matter what Miss Grutoff said, most of the girls did not think the nativity statues were singing "Joy to the World."

After we finished with those statues, there were no more idols to be changed to angels. By then, I too had changed, from tutor to teacher, from lonely girl to one who was in love with Teacher Pan's son.

The way we started was this.

Every year, during the small New Year, the students

painted good-luck banners for the temple fair in the Mouth of the Mountain. And so I was with Teacher Pan and our students in the classroom one day, painting the long red strips, which covered the desks and floors.

As usual, Kai Jing came by on his bicycle to take his father to his rooms. The ground at Dragon Bone Hill was frozen hard, so most of Kai Jing's time was devoted to drawing diagrams, writing reports, and making casts of different spots where bones were found. On this particular day, Kai Jing came early, and Teacher Pan was not ready to leave. So Kai Jing offered to help us paint banners. He stood next to me at my table. I was glad for the extra hands.

But then I noticed what he was doing. Whatever character or figure I drew, he would make the same. If I drew "fortune," he drew "fortune." If I wrote "abundance," he wrote "abundance." If I painted "all that you wish," he painted the same, stroke by stroke. He used almost the same rhythm, so that we were like two people performing a dance. That was the beginning of our love, the same curve, the same dot, the same lifting of the brush as our breath filled as one.

A few days later, the students and I took the banners to the fair. Kai Jing accompanied me, walking alongside, talking quietly. He held a little book of brush paintings done on mulberry paper. On the cover it said: *The Four Manifestations of Beauty.* "Would you like to know what's inside?" he asked. I nodded. Anyone who overheard us would have thought we were speaking of school lessons. But really, he was speaking of love.

He turned the page. "With any form of beauty, there are four levels of ability. This is true of painting, calligraphy, literature, music, dance. The first level is Competent." We were looking at a page that showed two identical renderings of a bamboo grove, a typical painting, well done, realistic, interesting in the detail of double lines, conveying a sense of strength and longevity. "Competence," he went on, "is the ability to draw the same thing over and over in the same strokes, with the same force, the same rhythm, the same trueness. This kind of beauty, however, is ordinary.

"The second level," Kai Jing continued, "is Magnificent." We looked together at another painting, of several stalks of bamboo. "This one goes beyond skill," he said. "Its beauty is unique. And yet it is simpler, with less emphasis on the stalk and more on the leaves. It conveys both strength and solitude. The lesser painter would be able to capture one quality but not the other."

He turned the page. This painting was of a single stalk of bamboo. "The third level is Divine," he said. "The leaves now are shadows blown by an invisible wind, and the stalk is there mostly by suggestion of what is missing. And yet the shadows are more alive than the original leaves that obscured the light. A person seeing this would be wordless to describe how this is done. Try as he might, the same painter could never again capture the feeling of this painting, only a shadow of the shadow."

"How could beauty be more than divine?" I murmured, knowing I would soon learn the answer.

"The fourth level," Kai Jing said, "is greater than this, and it is within each mortal's nature to find it. We can sense it only if we do not try to sense it. It occurs without motivation or desire or knowledge of what may result. It is pure. It is what innocent children have. It is what old masters regain once they have lost their minds and become children again."

He turned the page. On the next was an oval. "This painting is called *Inside the Middle of a Bamboo Stalk*. The oval is what you see if you are inside looking up or looking down. It is the simplicity of being within, no reason or explanation for being there. It is the natural wonder that anything exists in relation to another, an inky oval to a page of white paper, a person to a bamboo stalk, the viewer to the painting."

Kai Jing was quiet for a long time. "This fourth level is called Effortless," he said at last. He put the booklet back in his jacket and looked at me thoughtfully. "Recently I have felt this beauty of Effortlessness in all things," he said. "How about you?"

"It's the same for me," I said, and began to cry.

For we both knew we were speaking about the effortlessness with which one falls in love without intending to, as if we were two stalks of bamboo bent toward each other by the chance of the wind. And then we bent toward each other and kissed, lost in the nowhere of being together.

EFFORTLESS

The first night Kai Jing and I tried forbidden joy, it was summertime, a bright-moon night. We had slipped into a dark storage room at the abandoned end of a corridor, far from the eyes and ears of others. I had no shame, no guilty feelings. I felt wild and new, as though I could swim the heavens and fly through waves. And if this was bad fate, let it be. I was the daughter of Precious Auntie, a woman who also could not control her desires, who then gave birth to me. How could this be bad when the skin on Kai Jing's back was so smooth, so warm, so fragrant? Was it also fate to feel his lips on my neck? When he unbuttoned the back of my blouse and it fell to the floor, I was ruined, and I was glad. Then the rest of my clothing slipped off, piece by piece, and I felt I was growing lighter and darker. He and I were two shadows, black and airy, folding and blending, weak yet fierce, weightless, mindless of others—until I opened my eyes and saw that a dozen people were watching us.

Kai Jing laughed. "No, no, they're not real." He tapped one. They were the painted-over theater of hell, now converted to Merry Christmas.

"They're like an audience at a bad opera," I said, "not so pleased." There was Mother Mary with a screaming mouth, the sheepherders with pointed heads, and Baby

Jesus, whose eyes stuck out like a frog's. Kai Jing draped my blouse over the head of Mary. He covered Joseph with my skirt, while Baby Jesus received my slip. Then Kai Jing put his own clothes over the Three Wise Men and turned the sheepherders around. When all their eyes faced the wall, Kai Jing guided me to lie down in the straw, and once more we became shadows.

But what happened after that was not like a poem or a painting of the fourth level. We were not like nature, as beautifully harmonious as a leafy tree against the sky. We had expected all these things. But the straw made us itch and the floor stank of urine. A rat stumbled out of its nest, and this caused Kai Jing to roll off me and knock Baby Jesus out of his crib. The frog-eyed monster lay next to us, as if it were our love child. Then Kai Jing stood up and lighted a match, searching for the rat. And when I looked at Kai Jing's private parts, I saw he was no longer possessed. I also saw he had ticks on his thigh. A moment later, he pointed out three on my bottom. I jumped up and was dancing to shake them off. I had to try very hard not to laugh and cry as Kai Jing turned me around and inspected me, then burned off the ticks with the tip of a match. When I took back my blouse from Mary's head, she looked glad that I was ashamed, even though we had not fulfilled our desires.

As we quickly dressed, Kai Jing and I were too embarrassed to talk. He also said nothing as he walked me to my room. But at the door, he told me, "I'm sorry. I should have controlled myself." My heart hurt. I didn't want to hear his apology, his regrets. I heard him add: "I should have waited until we're married." And then I gasped and began to cry, and he embraced me and uttered promises that we would be lovers for ten thousand lifetimes, and I vowed the same, until we heard a loud "Shhhh!" Even after we quieted, Sister Yu, whose room was next to mine, kept grumbling: "No consideration for others. Worse than roosters . . ."

The next morning, I felt like a different person, happy but also worried. Sister Yu had once said that you could tell which girls in the lanes were prostitutes because they had eyes like chickens. What she meant by this, I didn't know. Did the eyes become redder or smaller? Would others see in my eyes that I had a new kind of knowledge? When I arrived in the main hall for breakfast, I saw that almost everyone was there, gathered in a circle, talking in serious voices. As I walked in, it seemed that all the teachers lifted their eyes to stare at me, shocked and sad. Then Kai Jing shook his head. "Bad news," he said, and the blood drained from my limbs so that even if I had wanted to run away I was too weak to do so. Would I be kicked out? Had Kai Jing's father refused to let him marry me? But how did they know? Who told? Who saw? Who heard? Kai Jing pointed to the shortwave radio that belonged to the scientists, and the others turned back to listen. And I wondered: Now the *radio* is announcing what we did? In English?

When Kai Jing finally told me, I didn't have even one moment to be relieved that the bad news was not about me. "The Japanese attacked last night," he said, "close to Peking, and everyone is saying it is war for sure."

Maku polo this, *maku polo* that, I heard the radio voice say. I asked: "What is this *maku* thing?"

Sister Yu said, "The *Maku Polo* Bridge. The island dwarves have captured it." I was surprised to hear her use this slur for the Japanese. In the school, she was the one who taught the girls not to use bad names, even for those we hated. Sister Yu went on: "Shot their rifles in the air—just for practice, they said. So our army shot back to teach the liars a lesson. And now one of the dwarves is missing. Probably the coward ran away, but the Japanese are saying one missing man is enough reason to declare war." With Sister Yu translating the English into Chinese, it was hard to tell which was the news and which were her opinions.

"This Maku Polo Bridge," I said, "how far away is it?"

"North of here, in Wanping," Miss Grutoff said, "close to the railway station."

"But that's the Reed Moat Bridge, forty-six kilometers from my village," I said. "When did they start calling it something else?"

"More than six hundred years ago," Miss Grutoff said, "when Marco Polo first admired it." And as everyone continued to talk about the war, I was wondering why no one in our village knew the bridge had changed its name so long before. "Which way are the Japanese advancing?" I asked. "North to Peking or south to here?"

Everyone stopped talking at once. A woman stood in the doorway. With the bright sun behind her, she was a shadow, and I could not make out who she was, only that she wore a dress. "Is Liu LuLing still living here?" I heard her say. I squinted. Who was asking this? I was already confused about so many things, now this as well. As I walked toward her, my confusion turned into a guess, then the guess into a certainty. *Precious Auntie.* I had often dreamed that her ghost would come back. As in dreams, she could talk and her face was whole, and as in dreams, I rushed toward her. And at last, this time she did not push me away. She threw open her arms and cried: "So you still recognize your own sister!"

It was GaoLing. We spun each other around, danced and

slapped each other's arms, taking turns to cry, "Look at you." I had not heard from her since she wrote me the letter four or five years before. In minutes, we were treating each other like sisters once again. "What's happened to your hair?" I joked, grabbing her messy curls. "Was it an accident, or did you do this on purpose?"

"Do you like it?"

"Not bad. You look modern, no longer the country girl."

"No flies circling your head, either. I heard rumors you're now a high-and-mighty intellectual."

"Only a teacher. And you, are you still—"

"Wife to Chang Fu Nan. Six years already, hard to believe."

"But what's happened to you? You look terrible."

"I haven't eaten since yesterday."

I jumped up, went to the kitchen, and brought her back a bowl of millet porridge, some pickles and steamed peanuts, and little cold dishes. We sat in a corner of the hall, away from news of the war, she eating with much noise and speed. "We've been living in Peking, Fu Nan and I, no children," she said between thick mouthfuls. "We have the back rooms of the ink shop. Everything's been re-built. Did I tell you this in my letter?"

"Some."

"Then you know that the Changs own the business, our family owns only the debt. Father and our uncles are back in Immortal Heart village, churning out ink till it sweats from their pores. And now that they're home all the time, they have bad tempers and argue constantly among themselves about who is to blame for this, that, and the weather."

"What about First Brother and Second Brother?" I asked. "Home, too?"

"The Nationalists conscripted First Brother five years ago. All the boys his age had to go. And Second Brother ran off to join the Communists two years after that. Big Uncle's sons followed, then Big Uncle cursed that all three should never come back. Mother didn't speak to him until the United Front was formed and Uncle apologized, saying now it didn't matter which side they were on."

"And Mother, how's her health?"

"Remember how black her hair used to be? Now it's like an old man's beard, white and wiry. She no longer dyes it."

"What? I thought it was naturally black from working with the ink."

"Don't be stupid. They all dyed their hair—Great-Granny, the aunts. But these days Mother doesn't care what she looks like. She claims she hasn't slept in two years. She's convinced the tenants are stealing from us at night and rearranging the furniture. And she also believes Great-Granny's ghost has returned to the latrine. She hasn't had a bowel movement bigger than a bean sprout in months. The shit's hardened to mortar, she says, that's why she's distended like a summer gourd."

"This is terrible to hear." Though this was the same Mother who had kicked me out, I took no pleasure in hearing about her difficulties. Perhaps a little bit of me still thought of Mother and Father as my parents.

"What about Precious Auntie's ghost? Did she ever come back?"

"Not a wail or a whimper, which is strange, since that Catcher of Ghosts turned out to be a fake, not a monk at all. He had a wife and three brats, one of whom was the assistant. They were using the same vinegar jar to catch other ghosts, just opened the lid, sealed it up, over and over. They caught a lot of foolish customers that way.

When Father heard this, he wanted to stuff the crook in the jar and plug it up with pony dung. I said to him, 'If Precious Auntie's ghost never came back, what does it matter?' But ever since, he's been muttering about the two ingots he lost, tallying their worth, which according to him was enough to purchase the sky."

My mind was a sandstorm: If the monk was a fake, did that mean Precious Auntie had escaped? Or was she never put in the jar? And then I had another thought.

"Maybe there never was a ghost because she never died," I said to GaoLing.

"Oh, she died for sure. I saw Old Cook throw her body in the End of the World."

"But perhaps she was not entirely dead and she climbed back up. Why else didn't I find her? I searched for hours, from side to side and top to bottom."

GaoLing looked away. "What a terrible day that was for you. . . . You didn't find her, but she was there. Old Cook felt sorry that Precious Auntie didn't get a proper burial. He pitied her. When Mother wasn't looking, he went down there and piled rocks on top of the body."

And now I pictured Precious Auntie struggling up the ravine, a rock rolling toward her, striking her, then another and another, as she tumbled back down. "Why didn't you tell me this sooner?"

"I didn't know until Old Cook died, two years after Precious Auntie. His wife told me. She said he did good deeds that no one even knew about."

"I need to go back and find her bones. I want to bury them in a proper place."

"You'll never find them," GaoLing said. "The cliff broke off again last year during the rainstorms, a ledge the length of five men. Collapsed all at once and buried everything along that side of the ravine with rocks and dirt three stories deep. Our house will be the next to go."

And I mourned uselessly: "If only you had come and told me sooner."

"What a pity, I know. I didn't think you'd still be here. If it weren't for Mr. Wei's gossipy wife, I wouldn't have known you were a teacher here. She told me when I came home for a visit during Spring Festival."

"Why didn't you come see me then?"

"You think my husband gives me permission to take a holiday when I want? I had to wait for the way of heaven to throw me a chance. And then it came at the worst time. Yesterday Fu Nan told me to go to Immortal Heart village to beg more money from his father. I said to him, 'Didn't you hear? The Japanese are parading their army along the railway.' *Fff*. He didn't care. His greed for opium is greater than any fear that his wife could be run through with a bayonet."

"Still eating the opium?"

"That's his life. Without it, he's a rabid dog. So I went to Wanping, and sure enough, the trains stopped and went no further. All the passengers got off and milled around like sheep and ducks. We had soldiers poking us to keep moving. They herded us into a field, and I was certain we were going to be executed. But then we heard *pau-pau-pau*, more shooting, and the soldiers ran off and left us there. For a minute, we were too afraid to move. The next I thought, Why should I wait for them to come back and kill me? They can chase me. So I ran away. And soon everyone did, scattering every which way. I must have walked for twelve hours."

GaoLing took off her shoes. The heels were broken, the sides were split, and her soles had bleeding blisters. "My feet hurt so much I thought they would kill me with the pain." She snorted. "Maybe I should let Fu Nan think I was killed. Yes, make him feel he is to blame. Though probably he'd feel nothing. He'd just go back to his cloudy dreams. Every day is the same to him, war or no war, wife or no wife." She laughed, ready to cry. "So Big Sister, what do you say? Should I go back to him?"

What could I do except insist four times that she stay with me? And what could she do except insist three times that she did not want to be a burden? Finally, I took her to my room. She wiped her face and neck with a wet cloth, then lay on my cot with a sigh, and fell asleep.

Sister Yu was the only one who objected to GaoLing's living with me at the school. "We're not a refugee camp," she argued. "As it is, we have no cots to take any more children."

"She can live in my room, stay in my bed."

"She is still a mouth to feed. And if we allow one exception, then others will want an exception, too. In Teacher Wang's family alone, there are ten people. And what about the former students and their families? Should we let them in as well?"

"But they're not asking to come here."

"What? Is moss growing on your brain? If we are at war, *everyone* will soon ask. Think about this: Our school is run by the Americans. The Americans are neutral on the Japanese. They are neutral on the Nationalists and the Communists. Here you don't have to worry which side wins or loses from day to day. You can just watch. That's what it means to be neutral."

For all these years, I had bitten back my tongue when Sister Yu was bossy. I had shown her respect when I felt none. And even though I was now a teacher, I still did not know how to argue with her. "You talk about kindness, you say we should have pity"—and before I could tell her what I really thought of her, I said, "and now you want to send my sister back to an opium addict?"

"My eldest sister also had to live with one," she replied. "When her lungs were bleeding, her husband refused to buy any medicine. He bought opium for himself instead. That's why she's dead—gone forever, the only person with deep feeling for me." It was no use. Sister Yu had found yet another misery to compare as greater than anyone else's. I watched her hobble out of the room.

When I found Kai Jing, we walked out the gate and around the back wall of the orphanage to snuggle. And then I told him my complaints about Sister Yu.

"You may not think so, but she really does have a good heart," he said. "I've known her since we were children together."

"Maybe you should marry her, then."

"I prefer a woman with ticks on her pretty bottom."

I slapped his hands away. "You mean to be loyal," he went on. "She means to be practical. Don't fight differences of meaning. Find where you mean the same. Or simply do nothing for now. Wait and see." I can honestly say I admired Kai Jing as much as I loved him. He was kind and sensible. If he had a fault, it was his foolishness in loving me. And as my head floated in the pleasure of this mystery and his caresses, I forgot about big wars and small battles.

When I returned to my room, I was startled to see Sister Yu there, shouting at GaoLing: "As hollow as a worm-eaten tree trunk!"

GaoLing shook her fist and said: "The morals of a maggot."

Then Sister Yu laughed. "I hate that man to the very marrow of my bones!"

GaoLing nodded. "Exactly my feeling, too."

After a while, I understood that they were not fighting with each other but in a contest to name the worst insult for the devils who had wronged them. For the next two hours, they tallied their grievances. "The desk that was in my father's family for nine generations," GaoLing said, "gone in exchange for a few hours of pleasure."

"No food, no coal, no clothes in winter. We had to huddle so tightly together we looked like one long caterpillar."

Later that night, GaoLing said to me, "That Sister Yu is very wise, also a lot of fun." I said nothing. She would soon learn this woman could also be like a stinging wasp.

The next day, I found them seated together in the teacher's dining room. Sister Yu was talking in a quiet voice, and I heard GaoLing answer her, "This is unbearable to even hear. Was your sister pretty as well as kind?"

"Not a great beauty, but fair," Sister Yu answered. "Actually, you remind me of her—the same broad face and large lips."

And GaoLing acted honored, not insulted at all. "If only I could be as brave and uncomplaining."

"She *should* have complained," Sister Yu said. "You, too. Why must those who suffer also be quiet? Why accept fate? That's why I agree with the Communists! We have to struggle to claim our worth. We can't stay mired in the past, worshipping the dead."

GaoLing covered her mouth and laughed. "Careful what you say, or the Japanese and Nationalists will take turns whacking off your head."

"Whack away," Sister Yu said. "What I say, I mean. The

Communists are closer to God, even though they don't believe in Him. Share the fish and loaves, that's what they believe. It's true, Communists are like Christians. Maybe they should form a united front with Jesus worshippers rather than with the Nationalists."

And GaoLing put her hand over Sister Yu's mouth. "Are all Christians as stupid as you are?" They were freely insulting each other, as only good friends can.

A few days after this, I found the two of them sitting in the courtyard before dinner, reminiscing like comrades stuck together through the ages like glue and lacquer. GaoLing waved me over to show me a letter with a red seal mark and the emblem of the rising sun. It was from the "Japanese Provisional Military Police."

"Read it," Sister Yu said.

The letter was to Chang Fu Nan, announcing that his wife, Liu GaoLing, had been arrested at Wanping as an anti-Japanese spy. "You were arrested?" I cried.

GaoLing slapped my arm. "You melonhead, read more."

"Before she escaped from the detention center, where she was awaiting execution," the letter said, "Liu GaoLing confessed that it was her husband, Chang Fu Nan, who sent her to the railway station to conduct her illegal mission. For this reason, the Japanese agents in Peking wish to speak to Chang Fu Nan of his involvement in her spying activities. We will be coming soon to Chang Fu Nan's residence to discuss the matter."

"I typed the words," Sister Yu boasted.

"And I carved the seals," GaoLing said.

"It's very realistic," I told them. "My heart went *peng-peng-peng* when I read it."

"Fu Nan will think firecrackers have exploded in his

chest," said GaoLing. She and Sister Yu squealed like schoolgirls.

"But won't Mother and Father be in agony when they hear you're missing?"

"I'll go see them next week if the roads are safe."

And that's what GaoLing did, went to Immortal Heart, where she discovered that Fu Nan had told no one about the letter. About a month later, she returned to the school as Sister Yu's helper. "Mother and Father knew only what the Chang father told him," she reported. " 'That husband of yours,' Father said to me. 'I thought he was all boast and no backbone. And then we hear he's joined the army—didn't even wait to be forced to go.'

"I also told Mother and Father that I ran into you at the railway station at the Mouth of the Mountain," GaoLing said. "I bragged you were an intellectual, working side by side with the scientists—and you'd soon be married to one."

I was glad she had said this. "Were they sorry about what they did to me?"

"Ha! They were proud," GaoLing said. "Mother said, 'I always knew we did well by her. Now you see the result.' "

The dew turned to frost, and that winter we had two kinds of weddings, American and Chinese. For the American part, Miss Grutoff gave me a long white dress she had made for her own wedding but never wore. Her sweetheart died in the Great War, so it was a bad-luck dress. But she had such happy tears when she gave me the gown, how could I refuse? For the Chinese banquet, I wore a red wedding skirt and head scarf that GaoLing had embroidered.

Since GaoLing had already told Mother and Father I was to be married, I invited them out of politeness. I hoped they would use the convenient excuse of war to not come. But Mother and Father did come, as did the aunts and uncles, big and little cousins, nephews and nieces. No one talked of the great embarrassment of what we all knew. It was very awkward. I introduced Mother and Father as my aunt and uncle, which would have been a true fact if I had not been a love child without proper claim to any family. And most everyone at the school acted politely toward them. Sister Yu, however, gave them critical stares. She muttered to GaoLing, loud enough for Mother to hear: "They threw her away, and now they stuff their mouths at her table." All day long, I felt confused—happy in love, angry with my family, yet strangely glad that they were there. And I was also worried about the white wedding dress, thinking this was a sign that my happiness would not last for long.

Only two of the scientists, Dong and Chao, came to our party. Because of the war, it was too dangerous for anyone to work in the quarry anymore. Most of the scientists had fled for Peking, leaving behind almost everything except the relics of the past. Twenty-six of the local workers stayed, as did Kai Jing, Dong, and Chao, who also lived on the former monastery grounds. Someone needed to keep an eye on the quarry, Kai Jing reasoned. What if the Japanese decided to blow up the hill? What if the Communists used the quarry as a machine-gun trench? "Even if they used it as an open pit toilet," I said to him, "how can you stop them?" I was not arguing that he and I should run to Peking as well. I knew he would never separate from his old father, and his old father would never separate from the school and the orphan girls. But I did not want my husband to go into the quarry as hero and come out as martyr. So much was uncertain. So many had already gone away.

And many of us felt left behind. As a result, our wedding banquet was like the celebration of a sad victory.

After the banquet, the students and friends carried us to our bedchamber. It was the same storeroom where Kai Jing and I had gone for that disaster of a first night. But now the place was clean: no rats, no urine, no ticks or straw. The week before, the students had painted the walls yellow, the beams red. They had pushed the statues to one side. And to keep the Three Wise Men from watching us, I had made a partition of ropes and cloth. On our wedding night, the students remained outside our door for many hours, joking and teasing, laughing and setting off fire-crackers. Finally they tired and left, and for the first time Kai Jing and I were alone as husband and wife. That night, nothing was forbidden, and our joy was effortless.

The next day, we were supposed to visit the houses of our in-laws. So we went to the two rooms at the other end of the corridor, where Teacher Pan lived. I bowed and served him tea, calling him "Baba," and we all laughed over this formality. Then Kai Jing and I went to a little altar I had made with the picture of Precious Auntie in a frame. We poured tea for her as well, then lighted the incense, and Kai Jing called her "Mama" and promised he would take care of my entire family, including the ancestors who had come before me. "I am your family now, too," he said.

All at once, a cold breath poured down my neck. Why? I thought of our ancestor who died in the Monkey's Jaw. Was that the reason? I remembered the bones that were never brought back, the curse. What was the meaning of this memory?

"There are no such things as curses," Kai Jing later told me. "Those are superstitions, and a superstition is a need-less fear. The only curses are worries you can't get rid of."

"But Precious Auntie told me this, and she was very smart."

"She was self-taught, exposed to only the old ideas. She had no chance to learn about science, to go to a university like me."

"Then why did my father die? Why did Precious Auntie die?"

"Your father died because of an accident. Precious Auntie killed herself. You said so yourself."

"But why did the way of heaven lead to these things?"

"It's not the way of heaven. There is no reason."

Because I loved my husband very much, I tried to abide by the new ideas: no curses, no bad luck, no good luck, either. When I worried over dark clouds, I said there was no reason. When wind and water changed places, I tried to convince myself that there was no reason for this as well. For a while, I had a happy life, not too many worries.

Every evening after dinner, Kai Jing and I paid a visit to his father. I loved to sit in his rooms, knowing this was my family home, too. The furnishings were plain, old, and honest, and everything had its place and purpose. Against the west wall, Teacher Pan had placed a cushioned bench that was his bed, and above that, he had hung three scrolls of calligraphy, one hundred characters each, as if done in one breath, one inspiration. By the south-facing window, he kept a pot of flowers in season, bright color that drew the eye away from shadows. Against the east wall were a simple desk and a chair of dark polished wood, a good place for thought. And on the desk were precious scholar-objects arranged like a still-life painting: a lacquered leather box, ivory brush holders, and an inkstone of *duan*, the best kind of stone, his most valuable possession, a gift from an old missionary who had taught him in his boyhood.

One night Teacher Pan gave me that *duan* inkstone. I was about to protest, but then I realized that he was my father now, and I could accept it openly with my heart. I held that circle of *duan* and ran my fingers over its silky smoothness. I had admired that inkstone since the days when I first came to the school as his helper. He had brought it to class once to show to the students. "When you grind ink against stone you change its character, from ungiving to giving, from a single hard form to many flowing forms. But once you put the ink to paper, it becomes unforgiving again. You can't change it back. If you make a mistake, the only remedy is to throw away the whole thing." Precious Auntie had once said words that were similar. *You should think about your character. Know where you are changing, how you will be changed, what cannot be changed back again.* She said that when I first learned to grind ink. She also said this when she was angry with me, during the last days we were together. And when I heard Teacher Pan talking about this same thing, I promised myself I would change and become a better daughter.

Much had changed, and I wished Precious Auntie could see how good my life was. I was a teacher and a married woman. I had both a husband and a father. And they were good people, unlike GaoLing's in-laws, the Changs. My new family was genuine and sincere to others, the same inside as they showed outside. Precious Auntie had taught me that was important. Good manners are not enough, she had said, they are not the same as a good heart. Though Precious Auntie had been gone for all these years, I still heard her words, in happy and sad times, when it was important.

* * *

After the Japanese attacked the Mouth of the Mountain, GaoLing and I climbed to the hilltop whenever we heard distant gunfire. We looked for the direction of the puffs of smoke. We noticed which way the carts and trucks were moving along the roads. GaoLing joked that we brought news faster than the ham radio that Kai Jing and Miss Grutoff sat in front of for half the day, hoping to hear a word from the scientists who had gone to Peking. I did not understand why they wanted the radio to talk back to them. It spoke only about bad things—which port city was taken, how nearly everyone in this or that town was killed to teach the dead people a lesson not to fight against the Japanese.

"The Japanese won't win here," GaoLing would say in the evenings. "They may be fast in the sea, but here in the mountains they're like fish flopping on the sand. Our men, on the other hand, are like goats." Every night she said this to convince herself it was true. And for a while, it was true. The Japanese soldiers could not push their way up the mountain.

While water couldn't run uphill, money did. All kinds of vendors from down below sneaked past the barricades and brought their goods up the mountain so that people from the hill towns could spend their money before they were killed. GaoLing, Kai Jing, and I would walk along the ridge road to buy luxuries. Sometimes I filled my tin with *shaoping*, the savory flaky buns coated with sesame seeds that I knew Teacher Pan loved so much. Other days I bought fried peanuts, dried mushrooms, or candied melon. There were many shortages during wartime, so any delicacies we could find were always an excuse for little parties.

We held them in Teacher Pan's sitting room. GaoLing and Sister Yu always joined us, as did the scientists—

Dong, the older man with a gentle smile, and Chao, the tall young one whose thick hair hung in front of his face. When we were pouring the tea, Teacher Pan would wind his phonograph. And as we savored our treats, we listened to a song by Rachmaninoff called "Oriental Dance." I can still see Teacher Pan, waving his hand like a conductor, telling the invisible pianist and cello players where to quiet down, where to come back with full feeling. At the end of the party, he would lie on the cushioned bench, close his eyes, and sigh, grateful for the food, Rachmaninoff, his son, his daughter-in-law, his dear old friends. "This is the truest meaning of happiness," he would tell us. Then Kai Jing and I would go for an evening stroll before we returned to our own room, grateful ourselves for the joy that exists only between two people.

Those were the small rituals we had, what comforted us, what we loved, what we could look forward to, what we could be thankful for and remember afterward.

Even in wartime and poverty, people must have plays and opera. "They are the speech and music of the soul," Kai Jing told me. Every Sunday afternoon, the students performed for us, and they were very enthusiastic. But to be honest, the acting and music were not very good, painful sometimes to listen to and see, and we had to be very good actors ourselves to pretend this was enjoyment beyond compare. Teacher Pan told me that the plays were just as bad when I was a student and performed in them. How long ago that seemed. Now Miss Towler was bent over with old age, almost as short as Sister Yu. When she played the piano, her nose nearly touched the keys. Teacher Pan had cataracts and worried that soon he would not be able to paint anymore.

When winter came, we heard that many of the Communist soldiers were falling sick and dying of diseases before they had a chance to fire a single bullet. The Japanese had more medicine, warmer clothes, and they took food and supplies from whatever villages they occupied. With fewer Communist troops to defend the hills, the Japanese were crawling up, and with each step, they chopped down trees so no one could hide and escape. Because they were coming closer, we could no longer safely walk the ridge road to buy food.

Yet Kai Jing and his colleagues still went to the quarry, and this made me crazy with anxiety. "Don't go," I always begged him. "Those old bones have been there for a million years. They can wait until after the war." That quarry was the only reason we had arguments, and sometimes when I remember this, I think I should have argued more, argued until he stopped going. Then I think, no, I should have argued less, or not at all. Then maybe his last memories of me would not have been those of a complaining wife.

When Kai Jing was not at the quarry, he taught the girls in my class about geology. He told them stories about ancient earth and ancient man, and I listened, too. He drew pictures on the chalkboard of icy floods and fiery explosions from underneath, of the skull of Peking Man and how it was different from a monkey's, higher in the forehead, more room for his changing brain. If Miss Towler or Miss Grutoff were listening, Kai Jing did not draw the monkey or talk about the ages of the earth. He knew that his ideas about life before and everlasting were different from theirs.

One day, Kai Jing told the girls how humans grew to be different from monkeys: "Ancient Peking Man could stand up and walk. We see this by the way his bones are formed, the footprints he left in the mud. He used tools. We see this by the bones and rocks he shaped to cut and smash. And Peking Man probably also began to speak in words. At least his brain was capable of forming a language."

A girl asked, "What words? Were they Chinese?"

"We don't know for certain," Kai Jing said, "because you cannot leave behind spoken words. There was no writing in those days. That happened only thousands of years ago. But if there was a language, it was an ancient one that likely existed only in that time. And we can only guess what Peking Man tried to say. What does a person need to say? What man, woman, or child does he need to say it to? What do you think was the very first sound to become a word, a meaning?"

"I think a person should always say her prayers to God," another girl said. "She should say thank you to those who are nice to her."

That night, when Kai Jing was already asleep, I was still thinking about these questions. I imagined two people without words, unable to speak to each other. I imagined the need: The color of the sky that meant "storm." The smell of fire that meant "Flee." The sound of a tiger about to pounce. Who would worry about such things?

And then I realized what the first word must have been: *ma,* the sound of a baby smacking its lips in search of her mother's breast. For a long time, that was the only word the baby needed. Ma, ma, ma. Then the mother decided that was her name and she began to speak, too. She taught the baby to be careful: sky, fire, tiger. A mother is always the beginning. She is how things begin.

One spring afternoon, the students were performing a play. I remember it well, a scene from *The Merchant of*

Venice, which Miss Towler had translated into Chinese. "Fall down on your knees and pray," they were chanting. And right then, my life changed. Teacher Pan burst into the hall, panting and shouting, "They've seized them."

Between broken breaths, he told us that Kai Jing and his friends had gone to the quarry for their usual inspection. Teacher Pan had gone along for the fresh air and small talk. At the quarry they found soldiers waiting. They were Communists, and since they were not Japanese, the men were not concerned.

The leader of the soldiers approached them. He asked Kai Jing, "Hey, why haven't you joined us?"

"We're scientists not soldiers," Kai Jing explained. He started to tell them about the work with Peking Man, but one of the soldiers cut him off: "No work has been going on here in months."

"If you've worked to preserve the past," the leader said, trying to be more cordial, "surely you can work to create the future. Besides, what past will you save if the Japanese destroy China?"

"It's your duty to join us," another soldier grumbled. "Here we are spilling our own blood to protect your damn village."

The leader waved for him to be quiet. He turned to Kai Jing. "We're asking all men in the villages we defend to help us. You don't need to fight. You can cook or clean or do repairs." When no one said anything, he added in a less friendly voice: "This isn't a request, it's a requirement. Your village owes us this. We order you. If you don't come along as patriots, we'll take you as cowards."

It happened that quickly, Teacher Pan said. The soldiers would have taken him as well, but they decided an old man who was nearly blind was more trouble than help. As the soldiers led the men away, Teacher Pan called out, "How long will they be gone?"

"You tell me, comrade," the leader said. "How long will it take to drive out the Japanese?"

Over the next two months, I grew thin. GaoLing had to force me to eat, and even then I could not taste anything. I could not stop thinking of the curse from the Monkey's Jaw, and I told GaoLing this, though no one else. Sister Yu held Praying for a Miracle meetings, asking that the Communists defeat the Japanese soon, so that Kai Jing, Dong, and Chao could return to us quickly. And Teacher Pan wandered the courtyards, his eyes misty with cataracts. Miss Grutoff and Miss Towler would not allow the girls to go outside the compound anymore, even though the fighting took place in other areas of the hills. They had heard terrible stories of Japanese soldiers raping girls. They found a large American flag and hung this over the gateway, as if this were a charm that would protect them from evil.

Two months after the men disappeared, Sister Yu's prayers were half answered. Three men walked through the gateway early in the morning, and Miss Grutoff beat the gong of the Buddha's Ear. Soon everyone was shouting that Kai Jing, Dong, and Chao had returned. I ran so fast across the courtyard I tripped and nearly broke my ankle. Kai Jing and I grabbed each other and gave in to happy sobs. His face was thinner and very brown; his hair and skin smelled of smoke. And his eyes—they were different. I remember thinking that at the time. They were faded, and I now think some part of his life force had already gone.

"The Japanese now occupy the hills," he told us. "They drove off our troops." That was how Sister Yu learned that the other half of her miracle prayer had not come true. "They'll come looking for us."

I heated water, made a bath, and washed his body with a cloth as he sat in the narrow wooden tub. And then we went to our bedchamber and I pinned a cloth over the lattice window so it would be dark. We lay down, and as he rocked me, he talked to me in soft murmurs, and it took all of my senses to realize that I was in his arms, that his eyes were looking at mine. "There is no curse," he said. I was listening hard, trying to believe that I would always hear him speak. "And you are brave, you are strong," he went on. I wanted to protest that I didn't want to be strong, but I was crying too much to speak. "You cannot change this," he said. "This is your character."

He kissed my eyes, one at a time. "This is beauty, and this is beauty, and you are beauty, and love is beauty and we are beauty. We are divine, unchanged by time." He said this until I promised I believed him, until I agreed it was enough.

The Japanese came for Kai Jing, Dong, and Chao that evening. Miss Grutoff was brave and declared that she was an American and they had no right to enter the orphanage. They paid no attention to her, and when they started to walk toward the rooms where the girls were hiding under their beds, Kai Jing and the other men came forward and said they did not need to look any further. I tried to follow.

A few days later, I heard wailing in the main hall. When GaoLing came to me with red eyes, I stopped her from saying what I already knew. For a month more, I tried to keep Kai Jing alive in my heart and mind. For a while longer, I tried so much to believe what he had said: "There is no curse." And then finally I let GaoLing say the words.

Two Japanese officers questioned the men day and night, tried to force them to say where the Communist troops had gone. On the third day, they lined them up, Kai Jing, Dong, and Chao, as well as thirty other villagers. A soldier stood nearby with a bayonet. The Japanese officer said he would ask them once again, one at a time. And one by one, they shook their heads, one by one they fell. In my mind, sometimes Kai Jing was first, sometimes he was last, sometimes he was in between.

I was not there when this happened, yet I saw it. The only way I could push it out of my mind was to go into my memory. And there in that safe place, I was with him, and he was kissing me when he told me, "We are divine, unchanged by time."

CHARACTER

GaoLing said the Japanese would soon come for all of us, so I should not bother to kill myself right away. Why not wait and die together? Less lonely that way.

Teacher Pan said I should not leave him for the other world. Otherwise, who would he have left as family to give him comfort in his last days?

Miss Grutoff said the children needed me to be an inspiration of what an orphan girl could become. If they knew I had given up hope, then what hope could they have?

But it was Sister Yu who gave me the reason to stay alive and suffer on earth. Kai Jing, she said, had gone to the Christian heaven, and if I did suicide, I would be forbidden by God to go see him. To me, the Christian heaven was like America, a land that was far away, filled with foreigners, and ruled by their laws. Suicide was not allowed.

So I stayed and waited for the Japanese to come back and get me. I visited Teacher Pan and brought him good things to eat. And every afternoon, I walked outside the school to the part of the hillside with many little piles of rocks. That was where the missionaries buried the babies and girls who had died over the years. That was where Kai Jing lay as well. In our room, I found a few dragon bones he had dug up in the last few months. They were nothing

304

too valuable, just those of old animals. I picked up one and with a thick needle carved words into it to make an oracle bone like the one Precious Auntie had given me. I wrote: "You are beauty, we are beauty, we are divine, unchanged by time." When I finished one, I began another, unable to stop. Those were the words I wanted to remember. Those were the morsels of grief I ate.

I put those oracle bones at Kai Jing's grave. "Kai Jing," I said each time I placed them there. "Do you miss me?" And after a long silence, I told him what had happened that day: who was sick, who was smart, how we had no more medicine, how it was too bad he wasn't there to teach the girls more about geology. One day I had to tell him that Miss Towler had not awakened in the morning and soon she would be lying next to him. "She went gently to God," Miss Grutoff had said at breakfast, and she acted glad that it was this way. But then she clamped her mouth shut and two deep lines grew down the sides, so I knew she was pitifully sad. To Miss Grutoff, Miss Towler had been mother, sister, and oldest friend.

After Miss Towler's death, Miss Grutoff began to make American flags. I think she made those flags for the same reason I made oracle bones for Kai Jing's grave. She was saving some memory, afraid of forgetting. Every day she would sew a star or a stripe. She would dye scraps of cloth red or blue. She had the girls in the school make flags, as well. Soon there were fifty flags waving along the outside wall of the old monastery building, then a hundred, two hundred. If a person did not know this was an orphanage for Chinese girls, he would think many, many Americans were inside having a patriotic party.

One cold morning, Japanese soldiers finally flocked onto the grounds. We were in the main hall for Sunday worship, although it was not Sunday. We heard gun sounds, *pau-pau*. We ran to the door and saw Cook and his wife lying facedown in the dirt, and the chickens squabbling nearby, pecking at a bucket of grain that had tipped over. The big American flag that used to hang over the gateway was now lying on the ground. The girls began to cry, thinking that Cook and his wife were dead. But then we saw Cook move a little, turn his head to the side, carefully looking to see who was around them. Miss Grutoff pushed past us to the front. I think we all wondered if she would order the Japanese soldiers to leave us alone, since she was an American. Instead, she asked us to be quiet. No one moved or talked after that. And then we watched, hands covering our mouths to keep from screaming, as the Japanese soldiers shot down the rest of those hundreds of flags, *pau-pau, pau-pau,* taking turns, criticizing if anyone missed. When all the flags were in pieces, they began to shoot at the chickens, which flapped and squawked and fell to earth. Finally, they took the dead chickens and left. Cook and his wife stood up, the remaining chickens clucked quietly, and the girls let out the wails they had kept locked inside.

Miss Grutoff asked everyone to return to the main hall. There she informed us in a shaky voice what she had learned on the ham and shortwave radios several days before: Japan had attacked the United States, and the Americans had declared war on Japan. "With America on our side, now China will be able to win the war more quickly," she said, and she led us to join her in clapping. To please her, we smiled to pretend we believed this good news. Later that night, when the girls had gone to their rooms, Miss Grutoff told the teachers and the cook and his wife what else she had heard from her friends at Peking Union Medical College.

"The bones of Peking Man are lost."

"Destroyed?" Teacher Pan asked.

"No one knows. They've disappeared. All the pieces of forty-one ancient people. They were supposed to be taken by train to be loaded on an American boat sailing from Tientsin to Manila, but the ship was sunk. Some say the boxes were never loaded onto the boat. They say the Japanese stopped the trains. They thought the boxes contained only the possessions of American soldiers, so they threw them on the tracks to let them get smashed by other trains. Now no one knows what to think. It's not good, either way." As I listened, I felt my own bones grow hollow. All of Kai Jing's work, his sacrifice, his last trip to the quarry— all was for nothing? I imagined those little pieces of skulls floating among the fish in the harbor, sinking slowly to the bottom, sea eels swimming over them, covering them with sand. I saw other fragments of bones thrown off the train like garbage, the tires of army trucks crushing them until the pieces were no bigger than grains of Gobi sand. I felt as if those bones were Kai Jing's.

The next day, the Japanese returned to take Miss Grutoff to a prisoner-of-war camp. She had known this would happen, and yet she had not tried to escape. "I would never willingly leave my girls," she told us. Her suitcases were already packed, and she was wearing her travel hat with a scarf that wrapped around her neck. Fifty-six weeping girls stood at the gate to say good-bye. "Teacher Pan, don't forget the lessons of the apostles," she called out, just before she boarded the back of the truck. "And please be sure to tell the others so they can pass on the good word." I thought it was a strange farewell. So did the others, until Teacher Pan showed us what she meant.

He took us to the main hall, to the statue of an apostle. He twisted off its hand. Inside was a hole that he and Miss Grutoff had carved out, where they had hidden silver, gold, and a list of names of former students in Peking. For the past month he and Miss Grutoff had been doing this, late at night. Each apostle had only part of her personal savings, so if the Japanese found money in one, as heathens they might not know which of hundreds of statues to search to find the rest.

If things became dangerous around the orphanage, we were supposed to use the money to take the girls to Peking, four or five at a time. There they could stay with former students and friends of the school. Miss Grutoff had already contacted these people, and they agreed that if the time came, they would willingly help us. We needed only to tell them by the ham radio when we were coming.

Teacher Pan assigned each of us—teachers, helpers, and four older students—to an apostle for our share of the refugee money. And from the day that Miss Grutoff left, Teacher Pan had us practice and memorize which apostle was which and where the wood had been dug out of its body. I thought it was enough that we recognized which was our own statue, but Sister Yu said, "We should say all the names out loud. Then the apostles will protect our savings better." I had to say those names so many times they are still in my head: *Pida, Pa, Matu, Yuhan, Jiama yi, Jiama er, Andaru, Filipa, Tomasa, Shaimin, Tadayisu,* and *Budalomu.* The traitor, *Judasa,* did not have a statue.

About three months after Miss Grutoff left us, Teacher Pan decided it was time for us to go. The Japanese had become angry that the Communists were hiding in the hills.

They wanted to draw them out by slaughtering people in the nearby villages. Sister Yu also told GaoLing and me that the Japanese were doing unspeakable acts with innocent girls, some as young as eleven or twelve. That was what had happened in Tientsin, Tungchow, and Nanking. "Those girls they didn't kill afterward tried to kill themselves," she added. So we knew what she was saying just by using the frightened parts of our imaginations.

Counting four older students who had stayed on through the war, we had twelve chaperones. We radioed Miss Grutoff's friends in Peking, who said the city was occupied, and although the situation was calm, we should wait to hear from them. The trains did not always run, and it would not be good for us to be stuck for days waiting at different cities along the way. Teacher Pan determined the order in which the groups would leave: first that led by Mother Wang, who could tell us how the journey went, then those of the four older girls, then those of Cook's wife, Teacher Wang, Cook, GaoLing, me, Sister Yu, and last, Teacher Pan.

"Why should you be last?" I asked him.

"I know how to use the radio."

"You can teach me just as easily."

"And me," said Sister Yu and GaoLing.

We argued, taking turns at being brave. And to do that, we had to be a little unkind and criticize each other. Teacher Pan's eyes were too poor for him to be left alone. Sister Yu was too deaf. GaoLing had bad feet and a fear of ghosts that made her run the wrong way. Plenty was wrong with me, as well, but in the end, I was allowed to go last so I could visit Kai Jing's grave as long as possible.

And now I can confess how scared I was those last few days. I was responsible for four girls: six years, eight, nine, and twelve. And while it was still comforting to think about killing myself, it made me nervous to wait to be killed. As each group of girls left, the orphanage seemed to grow larger and the remaining footsteps louder. I was afraid the Japanese soldiers would come and find the ham radio, then accuse me of being a spy and torture me. I rubbed dirt on the girls' faces and told them that if the Japanese came, they should scratch their heads and skin, pretending to have lice. Almost every hour, I prayed to Jesus and Buddha, whoever was listening. I lighted incense in front of Precious Auntie's photo, I went to Kai Jing's grave and was honest with him about my fears. "Where is my character?" I asked him. "You said I was strong. Where is that strength now?"

On the fourth day of our being alone, we heard the message on the radio: "Come quickly. The trains are running." I went to tell the girls, and then I saw that a miracle had happened, but whether this came from the Western God or the Chinese ones, I don't know. I was simply thankful that all four girls had swollen eyes, green pus coming out of the corners. They had an eye infection, nothing serious, but it was awful to see. No one would want to touch them. As for myself, I thought quickly and had an idea. I took some of the leftovers of the rice porridge we had eaten that morning, and drained off the watery portion and smeared this liquid onto my skin, my cheeks, forehead, neck, and hands, so that when it dried I had the leathery, cracked appearance of an old country woman. I put some more of the sticky rice water into a thermos and to that I added chicken blood. I told the girls to gather all the chicken eggs left in the pens, even the rotten ones, and put them in sacks. Now we were ready to walk down the hill to the railway station.

When we were about a hundred paces down the road, we

saw the first soldier. I slowed my pace and took a sip from the thermos. The soldier remained where he was, and stopped us when we reached him.

"Where are you going?" he asked. We five looked up and I could see an expression of disgust pass over his face. The girls started to scratch their heads. Before I answered, I coughed into a handkerchief, then folded it so he could see the blood-streaked mucus. "We are going to market to sell our eggs," I said. We lifted our sacks. "Would you like some as a gift?" He waved us on.

When we were a short distance away, I took another sip of the rice water and chicken blood to hold in my mouth. Twice more we were stopped, twice more I coughed up what looked like the bloody sputum of a woman with tuberculosis. The girls stared with their green oozing eyes.

When we arrived in Peking, I saw from the train window that GaoLing was there to meet us. She squinted to make sure it was I getting off the train. Slowly she approached, her lips spread in horror. "What happened to you?" she asked. I coughed blood one last time into my handkerchief. "Ai-ya!" she cried, and jumped back. I showed her my thermos of "Japanese chase-away juice." And then I began to laugh and couldn't stop. I was crazy-happy, delirious with relief.

GaoLing complained: "The whole time I've been worried sick, and you just play jokes."

We settled the girls in homes with former students. And over the next few years, some married, some died, some came to visit us as their honorary parents. GaoLing and I lived in the back rooms of the old ink shop in the Pottery-Glazing District. We had Teacher Pan and Sister Yu join us. As for GaoLing's husband, we all hoped he was dead.

Of course, it made me angry beyond belief that the Chang family now owned the ink shop. For all those years since Precious Auntie died, I had not had to think about the coffinmaker too much. Now he was ordering us to sell more ink, sell it faster. This was the man who killed my grandfather and father, who caused Precious Auntie so much pain she ruined her life. But then I reasoned that if a person wants to strike back, she must be close to the person who must be struck down. I decided to live in the ink shop because it was practical. In the meantime, I thought of ways to get revenge.

Luckily, the Chang father did not bother us too much about the business. The ink was selling much, much better than before we came. That was because we used our heads. We saw that not too many people had a use for inksticks and ink cakes anymore. It was wartime. Who had the leisure and calm to sit around and grind ink on an ink-stone, meditating over what to write? We also noted that the Chang family had lowered the quality of the ingredients, so the sticks and cakes crumbled more easily. Teacher Pan was the one who suggested we make quick-use ink. We ground up the cheap ink, mixed it with water, and put it in small jars that we bought for almost nothing at a medicine shop that was going out of business.

Teacher Pan also turned out to be a very good salesman. He had the manners and writing style of an old scholar, which helped convince customers that the quality of our quick-use ink was excellent, though it was not. To demonstrate it, however, he had to be careful not to write anything that could be interpreted as anti-Japanese or pro-feudal, Christian or Communist. This was not easy to do. Once he decided he should simply write about food. There was no danger in that. So he wrote, "Turnips taste best when pickled," but GaoLing worried that this would be taken either as a slur against the Japanese or as siding with the Japanese, since turnips were like radishes and radishes were what the Japanese liked to eat. So then he wrote, "Father, Mother, Brother, Sister." Sister Yu said that this looked like a listing of those who had died, that this was his way of protesting the occupation. "It could also be a throwback to Confucian principles of family," GaoLing added, "a wish to return to the time of emperors." Everything had dangers, the sun, the stars, the directions of the wind, depending on how many worries we each had. Every number, color, and animal had a bad meaning. Every word sounded like another. Eventually I came up with the best idea for what to write, and it was settled: "Please try our Quick Ink. It is cheap and easy to use."

We suspected that many of the university students who bought our ink were Communist revolutionaries making propaganda posters that would appear on walls in the middle of the night. "Resist Together," the posters said. Sister Yu managed the accounts, and she was not too strict when some of the poorer students did not have enough money to pay for the ink. "Pay what you can," she told them. "A student should always have enough ink for his studies." Sister Yu also made sure we kept some money for ourselves without the Chang father's noticing that anything was missing.

When the war ended in 1945, we no longer had to think about secret meanings that could get us in trouble with the Japanese. Firecrackers burst in the streets all day long and this made everyone nervously happy. Overnight the lanes grew crowded with vendors of every delicious kind of thing and fortune-tellers with only the best news. GaoLing thought this was a good day to ask her fortune. So Sister Yu and I went wandering with her.

The fortune-teller GaoLing chose could write three different words at one time with three different brushes held in one hand. The first brush he put between the tip of his thumb and one finger. The second rested in the web of his thumb. The third was pinched at the bend of his wrist. "Is my husband dead?" GaoLing asked him. We were all surprised by her bluntness. We held our breath as the three characters formed at once: "Return Lose Hope."

"What does that mean?" Sister Yu said.

"For another small offering," the fortune-teller answered, "the heavens will allow me to explain." But GaoLing said she was satisfied with this answer, and we went on our way.

"He's dead," GaoLing announced.

"Why do you say that?" I asked. "The message could also mean he's not dead."

"It clearly said all hope is lost about his returning home."

Sister Yu suggested: "Maybe it means he'll return home, then we'll lose hope."

"Can't be," GaoLing said, but I could see a crack of doubt running down her forehead.

The next afternoon, we were sitting in the courtyard of the shop, enjoying a new sense of ease, when we heard a voice call out, "Hey, I thought you were dead." A man was looking at GaoLing. He wore a soldier's uniform.

"Why are you here?" GaoLing said as she rose from the bench.

He sneered. "I live here. This is my house."

Then we knew it was Fu Nan. It was the first time I saw the man who might have been my husband. He was large like his father, with a long, wide nose. GaoLing rose and took his bundle and offered him her seat. She treated him extra politely, like an unwanted guest. "What happened to your fingers?" she asked. Both of his little fingers were missing.

He seemed confused at first, then laughed. "I'm a damn war hero," he said. He glanced at us. "Who are they?" GaoLing gave our names and said what each of us did to run the business. Fu Nan nodded, then gestured toward Sister Yu and said, "We don't need that one anymore. I'll manage the money from now on."

"She's my good friend."

"Who says?" He glared at GaoLing, and when she did not look away, he said, "Oh, still the fierce little viper. Well, you can argue with the new owner of this shop from now on. He arrives tomorrow." He threw down a document covered with the red marks of name seals. GaoLing snatched it.

"You sold the shop? You had no right! You can't make my family work for someone else. And the debt—why is it now even bigger? What did you do, gamble the money away, eat it, smoke it, which one?"

"I'm going to sleep now," he said, "and when I wake up, I don't want to see that woman with the hunchback. The way she looks makes me nervous." He waved one hand to dismiss any further protests. He left, and soon we smelled the smoke of his opium clouds. GaoLing began to curse.

Teacher Pan sighed. "At least the war is over and we can see if our friends at the medical school might know of rooms where we can squeeze in."

"I'm not going," GaoLing said.

How could she say this after all she had told me about her husband? "You'd stay with that demon?" I exclaimed.

"This is our family's ink shop. I'm not walking away from it. The war is over, and now I'm ready to fight back."

I tried to argue and Teacher Pan patted my arm. "Give her time. She'll come to her senses."

Sister Yu left that afternoon for the medical school, but soon she returned. "Miss Grutoff is back," she told us, "released from the war camp. But she is very, very sick." The four of us immediately left for the house of another foreigner, named Mrs. Riley. When we went in, I saw how thin Miss Grutoff had become. We used to joke that foreign women had big udders because of the cow's milk they drank. But now Miss Grutoff looked drained. And her color was poor. She insisted on standing up to greet us, and we insisted she sit and not bother to be polite with old friends. Loose skin hung from her face and arms. Her once red hair was gray and thin. "How are you?" we asked.

"Not bad," she said, cheerful and smiling. "As you can see, I'm alive. The Japanese couldn't starve me to death, but the mosquitoes almost had their way with me. Malaria."

Two of the little girls at the school had had malaria and died. But I did not tell Miss Grutoff. There would be plenty of time for bad news later.

"You must hurry and get well," I said. "Then we can re-open the school."

Miss Grutoff shook her head. "The old monastery is gone. Destroyed. One of the other missionaries told me."

We gasped.

"The trees, the building, everything has been burned to the ground and scattered." The other foreigner, Mrs. Riley, nodded.

I wanted to ask what had happened to the graves, but I could not speak. I felt as I had that day when I knew Kai

Jing had been killed. Thinking about him caused me to try to remember his face. But I saw more clearly the stones under which he lay. How long had I loved him when he was alive? How long had I grieved for him since he had died?

Mrs. Riley then said: "We're going to open a school in Peking once we find a building. But now we need to help Miss Grutoff get well, don't we, Ruth?" And she patted Miss Grutoff's hand.

"Anything," we took turns saying. "Of course we'll help. We love Miss Grutoff. She is mother and sister to us all. What can we do?" Mrs. Riley then said Miss Grutoff had to return to the United States to see the doctors in San Francisco. But she would need a helper to accompany her to Hong Kong and then across the ocean.

"Would one of you be willing to go with me? I think we can arrange for a visa."

"We can all go!" GaoLing answered at once.

Miss Grutoff became embarrassed. I could see this. "I wouldn't want to trouble more than one of you," she said. "One is enough, I think." And then she sighed and said she was exhausted. She needed to lie down.

When she left the room, we looked at one another, uncertain how to begin the discussion of who should be the one to help Miss Grutoff. America? Miss Grutoff did not ask this only as a favor. We all knew she was also offering a great opportunity. A visa to America. But only one of us could take it. I thought about this. In my heart, America was the Christian heaven. It was where Kai Jing had gone, where he was waiting for me. I knew this was not actually true, but there was a hope that I could find happiness that had stayed hidden from me. I could leave the old curse, my bad background.

Then I heard GaoLing say, "Teacher Pan should go.

He's the oldest, the most experienced." She had jumped in with the first suggestion, so I knew she wanted to go, as well.

"Experienced at what?" he said. "I can't be of much help, I'm afraid. I'm an old man who can't even read and write unless the words are as large and close as my shaky hands. And it would not be proper for a man to accompany a lady. What if she needs help during the night?"

"Sister Yu," GaoLing said. "You go, then. You're smart enough to overcome any obstacle." Another suggestion! GaoLing was desperate to go, to have someone argue that it should be she who went.

"If people don't trample me first," Sister Yu said. "Don't be ridiculous. Besides, I don't want to leave China. To be frank, while I have Christian love for Miss Grutoff and our foreign friends, I don't care to be around other Americans. Civil war or not, I'd rather stay in China."

"Then LuLing should go," GaoLing said.

What could I do? I had to argue: "I could never leave my father-in-law or you."

"No, no, you don't have to keep this old man company," I heard my father-in-law say. "I've been meaning to tell you that I may marry again. Yes, me. I know what you're thinking. The gods are laughing, and so am I."

"But who?" I asked. I could not imagine he had any time to court a woman. He was always at the shop, except when he went on brief errands.

"She lives next door to us, the longtime widow of the man who ran the bookshop."

"Wah! The man who sued my family?" GaoLing said.

"The books were fake," I reminded her. "The man lost the lawsuit, remember?" And then we remembered our manners and congratulated Teacher Pan by asking if she was a good cook, if she had a pleasant face, a kind voice, a family that was not too much trouble. I was happy for him but also glad that I no longer had to argue that I could not go to America.

"Well, it's clear to me LuLing should be the one to go to America with Miss Grutoff," Sister Yu said. "Teacher Pan will soon be bossed around by a new wife, so LuLing has less need to stay."

GaoLing hesitated a moment too long before saying, "Yes, that's the best. It's settled, then."

"What do you mean?" I said, trying to be bighearted. "I can't leave my own sister."

"I'm not even your real sister," GaoLing said. "You go first. Later, you can sponsor me."

"Ah, see! That means you want to go!" I could not help rubbing it in. But now that everything had been decided, I felt I could safely do this.

"I didn't say that," GaoLing said. "I meant only if things change and later I *need* to come."

"Why don't you go first, and later you can sponsor me? If you stay, that husband of yours will put you under his thumb and grind you to pieces." I was really being generous.

"But I can't leave my sister, any more than she can leave me," GaoLing said.

"Don't argue," I told her, "I'm older than you. You go first, then I'll go to Hong Kong in a month or so and wait for the sponsorship papers to come through."

GaoLing was supposed to argue that she should be the one to wait in Hong Kong. But instead she asked, "Is that how long it takes to sponsor another person? Only one month?"

And though I had no idea how long it took, I said,

"Maybe it's even quicker than that." I still thought she was going to agree to wait.

"That fast," GaoLing marveled. "Well, if it's that quick, I might as well go first, but only so I can leave that demon of a husband right away."

Just then Mrs. Riley came back to the room. "We've agreed," Sister Yu announced. "GaoLing will accompany Miss Grutoff to San Francisco."

I was too stunned to say anything. That night, I went over in my head how I had lost my chance. I was angry that GaoLing had tricked me. Then I had sisterly feelings and was glad she was going so she could get away from Fu Nan. Back and forth I went, between these two feelings. Before I fell asleep, I decided this was fate. Now whatever happened, that was my New Destiny.

Three days later, just before we left for Hong Kong, we had a little party. "There's no need for tears and good-byes," I said. "Once we're settled in the new country, we'll invite you all to come visit."

Teacher Pan said that he and his new wife would enjoy that very much, a chance to visit another country before their life was over. Sister Yu said she had heard much about dancing in America. She confessed that she had always wanted to learn how to dance. And for the rest of the evening, which was the last time we ever saw them, we took turns guessing and joking. Miss Grutoff would be healed, then come back to China, where she would make more orphan girls act in more bad plays. GaoLing would be rich, having finally found the right fortune-teller, one who could write with four brushes at once. And I would be a famous painter.

We toasted one another. Soon, maybe in a year or less, Sister Yu and Teacher Pan with his new wife would sail to

America for a holiday. GaoLing and I would come to the
harbor in San Francisco and wait for them in our new automobile, a shiny black one with many comfortable seats
and an American driver. Before we drove them to our man-
sion on top of a hill, we would stop at a ballroom. And to
celebrate our reunion, we all agreed, we would dance and
dance and dance.

FRAGRANCE

Each night when I returned to the rooming house in Hong Kong, I lay on a cot with wet towels over my chest. The walls were sweating because I couldn't open the windows for fresh air. The building was on a fishy street on the Kowloon side. This was not the part where the fish were sold. There it smelled of the morning sea, salty and sharp. I was living in Kowloon Walled City, along the low point in a wide gutter, where the scales and blood and guts gathered, swept there by the fishmongers' buckets of water at night. When I breathed the air, it was the vapors of death, a choking sour stink that reached like fingers into my stomach and pulled my insides out. Forever in my nose, that is the fragrance of Fragrant Harbor.

The British and other foreigners lived on the Hong Kong Island side. But in Kowloon Walled City, it was almost all Chinese, rich and raggedy, poor and powerful, everyone different, but we all had this in common: We had been strong, we had been weak, we had been desperate enough to leave behind our motherland and families.

And there were also those who made money from people's despair. I went to many blind seers, the *wenmipo* who claimed they were ghost writers. "I have a message from a baby," they called. "A message from a son." "A husband." "An ancestor who is angry." I sat down with one and she told me, "Your Precious Auntie has already been reincarnated. Go three blocks east, then three blocks north. A beggar girl will cry out to you, 'Auntie, have pity, give me hope.' Then you will know it is she. Give her a coin and the curse will be ended." I did exactly as she said. And on that exact block, a girl said those exact words. I was so overjoyed. Then another girl said those words, another and another, ten, twenty, thirty little girls, all without hope. I gave them coins, just in case. And for each of them, I felt pity. The next day, I saw another blind lady who could talk to ghosts. She also told me where to find Precious Auntie. Go here, go there. The next day was the same. I was using up my savings, but I didn't think it mattered. Soon, any day now, I would leave for America.

After I had lived a month in Hong Kong, I received a letter from GaoLing:

"My Own True Sister, Forgive me for not writing you sooner. Teacher Pan sent your address to me, but I did not receive it right away, because I was moving from one church lady's house to another. I'm also sorry to tell you that Miss Grutoff died a week after we arrived. Right before she flew to heaven, she said she made a mistake coming back to America. She wanted to return to China so her bones could rest there, next to Miss Towler's. I was glad to know how much she loved China, and sorry because it was too late to send her back. I went to her funeral, but not too many people knew her. I was the only one who cried, and I said to myself, She was a great lady.

"My other news is not so good, either. I learned I cannot sponsor you, not yet. The truth is, I almost was not able to stay myself. Why we thought it would be so easy, I don't know. I see now we were foolish. We should have asked many more questions. But now I have asked the questions, and I know of several ways for you to come later. How much later depends.

"One way is for you to apply as a refugee. The quota for Chinese, however, is very low, and the number who want to get in is beyond count. To be honest, your chances are like a leak moving against a flood.

"Another way is for me to be a citizen first so I can sponsor you as my sister. You will have to claim that Mother and Father are your real mother and father, since I cannot sponsor a cousin. But as a relative, you would be in a different line, ahead of ordinary refugees. For me to become a citizen, however, means I have to learn English first and get a good job. I promise you I am studying very hard, in case this is the means I have to turn to.

"There is a third way: I can marry a citizen and then become a citizen faster. Of course, it is inconvenient that I am already married to Chang Fu Nan, but I think no one needs to know this. On my visa papers, I did not mention it. Also, you should know that when I applied for the visa, the visa man asked for documents as proof of my birth, and I said, 'Who has documents for such things?' He said, 'Oh, were they burned during the war like everyone else's?' I thought that was the correct answer, so I agreed this was true. When you prepare your visa papers, you must say the same thing. Also make yourself five years younger, born 1921. I already did, born 1922, but in the same month as the old birthday. This will give you extra time to catch up.

"Mother and Father have already written to ask me to send them my extra money. I have had to write back and say I have none. If I do in the future, of course, I will send some to you. I feel so guilty that you insisted I come first and I gave in to your demands. Now it is you who are stuck, not knowing what to do. Don't mistake my meaning. Life here is not so easy. And making money is not like we imagined. All those stories of instant riches, don't believe them. As for dancing, that is only in the movies. Most of the day, I clean houses. I am paid twenty-five cents. That may sound like a lot, but it costs that much to eat dinner. So it is hard to save money. For you, of course, I am willing to starve.

"In his last letter, Father said he almost died of anger when he learned that Fu Nan lost the ink business in Peking. He said Fu Nan has returned to Immortal Heart and is lying around useless, but the Chang father is not being critical, saying Fu Nan is a big war hero, lost two fingers, saved lives. You know what I was thinking when I read that. Most terrible of all, our family still has to supply the inksticks and ink cakes, and we receive none of the profit, only a lesser debt. Everyone has had to take on various home businesses, weaving baskets, mending, doing menial labor that makes Mother complain that we have fallen as low as the tenants. She asks me to hurry and become rich, so I can pull her out of the bowels of hell.

"I feel a great burden of guilt and responsibility."

When I finished reading GaoLing's letter, I felt as if an ax were chopping my neck when I was already dead. I had waited in Hong Kong for nothing. I could wait a year, ten years, or the rest of my life, in this crowded city among desperate people with stories sadder than mine. I knew no one and I was lonely for my friends. There was no America for me. I had lost my chance.

The next day, I gathered my things and went to the train station to return to Peking. I put down my remaining money at the ticket booth. "The fare is higher now, miss," said the ticket man. How could this be? "Money is worth less now," he told me, "everything costs more." I then asked for a lower-class ticket. That's the lowest, he said, and pointed to a wall with fares written on a blackboard.

Now I was stuck. I wondered if I should write to Teacher Pan or perhaps Sister Yu. But then I thought, Oh, to give so much trouble to someone. No, you fix this problem yourself. I would pawn my valuables. But when I looked at them, I saw that these were treasures only to me: a notebook of Kai Jing's, the jacket GaoLing gave me before I went to the orphanage, the pages of Precious Auntie's and her photograph.

And there was also the oracle bone.

I unwrapped it from its soft cloth and looked at the characters scratched on one side. Unknown words, what should have been remembered. At one time, an oracle bone was worth twice as much as a dragon bone. I took my treasure to three shops. The first belonged to a bonesetter. He said the bone was no longer used as medicine, but as a strange curiosity it was worth a little money. He then offered me a price that surprised me, for it was almost enough to buy a second-class ticket to Peking. The next shop sold jewelry and curios. That shopkeeper took out a magnifying glass. He examined the oracle bone very carefully, turning it several times. He said it was genuine, but not a good example of an oracle bone. He offered me the price of a first-class ticket to Peking. The third place was an antique shop for tourists. Like the jeweler, this man examined the oracle bone with a special glass. He called another man over to take a look. Then he asked me many questions. "Where did you find this? . . . What? How did a girl like you find such a treasure? . . . Oh, you are the granddaughter of a bonesetter? How long have you been in Hong Kong? . . . Ah, waiting to go to America? Did someone else leave for America without this? Did you take it from him? There are plenty of thieves in Hong Kong these days. Are you one? Miss, you come back, come back, or I'll call the police."

I left that store, angry and insulted. But my heart was going *poom-poom-poom*, because now I knew that what was in my hand was worth a lot of money. Yet how could I sell it? It had belonged to my mother, my grandfather. It was my connection to them. How could I hand it over to a stranger so I could abandon my homeland, the graves of my ancestors? The more I thought these things, the stronger I became. Kai Jing had been right. This was my character.

I made a plan. I would find a cheaper place to live—yes, even cheaper than the stinky-fish house—and find a job. I would save my money for a few months, and if the visa still had not come through, I would return to Peking. There at least I could get a job at another orphanage school. I could wait there in comfort and companionship. If GaoLing got me the visa, fine, I would make my way back to Hong Kong. If she did not, fine, I would stay and be a teacher.

That day, I moved to a cheaper place to live, a room I shared with two women, one snoring, one sick. We took turns sleeping on the cot, the snoring girl in the morning, me in the afternoon, the sick one after me. Whichever two were not sleeping wandered outside, looking for take-home work: mending shoes, hemming scarves, weaving baskets, embroidering collars, painting bowls, anything to make a dollar. That's how I lived for a month. And when the sick girl didn't stop coughing, I moved away. "Lucky you didn't get TB like the other girl did," a melon vendor later told me. "Now they're both coughing blood." And I thought: TB! I had pretended to have this same sickness to escape from the Japanese. And would I now escape from getting sick?

Next I lived with a Shanghai lady who had been very, very rich but was no longer. We shared a hot little room above a place where we worked boiling laundry, dipping the clothes and plucking them out with long sticks. If she got splashed she yelled at me, even if it was not my fault. Her husband had been a top officer with the Kuomintang. A girl in the laundry told me he had been jailed for collaborating with the Japanese during the war. "So why does she act so uppity," the girl said, "when everyone looks down on her?" The uppity lady made a rule that I could not make any sounds at night—not a cough or a sneeze or a burst of gas. I had to walk softly, pretend my shoes were made of clouds. Often she would cry, then wail to the Goddess of Mercy what a terrible punishment it was that she had to be with such a person, meaning me. I told myself, Wait and see, maybe your opinion of her will change, as it did with Sister Yu. But it did not.

After that awful woman, I was glad to move in with an old lady who was deaf. For extra money, I helped her boil and shell peanuts all night long. In the morning, we sold the peanuts to people who would eat them with their breakfast rice porridge. During the heat of the afternoon, we slept. This was a comfortable life: peanuts and sleep. But one day a couple arrived, claiming to be relatives of the deaf lady's: "Here we are, take us in." She didn't know who they were, so they traced a zigzag relationship, and sure enough, she had to admit, maybe they were related: Before I left, I counted my money and saw I had enough for the train ticket to Peking at the lowest, lowest price.

Again I went to the railway station. Again I found out that the money value had gone down, down and the price of the ticket had gone up and up, to twice as much as before. I was like a little insect scurrying up a wall with the water rising faster.

This time I needed a better plan to change my situation, my *siqing*. In English and in Chinese, the words sound almost the same. On every street corner, you could hear people from everywhere talking about this: "My situation is this. This is how I can improve my situation." I realized that in Hong Kong, I had come to a place where everyone believed he could change his situation, his fate, no more staying stuck with your circumstances. And there were many ways to change. You could be clever, you could be greedy, you could have connections.

I was clever, of course, and if I had been greedy, I would have sold the oracle bone. But I decided once again I could not do that. I was not that poor in body and respect for my family.

As for connections, I had only GaoLing, now that Miss Grutoff was dead. And GaoLing was of no use. She did not know how to be resourceful. If I had been the one to go first to America, I would have used my strength, my character, to find a way to get a visa within a few weeks at the most. Then I wouldn't be facing the troubles I had simply because GaoLing didn't know what to do. That was the problem: GaoLing was strong, but not always in the right ways. She had forever been Mother's favorite, spoiled by pampering. And all those years in the orphanage, she had forever lived the easy life. I had helped her so much, as had

Sister Yu, that she never had to think for herself. If the river turned downstream, she would never think to swim upstream. She knew how to get her way, but only if others helped her.

By the next morning, I had devised a new plan. I took my little bit of money and bought the white smock and trousers of a *majie*. British people were crazy for that kind of maid—pious, refined, and clean. That was how I found a job with an English lady and her ancient mum. Their last name was Flowers.

They had a house in the Victoria Peak area. It was smaller than the others nearby, more like a cottage, with a twisty narrow path and green ferns that led to the front door. The two old English ladies lived on top, and I lived in a room on the basement floor of the cottage.

Miss Patsy was the daughter, seventy years old, born in Hong Kong. Her mother must have been at least ninety, and her name was Lady Ina. Her husband had been a big success in shipping goods from India to China to England. Sir Flowers was how Miss Patsy called him in memory, even though he was her father. If you ask me, the Flowers part of their name stood for the flowers that made opium. That was what the shipping business was a long time ago between India and Hong Kong, and that was how lots of Chinese people found the habit.

Because Miss Patsy had always lived in Hong Kong, she could speak Cantonese just like the local people. It was a special dialect. When I first went to live there, she spoke to me in the local talk, which I could not understand except for the words that sounded a little like Mandarin. Later she mixed in a bit of English, some of which I knew from living at the orphanage school. But Miss Patsy spoke

English like a British person, and at first it was very hard for me to understand.

Lady Ina's words were also hard to understand. The sounds spilled out as soft and lumpy as the porridge she ate every day. She was so old she was like a baby. She made messes in her panties, both kinds, stinky and wet. I know, because I had to clean her. Miss Patsy would say to me, "Lady Ina needs to wash her hands." And then I would lift Lady Ina from the sofa or bed or dining room chair. Lucky for me she was tiny like a child. She also had a temper like one. She would shout, "No, no, no, no, no," as I walked her to the bathroom, inch by inch, so slow we were like two turtles glued at the shells. She kept shouting this while I washed her, "No, no, no, no, no," because she did not like any water to touch her body and especially not her head. Three or four times a day, I changed and cleaned her and her panties, her other clothes, too. Miss Patsy did not want her mummy to wear diapers because that would be a big insult. So I had to wash, wash, wash, so many clothes, every day. At least Miss Patsy was a nice lady, very polite. If Lady Ina threw her temper, Miss Patsy had to say only three words in a happy voice, "Visitors are here!" and Lady Ina suddenly stopped what she was doing. She would sit down, her crooked back now very straight, her hands folded in her lap. That was how she had been taught from the time she was a young girl. In front of visitors, she had to be a lady, even if it was just pretend.

In that house, there was also a parrot, a big gray bird named Cuckoo—Cuckoo like the clock bird. At first I thought Miss Patsy was calling him *ku-ku*, like the Chinese word for crying, which is what he sometimes did, *ku! ku! ku!* as if he were wounded to near-death. And sometimes he laughed like a crazy woman, long and loud. He could copy any kind of sound—man, woman, monkey, baby. One day I heard a teakettle whistle. I went running, and the teakettle was Cuckoo rocking on his branch, stretching his neck, so delighted that he had fooled me. Another time I heard a Chinese girl cry, "Baba! Baba! Don't beat me! Please don't beat me!" and then she screamed and screamed, until I thought my skin would peel off.

Miss Patsy said, "Cuckoo was already bad when Sir Flowers bought him for my tenth birthday. And for sixty years, he has learned only what he wants, like so many men." Miss Patsy loved that parrot like a son, but Lady Ina always called him the devil. Whenever she heard that bird laugh she would waddle to his cage, shake her finger, and say something like, "*Ooh shh-duh,* you shut up." Sometimes she would raise her finger, but before any sounds could come out of her mouth, the bird would say, "*Ooh shh-duh,*" exactly like Lady Ina. Then Lady Ina would get confused. Wah! Had she already spoken? I could see these thoughts on her face, her head twisting this way, then that, as if two sides of her mind were having a fight. Sometimes she would go all the way to the end of the room, inch by inch, then turn around and walk back, inch by inch, raise her finger, and say, "*Ooh shh-duh!*" And then the bird would say the same. Back and forth they went: "You shut up! You shut up!" One day Lady Ina went up to the bird, and before she could say anything, Cuckoo said in Miss Patsy's singsong happy voice, "Visitors are here!" Right away, Lady Ina went to a nearby chair, sat down, took out a lacy handkerchief from her sleeve, crossed her hands in her lap, closed her lips, and waited, her blue eyes turned toward the door.

So that's how I learned to speak English. To my way of thinking, if a bird could speak good English, I could, too. I had to pronounce the words exactly right, otherwise Lady Ina would not follow my directions. And because Miss Patsy talked to her mother in simple words, it was easy for me to learn other new things to say: *Stand up, Sit down, Lunch is served, Time for tea, Horrid weather, isn't it.*

For the next two years or so, I thought my situation would never change. Every month, I went to the train station, only to find the fares had gone up again. Every month, I received a letter from GaoLing. She told me of her new life in San Francisco, how hard it was to be a burden on strangers. The church that sponsored her had found her a room with an old grandmother named Mrs. Wu who spoke Mandarin. "She is very rich but acts very cheap," GaoLing wrote. "She saves everything that she thinks is too good to eat right away—fruit, chocolates, cashews. So she puts them on top of her refrigerator, and when they are finally too rotten to eat, that's when she puts them in her mouth and says, 'Why does everyone say this tastes so good? What's so good about it?'" This was GaoLing's way of telling me how hard her life was.

One month, though, I received a letter from GaoLing that did not start with her complaints. "Good news," she wrote. "I have met two bachelors and I think I should marry one of them. They are both American citizens, born in this country. According to my passport with the new birth year, one is a year older than I am, the other is three years older. So you know what that means. The older one is studying to be a doctor, the younger a dentist. The older is more serious, very smart. The younger is more handsome, full of jokes. It is very hard for me to decide which one I should put all my attentions on. What do you think?"

When I read that letter, I had just finished cleaning up Lady Ina's bottom twice in one hour. I wanted to reach across the ocean and shake GaoLing by the shoulders and shout, "Marry the one who takes you the fastest. How can you ask which one, when I am wondering how I can live from day to day?"

I did not answer GaoLing at once. I had to go to the bird market that afternoon. Miss Patsy said that Cuckoo needed a new cage. So I went down the hill and crossed over the harbor in the ferry to the Kowloon side. Every day it was becoming more crowded there as people came in from China. "The civil war is growing worse," Sister Yu had written me, "with battles as fierce as those during the war with Japan. Even if you had enough money to return to Peking right now, you should not. The Nationalists would say you are a Communist because Kai Jing is now called one of their martyrs, and the Communists would say you are a Nationalist because you lived in an American orphanage. And whichever is worse changes with each town you pass through."

When I read this, I no longer had the worry of how to get back to Peking. I exchanged that for a worry over Sister Yu and Teacher Pan and his new wife. They, too, could be counted as enemies on either side. As I walked toward the bird market, these were the only thoughts I had. And then I felt a cold breeze run down my back, though it was a warm day. Like a ghost is right behind me, I thought. I kept walking, turning one corner, then another, and this feeling that someone was following me grew stronger. Suddenly I stopped and turned around, and a man said to me, "So it really is you."

There stood Fu Nan, GaoLing's husband, and now he was missing not only two fingers but his entire left hand. His face had a bad color, and his eyes were yellow and red. "Where's my wife?" he asked.

I stirred the question in my head. What was the danger in answering him one way or another? "Gone," I finally told him, and I was glad to be able to say these words: "Gone to America."

"America?" He looked astonished at first, and then he smiled. "I knew that. I just wanted to see if you would tell me the truth."

"I have nothing to hide."

"Then you aren't hiding the fact that you are trying to go to America, too?"

"Who says that?"

"The entire Liu family. They're panting like dogs for an opportunity to follow their daughter. Why should you go first, they say, when you aren't even really her sister? Only true relatives can be sponsored, not bastards." He gave me a smile of false apology, then added: "Husbands, of course, should be number one."

I began to walk away and he grabbed me. "You help me, I help you," he said. "Give me her address, that's all I want. If she doesn't want me to come, that's that, and you can be next in line. I won't tell the Liu family."

"I already know she doesn't want you to come. She went to America to run away from you."

"Give me her address, or I'll go to the authorities and tell them you aren't really sisters. Then you'll lose your chance to go to America as well, same as me."

I stared at that terrible man. What was he saying? What would he really do? I hurried away, weaving in and out of the busy crowds, until I was certain I had lost him. At the bird market, I watched from the corner of my eye. I did not spend too much time bargaining, and when I had bought the cage, I quickly made my way back to the Hong Kong side, holding on tight to my documents that showed where

I lived. What would Fu Nan do? Would he really tell the authorities? How smart was he? Which authorities would he tell?

That night, I wrote GaoLing a letter, telling her of Fu Nan's threats. "Only you know how tricky he is," I said. "He might also tell the authorities you are already married, and then you'll be in trouble, especially if you marry an American."

The next day, I left the house to post the letter. As soon as I stepped into the street, I felt the sudden chill again. I stuffed the letter in my blouse. Around the next corner, there he was, waiting for me.

"Give me some money," he said. "You can do this for your brother-in-law, can't you? Or aren't you really my wife's sister?"

For the next few weeks he popped up like that, every time I left the house. I could not call the police. What could I say? "My brother-in-law who is not really my brother-in-law is following me, asking me for money and the address of my sister who is not my true sister"? And then one day when I stepped outside to go to the market, he was not there. The entire time I was out, I expected I would see him, and I was prepared to be miserable. Nothing. When I returned home, I was puzzled and felt a strange relief. Perhaps he died, I allowed myself to hope. For the next week, I saw no sign of him. I felt no sudden cold breeze. Could it be that my luck had changed? When I opened the next letter from GaoLing, I was convinced this was true.

"I was so angry to hear that Fu Nan has been bothering you," she wrote. "That turtle spawn will stop at nothing to satisfy himself. The only way to get rid of him for a few days is to give him money for his opium. But soon this will no longer be a problem for you. Happy news has arrived! I have found another way you can come. Do you remember the brothers I told you about—one is studying to be a dentist, the other a doctor? Their family name is Young and the father said a person like you can come if a person like him sponsors you as a Famous Visiting Artist. This is like a tourist with special visiting privileges. The family is very kind to do this, since I am not yet related to them. Of course, I cannot ask them to pay your way. But they have already completed the application and supplied the documents. The next step is for me to earn more money so we can buy the boat passage. In the meantime, you must prepare yourself to leave at any moment. Obtain the boat schedules, have a doctor's examination for parasites. . . ."

I read the long list she provided, and was surprised at how smart she truly was. She knew so much, and I felt like a child now being guided by a worried mother. I was so happy I let tears fall right there as I rode the ferry home. And because I was on the ferry, I did not think to be afraid when I felt a breeze. To me it was a comfort. But then I looked up.

There was Fu Nan. One of his eyes was missing.

I nearly jumped off the boat I was so scared. It was as if I were seeing what would happen to me. "Give me some money," he said.

That night, I put Precious Auntie's picture on a low table and lighted some incense. I asked her forgiveness and that of her father. I said that the gift she had given me would now buy me my freedom and that I hoped she would not be angry with me for this, as well.

The next day, I sold the oracle bone to the second shop I had gone to all those months ago. With my savings as a maid, I had enough money to buy a ticket in steerage. I got the boat schedules and sent GaoLing a telegram. Every few days, I gave Fu Nan money for his habit, enough to put him into dreams. And then finally the visa was approved. I was a Famous Visiting Artist.

I sailed for America, a land without curses or ghosts. By the time I landed, I was five years younger. Yet I felt so old.

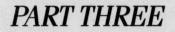

PART THREE

ONE

Mr. Tang was in love with LuLing, though he had never met her. Ruth could sense this. He talked as if he knew her better than anyone else, even her own daughter. He was eighty years old, a survivor of World War Two, the civil war in China, the Cultural Revolution, and a triple coronary bypass. He had been a famous writer in China, but here his work remained untranslated and unknown. A linguistics colleague of Art's had given Ruth his name.

"She is a woman of strong character, very honest," he said to Ruth on the telephone after he began to translate the pages Ruth had mailed to him. "Could you send me her picture, one when she was a young woman? Seeing her would help me say her words in English the way she has expressed them in Chinese."

Ruth thought that was an odd request, but she complied, mailing him scanned copies of the photo of LuLing and GaoLing with their mother when they were young, and another taken when LuLing first arrived in the United States. Later, Mr. Tang asked Ruth for a picture of Precious Auntie. "She was unusual," he remarked. "Self-educated, forthright, quite a rebel for her time." Ruth was bursting to ask him: Did he know whether Precious Auntie was indeed her mother's real mother? But she held off, wanting

341

to read his translation all at one time, not piecemeal. Mr. Tang had said he would need about two months to finish the job. "I don't like to just transliterate word for word. I want to phrase it more naturally, yet ensure these are your mother's words, a record for you and your children for generations to come. They must be just right. Don't you agree?"

While Mr. Tang translated, Ruth lived at LuLing's house. She had told Art of her decision when he returned from Hawaii.

"This seems sudden," he said as he watched her pack. "Are you sure you're not being rash? What about hired help?"

Had she downplayed the problems over the past six months? Or had Art simply not been paying attention? She was frustrated by how little they seemed to know each other.

"I think it would be easier if you hired help to take care of you and the girls," Ruth said.

Art sighed.

"I'm sorry. It's just that the housekeepers I get for my mother keep quitting, and I can't get Auntie Gal or anyone else to take care of her except for an occasional day here and there. Auntie Gal said that the one week she spent with her was worse than running after her grandkids when they were babies. But at least she finally believes the diagnosis is real and that ginseng tea isn't a cure-all."

"Are you sure something else isn't going on?" he asked, following Ruth into the Cubbyhole.

"What do you mean?" She took down diskettes and notebooks from the shelves.

"Us. You and me. Do we need to talk about something more than just your mother's mind falling apart?"

"Why do you say that?"

"You seem—I don't know—distant, maybe even a little angry."

"I'm tense. Last week I saw how she really is, and it frightened me. She's a danger to herself. She's far worse than I thought. And I realize the disease is further along than I first thought. She's probably had it six or seven years already. I don't know why I never noticed—"

"So your going to live there has nothing to do with us?"

"No," Ruth said firmly. And then in a softer voice, "I don't know." And after a long silence, she added, "I remember you asked me once what I was going to do about *my* mother. And it struck me. Yes, what am *I* going to do? I felt it was all up to me. I've tried to handle it the best I can, and this is it. Maybe my moving out does have to do with us, but now, if there's anything wrong with us, it's secondary to what's wrong with my mom. That's all I can handle right now."

Art looked uncertain. "Well, when you feel you're ready to talk . . ." He drifted off, so miserable, it seemed to Ruth, she was almost tempted to assure him that nothing was really wrong.

LuLing was also suspicious as to why Ruth needed to live with her.

"Someone asked me to write a children's book, with illustrations of animals," Ruth said. She was now accustomed to telling lies without feeling guilty. "I was hoping you'd do the drawings, and if you did, it would be easier if we worked together here, less noisy that way."

"How many animal? What kind?" LuLing was as excited as a child going to the zoo.

"Anything we want. You get to decide what to draw, Chinese style."

"All right." Her mother looked pleased at the prospect of being vital to her daughter's success. Ruth sighed, relieved yet sad. Why hadn't she ever asked her mother to make drawings before? She should have done it when her mother's hand and mind were still steady. It broke her heart to see her mother trying so hard, being so conscientious, so determined to be valuable. Making her mother happy would have been easy all along. LuLing simply wanted to be essential, as a mother should be.

Each day, she went to her desk and spent fifteen minutes grinding her inkstick. Luckily, many of the drawings she did were of subjects she had drawn many times for scroll paintings—fish, horse, cat, monkey, duck—and she executed them and the characters from a neuromotor memory of the strokes. The results were shaky yet recognizable renditions of what she once had done perfectly. But the moment LuLing attempted the unfamiliar, her hand flailed in synchrony with her confusion, and Ruth became as distressed as her mother, though she tried not to show it. Every time LuLing finished a drawing, Ruth praised it, took it away, then suggested a new animal to draw.

"Hippo?" LuLing puzzled over the word. "How you say in Chinese?"

"Never mind," Ruth said. "How about an elephant? Do an elephant, you know, the one with a long nose and big ears."

But LuLing was still frowning. "Why you give up? Something hard maybe worth more than easy. Hippo, what look like? Horn right here?" She tapped the top of her head.

"That's a rhinoceros. That's good too. Do a rhinoceros, then."

"Not hippo?"

"Don't worry about it."

"I not worry! You worry! I see this. Look your face. You not hiding from me. I know. I your mother! Okay-okay, you don't worry hippo anymore. I worry for you. Later I remember, then tell you, you be happy. Okay now? Don't cry anymore."

Her mother was good at being quiet when Ruth was working. "Study hard," she would whisper. But if Ruth was watching television, LuLing, as she always had, figured she was not doing anything important. Her mother then gabbed about GaoLing, rehashing her sister's greatest insults to her over the years. "She want me to go love-boat cruise to Hawaii. I ask her, Where I have this kind money? My Social Security only seven hundred fifty dollar. She tell me, You too cheap! I tell her, This not cheap, this *poor*. I not rich widow. Hnh! She forget she once want marry my husband. Tell me when he die, *lucky* she choose other brother. . . ."

Sometimes Ruth listened with interest, trying to determine how much of the story LuLing changed in each retelling, feeling reassured when she repeated the same story. But other times Ruth was simply irritated by having to listen, and this irritation made her feel strangely satisfied, as if everything was the same, nothing was wrong.

"That girl downstair eat popcorn almost every night! Burn it, fire alarm go off. She don't know, I can smell! Stink! Popcorn all she eat! No wonder skinny. Then she tell me, this not work right, that not right. Always complaining, threat me 'lawsuit *in*-jury, code vio-*la*-tion' . . ."

At night, as Ruth lay in her old bed, she felt she had come back to her adolescence in the guise of an adult. She was the same person and yet she was not. Or perhaps she was two versions of herself, Ruth 1969 and Ruth 1999, one more innocent and the other more perceptive, one needier, the other more self-sufficient, both of them fearful. She was her mother's child, and mother to the child her mother had become. So many combinations, like Chinese names and characters, the same elements, seemingly simple, re-configured in different ways. This was the bed from her childhood, and still within were those youthful moments before dreams, when she ached and wondered alone: What's going to happen? And just as in childhood, she listened to her breathing and was frightened by the idea that her mother's might one day stop. When she was conscious of it, each inhalation was an effort. Expiration was simply a release. Ruth was afraid to let go.

Several times a week, LuLing and Ruth would talk to ghosts. Ruth pulled out the old sand tray stored on top of the refrigerator and offered to write to Precious Auntie. Her mother reacted politely, the way people do when of-fered a box of chocolates: "Oh! . . . Well, maybe just little." LuLing wanted to know if the children's book was going to make Ruth famous. Ruth had Precious Auntie say that LuLing would be.

LuLing also asked for updates on the stock market. "Dow Jones go up or down?" she asked one day.

Ruth drew an upward arrow.

"Sell Intel, buy Intel?"

Ruth knew her mother watched the stock market mostly just for fun. She had not found any letters, junk mail or otherwise, from brokerage firms. *Buy on sale,* she decided to write.

LuLing nodded. "Oh, wait till down. Precious Auntie very smart."

One night, as Ruth held the chopstick in her hand, ready

to divine more answers, she heard LuLing say: "Why you and Artie argue?"

"We're not arguing."

"Then why you not live together? This because me? My fault?"

"Of course not." Ruth said this a bit too loudly.

"I think maybe so." She gave Ruth her all-knowing look. "Long time 'go, you first meet him, I tell you, Why you live together first? You do this, he never marry you. You remember? Oh, now you thinking, Ah, Mother right. Live together, now I just leftover, easy throw away. Don't be embarrass. You be honest."

Her mother had said those things, Ruth recalled with chagrin. She busied her hands, brushing off stray grains of sand from the edges of the tray. She was both surprised by the things her mother remembered and touched by her concern. What LuLing had said about Art was not exactly right, yet she had pierced the heart of it, the fact that Ruth felt like a leftover, last in line to get a helping of whatever was being served.

Something was terribly wrong between Art and her. She had sensed that more strongly during their trial separation—wasn't that what this was? She saw more clearly the habits of emotion, her trying to accommodate herself to him even when he didn't need her to. At one time she had thought that adjustment was what every couple, married or not, did, willingly or out of grudging necessity. But had Art also accommodated to her? If so, she didn't know how. And now that they had been apart, she felt unweighted, untethered. This was what she had predicted she might feel when she lost her mother. Now she wanted to hang on to her mother as if she were her life preserver.

"What bothers me is that I don't feel lonelier without Art," she told Wendy over the phone. "I feel more myself."

"Do you miss the girls?"

"Not that much, at least not their noise and energy. Do you think my feelings are deadened or something?"

"I think you're worn out."

Twice a week, Ruth and her mother went to Vallejo Street for dinner. On those days, Ruth had to finish her work early and shop for groceries. Since she did not want to leave her mother alone, she took her along to the store. While they shopped, LuLing commented on the cost of every item, questioning whether Ruth should wait until it was cheaper. Once Ruth arrived home—and yes, she reminded herself, the flat on Vallejo Street was still her home—she seated LuLing in front of the television, then sorted through mail addressed to her and Art as a couple. She saw how little of that there was, while most of the repair bills were in her name. At the end of the night, she was frazzled, saddened, and relieved to go back to her mother's house, to her little bed.

One night, while she was in the kitchen cutting vegetables, Art sidled up to her and patted her bottom. "Why don't you get GaoLing to baby-sit your mom? Then you can stay over for a conjugal visit."

She flushed. She wanted to lean against him, wrap her arms around him, and yet the act of doing so was as scary as leaping off a cliff.

He kissed her neck. "Or you can take a break right now and we can sneak into the bathroom for a quickie."

She laughed nervously. "They'll all know what we're doing."

"No they won't." Art was breathing in her ear.

"My mother knows everything, she sees everything."

With that, Art stopped, and Ruth was disappointed.

During the second month of their living apart, Ruth told Art, "If you really want to have dinner together, maybe you should come over to my mother's for a change, instead of my schlepping over here all the time for dinner. It's exhausting to do that all the time."

So Art and the girls started to go twice a week to LuLing's house. "Ruth," Dory whined one night as she watched her making a salad, "when are you coming home? Dad is like really boring and Fia is all the time like, 'Dad, there's nothing to do, there's nothing good to eat.' "

Ruth was pleased that they missed her. "I don't know, honey. Waipo needs me."

"We need you too."

Ruth felt her heart squeeze. "I know, but Waipo's sick. I have to stay with her."

"Then can I come and stay here with you?"

Ruth laughed. "I'd like that, but you'll have to ask your dad."

Two weekends later, Fia and Dory came with an inflatable mattress. They stayed in Ruth's room. "Girls only," Dory insisted, so Art had to go home. In the evening, Ruth and the girls watched television and drew mehndi tattoos on each other's hands. The next weekend, Art asked if it was boys' night yet.

"I think that can be arranged," Ruth said coyly.

Art brought his toothbrush, a change of clothes, and a portable boombox with a Michael Feinstein CD, Gershwin music. At night, he squeezed into the twin bed with Ruth. But she did not feel amorous with LuLing in the next room. That was the explanation she gave Art.

"Let's just cuddle, then," he suggested. Ruth was glad he did not press her for further explanations. She nestled against his chest. Deep into the night, she listened to his sonorous breathing and the foghorns. For the first time in a long while, she felt safe.

Mr. Tang called Ruth at the end of two months. "Are you sure there aren't any more pages?"

"Afraid not. I've been cleaning out my mother's house, drawer by drawer, room by room. I even discovered she put a thousand dollars under a floorboard. If there was anything else, I'm sure I would have found it."

"Then I've finished." Mr. Tang sounded sad. "There were a few pages with some writing on them, the same sentences over and over, saying she was worried that she was already forgetting too many things. The script on those was pretty shaky. I think they were more recent. It may upset you. I'm just telling you now, so you know."

Ruth thanked him.

"May I come over now to deliver my work to you?" he asked formally. "Would that be all right?"

"Is it too much trouble?"

"It would be an honor. To be honest, I would dearly like to meet your mother. After all this time of reading her words, day and night, I feel I know her like an old friend and miss her already."

Ruth warned him: "She won't be the same woman who wrote those pages."

"Perhaps . . . but somehow I think she will be."

"Would you like to come for dinner tonight?"

Ruth joked with her mother that an admirer was coming to see her and she should put on her pretty clothes.

"No! No one coming."

Ruth nodded and smiled.

"Who?"

Ruth answered vaguely. "An old friend of an old friend of yours in China."

LuLing pondered hard. "Ah, yes. I remember now."

Ruth helped her bathe and dress. She tied a scarf around her neck, combed her hair, added a touch of lipstick. "You're beautiful," Ruth said, and it was true.

LuLing looked at herself in the mirror. "Buddha-full. Too bad GaoLing not pretty like me." Ruth laughed. Her mother had never expressed vanity about her looks, but with the dementia, the modesty censors must not have been working. Dementia was like a truth serum.

At seven exactly, Mr. Tang arrived with LuLing's pages and his translation. He was a slender man with white hair, deep smile lines, a very kind face. He brought LuLing a bag of oranges.

"No need to be so polite," she said automatically as she inspected the fruit for soft spots. She scolded Ruth in Chinese: "Take his coat. Ask him to sit down. Give him something to drink."

"No need to trouble yourself," Mr. Tang said.

"Oh, your Chinese is the Beijing dialect, very elegant," LuLing said. She became girlish and shy, which amused Ruth. And Mr. Tang in turn poured on the charm, pulling out LuLing's chair to seat her, serving her tea first, filling her cup when it was half empty. She and Mr. Tang continued to speak in Chinese, and to Ruth's ear, her mother began to sound more logical, less confused.

"Where in China are you from?" LuLing asked.

"Tianjin. Later I went to school at Yenching University."

"Oh, my first husband went there, a very smart boy. Pan Kai Jing. Did you know him?"

"I've heard of him," Ruth heard Mr. Tang answer. "He studied geology, didn't he?"

"That's right! He worked on many important things. Have you ever heard of Peking Man?"

"Of course, Peking Man is world-famous."

LuLing looked wistful. "He died watching over those old bones."

"He was a great hero. Others admired his bravery, but you must have suffered."

Ruth listened with fascination. It was as if Mr. Tang had known her mother years before. He easily guided her to the old memories, to those that were still safeguarded from destruction. And then she heard her mother say, "My daughter Luyi also worked with us. She was at the same school where I lived after Precious Auntie died."

Ruth turned, startled then touched that her mother included her in the past.

"Yes, I was sorry to hear about your mother. She was a great lady. Very smart."

LuLing tilted her head and seemed to be struggling with sadness. "She was the daughter of a bonesetter."

Mr. Tang nodded. "A very famous doctor."

At the end of the evening, Mr. Tang thanked LuLing elaborately for some delightful hours of remembering the old times. "May I have the honor of visiting you again soon?"

LuLing tittered. She raised her eyebrows and looked at Ruth.

"You're welcome to come anytime," Ruth said.

"Tomorrow!" LuLing blurted. "Come tomorrow."

Ruth stayed up all night to read the pages Mr. Tang had translated. "Truth," the account began. She started to enumerate all the true things she was learning, but soon lost count, as each fact led to more questions. Her mother was really five years older than Ruth had always thought. So that meant she had told Dr. Huey the truth about her age! And the part about not being GaoLing's sister, that was true as well. Yet her mother and GaoLing *were* sisters, more so than Ruth had ever thought. They had had more reason than most sisters to disavow their relationship, yet they had been fiercely loyal, had remained irrevocably bound to each other by grudges, debt, and love. She was elated to know this.

Parts of her mother's story saddened her. Why did she feel she could never tell Ruth that Precious Auntie was her mother? Did she fear that her own daughter would be ashamed that LuLing was illegitimate? Ruth would have assured her that there was no shame, that it was practically fashionable these days to be born a love child. But then Ruth remembered that as a girl she had been terrified of Precious Auntie. She had resented her presence in their lives, had blamed her for her mother's quirkiness, her feelings of doom. How misunderstood Precious Auntie had been—by both her daughter and her granddaughter. Yet there were moments when Ruth sensed that Precious Auntie had been watching her, that she knew when Ruth was suffering.

Ruth mused over this, lying in her childhood bed. She understood more clearly why her mother had always wanted to find Precious Auntie's bones and bury them in the proper place. She wanted to walk through the End of the World and make amends. She wanted to tell her mother, "I'm sorry and I forgive you, too."

* * *

The next day, Ruth telephoned Art to tell him what she had read. "It feels like I've found the magic thread to mend a torn-up quilt. It's wonderful and sad at the same time."

"I'd like to read it. Would you let me?"

"I want you to." Ruth sighed. "She should have told me these things years ago. It would have made such a difference—"

Art interrupted: "There are things I should have said years ago too."

Ruth fell silent, waiting.

"I've been thinking about your mother, and I've also been thinking about us."

Ruth's heart started to race.

"Remember what you said when we first met, about not wanting to have assumptions about love?"

"I didn't say that, you did."

"I did?"

"Absolutely. I remember."

"Funny, I thought you did."

"Ah, you assumed!"

He laughed. "Your mother isn't the only one with memory problems. Well, if I said it, then I was wrong, because I do think it's important to have certain assumptions— for one thing, that the person who's with you is there for the long haul, that he'll take care of you and what comes with you, the whole package, mother and everything. For whatever reason—my having said that about assumptions, and your going along with it—well, I guess I thought it was great at the time, that I had love on a free ride. I didn't know what I was going to lose until you moved out."

Art paused. Ruth knew he was waiting for her to respond. In part, she wanted to shout with gratitude that he had said what she had been feeling and could not express. Yet she was scared that he was saying this too late. She felt no joy in hearing his admission. She felt sad.

"I don't know what to say," she finally admitted.

"You don't have to say anything. I just wanted you to know. . . . The other thing is, I really am worried about your taking care of your mother over the long term. I know you want to do this, that it's important, and she needs someone around. But you and I know she's going to get worse. She'll require more and more care, and she can't do it alone, and neither can you. You have your work and a life too, and your mother would be the last person to see you give that up for her sake."

"I can't keep hiring new housekeepers."

"I know. . . . That's why I've been reading up on Alzheimer's, stages of the disease, medical needs, support groups. And I've thought of an idea, a possible solution . . . an assisted-living residence."

"That's not a solution." Ruth felt as she had when her mother showed her the ten-million-dollar check from the magazine sweepstakes.

"Why not?"

"Because my mother would never go for it. *I* wouldn't go for it. She'd think I was sending her to the dog pound. She'd threaten to kill herself every single day—"

"I'm *not* talking about a nursing home and bedpans. This is assisted living. They're the latest concept, the wave of the baby-boomer future, like senior Club Meds—meals, maid service, laundry, transportation, organized outings, exercise, even dancing. And it's supervised, twenty-four hours. It's upscale, not depressing at all. I've already looked at a bunch of residences, and I've found a great one, not far from where your mother lives now—"

"Forget it. Upscale or not, she would never live in a place like that."

"All she has to do is try it."

"I'm telling you, forget it. She won't do it."

"Whoa, whoa. Before you dismiss the idea outright, tell me the specific objections. Let's see if we can move forward from there."

"There's nothing to move forward. But if you must know, for one thing, she'd never leave her own home. And second, there's the cost. I assume these places aren't free, which is what it would have to be for her to even consider it. And if it *were* free, she'd think it was welfare, so she'd refuse on those grounds."

"All right. I can deal with those factors. What else?"

Ruth took a deep breath. "She'd have to love it. She would have to *want* to live there as her choice, not yours or mine."

"Done. And she can come stay with you and me anytime she wants."

Ruth noted that he said "you and me." She let down her guard. Art was trying. He was telling her he loved her in the best way he knew possible.

Two days later, LuLing showed Ruth an official-looking notice from the California Department of Public Safety, on letterhead generated from Art's computer.

"Radon leak!" LuLing exclaimed. "What this mean, radon leak?"

"Let me see," Ruth said, and scanned the letter. Art had been very clever. Ruth played along. "Mm. It's a heavy gas, it says, radioactive, dangerous to your lungs. The gas company detected it when they did a routine inspection for earthquake dangers. The leakage isn't from a pipe. It comes from the soil and rocks under the house, and they need to have you move out for three months while they do an environmental assessment and hazard removal via intensive ventilation."

"Ai-ya! How much cost?"

"Hm. Nothing, it says. The city does it for free. Look, they even pay for the place where you stay while they do the ventilation. Three months' free rent . . . including food. The Mira Mar Manor—'located near your current residence,' it says, 'with amenities typical of a five-star hotel.' That's the highest rating, five stars. They're asking you to go there as soon as possible."

"Free five-star? For two people?"

Ruth pretended to search the fine print. "No. Looks like it's just for one person. I can't go." She sighed, sounding disappointed.

"Hunh! I don't mean you!" her mother exclaimed. "What about that girl downstair?"

"Oh, right." Ruth had forgotten about the tenant. So had Art, evidently. But her mother, brain disease and all, hadn't let that slip by.

"I'm sure she got a similar notice. They wouldn't let anyone remain in the building, not if it can give them lung disease."

LuLing frowned. "Then she live my *same* hotel?"

"Oh! . . . No, it's probably different, a place that isn't as nice, I'm sure, since you're the owner and she's only the renter."

"But she still pay *me* rent?"

Ruth looked at the letter again. "Of course. That's the law."

LuLing nodded with satisfaction. "Okay, then."

By phone, Ruth told Art that his plan seemed to have worked. She was glad that he didn't sound smug.

"It's kind of scary how easily fooled she was," he said. "That's how a lot of old people get swindled out of their homes and savings."

"I feel like a spy right now," Ruth added. "Like we succeeded at a covert mission."

"I guess she and a lot of other people will buy into any idea that involves getting something for nothing."

"Speaking of which, how much will this Mira Mar place cost?"

"Don't worry about it."

"Come on. Tell me."

"I'll take care of it. If she likes it and stays, we'll figure it out later. If she hates it, the three months are on me. She can move back into her old place, and we'll think of something else."

Ruth liked that he was thinking "we" again. "Well, we'll share the cost of the three months, then."

"Just let me do this, okay?"

"Why should I?"

"Because it feels like the most important thing I've done in a long time. Call it a Boy Scout good deed for the day. Mitzvah-gathering, mensch remedial training. Temporary insanity. It makes me feel good, like a human being. It makes me happy."

Happy. If only her mother could be happy as well, living in a place like the Mira Mar. Ruth wondered what made people happy. Could you find happiness in a place? In another person? What about happiness for herself? Did you simply have to know what you wanted and reach for it through the fog?

As they parked in front of the three-story shingled building, Ruth was relieved to see that it did not look like an asylum. LuLing was at her sister's for the weekend, and it was Art's idea that they visit Mira Mar Manor without her, so that they could anticipate what objections she might raise. Mira Mar Manor was flanked by windswept cypress trees and looked out on the ocean. The wrought-iron fence held a plaque declaring that this was a San Francisco landmark, erected as an orphanage after the Great Earthquake.

Ruth and Art were ushered into an oak-paneled office and told that the director of care services would be with them soon. They sat stiffly on a leather sofa, facing a massive desk. Framed diplomas and health certifications hung on the wall, as well as old photographs of the building in its original incarnation, with beaming girls posed in white frocks.

"Sorry to keep you waiting," she heard someone say in a British accent. Ruth turned and was surprised to see a polished-looking young Indian man in suit and tie. "Edward Patel," he said, smiling warmly. He shook hands and handed them each a business card. He must be in his early thirties, Ruth thought. He looked like a stockbroker, not someone who concerned himself with laxatives and arthritis medication.

"I'd like to start here," Patel said, taking them back to the foyer, "because this is what our seniors first see when they arrive." He began what sounded like an oft recited spiel: "Here at Mira Mar Manor, we believe home is more than a bed. It's a whole concept."

Concept? Ruth looked at Art. This would never work.

"What does the 'P and F' in P and F HealthCare stand for?" Art asked, looking at the business card.

"Patel and Finkelstein. One of my uncles was a founding partner. He's been in the hospitality business a long time, hotels. Morris Finkelstein is a doctor. His own mother is a resident here."

Ruth marveled that a Jewish mother would allow her son to put her in a place like this. Now *that* was an endorsement.

They stepped through French doors into a garden surrounded by hedges. On each side was a shady arbor with a latticed covering of jasmine. Underneath were cushioned chairs and opaque glass-topped tables. Several women glanced up from their conversations.

"Hello, Edward!" three of them sang out in turn.

"Morning, Betty, Dorothy, Rose. Wow, Betty, that's a spectacular color on you!"

"You watch it, young lady," the old woman said sternly to Ruth. "He'll sell the pants off you, if he can." Patel laughed easily, and Ruth wondered whether the woman was only joking. Well, at least he knew their names.

Down the middle of the garden was a reddish pathway lined with benches, some shaded by awnings. Patel pointed out amenities that might have gone unnoticed to an untrained eye. His voice was resonant, familiar, and knowledgeable, like that of an English teacher Ruth had once had. The strolling path, he explained, had the same covering used for indoor running tracks, no loose bricks or stones to catch a feeble walker off guard, no hard concrete. Of course, if a senior fell, she could still break a hip, he said, but it was less likely to shatter into a million pieces. "And studies show that's what is so deadly to this population. One fall, boom!" Patel snapped his fingers. "Happens a lot when the elderly live alone and in the old family home that hasn't been adapted to their needs. No rampways, no handrails."

Patel gestured to the flowers in the garden. "All thorn-free and non-toxic, no deadly oleander or foxglove that a confused person might nibble on." Each plant was identified by staked marker at eye level—no bending down necessary. "Our seniors really love naming the herbs. On Mondays, the afternoon activity is herb collecting. There's rosemary, parsley, oregano, lemon thyme, basil, sage. The word 'echinacea' gives them a hard time, though. One lady calls it 'the China Sea.' Now we all call it that."

The herbs from the garden, Patel added, were used in the meals. "The ladies still pride themselves on their cooking abilities. They love to remind us to add only a pinch of oregano, or to rub the sage on the inside not the outside of the chicken, that sort of thing." Ruth could picture dozens of old ladies complaining about the food, and her mother yelling above the rest that everything was too salty.

They continued walking along the path toward a greenhouse at the back of the garden. "We call this the Love Nursery," Patel said, as they stepped into a blast of color—shocking pink and monk-robe saffron. The air was moist and cool.

"Each resident has an orchid plant. The flower pots are painted with the names they've given their orchids. As you may have already noticed, about ninety percent of our residents are women. And no matter how old they are, many still have a strong maternal instinct. They adore watering their orchids every day. We use a dendrobium orchid known as *cuthbertsonii*. Blooms nearly year-round, nonstop, and unlike most orchids, it can take daily watering. Many of our residents have named their orchids after their husbands or children or other family members who've already passed. They often talk to their plants, touch and kiss the petals, fuss and worry over them. We give them tiny eye-droppers and a bucket of water we call 'Love Potion.' 'Mother's coming, Mother's coming,' you'll hear them say. It's quite touching to watch them feeding their orchids."

Ruth's eyes welled up. Why was she crying? Stop this, she told herself, you're being stupid and maudlin. He's talking about a business plan, for God's sake, concept-sanctioned forms of happiness. She turned away as if to inspect a row of orchids. When she had collected herself, she said, "They must love it here."

"They do. We've tried to think of everything that a family would think about."

"Or wouldn't," Art said.

"There's a lot to think about," Patel said with a modest smile.

"Do you ever find any of them reluctant to be here, especially in the beginning?"

"Oh, yes indeed. That's expected. They don't want to move out of their old homes, because that's where all the memories are. And they don't want to spend down their kids' inheritance. Nor do they think they're old—certainly not *that* old, they'll say. I'm sure we'll be saying the same thing when we're their age."

Ruth laughed to be polite. "We may have to trick my mother into coming here."

"Well, you won't be the first family members to do so," Patel said. "The subterfuges people have used to get their parents here—wow, pretty ingenious. It could fill a book."

"Like what?" Ruth asked.

"We have quite a few folks here who don't know it costs anything to live here."

"Really!" Art exclaimed, and gave Ruth a wink.

"Oh, yes. Their sense of economy is strictly Depression-era. Paying rent is money down the drain. They're used to owning a house, paid free and clear."

Ruth nodded. Her mother's building had been paid up last year. They continued along the walkway and went inside and down a hall toward the dining room.

"One of our residents," Patel added, "is a ninety-year-old former sociology professor, still fairly sharp. But he thinks he's here on a fellowship from his alma mater to study the effects of aging. And another woman, a former piano teacher, thinks she's been hired to play music every night after dinner. She's not too bad, actually. We direct-bill most families, so their parents don't even know what the fees are."

"Is that legal?" Ruth asked.

"Perfectly, as long as the families have conservatorship or power of attorney over the finances. Some of them take out loans against the principal on the house, or they've sold their parents' homes and use the money in trust to make the payments. Anyway, I know all about the problems of getting seniors to accept the idea of even considering living in a place like this. But I guarantee you, once your mother has lived here for a month, she'll never want to leave."

"What do you do," Ruth joked, "spike the food?"

Patel misunderstood. "Actually, because of all the dietary needs of our population, we can't prepare anything too spicy. We do have a nutritionist who makes up the monthly menu. Many of the choices are low-fat, low-cholesterol. We also offer vegan. The residents receive printed-out menus every day." He picked one off a nearby table.

Ruth scanned it. The choice today was turkey meatloaf, tuna casserole, or tofu fajitas, accompanied by salad, rolls, fresh fruit, mango sorbet, and macaroons. Suddenly another problem loomed: No Chinese food.

But when she brought it up, Patel was ready with an answer: "We've encountered that issue in the past. Chinese, Japanese, kosher food, you name it. We have a delivery service from approved restaurants. And since we have two other Chinese residents who get takeout twice a week, your mother can share the selections we get for them. Also, one of our cooks is Chinese. She makes rice porridge on the weekends for breakfast. Several of our non-Chinese residents go for that as well." Patel returned smoothly to his rehearsed patter: "Regardless of special diets, they all love the waiter service, tablecloths at the meals, just like a fine restaurant. And no tipping is necessary or allowed." Ruth nodded. LuLing's idea of a big tip was a dollar.

"It's really a carefree life, which is how it should be when you're this age, don't you agree?" Patel looked at Ruth. He must have picked her as the stumbling block. How could he tell? Did she have a crease in the middle of her brow? It was obvious that Art thought the place was great.

Ruth decided she should get hard-nosed. "Are any of the people here, you know, like my mother? Do any of them have, well, memory problems of some sort?"

"It's safe to assume that half the general population over age eighty-five likely has some memory problems starting to show. And after all, our average age here is eighty-seven."

"I don't mean just memory problems. What if it's something more . . ."

"You mean like Alzheimer's? Dementia?" Patel motioned

them into another large room. "I'll get back to your question in just a minute. This is the main activity hall."

Several people looked up from a bingo game being conducted by a young man. Ruth noticed that most were nicely dressed. One was wearing a powder-blue pantsuit, a pearl necklace and earrings, as if she were going to Easter services. A beak-nosed man in a jaunty beret winked at her. She imagined him at thirty, a brash businessman, confident of his position in the world and with the ladies.

"Bingo!" a woman with almost no chin shouted.

"I haven't called enough numbers yet, Anna," the young man said patiently. "You need at least five to win. We've only done three so far."

"Well, I don't know. Just call me stupid, then."

"No! No! No!" a woman in a shawl yelled. "Don't you dare use that word in here."

"That's right, Loretta," the young man added. "No one here is stupid. Sometimes we get a little confused, that's all."

"Stupid, stupid, stupid," Anna muttered under her breath, as if she was cursing. She gave Loretta the evil eye. "Stupid!"

Patel did not seem perturbed. He quietly led Ruth and Art out of the room and to an elevator. As they ascended, he spoke. "To answer your question, most of the residents are what we call 'frail elderly.' They may have problems seeing or hearing or getting around without a cane or a walker. Some are sharper than you or I, others are easily confused and have signs of dementia due to Alzheimer's or what have you. They tend to be a little forgetful about taking their pills, which is why *we* dispense all medications. But they always know what day it is, whether it's movie Sunday or herb-picking Monday. And if they don't remember the year, why should they? Some notions of time are irrelevant."

"We might as well tell you now," Art said. "Mrs. Young thinks she's coming here because of a radon leak in her home." He presented a copy of the letter he had created.

"That's a new one," Patel conceded with an appreciative chuckle. "I'll keep that in mind for other family members whose parents need a nudge. Ah yes, free rent, courtesy of the California Department of Public Safety. Quite good to make it official, mark of authority, like a summons." He swung open a door. "This is the unit that just became available." They walked into an apartment overlooking the garden: a compact living room, bedroom, and bathroom, empty of furnishings, smelling of fresh paint and new carpets. It occurred to Ruth that what Patel meant by "just became available" was that the last resident had died. The cheeriness of the place now seemed ominous, a façade hiding a darker truth.

"This is one of the nicest units," Patel said. "There are smaller, less expensive rooms, studios, and some without an ocean or garden view. We should have one of those available, oh, in about another month."

My God! He expected someone else to die soon. And he said it so casually, so matter-of-factly! Ruth felt trapped, frantic to escape. This place was like a death sentence. Wouldn't her mother feel the same way? She'd never stay here for a month, let alone three.

"We can provide the furniture at no extra charge," Patel said. "But usually the residents like to bring their own things. Personalize it and make it their home. We encourage that. And each floor is assigned the same staff, two caretakers per floor, day and night. Everyone knows them by name. One of them even speaks Chinese."

"Cantonese or Mandarin?" Ruth asked.

"That's a good question." He pulled out a digital recorder and spoke into it: "Find out if Janie speaks Cantonese or Mandarin."

"By the way," Ruth asked, "how much are the fees?"

Patel answered without hesitation: "Thirty-two to thirty-eight hundred a month, depending on the room and level of services needed. That includes an escort to a monthly medical appointment. I can show you a detailed schedule downstairs."

Ruth couldn't keep from gasping over the cost. "Did you know that?" she asked Art. He nodded. She was both shocked at the expense and amazed that Art would be willing to pay that for three months, nearly twelve thousand dollars. She stared at him, openmouthed.

"It's worth it," he whispered.

"That's crazy."

She repeated this later, as he drove her to her mother's.

"You can't think of it the same way you think of rent," Art replied. "It includes food, the apartment, a twenty-four-hour nurse, help with medication, laundry—"

"Right, and a very expensive orchid! I can't let you pay that, not for three months."

"It's worth it," he told her again.

Ruth exhaled heavily. "Listen, I'll pay half, and if it works out, I'll pay you back."

"We already went through this. No halves and there's nothing to pay back. I have some money saved and I want to do this. And I don't mean it as a condition for us getting back together or getting rid of your mother or any of that. It's not a condition for anything. It's not pressure for you to make a decision one way or the other. There are no expectations, no strings attached."

"Well, I appreciate the thought, but—"

"It's more than a thought. It's a gift. You have to learn to take them sometimes, Ruth. You do yourself wrong when you don't."

"What are you talking about?"

"The way you want something from people, some kind of proof of love or loyalty or belief in you. But you expect it won't come. And when it's handed to you, you don't see it. Or you resist, refuse."

"I do not—"

"You're like someone who has cataracts and wants to see, but you refuse to have an operation because you're afraid you'll go blind. You'd rather go blind slowly than take a chance. And then you can't see that the answer is right in front of you."

"That's not true," she protested. Yet she knew there was some validity to what Art was saying. It was not exactly right, but parts of it were as familiar as the tidal wave in her dreams. She turned. "Have you always thought this of me?"

"Not in so many words. I didn't really think about it until these past few months you've been gone. And then I started wondering if what you said about me was true. I realized I *am* self-centered, that I'm used to thinking about me first. But I also realized that you tend to think about you second. It's as though I had permission from you to be less responsible. I'm not saying it's your fault. But you have to learn to take back, grab it when it's offered. Don't fight it. Don't get all tense thinking it's complicated. Just take it, and if you want to be polite, say thank you."

Ruth was tumbling in her head. She was being swept and tossed, and she was scared. "Thank you," she finally said.

* * *

To Ruth's surprise, her mother seemed to have no objection to staying at Mira Mar Manor. Then again, why would she? LuLing thought it was temporary—and free. After she had toured the place, Ruth and Art took her to a nearby deli to have lunch and hear her reactions.

"So many old people have radon leak," she murmured with awe.

"Actually, not all of them are staying there because of radon leaks," Art said. Ruth wondered where this was leading to.

"Oh. Other problem their house?"

"No problem at all. They just like living there."

LuLing snorted. "Why?"

"Well, it's comfortable, convenient. They have plenty of company. In a way, it's like a cruise ship."

LuLing's face broke into a look of disgust. "Cruise ship! GaoLing always want me go cruise ship. You too cheap, she tell me. I not cheap! I poor, I don't have money throw in ocean. . . ."

Ruth felt Art had blown it. Cruise ship. If he had been listening to her mother's complaints these last few years, he'd have known this was precisely the wrong comparison to make.

"Who can afford cruise ship?" her mother groused.

"A lot of people find staying at the Mira Mar cheaper than living at home," Art said.

One of LuLing's eyebrows rose. "How cheap?"

"About a thousand dollars a month."

"T'ousand! Ai-ya! Too much!"

"But that includes housing, food, movies, dancing, utilities, *and* cable TV. That's thrown in for free."

LuLing did not have cable TV. She often talked about

getting it, but changed her mind when she found out how much it cost.

"Chinese channel too?"

"Yep. Several of them. And there are no property taxes."

This also captured LuLing's interest. Her property taxes were in fact low, stabilized by a state law that protected the holdings of the elderly. Nonetheless, each year when LuLing received her tax bill, the sum seemed agonizingly huge to her.

Art went on: "Not all of the units are a thousand a month. Yours is more expensive because it's the number-one unit, the best view, top floor. We're lucky that we got it for free."

"Ah, best unit."

"Number one," Art emphasized. "The smaller units are cheaper. . . . Honey, what did Mr. Patel say they were?"

Ruth was taken by surprise. She pretended to recollect. "I think he said seven hundred fifty."

"That how much I get Social Security!" LuLing said smugly.

And Art added: "Mr. Patel also said people who eat less can get a discount."

"I eat less. Not like American people, always take big helping."

"You'd probably qualify, then. I think you're supposed to weigh less than a hundred and twenty pounds—"

"No, Art," Ruth interrupted. "He said the cutoff was a hundred."

"I only eighty-five."

"Anyway," Art said offhandedly, "someone like you could live in the number-one unit for the same as what you get each month for Social Security. It's like living there for free."

As they continued with lunch, Ruth could see her mother's mind adding up the *free* cable TV, the *big discounts*, the *best* unit—all irresistible concepts.

When LuLing next spoke, she gloated: "Probably Gao-Ling think I got lots money live this place. Just like cruise ship."

TWO

They were celebrating Auntie Gal's seventy-seventh birthday—her eighty-second if the truth be known, but only she, LuLing, and Ruth knew that.

The Young clan was gathered at GaoLing and Edmund's ranch-style house in Saratoga. Auntie Gal was wearing a silk-flower lei and a hibiscus-patterned muumuu, in keeping with the luau theme of the party. Uncle Edmund had on an aloha shirt printed with ukuleles. They had just returned from their twelfth cruise to the Hawaiian Islands. LuLing, Art, Ruth, and various cousins were sitting poolside in the backyard—or lanai, as Auntie Gal referred to it—where Uncle Edmund had fired up a grill to barbecue enough slabs of spare ribs to give everyone indigestion. The outdoor gas-fueled tiki torches were wafting warmth, making the outdoors seem balmy. The kids weren't fooled. They decided the pool was too cold and improvised a game of soccer on the lawn. Every few minutes they had to use the long-handled net to fish the ball out of the water. "Too much splash," LuLing complained.

When GaoLing went to the kitchen to prepare the last side dishes, Ruth followed. She had been waiting for an opportunity to talk to her aunt privately. "Here's how you make tea eggs," Auntie Gal said, as Ruth shelled the hard-boiled eggs. "Use two big pinches black tea leaves. It must be black, not Japanese green, and not the herbal kind all you kids like to drink for health purposes. Put the leaves in the cheesecloth, tie it tight.

"Now put these cooked eggs in the pot with the tea leaves, a half-cup soy sauce for twenty eggs, and six star anise," GaoLing continued. She sprinkled the mixture with liberal amounts of salt. Her longevity was obviously a tribute to her genetics and not her diet. "Cook for one hour," she said, and set the pot on the stove to simmer. "When you were a little girl, you loved to eat these. Lucky eggs, we called them. That's why your mommy and I made them. All the kids liked them better than anything else. One time, though, you ate five and got very sick. Big mess all over my sofa. After that, you said no eggs, no more eggs. You wouldn't eat them the next year either, not you. But the year after that, eggs were okay again, yum-yum."

Ruth didn't remember any of this, and wondered whether GaoLing was confusing her with her daughter. Was her aunt also showing signs of dementia?

She went to the refrigerator and took out a bowl of scalded celery, cut into strips. Without measuring, she doused the celery with sesame oil and soy sauce, chatting as if she were on a talk show for cooks.

"I've been thinking one day I might write a book. The title is this, *Culinary Road to China*—what do you think, good? Easy recipes. Maybe if you're not too busy, you can help me write it. I don't mean for free, though. Course, most of the words are already in my head, right here. I just need someone to write them down. Still, I'd pay you, doesn't matter that I'm your auntie."

Ruth did not want to encourage this line of thinking.

"Did you make those same eggs when you lived in the orphanage with Mom?"

GaoLing stopped stirring. She looked up. "Ah, your mother told you about that place." She tasted a piece of celery and added more soy sauce. "Before, she never wanted to tell anyone why she went to the orphan school." GaoLing paused and pursed her lips, as if she had already divulged too much.

"You mean that Precious Auntie was her mother."

GaoLing clucked her tongue. "Ah, so she told you. Good, I'm glad. Better to tell the truth."

"I also know both you and Mom are five years older than what we always thought. And that your real birthday is what, four months earlier?"

GaoLing tried to laugh, but she also looked evasive. "I always wanted to be honest. But your mommy was afraid of so many things—oh, she said the authorities would send her back to China if they knew she wasn't my real sister. And maybe Edwin wouldn't marry her, because she was too old. Then later you might be ashamed if you knew who your real grandmother was, unmarried, her face ruined, treated like a servant. Me? Over the years, I've become more modern-thinking. Old secrets? Here nobody cares! Mother not married? Oh, just like Madonna. But still your mommy said, No, don't tell, promise."

"Does anyone else know? Uncle Edmund, Sally, Billy?"

"No, no, no one at all. I promised your mother. . . . Of course Uncle Edmund knows. We don't keep secrets. I tell him everything. . . . Well, the age part, he doesn't know. But I wasn't lying. I forgot. It's true! I don't even feel like I'm seventy-seven. In my mind, the most is sixty. But now you remind me, I'm even older—how old?"

"Eighty-two."

THE BONESETTER'S DAUGHTER 375

"Wah." Her shoulders slumped as she pondered this fact. "Eighty-two. It's like less money in the bank than I thought."

"You still look twenty years younger. Mom does too. And don't worry, I won't tell anyone, not even Uncle Edmund. Funny thing is, last year when she told the doctor she was eighty-two, I thought that was a sure sign something was wrong with her mind. And then it turned out she did have Alzheimer's, but she was right all along about her age. She just forgot to lie—"

"Not lying," GaoLing corrected. "It was a secret."

"That's what I meant. And I wouldn't have known her age until I read what she wrote."

"She wrote this down—about her age?"

"About a lot of things, a stack of pages this thick. It's like her life story, all the things she didn't want to forget. The things she couldn't talk about. Her mother, the orphanage, her first husband, yours."

Auntie Gal looked increasingly uncomfortable. "When did she write this?"

"Oh, it must have been seven, eight years ago, probably when she first started worrying that something was wrong with her memory. She gave me some of the pages a while back. But it was all in Chinese, so I never got around to reading them. A few months ago, I found someone to translate."

"Why didn't you ask me?" GaoLing pretended to be insulted. "I'm your auntie, she's my sister. We are still blood-related, even though we don't have the same mother."

The truth was, Ruth had feared her mother might have written unflattering remarks about GaoLing. And it occurred to her now that GaoLing might have also censored the parts that dealt with her own secrets, her marriage to the opium addict, for instance. "I didn't want to bother you," Ruth said.

Her aunt sniffed. "What are relatives for if you can't bother them?"

"That's true."

"You call me anytime, you know this. You want Chinese food, I cook for you. Translate Chinese writing, I can do this too. You need me to watch your mommy, no need to ask, just drop her off."

"Actually, remember how we talked about Mom's future needs? Well, Art and I looked at a place, Mira Mar Manor, it's assisted living, really nice. They have staff twenty-four hours a day, activities, a nurse who helps with medication—"

GaoLing frowned. "How can you put your mommy in a nursing home? No, this is not right." She clamped her mouth shut and shook her head.

"It's not what you think—"

"Don't do this! If you can't take care of your mommy, let her come live here with me."

Ruth knew that GaoLing was barely able to handle LuLing for a couple of days at a time. "Nearly gave me a heart attack," was how she had described LuLing's last visit. Still, Ruth was ashamed that her aunt saw her as neglectful, uncaring. All the doubts she had about the Mira Mar bobbed to the surface, and she felt unsteady about her intentions. Was this really the best solution for her mother's safety and health? Or was she abandoning her mother for convenience' sake? She wondered whether she was simply going along with Art's rationale, as she had with so many aspects of their relationship. It seemed she was always living her life through others, for others.

"I just don't know what else to do," Ruth said, her voice full of the despair she had kept pent up. "This disease, it's awful, it's progressing more quickly than I thought. She can't be left alone. She wanders away. And she doesn't know if she's eaten ten minutes ago or ten hours ago. She won't bathe by herself. She's afraid of the faucets—"

"I know, I know. Very hard, very sad. That's why I'm saying, you can't take it anymore, you just bring her here. Part-time my place, part-time your place. Easier that way."

Ruth ducked her head. "Mom already went for a tour of the Mira Mar. She thought it was nice, like a cruise ship."

GaoLing gave a doubting sniff.

Ruth wanted her aunt's approval. She also sensed that GaoLing wanted her to ask for it. She and her mother had taken turns protecting each other. Ruth met GaoLing's eyes. "I won't make any decision until you think it's the right thing. But I would like you to look at the place. And when you do, I can give you a copy of what Mom wrote."

That got GaoLing's interest.

"Speaking of which," Ruth went on, "I was wondering whatever happened to those people you and Mom knew in China. Mom didn't say anything about her life after she left Hong Kong. What happened to that guy you were married to, Fu Nan, and his father? Did they keep the ink shop?"

GaoLing looked to the side to make sure no one was close enough to hear. "Those people were *awful*." She made a face. "So bad you can't even imagine how bad. The son had many problems. Did your mother write about this?"

Ruth nodded. "He was hooked on opium."

GaoLing looked momentarily taken aback, realizing that LuLing had been thorough in her account. "This is true," she conceded. "Later he died, maybe in 1960, though no one is sure-for-sure. But that was when he stopped writing and calling different people, threatening this and that to get them to send money."

"Uncle Edmund knows about him?"

GaoLing huffed. "How could I tell him that I was still married? Your uncle would then question if we are really married, if I am a bigamist, if our children are—well, like your mother. Later, I forgot to tell him, and when I heard my first husband was probably dead, it was too late to go back and explain what should be forgotten anyway. You understand."

"Like your age."

"Exactly. As for the Chang father, well, in 1950, the Communists cracked down on all the landlords. They put the Chang father in jail and beat a confession from him for owning many businesses, cheating people, and trading in opium. Guilty, they said, and shot him, public execution."

Ruth pictured this. She was against the death penalty in principle, but felt a secret satisfaction that the man who had caused her grandmother and mother so much misery had met a fitting end.

"The people also confiscated his house, made his wife sweep the streets, and all his sons were sent to work outdoors in Wuhan, where it's so hot most people would rather bathe in a vat of boiling oil than go there. My father and mother were glad they were already poor and didn't have to suffer that kind of punishment."

"And Sister Yu, Teacher Pan. Did you hear from them?"

"My brother did—you know, Jiu Jiu in Beijing. He said Sister Yu was promoted many times, until she was a high-position Communist Party leader. I don't know her title, something to do with good attitude and reforms. But during the Cultural Revolution, everything got turned around, and she became an example of bad attitude because of her background with the missionaries. The revolutionaries put her in jail for a long time and treated her pretty hard. But when she came out, she was still happy to be a Communist. Later, I think she died of old age."

"And Teacher Pan?"

"Jiu Jiu said the country one year held a big ceremony for the Chinese workers who helped discover Peking Man. The newspaper article he sent me said Pan Kai Jing—the one your mother married—died as a martyr protecting the whereabouts of the Communist Party, and his father, Teacher Pan, was present to receive his honorable-mention award. After that, I don't know what happened to Teacher Pan. By now, he must be dead. So sad. We once were like family. We sacrificed for each other. Sister Yu could have come to America, but she let your mommy and me have this chance. That's why your mommy named you after Sister Yu."

"I thought I was named after Ruth Grutoff."

"Her too. But your Chinese name comes from Sister Yu. Yu Luyi. Luyi, it means 'all that you wish.' "

Ruth was amazed and gratified that her mother had put so much heart into naming her. For most of her childhood, she had hated both her American and her Chinese names, the old-fashioned sound of "Ruth," which her mother could not even pronounce, and the way "Luyi" sounded like the name of a boy, a boxer, or a bully.

"Did you know your mommy also gave up her chance to come to America so I could come first?"

"Sort of." She dreaded the day GaoLing would read the pages describing how she had wangled her way to the States.

"Many times I've thanked her, and always she said, 'No, don't talk about this or I'll be mad at you.' I've tried to repay her many times, but she always refused. Each year we invite her to go to Hawaii. Each year she tells me she doesn't have the money."

Ruth nodded. How many times she had had to suffer listening to her mother complain about that.

"Each time I tell her, I'm inviting you, what money do you need? Then she says she can't let me pay. Forget it! So I tell her, 'Use the money in the Charles Schwab account.' No, she doesn't want that money. She *still* won't use it."

"What Charles Schwab account?"

"*This* she didn't tell you? Her half of the money from your grandparents when they died."

"I thought they just left her a little bit."

"Yes, that was wrong of them to do. Very old-fashioned. Made your mommy so angry. That's why she wouldn't take the money, even after your Uncle Edmund and I said we could divide it in half anyway. Long time ago, we put her half in T-bills. Your mommy always pretended she didn't know about it. But then she'd say something like, 'I hear you can make more money investing in the stock market.' So we opened a stock market account. Then she said, 'I hear this stock is good, this one is bad.' So we knew to tell the stockbroker what to buy and sell. Then she said, 'I hear it's better to invest yourself, low fees.' So we opened a Charles Schwab account."

A chill ran down Ruth's arms. "Did some of those stocks she mentioned include IBM, U.S. Steel, AT&T, Intel?"

GaoLing nodded. "Too bad Uncle Edmund didn't listen to her advice. He was always running after this IPO, that IPO."

Ruth now recalled the many times her mother had asked Precious Auntie for stock tips via the sand tray. It never occurred to her that the answers mattered that much, since her mother didn't have any real money to gamble with. She thought LuLing followed the stock market the way some people followed soap operas. And so when her mother presented her with a choice of stocks, Ruth chose whichever was the shortest to spell out. That was how she decided. Or had she? Had she also received nudges and notions from someone else?

"So the stocks did well?" Ruth asked with a pounding heart.

"Better than S and P, better than Uncle Edmund—she's like a Wall Street genius! Every year it's grown and grown. She hasn't touched one penny. She could have gone on lots of cruises, bought a fancy house, nice furniture, big car. But no. I think she has been saving it all for you. . . . Don't you want to know how much?"

Ruth shook her head. This was already too much. "Tell me later." Instead of feeling excited about the money, Ruth was hurt to know that her mother had denied herself pleasure and happiness. Out of love, she had stayed behind in Hong Kong, so GaoLing could have a chance at freedom first. Yet she would not take love back from people. How did she become that way? Was it because of Precious Auntie's suicide?

"By the way," Ruth now thought to ask, "what was Precious Auntie's real name?"

"Precious Auntie?"

"Bao Bomu."

"Oh, oh, oh, *Bao Bomu*! You know, only your mother called her that. Everyone else called her Bao Mu."

"What's the difference, 'Bao Bomu' and 'Bao Mu'?"

"*Bao* can mean 'precious,' or it can mean 'protect.' Both are third tone, *baaaaooo*. And the *mu* part, that stands for 'mother,' but when it's written in *bao mu*, the *mu* has an extra piece in front, so that the meaning is more of a female servant. *Bao mu* is like saying 'baby-sitter,' 'nursemaid.' And *bomu*, that's 'auntie.' I think her mother taught her to say and write it this way. More special."

"So what was her real name? Mom can't remember, and it really bothers her."

"I don't remember either. . . . I don't know."

Ruth's heart sank. Now she would never know. No one would ever know the name of her grandmother. She had existed, and yet without a name, a large part of her existence was missing, could not be attached to a face, anchored to a family.

"We all called her Bao Mu," GaoLing went on, "also lots of bad nicknames because of her face. Burnt Wood, Fried Mouth, that sort of thing. People weren't being mean, the nicknames were a joke. . . . Well, now that I think of this, they were mean, very mean. That was wrong."

It pained Ruth to hear this. She felt a lump growing in her throat. She wished she could tell this woman from the past, her grandmother, that her granddaughter cared, that she, like her mother, wanted to know where her bones were. "The house in Immortal Heart," Ruth asked, "is it still there?"

"Immortal Heart? . . . Oh, you mean our village—I only know the Chinese name." She sounded out the syllables. "*Xian Xin*. Yes, I guess that's how it might translate. The immortal's heart, something like that. Anyway, the house is gone. My brother told me. After a few drought years, a big rainstorm came. Dirt washed down the mountain, flooded the ravine, and crumbled the sides. The earth holding up our house broke apart and fell, bit by bit. It took with it the back rooms, then the well, until only half the house was left. It stood like that for several more years, then in 1972, all at once, it sank and the earth folded on top of it. My brother said that's what killed our mother, even though she had not lived in that house for many years."

"So the house is now lying in the End of the World?"

"What's that—end of what?"

"The ravine."

She sounded out more Chinese syllables to herself, and laughed. "That's right, we called it that when we were kids. End of the World. That's because we heard our parents saying that the closer the edge came to our house, the faster we'd reach the end of this world. Meaning, our luck would be gone, that was it. And they were right! Anyway, we had many nicknames for that place. Some people called it 'End of the Land,' just like where your mommy lives in San Francisco, Land's End. And sometimes my uncles joked and called that cliff edge *momo meiyou*, meaning 'rub sink gone.' But most people in the village just called it the garbage dump. In those days, no one came by once a week to take away your garbage, your recycling, no such thing. Course, people then didn't throw away too much. Bones and rotten food, the pigs and dogs ate that. Old clothes we mended and gave to younger children. Even when the clothes were so bad they couldn't be repaired, we tore them into strips and weaved them into liners for winter jackets. Shoes, the same thing. You fixed the holes, patched up the bottoms. So you see, only the worst things were thrown away, the most useless. And when we were little and bad, our parents made us behave by threatening to throw us in the ravine—as if we too were the most useless things! When we were older and wanted to play down there, then it was a different story. Down there, they said, was everything we were afraid of—"

"Bodies?"

"Bodies, ghosts, demons, animal spirits, Japanese soldiers, whatever scared us."

"Were bodies really thrown in there?"

GaoLing paused before she answered. Ruth was sure she was editing a bad memory. "Things were different then. . . . You see, not everyone could afford a cemetery or funeral. Funerals, those cost ten times more than weddings. But it wasn't just cost. Sometimes you couldn't bury someone for other reasons. So to put a body down there, well, this was bad, but not the same way you think, not as though we didn't care about who died."

"What about Precious Auntie's body?"

"Ai-ya. Your mommy wrote everything! Yes, that was very bad what my mother did. She was crazy when she did that, afraid that Bao Mu put a curse on our whole family. After she threw the body in there, a cloud of black birds came. Their wings were big, like umbrellas. They nearly blocked out the sun, there were so many. They flapped above, waiting for the wild dogs to finish with the body. And one of our servants—"

"Old Cook."

"Yes, Old Cook, he was the one who put the body there. He thought that the birds were Bao Mu's spirit and her army of ghosts and that she was going to pick him up with her claws and snatch him up if he did not bury her properly. So he took a large stick and chased the wild dogs away, and the birds stayed there above him, watching as he piled rocks on top of her body. But even after he did all that, our household was still cursed."

"You believed that?"

GaoLing stopped to think. "I must have. Back then I believed whatever my family believed. I didn't question it. Also, Old Cook died only two years later."

"And now?"

GaoLing was quiet for a long time. "Now I think Bao Mu left a lot of sadness behind. Her death was like that ravine. Whatever we didn't want, whatever scared us, that's where we put the blame."

Dory flew into the kitchen. "Ruth! Ruth! Come quick! Waipo fell in the pool. She almost drowned."

By the time Ruth reached the backyard, Art was carrying her mother up the steps of the shallow end. LuLing was coughing and shivering. Sally ran from the house with a pile of towels. "Wasn't anyone watching her?" Ruth cried, too upset to be more tactful.

LuLing looked at Ruth as though she were the one being chastised. "Ai-ya, so stupid."

"We're okay," Art told LuLing in a calming voice. "Just a little whoopsie-daisy. No harm done."

"She was only ten feet away from us," Billy said. "Just walked in and sank before we knew it. Art dove in, beer and all, as soon as it happened."

Ruth swaddled her mother in towels, rubbing her to stimulate her circulation.

"I saw her down there," LuLing moaned in Chinese between more coughs. "She asked me to help her get out from under the rocks. Then the ground became sky and I fell through a rain cloud, down, down, down." She turned to point to where she saw the phantom.

As Ruth glanced where her mother gestured, she saw Auntie Gal, her face stricken with new understanding.

* * *

Ruth left her mother at Auntie Gal's and spent the next day at her house sorting out what should be moved to Mira Mar Manor. On the take list she included most of her mother's bedroom furniture, and the linens and towels LuLing had never used. But what about her scroll paintings, the ink and brushes? Her mother might feel frustrated looking at these emblems of her more agile self. One thing was for certain: Ruth was not moving the vinyl La-Z-Boy. That was destined for the dump. She would buy her mother a new recliner, a much nicer one, with supple burgundy leather. Just thinking about this gave Ruth pleasure. She could already envision her mother's eyes aglow with wonder and gratitude, testing the squishiness of the cushion, murmuring, "Oh, so soft, so good."

In the evening, she drove to Bruno's supper club to meet Art. Years before, they often went there as prelude to a romantic night. The restaurant had booths that allowed them to sit close and fondle each other.

She parked around the corner a block away, and when she looked at her watch, she saw she was fifteen minutes early. She did not want to appear too eager. In front of her was the Modern Times bookstore. She went in. As she often did in bookstores, she headed to the remainder table, the bargains marked down to three ninety-eight with the lime-green stickers that were the literary equivalent of toe tags on corpses. There were the usual art books, biographies, and tell-alls of the Famous for Fifteen Minutes. And then her eyes fell on *The Nirvana Wide Web: Connections to a Higher Consciousness*. Ted, the *Internet Spirituality* author, had been right. His was a time-sensitive topic. It was already over. She felt the thrill of guilty glee. On the fiction table were an assortment of novels, most of them contemporary literary fiction by authors not well known

by the masses. She picked up a slim book that lay oblig-
ingly in her hands, inviting her to cradle it in bed under a
soft light. She picked up another, held it, skimmed its
pages, her eye and imagination plucking a line here and
there. She was drawn to them all, these prisms of other
lives and times. And she felt sympathetic, as if they were
dogs at the animal shelter, abandoned without reason,
hopeful that they would be loved still. She left the store
carrying a bag with five books.

Art was sitting in the bar at Bruno's, a retro expanse of
fifties glamour. "You're looking happy," he said.

"Am I?" She was instantly embarrassed. Lately, Wendy,
Gideon, and others had been telling her what she appeared
to be feeling, that she seemed bothered or upset, puzzled
or surprised. And each time, Ruth had been unaware of
any feelings in particular. Obviously she was showing
something on her face. Yet how could she not know what
she was feeling?

The maître d' seated them in a booth that had recently
been redone in clubby leather. Everything in the restaurant
had managed to stay as though nothing had changed for
fifty years, except the prices and the inclusion of *uni* and
octopus appetizers. As they looked over the menu, the
waiter came with a bottle of champagne.

"I ordered it," Art whispered, "for our anniversary. . . .
Don't you remember? Nude yoga? Your gay buddy? We
met ten years ago."

Ruth laughed. She had not remembered. As the waiter
poured, she whispered back, "I thought you had nice feet
for a pervert."

When they were alone, Art lifted his flute. "Here's to ten
years, most of it amazing, with a few questionable parts,
and the hope that we'll get back to where we should be."

He pressed his hand on her thigh and said, "We should try it some time."

"What?"

"Nude yoga."

A rush of warmth flooded her. The months of living with her mother had left her feeling like a virgin.

"Hey, baby, want to come back to my place afterward?" She was thrilled at the prospect.

The waiter stood before them again, ready to take orders. "The lady and I would like to begin with oysters," Art said. "This is our first date, so we'll need the ones that have the best aphrodisiac effects. Which do you recommend?"

"That would be the Kumamotos," the waiter said without a change of expression.

That night, they did not make love right away. They lay in bed, Art cuddling her, the bedroom window open so they could listen to the foghorns. "In all these years we've been together," he said, "I don't think I know an important part of you. You keep secrets inside you. You hide. It's as though I've never seen you naked, and I've had to imagine what you look like behind the drapes."

"I'm not consciously hiding anything." After Ruth said that, she wondered whether it was true. Then again, who revealed everything—the irritations, the fears? How tiresome that would be. What did he mean by secrets?

"I want us to be more intimate. I want to know what you want. Not just with us, but from life. What makes you happiest? Are you doing what you want to do?"

She laughed nervously. "That's what I edit for others, that intimate-soul stuff. I can describe how to find happiness in ten chapters, but I still don't know what it is."

"Why do you keep pushing me away?"

Ruth bristled. She didn't like it when Art acted as if he

knew her better than she knew herself. She felt him shaking her arm.

"I'm sorry. I shouldn't have said that. I don't want to make you tense. I'm just trying to get to know you. When I told the waiter this was our first date, I meant it, in a way. I want to pretend I've just met you, love at first sight, and I want to know who you are. I love you, Ruth, but I don't know you. And I want to know who this person is, this woman I love. That's all."

Ruth sank against his chest. "I don't know, I don't know," she said softly. "Sometimes I feel like I'm a pair of eyes and ears, and I'm just trying to stay safe and make sense of what's happening. I know what to avoid, what to worry about. I'm like those kids who live with gunfire going off around them. I don't want pain. I don't want to die. I don't want to see other people around me die. But I don't have anything left inside me to figure out where I fit in or what I want. If I want anything, it's to *know* what's possible to want."

THREE

In the first gallery of the Asian Art Museum, Ruth saw Mr. Tang kiss her mother's cheek. LuLing laughed like a shy schoolgirl, and then, hand in hand, they strolled into the next gallery.

Art nudged Ruth and crooked his arm. "Come on, I'm not about to be outdone by those guys." They caught up with LuLing and her companion, who were seated on a bench in front of a display of bronze bells hung in two rows on a gargantuan frame, about twelve feet high and twenty-five feet long.

"It's like a xylophone for the gods," Ruth whispered, taking a seat beside Mr. Tang.

"Each bell makes two distinct tones." Mr. Tang's voice was gentle yet authoritative. "The hammer hits the bell on the bottom and the right side. And when there are many musicians and the bells are struck together, the music is very complex, it creates tonal layers. I had the pleasure of hearing them played recently by Chinese musicians at a special event." He smiled in recalling this. "In my mind, I was transported back three thousand years. I heard what a person of that time heard, experiencing the same awe. I could imagine this person listening, a woman, I think, a very beautiful woman." He squeezed LuLing's hand. "And

390

I thought to myself, in another three thousand years, perhaps another woman will hear these tones and think of me as a handsome man. Though we don't know each other, we're connected by the music. Don't you agree?" He looked at LuLing.

"Buddha-ful," she answered.

"Your mother and I think alike," he said to Ruth. She grinned back. She realized that Mr. Tang translated for LuLing, as she once had. But he knew not to be concerned with words and their precise meanings. He simply translated what was in LuLing's heart: her better intentions, her hopes.

For the past month, LuLing had been living at Mira Mar Manor, and Mr. Tang went several times a week to visit. On Saturday afternoons, he took her on outings—to matinees, to free public rehearsals of the symphony, for strolls through the arboretum. Today it was an exhibit on Chinese archaeology, and he had invited Ruth and Art to join them. "I have something interesting to show you," he had said mysteriously over the phone, "very much worth your while."

It was already worth Ruth's while to see her mother so happy. *Happy.* Ruth pondered the word. Until recently, she had not known what that might encompass in LuLing's case. True, her mother was still full of complaints. The food at the Mira Mar was, as predicted, "too salty," the restaurant-style service was "so slow, food already cold when come." And she hated the leather recliner Ruth had bought her. Ruth had to replace it with the old vinyl La-Z-Boy. But LuLing had let go of most worries and irritations: the tenant downstairs, the fears that someone was stealing her money, the sense that a curse loomed over her life and disaster awaited her if she was not constantly on guard. Or had she simply forgotten? Perhaps her being in love was the tonic. Or the change of scenery had removed reminders of a more sorrowful past. And yet she still recounted the past, if anything more often, only now it was constantly being revised for the better. For one, it included Mr. Tang. LuLing acted as if they had known each other many lifetimes and not just a month or so. "This same thing, he and I see long time 'go," LuLing said aloud as they all admired the bells, "only now we older."

Mr. Tang helped LuLing stand up, and they moved with Ruth and Art to another display in the middle of the room. "This next one is a cherished object of China scholars," he said. "Most visitors want to see the ritual wine vessels, the jade burial suits. But to a true scholar, this is the prize." Ruth peered into the display case. To her, the prize resembled a large wok with writing on it.

"It's a masterly work of bronze," Mr. Tang continued, "but there's also the inscription itself. It's an epic poem written by the great scholars about the great rulers who were their contemporaries. One of the emperors they praised was Zhou, yes, the same Zhou of Zhoukoudian— where your mother once lived and Peking Man was found."

"The Mouth of the Mountain?" Ruth said.

"The same. Though Zhou didn't live there. A lot of places carry his name, just like every town in the United States has a Washington Street. . . . Now come this way. The reason I brought you here is in the next room."

Soon they were standing in front of another display case. "Don't look at the description in English, not yet," Mr. Tang said. "What do you think this is?" Ruth saw an ivory-colored spadelike object, cracked with lines and blackened with holes. Was it a board for an ancient game of go? A cooking implement? Next to it was a smaller object, light brown and oval, with a lip around it and writing instead of holes. At once she knew, but before she could speak, her mother gave the answer in Chinese: "Oracle bone."

Ruth was amazed at what her mother could recall. She knew not to expect LuLing to remember appointments or facts about a recent event, who was where, when it happened. But her mother often surprised her with the clarity of her emotions when she spoke of her youth, elements of which matched in spirit what she had written in her memoir. To Ruth this was evidence that the pathways to her mother's past were still open, though rutted in a few spots and marked by rambling detours. At times she also blended the past with memories from other periods of her own past. But that part of her history was nonetheless a reservoir which she could draw from and share. It didn't matter that she blurred some of the finer points. The past, even revised, was meaningful.

In recent weeks, LuLing had related several times how she received the apple-green-jade ring that Ruth had retrieved from the La-Z-Boy. "We went to a dance hall, you and I," she said in Chinese. "We came down the stairs and you introduced me to Edwin. His eyes fell on mine and did not turn away for a long time. I saw you smile and then you disappeared. That was naughty of you. I knew what you were thinking! When he asked me to marry, he gave me the ring." Ruth guessed that GaoLing had been the person who did the introductions.

Ruth now heard LuLing speaking in Mandarin to Art: "My mother found one of these. It was carved with words of beauty. She gave it to me when she was sure I would not forget what was important. I never wanted to lose it." Art nodded as if he understood what she had said, and then LuLing translated into English for Mr. Tang: "I telling him, this bone my mother give me one."

"Very meaningful," he said, "especially since your mother was the daughter of a bone doctor."

"Famous," LuLing said.

Mr. Tang nodded as if he too remembered. "Everyone from the villages all around came to him. And your father went for a broken foot. His horse stepped on him. That's how he met your mother. Because of that horse."

LuLing went blank-eyed. Ruth was afraid her mother was going to cry. But instead, LuLing brightened and said, "Liu Xing. He call her that. My mother say he write love poem about this."

Art looked at Ruth, waiting for her to acknowledge whether this was true. He had read some of the translation of LuLing's memoir, but could not connect the Chinese name to its referent. "It means 'shooting star,'" Ruth whispered. "I'll explain later." To LuLing she said, "And what was your mother's family name?" Ruth knew it was a risk to bring this up, but her mother's mind had entered the territory of names. Perhaps others were there, like markers, waiting to be retrieved.

Her mother hesitated only a moment before answering: "Family name Gu." She was looking sternly at Ruth. "I tell you so many time, you don't remember? Her father Dr. Gu. She Gu doctor daughter."

Ruth wanted to shout for joy, but the next instant she realized her mother had said the Chinese word for 'bone.' Dr. Gu, Dr. Bone, bone doctor. Art's eyebrows were raised, in expectation that the long-lost family identity had been found. "I'll explain later," Ruth said again, but this time her voice was listless.

"Oh."

Mr. Tang traced characters in the air. "*Gu*, like this? Or this?"

Her mother put on a worried face. "I don't remember."

"I don't either," Mr. Tang said quickly. "Oh well, doesn't matter."

Art changed the subject. "What's the writing on the oracle bone?"

"They're the questions the emperors asked the gods," Mr. Tang replied. "What's the weather going to be like tomorrow, who's going to win the war, when should the crops be planted. Kind of like the six-o'clock news, only they wanted the report ahead of time."

"And were the answers right?"

"Who knows? They're the cracks you see next to the black spots. The diviners of the bones used a heated nail to crack the bone. It actually made a sound—*pwak!* They interpreted the cracks as the answers from heaven. I'm sure the more successful diviners were skilled at saying what the emperors wanted to hear."

"What a great linguistic puzzle," Art said.

Ruth thought of the sand tray she and her mother used over the years. She too had tried to guess what might put her mother at ease, the words that would placate but not be readily detected as fraudulent. At times she had made up the answers to suit herself. But on other occasions, she really had tried to write what her mother needed to hear. Words of comfort, saying that her husband missed her, that Precious Auntie was not angry.

"Speaking of puzzle," Ruth said, "the other day you mentioned that no one ever found the bones of Peking Man."

LuLing perked up. "Not just man, woman too."

"You're right, Mom—Peking Woman. I wonder what happened to her? Were the bones crushed on the train tracks on the way to Tianjin? Or did they sink with the boat?"

"If the bones are still around," Mr. Tang replied, "no one's saying. Oh, every few years you read a story in the paper. Someone dies, the wife of an American soldier, a former Japanese officer, an archaeologist in Taiwan or Hong Kong. And as the story goes, bones were found in a wooden trunk, just like the trunks used to pack the bones back in 1941. Then the rumors leak out that these are the bones of Peking Man. Arrangements are made, ransoms are paid, or what have you. But the bones turn out to be oxtails. Or they are casts of the original. Or they disappear before they can be examined. In one story, the person who had stolen the bones was taking them to an island to sell to a dealer, and the plane went down in the ocean."

Ruth thought about the curse of ghosts who were angry that their bones were separated from the rest of their mortal bodies. "What do you believe?"

"I don't know. So much of history is mystery. We don't know what is lost forever, what will surface again. All objects exist in a moment of time. And that fragment of time is preserved or lost or found in mysterious ways. Mystery is a wonderful part of life." Mr. Tang winked at LuLing.

"Wonderful," she echoed.

He looked at his watch. "How about a wonderful lunch?"

"Wonderful," they said.

As Ruth and Art lay in bed that night, she pondered aloud over Mr. Tang's romantic interest in her mother. "I can understand that he's intrigued with her since he's done this work on her memoir. But he's a man who's into culture, music, poetry. She can't keep up, and she's only going to get worse. She might not even know who he is after a while."

"He's been in love with her since she was a little girl," Art said. "She's not just a source of temporary companionship. He loves everything about her, and that includes who she was, who she is, who she will be. He knows more about her than most couples who are married." He drew Ruth closer to him. "Actually, I'm hoping we might have that. A commitment through time, past, present, future . . . marriage."

Ruth held her breath. She had pushed the idea out of her head for so long she still felt it was taboo, dangerous.

"I've tried to legally bind you in the past with ownership in the house, which you've yet to take."

That's what he had meant by a percentage interest in the house? She was baffled by the mechanisms of her own defenses.

"It's just an idea," Art said awkwardly. "No pressure. I just wanted to know what you might think."

She pressed closer and kissed his shoulder. "Wonderful," she answered.

"The name, I know your mother's family name." GaoLing was calling Ruth with exciting news.

"Oh my God, what is it?"

"First you have to know what trouble I had trying to find out. After you asked me, I wrote Jiu Jiu in Beijing. He didn't know, but wrote back that he would ask a woman married to a cousin whose family still lives in the village where your grandmother was born. It took a while to sort out, because most people who would know are dead. But finally they tracked down an old woman whose grandfather was a traveling photographer. And she still had all his old glass plates. They were in a root cellar and luckily not too many were damaged. Her grandfather kept excellent records, dates, who paid what, the names of the people he photographed. Thousands of plates and photos. Anyway, the old lady remembered her grandfather showing her the photo of a girl who was quite beautiful. She had on a pretty cap, high-neck collar."

"The photo Mom has of Precious Auntie?"

"Must be the same. The old lady said it was sad, because soon after the photo was taken, the girl was scarred for life, the father was dead, the whole family destroyed. People in the village said the girl was jinxed from the beginning—"

Ruth couldn't stand it any longer. "What was the name?"

"Gu."

"Gu?" Ruth felt let down. It was the same mistake. "*Gu* is the word for 'bone,'" Ruth said. "She must have thought 'bone doctor' meant 'Dr. Bone.'"

"No, no," GaoLing said. "*Gu* as in 'gorge.' It's a different *gu*. It sounds the same as the bone *gu*, but it's written a different way. The third-tone *gu* can mean many things: 'old,' 'gorge,' 'bone,' also 'thigh,' 'blind,' 'grain,' 'merchant,' lots of things. And the way 'bone' is written can also stand for 'character.' That's why we use that expression 'It's in your bones.' It means, 'That's your character.'"

Ruth had once thought that Chinese was limited in its sounds and thus confusing. It seemed to her now that its multiple meanings made it very rich. *The blind bone doctor from the gorge repaired the thigh of the old grain merchant.*

"You're sure it's Gu?"

"That's what was written on the photographic plate."

"Did it include her first name?"

"Liu Xin."

"Shooting Star?"

"That's *liu xing*, sounds almost the same, *xing* is 'star,' *xin* is 'truth.' Liu Xin means Remain True. But because the words sound similar, some people who didn't like her called her Liu Xing. The shooting star can have a bad meaning."

"Why?"

"It's confusing why. People think the broom star is very bad to see. That's the other kind, with the long, slow tail, the comes-around kind."

"Comet?"

"Yes, comet. Comet means a rare calamity will happen. But some people mix up the broom star with the shooting star, so even though the shooting star is not bad luck, people think it is. The idea is not so good either—burns up quick, one day here, one day gone, just like what happened to Precious Auntie."

Her mother had written about this, Ruth recalled, a story Precious Auntie told LuLing when she was small— how she looked up at the night sky, saw a shooting star, which then fell into her open mouth.

Ruth began to cry. Her grandmother had a name. Gu Liu Xin. She had existed. She still existed. Precious Auntie be-longed to a family. LuLing belonged to that same family, and Ruth belonged to them both. The family name had been there all along, like a bone stuck in the crevices of a gorge. LuLing had divined it while looking at an oracle in the museum. And the given name had flashed before her as well for the briefest of moments, a shooting star that entered the earth's atmosphere, etching itself indelibly in Ruth's mind.

EPILOGUE

It is the twelfth of August and Ruth is in the Cubbyhole, silent. Foghorns blow in the night, welcoming ships into the bay.

Ruth still has her voice. Her ability to speak is not governed by curses or shooting stars or illness. She knows that for certain now. But she does not need to talk. She can write. Before, she never had a reason to write for herself, only for others. Now she has that reason.

The picture of her grandmother is in front of her. Ruth looks at it daily. Through it, she can see from the past clear into the present. Could her grandmother ever have imagined she would have a granddaughter like her—a woman who has a husband who loves her, two girls who adore her, a house she co-owns, dear friends, a life with only the usual worries about leaks and calories?

Ruth remembers how her mother used to talk of dying, by curse or her own hand. She never stopped feeling the urge, not until she began to lose her mind, the memory web that held her woes in place. And though her mother still remembers the past, she has begun to change it. She doesn't recount the sad parts. She only recalls being loved very, very much. She remembers that to Bao Bomu she was the reason for life itself.

The other day Ruth's mother called her. She sounded like her old self, scared and fretful. "Luyi," she said, and she spoke quickly in Chinese, "I'm worried that I did terrible things to you when you were a child, that I hurt you very much. But I can't remember what I did. . . ."

"There's nothing—" Ruth began.

"I just wanted to say that I hope you can forget just as I've forgotten. I hope you can forgive me, because if I hurt you, I'm sorry."

After they hung up, Ruth cried for an hour she was so happy. It was not too late for them to forgive each other and themselves.

As Ruth now stares at the photo, she thinks about her mother as a little girl, about her grandmother as a young woman. These are the women who shaped her life, who are in her bones. They caused her to question whether the order and disorder of her life were due to fate or luck, self-determination or the actions of others. They taught her to worry. But she has also learned that these warnings were passed down, not simply to scare her, but to force her to avoid their footsteps, to hope for something better. They wanted her to get rid of the curses.

In the Cubbyhole, Ruth returns to the past. The laptop becomes a sand tray. Ruth is six years old again, the same child, her broken arm healed, her other hand holding a chopstick, ready to divine the words. Bao Bomu comes, as always, and sits next to her. Her face is smooth, as beautiful as it is in the photo. She grinds an inkstick into an inkstone of *duan*.

"Think about your intentions," Bao Bomu says. "What is in your heart, what you want to put in others'." And side by side, Ruth and her grandmother begin. Words flow. They have become the same person, six years old, sixteen, forty-six, eighty-two. They write about what happened, why it happened, how they can make other things happen. They write stories of things that are but should not have been. They write about what could have been, what still might be. They write of a past that can be changed. After all, Bao Bomu says, what is the past but what we choose to remember? They can choose not to hide it, to take what's broken, to feel the pain and know that it will heal. They know where happiness lies, not in a cave or a country, but in love and the freedom to give and take what has been there all along.

Ruth remembers this as she writes a story. It is for her grandmother, for herself, for the little girl who became her mother.

The Hundred Secret Senses

"Tan is a wonderful storyteller."
—*USA Today*

"Tan has produced a novel wonderfully like a hologram: Turn it this way and find Chinese Americans shopping and arguing in San Francisco; turn it that way and the Chinese in Chagmian Village in 1864 are fleeing into the hills to hide from the rampaging Manchus."
—*Newsweek*

"No one will deny the pleasure of Tan's seductive prose and the skill with which she unfolds the many-layered narrative."
—*Publishers Weekly* (starred review)

Published by Ballantine Books.
Available at bookstores everywhere.

The Joy Luck Club

"Beautifully written. . .A jewel of a book."
—*The New York Times Book Review*

"Vivid. . .Wondrous. . .What it is to be American, and a woman, mother, daughter, lover, wife, sister, and friend—these are the troubling, loving alliances and affiliations that Tan molds into the sixteen intricate interlocking stories that constitute this remarkable first novel."
—*San Francisco Chronicle*

"Intensely poetic, startlingly imaginative and moving, this remarkable book will speak to many women, mothers and grown daughters, about the persistent tensions and powerful bonds between generations and cultures. . . .Tan's first novel is a major achievement."
—*Publishers Weekly*

Published by Ballantine Books.
Available at bookstores everywhere.

The Kitchen God's Wife

"Remarkable. . .Mesmerizing. . .compelling. . .
An entire world unfolds in a Tolstoyan tide of
event and details. . .Give yourself over to
the world Ms. Tan creates for you."
—*The New York Times Book Review*

"An absorbing narrative of Winnie Louie's life,
which she tells—or offers—as a gift to her
daughter Pearl. Much happens in the telling:
Long-held secrets are revealed, and a family's
myths are transferred ceremoniously to the
next generation. . . .Tan returns to the richly
textured world of California's immigrant
Chinese. . .with its brilliant tapestry of characters and conflicts here and overseas. . . .She is a
wonderful writer with a rare power to
touch the heart."
—*Newsweek*

Published by Ballantine Books.
Available at bookstores everywhere.

The Spanish Press
1470 • 1966

The Spanish Press

1470 · 1966

PRINT, POWER, AND POLITICS

HENRY F. SCHULTE

UNIVERSITY OF ILLINOIS PRESS   URBANA, CHICAGO, LONDON   1968

To Irene and Emilio

Preface and Postscript

The word "press" is used in this work in the traditional sense, to indicate the Fourth Estate, or, as the Spanish say, *el cuarto poder*. It embraces that sphere of human activity which involves editing and producing periodicals, and reporting or writing for them, and includes the periodicals themselves. That it is so used in an age when the representatives of radio and television are included among "the gentlemen of the press" does not indicate that the role of the electronic media is unimportant. One would be ill-informed to minimize their impact, yet one can argue that in the Spain of 1966 neither radio nor television had the social or political impact it has in more audio- and video-oriented countries. This book deals with Spain's periodical press, primarily newspapers, for two reasons: because, in the political sense, they are the key medium of mass communications; and because, unlike the other media, they carry the burden of history. The omission of analysis or criticism of Spanish radio and television, therefore, is not an oversight. Perhaps the next time around they will have come of age and will cry out for inclusion in a work on the Spanish press. More likely, they will merit their own study.

Even before finishing this book, a few months ago, I sent up a few "trial balloons" in the form of a short magazine article and some lengthy letters to friends, Spaniards and Americans who know Spain at least as well as I do. The reactions have varied—depending on the individual's attitude toward this country and the Franco regime—from laudatory to abusive. These passionate extremes of feeling are something with which I am familiar. During more than six years as a correspondent headquartered in Madrid and responsible for the news from Spain and its possessions, I found myself accused, on occasion, of being "tendentious," a favorite term for describing a reporter whose dispatches do not find favor with the government; described as a "communist," a label applied not to followers of the Marxist-Leninist doctrine but rather to anyone considered to be in opposition to the regime; and called a "damned nuisance." When I returned to the United States and expressed exactly the same ideas in conversations with friends and colleagues, I was often characterized as "pro-Franco" and an "authoritarian." There seems to be no middle ground when considering Spain and, though I painstakingly sought it in the chapters that follow, there will be some who deny that the attempt was successful. *¡Es la vida!*

The events with which this book deals carry through to the end of 1966. They tell the story I intended to tell. However, the newsman's instinct is strong, and I am going to take advantage of this preface to update briefly my material, to write a "new lead" as it were, which is why this is both preface and postscript.

A few days ago I strolled around the arcaded Plaza Mayor of Salamanca, that Castilian city famed since the thirteenth century for its university. My companion was a professor at the university, a gentleman and scholar, and a political liberal. Though spring should have been advanced, gray clouds hid the sky, as they had for days, and shut out the warmth of the sun. We jammed our hands into our coat pockets, hunched slightly against the chill, and talked of Spain and, naturally for me, of its press. Briefly—I somehow managed to do it in one turn around the plaza—I tried to sum up the conclusions I had reached in this book. It was a dangerous thing to do, for conclusions without the evidence upon which they are based are infirm things in an argument. When I had finished, or perhaps had only paused to collect my thoughts, my companion reacted with one word, *"ingenuo,"* which means "simpleton."

"Things are worse now than ever before," he said. "There is less press freedom than during the years you worked here.

"Before, there was censorship and a newspaper knew what it could print and what it could not print. The worst that could happen would be to have the censors order the deletion of a few paragraphs before the paper was printed. Today, there is no censorship, yet the government, if it is displeased with something, can confiscate the total press run of a paper, thousands of copies. Yes, things are worse."

He ticked off a list of official acts against the press, all of which had taken place within the past year, after a new and presumably much more liberal press law had come into being. His list included: the confiscation of one issue of the Madrid newspaper *ABC* because it had published a pro-monarchist editorial; the seizure, on three occasions, of the magazine *Juventud Obrera*; the official dismissal of the editorial staff of another magazine, *Signo*; the beating of an American wire service correspondent by police; the ouster of the correspondent for the French newspaper, *Le Figaro*; and the detention of two American network reporters who were covering student riots early in the year in Barcelona.

We paused, pushed our way into a café, and found some warmth in coffee. He sipped and then resumed, mentioning a recent editorial in a regional newspaper which had spoken of the danger of the "silence of fear" and the "threat of conformity" which might come to dominate the nation's press—fear and conformity induced by the government.

I countered by asking him if the newspaper would have been permitted to publish such an editorial five or six years ago. "No, it would not have," he admitted.

"Things are looking up, then," I said.

"No, they are not! A short time ago, some colleagues and I signed a petition and carried it to our newspaper here. Do you think the newspaper would publish it? No, it would not. There is no freedom." He shrugged.

Did he and his colleagues expect the newspaper to print the petition, which was, it turned out, a protest against the provincial authorities?

"We hoped it would."

"Would you have had any such hope five years ago?" I asked.

"No, none whatsoever."

"Then aren't things better than they were? At least the possibility of publication existed. That is better somehow, isn't it, than no possibility at all?"

"Perhaps there is a very slight improvement," he conceded.

It would have been possible to help him in his argument, for I had in my pocket a copy of a proposed revision in the nation's penal codes which could mean trouble for the press. I did not bring it up then.

The proposed law, already approved by a parliamentary committee, provided for fines of from 5,000 ($83) to 50,000 *pesetas* ($834) for journalistic acts that

violate the limits imposed by the laws on freedom of expression and the right of diffusion of information through the publication of false news stories or of information dangerous to that which is moral or to good customs; [or] is contrary to the demands of national defense, the security of the state and the maintenance of internal public order or external peace; or which attacks the principles of the national movement or the fundamental laws, lacks respect owing to institutions or individuals when criticizing political or administrative actions, or endangers the independence of the courts.

When, in the judgment of the courts, the acts have obvious gravity, the applicable penalty will be imprisonment and a fine of from 10,000 to 100,000 pesetas.[1]

Despite the threat inherent in such a law, there was still cause for some optimism, as the newspaper *ABC*—mentioned by my friend and which appears in the pages of this book—had pointed out on April 9, the first anniversary of the new press law. "The balance sheet for this year," an *ABC* editorial said, "which has bright and dark spots, is [on the whole] very estimable. In addition, it gives us an ample credit of hope. The press law inaugurated a road which is, by its very nature, evolutionary and capable of being perfected in the future." [2]

On that note of hope, however vague, this preface and postscript could end. However, there is one more explanation to be made. The Spanish language, like all living languages, changes over time. In the recording of the titles of Spanish publications, old and new, I have attempted to follow precisely the original. Thus one will encounter the word *muger*, a now out-of-date spelling of *mujer*, the use of *buelta* for *vuelta*, and many other orthographic oddities. They are there, not because of editorial oversight, but because the men of the time so wrote them. The word for "gazette," which appears here as both *gazeta* and *gaceta*, caused some concern to the editors. *Gazeta* is a direct borrowing from the Italian where it originated. Since in Spanish *c* and *z* are pronounced the same when they appear before *e*, the difference in spelling would make no

[1] *Código Penal, Artículo 165-bis.*
[2] *ABC* (Madrid), April 9, 1967, p. 60.

difference in pronunciation. Both forms of the word were used until the Spanish Academy ruled in favor of *gaceta*. Both forms appear in this book because both have appeared on the mastheads of newspapers.

In conclusion, let me say that no volume could be long enough for me to record my debt to those individuals who have contributed in some way to this book. It would not have been written without them and, depending upon who they were, their assistance, insistence, or resistance.

MADRID AND SALAMANACA
Spring, 1967

Contents

 Newsman's View

On April 9, 1966, a professional soldier from Galicia in northern Spain signed his name to a series of documents which officially launched the Spanish press on what can be described only as an experiment in liberalization. The soldier was Francisco Franco Bahamonde, an infantry officer from an obscure, middle-class Spanish family, then in his thirtieth year as dictator of the nation. The documents constituted a complex body of laws regulating the nation's press and replacing an earlier law drawn up in 1938 during the Spanish Civil War and unamended despite twenty-seven years of domestic peace.

The new Press and Print Law (*Ley de Prensa e Imprenta*) was accepted, if not hailed, by the nation's newsmen, whose representatives had helped forge its articles. It was accepted because it represented, for the nation's newspapers, a step toward self-management. That it was not hailed was due to the fact that it left powers of control and punishment in the hands of the government. Some officials, aware of the law's shortcomings in terms of press freedom, saw it not as the final word but rather as one carefully considered step in the direction of a free and responsible press. Those men whose advocacy had made the law possible considered the powers it delegated to them less as controls abridging freedom of the press than as instruments insuring the press's responsible functioning in a nation suffering the throes of great economic and social changes and nearing the day when Franco's death or retirement would inevitably bring about changes in the national political structure.

Reaction on a political level was different. Those of liberal persuasion viewed the new law with distaste, objecting to the restraints on news media activities and the controls retained by the government. Conservatives condemned it, arguing that the elimination of prepublication censorship would endanger the sometimes precarious peace that had existed since the Civil War ended in 1939, for traditionally periods of press freedom had coincided with periods of general unrest. Liberals would have "gone all the way," creating a press free from any restraints other than those imposed by libel and morality. Theirs was a dream dating back to the first decade of the nineteenth century. The conservatives, whose rearguard action had delayed by months and years the law's metamorphosis from ideas into concrete rules, would have blocked its passage entirely. They represented a nearly 500-year-old tradition, which had dominated Spain until the early 1960's.

The two conflicting positions were firmly ingrained, and both tended toward extremism. In fact, they were so much a part of the fabric of Spanish history that the nation's press has been likened to a pendulum swinging at irregular intervals between oppressive government controls and liberty quickly distorted into license and gross irresponsibility. "Sometimes," it has been said, "there has been free expression to the point of anarchy: at other times, previous censorship to the point of a padlock on the mouth." [1]

This is the history of that pendulum—of the oscillations between strict controls, rigorously applied, and libertine freedom—and of the efforts which culminated in early 1966 in the new press laws, an attempt to bring it to permanent rest at a point between the two extremes.

The Spanish press, that is, the nation's periodicals, particularly its newspapers, has suffered no indignities unknown to the presses of other lands, but it has suffered them more often. It has been guilty of no acts of irresponsibility greater than those committed by its counterparts elsewhere, but perhaps it has committed more, and in an environment more susceptible to influence by irresponsi-

---

[1] Juan Beneyto, *Ordenamiento Jurídico de la Información* (Madrid, 1961), p. 18. William C. Atkinson notes that such polarity has marked the political history of the past century and a half, the nation alternating between the extremes of "anarchy" and "hierarchy." See *A History of Spain and Portugal* (London, 1960), p. 12.

bility. Its pattern of growth has been unusual, for it has as yet not reached the even limited maturity elsewhere associated with the press. The 1966 attempt to achieve an equilibrium is unique—an experiment in a government-directed movement toward responsible freedom.

The art of printing, which fathered the periodical press, was introduced into Spain two decades before Columbus sailed forth on his first voyage of discovery. At first it was welcomed as a means of spreading knowledge, but the welcome quickly degenerated into distrust as its potential as a political and religious instrument became apparent. Controls were quickly imposed, first by the government and then by the Inquisition, the agent of the Catholic church. During the five centuries following, the role of the press was largely defined in terms of controls and regulations, and no tradition of freedom was delineated. Its history is dotted with intrigue and subversion, self-seeking and polemics, and is populated by cynics, hypocrites, manipulators, denouncers, praisers, and, occasionally, visionaries. Its language has been that of royalty, philosophers, scholars, statesmen, political infighters, and literate guttersnipes. Its role has been that of public mouthpiece for the nation's rulers or political podium for narrow, partisan interests. It has been the weapon of those grasping for power and a tool for consolidating power once it was gained. Its history, so far as it has been revealed, reached a "moment of truth," to borrow from the language of the Spanish bullring, in April, 1966, when Generalísimo Franco signed the *Ley de Prensa e Imprenta.*

If the men who framed the new law and maneuvered it past the obstacles of traditional conservatism are correct, and the law is revealed by time to be a step toward complete freedom of the press from government controls, then the pattern of history will have been reversed, for if one traces the development of the press in Spain, and of its interaction with other parts of the political-social order, a definite pattern does emerge. Four factors are interwoven in that pattern and dominate it.

1. Authoritarianism—government controls, direction, regulation—has been the mainstream of Spanish policy in dealing with the press.

2. The social, political, and economic consequence of the intermittent swings to freedom of the press have reinforced the arguments upon which the authoritarian philosophy is based.

3. The press, regardless of the temper of the times, has been used as a political instrument—either by those in power or by those desiring power—and not as a social instrument: that is, it has been used either to reinforce the status quo or to reshape the status quo in accordance with the desires of self-interested individuals or minority groups.

4. The practice of journalism has been considered, historically, not as a goal in itself but rather as a stepping-stone to other careers, generally within the official hierarchy.

The very fact that many Spaniards assume that the press can be channeled toward freedom by the government, however paternal it may be, suggests continued faith in the efficacy of authoritarianism.[2] It represents an unusual ambivalence, the conflict between intellectual commitment to some of the ideals of press freedom and an almost conditioned authoritarian response when faced with any of the problems created by press freedom. Such an ambivalence was especially apparent during the four years immediately preceding the signing by Franco of the 1966 law.

For the sake of convenience, one could suggest that the law began its journey toward reality in 1962 with Franco's appointment of Manuel Fraga Iribarne to the post of Minister of Information and Tourism. Yet such a suggestion is fraught with danger, for the law gained momentum over time—it was a product of the total history of the Spanish press—rather than impulse at any moment in time. It can be said that during the summer months a bullfight in Madrid begins at six P.M., yet generations of breeding went into the production of the bulls, thousands of hours of practice into the development of the bullfighters' skills, and centuries of cultural patterning into a heritage which considers the bullfight as the "national fiesta." It is only in that sense that one can date the press law from Fraga's

---

[2] In other societies, grounded in different historical traditions, government controls and press freedom are held to be antithetical. For example, compare the First Amendment of the Constitution of the United States which says, "Congress shall make no law . . . abridging the freedom of speech, or of the press . . . ." with the second article of the *Ley de Prensa e Imprenta* which states that freedom of expression in Spain "shall have no limits other than those imposed by considerations of morality and truth; respect for existing public and constitutional order; the demands of national defense, of the security of the State and of internal and external public peace; the reserve owing to the actions of the government, of the Cortes, and of the administration; the independence of the tribunals in the application of the laws; and the safeguarding of private affairs and honor."

appointment. There is a second danger inherent in suggesting that the law had its inception in the appointment. It is the implication that the individual is somehow solely responsible for the law, that he deserves all the credit or responsibility. Such is not the case, for Fraga, though ambitious to be instrumental in changing and guiding Spain and the possessor of a superb background in the theoretical and technical problems of the press, arrived on the scene long after the first demands for a new press law had been made. From 1938 until Fraga's appointment, the national press had been governed by wartime regulations, created during a period of emergency and designed to cope with the problems of military conflict. By the time Fraga took over, there was widespread agreement in Spain that the 1938 law was not only outdated but also positively damaging to the nation. Though there was political and social unrest, which manifested itself in strikes and demonstrations, there was no danger of armed upheaval. A creaky, antiquated economy was being modernized. Though poverty continued to be endemic, wealth was pouring into the country from abroad. In the large metropolitan areas and Spain's magnificent tourist areas, there was every evidence of prosperity—traffic jams, hotels that could not accept reservations because no space was available, long lines outside cinema box offices, and "sold out" signs on bullrings and theaters. The basis for a solid internal stability built on a burgeoning middle class was being laid.

Meanwhile, a growing internationalization—which dated from 1953 when Spain and the United States signed a joint defense pact and which had been fostered by Spain's growing participation in international affairs and nourished by increasing tourism, diminishing illiteracy, and mounting prosperity—cast the wartime press controls in a bad light, both at home and abroad. The image of the police state carried into the country by a visitor did not jibe with the sight of an apparently content people crowding into restaurants and cafés, drinking in comfortable moderation, jamming soccer and bullfight stadiums, downing shrimp in seafood bars, promenading the streets at dusk, filling the air with animated conversation, and even criticizing the government with no apparent fear of reprisal from "big brother." The freedom from political fear, at least for the nonmilitant anti-Francoist, was evident in a joke making the rounds of the cafés—a joke which began with a tourist asking a Spanish friend, as had thousands of visitors over the years, "Confidentially, just what do you think of Franco?" The Spaniard glanced around the crowded bar in which they were sipping a pre-dinner drink and, obviously unwilling to express himself within hearing distance of so many unknown ears, asked the visitor to follow him outside. Once on the street, crowded with evening strollers, the foreigner repeated his question: "What do you think of Franco?" Again the Spaniard glanced around and, finding himself closed in by the stream of humanity moving up and down the avenue, guided his friend to the Retiro, the sprawling park in Madrid's center. He led the way to an open glen where the two were absolutely alone. "What do you think of Franco?" the question came again. The Spaniard looked around one final time to insure that no one could hear, leaned toward his questioner, and whispered, "I like him."

The average Spaniard could joke, grumble, or complain, but not the press. There was always censorship, heavy-handed, evident to anyone who read Spanish newspapers, and worth at least a mention in stories filed by foreign newsmen. In the Spain of the 1960's, a nation more and more conscious of its international image, censorship muddied some otherwise glowing colors and tarnished the general glow. As Dionysio Ridruejo, a poet, political commentator, and onetime staunch supporter of Franco who had turned against the regime in the 1950's, saw it, "The present government can no longer exert the control it once did over communications . . . [for the government] depends in large measure upon the good will of international opinion." [3]

But the issue of the image was not the sole factor working for the new press laws. More than twenty years of controls had seen a new generation of journalists move into key positions and staff the lower echelons of the news business—a generation to which the bitterness of the Civil War was merely history and which wanted more freedom, not to involve itself in politics, but to accept the challenge of responsibility and try out its wings in the decision-making arena. The members of that generation argued—among themselves, in discussions with foreigners, and before the massive desks of the Ministry of Information officials—that the press had matured and could better perform its functions, within the framework of the socioeconomic structure, if it operated in a freer atmosphere. They argued also that the Spanish people, who were expected to function in a highly complex society which was under-

[3] "Spain's Restless Voices," *Catholic World*, no. 197 (May, 1963), p. 91.

going drastic changes, deserved to be better informed. They asked not for unlimited freedom of the press but for greater mobility within well-defined boundaries. The newspaper *ABC*, for example, called for press "liberty within a framework of order," and asked for a new press law which would "return to the periodicals all their authority, but also all their responsibility." [4]

These arguments found their counterparts in the chambers of government, albeit counterparts which tended to touch the problem of relaxation of controls rather gingerly. Spanish officialdom admitted that there was a social need for better and broader information to be disseminated by the mass media. "Information and communication today constitute basic fundamentals of society," a publication of the Falange, the nation's only legal political organization, declared. "Dependent upon their adequate ordering and efficient exercise are, in the first place, the preparation of citizens so that they can play incisive roles in the affairs that concern them, and, in the second place, the very existence of a fundamental democratic order." [5] But it was not a simple matter: the mere elimination of controls might not achieve the desired goals. A high official of the Ministry of Information summed it up thus: " . . . the right of contemporary man to be well-informed is not guaranteed by the simple opening up of the new informational possibilities, just as the right to work is not guaranteed by pure faith in the dynamics of economic growth. The right to be informed demands adequate juridical structures and, to prepare them, a clear awareness of the permissible and of that which is not allowable, of the instrumental and the fundamental." [6] Professor Juan Beneyto, a former Director-General of the Press and an expert on press law, added a footnote indicating the complexities when he wrote: "Obvious changes [in the whole sociopolitical structure] make it necessary to remove the press from traditional regulations and submit it to those norms which are based on a new reality." [7]

The "old reality," at least so far as the press was concerned, had involved two factors—the 1938 Press Law and Gabriel Arias Sal-

---

[4] "La píldora endulzada," *ABC* (Madrid), quoted by Manuel Fraga Iribarne in *Horizonte Español* (Madrid, 1965), p. 225.
[5] Delegación Nacional de Prensa, Propaganda y Radio del Movimiento, *Nuevo Horizonte de la Información* (Madrid, 1962), p. 13.
[6] Gabriel Eloriaga, *Información y Política* (Madrid, 1964), p. 25.
[7] *Ordenamiento Jurídico*, p. 8.

gado, Minister of Information and Tourism, who had been charged with the direction of the press from 1941 to mid-1962. Arias Salgado, an advocate of the most rigid government controls, ruled the press with an iron hand in the belief that it was a public service like the post office or, in Spain, the national railways. Arias Salgado's attitude, his absolute hewing to the authoritarian tradition, without doubt reflected personal orientation. But it also represented the prevailing climate of opinion. The 1938 Press Law had stated: "The existence of a fourth estate cannot be tolerated. It is inadmissible that the press can exist outside the State. The evils that spring from 'freedom of the democratic kind' must be avoided. . . . The press should always serve the national interests; it should be a national institution, a public enterprise in the service of the State." [8] There was nothing positive in the way Arias Salgado defined the press's role as a "national institution." He used his powers, first as director of "Press and Propaganda" for the Falange, when the party was charged with press direction, and later as Minister of Information, when the Ministry was established, to muzzle the press, stifle initiative and independence, and use the media of mass communications as vehicles for the clumsiest propaganda.

As Minister of Information, Arias Salgado treated the Spanish press with scorn and contempt and the foreign press with condescension and distrust. Any foreign newsman who had prolonged contact with the Spanish government during the 1940's and 1950's was exposed to that distrust.[9] It was certainly apparent when this writer paid a courtesy call on Arias Salgado. The writer, just named United Press bureau chief in Madrid, assured the Minister that U.P. coverage out of Spain would always toe the line of "truth." That comment, surely naive in the view of the Minister, elicited the resigned expression of a schoolmaster dealing with an unruly, backward pupil. "There are many ways of telling the truth," Arias Salgado replied wearily. Unstated, but implicit in the Minister's attitude during the meeting, was the assumption that the "truth" would inevitably be anti-Franco, anti-regime, and anti-Spain. Admittedly there was some basis for that assumption, but the fault

---

[8] Quoted by the International Commission of Jurists, *Spain and the Rule of Law* (Geneva, 1962), p. 48.
[9] Charles Foltz, Jr., an Associated Press correspondent in Spain during World War II, has reported his experiences in *The Masquerade in Spain* (Boston, 1948).

lay more with the Spanish government than with the foreign correspondents, resident and visiting. Though it was officially the Ministry of Information, it was nicknamed the "Ministry of Non-Information." One could and would dutifully call to ask something. There were three categories of response: a blunt "no comment," a condescending "but you're really not interested in that," or a promise to find out and call back the initiator of the query, a promise rarely kept. Foreign newsmen were even excluded from the regular press briefing held after each meeting of Franco's cabinet. As a result, newsmen who needed information or opinion quickly learned to seek it from members of the nation's loosely knit anti-Franco opposition, always willing to cooperate when a chance to break into print abroad presented itself. One made the "rounds," one took visiting reporters on the "rounds," and the mere mention of "making the rounds" conjured up visions of a well-defined series of visits to members of the opposition including Dionysio Ridruejo, once known as "The Poet of the Falange" and therefore a supporter of the regime, whose political philosophy had diverged from that prevailing in the government, and Joaquín Satrústegui, a member of a wealthy and powerful family, who headed a nebulous political group called the Unión Española (Spanish Union) and spouted a startling mixture of monarchist, democratic, and socialist doctrines.

Franco himself was one of the very few constructive official sources for the foreign newsman, but, while he was perhaps more available than many chiefs of state, he was not the type of source contacted during the run-of-the-mill, daily business of carrying out a news-gathering operation. Whether Franco's relative accessibility was due to a more enlightened view of the press than that held by his Minister of Information is a moot question. It may have been no more than the end product of a totalitarian system in which all underlings refused to deal with the press for fear of reprisals from above, which left, obviously, only one man not subject to such fear. There is little evidence to indicate that Franco gave much thought to the problems and potential of the media of mass communications. Yet he was aware that, at least at times, the national interest could be served best by an informed people. Such was the case on Christmas Eve in 1961 when one barrel of Franco's English-made shotgun exploded during an informal hunt on the grounds of his residence near Madrid. Only Franco's left hand was injured, but rumors began to spread through the capital that he had been killed. Even before doctors finished treating the damaged member, Franco had personally issued orders that a detailed report on the accident be broadcast nationally. It is possible that his prompt action forestalled an attempt by the Falange to take over national control in the presumed vacuum left by his death. Franco's direct intervention in the area of news dissemination was the exception rather than the rule, however. Normally, the texts of his own speeches and other public pronouncements were subjected to special censorship before being released to the press.

The extent to which the subjugation of the press between 1941 and 1962 represented the will of Franco is also open to question. Evidence suggests that he gave Arias Salgado a blank check to run things as he saw fit. Had there been any disagreement over Arias Salgado's handling of press affairs, Franco could have named a new Minister of Information, just as he replaced all other members of his cabinet at one time or another. It is most likely that Franco was satisfied with the role Arias Salgado played as Minister, at least until the very late 1950's and early 1960's. To Franco, a professional soldier and a product of a tradition in which press freedom was usually equated with disorder and unrest, a rigidly controlled press must have seemed logical. There is no evidence to suggest, during the first two decades of his rule, that Franco ever considered that the role of the press might be constructive, if he ever considered it at all.

But the very fact that, in 1962, Franco ousted Arias Salgado, not only a trusted aide but also a close family friend, does suggest that the *Caudillo*'s ("Leader's") position was being modified. By that time, Franco had come a long way.

He was born in Galicia, on Spain's verdant Atlantic Coast, in 1893, the second son of a naval officer. One brother, Ramón, achieved fame as the pilot of the first plane to fly from Europe to South America; another, Nicolás, had a successful career as a businessman and diplomat. In 1907, Franco entered Spain's infantry academy in Toledo and, five years later, was assigned to active duty in Morocco, at that time the scene of fighting between Moroccans and the Spanish and French armies. In 1920, he helped organize the Spanish Foreign Legion, with which he served until the end of the desert war. He was appointed a brigadier general at the age of thirty-three. When the monarchy fell in 1931, he was commandant of a military academy in Saragossa. Despite apparently loyal service to the Republic that followed the monarchy, Franco came under suspicion and was sent off to the Canary Islands, where he served as captain-general. In 1936, as the Republic gradually disintegrated and upheaval spread, he joined the forces plotting a coup d'état. However, changing circumstances forced the plotters to switch to open military uprising. In a dramatic flight aboard a chartered plane piloted by an English adventurer, Franco was flown to Morocco where he assumed command of troops stationed there.

The death of two officers above him in the official hierarchy— one in a plane crash, the other executed after capture by Republican forces—vaulted him into the role of leader of the Nationalist forces. Late in the year, he was named chief of state as well as supreme military commander, the dual roles he has kept since.

During the early years of his rule, he was described as "the world's greatest sixteenth-century politician," as much a criticism of the system that produced him as of the man himself. However, by the mid-1950's he began to show signs of flexibility as Spain moved away from isolation and toward close cooperation with the United States and other nations of the Western bloc. He appeared less often in the decoration-bedecked uniforms that had earned him the not altogether flattering nickname *Paco de las Medallas* ("Frankie of the Medals"), switching to double-breasted business suits, designed to hide a growing paunch. He replaced pictures of other dictators and military leaders, which lined the table behind his desk, with photographs of civilians, including United States President Eisenhower. In 1957 and 1958, he slowly converted the Falange, until then one of the basic supports of his regime, from an elite, jackbooted, pistol-carrying, quasi-military organization into the all-embracing social action group it is today. He revamped his cabinet to include economic and trade experts who moved the nation through a period of crisis toward prosperity and growth. During all that time, he continued to function as doting father, then grandfather; devout Catholic; and enthusiastic hunter and fisherman, equally at home in a trout stream or behind the harpoon on a whaling vessel. The image of the fascist dictator of the 1940's was changing, being replaced by that of the progressive, moderate head of state. But the image and methods of his Minister of Information were not keeping pace with the times. And neither was the press.

CHAPTER TWO

ℭhe Franco Years:

The Padlocked Mouth

Viewed from the perspective of the mid-1960's, four dates loom as important in the history of the Spanish press. The first is 1470, when printing with movable type was introduced into Spain. The second is 1502, the year in which Ferdinand and Isabella put into effect the first law regulating the product of the press and the import of printed matter. The third is 1810, when, for the first time, the concept of freedom of the press was incorporated into the legal fabric of the nation. The fourth is 1938, the year from which the press of the Franco years may be said to date.

By spring of that year, the Nationalist forces, those commanded by Franco and aided by the Nazi military might of Adolf Hitler's Germany and Italian troops from the Fascist Italy of Benito Mussolini, were beginning to scent victory in the Spanish Civil War. The Republican forces, which counted on the support of Communist Russia, were falling more and more into defensive positions. In March, Franco began a long-planned offensive, striking first north and then south in the area west of Barcelona, between Lérida and the sea. His attacks cut in two the territory then held by the Republic and, for a moment, it appeared that he held victory in his grasp.

With the successful end of the war looming on the horizon, the wartime government headed by Franco, which was meeting in the ancient cathedral city of Burgos, turned its attention to the future —outlining the sociopolitical organization of postwar Spain, the "new Spain." The press came under consideration immediately. "One of the old concepts," the government decided, "which the new Spain has most urgently to revise is that of the press." [1] On April 22, Franco decreed into existence a new press law which had been hammered out by the Council of Ministers (Cabinet) under the direction of Ramón Serrano Suñer, Franco's brother-in-law and then Minister of the Interior.[2] The new law described itself as designed "to awaken in the press the idea of service to the State and to return to the men who live from the press the dignity which is merited by anyone who dedicates himself to such a profession." [3] It delegated to the State, and specifically to the Ministry of the Interior (Ministerio de Gobernación), "the organization, supervision, and control of the national institution of the periodic press." [4] The government was given the right of:

1. Regulating the number and size of periodical publications.
2. Participating in the designation of directive personnel.
3. Ordering the journalistic profession.
4. Supervising press activity.
5. Censoring all publications.[5]

The concept of the "responsible editor," dating from the previous century, was resurrected. In essence, it made a periodical's director the legal scapegoat in case of any real or fancied transgressions on the part of any member of the periodical's staff. "The director," the law said, "who must be enrolled in the National Registry of Journalists . . . and who must be approved for the post by the Minister, is responsible for the whole newspaper."[6] In addition, the company running the periodical was given "broad responsibility for the performance, whether by commission or omission, of the director."[7] The Ministry was delegated the power to punish all writings which, "directly, or indirectly, may tend to reduce the prestige of the Nation or Regime, to obstruct the work of the government of the new State, or sow pernicious ideas among the intel-

[1] *Ley de Prensa de 22 de abril de 1938, Preámbulo.*
[2] Suñer, who served as Spanish Foreign Minister during part of World War II, is best remembered for his staunch support of the Axis cause, a sympathy that died hard for him. This writer called on Suñer in the late 1950's and was amused to find a signed photograph of Mussolini displayed prominently on Suñer's desk.
[3] *Ley de Prensa de 22 de abril de 1938, Preámbulo.*
[4] *Ibid., Artículo 1.*   [5] *Ibid., Artículo 3.*
[6] *Ibid., Artículo 8.*   [7] *Ibid., Artículo 9.*

lectually weak." Such powers were in addition to those granted to punish acts defined as illegal by criminal codes.[8] Futhermore, the Ministry was authorized to act against the offenses of disobedience, passive resistance, and, in general, deviation from the norms laid down by the competent authorities in press matters.[9] Punishment could consist of a fine, the removal of the director of the periodical from his post, his removal and official ouster from the profession, or the confiscation of the periodical, depending upon the gravity of the deed.[10]

The law represented no more than a swing of the pendulum to which the press has been likened. The voices of the Republic, as we shall see in a later chapter, had practiced controls but preached press freedom. The "new Spain" minced no words about controls. The press would serve the interests of the state; the state had the power to insure that. A more liberal approach had been tried and, in the eyes of the nation's new rulers, had been found wanting. It was not the first, nor the second, nor the third time that a new regime had initiated its span of life by spelling out the press's role in terms of stringent controls and narrow limitations. That was already part of the Spanish tradition.

The Nationalist forces had rebelled against the Second Republic which, the Nationalists claimed, had led the nation to the brink of chaos. The Republic and its attempts at liberal constitutional rule had ended in failure, as had earlier similar attempts, and had come close to spelling disaster for the country—disaster from which Spain had been rescued by the Civil War, according to the Nationalist position. The idea of a press freed in theory, if not in practice, had been too closely associated with the power structure of the Republic to escape being tarred by the same brush. And, according to the nation's new rulers, it did not deserve to escape, for the press had done more than merely record in its news columns the "chaos" of constitutional rule: it had contributed to that chaos.

One thing must be made clear. Though the Nationalists spoke of "national revolution," and intimated that major changes were in the offing, their revolt was one of reaction, reimposing authoritarianism and arresting any modifications in the socioeconomic structure that might have grown out of the Republic if there had

---

[8] *Ibid., Artículo 18.*
[9] *Ibid., Artículo 19.*
[10] *Ibid., Artículo 20.*

been any consensus and stability. The revolt led by Franco did not herald a period of social change but rather a period of stability—"twenty-five years of peace," in the words of the slogan coiners of 1964.

Franco's rise to power followed a precise, well-defined course. Hans Gerth and C. Wright Mills, for example, could have been describing Spain and Franco when they wrote:

Modern dictators are revolutionary usurpers, usually going against a center which is faction-ridden. Their usurpation is usually preceded by a condition in which there is a plurality of pressure groups and parties, and no chance to establish a stable government. [An apt description of the Republic.] The individual experiences fully his inability to meet the public crises which intensify his anxieties. He longs for a center of management. Nobody seems to do anything, although everybody is busy. Both the right and the left may unite against the middle, but they cannot form a stable government. So, the dictator—the conspicuous man thrown up by the crisis and eager to assume emergency powers and responsibility for all public affairs—arises on the basis of a party and establishes a one-party rule.[11]

On March 29, 1939, the final remnants of the Republican army, the forces occupying the city of Madrid, surrendered, ending a prolonged siege. The Spanish Civil War, a three-year ordeal of blood, was over, but the hate would linger, as would the scars of battle. Among the battle-scarred were the newspapers of Madrid. Two of the city's most famous newspapers—*El Sol*,[12] which had numbered among its contributors and editors some of the great names of Spanish arts and letters, and *El Heraldo* [13]—had died during the war. *El Sol*'s physical plant had already been turned over to *Arriba*,[14] a Falangist organ founded in 1935 and suspended by the Republic a year later. *El Heraldo*'s offices and presses would soon become the property of *Madrid*.[15]

Arriba put out its first postwar edition on March 29, the day of the surrender. Three other newspapers resumed operations within the next hours. They were *ABC*,[16] *Ya*,[17] and *Informaciones*,[18] which were able, on April 1, to join in welcoming the troops of

---

[11] *Character and Social Structure* (New York, 1953), p. 212.
[12] *El Sol* ("The Sun") (Madrid, 1916-37).
[13] *El Heraldo* ("The Herald") (Madrid, 1890-1936).
[14] *Arriba* ("Hurrah") (Madrid, 1935-36, 1939–in operation).
[15] *Madrid* (Madrid, 1939–in operation).
[16] *ABC* (Madrid, 1930–in operation).
[17] *Ya* ("Now" or "Already") (Madrid, 1935–in operation).
[18] *Informaciones* ("Information") (Madrid, 1922–in operation).

Generalísimo Franco as they made their triumphal entry into the city, where life began to return to normal along the avenues and in the shadows of bullet-pocked buildings. The newspapers found space among their glowing reports of the Nationalist victory, their praise of Franco, and their bitter condemnation of the Republicans, to announce that cafés and bars, closed during the final days of the siege of Madrid, would reopen the following day, Sunday, and would serve, among other things, "coffee made from real coffee" rather than the ersatz product available during the siege.

ABC, which had been published by the Republicans during the war, was back under the direction of Juan Ignacio Luca de Tena, a member of the paper's founding family. *Informaciones* struggled onto the streets from a temporary printing plant, its own building a war casualty. During that year, 1939, eighty-four dailies were published in Spain.[19] Some had gone through the war unscathed; some had been operated by the opposing military forces; others merely reappeared after varying periods of suppression or voluntary hiatuses. Still others had been born, either naturally or by political cesarian sections, during the war; namely, the twenty-eight Falangist organs founded since 1935. In addition, there was a "vast purge of journalists: a large number of them were arrested and about forty were condemned to death."[20]

There are two views of what the Nationalist victory meant to the press. The International Press Institute terms it "fatal to the freedom of the press."[21] The Spanish position is that only the free-wheeling political press, "the capitalist servant of reactionary clients or of marxists,"[22] had expired during the war years, its death knell sounded by the Press Law of April 22, 1938. The wartime controls represented no more than a means of imposing a period of readjustment on the press. Inherent in the Spanish argument, as we shall see, is the assumption that the role of the press has been changed by the complexities of twentieth-century life. While no one can argue with the I.P.I. appraisal, any understanding of the position of the

---

[19] In addition, there were four dailies in Spanish Africa: *Bard-es Sabah* of Tetuan, founded in 1939; *Ebano* of Santa Isabel de Fernando Póo; the prestigious *España* of Tangier; and *El Faro* of Ceuta. In subsequent years, two more were founded: *Aj-Bar* of Tetuan and *El Telegrama del Rif* of Melilla.
[20] International Press Institute, *The Press in Authoritarian Countries* (Zurich, 1959), p. 139.
[21] *Ibid.*
[22] *Ley de Prensa de 22 de abril de 1938, Preámbulo.*

press in Spain today is contingent on some comprehension of the official Spanish point of view, whether it be considered as no more than an excuse or as a sincere attempt to analyze and cope with the realities of a sociopolitical situation.

It has been argued that press controls were innovated in Spain by Franco, yet government supervision and control of the press have been woven into the thread of the nation's mass communications since the introduction of printing. The Franco government merely followed one well-traveled path, that of controls, while rejecting the other alternative, a press free of restrictions. Without becoming involved in an argument over the pros and cons of the system accepted, one can suggest that, to at least some degree, the course followed was determined by history as well as by the political and social realities of the moment and the beliefs of Franco and the men surrounding him. The press law was created in the heat of war by military men and at a time of instability. " . . . the military politicians," Spain's historian-in-exile Salvador de Madariaga suggests, "object to freedom of the press. . . . All military politicians, even those who entered politics through the Liberal gates, have revealed themselves unable to govern without the censor. Instinctively, they limit the political field to the arena of material forces, in which they feel stronger." [23] Added to that is a natural tendency to restrict the area of freedom "as stresses on the stability of the government and of the structure of society increase." [24] Philip II had turned to such restricting of the area of freedom in the sixteenth century when he found his empire and his faith threatened. So did Charles IV when he recognized the menace to absolutism inherent in the French Revolution. So, in fact, did the Republicans when they saw danger in the activity of the press. "The Spain of 1939-1949," historian Richard Pattee has written, "is not an arbitrary thing, conjured up in the mind of General Francisco Franco. It is not the creation of the civil war, for the simple reason that a large number of the more pressing difficulties of today are problems that Spain has grappled with for centuries and constitute a direct heritage from the past." [25]

One other factor may well be added to those already mentioned.

[23] *Spain: A Modern History* (New York, 1958), p. 65.
[24] Frederick S. Siebert, *Freedom of the Press in England, 1476-1776: The Rise and Decline of Government Controls* (Urbana, Ill., 1952), p. 10.
[25] *This is Spain* (Milwaukee, 1951), p. 88.

Franco and his followers emerged victorious from the Civil War, but with an international image that was dark and tarnished, an image that was to suffer even more during the post-Spanish-war period, especially during World War II. In three years of internal strife, the Spanish "black legend" (*Leyenda negra*)—a set of adverse foreign attitudes that have plagued the country across the centuries —found new fuel. The factual merits of the "legends" are not a part of the analysis of this work. The extent to which they reflect the reality of Spanish history is a matter for scholars concerned with broader aspects of the nation's history, for, in some cases, it has been the historians who generated and perpetuated the *Leyendas negras*, "especially those historians who maligned the dominant and hated Spaniards of the sixteenth century."[26] Regardless of origin, the "black legends" do exist and do structure not only the attitudes toward Spain but also Spain's attitudes toward other nations and cultures and even, perhaps, toward itself. Franco himself has expressed preoccupation with the *Leyenda negra*, which he has defined as the "distorted dissemination of any incident . . . with the exclusive end of blackening the good name of the Spanish people or of the system of government which they have given themselves." [27] Pattee has suggested that some of the present-day attitudes toward Spain and its regime are grounded in the "black legends" of the past. He writes, " . . . the present day adverse opinion regarding the regime of General Francisco Franco is no different in essence than the views held contemporaneously regarding Philip II, Charles V, or other Spanish rulers." [28]

At the end of the Civil War, the voices raised in public outside of Spain were not those of the victors, but rather those of the losers, the Republicans. At the beginning of the war, British, French, and American sympathies were with the Republicans, especially the sympathies of the intellectuals because "most Spanish intellectuals were Republicans. . . ." [29] During the war, which fired the imagination of the whole world, a great mass of literature had been turned

---

[26] Charles E. Chapman, *A History of Spain Founded on the Historia de España y de la Civilización Española of Rafael Altimira* (New York, 1922), p. 517.
[27] "Mensaje al Pueblo Español," a nationwide radio-television address originated in Madrid, Dec. 30, 1963, in *Pensamiento Político de Franco*, published by the Spanish Information Service (Madrid, 1964), p. 10.
[28] *This is Spain*, p. 17.
[29] Arthur P. Whitaker, *Spain and the Defense of the West* (New York, 1961), p. 88.

out by Republican sympathizers. The roster of writers who covered parts of the war or built works around it reads like a twentieth-century literary hall of fame: Ernest Hemingway, John Dos Passos, Upton Sinclair, André Malraux, Palmiro Togliatti, Pietro Nenni, Ilya Ehrenburg, George Orwell, Stephen Spender, W. H. Auden, Arthur Koestler, Louis Fischer, Simone Weil, C. Day Lewis, Louis MacNeice, Jacques Maritain, François Mauriac, Ludwig Renn, and Bertolt Brecht.[30]

As a result of the outpouring of material about the war and postwar mass media opposition to Franco, many Spaniards developed a "chip on the shoulder" attitude, especially when considering foreign newspapers, magazines, radio, and, later, television. There was, and is, a widespread belief, nurtured admittedly by the government, that a mass media conspiracy existed against Spain, which was "a victim . . . of distortion and falsity." [31] The war itself, according to Spaniards, had been covered abroad as if it were a "fight between the republican forces—made up of Russians, Mexicans,[32] French, and the international brigades supplied by the English—and the opposing forces, composed of millionaires, landlords, bullfight entrepreneurs, and members of groups harmonious to them."[33] The treatment the regime received in the foreign press most certainly reinforced the regime's decision to maintain its press controls, for it aroused the fear that the "sins" of the foreign press might be manifest in a free Spanish press. It was not until the 1950's that any suggestion was made to moderate the 1938 law. This treatment also colored the government's dealings with foreign newsmen. The law gave the government " 'the sole authority to organize, watch over and control the press as a national institution.' In this sense, its regulation is incumbent on the minister in charge of the 'National Press Service.' The minister appoints the editors and chief staff members

---

[30] For a discussion of this aspect of the Civil War, written from the point of view of the victors, see Rafael Calvo Serer, *La Literatura universal sobre la Guerra de España* (Madrid, 1962).

[31] *Arriba* (Madrid), Apr. 6, 1965: a front-page editorial on the use by *La Razón* of Buenos Aires of photographs taken during a taxi strike in Athens, Greece, to illustrate reports of student demonstrations in Madrid.

[32] As this was being written, Spain and Mexico had not renewed diplomatic relations, broken off as a result of the Spanish Civil War.

[33] *ABC* (Madrid), Mar. 17, 1965, p. 54: an article in which the newspaper attacked Britain's Independent Television Service for airing a program on Spanish education which *ABC* called "truly insulting to Spain" and which, it said, "defamed our authorities and falsified historical facts."

of all newspapers, he dismisses them when he so wishes." [34] Wielding such powers in dealings with the domestic press, government officials developed autocratic habits of behavior which ill-equipped them to handle foreign newsmen. The government could not tell the *New York Times, Le Monde,* the *Christian Science Monitor,* or the *Times* of London what to publish as it did *ABC, Arriba,* or *La Vanguardia.* Nor could it dictate to a foreign correspondent, especially a national of a major power. The government's authority was limited; its sole means of control, besides minor harassment, was the threat of ouster from Spain, a recourse that would involve international publicity and further tarnishing of the Spanish image. As a result, foreign newsmen were treated, in turn, with scorn, condescension, and attempts at syrupy ingratiation, though recently officials charged with press relations have developed more sophistication in their field of endeavor and tend to be much more cooperative.[35]

The press recovered slowly from the Civil War, as did Spain in general. The country's recovery was inhibited by three factors: its own economic underdevelopment; World War II, which exploded only months after the termination of hostilities on the Iberian Peninsula; and a later United Nations economic and diplomatic boycott directed at the Franco regime. The 1938 Press Law hindered the recovery of the press, dictating its content and limiting its growth. Though the law was created as an emergency measure, it remained in effect for twenty-eight years, less thirteen days. A decade and a half passed before the idea that it might be changed gained even slight momentum, and more than twenty years passed before it was officially suggested that it was established "with no intention of permanency."[36]

Between the end of the Civil War and 1944, the number of dailies in Madrid, for example, had risen from four to nine, the peak for

---

[34] Madariaga, *Spain: A Modern History,* p. 607.
[35] One can cite several outstanding examples, among them Adolfo Martín Gamero, press officer of the Foreign Ministry, a hardworking, capable information specialist; Manuel Jiménez Quíles, Director-General of the Press; and Jesús Gorrity, chief of the Foreign Press section of the Ministry of Information and Tourism. The last two were brought into the Ministry by Manuel Fraga Iribarne when he was named Minister of Information and Tourism in 1962 and appear to operate on the assumption that more can be accomplished by cooperation than by hindrance.
[36] Gabriel Eloriaga, "Los Principios sobre la Libertad de la Información en la España actual," *Working Paper No. 9, United Nations Conference on the Freedom of Information* (Rome, 1964), pp. 6-7.

the 1939-65 period.[37] They were *ABC, Arriba, Gol,*[38] *Informaciones, Madrid, Marca,*[39] *Ya, Pueblo,*[40] and *El Alcázar,*[41] founded in Toledo during the siege of the fortress and moved to Madrid in July of 1939. Barcelona had six dailies, including the historic *Diario de Barcelona, Solidaridad Nacional,*[42] *El Mundo Deportivo,*[43] *La Prensa,*[44] and *La Vanguardia Española,* which had added the *Española* to its name at the end of the war. There were, in all, 104 newspapers in Spain, plus six in the African colonies. Only twenty new dailies had been founded in Spain proper in the four years following the war. Nine of those were Falangist organs, which swelled the network of party newspapers to thirty-seven, all under the control of the Secretary-General of the National Movement (Movimiento Nacional). A century before, Madrid had claimed at least three times as many dailies.[45] In 1920, one of the rare years when official press statistics were compiled, Madrid had forty-one dailies, Barcelona had twenty-two, and Spain as a whole had 290.[46]

During the postwar period, an "official theory of news reporting" was being developed—a theory based on the 1938 Press Law and "derived from the legal order and social reality of the country in the post-war political conditions."[47] The press law had stated: "The existence of a fourth estate cannot be tolerated. It is inadmissible that the press can exist outside the State. The evils that spring from 'freedom of the democratic kind' must be avoided. . . . The press should always serve the national interests; it should be a national institution, a public enterprise in the service of the State." [48] Ac-

---

[37] Delegación Nacional de Prensa, *Anuario de la Prensa Española,* I (Madrid, 1944), 19–56.
[38] *Gol* ("Goal") (Madrid, 1940–45).
[39] *Marca* ("The Score") (Madrid, 1938–in operation)
[40] *Pueblo* ("The People") (Madrid, 1940–in operation).
[41] *El Alcázar* ("The Fortress") (Toledo, 1936, Madrid, 1939–in operation).
[42] *Solidaridad Nacional* ("National Solidarity") (Barcelona, 1936–in operation).
[43] *El Mundo Deportivo* ("The Sports World") (Barcelona, 1906–in operation).
[44] *La Prensa* ("The Press") (Barcelona, 1941–in operation).
[45] Eugenio Hartzenbusch é Hiríart, *Apuntes para un Catálogo de periódicos madrileños desde el año 1661 al 1870* (Madrid, 1894), pp. 317–318.
[46] Instituto Geográfico y Estadístico, quoted in the *Enciclopedia Universal Ilustrada* (Barcelona, 1923), XXI, 1481.
[47] Ángel Benito, "The Training of Journalists," *L'Enseignement du Journalisme,* XIII (Spring, 1962), 87.
[48] Quoted by the International Commission of Jurists, *Spain and the Rule of Law,* p. 48.

cording to the "theory of news reporting," as formulated in 1962, "The press is not an institution of private nature, but a social institution. In this way, the State makes use of its right to control the organs of news of the country." [49] As a result of the original press law and the maturing "theory," political news was suppressed, except for driblets passed by the censor or which originated with the government and which the newspapers were compelled to publish, pretending that "it . . . was put out by the newspaper office itself." [50] The deception, as practiced in Spain, has been called by the International Press Institute "one of the worst abuses of power." [51]

Newspapers in present-day Spain differ from those in countries with free presses. Until recently, at least, they devoted practically no space to political news and less space to local and national news. Cultural, religious, and sports news was given much more prominence and importance, a fact which accounts for the success of sports newspapers such as *Marca*, which has the third daily highest circulation of any newspaper in Spain.[52] As a result, according to historian James Cleugh,

[Newspapers] are not read for enlightenment, nor even primarily for information about happenings at home. . . . They are read for foreign news, which is usually printed without comment, and above all for their numerous and judicious articles of a non-political, mainly cultural kind. In Spain, the newspaper reader has a host of opinions on every subject but politics. In the Anglo-Saxon and French press, the reader has a host of views on the political party which he favors, but lacks information on other subjects.[53]

A study done by this writer comparing the space devoted to various categories of news by *La Vanguardia* and the *New York Times* shows that the Barcelona morning newspaper, during one week in 1960, used 27.3 per cent of its available editorial space for foreign news, while the New York paper used 13.3 per cent of its available space for news from abroad. National and local political

---

[49] Benito, "The Training of Journalists," p. 87.
[50] International Press Institute, *Government Pressures on the Press,* I.P.I. Survey No. IV (Zurich, 1955), p. 99.
[51] *Ibid.*
[52] *Marca* (Madrid) prints 145,000 copies daily and ranks behind only *ABC* and *La Vanguardia* in circulation, according to the *Estudio sobre los Medios de Comunicación de Masas en España,* published in 1964 by Madrid's Instituto de la Opinión Pública, I, 8–11. A special Monday supplement of *Marca* tops the nation's circulation figures with an estimated 300,000 copies.
[53] *Spain in the Modern World* (New York, 1953), pp. 139–140.

news took up 10.5 per cent of the *Times*'s space, while roughly 2 per cent of *Vanguardia*'s columns carried what might be considered political news. *Vanguardia* devoted 34.7 per cent of available space to sports, cultural, religious, and entertainment news. The *Times* gave only 20.7 per cent of its space to that type of news coverage.[54] It is interesting to note that the Spanish newspaper, published in a nation that had not yet begun the rapid economic development that has marked the past five or six years, allotted only 7.8 per cent of its editorial space to financial news, while the New York paper, published in the financial capital of the world, devoted 33.6 per cent of its space to coverage of economic matters.

That difference in the Spanish press is traceable, obviously, to government controls, to direct and indirect censorship which allows only one public political attitude and encourages emphasis on nonpolitical interests. Until 1962, all news copy in Spain was "blue-penciled" by censors, either those in Madrid's Ministry of Information and Tourism, or those charged with supervising the provincial press. With the appointment of Manuel Fraga Iribarne as head of the Ministry, prepublication censorship was eliminated outside of Madrid and Barcelona. However, as we shall see later, pressures were still exerted on provincial newspapers. The Director-General of Information supervised book censorship; the Director-General of the Press oversaw magazine and newspaper censorship. It must be noted that no section of the Ministry was publicly charged with the censorship function. There were no doors bearing the title "Censor" nor any official paper which incorporated the word in its letterhead. For that matter, there were few legal references to censorship and no regulations providing for recourse against the censor's decision. The only written rules for the guidance of censors dealt with immorality and attacks on the head of state. One of the rare official references to the function of the censor was contained in

---

[54] The comparison was based on issues of the two newspapers for the week of March 4–10, 1960. The method followed was that used by UNESCO in 1953 and reported by Jacques Kayser in *One Week's News: Comparative Study of 17 Major Dailies for a Seven-Day Period* (Paris, 1953). Linear inches of space devoted to each type of news were counted and, to compensate for a difference in column width, the totals were converted to square inches. Since the *Times* was about twice as large as *Vanguardia*, the daily totals were summed, then divided to produce an average percentage distribution for the period. *La Vanguardia* and the *New York Times* were selected because they are representative national newspapers, published in major, non-capital cities in the two countries.

a 1941 order exempting the Falange press from censorship.[55] Enemies of the regime charged that "Francoist censorship is a censorship which is ashamed, one which never admits its own existence." [56]

The regulation of the press was incumbent on the official in charge of the National Press Service who worked directly under the Director-General of the Press, who, in turn, was responsible to the Minister. The censors themselves were drawn from all walks of life and won their jobs by means of the same competitive tests given all Ministry employees. They needed no special technical or professional qualifications. A member of the Spanish opposition has described the censors as "all the more zealous in their duties knowing that should they allow any heterodox text to slip by or should anything untoward escape their scrutiny, it would cost them their jobs and they would remain unemployed, marked forever as suspect persons."[57] Spanish newsmen, however, claim that the penalties for careless censoring were not so stiff, consisting of transfer to another post in the Ministry and, rarely, reduction in grade. At least one inattentive censor, it is known, was suspended without pay for fifteen days.

Until 1962, all newspapers were compelled to submit all copy to the censors. In addition, foreign news received by the Spanish news agency EFE was sent to the censors before being distributed to newspapers and other news outlets. Little news of foreign origin, with the exception of that dealing with Spain or Spanish affairs, was censored, though items from behind the Iron Curtain were rewritten to indicate that the news had been received from a non-Communist point, usually Stockholm or Helsinki. The practice reflected resentment at Russian intervention on the Republican side during the Civil War and was part of a policy of complete nonrecognition of Communist governments, only recently undergoing modification.

In addition to censorship, the press was subjected to the controls

---

[55] Ministerio de Interior, *Orden del 1 de mayo de 1941*.
[56] Fernando Entrerio (pseud.), "The Peculiarities of Censorship Under the Franco Regime," *Iberica: For a Free Spain*, X, no. 5 (May 15, 1962), 5. There is no department of press censorship listed in an official Ministry of Information and Tourism guide published in 1965, but there is a section of the Dirección General de Radiodifusión y Televisión devoted to "Control, Censorship, and Coordination." Ministerio de Información y Turismo, *1965 Guía del Ministerio de Información y Turismo* (Madrid, 1965), p. 51.
[57] Entrerio, "The Peculiarities," p. 5.

inherent in government direction of newsprint allocations, which were used to enforce the official will. The newsman himself was incorporated into the official system, being forced to swear allegiance to the State before being granted his press credentials, an absolute requisite to finding and keeping a job. The oath, reproduced on all Spanish newsmen's press cards, read: "I swear before God, for Spain and its leader, to serve the Unity, the Greatness and the Freedom of the Fatherland with complete and total faithfulness to the principles of the Spanish State, without ever permitting falsehood, craft or ambition to distort my pen in its daily labor." [58] The incorporation of the journalist into the service of the State created an amorphous, uncomfortable situation for the newsman. He had constantly to ask himself what constituted "complete and total faithfulness to the principles of the Spanish State . . . " and at what point a desire to achieve high professional standards and distinguish oneself became "ambition" capable of "distorting my pen in its daily labor." In a series of cases reported by the International Commission of Jurists, one newsman found that he transgressed against his duties by reporting a deficit in an orange crop. Another was arrested and fined for publishing a story about a poliomyelitis epidemic. A third was arrested for criticizing defects in a public housing project.[59]

Thus the newsman's official role inhibited individual initiative, just as censorship controlled the content of newspapers. In addition, a virtual monopoly on foreign news given to a semi-national news agency, plus a priority on domestic news, tended to regulate the flow of information into and within the nation.

That news agency, EFE, the number one "wholesaler" of news in Spain, is, as are the press laws, a product of the Civil War. It had been founded in 1938 in Burgos, headquarters of the Nationalist armies, by Vicente Gallego Castro with the official backing of Ramón Serrano Suñer. In 1939, at the end of the war, EFE was moved to Madrid. Though it has been claimed that the name EFE represents the phonetic spelling of *F*, the first letter of "Falange," [60]

---

[58] "Juro ante Dios, por España y su Caudillo, servir a la Unidad, a la Grandeza y a la Libertad de la Patria con fidelidad integra y total a los principios del Estado español, sin permitir jamás que falsedad, la insidia, o la ambición tuerzan mi pluma en la labor diario."
[59] *Spain and the Rule of Law*, p. 49.
[60] Marvin Alisky, "Spain's Press and Broadcasting: Conformity and Censorship," *Journalism Quarterly*, XXXIX, no. 1 (Winter, 1962), 68.

executives of the agency deny that is the source of the title, claiming that "EFE" is a symbol without meaning. Gallego's intention, originally, had been to set up a nonofficial news agency, which could be linked eventually to international news agencies on a cooperative basis. With that in mind, he built up a network of foreign correspondents which included some of the nation's present journalistic luminaries.

The company itself was private, its stock held by banks or individuals. In May, 1940, Gallego received permission to expand his operations by publishing *El Mundo*,[61] a weekly devoted to international affairs and put out as a dependency of EFE. However, Gallego's dream of developing a private, independent company devoted to gathering and presenting news was soon to fade. In 1941, Gabriel Arias Salgado was named Vice-Secretary of National Education when that post was created within the Falange party to handle "press and propaganda," functions performed up until then by the Ministerio de Gobernación.[62] As already noted, Arias Salgado ruled the press with an iron hand. Whether he was a "stooge" executing the orders of Franco, as some have charged,[63] or exploited his close personal ties with the *Caudillo* to impose his will on the government, is a matter for conjecture. It is known, however, that there was, and still is, an influential group within the government, with strong representation in the cabinet, which opposed any trend toward relaxing press controls. Arias Salgado was most certainly aligned with that element. Franco himself has made few public pronouncements on the question of press liberty or on the role of mass communications, though he has declared that he does not consider freedom of the press an absolute principle.[64] He has manifested a basic preoccupation with the necessity of "avoiding an excess of illicit liberty which can cause the loss of freedom." [65] Presumably, freedom of the press during liberal periods would be considered a dangerous "illicit liberty." Arias Salgado, on the other hand, was both outspoken and specific. "Freedom of information," he said, "has installed the freedom of error. . . . The consequences of libertinism of information in

[61] *El Mundo* ("The World") (Madrid, 1940–in operation).
[62] *Ley de 20 de mayo de 1941* (transferring press control from the Ministerio de Gobernación to the Falange Española Tradicionalista y de la JONS), *Artículo 1.*
[63] A.F.L., "The Press in Spain: Complete Government Control," *Winnipeg Free Press*, Sept. 5, 1960.
[64] I.P.I., *The Press in Authoritarian Countries*, p. 140.
[65] Spanish Information Service, *Pensamiento Político de Franco*, p. 226.

Spain during the period of political liberalism, and today in the world at large, are bitter and visible signs of social and political decomposition. . . ." [66] Until the unlikely moment when evidence is presented to the contrary, one must assume that Arias Salgado's execution of press policy as Vice-Secretary of National Education and later as Minister of Information did not run counter to Franco's wishes, regardless of which man formulated the policy. Arias Salgado's successor, Manuel Fraga Iribarne, an advocate of relaxed press controls and greater editorial latitude, has expressed disagreement with the policies of his predecessor. He did so within days of being named Minister of Information by promising to liberalize the national press laws. Moreover, there has been some criticism implicit in his public statements, though he does, at least partially, excuse his predecessor on the grounds that Arias Salgado ran the press at a time when Spain "was impoverished by a cruel conflict and repressed by a hostile external world. . . ." [67]

Regardless of Arias Salgado's motives and role, he quickly recognized the potential power of the news agency EFE and started a campaign to gain control of it. Vicente Gallego realized he could not stop the government encroachment and, in 1944, resigned, turning his attentions exclusively to El Mundo. Pedro Gómez Aparicio, then subdirector, was named director. From then on, the agency received subsidies of varying amounts and in various forms from the government. The process of taking over the agency continued as late as 1965, when Franco authorized the government to buy up outstanding shares of the agency, including, among others, 100 shares held by the newspaper La Gaceta del Norte, 594 held by the Bank of Vizcaya, and 1,520 by the Spanish American Bank. [68]

During the early stages of World War II, until November, 1942, Spain played the role of "pro-Axis neutral." [69] After 1942, when the tide began to turn against Hitler and Mussolini, Spain assumed a role of stricter neutrality. However, all foreign news arriving in the country was distributed by EFE and originated by the German Transocean agency. The result was that "the Spanish press never published a word of criticism of Germany from 1939 to the end of

---

[66] A speech delivered before the National Council of the Spanish Press in December, 1954.
[67] Fraga Iribarne, quoted by Informaciones (Madrid), Mar. 14, 1965, p. 9.
[68] Decretos 421, 422, and 423 of the Ministerio de Hacienda, Boletín Oficial del Estado, Mar. 8, 1965, p. 3557.
[69] Whitaker, Spain and Defense, p. 8.

the war in Europe." [70] Only after the fall of Mussolini and as the result of United States protests was there an improvement. The press, according to foreign observers in Spain at the time, was far from neutral, but it did, after 1942, publish an occasional United States or British war communiqué.[71]

With the end of hostilities in Europe and an Allied victory assured in the Pacific, Franco moved to blunt criticism of his regime. He issued, through the Cortes (Parliament), the "Spanish Bill of Rights" (*Fuero de los Españoles*). One provision stipulated that "All Spaniards will be able to express freely their ideas as long as they do not attack the fundamental principles of the State." [72] However, there was a kicker attached—a provision that permitted the arbitrary "temporary suspension" by the government of that and other key articles during any period of crisis.[73] At the same time, the *Caudillo* reorganized his cabinet, shifting its emphasis from the totalitarian Falange to the Catholic Action group which was headed by Alberto Martín Artajo, the new Minister of Foreign Affairs.

The press was also incorporated into the campaign to gain "free world" favor. The Spanish news agency EFE was encouraged, if not ordered, to create ties with major Western wire services. Its first was with the British agency Reuters. In 1945, it was decided to add an American agency, and a detailed study was undertaken of the relative merits of Associated Press and United Press. Finally, in a decision influenced by José Félix de Lequerica, then Foreign Minister and later Spain's Ambassador to the United States and United Nations, EFE signed a contract with U.P. One can only conjecture that the Spanish government was hopeful that United Press, a privately owned news agency obligated only by business ties to clients, would be more malleable and less likely to be anti-Franco than Associated Press, which, as an organization constituted by member U.S. newspapers, might be inclined to reflect the anti-Francoism believed rampant in the United States. The feeling that the purchase of the U.P. service entitled Spain to favorable treatment certainly permeated some areas of government and did, to this writer's personal knowledge, enter into exchanges between government officials and U.P. correspondents. Whether it ever influenced U.P. news re-

---

[70] Charles Foltz, Jr., *The Masquerade in Spain* (Boston, 1948), p. 146.
[71] *Ibid.*, p. 198.
[72] *Fuero de los Españoles, Ley de 17 de julio de 1945, Artículo 12.*
[73] *Ibid., Artículo 35.*

ports on Spanish subjects is a moot question, one which personally would have to be answered in the negative. In all fairness, it must be made clear that there were government officials who often served as buffers against pressures exerted on foreign newsmen.

As an aid to EFE, which was in shaky financial condition, the government had agreed to pay for news distributed to official agencies. It also arranged a system whereby EFE payments to U.P., made in Spanish *pesetas*, would be converted into dollars at a favorable rate of exchange. Reuters already had a similar arrangement. The special exchange considerations were to last for a decade and a half, becoming increasingly unrealistic as the *peseta*'s value in relation to the dollar dropped. The U.P. news was supplied to EFE by means of radio teletype broadcasts, some originating in London, which were received direct, and some originating in New York, which were relayed by a Mackay station in Tangier.

Despite the moves designed to stem the international tide of anti-Spanish feeling, Franco's prestige outside of Spain did not rise. In the United Nations, Luis Quintanilla of Mexico introduced a motion—unanimously adopted—that barred Spain from U.N. membership. On March 4, 1946, the United States, France, and Britain issued a Tripartite Declaration stating that Spain would remain ostracized so long as Franco was in control. Later that year, during meetings of the Security Council and General Assembly, Poland introduced a resolution calling for complete severance of normal diplomatic relations with Spain and branding the Franco regime a threat to international peace.[74] The measure was defeated, but a compromise, proposed by Belgium and backed by the United States, that heads of mission be withdrawn from Madrid was approved on December 12, 1946. The opposition to such censure of Franco was led by Argentina, where Juan Perón was at the height of power and prestige.[75]

Spain's rejection by the United Nations and its subsequent diplomatic and economic ostracism had two consequences. In the first place, the nation's recovery from the Civil War was retarded. The war losses had included two-thirds of the national transport, one-third of the merchant marine, and almost all of its gold reserves, raw materials, and consumer goods. In addition, one million Spaniards

---

[74] Whitaker, *Spain and Defense*, p. 345.
[75] Franco subsequently showed his gratitude to Perón by granting him asylum after his flight from Argentina.

had been killed and another 500,000 were in exile.[76] It had been expected that recovery would accelerate when normal international commercial and financial intercourse was resumed after World War II. The United Nations dashed those hopes.

In the second place, Franco's position was strengthened, if not with the rank-and-file Spaniards, at least with those members of the official hierarchy whose future depended on the stability of his regime. His own determination to follow the political path already embarked upon was also reinforced. The world attitude, reflecting the views of "communists" and exponents of the "liberal-capitalist system," as he called them, was a vindication of his "crusade" against communism, already a cornerstone of his propaganda, and his rejection of liberalism. His system of "organic" or "vertical democracy" would allow no modification, for modification would of necessity move it in the direction of either communism or "liberal capitalism," which, though responsible for technical and material miracles, had created no moral progress. His distrust of the "liberal-capitalist" system was obvious in 1946, for example, when he told the nation's deputies, "If we can say that to a great extent we owe the multiplication of benefits to the great liberal century, we must, in all justice, also blame it for the multiplication of miseries." [77]

The international pressures on Spain were reflected in the press. A dominant theme in any political commentary was the determination that "We, the Spanish, can go it alone." The quality of newsprint was low, the amount available limited—before the boycott nearly 50 per cent of the national supply was imported—and press machinery was antiquated. In 1943, the average press run of all the dailies in the country was 1,467,000 copies, 12,200 per paper.[78] That remained static until the early 1950's, when a change in the international scene permitted economic expansion and technical modernization, which were reflected in the easing of newsprint restrictions and a concomitant increase in circulations. By the mid-1950's, according to UNESCO estimates, the national circulation of dailies had grown to 2,450,000 copies.[79] At that point, if available estimates are correct, growth stopped and circulations even showed

[76] Whitaker, *Spain and Defense*, p. 33.
[77] Address to the Cortes, May 14, 1946.
[78] Delegación Nacional de Prensa, *Anuario*, I, 417–421.
[79] UNESCO, Department of Mass Communications, *World Communications* (Paris, 1956), p. 216.

some decline.[80] In 1964, total daily circulation was estimated at about 2,295,000,[81] some 155,000 less than a decade before.

The ostracism of Spain remained complete until 1948, though Franco had begun to chip away at his foreign opposition by suggesting that Spain could play an important role in the cold war against Communism. By 1948, this campaign began to pay off with indications of mounting U.S. interest in Spain's strategic potential, an interest which continued despite Spain's exclusion from NATO in 1949. In 1950, tentative financial feelers were put out by major U.S. companies, and Secretary of State Dean Acheson called for repeal of the U.N. resolution on the withdrawal of chiefs of mission from Madrid.[82]

It was in 1950, also, that the first tentative suggestions were made that the 1938 Press Law should be amended and the press liberalized. In that year, Spain's Primate, Enrique Cardinal Pla y Deniel, published a pastoral calling for some modifications in existing regulations. "It is highly deplorable," the Cardinal wrote, "that it is not recognized that between the liberties of damnation—the unrestrained license of the press for cheating and corrupting the public, always condemned by the Church—and the absolute state control of the press, exists a happy medium of a responsible freedom of the press, proper to a Christian and civilized society, such as that defined in the Christian Rights of the Spanish." [83]

That touched off an occasional and usually halfhearted exploration by the Spanish government of ways and means of achieving press "liberalization" within the framework of the existing political order. Such "liberalization" could mean only one thing in Franco Spain, a middle-of-the-road approach, the "responsible freedom" of which the Cardinal wrote. Complete freedom was ruled out. The history of the Spanish press had been that of an institution either interacting intimately with the political system or being acted upon by the political system. As viewed from the perspective of Franco and his aides, the periods of interaction resulted in threats to the national stability. A restoration of the conditions conducive

---

[80] Juan Beneyto, a top student of the Spanish press, attributes the decline to the increase in radio and television receivers, especially of small transistor radios. Interview, Feb. 18, 1965.
[81] Instituto de la Opinión Pública, *Estudio,* I, 18.
[82] Whitaker, *Spain and Defense,* p. 37.
[83] Quoted by Eloriaga, "Principios sobre la Libertad," pp. 10–11.

to such interaction would be unthinkable, meaning a return to "free expression to the point of anarchy. . . ." [84] Thus "liberalization of the press" was interpreted as a redefinition of the rules governing play rather than a complete relaxation of controls: it implied a broadening of the area in which decisions could be made by editors rather than in the censors' sanctum, but not an erasing of the lines beyond which an umpire calls "foul." The history of the Spanish press after 1950 was the history of the movement toward "liberalization."

Spain's reincorporation into the "family of nations" was speeded by the outbreak of the Korean War in June, 1950, which immediately highlighted the strategic value of the country's geographic location. In July, 1951, the United States began preliminary talks leading to the signing, on September 26, 1953, of the Pact of Madrid, which embraced three separate agreements between Spain and the U.S.—a Defense Agreement, an Economic Aid Agreement, and a Mutual Defense Assistance Agreement. Spanish-U.S. relations had been defrosted, and with them, relations between Spain and much of the Western World.[85]

In 1954, the number of daily newspapers in Spain still stood at 110.[86] Of that number, thirty-eight were Falangist organs. The stabilization of the number of newspapers at that level must be attributed to government policy, made by the Ministry of Information and Tourism which had been created in 1951 as an umbrella for the various agencies handling press, propaganda, and tourism. The reasons for limiting the number of dailies have never been publicly formulated, though it is assumed that they involve questions of control—a limited number of periodicals being more easily overseen—and economic realities. It may partially be explained also as an attempt to introduce stability into the Spanish social structure, for in Spain there is a tendency to equate large-scale changes in periodical reading habits with social unrest. According to the theory, as formulated by José Bugeda, a professor at Madrid's official Journalism School and a Ministry of Information official, "A stable society is always a society of unchangeable readers. Great fluctuations in readers are, on the contrary, the best index which

---

[84] Juan Beneyto, *Ordenamiento Jurídico de la Información* (Madrid, 1961), p. 18.
[85] There are still some holdouts, including, for example, Norway, which have successfully blocked Spain's incorporation into NATO.
[86] *The New York Times*, Dec. 16, 1954, p. 18, col 4.

a sociologist can find to diagnose a society on the point of explo-
sion." [87] One would assume that the more limited the range of alternatives, the less the changes in readership. One way to limit the
range of alternatives available to the newspaper reader is to control
their number.

Though the number of newspapers remained static, circulations,
as already noted, increased. A combination of three factors was
responsible:

1. Some slight increase in disposable income, which was not
matched by increases in the per-issue cost of newspapers to readers.
The price of dailies was set by the government—at present, 1.50
pesetas per weekday copy, two *pesetas* on Sunday—and figured in
the national cost-of-living index, along with the fares of the govern-
ment-operated transit system, for example. The cost of other forms
of entertainment—films, bullfights, and football—soared.

2. An increase of interest in international events as a result of the
easing of the boycott against Spain and its gradual incorporation
into the Western bloc, plus an increase in the number of tourists,
bringing new ideas into the country. Between 1940 and 1953, the
annual flow of visitors into the country rose from 22,700 to
1,710,000.[88]

3. An increase in literacy which expanded the reading public. In
1940, 18.68 per cent of those over ten years of age were illiterate.
By 1950, that had been reduced to 14.24 per cent and, by 1960, had
dropped to 10.35 per cent.[89] The increase in literacy between 1940
and 1950, for example, added more than one million persons to the
rolls of those who could read.

Meanwhile, the question of press liberalization appears to have
lain dormant. The Cardinal Primate's 1950 call for modifications
in the systems of controls had either fallen on deaf ears or been
pigeonholed in a compartment marked "for future consideration."
In 1952, the National Council of the Catholic Press submitted a list
of demands calling for general press reforms. Among the demands
were those for reorganization of censorship along lines that would
eliminate harm to newspapers and the creation of a special tribunal
to consider press offenses. In 1953, the National Congress of the
Spanish Press met in Madrid, and newspaper editors used the meet-

---

[87] *Una Sociología del Periódico* (Madrid, 1963), p. 7.
[88] Ministerio de Información y Turismo, *España Hoy* (Madrid, 1964), p. 62.
[89] *Ibid.*, p. 21.

ing as a forum for denunciations of censorship abuses. They complained "of the extension of censorship to non-political news items . . . and insisted on the elimination of controls and the elaboration of a new law." [90] In 1954, the call for press liberalization was picked up by the editor-in-chief of *Ecclesia*, the official Catholic organ. Its editor, Father Jesús Iribarren, wrote in May, "How can we consider our press regime as ideal when it obliges people to look elsewhere for the news that is the newspaper's 'raison d'être'?" [91] Iribarren was forced to resign shortly thereafter.

Toward the end of the year, the government itself resurrected the question of the press amid a flurry of confusion that never filtered down to the Spanish reading public. On December 10, at a regular bimonthly meeting of the Consejo de Ministros (Franco's cabinet), Minister of Information Arias Salgado presented a new press law. The *New York Times* reported that the "bill would empower the Government not only to control but actually to manage all Spain's privately owned newspapers. . . ." [92] According to the *Times* report, the draft of the new law—which was never made public—contained a preamble plus twenty-eight articles which, among other things, provided that: the publisher of a newspaper submit to the Minister of Information the names of three candidates for the post of editor-in-chief, with the Minister having the right to reject all three and name his own man to the job; the editor-in-chief have the power to decide not only what news would be published in the newspaper, but also the amount of advertising to be published, and the number of copies to be sold; and the editor-in-chief be responsible to the government for the management of the newspaper, not to the publisher, and also be responsible for the "doctrinal orientation of the newspaper which must not harm the fundamental principles of the State and the spiritual, national and social unity of Spain."

The following day, the *Times* carried a dispatch from Washington quoting then Spanish Ambassador to the U.S.A. José María de Areliza to the effect that the December 16 dispatch had "surprised him."[93] The Ambassador, according to the *Times*, hinted that the

---

[90] I.P.I., *The Press in Authoritarian Countries*, p. 151.
[91] *Ibid.*, p. 150.
[92] Camille M. Cianfarra, "Tight Press Curb Mapped by Spain," *The New York Times*, Dec. 16, 1954, p. 18, col. 3.
[93] *The New York Times*, Dec. 17, 1954, p. 9, col. 3.

report originating in Madrid had been incorrect. The regime, he conceded, planned a new press code which would end censorship, but the only rights the government would reserve to itself in connection with the appointment of editors-in-chief would be that of "veto" of "Communist or revolutionary appointments." He concluded by noting that the issue of the New York Times carrying the original story would be allowed to circulate in Spain, where, he said, "it will arouse great curiosity." He was wrong, as the Times was to find out.

On December 18, the Spanish press again figured in the columns of the New York Times, which reported that the monarchist newspaper ABC had been "punished" because of the political activity of a member of the family which owned it. The offending family member, the Marqués Torcuata Luca de Tena, had been dismissed as editor-in-chief of the daily a year before, ostensibly for defying censorship by reporting, despite an official denial, the arrival in Spain of Soviet Police Chief Laventry Beria, supposedly an escapee from the post-Stalinist purge. However, the real reason for his removal was apparently an article on the personality cult of the Kremlin—an article which alluded to the possibility of a similar situation in Franco's Pardo Palace. Luca de Tena had compounded his fall from grace by joining three other monarchists in opposing Falangist candidates in a nationwide administrative election in October, 1954. As a result, according to the Times, the National Syndicates had, on December 15, reduced ABC's newsprint quota by fifty tons, which amounted to a fine of $4,000.[94] Ten days later, the Times revised the estimate of the monetary value of the punishment to $40,000.[95]

Meanwhile, on December 22, the Times reported that Ambassador Areliza had been far off base when he predicted that the report of the press law would be allowed to circulate in Spain. The issue containing that story, as well as the one reporting the sanctions against ABC, had been excluded from Spain "presumably because

---

[94] Camille M. Cianfarra, "Spain Punishes Monarchist Paper by Reducing Its Newsprint Quota," The New York Times, Dec. 18, 1954, p. 4, col. 5.
[95] The New York Times, Dec. 28, 1954, p. 7, col. 6. The International Press Institute report on the sanctions in The Press in Authoritarian Countries, p. 149, differs from that of the Times. According to the I.P.I., the "punishment" consisted of the provisional withdrawal of a general exemption from taxes on newsprint exceeding fifty tons a month. The withdrawal of the exemption added $400 a month to ABC's newsprint costs, the I.P.I. report said.

they contained news displeasing to government policy." [96] It was not an uncommon occurrence, for, during 1954 alone, twenty issues of the *Times* were banned from Spain, "including copies mailed to diplomats. . . ." [97]

Early in 1955, the Church returned to the fray, renewing its demands for modification of the press law. *Ecclesia*, using the freedom from censorship granted it by a special agreement between Franco and the Cardinal Primate,[98] called for an end to the system of directives which "oblige newspapers to publish as their opinions the views of ruling circles, a practice that is an outrage to the rights of human beings." [99] It was no call for freedom of the press, however, for *Ecclesia*, according to Herbert L. Matthews, a longtime student of Spanish affairs, while free from censorship itself, "applauds censorship of everything and everyone else."[100]

The editorial was seconded by the Bishop of Málaga, Ángel Herrera Oria, onetime editor-in-chief of *El Debate*. In an open letter, the Bishop admitted that censorship was legitimate but urged that it be used judiciously and not to force a journalist to publish that which he did not believe. Herrera proposed several points as an outline for a press law. They included:

1. The maintenance of prepublication censorship, but censorship limited by law.

2. The reorganization of the censorship function to keep it from harming a newspaper.

---

[96] *The New York Times*, Dec. 22, 1954, p. 8, col. 2.
[97] *Ibid.* The *New York Times* was not the only foreign periodical regularly banned from Spanish newsstands. Reprisals against periodicals carrying reports displeasing to the regime were common. Between 1947 and 1963, for example, Spain acted against the international editions of *Time* and *Life* on 113 occasions, confiscating copies sent into the country fifty times and banning fifty-six other issues. On five occasions, the editors of the magazines, anticipating government action, did not bother to ship the publications into Spain. Copies of one issue were clipped to remove an item offensive to official sensibilities, and one issue was held up for some time before being allowed to appear. For a complete discussion of foreign censorship of *Time* and *Life*, including that of the Spanish government, see Michael A. Barkocy, "Censorship Against *Time* and *Life* International Editions," *Journalism Quarterly*, XL, no. 4 (Autumn, 1963), 517–524.
[98] The Church's right to publish freely any matter relating to religion or the organization or management of the Church is guaranteed by a Concordat between the Holy See and the Spanish government which was signed on Aug. 27, 1953.
[99] Quoted by the International Commission of Jurists, *Spain and the Rule of Law*, p. 50.
[100] *The Yoke and the Arrows: A Report on Spain* (New York, 1957), p. 101.

3. The creation of a special tribunal to hear press offenses.[101]

On April 28, 1955, the government ratified a code of professional ethics for journalists which had been drawn up by the Spanish Federation of Press Associations and the Directorate-General of the Press. The code, which outlined principles governing professional conduct, stated, in part:

As Spaniards of the Catholic faith and as defenders of principles of the glorious National Movement, we have the duty to serve this religious truth as well as this political truth with fervor for our task of information and orientation. . . . The journalist owes allegiance to the newspaper to which he lends his services within the framework of those principles previously declared. Service to the interests of the newspaper is obligatory. Service to the personal interests of the journalist is lawful, providing that these interests are not incompatible with the ethic inspired by the Catholic faith, the doctrine of the Movement, and the general needs of the community. . . . Each news item should be judged at its proper value. In its manner of presentation and in the title under which it is published, truth and justice must be respected and prudence must be exercised on account of the power of the press on public opinion. All conscious changes in the content of the news item, all equivocal playing up of news, all sensationalism must be avoided.[102]

Two weeks later, the Ministry of Information created special journalist tribunals to try cases of "dishonorable acts committed by those holding official press cards. . . ." [103] The official action may have been in response to Herrera's demands, a concession to the distinguished newsman turned churchman. The tribunal's juridical authority was sharply limited. It had two alternatives in considering the case of a remiss journalist: absolving the defendant of guilt or voting for his "definitive separation from the journalistic profession." [104] There was no middle course of minor punishment for minor offenses.

Meanwhile, some serious attempts, stimulated by Herrera's needling, had been made to hammer out a workable press law. There was even a public interchange of points of view between the Bishop and Minister Arias Salgado. However, the attempts met with no success, for no one was able to reconcile the position of the newspaper publishers with that of the government, and the drive for

---

[101] I.P.I., *The Press in Authoritarian Countries*, p. 151.
[102] Quoted by the International Commission of Jurists, *Spain and the Rule of Law*, p. 51.
[103] *Normas reglamentarias de los Tribunales de honor en la profesión periodística, Artículo 2.*
[104] *Ibid., Artículo 5.*

changes petered out. Government control of the press continued without modification. The government used its power to allocate the distribution of newsprint for "favoring the Falangist press, which also . . . [enjoyed] fiscal and postal privileges . . . and for silencing nonconformist publications." [105] One could cite many examples of how government control worked and with what results. A few must suffice.

At the beginning of 1956, the government closed down the literary reviews *Índice* [106] and *Ínsula* [107] on the grounds that they had violated newsprint regulations. Prior to 1956, the two magazines had courted official disfavor by publishing, with laudatory comments, the work of exiled Spanish writers. In 1955, when philosopher José Ortega y Gasset died, the Ministry of Information issued an order outlining coverage of his death. "Each newspaper," the order said, "may publish up to three articles relative to the death of Ortega y Gasset: a biography and two commentaries. Every article on the writer's philosophy must underline his errors in religious matters. It is permissible to publish photographs of the mortuary on the front page, of the death mask or body of Ortega, but no photographs made during his lifetime." [108] *Índice* and *Ínsula* exceeded their authorized number of pages in issues devoted to Ortega y Gasset and were closed. *Índice* reappeared at the end of 1956, *Ínsula* the following year.

In the summer of 1958, the Ministry of Information informed the Madrid morning paper, *Informaciones*, that its newsprint allotment would be cut by 10 per cent because its "political nuances" were offensive to the government. The newsprint taken from *Informaciones*, the government said, would be divided between *ABC* and *Madrid*.

The government had consistently exercised its right to order a newspaper to print certain official copy as if it had been originated by the newspaper.[109] The practice is most apparent on July 18, the

[105] I.P.I., *The Press in Authoritarian Countries*, p. 147.
[106] *Índice* ("Index") (Madrid, 1945–in operation).
[107] *Ínsula* ("Island") (Madrid, 1945–in operation).
[108] Quoted by the International Commission of Jurists, *Spain and the Rule of Law*, p. 49.
[109] The new press law modified the practice. *Artículo 6* of the *Ley de Prensa e Imprenta* states: "Periodical publications will have to insert and news agencies distribute, *with an indication of their origin* [italics added], the notes, communications, and news items of general interest which the Administration and public bodies consider necessary to divulge. . . ."

anniversary of the "National Revolution," when most editorial space in the daily press is devoted to recapitulation of the Nationalist victory in the Civil War and a review of the events of the peace that had followed. In 1958, the government involved the foreign press in its output of "custom-made" news. Within a space of two weeks, it distributed to newspapers reports of a United Press interview with the Foreign Minister, Fernando María Castiella, and an Associated Press interview with Franco. Neither Louis Nevin of Associated Press nor this writer, the U.P. Madrid bureau chief, had solicited or been a party to the interview.

The same year, the newspaper *ABC* was authorized to give a detailed report of a meeting between Mrs. Franco and Don Juan, Count of Barcelona and Pretender to the Spanish throne, but the weekly *SP* [110] was forbidden to report on the event. The reason given by the government for its decision was that the two periodicals appealed to different classes of readers.

In 1959, the government set up a special commission to study reform of the press law. The regime's enemies charged that the existing regulations were "harmful and oppressive." [111] Regime spokesmen, however, suggested that reform was necessary only because the 1938 Press Law was "somewhat out of date, considering the dynamism and the needs of modern journalism." [112] By 1960, some form of concrete draft had been worked out. According to official spokesmen, the projected law provided that "the press and all other mass communication media will cease to be under the control of the state, which in the future will merely have a complementary role of assistance to private press undertakings. In this way, the conception of state control over news disappears." [113] Critics of the regime viewed the proposed law in a different light. One summed it up:

. . . it is so ridiculous that one wonders if it is possible that it could really become law in a modern state in the middle of the twentieth century. It provides, basically, for the following: pre-publication censorship of the press and magazines is ended, but it defines a most detailed and endless series of "Crimes of the Press," so unprecedented that were they to be applied in any other country of the so-called free world, like

110 *SP* (Madrid, 1958–in operation).
111 "Press Law in Spain," *America: National Catholic Weekly Review,* CV, no. 2 (Apr. 8, 1961), 47.
112 Angela Martínez de Banos, "The Organization of the Profession," *L'Enseignement du Journalisme,* XIII (Spring, 1962), 92.
113 Benito, "The Training of Journalists," p. 88.

France, England or the United States, it would mean the end of all publications. The list includes "crimes" of action and omission, and they range to everything from criticizing the regime or its officials to failing to give adequate importance to a speech by Franco or some "success" of the regime.[114]

Early in 1960, work on the new press law ran into an unexpected snag—a bitter disagreement between Church officials, who were represented on the commission, and Ministry of Information officials over regulations governing a Church-run journalism school in Pamplona. In 1941, the government had set up in Madrid an Official School of Journalism (Escuela Oficial de Periodismo) which was to be the "only authorized center for the training of journalists." [115] Admission to the school was strictly controlled; applicants had to file, among other things, certificates from the police indicating a clean record and letters of reference. The faculty was appointed by the Ministry of Information. The courses included traditional technical training to which was added indoctrination in the philosophy of the National Movement as well as grounding in history, literature, and economics. In subsequent years, a branch was opened in Barcelona, but the right of final examination was reserved to the central school in Madrid.

When the Church opened its journalism school in Pamplona, the government "recognized the right of the Spanish ecclesiastic hierarchy . . . to create its School of Journalism." [116] The Church would be allowed to appoint the school's faculty, but the Ministry of Information reserved the right to check appointees in case there were "difficulties of a general political character." [117] So far, all was fine. The catch came in provisions which limited graduates to working on Church publications unless they passed tests administered by the Official School. The Church protested that such discrimination against its school violated the rights granted it by the 1953 Concordat.

To dramatize that protest, Church members of the commission charged with drawing up a new press law refused to attend a commission meeting in February, 1961. The Church representatives—

---

[114] Entrerio, "The Peculiarities of Censorship," p. 7.
[115] *Orden de 17 de noviembre de 1941.*
[116] Ministerio de Información y Turismo, *Decreto de 7 de septiembre de 1960, Artículo 1.*
[117] *Ibid., Artículo 4.*

Bishop Herrera; Juan Hervas, Bishop of Ciudad Real; and Antonio Ona de Chave, Bishop of Lugo—used the alleged illness of Herrera as their excuse. At the same time, word was leaked that they found the draft upon which the commission was working "ideologically unacceptable and incompatible with the teachings of the Church." [118] With that, work on the new press law lapsed. The roadblock was not immediately to be removed. And yet the conditions that spurred interest in a revision of the press code and the need for such revisions did not cease to exist.

In a sense, in 1961, an era was drawing to a close—the era of Arias Salgado, the "Minister of Non-Information," who "believed it his duty to pretend that nothing ever happened anywhere . . . [and who saw his role as] that, not of a responsible censor, but of a man whose aim in life was to save souls." [119]

For years, Arias Salgado's name had figured in every rumor about possible changes in the cabinet, but each time Franco made changes Arias Salgado stayed on at his post. The rumors of 1962 included the usual speculation about a change at the top in the Ministry of Information and Tourism. The realities of a fresh cabinet in July, 1962, confirmed the rumors. Arias Salgado was retired, and Manuel Fraga Iribarne replaced him. Within two weeks, Arias Salgado died.

---

[118] United Press International, *Dispatch No. 5*, Madrid, Feb. 5, 1961.
[119] Robert E. G. Harris, *A Report from Spain—The Press in an Authoritarian State* (Los Angeles, 1964), p. 29.

he Franco Years:

The Loosened Padlock

The appointment on July 10, 1962, of Manuel Fraga Iribarne as Minister of Information and Tourism ushered in a new era for the Spanish press. It could not have been otherwise. Economically and socially the country was not the same as it had been five years before. There were bikinis on the beaches along the Mediterranean and smoke belching from the factories in the industrial north. Large English, French, and American cars clogged city streets where chauffeur-driven Volkswagens had once been a status symbol. The *señorito,* the well-off Spanish male who played during the night and slept during the day, ceased to be an object of awe and respect, replaced in that role by the aggressive entrepreneur with an eye on the fast *peseta.* Spain was still a dictatorship, a totalitarian state, but absolute power was less concentrated in the hands of the top few men in government. More and more businessmen and economic experts were shaping policy. In addition, economic and military dependence on its neighbors and on the United States had forced Spain to temper its uses of power. The desire for international approval had enclosed the iron fist in a velvet glove.

Fraga's appointment as Minister of Information cast him in the role not only of administrator of the press but also of public articulator of the ideas underlying demands for a change. He brought to his new post a background in diplomacy, education, and law; he had written on political theory and, as would become apparent, had a wide-ranging knowledge of the problems involved in fitting the media of mass communications into the total social, political, and economic framework. His writings and speeches were studded with references to sociologists who had explored the problems of social interaction and public opinion, to philosophers who had discussed mass society, and to those from diverse disciplines who had attempted to analyze the media themselves and their effects on their mass audiences. For example, in a work published in 1965, *Horizonte Español*, in which he attempted to appraise the nation's problems of the moment and its future course, he cited, among others, such varied works as Bernard Berelson's *Content Analysis in Communication Research*, Robert Park's *Society*, Bernard Voyenne's *La Presse dans la société contemporaine*, L. W. Doob's *Public Opinion and Propaganda*, C. H. Cooley's *Social Process*, Karl Popper's *The Open Society and Its Enemies*, Pitirim A. Sorokin's *Society, Culture, and Personality*, and Joseph Klapper's *The Effects of Mass Communications*.[1] At least he had done his "homework."

Within days after his appointment to the post of Minister, Fraga had moved to "liberalize" the press by ending censorship in all of Spain, except Madrid and Barcelona. He also promised in an interview with Jean Creach, a correspondent for the Parisian newspaper *Combat*, that a new press law would be in effect before the year's end. But, as he was to discover, his enthusiasm outran the bounds of the possible. The conservative tradition worked against sudden or drastic change. By 1965, Fraga was calling for "patience and equanimity" in the process of press liberalization. In a book published in that year, he wrote:

We live during a transcendental experiment for the Spanish society, and prudence and good sense must prevail. We do not wish to put the cart before the oxen. Before the press can exercise a freedom, which is an ordered liberty and not libertinism, it is necessary to follow a long road—the progressive education of journalists, the public, and the government. It is a process of adaptation which is basic to preparing adequate foundations for a responsible public opinion and an awareness of the limits which cannot be passed without endangering our ability to live peacefully together with a reasonable degree of harmony and satisfaction (*convivencia*).

It is a difficult path which does not admit false steps and where every movement must be calculated with precision. It is preferable to walk at a slow but sure pace which will lead us, progressively, to the freedom

---

[1] Manuel Fraga Iribarne, *Horizonte Español* (Madrid, 1965), pp. 224, 221, 219, 217, 214, 209, 207.

of the press in a country which has the proper structures to permit profiting from it.[2]

In other writings and public utterances, Fraga stressed the dangers inherent in man's ability to communicate rapidly with large masses of other men and, at the same time, expressed his recognition of its potentials for the enrichment of the individual and society. These themes appeared again and again, interwoven with a continuing public discussion of the role government should play. "Should regulation be simply limiting or negative, reduced to prohibiting those things which are considered prejudicial," he asked, "or should it, on the contrary, be of a positive and creative character. . . ?" His own answer was that the state "not only has the obligation to eliminate that which is considered prejudicial in the use of the media of mass communications, but also has the positive obligation of fostering in every possible way the 'development of the individual and collective conscience' through the use of these media." [3]

Fraga also noted the dangers that could be created by pressures exerted on the press by special interest groups, whether political or economic, including those created by advertising or the involvement of newspaper publishers in other business activities.[4] He even referred to the potential danger of government manipulation of the media of mass communications and cited the "predictions" of Aldous Huxley and George Orwell of what might follow if a government exercised no self-restraint and usurped all media control from private enterprise. The law, he suggested, should be a "bridge" or arbiter between the public and the press. "The juridical statute for information," he said, "is a bridge between the public and private [interests] in which the right of the individual to express his ideas freely cannot be ignored nor can the fact be disregarded that information, and especially the press, moves directly in the public

---

[2] *Ibid.*, pp. 226–227.
[3] Manuel Fraga Iribarne, *Discurso de Excmo. Sr. Ministro del Departamento en el Acto de Clausura de la II Asamblea del Consejo Nacional de "Festivales de España,"* a speech given in November, 1964, and published in pamphlet form (Madrid, 1964), p. 12.
[4] *Horizonte Español,* p. 220. Fraga's top press official, Manuel Jiménez Quílez, Director-General of the Press, expressed the idea in the course of an exchange of written questions and answers between April 5 and April 27, 1965: "The reader who can easily recognize official censorship can not as easily see another class of censorship, more subtle and hidden, which acts on the information he reads. This class of pressure seeks only to benefit special interests, which are, most of the time, unknown to the public."

sphere, gathering and expressing opinions, predominantly of groups, about public affairs of the greatest social importance." [5]

The announcement of his appointment, on July 10, 1962, was heralded as a step toward relaxation of press controls and the over-haul or elimination of existing controls. He was characterized, by at least one foreign news agency, as "more liberal than his predecessor and more in favor of a democratic press system for Spain." The same agency suggested that his appointment "might bring about a gradual elimination of press censorship." [6]

In the months before his appointment there had been a series of events which indicate the role in which the Spanish press had been cast. They merit examination as points of departure for an examination of what changes did take place after Fraga's elevation to the post of Minister of Information.

Late in January of 1962, the Madrid newspaper *ABC* rocked the surface serenity of U.S.-Spanish relations by charging that those who governed the United States were "hypocrites." The newspaper lashed out against the U.S.A. for "abandoning its allies" as the result of "infantile policies," and raked it over the editorial coals for twenty-four acts of hypocrisy.[7] *New York Times* correspondent Benjamin Welles called it "a string of the most vitriolic accusations at the United States that diplomats and observers can recall in recent times." Welles pointed out, as did other American correspondents, that it seemed unlikely that the editorial could have been published without authorization from the Minister of Information and Tourism, Gabriel Arias Salgado.[8] The conclusion arrived at by foreign correspondents and, unofficially, by U.S. diplomats, was that the attack in *ABC*, as well as subsequent comments on radio and re-publication of the *ABC* editorial in provincial newspapers, was part of a government campaign aimed at strengthening Spain's bargaining position in upcoming negotiations for the renewal of the military pacts with the United States and an attempt to force the U.S.

---

[5] *A resume of the speech given by the Minister of Information and Tourism before the National Council of the Movement, April 8, 1964,* distributed by the Servicios Informativos de la Dirección General de Prensa (Madrid, 1964), p. 2.
[6] United Press International, *Dispatch No. 55*, Madrid, July 10, 1962.
[7] "Hipócritas," *ABC* (Madrid), Jan. 19, 1962, p. 3.
[8] "U.S. Disturbed by Spain's Press," *The New York Times*, Jan. 21, 1962, p. 27, col. 1.

to revise its policy in reference to Portugal's colonies of Angola and Mozambique in Africa.

The Spanish government denied this interpretation. "In some cases," an official note said, "political and diplomatic observers as well as the press of foreign countries erroneously think there is official inspiration to news items and commentaries on international politics appearing in Spanish newspapers and magazines. In this respect, it must be repeated that the Spanish press spontaneously informs and expresses its opinion even on questions of international politics." [9] Despite that denial, government sources leaked to foreign press representatives the information that the *ABC* editorial had been submitted, before publication, to both the Minister of Information and Tourism and the Minister of Foreign Affairs.[10] The attacks, the "spontaneous" expression of the press's opinions, continued for one week and then halted abruptly—on orders from the Ministry of Information.[11]

In early April, 1962, a handful of miners laid down their picks in one mine in northern Spain. The strike spread, and by late May, an estimated 80,000 workers in the nation were on strike, while another 80,000 had struck for varying periods of time and then returned to work, costing the country an estimated $250 million and some 15,000,000 man-hours of production. The strike had begun as a demand for higher wages but turned into a social protest. It was an event that merited coverage in the mass media—especially because Spanish law made strikes illegal. However, the press, which the government had said "spontaneously informs and expresses its opinion," carried no word of the strikes until May 5, when the government was forced to declare a limited state of emergency and suspend certain of the basic rights of the Spanish people (*Fuero de los Españoles*). On that day Spanish newspapers reported: "The illegal paralyzation of work in certain coal mines and other business imposes the necessity to safeguard, within the law, the general interest: therefore, the government must apply the provisions of Article 35 [12] of the rights of the Spaniards." The articles then re-

---

[9] Ministerio de Información y Turismo, quoted by United Press International, *Dispatch No. 30*, Madrid, Jan. 22, 1962.
[10] United Press International, *Dispatch No. 10*, Madrid, Jan. 21, 1962.
[11] United Press International, *Dispatch No. 30*, Madrid, Jan. 29, 1962.
[12] *Artículo 35* of the *Fuero de los Españoles* gives the government the power

peated the official announcement.[13]

The following day, there was no news about the strikes in the Spanish press. The major domestic story was one reporting on the celebration in Spain of an international "accident-free day." Not until May 17 did news of the strikes again appear in the press. On that day, *ABC* devoted two columns to reports of international agitators at work in Asturias, the center of Spain's coal-mining industry. The story emphasized the role played by Radio Prague, a station which transmitted news about Spain to Spain from behind the Iron Curtain.[14] Meanwhile, despite the almost total blackout on news of the strike within Spain, dispatches were flowing out of the country and appearing in newspapers throughout the world.[15] Such was the coverage that there were public demonstrations of sympathy for the strikers and their goals in at least thirteen European and American cities. On May 19, *ABC*, with the approval of the government, printed a list of the demonstrations, which ranged from silent protest marches to attempts to burn Spanish embassies or consular buildings in Copenhagen and Athens and shots fired into Spanish cultural exchange offices in Buenos Aires.[16]

Meanwhile, those who opposed the Franco government created their own substitutes for the mass media, to which they were denied access, in an attempt to spread news about the strike and to foment additional disturbances. Hidden mimeograph machines poured out copy, which arrived in plain envelopes or was slid under the doors of foreign newsmen, presumed sympathizers with the strikers' cause, and key figures among the nation's intellectuals. One unnamed group reported in detail, but with a notorious lack of accuracy, on strike developments, including government efforts to bring it to an end. In Madrid, a self-styled "Syndical Opposition" called for a union of "Catholics, Communists, Socialists, Liberals, Anarchists, and those without affiliation." A group of Spanish in-

---

to suspend other articles of the *Fuero*, including that which guarantees that Spaniards "shall be able to express freely their ideas so long as they do not undermine the fundamental principles of the state."

[13] *ABC* (Madrid), May 5, 1962, p. 31. All Madrid newspapers carried exactly the same account.

[14] *Ibid.*, May 19, 1962, p. 58.

[15] The author's dispatches were published, for example, in the *New York Times, Washington Post*, Omaha *World Herald, El Universal* and *Ovaciones* of Mexico City, and *La Prensa* of Buenos Aires.

[16] *ABC* (Madrid), May 19, 1962, p. 58.

tellectuals distributed an open letter to "friends and colleagues," calling on them to urge the Franco regime to inform the people of the strikers' grievances and to legalize strikes. Among those who signed the letter were Ramón Menéndez Pidal, president of the Spanish Academy; José María Gil Robles, a cabinet minister during the Republic and onetime leader of the Catholic Action party; and, of course, Dionysio Ridruejo, one of Franco's most voluble critics.

In early June, the strikes finally petered out. During the time they had lasted, *ABC*, whose coverage was typical, contented itself with publishing official handouts and some related material originating abroad. The newspaper itself, according to members of its staff, made no independent effort to gather together any information. The assumption is that it could not have published any reports it might have originated. The news agency EFE supplied its clients with brief daily wrap-ups of strike activity—reports labeled "confidential" and destined for the attention of newspaper editors and publishers, not for public consumption. During the most critical period of the strike—between late April and the last day in May— *ABC* published a total of six and a half columns of material about the strikes or related to the strikes, a total of roughly 2,500 words. That was only little more than the total words carried each day of the strike by each of the major foreign news agencies operating out of Spain.

Viewed from the perspective of Spanish officialdom, the weeks of labor unrest had been doubly trying—as an internal problem which defied simple solutions and as a prolonged period during which international attention had been focused on Spain and its domestic stresses and strains. It may even be—and some government officials suggested it was so—that there was a positive relationship between the intensity of foreign attention directed at Spain and the difficulty with which the government settled the strike and restored normalcy. The strike could have been ended by force at any stage of its development. Instead, the Spanish government, conscious of its international "image," [17] chose to use persuasion and negotiation. As one government official told this author at the time of the strikes, "It is too late now to put the brakes on, though we

[17] In late 1961, an "image" expert was sent into Spain by Communications Counselors, a subsidiary of McCann, Erickson, to advise government officials. He was Percy Winner, a psychological warfare expert on leave from the U.S. Department of Defense.

could. We just have to wait and see what will happen. If we do otherwise, every one of our enemies is going to scream 'repression' and write about policies dating from the Middle Ages."

The handling of news about the strike had been a good example of the policy of withholding news. In June, the government resorted to the other extreme to deal with a delicate situation: it manufactured a news story and ordered newspapers to publish it. On June 7 and 8, eighty members of the anti-Franco opposition attended a Congress of the European Movement in Munich. While there, they met with thirty-eight exiled Spaniards and drew up a resolution demanding the recognition of certain rights by the Spanish government. One of the demands was for the "effective guarantee of all Human Rights, in particular those of personal liberty and freedom of opinion and the suppression of government censorship." [18] When the participants, including some major opposition spokesmen, returned to Spain, they were either jailed or exiled. Even before that, though, the government had fabricated a news report which supposedly was originated in Munich by EFE, the Spanish national news agency, or by Reuters, UPI, or Agence France-Presse, which supplied news to EFE. The government "sent out very detailed telegraphic instructions to all newspapers and ordered the obligatory publication of the 'reportage' of the official news agency, EFE, on the 'conspiracy of Munich.' " [19] The report called the congress communist-dominated and said the Spaniards who attended were traitors.

There were repercussions to these events—the strike and the Munich meeting—which had kept Spain in the public eye. On June 15, the Ministry of Information informed Richard Scott Mowrer, one of six full-time American correspondents in Madrid, that his press credentials, normally revalidated every six months, would not be renewed. "I was notified by letter of the government's decision," Mowrer explained. "I asked for a reason and was given none." A spokesman for the Ministry of Information, the department of government charged with issuing press credentials, told the foreign press the following day, "I have no comment to make on the de-

[18] International Commission of Jurists, *Spain and the Rule of Law* (Geneva, 1962), p. 42.
[19] "Uncensored" (a report from an anonymous correspondent), *Iberica: For a Free Spain*, X, nos. 7-8 (July-August, 1962), 13.

cision to discontinue his credentials. As far as we are concerned, we no longer recognize Mr. Mowrer as being accredited here." [20]

At about the same time, the author, then United Press International manager in Spain, was threatened with expulsion from the country. The threat came, not from the Ministry of Information, but from the Director-General of Security, Carlos Arias Navarro, the nation's number one police officer. This writer had reported that crowds lining the route of the annual "Victory Day Parade," celebrating the end of the Civil War, had made derisive sounds as police units marched past.

The parade had taken place Sunday, June 3. The following Thursday, this writer was ordered to report to Arias Navarro's office. Without prelude, Arias Navarro charged that the report was erroneous and ordered me to write a retraction for distribution by UPI. When I refused, the Director-General threatened, "You will print a complete retraction or be expelled from Spain." Finally, after some argument, we agreed to refer the matter to the Spanish Foreign Office—Arias Navarro being presumably more reluctant to expel an American newsman than I was to be expelled. At that point, Arias Navarro admitted that my offense had not been as great as he had originally suggested. There were other reasons for his attitude. "We are fed up with the way you Americans are treating us in your press," he explained, adding that part of his indignation stemmed from the actions of American visitors to Spain and American students. Recently, he explained, an American tourist had torn down a picture of Franco and spat on it. "What would you do," he asked, "if a Spaniard were to spit on a picture of President Kennedy?" He noted also that American students had recently been involved in demonstrations against the regime. We shook hands as I prepared to leave. Another senior police officer who had been present and who had appeared to view with distaste the whole scene, especially the Director-General's anger during the initial stages of the meeting, took my hand a second time. "The first handshake was protocol," he said, "this one is for friendship."

Before the end of the month, Mr. Mowrer's credentials were renewed, without explanation, and the threat to declare this author *persona non grata* was pigeonholed.

Shortly thereafter, on July 10, Fraga was named Minister of In-

---

[20] United Press International, *Dispatch No. 18,* Madrid, June 18, 1962.

formation and Tourism. There was a mood of change in the air. After the first meeting of the new cabinet, Fraga announced that the government was prepared to move in the direction of a "new policy of information." Franco himself approved and, according to Fraga, had told the ministers, "The past years and the undeniable improvement in the social structure of our country have produced today a vigorous social reality, distinct from and better than that which existed thirty years ago." Such new conditions permitted changes.[21]

Before the month was over, Fraga had crystallized the vague hints of the past and the new climate of opinion into a public promise that new press laws would be drawn up and in force by the end of the year.[22] Even before there was a change in statutes, he began a process of "liberalizing" the press. He ordered the gradual end of prepublication censorship everywhere in Spain, except in Madrid and Barcelona, and admitted more flexibility and wider coverage for newspapers in those two major cities. By October, the process had accelerated, Fraga claimed, "to the extent that state censors are unemployed."[23] He emphasized the trend toward liberalization by restoring the Marqués de Luca de Tena to the post of editor of *ABC*, from which Arias Salgado had earlier removed him.[24]

In his first year as Minister, Fraga authorized the reopening of a liberal newspaper, ordered closed in 1939,[25] and the founding of a new daily.[26] Arias Salgado had permitted only three dailies to begin operations between 1951 and 1962. In addition, the new Minister gave the "go" signal to 654 magazines in the period between his appointment and the end of March, 1964,[27] more than his predecessor had authorized during the entire decade beginning in 1950.[28] By early 1965, the number of new magazines approved by Fraga had risen to approximately 1,250, according to Gabriel

[21] Fraga Iribarne, *Horizonte Español*, pp. 249–250.
[22] In an interview with Jean Creach, correspondent of *Le Combat* of Paris.
[23] *The New York Times*, Oct. 10, 1962, p. 10, col. 1.
[24] *Ibid.*, Oct. 8, 1962, p. 3, col. 8.
[25] *Diario de Pontevedra* ("Pontevedra Daily") (Pontevedra, 1887-1939, 1962– in operation).
[26] *Majorca Daily Times* (Palma, 1962–in operation), an English-language daily run by Spaniards.
[27] *Gaceta de la Prensa Española*, May 15, 1964, p. 45.
[28] Instituto de la Opinión Pública, *Estudio sobre los Medios de Comunicación de Masas en España* (Madrid, 1964), I, 67.

Cañadas, a top official of the Ministry of Information and Tourism, who suggested that the increase in periodicals could be construed as a sign of liberalization.[29]

There was also a decided liberalization in book publishing and import, according to Luis G. Seara, director of Spain's relatively new Public Opinion Institute (Instituto de la Opinión Pública). Seara cited, as examples, the appearance in bookstores of Vladimir Nabokov's *Lolita* and various works by Alberto Moravia and D. H. Lawrence. He also noted a relaxation in censorship of the works of Spanish authors. The same relaxation was apparent in the treatment of films and theatrical productions.[30]

By mid-1964, the changes caused one foreign observer, Terrance Prittie of the Manchester *Guardian*, to write of "a liberal wind blowing in Spain at present. . . ." Prittie reported: "Ministry of Information officials have been instructed to cease their scrutiny of papers, 95 per cent of whose contents are 'passed' without any comment. Criticism of the Government is now regarded as allowable, as long as its intention is not manifestly to 'undermine' the regime. Fraga puts it this way: 'We want to encourage all free discussion which is in the national interest.' "[31]

Yet the reaction to Fraga's liberalization was not all positive. Dionysio Ridruejo charged that "liberalization means much more than allowing a few privileged papers to print uncensored news." He suggested that it involved a mode of thinking and reacting that must permeate not only the ranks of those who are connected with

---

[29] Gabriel Cañadas Nouvilas, Secretario-General Técnico of the Ministry, an interview on Feb. 12, 1965.
[30] Luis G. Seara, an interview on Feb. 25, 1965. One of the Spanish books cited by Seara as an indication of the relaxation of censorship was *Paralelo Cuarenta*, in which the author, José Luis Castillo Puche, calls the mayor of Madrid a "fool." Seara noted also that a study of Spain's mass communications media, prepared by his institute, had included "attacks" on departments within the Ministry of Information and Tourism, "yet everything we gathered was published and the Ministry paid." See *Estudio sobre los Medios*, II, 1, 700, 814, and 995. However, some of the old ways of approaching a problem did linger. When Columbia Pictures announced its intention of making *Behold a Pale Horse*, which involved the portrayal of Spanish Republicans in exile and officials of the present regime, the Ministry of Information objected to the representatives of the film company, asking that the project be given up. Columbia ignored the objections and produced the picture; the Spanish government, in retaliation, banned all Columbia films from Spain. The ban lasted until early 1966.
[31] "Franco's Finesse," *The Guardian* (Manchester ed.), June 5, 1964.

the press but also all levels of the official hierarchies.[32]

The clash of the old modes of authoritarian action with the basic concepts of liberalization exhibited itself in many ways. In an interview with this writer, Spain's Director-General of the Press, Manuel Jiménez Quílez, noted, as a sign of liberalization, a relaxation of the censorship of imported publications. "You can see that the foreign magazines and newspapers are distributed without limitation in the kiosks of our cities. Not too long ago, all magazines bore a stamp of approval. Now there are more than 300 foreign publications which enter without that red tape." [33] At about the same time, April, 1965, another official of the Ministry of Information said that foreign newspapers were no longer censored. Yet, on April 28, the Ministry of Information banned the Swedish morning newspaper, *Dagens Nyheter*, from the country. The newspaper was informed of the Spanish government's decision by cable, and no explanation was given, but *Dagens Nyheter* officials assumed it was because of coverage of events within Spain.[34]

There were many such contradictions. Newspapers were allowed to print more "political news," yet such news lacked the elements of controversy or conflict generally associated with politics. A typical column of news, published under the heading of "Political Information" ("Información política"), might include items, as one column did, about the movements of the Minister of the Army; a visit paid by Madrid's mayor to the Minister of Agriculture; and a report on a meeting of provincial governors, a report devoted entirely to listing the participants' names and noting the hours at which the meeting began and ended.[35]

The press was allowed wider scope in its editorial columns, being permitted to discuss matters which had hitherto been sacrosanct— those related to municipal and national government. It was even free to call for some fundamental changes, such as the revision of the press laws,[36] a greater equality of economic opportunity for all Spaniards, or the legalizing of formal opposition parties.[37] But there was no unrestricted freedom. The press could not discuss such

---

[32] "Spain's Restless Voices," *Catholic World*, no. 197 (May, 1963), p. 91.
[33] Written answers to questions submitted by the author on Apr. 7, 1965.
[34] United Press International, *Dispatch No. 10*, Stockholm, April 29, 1965.
[35] *Arriba* (Madrid), Feb. 26, 1965, p. 14.
[36] *Ya* (Madrid), Feb. 24, 1964, p. 7.
[37] *Arriba* (Madrid), Mar. 24, 1965, p. 2.

matters as agrarian reform, religious freedom, academic freedom, or the transfer of power. In Madrid and Barcelona, the censors made sure newspapers did not. A Madrid newspaper executive complained, in early 1965, that some of his editorials, which had been sent to the Ministry of Information eight months before, had not been returned—editorials which noted a nationwide feeling of "intranquillity" because no apparent provisions had been made for a government to succeed that of Franco, then in his seventies.

The provincial press was left to make its own decisions about what could be discussed in print and what should be left untouched. There were dangers for those editors who interpreted "liberalization" too broadly. In 1964, for example, the director of *El Norte de Castilla* [38] wrote a series of articles about the need for agrarian reform, flood-control problems, poverty, and farm subsidies. The government did not approve, and the Ministry of Information asked the newspaper to discharge the author of the offending articles, threatening to withdraw newsprint subsidies if it did not. The company refused, but did remove the writer from the directorship.

Nowhere, perhaps, were the contradictions between the concept of liberalization and the ingrained authoritarian responses more clearly delineated than in the case of Manuel Fernández Areal. On November 6, 1964, the *Diario Regional* of Valladolid [39] published an editorial written by Fernández Areal, its director, in which he called for a modernization of Spain's program of compulsory military training. In the editorial, entitled "A Realistic Project" ("Un Proyecto Realista"), he asked:

What would happen if Spain were to do away with some of those large, dark, disintegrating barracks which are so difficult to keep clean and maintain in the "perfect state for inspection," barracks which are so costly and often vacant? What would happen if Spain were to shorten the period of military service [from eighteen months] so that a young Spaniard could, in three months of intensive training, learn how to manage his weapons, be grounded in hygienic practices, master close order drill, and learn whatever else that is absolutely necessary? The time would be used to better advantage and less money would be spent. . . . [40]

---

[38] *El Norte de Castilla* ("The North of Castile") (Valladolid, 1853–in operation).
[39] *Diario Regional* ("Regional Daily") (Valladolid, 1908–in operation).
[40] *Diario Regional* (Valladolid), Nov. 6, 1964.

On the day the editorial appeared, Fernández Areal was called to the office of the provincial captain-general, questioned, and then jailed. The same day, the Ministry of Information telephoned the *Diario Regional* and ordered his suspension from his post. He was held in jail for twenty-eight hours, eighteen incommunicado. While he was in jail, the Ministry of Information prepared and transmitted to the *Diario Regional* a reply to the offending editorial, an unsigned reply whose publication was made a condition for Fernández Areal's temporary release from jail. The reply was published. The following day, Fernández Areal, by then released, was formally charged with "insulting the army." For nineteen days, he pleaded his case with military and Ministry of Information officials, but to no avail. He was brought to trial early in February and a panel of four generals sentenced him to six months and one day in jail, despite his contention that "constructive criticism" had been the sole intent of the editorial. It was a momentary triumph for the traditional approach. However, the sentence was not carried out. Early in March, it was announced that Fernández Areal had been pardoned and, on March 18, Madrid newspapers noted laconically that he had been "restored to his post as director of the *Diario Regional*." [41]

In general, it was a period of confusion for newspapermen. The strict censorship of the past years had been an irritation or worse, an ever present chain that had shackled the energies and initiative of the press. But there had been no confusion, no uncertainty; the censors saw to that, making the decisions about what should be published and what should be rejected. Liberalization, which did not mean freedom but rather more flexibility and a broadening of the scope of editorial and newsgathering activities, brought insecurity. It was viewed as the first in a long series of steps that might, someday, lead to freedom—steps, as Fraga had said, "where every movement must be calculated with precision." There were still limits, which were, at best, imprecisely defined. As one newspaper executive confided early in 1965, "We lack norms. We don't know what to publish and what not to publish. There are no guidelines. We used to get written orders. Now we get only vague verbal instructions or no instructions at all." [42] Other newspapermen declared that

---

[41] *Ya* (Madrid), Mar. 18, 1965, p. 32.
[42] The speaker asked that his identity be kept secret.

what was most needed was a new press law. Fraga had promised a new press law when he became Minister and had implemented his promise by increasing membership in the National Press Council (Consejo Nacional de Prensa) and entrusting to it the task of preparing the draft of a new law. By mid-1964, a draft had been drawn up. Its provisions included one which stated: "The administration will not be able to apply previous censorship nor impose obligatory consultation except in exceptional cases expressly foreseen in the Laws." [43]

There was, however, official opposition to the new law and to liberalization of the press; and the press's insecurities and uncertainties were without doubt the indirect result of that opposition. The government's attitude to the whole subject was ambivalent. Liberalization was approved by only a segment of those in power. There were many, including influential members of Franco's cabinet, who bitterly opposed any change, and their opposition blocked the movement of the new law through legislative channels, thus tending to put Fraga's liberalization on a somewhat experimental basis. If the Spanish press, partially freed from controls, operated responsibly, then their opposition to liberalization in general, and in particular to a formal end to prepublication censorship as spelled out in the draft of the new law, might be withdrawn. But if the press were to transgress during the experimental period, then opposition to change would harden, its arguments fortified by evidence other than that drawn from the experiences of the pre–Civil War period.

Fraga, and those who backed him, were caught in the middle. They desired liberalization and its formal legalization. Yet they knew that if experimental liberalization resulted in dramatic changes in the content of the Spanish press, they might not be able to achieve their goals. In order to insure that the press did not rock the boat, and thus set back its own cause, they were forced to resort to some of the controls which the concept of liberalization rejected. It is probable, also, that those who favored liberalization were caught in the middle historically, dedicated to the principles of liberalization and yet conditioned by experience to seek simple, direct authoritarian solutions to any problems caused by the liberalization which they espoused.

---

[43] Ministerio de Información y Turismo, *Anteproyecto de Ley de Prensa e Imprenta* (Madrid, undated), pp. 5–6.

It has been suggested that the case of Fernández Areal, the director of the *Diario Regional*, reflected some of the official ambivalence. His trial and conviction were ordained by the Spanish Army, one of the groups in opposition to liberalization. His subsequent pardon and restoration to work were engineered by those who favored liberalization, including Fraga.

Some forms of direction persisted, direction incompatible with the ideals presumably associated with liberalization. On February 10, 1965, a Spanish passenger train went off the rails and burned near Saragossa. Thirty-four persons died, probably because they were riding in outdated wooden coaches. José Luis Cebrian, editor of the Madrid evening newspaper *El Alcázar*, reported that he had received instructions to print no more than two columns of news and pictures of the event. Some subjects were banned from print. The press was not allowed to print news or articles about Prince Carlos Hugo, heir to the Carlist claim to the Spanish throne, or of his marriage to Princess Irene of the Netherlands. His name was not to be mentioned, not even unfavorably, according to Vicente Royo Masia, editor of the weekly magazine *Confidencial*,[44] who had tried vainly in 1964 to obtain permission to publish a highly critical analysis of the Prince.

The ambivalence also appeared in the government's relationship with the foreign press. Under the direction of Fraga, Ministry of Information personnel cooperated more with foreign correspondents, providing information that would have been unavailable during the period when Arias Salgado was director. Fraga himself held regular press conferences and took over some of the responsibilities of government spokesman, a role ignored by his predecessor. He also made himself available for interviews. But, despite the cooperation of Ministry personnel and his own accessibility, Fraga's attempts at working closely with the foreign press were not completely successful. At least two foreign correspondents, Harold Milks of Associated Press and Pierre Brisard of Agence France Presse, refused to attend briefings, claiming, as Milks put it, that "we are insulted if we ask a pertinent question." [45] Brisard, who had been assigned to Spain by his agency in February, 1963, reported that he had been under pressure during his first year in Madrid to submit his dispatches to the Ministry of Information before sending

---

[44] *Confidencial* ("Confidential") (Madrid, 1964–in operation).
[45] An interview on Apr. 13, 1965.

them. However, he refused, and by late 1963 or early 1964, the pressure was relaxed.[46] Brisard's presence in Spain was the result of a "deal" between the government and AFP. The agency had been awarded a contract to supply news to EFE in return for the transfer out of Spain of its resident correspondent, Jacqueline Darricarére d'Etchevers, Brisard's predecessor, who was considered by the government to be unduly critical of the regime.[47]

In November, 1964, Fraga withdrew the credentials of Gustave Hermann, who covered Spain for several German periodicals, including the *Wiener Zeitung* and the *Frankfurter Rundschau.* The Minister acted only after much consideration and as the result of "sufficient provocation," Ministry officials said. Early the following year, he also canceled the accreditation of José Antonio Novais, a Spanish newsman who served as correspondent for *Le Monde* of Paris and *O Estado* of Sao Paulo, Brazil. Fraga acted against Novais with a blare of publicity, attacking him publicly for having "deformed" the news in his dispatches to *Le Monde.*[48] The weekly magazine *El Español,*[49] published in the Ministry of Information and Tourism, amplified the attack. It dug up and printed a two-year-old accident report as evidence that Novais was an "alcoholic."[50] It also reached deep into Falange party records to turn up the information that Novais had professed undying loyalty to the party and the regime in an application for a scholarship in 1951. Yet, the magazine said, his reports to *Le Monde* had been very critical of the Falange and the regime, which made Novais a hypocrite.[51] The article suggested that Novais had been a source of irritation for some time, though the precise reason given for the withdrawal of his credentials was his report that twenty students had been injured in a clash with police and one was in "very serious condition."[52] Novais had been notified on February 26, by telephone, that his credentials had been withdrawn. Early in March, during an

---

[46] An interview on Apr. 20, 1965.
[47] Carlos Mendo, now director of EFE, an interview on Mar. 19, 1965.
[48] "Declaraciones del Ministro de Información a un periódico danés," *Ya* (Madrid), Mar. 14, 1965, p. 9.
[49] *El Español* ("The Spaniard") (Madrid, 1962–in operation).
[50] "El Caso Novais," *El Español,* Mar. 20, 1965, pp. 6–7.
[51] *Ibid.,* p. 8.
[52] A Ministry of Information and Tourism note, published in *Arriba* (Madrid), Feb. 27, 1965, p. 5. Other Spanish newspapers carried the same note on the same day.

interview with a correspondent from the Danish newspaper *Ekstrabladet*, Fraga made his charge that Novais had "deformed" the news by reporting that one student had been killed and twenty injured. The interview was widely published in Spain, the local accounts noting that the "Danish newspaper, by mistake, had given the number of injured as forty." [53]

In April, Novais, smarting under Fraga's attack, brought a suit for libel against the Minister. Fraga failed to appear in court and was fined 300 pesetas, about $5.00, for his nonappearance, and the matter apparently was dropped.

The incident which led to the withdrawal of Novais' credentials was only a sidelight of an overall event whose coverage in the Spanish press lends itself to comparison with coverage of the 1962 strikes. In that year, as noted earlier, a series of illegal work stoppages, lasting for about three months, had idled factories and mines across Spain and had involved, at one time or another, about 160,-000 workers. That was before Fraga had been named Minister and initiated liberalization. Press coverage had been limited: *ABC*, for example, published only about 2,500 words during the walkouts.

In February, 1965, students at the University of Madrid launched a series of protests against the official and obligatory student union, the Sindicato Español Universitario (Spanish University Syndicate). On February 24, 3,000 students, led by professors, staged a protest march followed by a sit-in in the university's Faculty of Philosophy and Letters, the first of a series of demonstrations which continued sporadically until early April. According to foreign press dispatches, 350 police were called in and used jets of water and clubs to disperse the demonstrators.[54] Madrid newspapers reported in some detail on the events.[55] The government ordered the faculty to close and suspend four professors allegedly involved in the demonstrations. This was duly reported. Each day and in every paper, there was a report on the student protests, or events related to them. The press even editorialized, its comments ranging from charges that the students had committed an "abuse of confidence" [56] to a call for "highly skillful and extremely clear handling" of the

---

[53] *Ya* (Madrid), Mar. 14, 1965, p. 9.
[54] United Press International, *Dispatch No. 29*, Madrid, Feb. 24, 1965.
[55] *ABC* (Madrid), Feb. 25, 1965, p. 49; *Ya* (Madrid), the same date, p. 1; *Arriba* (Madrid), the same date, p. 23.
[56] *Arriba* (Madrid), Feb. 25, 1965, p. 1.

situation.[57] As it became evident that the period of protest would be prolonged, the newspapers devoted more attention to reports of "agitators" at work in stirring up trouble,[58] a suggestion reinforced by sympathy demonstrations organized in France, Italy, and Germany. In addition, attention was focused on student protests outside the country, in Rome, Rabat, Paris, Lagos, Cuernavaca, and New York. Prominence given to demonstrations of student dissatisfaction elsewhere presumably tended to minimize the importance of the local disorders.

The students' request for a reorganization of their "syndicate"—a reorganization which would allow them more right to participate in the selection of officers and the making of policy decisions—was considered favorably by the government and concessions were granted. That development was reported in detail. In all, during the six-week period of demonstrations and events related to the demonstrations, *ABC* published at least 20,000 words, eight times the number it used to report the strikes of 1962, which lasted nearly twice as long.

Insofar as the space devoted to the two events is an indicator, liberalization meant that the press was doing a more extensive job of informing the Spanish people. However, one Spanish newsman, who must remain anonymous, reported that the amplitude of coverage and the prominence given to the coverage had been "suggested by the Ministry of Information." It was even claimed that the Ministry prepared news releases which the press printed verbatim, and the fact that many of the stories carried by Madrid newspapers were identical does indicate a common source. For example, the three morning newspapers in Madrid all carried reports of equal length which described the outbreak of demonstrations in identical terms: "Yesterday a group of students and uncontrolled persons provoked a tumultuous meeting in the lobby of the Faculty of Philosophy and Letters in University City." [59] The uniformity of coverage led graduates of the nation's official school of journalism to complain to Fraga about strike coverage, a fact which was not reported in the newspapers. The newspaper *La Nueva España* [60] of Oviedo did report that faculty members at the Uni-

---

[57] *ABC* (Madrid), Mar. 3, 1965, p. 32.
[58] *Ibid.*, Mar. 14, 1965, p. 79; *Ya* (Madrid), the same date, p. 6.
[59] Editions of Feb. 25, 1965: *ABC*, p. 49; *Arriba*, p. 23; *Ya*, p. 1.
[60] *La Nueva España* ("The New Spain") (Oviedo, 1936–in operation).

versity of Oviedo had drawn up a protest against press coverage
of the demonstrations, which had been reflected on a very minor
scale at their school. The news agency EFE, in a short, nationally
distributed dispatch, suggested that *La Nueva España* had been
"officious" (*oficioso*) in reporting such a development.[61]

Some events related to the demonstrators, judged newsworthy
by the foreign press, were not reported in Spain. Such was the
case on February 26, when police picked up four British television
newsmen, in Spain to interview Fraga; held them for several hours;
and finally released them after confiscating their film. The same
news blackout prevailed several days later when United Press International news editor Harry Debelius was held for part of a day,
and it continued on March 9, when authorities detained Mrs. Elna
Álvarez Prida, sister-in-law of Spain's historian-in-exile, Salvador
de Madariaga, for questioning. The Spanish press did not report
the arrest of twenty-five persons, mainly students, on March 2,
though the arrests were covered in detail by foreign correspondents.[62] There were other omissions, far too many to list.

In looking back over the coverage of the two events—the 1962
strikes and 1965 student demonstrations—one is tempted by the
marked difference in domestic coverage to conclude, as do Ministry
of Information and Tourism officials, that the difference was due
to that change in policy which has been called "liberalization." But
to be content with one explanation might well mean settling for an
oversimplification. The press was permitted, even encouraged, to
publish more, but much of what was published originated from
within the official power structure and thus did not represent an
increased freedom of selection on the part of the press. Certain facets
of the student demonstration which appeared newsworthy to non-
Spaniards were not reported. Other facets—the suggestions that
professional agitators were at work and the reports of student protests elsewhere in the world—were given a prominence that suggests a deliberate policy designed to minimize the domestic disturbances. If the increased coverage can be attributed solely to the
process of liberalization, then the press's reliance on handouts and
the gaps in its coverage can be assumed to illustrate the limitations
of the liberalizing process and the ambivalence of the official atti-

[61] *ABC* (Madrid), Mar. 4, 1965, p. 49.
[62] United Press International, *Dispatch No. 24*, Madrid, Mar. 2, 1965.

tude toward it. Explanations other than liberalization have been suggested by those who are critical of the regime and skeptical of its sincerity. According to such critics, the increased coverage of 1965 might have resulted from the fact that the government was aware of the cause of the student protests—the student's complaints had been aired before—and was prepared, from the beginning, to grant the demanded concessions. If so, their argument goes, the government encouraged the mass media to focus attention on the demonstrations since they provided the regime an opportunity to demonstrate publicly its flexibility. Other skeptics viewed the press coverage as manipulated evidence of the progress of the process of liberalization. And still others wrote it off as an attempt to project a more favorable international image. It may be possible that all those reasons, and others less apparent, contributed to some degree.

Meanwhile, work on the new press law had progressed. The National Press Council had drawn up a draft of a press and print law (*Anteproyecto de la Ley de Prensa e Imprenta*), which was distributed to members of the government and to newspaper executives. In its preamble, the draft reaffirmed "liberty of expression in the print media." [63] Its second article, however, defined, in general terms, the limits to that right: "The freedom of expression affirmed in Article 1 shall have no limits other than those imposed by the considerations of morality and truth; respect for existing public and constitutional order; the demands of national defense, of the security of the State and of internal and external public peace; the reserve owing to the action of the government, of the Cortes, and of the administration; the independence of the tribunals in the application of the laws; and the safeguarding of private affairs and honor." [64] It also prohibited prepublication censorship,[65] which aroused the vehement objections of many influential individuals and groups within the government—individuals and groups who feared that the legal lifting of censorship would lead to the return of the excesses that had marked some periods of press freedom.[66]

---

[63] Ministerio de Información y Turismo, *Anteproyecto de Ley, Preámbulo.*
[64] *Ibid., Artículo 2.*
[65] *Ibid., Artículo 3.*
[66] The author asked the opinions of several Spanish lawyers, all of whom agreed that the provisions of Article 2, which limited the area of discussion of the press, were sufficiently broad to allow the government the means of effective control.

The law also proposed to return to the enterprises the right to select their own directors, rather than reserve that right to the government as did the existing law. Article 46 stated flatly that "the director will be appointed by the enterprise, complying with the formalities established in this law." The formalities included certification of certain legal requisites. "In order to fill the post of director," the law stated ". . . [the individual must] have Spanish nationality, be in full exercise of civil and political rights [i.e., not have been convicted of a crime nor be charged at the time of appointment with a crime], be domiciled in the place where the periodical is published, and be enrolled as a journalist in the official register of journalists." [67] The law specified also that the director of a periodical could not become involved in any "public post or private activity which might restrict his liberty or independence in the performance of his functions or limit his dedication to them," [68] and stipulated that only Spanish nationals could own, fully or partially, a periodical,[69] but that the right to found a periodical could be denied to no Spaniard in possession of national citizenship.[70] And finally, it cast the government in the role of defender and protector of "the liberties which are specified in this law" and gave it the right to bring charges whenever "pressure is illegally exercised against them, particularly that pressure which through monopolies or by other means tries to deform public opinion or impede the free flow of information." [71]

Just as some officials had objected to ending censorship, some newspaper executives objected to other provisions in the draft, especially one that gave the Ministry of Information and Tourism the right to impose fines of between 100,000 and one million *pesetas* and suspend newspapers for periods of up to six months.[72] The newspapermen argued that such a provision gave the Ministry too much arbitrary power which could be used to force a newspaper out of business by strangling it economically.

For some months in 1964, the draft lay dormant, partly because Manuel Aznar, president of the National Press Council, was out of

[67] Ministerio de Información y Turismo, *Anteproyecto de Ley, Artículo 43.*
[68] *Ibid., Artículo 49.*
[69] *Ibid., Artículos 22* and *24.*
[70] *Ibid., Artículo 17.*
[71] *Ibid., Artículo 5.*
[72] *Ibid., Artículo 70.*

the country much of the time, involved with his duties as a member of the Spanish mission to the United Nations. In October, Fraga visited the United States and, during his visit, accepted Aznar's resignation. When Fraga returned to Spain, he named Juan Beneyto, a former Director-General of the Press, to the press council's presidency. Under Beneyto's direction, criticism of the draft was reviewed. In early 1965, Fraga turned over the original draft and extensive notes on its criticism to Pío Cabanillas Gallas, the Undersecretary of Information and Tourism. Cabanillas, a legal expert, went into seclusion in February and drew up a new draft, which was submitted to the Cortes for its approval.

Shortly before the draft went to the Cortes, the pending step of submitting it to the legislature was hailed by the newspaper *Pueblo* as "one step more in the institutionalization of the traditional liberties within the juridic scope of the Spanish state, another indication of political maturity, and, as Fraga Iribarne said, 'a show of confidence in the press, which should greet the law with great satisfaction.' " [73]

The draft was sent first to the Information Commission of the Cortes, a fifty-three-member body, which discussed it with a freedom unusual in Spain's normally rubber-stamp parliament. During an eighteen-day period, beginning the morning of January 17 and ending in the evening of February 3, the Commission met twelve times, devoting eighty hours to the consideration of the bill. A total of 909 speeches were given, and to record them shorthand experts filled 3,000 pages with notes. By the time the Commission had finished its work, it had considered 367 amendments to the press bill and had actually changed fifty-two of its seventy-two articles, though not fundamentally. For example, the second article of the draft had stated that "freedom of expression shall have no limitations other than those imposed by the laws"; the revised text amended that to read "freedom of expression and the right to spread information. . . ." [74] Article 17 of the draft had reserved ownership of periodicals to Spaniards who actually live in Spain; the final bill amended that to allow Spaniards living abroad to own up to 30 per cent of a periodical.[75] Another article had specified

---

[73] Quoted in *Guidepost: Spain's American Weekly* (Madrid), Aug. 20, 1965, p. 10.
[74] *Ley de Prensa e Imprenta, Artículo 2.*
[75] *Ibid., Artículo 17.*

that the source of any news item published in a newspaper must be stated within the story; the revised, final product added to that the specification that any advertising "which expressed opinion about affairs of public interest must include the name and address of the advertiser." [76]

On the morning of March 15, 1966, the deputies of Spain streamed into the Cortes building to vote on the press and print law. Before the vote, they were addressed by the Minister of Information, Fraga Iribarne, who outlined the purposes and reasoning behind the bill. It was, he said, an attempt to find a middle way between the extremes of "an absolute and unlimited freedom of the press and . . . State control imposed under the pretext of enabling it to serve the people better. . . ." The law, he explained, represented an attempt to take into consideration certain "general factors, economic, social, and political, in the informative process." Those factors, he said, included "the general tendency towards concentration, which reduces the real ability to operate the channels of information to a small number of business enterprises; the weight of advertising interests in the running of ever more expensive technical media; the liability to try to increase circulation through a facile recourse to sensationalism or the exciting of all kinds of passion, etc." As a result, he said, the law had grown out of Spain's need for more press liberty and, at the same time, the necessity "for public control and responsibility to keep abuses to a minimum, to regulate the employment of the media, facilitating the access to them of the greatest number [of individuals], and the maximum participation of the public in general." [77]

At a few minutes past noon, the voting began. Only three of more than 500 deputies voted against the bill, a fact which may be interpreted as enthusiastic support for the law or merely as typical of the tradition of the Cortes, which, since the Civil War, had served the function of rubber-stamping foregone conclusions.

On March 25, the Spanish cabinet met under the direction of Generalísimo Franco. It was a regular, biweekly meeting, a marathon session lasting from early afternoon until late in the evening. During the meeting, Franco, the disciplined soldier, remained in his chair at the head of the conference table, listening impassively

[76] Ibid., Artículo 38.
[77] "Press and Printing Bill Passed by Cortes," ES: The Week in Spain, Mar. 28, 1966, p. 2.

as his ministers discussed current problems and the future of the state. He noted as one by one they stole from the meeting room to gulp a soft drink, smoke a hasty cigarette, or relieve themselves, but he barely stirred. Out of that meeting emerged fourteen supplementary laws, spelling out in detail the administration of the new press law. Two weeks later, on April 9, Franco signed the bill, which had passed the Cortes, and with that flourish it became the law of the land.

As already noted, the new law eliminated the worst repressions of the regulations it superseded. It did away with prepublication censorship, withdrew from the government the right to be consulted over the appointment of top newspaper officials, and made it possible for any Spaniard in good standing to start a periodical without government permission. As Harold Milks, the Associated Press bureau chief in Madrid, saw it, the new law "gives the Spanish people freedom of expression unknown previously under the Franco regime, the Republic, or the Spanish monarchy." [78]

---

[78] Quoted by Virginius Dabney, "A Report on the Press in Spain and Portugal," *Saturday Review*, July 9, 1966, p. 50.

he Pattern Is Set:

The Padlock Applied

Printing was introduced into Spain in 1470,[1] the year following the marriage of Isabella and Ferdinand. Spain was not yet a nation, merely a cluster of kingdoms. Castile, to whose throne Isabella succeeded in 1474, lay in the peninsula's center and embraced Old Castile, Leon, Galicia, Asturias, the Basque provinces, Toledo, Estremaduras, and Andalusia. To the east lay the kingdom of Aragon; Navarre, under French rule since 1234; and the principality of Catalonia. To the west was the kingdom of Portugal. In the south, the last Moors lived out their numbered days in Europe on lands stretching east and north from Ronda to Murcia and embracing the lush valley dominated by their stronghold capital of Granada. In 1479, Ferdinand became King of Aragon, and the unification of Spain was begun. In 1492, Ferdinand and Isabella, driving south, captured Granada and thus ended seven centuries of Moorish occupation of the Iberian Peninsula. The same year, Christopher Columbus, sailing west on uncharted seas, reached the New World and helped lay the foundations for Spain's reign as the great world power. As the nation crossed the threshold of its Golden Century, the art of printing spread. In 1474, a nameless printer in Valencia produced an edition of the *Certamen poetich en*

---

[1] Antonio Palau y Dulcet, *De los origenes de la imprenta y su introducción en España* (Barcelona, 1952), p. 13.

lohor de la Concecio,[2] the first work of which a copy exists to this day. Later in the same year, Lambert Palmart, a German living in Spain, published a 334-page folio edition of the *Comprehensorium* of Johannes.

A portable printing press, one of several in the country, followed the victorious armies of Ferdinand and Isabella as they moved south in 1492 against the Moors at Granada, the last stronghold of Islam on the Iberian Peninsula. In 1493, at least three different Latin editions of a report on the discovery of the New World appeared in Spain and, by the year 1500, two Spanish editions of Columbus' letter describing his first voyage of discovery had been printed— one in Barcelona and another in Valladolid.[3]

Printing and printed works were, at first, welcomed into Spain. In 1480, Ferdinand and Isabella decreed that all foreign books should be exempt from duty and other taxes "in consideration of the profit and honor accruing from the bringing to these kingdoms of books from abroad, so that men may thereby become learned."[4] However, the proliferation of printing facilities in Spain was accompanied by a growing recognition on the part of both Church and State of the press's potential danger to established institutions. In 1490, the Inquisition began burning books, primarily Hebrew Bibles and other Jewish works. In Salamanca, some 6,000 volumes on Judaism and sorcery were consigned to the flames. However, those acts were, in a sense, extra-official. It was not until 1494 that a manual for the guidance of inquisitors, printed in Valencia, noted that any heretical work should be either burnt or delivered to the nearest Church official.[5]

In 1502, Ferdinand and Isabella, acting to preserve the outlines of the authoritarian state they were shaping, issued a Pragmatic-Sanction (*Pragmatica-Sanción*) regulating the printing of books. The law, which has formed the basis of much subsequent legislation, stipulated that books be neither published nor imported without a royal license, which could be conferred by the presidents of the

---

[2] Eduardo Martínez de Salinas y Mendoza, *Textos Legales: Prensa* (Madrid, 1958), p. 1.
[3] Frank H. Robbins, *The Columbus Letter of 1493: A Facsimile of the Copy in the William L. Clements Library with a New Translation into English* (Ann Arbor, 1952), p. 4.
[4] *Novísima Recopilación, Libro VIII, Titulo XV, Ley 1.*
[5] Henry Charles Lea, *A History of the Inquisition of Spain* (New York, 1922), III, 480.

audiencias ("royal courts"), by archbishops, or by certain selected bishops. Each official authorized to issue licenses was aided by examiners, whose salaries were paid by printers and booksellers. The examiners were charged with reading imported books before their distribution and examining manuscripts before publication. In addition, they were ordered to make detailed comparisons between manuscripts and the printed works based on them. The examiners themselves were to be "learned persons, faithful and of good background in the area of learning of the books." [6] The law provided for the seizure and destruction of any work imported or printed without a license or which deviated from an approved manuscript. The printer or bookseller who dealt in unlicensed works was to be penalized by ouster from his profession and a fine double the amount received for any copies sold. The order, issued July 8, 1502, antedated by more than thirty years the imposition of censorship and licensing on England's printing trade.

Despite the controls, printing flourished on the Iberian Peninsula. Before the end of the first decade of the sixteenth century, there were thirty-one permanent printing shops, primarily in monasteries, plus several mobile presses, transported from town to town by mules.[7] The relative simplicity of the equipment made possible such wandering printing plants. Among the more popular works produced in Spain during the infancy of printing were romances of chivalry. Historian J. H. Elliott suggests that these tales, which had wide circulation, may have fired the imaginations of the men of Andalusia and Estremaduras, stirring them to seek their own adventures in the New World. "Their heads filled with fantastic notions, their courage spurred by noble examples of the great heroes of chivalry, the *conquistadores* were prepared to undergo every kind of hardship and sacrifice as they penetrated through swamps and jungles into the heart of the new continent." [8]

Spain's printers did not confine themselves, however, to book publishing. Off their presses poured a stream of *relaciones*—literally, "accounts." Even though these were irregular in publication, appearing only when there was news of some importance, and were usually put together by one man, in them can be found the origins

---

[6] *Novísima Recopilación, Libro VIII, Titulo XVI, Ley 1.*
[7] "La imprenta en España," *Enciclopedia Universal Ilustrada* (Barcelona, 1923), XXI, 1491.
[8] *Imperial Spain: 1469-1716* (New York, 1963), pp. 52–53.

of modern journalism in Spain.[9] The Biblioteca Nacional possesses copies dating from the reign of Charles V (1517-56), though the greatest number of examples still extant comes from the end of the sixteenth century and beginning of the seventeenth.[10]

Paralleling the growth of printing in the sixteenth century was a prolonged process of centralization of power. Ferdinand and Isabella had begun the process while unifying Spain. Charles V continued it, but it was Philip II (1556-98) who carried it to its ultimate end—the consolidation of absolute authority in one person and the personal overseeing of every administrative detail. His authority "was uncontested and absolute." [11] During the summer of 1554, the Council of Castile (Consejo Real) had been invested with "the increasingly important function of censorship and regulation of the press." [12] The King, Charles V, acting in concert with his son, Prince Philip, ordered that "the licenses given in the future for the publication of any new books of any kind whatsoever, shall be given by the President and members of our Council and by no one else." The order also stipulated that copies of manuscripts or of books to be reprinted be deposited with the Council, which was charged with insuring that "no alterations or additions be made in the process of printing." [13] The Inquisition retained the right to halt publication of any book it judged heretical.

Within two years after becoming King of Spain, Philip completed the process of the secular regulation of the press.[14] A Pragmatic-Sanction, issued September 7, 1558, in Philip's name by his sister, the Infanta Juana, forbade the import of foreign books and reaffirmed the Council of Castile as the licensing agency for domestically printed works. All persons, including booksellers, possessing works condemned by the Inquisition were ordered, on pain of death, to burn publicly the offending volumes. The death penalty was also

---

[9] Florentino Zamora Lucas and María Casada Jorge, *Publicaciones periódicas existentes en la Biblioteca Nacional* (Madrid, 1952), p. x.
[10] A list of *relaciones* in the National Library, compiled in 1857 and considered very incomplete by modern experts, describes 159 printed between 1599 and 1614.
[11] Louis Bertrand and Sir Charles Petrie, *The History of Spain*, 2nd ed. (London, 1952), p. 235.
[12] Roger Bigelow Merriman, *The Rise of the Spanish Empire in the Old World and in the New*, vol. IV: *Philip the Prudent* (New York, 1934), p. 415.
[13] *Novísima Recopilación, Libro VIII, Título XVI, Ley 2.*
[14] Juan Beneyto, *Ordenamiento Jurídico de la Información* (Madrid, 1961), p. 17.

ordered for anyone circulating a banned book or owning a manuscript on a religious subject without submitting it to the Council for licensing or destruction.[15] The following year, the Spanish Inquisition, encouraged by Philip's law, issued its first indigenous Index, which was distributed to Church tribunals. Inquisition agents were ordered to seize all prohibited books, including those found in private collections, which were subject to inspection; burn those considered heretical; and store the rest, pending action by the organization's Supreme Junta.[16] In 1568, Philip, reacting with "acute sensitivity" to the spread of Protestantism, especially the possibility of French Huguenot influence penetrating into the principality of Catalonia, decreed special measures in the areas bordering on France—measures which included stricter censorship, prohibition of travel into France by residents of the area, and a ban on Frenchmen teaching in the Catalan schools.[17]

In 1588, Spain's "Invincible Armada," after being pounded by gales off Cape Finisterre, was defeated by an English fleet. In 1596, another English fleet, commanded by the Earl of Essex, dealt a second major blow to Spain's sea power in an engagement off Cádiz. In 1598, Philip died, and Spain passed from its Golden Century into what French historian Jean Descola calls the "Twilight Epoch," [18] the decline from ascendency. Philip II left to his heir, Philip III, an immense complex of kingdoms. "For the first time all the realms of the Peninsula, Castile, Portugal, Navarre, Aragon, Catalonia, and Valencia, had done homage to a single heir." [19] In addition, Philip III ruled Flanders, the Franche-Comté, and Artois. He was King of Naples and Sicily, and controlled Sardinia. He dominated Oran, Ceuta, and Tangier in North Africa, and the Canary Islands off the African coast. As King of Portugal, he ruled the Portuguese African and Atlantic possessions. In the New World the Spanish territories stretched from California to the southern tip of South America, and in Asia they included the Philippines.

Though unrecognized at the time, the seeds of decline were sprouting. The British had successfully challenged Spain's sea might.

---

[15] Novísima Recopilación, Libro VIII, Titulo XVI, Ley 3.
[16] Lea, Inquisition, pp. 483–484
[17] Elliott, Imperial Spain, p. 227.
[18] A History of Spain, trans., Elaine P. Halperin (New York, 1963), p. 479.
[19] Harold Livermore, A History of Spain (New York, 1960), p. 285.

By the end of the seventeenth century, Portugal would be free; Spain's continental possessions would be shrunken by losses to France, racked by rebellion, or inflamed by conspiracy against the crown; and Spanish territories in the New World would be diminished by the loss of Brazil.

It was a time of political and diplomatic crises and the "people demanded, with insatiable urgency, information about the movements of the royal armies and the complicated diplomatic changes of circumstances." [20] The *relaciones*, however primitive they may have been, supplied the information and flourished. Viewed from the perspective of historians, many of those of the sixteenth century "were vivid documents which reported with accuracy and responsibility." [21] Typical of the period were such titles as "Account of what happened to the Emperor while in Worms with Luther in 1521" [22] and "The entry which the Rulers made into Madrid on returning from their marriage in the kingdoms of the Crown of Aragon, Sunday, the twenty-fourth of October, 1599."[23] They provide data of much interest to the historian, such as exact dates and times, details of the protocol of the period, and insights into the tastes and styles of the century.

However, during the early years of the seventeenth century, a change appeared in the *relaciones*. Instead of contenting themselves with factual accounts of events, some editors introduced elements of opinion or judgment or used their sheets as vehicles for political or personal attacks, or for praising persons in a position to help them—characteristics which appear again and again in the Spanish press of later years. The publications could and did range from the "inoffensive and innocuous to the cruelest libels. . . ." [24] As a result, the official controls, limited to books in the previous century, so far as is known, were extended to the *relaciones*. The editor found himself, on occasion, "compelled by inescapable in-

[20] Eulogio Varela Hervías, *Gazeta Nueva: 1661-1663* (Madrid, 1960), p. xi.
[21] *Ibid.*, p. xviii.
[22] *Relación de lo que pasó al Emperador en Bornes con Luthero en 1521*, cited by Marcel Bataillon in *Erasmo y España: Estudios sobre la historia espiritual del siglo XVI*, trans., Antonio Alatorre (Mexico City, 1950), pp. 373-379, n. 21.
[23] *La entrada que los Reyes hizieron en Madrid de buelta* [sic] *de su casamiento, de los reinos de la Corona de Aragon, domingo veinte y cuatro de Octubre de 1599* (Madrid, 1600).
[24] "El periodismo en España," *Enciclopedia Universal Ilustrada*, XXI, 1481.

structions from above—the embryo of present state censorship—
to touch up the coloring and naturalness of the news, thus modifying its meaning, or which demanded its suppression when it was
adverse to determined political goals." [25] The extent to which the
embryonic censorship of the early seventeenth century was a
response to the excesses of the editors of the *relaciones* and the
degree to which it was an instrument of state policy is not known.
Nor is there any indication of the way in which censorship worked.
"One does not know the manner and means used by the state or-
ganisms to carry out censorship in Spain at this time." [26] Only one
law dates from the period—a Royal Order of June 13, 1627, which
prohibited the publication of court reports or other legal information without permission from the government; authorized the Royal
Council to delegate licensing responsibilities to one of its members;
and granted universities permission to print classroom exercises
and scholarly papers.[27] However, the importance sometimes attached to censorship is indicated by a proof copy of an account
of the wedding of the Spanish Infanta, María Teresa, to Louis XIV.
The proof was scrutinized by Philip IV, King of Spain from 1621
and father of the bride, who scribbled short notes in the margin
indicating where changes or additions should be made.[28]

In 1682, Charles II issued an order dealing with printing, which
did no more than reaffirm the regulations established by his predecessors.

As noted earlier, during the seventeenth century the objective
presentation of "news" ceased to be the sole reason for the existence
of the *relaciones*, and the editor's personal gain or biases, as well as
state policy, began to exert an influence on content. Another gradual
change took place about the same time. The whole concept of the
relación was modified. In imitation of the gazettes founded in
Antwerp in 1605, in Frankfurt in 1616, and in Paris in 1631, the
editors of the *relaciones* began publishing with some regularity
under a fixed title which usually incorporated some term such as
Correo ("The Mail"), *Gazeta* or later *Gaceta* ("Gazette"), or
Noticias ("The News"). In 1621, one Andrés de Almansa y Men-

---

[25] Varela Hervías, *Gazeta*, p. xv.
[26] *Ibid.*, p. xxiii.
[27] Antonio Rumeu de Armas, *Historia de la censura literaria gubernativa en España* (Madrid, 1940), pp. 18–20.
[28] Varela Hervías, *Gazeta*, pp. xxiii-xxiv, n. 25.

doza began the *Correos de Francia, Flandes y Alemania*,[29] a four-to-six page paper which appeared every three months. The *Correos* carried no Spanish news, devoting itself to translations from publications elsewhere in Europe.

In May of 1641, a Barcelona printer, Jaume Romeu, began publishing a weekly, the first issue of which was called *Gaceta vinguda a esta ciutat de Barcelona a 28 de maig 1641*.[30] It carried news from Naples dated May 12 and from Rome dated May 14. The success of Romeu's *Gaceta vinguda* touched off a flurry of imitators in Catalonia, including, for example, the *Gaceta enviada de Roma de tot lo succehit en Italia en tot lo mes de agost y setembre del present any 1641*.[31] Many of the imitators were successful on a short-term basis, appearing, as they did, at a time when Catalonia was in open revolt against Philip IV and the people demanded news. A number of the papers were carefully encouraged by the leaders of the anti-Castilian movement who used them as propaganda organs designed to "keep red-hot a state of opinion favorable to the political propositions of the moment." [32]

Each of the *relaciones* was the work of one man, and so usually were the *gacetas*, though in some cases an editor and printer joined forces in a publishing venture, the forerunners of the modern newspaper organization. The *relaciones*, which survived throughout the seventeenth century and well into the eighteenth, appeared only when an event was judged to merit being recorded in print. Their sources of information were limited, generally, to foreign gazettes, translated for publication, plus letters, and word-of-mouth accounts brought back by travelers. Thus, the news publishing businesses were largely dependent on the irregular and unreliable mail systems of the day, which were subject to the whims of local authorities, delayed by storms, and disrupted by internal and international

---

[29] *Correos de Francia, Flandes y Alemania* ("Mail from France, Flanders and Germany") (Madrid, 1621-?). The *Correos* appeared for some years. Two copies dating from 1638 are preserved in the collection of the National Library in Madrid. Press historian Aurelio Fernández Guerra, writing in the January 1, 1860, issue of the *Gazeta de Madrid*, suggests that it appeared, under the direction of various editors, throughout the seventeenth century.
[30] *Gaceta vinguda a esta ciutat* . . . ("News arriving in this city of Barcelona the 28th of May 1641") (Barcelona, 1641).
[31] *Gaceta enviada de Roma* . . . ("News sent from Rome of all that occurred in Italy in the months of August and September of the present year, 1641") (Barcelona, 1641).
[32] Varela Hervías, *Gazeta*, p. xxvii.

strife. For the growing number of periodicals this presented a source of preoccupation, often reflected in print. The *Noticias Principales y Verdaderas* of San Sebastián noted in 1688 that "the mail did not arrive Saturday from either Catalonia or Aragon from which fact the populace infers great events." [33] Earlier that year, the same periodical had reported: "Because of the severity of the weather, so rainy that one can hardly travel, the post from Germany has not arrived, leaving us deprived of the much-desired notice of the confirmation and circumstances of the exit of the Turks from Agria and the entry of the most victorious armies into a place of such importance." [34]

Clever editors learned to exploit potential sources of news, and some left records of their newsgathering. One in Saragossa, for example, reported in some detail on military movements along the Mediterranean between Barcelona and Tarragona, information gleaned "yesterday from a courier sent from Catalonia to Madrid by the viceroy. . . ." [35] Once the news was at hand, the pressure did not abate. Deadlines had to be met. Varela Hervías cites the case of one editor who reported the receipt of a letter containing news and added, "I was limited to one hour in which to make a copy." [36] The combination of not altogether unimpeachable sources and the pressure under which the editor worked led to errors and corrections—for example, a notice published in 1688, which reads, "To the reader: It being impossible always to satisfy quickly the public curiosity without sometimes making mistakes, you are advised that the Document entitled *First news item, etc.*, letter LII, was based on an erroneous report, even though from a hitherto good source, who will be believed in the future only when confirmed by other, posterior sources." [37]

The year 1629 assumes some importance in the history of the Spanish press, for during it was born Juan José of Austria, the bastard son of Philip IV. Juan José, so far as is known, was the first Spaniard of high estate to use the printing press as an instrument of policy in a prolonged campaign aimed at personal aggrandizement. In addition, he encouraged the founding of the nation's most

---

[33] March, 10, 1688.
[34] January 19, 1688.
[35] *Gazeta de Zaragoza*, May 11, 1967.
[36] Varela Hervías, *Gazeta*, p. xiv.
[37] *Gazeta de Zaragoza*, May 6, 1688.

enduring periodical, the *Gazeta Nueva,* which exists today as the *Boletín Oficial del Estado,* and introduced into Spain Francisco Fabro Bremundan, "the first 'journalist' that we had. . . ." [38]

Juan José, as the son of the King, rose to high positions in the government, but aspired to the highest, driven by an "insatiable vanity for fame. . . ." [39] At the age of twenty-two, he commanded part of a Spanish army that invested Barcelona, starving it into submission on October 31, 1651, and thus restoring Catalonia to Spain after a twelve-year separation. In 1656, he was named governor of Flanders, where he met the Burgundian, Fabro Bremundan, a noted linguist, who began as his German teacher and, in time, became his secretary and confidant. Fabro Bremundan eventually rose to positions of trust in the Court, first as perpetual secretary to Charles II and his mother, Queen Mariana of Austria, and, in 1677, as official court translator in Latin, French, and Italian. He left behind a body of books written in elegant, incisive Spanish, though that was not his mother tongue.

In 1659, Juan José ended his tour as governor of Flanders and returned to Spain, taking Fabro Bremundan with him. On November 17 of that year, the Franco-Spanish War was ended with the signing of the Treaty of the Pyrenees. For some time, Spain's Secretary of State, Pedro Fernández del Campo y Angulo, had been urging Philip IV to create a *gaceta* with an official character. Philip appeared reluctant, presumably afraid that such a publication "might be converted into an instrument of subversion . . . ," [40] an apprehension shared by his successors as head of state. Juan José joined the backers of the project and, to please his son, Philip finally agreed, in 1660, to authorize the new publication. Juan José arranged to have Fabro Bremundan appointed editor of the periodical.

It was not until late in the year that Fabro Bremundan completed his preparations and the first issue of the *gazeta* appeared in January 1661 under the title, *Relación o Gazeta de Algunos Casos particulares, assi Politicos, como Militares, sucedidos en la mayor parte del Mundo, hasta fin de Diziembre de 1660.* [41] It began:

---

[38] Varela Hervías, *Gazeta,* p. xxix.
[39] Pedro Gómez Aparicio, "Apuntes para una historia del periodismo Español," *Gaceta de la Prensa Española,* Dec. 15, 1963, p. 18.
[40] *Ibid.,* p. 16.
[41] *Relación o Gazeta . . .* ("Account or Gazette of Some Special Things, Political as well as Military, which occurred in the greater part of the World up to the end of December of 1660") (Madrid, 1661).

Inasmuch as in the most populous cities of Italy, Flanders, France and Germany there are printed each week (in addition to the *Relaciones* of special events) others with the title of Gazettes, in which is given news of the most notable things, Political as well as Military, which have occurred in the greater part of the globe, there is reason that this kind of printed matter be introduced into Spain, if not every week at least every month, so that the curious may have word of said events, and the Spaniards not lack the news which abounds in Foreign Nations. And, as for the first, we shall begin with the Provinces of Italy.[42]

The first item of the eight-page, quarto-sized paper reported the death in Rome of Cardinals Juan de Lugo and Christobal Widman. It was followed by reports from Venice, Vienna, Sweden, France, and England. The second issue, which appeared in February, forever dropped the term *Relación* from the title. It became simply the *Gazeta* and, according to its title, dealt with "political and military events in the main part of the world, until the month of January of this year, 1661." [43] The paper appeared twelve times in 1661 and eight in 1662. Its title varied with each issue as did the self-proclaimed scope of its news coverage. It opened 1662, for example, by reporting on "political and military events from the main part of Europe, until the end of February of this year of 1662." [44] The next month, its scope was expanded "to the main part of Europe and Africa. . . ," [45] while the third issue embraced "Africa, Asia, and Europe. . . ." [46] It is interesting to note that, despite Spain's position of dominance in the Americas, not one word of news from the New World appeared in the *Gazeta* during its first two years of existence.

Meanwhile, early in August of 1661, Juan José had been named commander of the force with which Philip was attempting to reconquer Portugal, free from Spanish rule since 1639. Fabro Bremundan, mindful of his debt to his patron, to whom the fortunes of the *Gazeta* were linked, devoted the next issue of the periodical to news of the Portuguese campaign, highlighting the role of the commander-in-chief. The rest of the world was excluded from the issue which was devoted to "that which happened to the Catholic

---

[42] *Relación o Gazeta*, I (1661).
[43] *Gazeta*, II (1661). *Gazeta de los Sucesos Politicos y Militares de la mayor parte del mundo, hasta el mes de Enero deste año de mil y seiscientos sesenta y uno.*
[44] *Gazeta*, I (1662).
[45] *Gazeta*, II (1662).
[46] *Gazeta*, III (1662).

Arms of His Majesty in the armies of Estermadura, Castile, and the Kingdom of Galicia, until the twentieth of August of this year of 1661." [47] However, after that editorial genuflection to Juan José, Fabro Bremundan again turned the attention of the *Gazeta* to news from outside Spain, limiting himself to brief chronicling of the fortunes of Juan José's army. But his patron was not forgotten, for during 1662 Fabro Bremundan published possibly as many as six *relaciones*, independent of the *Gazeta*, which reported on the progress of the war in Portugal and Juan José's successes.[48]

By the end of 1662, however, Juan José was suffering military setbacks in Portugal. Until then, he had been, "for many Spaniards, a hope and a solution who could halt the drift of the nation toward nothingness," [49] but his lack of success on the battlefield caused his popularity to plummet at home. Spanish press historian Pedro Gómez Aparicio suggests that the cessation of publication of the *Gazeta* in January of 1663 was a result of Juan José's decline in public esteem.[50] The edition covering events through December of 1662 was the last of this first of many series of Madrid *Gazetas*. On June 6, 1663, the army, led by Juan José, was defeated at Ameixial by combined British-French armies under the command of Marshal Schomberg. A new army was put into the field, but it was defeated at Montes Claros in 1665—a defeat which led to recognition of Portugal's independence in 1668.

Though there was a hiatus in the life of the *Gazeta*, its imitators throughout Spain continued to thrive. The foremost was the *Gazeta Nueva* of Seville, published by Juan Gómez de Blas, who had begun producing *relaciones* in 1638. It was a copy of Fabro Bremundan's publication, but not a literal transcription, for Gómez de Blas added news not appearing in the Madrid original. The *Gazeta Nueva* of Seville continued publishing after the Madrid *Gazeta* closed down, even though its editor found himself cut off from much of the international information available to Fabro Bremundan through his official position in Madrid. In 1667, Gómez de Blas died and proprietorship of the paper passed to his son,

---

[47] *Gazeta*, X (1661). *Gazeta Nueva de lo Sucedido a los Católicos Armas de su Magestad* [sic] *en los Exércitos de Estremadura, Castilla, y Reino de Galicia, hasta veinte de Agosto deste año de 1661.*
[48] Juan Pérez de Guzmán y Gallo, *Bosquejo histórico-documental de la Gaceta de Madrid* (Madrid, 1902), p. 44.
[49] Varela Hervías, *Gazeta*, p. xxviii.
[50] "Historia del periodismo," *GPE*, Dec. 15, 1963, p. 18.

Juan Francisco de Blas, who continued it until 1680 when Charles II prohibited its further publication.[51]

Another *Gazeta Nueva* appeared in Saragossa in 1661, three months after the original of Madrid. There seems to have been no editor, merely printers who reproduced the content of the Madrid prototype. No copy exists of any issue after that of July, 1662, which suggests a limited life span. A *Nueva Gazeta* appeared in Valencia in June, 1661; it used Fabro Bremundan's paper as its source but condensed the news from eight to four pages.

Within five years, the influence of Fabro Bremundan's *Gazeta* had reached the New World via Seville. In Mexico City, where the first printing press in the hemisphere had been established in 1539, it flowered in 1666 as the *Gazeta General. Sucesos de este año de 1666. Provisiones y Mercedes, en los Reynos de España, Portugal y Nueva-España.*[52] The *Gazeta General* used as its source and model the Sevillian gazette, which had been inspired by Fabro Bremundan. Copies of the Seville paper were rushed to the port of Cádiz where they were dispatched by sailing vessel to the Mexican coast and thence overland to the capital.[53]

For a decade following the demise of the Madrid *Gazeta*, Fabro Bremundan disappeared from the spotlight of the theater of history. His patron, Juan José, however, stayed on stage and it may be supposed that Fabro Bremundan remained in the shadows at his side, serving as the Hapsburg bastard's propaganda expert. In 1665, three months after the Portuguese victory at Montes Claros, Philip IV died. Before his death, he had excluded Juan José from the government, which he left to his four-year-old son, Charles II. But Juan José was not long on the political sidelines. The power, which was

---

[51] Manuel Chaves, *Historia y Bibliografía de la Prensa sevillana* (Seville, 1896), pp. xvi-xvii.

[52] *Gazeta General* . . . ("General Gazette. Events of this year of 1666. Decrees and Benefices, in the Kingdoms of Spain, Portugal and New Spain") (Mexico City, 1666).

[53] The title of a Mexico City paper of the period indicates the sense of urgency attached to the operation: *Primera Gazeta Nueva del Aviso que salió del Puerto de Cádiz a primero de Julio y llegó al Puerto de San Juan de Ulúa a veinte y siete de Agosto, y la nueva a esta ciudad, Martes 30 de dicho mes a la siete de la mañana de este año 1689* ("First New Gazette of Announcement which left the Port of Cádiz, on the first of July and arrived at the Port of San Juan de Ulúa on the twenty-seventh of August, and on the [twenty-] ninth at this city, Tuesday, 30th of said month at seven in the morning of this year 1689") (Mexico City, 1689).

supposed to reside in a five-man ministerial Junta de Gobierno, set up to advise the Queen-Regent, Mariana, until Charles reached the age of fourteen, was quickly lost to the Queen's confessor, the Austrian Jesuit Father Juan Everado Nithard. A large opposition group formed around Juan José, the leader of court intrigue against Father Nithard. Juan José flooded the Court with polemical and informative papers, printed clandestinely in Guadalajara and Madrid and smuggled into influential circles by his adherents. The papers primarily outlined Juan José's program of political reform. He denounced taxation, the concession of favors, and the maladministration of justice, and recommended the formation of an advisory committee of ministers to aid the Queen-Regent. A modern judgment that the propaganda showed Juan José as "expert in these campaigns which we call today press campaigns" [54] suggests that the editorial genius of Fabro Bremundan may have been at work.

Juan José appears to have carried his attacks on Nithard too far, for in October, 1668, fearing arrest, he fled to Aragon and from there to Catalonia. During the winter, he enlisted much anti-Castilian sentiment, traditional in Catalonia, to his cause and, in early 1669, set out at the head of an army on the return trip to Madrid. His passage along the road from Barcelona to the capital was triumphal: at every stop he was hailed as a hero. On February 24, he reached Torrejón de Ardoz, not far from Madrid, and there demanded that the Queen dismiss Nithard. She did, and the next day the Jesuit left Spain for Rome.

Juan José failed to exploit his victory, hesitating to assume supreme power, and a stalemate resulted. Eventually, the Queen succeeded in appointing Juan José Viceroy of Aragon, thus removing him from the capital. Power fell into the hands of Fernando de Valenzuela, the son of an Andalusian army captain and the Queen's favorite. In 1675, when Charles reached fourteen, it was expected that Valenzuela would be replaced by Juan José, but he and the Queen Mother clung to power. From his headquarters, Juan José hurled himself into conspiratorial activity; to silence him, the Queen named him Viceroy to Naples. Rather than assume the post and renounce his ambitions, he lingered in Spain.

In 1672, war had broken out again between Spain and France, touched off by a French invasion of the Low Countries. Spain allied

---

[54] Gabriel Maura y Gamazo, *Carlos II y su Corte*, II (Madrid, 1915), 31.

itself with the Dutch against the forces of Louis XIV, who turned his armies against the Franche-Comté, where, within two years, the Spanish were defeated. In 1676, Juan José began a newspaper in Saragossa, which he entrusted, as before, to Fabro Bremundan. The new periodical, *Avisos ordinarios de las cosas del Norte*,[55] was of an "exclusively political and polemic character, whose final goal was to defend the interests of the coalition formed by Spain, Germany, Denmark, and Brandenburg against the hostile bloc of France, England, and Sweden." [56] The *Avisos ordinarios* devoted itself strictly to foreign affairs; not one note of domestic news appeared in the thirty-six numbers published between its first issue on January 7, 1676, and its last on September 15. Nowhere is Fabro Bremundan's genius as an editor and penetrating analyst of political and diplomatic complexities more apparent than in the pages of the short-lived Saragossa periodical. In less than a year, he earned himself the right to be considered, in the eyes of Spain's press historians, the country's first foreign news expert.[57] During the period, Fabro Bremundan assumed a pacifist position and urged his readers to "implore divine aid for negotiations being directed toward that great goal [the establishment of a just peace]." [58] He defined the function of the weekly *Avisos ordinarios* as that of presenting the facts that would enable his readers to distinguish between "the believable and the false," an endeavor involving repeated attacks on the *Gazette de Paris* which Fabro Bremundan considered no more than a propaganda sheet and which he labeled the product of men "whose work could only be worthily rewarded with a lifetime detention in the *little houses* of Paris, which (for those who do not know) is the insane asylum." [59]

Despite Fabro Bremundan's excellence as an editor, there is no doubt that the *Avisos ordinarios* reflected, to a great extent, the policies and aspirations of Juan José. In September, a series of upheavals in Spain made it apparent that the time was nearly ripe for the Hapsburg bastard's return to Madrid. The *Avisos ordinarios* ceased publication. In December, answering the call of the Court's

---

[55] *Avisos ordinarios* . . . ("Regular notices of the things of the North") (Saragossa, 1676).
[56] Varela Hervías, *Gazeta*, pp. lxi-lxii.
[57] *Ibid.*, p. lxiii.
[58] *Avisos ordinarios* (Saragossa), Jan. 7, 1676.
[59] *Ibid.*, July 7, 1676.

grandees, who had turned against Valenzuela, Juan José marched toward Madrid at the head of an army that, until recently, had been fighting the French in Catalonia. On January 2, 1677, Juan José, accompanied by Fabro Bremundan, entered Madrid where he was named Prime Minister, and Valenzuela was exiled to the Philippines. In less than four months, the journalist was back in Saragossa, this time as part of the retinue of Charles II, who had been persuaded by Juan José that a visit to Aragon would be politic. The King stayed from April 21 to June 12. Three years later—not long after the death on September 17, 1679, of his patron, Juan José—Fabro Bremundan published a detailed account of that visit, full of flattery for Charles II. The account, printed in Madrid in 1680, was entitled: "The Trip of Our King Señor Don Carlos the Second to the Kingdom of Aragon. Entry of His Majesty into Saragossa. Solemn Oath to the Rights and principles of the General Courts of the same Kingdom, the year 1677.—In a daily account. Written by Don Francisco Fabro Bremundan, of the Council of His Majesty, his Secretary, Interpreter of the Latin Language, in the office of the Secretary of State of the North: And dedicated to His Majesty by the hand of the Señor Marqués de Canales, Knight of the Order of Calatrava, of the Council of His Majesty, and his Secretary of State for Spain and the North." [60]

The timing of the publication raises a question about Fabro Bremundan's intentions: was it designed to curry favor with Charles II after the death of his original patron, Juan José? One is inclined to that inference, for, in 1678, shortly after Juan José became Prime Minister, Fabro Bremundan had published an account of his patron's role as an army commander in the campaign of 1651 against the insurgent Catalans: "History of the acts of the Most Serene Señor Don Juan of Austria, in the Principality of Catalonia. Part I. Written by Don Francisco Fabro Bremundan, Servant of His Majesty and senior Language Official of the Secretariats of State and War of His Highness." [61]

---

[60] *Viaje de Rey Nuestro Señor Don Carlos Segundo Al Reyno de Aragón. Entrada de su Magestad en Zaragoza. Iuramento solemne de los Fueros y principios de las Cortes Generales del mismo Reyno, el Año M.DC.LII.—En relación diaria. Escrita por Don Francisco Fabro Bremundan, del Consejo de su Magestad, su Secretario, Intérprete de la Lengua latina, en la Secretaria del Norte: Y dedicada a Su Magestad por mano del Señor Marqués de Canales, Cavallero de la Orden de Calatrava, del Consejo de Su Magestad, y su Secretario de Estado de España el Norte* (Madrid, 1680).

[61] *Historia de los hechos del Serenissimo Señor Don Juan de Austria, en el*

During the two years of Juan José's service as Prime Minister, Fabro Bremundan's fortunes soared. His patron allowed him to buy the post of Gazetero del Reino (Gazetteer of the Kingdom), a title which, according to contemporary documents, gave him a monopoly on *Gazetas*: ". . . no one without his license may imprint *Gazetas* elsewhere, under grave penalties, expressed in the letter of sale. . . ." [62] On July 4, 1677, Fabro Bremundan resumed publication of the *Gazeta* of Madrid, this time as the weekly *Gazeta Ordinaria de Madrid*.[63] That the new *Gazeta* was subjected to careful scrutiny by the Royal Council is attested to by a handwritten note on a copy of its second number: "Author D. Francisco Fabro, Secretary to His Highness, and, before being printed, seen by the Council." [64] The paper was divided into two sections. The first section was devoted to international news and the second to news of the Court, especially the activities of Charles II, as well as the announcement of military, religious, and civil appointments.

Fabro Bremundan almost at once resumed his attacks on the *Gazette de Paris*. In the third issue of the Madrid *Gazeta* he felt compelled to "make reparations in an account in the *Gazette de Paris*" of a clash between Spanish and French troops.[65] Certainly such an editorial approach must have pleased the censors who exercised "a vigilant and assiduous caution aimed at eliminating or palliating, whenever possible, all the news which it was not convenient to divulge, and, also, the neutralizing of certain political stories which, because of their origin or intention, were not pleasing." [66] Fabro's treatment of the Court tended toward the syrupy, especially his editorial handling of the King. The *Gazeta*'s initial reference to Charles II stated: "The King, our Señor, since his happy and applauded trip to Aragon, has continued to make, with untiring application, the dispositions which the occurrences of the Monarchy require." [67]

On September 17, 1679, Juan José died. Whatever his motives

Principado de Cataluña. Parte I. Escrivióla Don Francisco Fabro Bremundan, Criado de su Magestad, y Oficial mayor de Lenguas de las Secretarias de Estado y Guerra de su Alteza (Madrid, 1678).
[62] Cited by Pérez de Guzmán, *Bosquejo histórico-documental*, p. 53.
[63] *Gazeta Ordinaria de Madrid* ("Ordinary Gazette of Madrid") (Madrid, 1677–80, 1683–84).
[64] In the collection of *Gacetas* of Madrid's Hemeroteca Municipal.
[65] *Gazeta Ordinaria*, July 28, 1677.
[66] Varela Hervías, *Gazeta*, p. lxiv.
[67] *Gazeta Ordinaria*, July 4, 1677.

may have been—political propaganda or self-glorification—he had encouraged the development of the press in Spain. Within less than two weeks, the government, once again in the hands of the Queen Mother, issued an edict which strengthened existing regulations for licensing printers. Until then, the Council of Castile had been unable to enforce such regulations. But, on September 29, 1679, the occasion of the betrothal of Charles II to Maria-Luisa of Orleans, Louis XIV's niece, the King's Council and burgesses ordered:

All couplets and *relaciones* which have appeared and which are sold by the blind and in which is treated the journey of their majesties, God guard them, should be gathered up and not sold. They also order that the printers be notified that, under penalty of a fine of 50 ducats, they should neither print nor sell them without having first registered them with the Señor Protector from whom license to print and sell must be obtained.[68]

Left by Juan José's death without an advocate at court, the press suffered. In April of the following year, the government ordered the suspension of the *Gazeta Ordinaria*. The final issue noted that effective the following week, on Monday, April 8, 1680, "it is ordered that no more gazettes be distributed or printed, which puts an end to this one." [69] On November 11, the prohibition was extended to all printed publications in the country. A Royal Decree of that date stated:

The gentlemen Mayors of the House and Court of his Majesty, now holding audience in the Royal Prison of this Court, order that all printers of this Court be notified that they should print neither *relaciones* nor other papers in small or large quantities without the license of the Council. The punishment for those who do the contrary shall be a fine of 100 ducats and four years in prison in Africa.[70]

It was the same decree that ended, as noted earlier, the nineteen-year life of the *Gazeta Nueva* of Seville.

Despite the decree, printers of *relaciones* continued to operate with relative freedom, except on the rare occasions when pressure from above caused authorities to enforce the regulations. But for three years Spain had no legally published newspapers. The journalistic drought ended on November 16, 1683, when the Court once again authorized *gacetas*. Fabro Bremundan—to whom the

---

[68] *Real Orden del 29 de septiembre de 1679.* Quoted by Varela Hervías, *Gazeta*, p. xii.
[69] *Gazeta Ordinaria*, April 2, 1680.
[70] *Decreto real del 11 de noviembre de 1680.*

new decree restored the *privilegio* granted by Juan José in 1677 as well as his official posts as Council secretary and court translator —must have had foreknowledge of the relaxation of the ban, for his *Gazeta Ordinaria de Madrid* appeared the same day as the decree. But one thing had been lost to Fabro Bremundan, his right to exclusivity. On January 4, 1684, Sebastián de Armendáriz, bookseller to the king, issued the first number of the *Nuevas Singulares del Norte.*[71] In addition, Lucas Antonio de Bedmar y Valdivia, royal printer in the kingdoms of Castile and Leon, began, on January 18, 1684, the short-lived *Gazeta General del Norte, Italia y otras partes.*[72] The proliferation of newspapers caused some second thoughts in government circles, for, on January 22, 1684, the Royal Council reiterated previous orders that all printers be licensed. A decree of that date stated that "no printer of this Court shall print nor impress any paper without the license from the gentlemen of the Council and no person may sell them on the streets or in any other manner, under pain of six years exile to a distance of 10 leagues from this Court and whatever else may be deemed suitable by the members of this Court."[73]

The competition between Armendáriz, Fabro, and Bedmar y Valdivia lasted until late May of 1684, when Armendáriz and Fabro merged their papers. The combined publication appeared each week until September 12, 1690, when Fabro died. His legacy to the Spanish press was great, for he had fostered in it a respect for accuracy and speed and had pioneered in the use of mixed type faces to attract the interest of the reader. With his death, the title of Gazetteer of the Kingdom was transferred to the King's Priest and Chaplain, Juan de las Herbas, but the printing *privilegio* went to the General Hospital of Madrid.

The *Gazeta* failed to flourish under the auspices of the General Hospital; ". . . bureaucratized and lacking interest, it decayed rapidly and with it the income destined for supporting that worthy center."[74] The Queen's Treasurer, Juan de Goyeneche, noting the decline in the fortunes of the *Gazeta*, proposed to the Hospital's

---

[71] *Nuevas Singulares del Norte* ("Strange New Things from the North") (Madrid, 1684).
[72] *Gazeta General del Norte* . . . ("General Gazette from the North, Italy and other parts") (Madrid, 1684).
[73] *Real decreto del 22 de enero de 1684.*
[74] Gómez Aparicio, "Historia del periodismo," *GPE*, Dec. 15, 1963, p. 20.

trustees that publication of the paper be turned over to him, offering to pay 400 ducats annually for the right. Hospital officials, tempted by the idea, called for public bidding for the rights. Goyeneche's offer was not bettered and, on March 23, 1697, he was granted the concession, which was confirmed on October 22, 1701, in a royal order issued by Philip V, the French duke who succeeded Charles II as King of Spain. The order gave Goyeneche not only the right to publish the *Gazeta* in Madrid but also exclusivity to such publications in the rest of Spain. Goyeneche changed the title to *Gazeta de Madrid*, which it appeared as until November 30, 1808. On September 11, 1778, it was converted from a weekly into a biweekly and, on June 18, 1808, it became a daily.

In 1711, Rafael Figueró, a printer in Barcelona, founded the *Gazeta de Barcelona*, which, modeled on the Madrid *Gazeta*, survived into the next century, first as a weekly and later as a biweekly. In 1732, the Franciscan priest José Álvarez de la Fuente, Predicant-General of the order and of the king, put out the first new periodical to appear in Madrid since 1684. Despite its title, *Diario Histórico, Político-canónico y Moral*,[75] the paper appeared monthly. In a "Prologue to the Reader," which appeared in the first issue, Father Álvarez de la Fuente explained the use of "daily" in the title of a monthly periodical. "Dailies have to be distinguished from Annuals, which pay attention only to the successive order of the years, disregarding the days," he wrote, "and the Dailies paying attention only to the ordering of the days, without regard to the years." Each issue ran to about 600 pages and approached the encyclopedic in scope. Historical notes were mixed with reports of the contemporary scene. The first two pages of each issue discussed the origin of the month and the name given it by the Egyptians, Hebrews, Greeks, Germans, English, Arabs, and so on. The rest of the *Diario* was devoted to the days of the month, about twenty pages for each day. The historical events which fell on each particular date were chronicled in some detail—histories of saints; deaths of important persons; biographies of artists, soldiers, and religious leaders; military actions; natural disasters; and so on. To this compilation of fact, Álvarez de la Fuente added aphorisms, commentaries, and explications. The *Diario Histórico, Político-*

---

[75] *Diario Histórico* . . . ("Historical, Politico-canonical and Moral Daily") (Madrid, 1732).

canónico y Moral, which began with the January, 1732, issue, ended with that of December of the same year. Within the next five years, Spain's first scientific and cultural periodicals were founded. In 1734, members of the Academy of Medicine and Surgery, authorized in that year by Royal Decree, began publishing the *Efemérides Barométrico-medicas Matritenses*,[76] which appeared monthly and was made up usually of translations of medical articles from abroad and resumes of foreign books. On January 1, 1737, a group of "well-known writers, desirous of reforming . . . the decadent literature of the eighteenth century, published a kind of magazine, which merited the protection of Philip IV . . ."[77] and which was called the *Diario de los literatos de España*.[78] The *Diario de los literatos* modeled itself after the Parisian *Journal de Savants*, which antedated it by sixty-two years, and its goal was to "reduce to summary the writings of Spanish authors and judge their works."[79] To do so, the quarterly published "long extracts, analyses and critiques, both measured and severe, of all the works worthy of attention that were appearing."[80]

In January of 1738, the year following the appearance of the *Diario de los literatos*, Salvador José Mañer founded the *Mercurio histórico y político*.[81] The *Mercurio histórico* began as a monthly, converted to a quarterly in 1759, reconverted to a monthly in the same year, and in 1804 became a bimonthly. Mañer was granted a royal *privilegio* to publish for six years with exclusive rights to such periodicals throughout Spain. In 1744, the term of the *privilegio*

---

[76] *Efemérides Barométrico-medicas Matritenses* ("Madrid Barometrical-medical Almanac") (Madrid, 1734–47).

[77] Eugenio Hartzenbusch é Hiríart, *Apuntes para un Catálogo de periódicos madrileños desde el año 1661 al 1870* (Madrid, 1894), p. 4.

[78] *Diario de los literatos de España, en que se reducen a compendio los escritos de los autores españoles, y se hace juicio de sus obras* ("Daily of the learned of Spain, in which the writings of Spanish authors are summarized, and their works judged") (Madrid, 1737–42).

[79] *Diario de los literatos de España* (Madrid), Jan., 1737.

[80] Marcelino Menéndez y Pelayo, *Historia de las ideas estéticas en España*, 3rd ed. (Madrid, 1909–12), V, 149.

[81] *Mercurio histórico y político en que se contiene el estado presente de la Europa; lo que pasa en todas sus Cortes; los intereses de los Príncipes, y todo lo que conduce de más curioso para él. Con las reflexiones políticas sobre cada Estado* ("Historical and Political Mercury, which contains the present state of Europe, that which happens in all its Courts, the interests of the Princes, and all which he finds curious. With political thoughts on each state") (Madrid, 1738-1830).

expired, and one Miguel José de Aoiz, to whom the King was indebted, offered 1,000 doubloons for the concession. Mañer, unable to retain control of his periodical, presented it to Madrid General Hospital and retired to a convent, where he died in 1751. Under a series of officially named editors, the *Mercurio histórico y político* continued publishing until 1830.

Both the *Diario de los literatos* and the *Mercurio histórico y político* were typical of their times. They were products of the intellectual climate which produced the English encyclopedias and was to produce the great French encyclopedists. They did obeisance to erudition and pedantry and reflected a strong French influence which had been introduced into the country at the turn of the century when a Bourbon dynasty had replaced the Hapsburgs on the Spanish throne. Philip V was a Frenchman who longed for his native land, and his influence "frenchified" the Spanish court. Royal buildings imitated French architecture. Philip's summer palace at La Granja, built in 1721, was modeled after Versailles, as were the royal buildings at Aranjuez, which date from 1727. Following the lead of the French *Academie*, a Royal Academy of History was founded in Spain in 1738. A Royal Academy of Language followed in 1739, and in 1744 an Academy of Noble Arts was created. Even Mañer headed his *Mercurio histórico y político* with the announcement that it was "Translated from the French . . . by Monsieur Le-Margne," his nom de plume.

For five months in late 1735 and early 1736, the hitherto ponderous Spanish press was enlivened by the appearance of a clandestinely published and circulated sheet called *El Duende de Madrid.*[82] The one-sheet broadside was never printed, but "was multiplied by hand into innumerable copies," which found their way under the Queen's napkin in the palace dining room, into the throne room, and even into the pockets of José Patiño, who held the posts of Minister of Marine and the Indies and of Finance, and was one of its chief targets.[83] It appeared eighteen times between December 8, 1735, and April 12, 1736, and in its first issue characterized itself in a verse that quickly became popular:

> I am, in the Court,
> A ghostly critic,

---

[82] *El Duende de Madrid* ("The Madrid Ghost") (Madrid, 1735–36).
[83] Hartzenbusch, *Periódicos madrileños*, p. 5.

Read by all, but
Understood by none.
When my way I find
Into the Cabinet
I frighten Patiño
And enrage the King.[84]

After an extensive investigation, which involved the arrest and imprisonment of several innocent persons, blame for *El Duende* was finally pinned on Manuel Preyre da Sílva, a Portuguese captain of dragoons turned Carmelite monk. Da Sílva was arrested on May 31, 1736. On March 17, 1737, he escaped from prison and was lost from the pages of history.

Da Sílva's *El Duende* was not an isolated phenomenon in the history of Spanish communications. Similar handwritten and copied attacks had been distributed in almost epidemic proportions during the troubled reign of Henry IV, "The Impotent" (1454-74). The tradition of the clandestine attempt at widespread communication appears to have been resurrected periodically at times of crisis or tension. With the introduction of mechanical means of reproduction, the mimeograph and other machines replaced handwriting. As recently as February and March of 1965, such clandestine documents were widely circulated in Spain, urging sympathy strikes to back the demands of demonstrating university students.

In 1749, Ferdinand VI, who had succeeded to the throne in 1746, took note of the occasional use to which printing was put in Spain. A decree of December 6 stated:

The facility with which one can print and distribute many papers, which, under the title of manifestoes, legal defenses, or other similar titles, contain satires and passages which defame the honor and position of persons of all classes and all estates . . . demands that attention be turned to uprooting an abuse so prejudicial and contrary to Christian charity. . . . Therefore, in the future, no paper of any kind, whether large or small, may be printed unless its manuscript is first presented to the Council or Tribunal charged with such matters. . . . After examination, if it is approved, a license for printing will be granted. The license must be turned over to the printer and without it he shall print no paper or papers.[85]

The decree set up, as punishment for authors and printers who vio-

---

[84] *El Duende de Madrid*, Dec. 8, 1735.
[85] *Real decreto del 15 de diciembre de 1749*.

lated the regulation, a fine of 200 ducats and disbarment from further professional activities.

In 1752, two new periodicals appeared: *Memorias para la historia de las ciencias y bellas artes*,[86] published by José Vicente de Rustant; and *Discursos mercuriales políticos*,[87] written by Joaquín Enrique de Graef. But the major work of the second half of the eighteenth century was that of Nipho, one of the towering figures of Spanish journalism and the dominant influence on the Spanish press for more than three decades.

---

[86] *Memorias para la historia* . . . ("Notes for the history of the sciences and fine arts") (Madrid, 1752).
[87] *Discursos mercuriales políticos* ("Mercurial political discourses") (Madrid, 1752 and 1755–56).

CHAPTER FIVE

ᴛ̲he Nipho Years

Francisco Sebastián Manuel Mariano Nipho y
Cagigal exerted on the press of his time an influence as great as,
if not greater than, that of Fabro Bremundan, the Gazetteer of the
Kingdom, in the preceding century. Among the more than twenty
periodicals he founded was the nation's first daily. In the opinion of
Spanish press historian Luis Miguel Enciso Recio, "one must attribute to Nipho the creation, in Spain, of the daily press and with
it, commercial news and advertising, the establishment of the subscription system for private newspapers and the street sale of newspapers as we know it today. . . ." [1] In addition, he converted the
newspaper "into an instrument accessible to all people and infused
it with the pleasantness which the former erudite press lacked. . . ." [2]
Nipho himself disclaimed any intention or desire to carry on the
tradition of the erudite press in Spain. "I write not for the
learned. . . ," he said.[3] Though what he created was far from
the popular press of the mid-twentieth century, Nipho contributed
much to popularizing the press of his time.

He began his journalistic career in 1754, when thirty-six years
old, by founding the weekly *Varios discursos elocuentes y políticos*.[4] Nipho's permission to publish the *Varios discursos* was

---

[1] *Nipho y el periodismo español del siglo XVIII* (Valladolid, 1956), p. 337.
[2] *Ibid.*, p. 335.
[3] *Correo General de Europa* (Madrid), 1763, II, 337.
[4] *Varios discursos elocuentes y políticos sobre las acciones más heroicas de*

granted on December 22, 1754, after his outline for the first issue had been approved by Father Agustín Sánchez, censor of the publication, but was not delivered to him until January 8 of the new year. On January 14, the government authorized him to charge at the rate of six *maravedis* per sheet of paper used or one and a half *maravedis* per page. Its prices, therefore, ranged from seven and a half to fifteen *maravedis*.

In the prologue to the first issue, Nipho noted that it would appear every Thursday if "chance does not introduce some forced parenthesis." [5] It continued for nine issues before Nipho dropped the operation as uneconomic.

In 1757, Nipho began preparing for his most ambitious undertaking, the *Diario Noticioso, curioso-erudito y comercial, público y económico*.[6] Late in that year, he and his partner in the venture, Juan Antonio Lozano Yuste, petitioned the Royal Council for permission to publish a daily newspaper. The petition was signed by Manuel Ruiz de Uribe, a business pseudonym used, for reasons nowhere explained, by Nipho. The Royal Council referred the petition to Juan Curiel, Judge-Superintendent of Printing, who offered no objection to the granting of the necessary licenses if the publication was subjected to regular censorship. On December 15, 1757, Ferdinand VI, who had become King in 1746, granted the rights of printing and sale. The draft of the first number was sent to Miguel Pérez Pastor of the Royal Spanish Academy, who reported to the King in January, 1758, "I have studied the *Diario Nuevo* [sic] *Curioso, Erudito*, etc., which Your Highness sent me to censor and which Manuel Ruiz de Uribe and Company wish to publish and it seems to me that it would be a very useful work for the public if they carry out their proposals. The present example contains nothing against our religion, good customs and the prerogatives of Your Majesty, therefore it seems to me that Your

---

diferentes personajes antiguos y modernos, en los que, por medio de prudentes avisos, puede lograr el hombre el verdadero modo de gobernarse, según los preceptos de las tres partes constitutivas de la sabiduría humana, en a saber Etica, Política y Economía ("Various eloquent and political discussions about the most heroic actions of different ancient and modern personages, in which, by means of wise counsel, man may gain the real means of governing himself according to the precepts of the three constituent areas of human wisdom: the knowledge of ethics, politics and economics") (Madrid, 1755).
[5] *Varios discursos* (Madrid), 1755, no. I.
[6] *Diario Noticioso* . . . ("Daily news, curious-erudite and commercial, public and economic") (Madrid, 1758).

Highness will be able to grant the license which is solicited." [7]

On January 17, Ferdinand VI signed the *privilegio* for the *Diario Noticioso*. His decree, addressed to all the officials of the kingdom, stated:

I have taken into consideration that which Don Manuel Ruiz de Uribe and Company have shown to me and the benefits that can accrue to the Public by giving it a Daily with news of all important occurrences in trade, as much literary as civil and economic. In a decree signed by my Royal Hand the fifteenth of the December just past, I have granted a privilege to the aforementioned Don Manuel Ruiz de Uribe and Company so that the cited Daily may be printed and sold by them or the person who may have their power and no other of whatever class. Therefore, I command you all, and each one of you in your places, districts, and jurisdictions, that, it being shown to you, you should read my Royal Resolution, and observe, keep, and carry it out, and make sure it is kept, and carried out, and executed as it corresponds to each one, without contravening it, or permitting or allowing that it be contravened in any way. And I wish that no person, without license from the aforementioned Don Manuel Ruiz de Uribe and Company, or from whoever may have their power, may put together, print, or sell the cited Daily, and whoever may be apprehended in the very act shall lose all books, forms, and implements which he may have and, in addition, incur [a fine] of fifty thousand *maravedis*, one third going to my house, another third to the sentencing judge, and the other part to the denunciator. It is my wish that you should neither tolerate nor consent to tolerate anything, however small, against the tenor and form of all herein referred to.[8]

A copy of the license was delivered to Nipho on January 20. To it was appended a note which said that "the *Diario* can be printed in the future without a new license, [provided it is] marked or signed by the censor named by the Council." [9] Miguel Pérez Pastor, who had been charged with the prepublication appraisal of the *Diario*, was named censor.[10]

The first issue appeared on Wednesday, February 1, 1758. It

---

[7] National Historical Archives, Court and Commission of Printing, quoted by Enciso Recio, *Nipho*, p. 166, n. 20.
[8] Francisco Sebastián Manuel Mariano Nipho y Cagigal, *Prospecto para el Diario Noticioso, curioso-erudito y comercial, público y económico* (Madrid, 1758).
[9] Enciso Recio, *Nipho*, pp. 166–167.
[10] In 1756, Charles III had authorized the employment of paid censors. Until that time, the censorship function had been performed by government officials who had other, sometimes conflicting, responsibilities. See Antonio Rumeu de Armas, *Historia de la censura literaria gubernativa en España* (Madrid, 1940), p. 47.

began with a long article addressed to the "well-intentioned Wise, Learned, and Erudite of Spain." [11] In it, Nipho outlined the *Diario*'s intent and asked for its readers' benevolence. The final section of the four-page paper was devoted to "News of Commerce" and "Public Notices," a forerunner of modern "want ads." The first "Public Notice" read, "The house of a person of circumstances needs a Servant who knows how to sew well, irons with cleanliness, and cooks without filth. If you are unemployed and wish to find employment, come to the house in which this Gentleman lives, which is in front of the Monastery of Sacramento, fourth floor second, in a large building which has various shops downstairs, a Glazier, Pastry shop, and a Barber." [12]

Nipho's *Diario Noticioso* was the first daily newspaper to appear on the continent and was antedated only by the *Daily Courant*, which had been published in London between 1702 and 1735. Its impact on the readers of Madrid must have been great, or so Nipho imagined it, for in the second issue, still using the pseudonym "Manuel Ruiz de Uribe," he wrote:

The *Diario* is already in the palestra. There is angry grumbling; much envy of it; lack of confidence, partly from suspicion; the people divided into camps and I aware of the commotion of all. Some say that this *Diario* is a very laudable invention; some, that it cannot be lasting; some, that it is a source of much mischief; some, that it is for the benefit and use of all; some, that it is a taker-of-money and a cheater of youth; some, that it cannot carry out what it promises; some, that to please so many, one man is not enough. [13]

The editor's delight at the controversy over the *Diario* was not shared by the nation's authorities. In March, a month after it first appeared, the kingdom's Judge-Superintendent of Printing, Juan Curiel, moved to limit Nipho's operations by precisely defining the rights that went with the newspaper's *privilegio* and licenses. He ordered one Phelipe de Castilblanque to "go to the plant of the *Diario* and notify the printer that he should not print, without a license, a supplement to the *Diario* nor any thing other than the said *Diario* in four pages, as has been done until now, under pain of the penalties imposed on those who print without a license, and make the same known to the editors of the *Diario*." [14] There was

---

[11] *Diario Noticioso* (Madrid), Feb. 1, 1758, p. 2.
[12] *Ibid.*, p. 4.
[13] *Diario Noticioso*, (Madrid), Feb. 2, 1758, p. 2.
[14] Enciso Recio, *Nipho*, p. 169.

no desire that this newspaper—which, in the words of the King, could give so much benefit to the public, and which had stirred so much controversy—should escape the vigilance or control of the government.

The price per copy of the *Diario Noticioso* was two *cuartos*, the equivalent of six modern Spanish *céntimos* (one-tenth of a U.S. cent), and no charge was made for the insertion of "public notices." With the third issue, the title was reduced from *Diario Noticioso, curioso-erudito y comercial, público y económico* to the simpler *Diario Noticioso* in an attempt to popularize the publication. On January 1, 1759, it was changed to *Diario Noticioso Universal*.

As Nipho admitted in a later publication, the profits realized from the *Diario Noticioso* were unsatisfactory.[15] In addition, there is evidence to suggest that the personal relationship between Nipho and Lozano Yuste was deteriorating.[16] So, disillusioned by the newspaper's failure to produce economic rewards and plagued by friction with his partner, Nipho sold out. Lozano paid him 14,000 *reales*[17] for his share of the *Diario Noticioso Universal* and, on May 29, 1759, took over the publication.

In that year, Ferdinand VI died after a ten-month attack of manic melancholy that terminated his active rule.[18] His successor was Charles III, Duke of Parma and King of Naples. In October, 1759, Charles arrived in Spain and by early the next year had begun an overhaul of the government, especially the municipal divisions which he hoped to free from the absolute control exercised by the Court. He ended Ferdinand's indecisive vacillation between England and France and allied Spain with the French. His own enlightened cultural tastes, fostered in the less traditional atmosphere of the Italian kingdoms, led him to encourage the arts. His reforms, and a period of peace, led to economic development and increasing prosperity. It was in such an environment of change, of emphasis on culture, of encouragement of the theater, of litera-

---

[15] In 1763, he wrote, "I began with a lively desire to make money with the *Diario Noticioso*, which was seen at the beginning as more than a mere profit of a thousand ducats. I quit this work for good reasons, stayed quiet for some days, and meanwhile some *pesetas* from the sale of the work lasted me." *Correo General de Europa* (Madrid), 1763, II, 218.
[16] See the *Diario Noticioso Universal* (Madrid), May 29, 1759, p. 2.
[17] A *real* is one quarter of a *peseta*, or 25 *céntimos*, and had a value of slightly more than six U.S. cents.
[18] Harold Livermore, *A History of Spain* (New York, 1960), pp. 335–336.

ture, and of the arts, that Nipho resumed his journalistic activities. In late 1760, he began the *Caxón de Sastre*.[19] The merits of the *Caxón de Sastre* rest more on its innovations than on its content. It devoted its pages to rare or hitherto unpublished works by Spanish authors and introduced some major foreign writers of the period to its readers. But, of more importance, with it Nipho introduced the use of subscriptions into Spain and, for the first time, used the mails to distribute an unofficial publication.

In theory the *Caxón de Sastre* was a weekly, but in practice it had a periodicity of its own. Octavo in size, each paper was published in two sections, and separate press runs were made for subscribers and for regular sales. The two parts of each issue appeared on Mondays and Thursdays for those who subscribed and Tuesdays and Fridays for direct sale customers, who picked up their copies at the printer's shop or in bookstores. Nipho told his readers that the presentation of the weekly in split form made "reading less bothersome and acquisition of the paper easier. . . ."[20] In the beginning, he charged twenty-four *reales* (six *pesetas*) for a six-month subscription, but, in early 1761, he raised the rate to thirty *reales*. In all, sixty issues of the *Caxón de Sastre* appeared, varying in length from sixteen to fifty-four pages. Nipho brought the *Caxón de Sastre* to an end in October, 1761, though it was reprinted in collected form in January of 1762 and again in 1781.

Even before dropping the *Caxón de Sastre*, Nipho had launched at least one other venture and possibly two. On June 5, 1761, a weekly called *El Duende especulativo sobre la vida civil* first appeared.[21] The editor was listed as one Juan Antonio Mercadal, but Spanish press historian Eugenio Hartzenbusch states that Mercadal was merely one of Nipho's many pseudonyms.[22] The paper appeared seventeen times.

In addition, he published the weekly *El Murmurador Imparcial*

---

[19] *Caxón de Sastre o montón de muchas cosas buenas, mejores y medianas, útiles, graciosas y modestas, para ahuyentar el ocio sin las rigideces del trabajo, antes bien a caricias del gusto* ("The Tailor's Scrap Box or pile of many good, better, and average things which are useful, amusing, and modest, for the purpose of driving away boredom without the strictness of work, even with the caresses of pleasure") (Madrid, 1760–61).
[20] *Caxón de Sastre* (Madrid), 1761, no. 41 (page unnumbered).
[21] *El Duende especulativo* . . . (" The Spirit speculative about civil life") (Madrid, 1761).
[22] *Unos cuantos seudónimos de escritores españoles con sus correspondientes nombres verdaderos* (Madrid, 1904), p. 7. Enciso Recio also attributes *El Duende especulativo* to Nipho. See *Nipho*, p. 317.

y observador despacionado de las locuras y despropósitos de los hombres.[23] Few copies of the periodical, which was twenty-four pages in length, are to be found today, though historians suggest it appeared until late in the year.[24] It dealt primarily with discussions and criticisms of literature and customs.

Despite the fact that 1761 had seen the end of two periodicals, Nipho's professional enthusiasm did not lessen and, in 1762, he began a new weekly, the *Estafeta de Londres.*[25] The periodical, which began with the issue of September 14, 1762, and ended with that of December 28, 1762, appeared each Tuesday. It took the form of "letters," written by Marciano de la Giga, one of Nipho's many pen names.

In the first issue, Nipho outlined the project:

This new work will consist of various letters written from London to different persons and of some observations from various men of affairs about the customs, government, popular skill, and discretion of the English. These letters will be distributed once a week so that they will form a collection of political investigations in which the curious will find: 1) extraordinary events and all that which is most valuable which may stem from history, customs and humanity; 2) all those acts which are related to history, laws, the revenue of the kingdom, the navy and the army, most careful consideration being given to the most useful knowledge of England; 3) the letters will show the English, with all the self-interested connections they have made, as rivals and competitors of all the kingdoms of the world. Finally, a great many of these letters will offer the examples which the English give each other to inspire themselves to the useful and valuable. In addition, the sciences and arts, in all their usual meanings, will form a principal part of this treatise. In it, I suppose myself a resident of London and observe the good and the evil of their customs.[26]

The work was primarily political in nature though it offered its readers large doses of history and economic and financial news.[27]

---

[23] *El Murmurador Imparcial* . . . ("The Impartial Gossip and dispassionate observer of the madnesses and absurdities of men") (Madrid, 1761).
[24] Martín Alonso, "Bibliografía especializada sobre periodismo español e hispanoamericano," *Ciencia de lenguaje y arte del estilo* (Madrid, 1953), p. 606.
[25] *Estafeta de Londres: Obra periódica repartida en diferentes cartas, en las que se declara el proceder de la Inglaterra respecto a sus costumbres, industria, artes, literatura, comercio y marina* ("The Courier of London: A periodic work divided into different letters in which is outlined the conduct of England in respect to its customs, industry, art, literature, commerce, and navy") (Madrid, 1762).
[26] *Estafeta de Londres* (Madrid), Sept. 14, 1762, pp. xix-xx.
[27] Florentino Zamora Lucas and María Casada Jorge, *Publicaciones periodicas existentes en la Biblioteca Nacional* (Madrid, 1952), pp. 162, 428.

Nipho was not the only newspaper founder at work in Spain. On April 1, 1758, the *Hebdomadario Útil Sevillano* [28] first appeared. Despite the "Weekly" (*Hebdomadario*) in its title, it was published twice a week, on Fridays and Tuesdays.[29] In 1762, José de Clavijo y Fajardo began a weekly called *El Pensador*, which he published until the end of 1763 and then resumed during 1766 and 1767. For Clavijo y Fajardo, a protegé of Charles III, *El Pensador* served as a stepping-stone to official posts, including that of Secretary of the Royal Cabinet of Natural History, Director of Court Theaters, and the editorship of the *Mercurio Histórico y Político* when that monthly was made an official publication in 1773.

In mid-1761, Pedro Ángel de Tarazona, a Barcelona businessman, petitioned the government for permission to begin in his city a daily similar to the *Diario Noticioso Universal* of Madrid. Despite the fact that he had obtained advance permission from Juan Antonio Lozano, Nipho's partner in the founding of the Madrid daily and holder of the *privilegio*, traditional court conservatism prevailed and the petition was denied. On November 10, he reapplied. His position was reappraised in the light of the changing times in Spain. The Royal Council decided that the *privilegio* was for one Madrid newspaper and announced that there was "no reason that the privilege should create a monopoly of all those [newspapers] which might be particularly useful to the other parts of Spain, which might wish to equip themselves, by means of the Council's license, with similar dailies." [30] The license was granted to Ángel de Tarazona on December 2, 1761, with the condition that the newspaper adhere to the same regulations as the Madrid *Diario Noticioso Universal* and, in line with Spain's newly active interest in economic development, serve as an aid "to the growth of commerce, as much by land as by sea. . . ." [31] The new essay into the field of daily journalism, the *Diario Evangélico, Histórico-Político*,[32] appeared on Thursday, January 7, 1762. It was not long before Ángel de Tarazona manifested a now familiar dissatisfaction

---

[28] *Hebdomadario Útil Sevillano* ("Useful Sevillian Weekly") (Seville, 1758).
[29] During 1710 and 1711, Seville produced a periodical with the extravagant title, *Gaceta de Gacetas, Noticia de Noticias, Cuenta de Cuentas* ("Gazette of Gazettes, News Item of News Items, Tale of Tales").
[30] Quoted in Enciso Recio, *Nipho*, p. 192.
[31] *Ibid.*
[32] *Diario Evangélico, Histórico-Político* ("The Evangelical, Historical-Political Daily") (Barcelona, 1762-73).

with the title of his daily. Beginning with the seventy-second number, he halved the paper's size to four pages and expanded the title to *Diario Curioso, histórico, erudito, comercial y económico.*[33] In late 1762, Charles III acted to extend the use of print as a means of popular education. He did so by removing obstacles to the growth of the medium. A Royal Order, issued November 14, 1762, suppressed "the regulation, the requirement of soliciting permission to print, the privileges for books, the correctors, the laws of censorship, the publication of approvals, and all the other turns of the labyrinthian gears which chain the cultural intelligence transmitted by the vehicles of public communication." [34] However, not all the liberalizing measures applied to the periodical press, which continued to be licensed and subject to censorship. But the relaxation of restrictions did make its impression on newspapers, as publishing activity in the following year indicates.

In the months following the royal liberalization of print controls, Nipho announced his intention of founding a new weekly, the *Correo General, histórico, literario y económico de la Europa.*[35] He noted in the final issue of the *Estafeta de Londres*:

The new work which I am going to begin in continuation of this periodical, under the title of *Correo General, Histórico, Literario y Económico de la Europa y particularmente de nuestra Península* is vast in scope and we must all help jointly in its shaping, for which reason I beg all those who believe themselves capable or who find themselves with opportune material to favor me with their items, and I will happily

---

[33] *Diario Curioso* . . . ("Curious, historical, erudite, commercial, civil, and economic Daily").
[34] *Real Orden del 14 de noviembre de 1762.*
[35] *Correo General, histórico, literario y económico de la Europa (en continuación de la Estafeta de Londres), donde se contienen memorias útiles sobre las ciencias, agricultura, artes y comercio de Francia, Holanda, Alemania, Italia y demás reinos y provincias europeas que saben sacar su felicidad de una prudente y bien dirigida economía pública. También, y por ser más necesarias, se darán las noticias recientes, regulares o imprevenidas que sobre todo lo expresado y de la Historia natural, literaria e industriosa ofreciesen los reinos y provincias de España* ("General, Historic, Literary, and Economic Mail from Europe [in continuation of the *Estafeta de Londres*], which will contain useful notes about the sciences, agriculture, arts, and commerce of France, Holland, Germany, Italy, and other European kingdoms and provinces which know how to draw happiness from a prudent and well-directed public economy. In addition, and being more necessary, it will give recent, regular, or unforeseen news, above all about that which is discussed, and about the natural, literary, and industrial history offered by the kingdoms and provinces of Spain") (Madrid, 1763).

concede my place to all who wish to so aid me, putting their names [on the items] or masking them behind the cloak of anonymity. This work is nothing more than love of the Fatherland, and, in order that its fortunes may rise, let there be greater interest, let there be more glory.[36]

The goals of the *Correo General de Europa* were no less than the general improvement of Spain, or so Nipho declared in the first issue. "That which I intend to do in this work is absolutely useful and necessary for the Fatherland; not correcting unimportant or variable customs, but rather returning it to a lapsed splendor and a timely and unique felicity which has fled from our soil, vomited up and thrown out by laziness and the gross inattention of neglect." [37] Throughout the successive issues, there was a preoccupation with economic matters. Nipho attacked Spain for its economic decadence which he blamed on a failure to cultivate its commerce and industry, a lack of consumers, and an unfavorable balance of trade. His cure included the standardization of customs practices, special treatment for Spanish ships, an increase in export taxes on such primary materials as wool and silk, and government aid to exporters of highly competitive foodstuffs, including raisins, olive oil, and wine. But, above all, he called for study and adoption of commercial techniques being used in the rest of Europe, where the industrial revolution was just being born.

The *Correo General de Europa* was the first of four publications begun by Nipho in 1763. In addition, six other periodicals appeared in Madrid that year, bringing to ten the number started in the months following the relaxation of print controls decreed by Charles III in November of 1762. One can only surmise that there was a relationship between the burst of publishing activity and the change in the control structure, the greater degree of freedom encouraging entrepreneurial enterprise by reducing the difficulties confronting the founder of a periodical. Nor is it possible to do more than conjecture about the influence that Nipho and Clavijo y Fajardo, editor of *El Pensador,* may have had on the decision to relax press controls. They presided over a press which was not critical in its treatment of official Spanish institutions. It is certain that Nipho's political views represented a source of neither danger nor embarrassment to the Monarch. His political philosophy was conservative and absolutist. To him, Charles III was "a sovereign

---

[36] *Estafeta de Londres* (Madrid), Dec. 28, 1762, Letter XV, p. 446.
[37] *Correo General de Europa* (Madrid), Jan. 11, 1763, p. iii.

so fond of his subjects that he treated them all like sons . . . to such a degree that if it were proposed to him that it was necessary to give up all that constitutes the glory and splendor of the position of majesty for the universal good of the Spanish [people], he would retire to the life of a private gentleman." [38] Liberalism was anathema to Nipho, especially the English variety which created a form of government in which "the poorest, most mechanical official is believed to be a judge, able, capable, and competent to control the conduct of the most respectable personage. Ministers of the first order, the most courageous and prudent generals, the most expert admirals, all faithful and vigilant, are subject to the caprices of the vilest vassals. Everything in England is a monstrosity and in nothing are the English like the rest of the great mass of men." [39]

A month after the first appearance of the *Correo General de Europa*, Nipho began *El Pensador Cristiano: Meditaciones provechosas para todos los días de Cuaresma.*[40] The first number appeared on Friday, February 11, and the publication lasted through Lent. As its title suggested, it consisted of a series of religious "meditations," one for each day of the week covered by the current number. Also during the year, he published a few numbers of *El Amigo de Mugeres*,[41] a periodical designed for female readers. But, next to the *Correo General de Europa*, his most important project was the weekly *Diario Estrangero*,[42] which first appeared on Tuesday, April 5, cost eight *cuartos* (twenty-four *céntimos*), and in which Nipho attempted to complement the economically oriented *Correo General de Europa* with a publication devoted to culture. It was normally divided into two sections: "Literary news" and "Fashionable news." The first section was quite flexible, being devoted in various issues to discussions of morals, economics, politi-

---

[38] *Estafeta de Londres* (Madrid), Jan. 11, 1762, p. xv.
[39] *Ibid.*, pp. xiii-xiv.
[40] *El Pensador Cristiano* . . . ("The Christian Thinker: Profitable meditations for each day of Lent") (Madrid, 1763).
[41] *El Amigo de Mugeres* ("The Friend of Women") (Madrid, 1763).
[42] *Diario Estrangero: Noticias importantes y gustosas para los verdaderos apasionados de artes y ciencias que ofrecen en el día los reinos civilizados de Europa. Añadidos muchos secretos para las artes, agricultura y mecánica aprovechadora* ("The Foreign Daily: Important and pleasant news for the true devotees of the arts and sciences offered today by the civilized kingdoms of Europe. Many secrets of the arts, agriculture, and beneficial machinery added") (Madrid, 1763).

cal philosophy, and jurisprudence. The "Fashionable news" ("Noticias de moda") served as a sounding board for Nipho's comments on the theater which were, according to historian Marcelino Menéndez y Pelayo, "sensible enough, though not very original." [43] The *Diario Estrangero* appeared twenty-two times, the last issue being that of August 30, 1763.

The year 1763 also witnessed the founding of such other papers as the *Aduana Crítica*,[44] a weekly published by Miguel de la Barrera; Juan Cristóval Romea y Tapia's *El Escritor sin título*,[45] a collection of comments on literary matters and customs published bimonthly; *El Hablador judicioso y crítico imparcial*,[46] a weekly comment on literary affairs by one J. Langlet, a priest and member of the Royal Academy of Antwerp; and *La Pensadora Gaditana*,[47] published by Doña Beatriz Cienfuegos, the second woman in Spanish history to put out a periodical.[48] In addition, there was *El Amigo del público*,[49] a paper published at irregular intervals by Juan Antonio Aragonés, a legal consultant to the Royal Council, and *El Amigo y corresponsal del Pensador*,[50] which ceased publication after two issues.

The following year, 1764, Nipho's activity slackened, but he did publish the winning entries in a literary contest he had sponsored in mid-1763. The contest results appeared at irregular intervals during the year under the title, *Discursos eruditos de varios ingenios españoles*.[51] Nipho's contribution was limited to assembling the

---

[43] *Historia de las ideas estéticas en España*, vol. III; *Obras Completas de Menéndez y Pelayo* (Santander, 1940), p. 284.
[44] *Aduana Crítica* ("Critical Customhouse") (Madrid, 1763–64).
[45] *El Escritor sin título* ("The Writer without title") (Madrid, 1763).
[46] *El Hablador judicioso* . . . ("The judicious speaker and impartial critic") (Madrid, 1763).
[47] *La Pensadora Gaditana* ("The Thinker from Cádiz") (Madrid and Cádiz, 1763–64).
[48] Spain's first newspaper woman was Doña Francisca de Aculodi who, between 1687 and 1689, published in San Sebastián a bimonthly translation of a Spanish-language publication in Brussels, then the capital of Spanish Flanders.
[49] *El Amigo del público* ("The Friend of the public") (Madrid, 1763).
[50] *El Amigo y corresponsal del Pensador* (" The Friend and correspondent of the Thinker") (Madrid, 1763).
[51] *Discursos eruditos de varios ingenios españoles que, en desagravio de la patria ofendida por algunos escritores de moda, ofrecen sobre algunos asuntos de los propuestos en 4 de junio de 1763* ("Erudite discourses about some of the topics proposed on June 4, 1763, which are presented by various Spanish geniuses in vindication of the fatherland, which has been offended by some fashionable writers") (Madrid, 1764).

works and adding some personal notes and rather disillusioned advice to the "Spanish geniuses," who, he suggested, should avoid writing about serious matters and stick to "mockeries and jests." [52]
The same year, Nipho published a collection of short novels by Spanish and French authors [53] using the pseudonym Antonio Ruiz y Minondo. On April 9, Friar Antonio de la Chica Benavides began Granada's first newspaper, the *Gazetilla Granadina: Noticioso y útil para el bien común*,[54] which continued until his death the following year.

In 1765, the *Semanario Económico, compuesto de noticias prácticas de todas ciencias, artes y oficios*,[55] an imitation of Nipho's *Estafeta de Londres* and *Correo General de Europa*, began a life that extended over a thirteen-year period, despite a prolonged and unexplained interruption. Two years later, Nipho founded *El Bufón de la Corte*,[56] a partly humorous, partly literary weekly. He called himself Joseph de Serna. The *Bufón*, which appeared sixteen times and was collected into a 250-page volume, was not dated and the months of its publication are not known. Shortly after its appearance, one Joseph Nuaño put out several issues of *El Bufón de Ballecas*,[57] also a weekly, which satirized Nipho's *Bufón*. Ballecas, or today Vallecas, is a lower class area of Madrid.

In the same year, 1767, Nipho began one of his more successful publications, the *Guía de Litigantes y Pretendientes*,[58] a list of legal proceedings and government appointments modeled after the *Almanac Royal de France*. The idea of an annual *Guía* was well received by the Royal Council which granted him, on January 11, 1767, the exclusive *privilegio* for its publication. However, Nipho ran into difficulties in securing the information he needed from government officials. In the end, it took top-level intervention to release the details Nipho demanded for the *Guía* of 1768. On January 18 of that year, the Council's *agente fiscal* gave orders, in the

---

[52] *Discursos eruditos de varios ingenios españoles*, I (Madrid, 1764), 3.
[53] *El novelero de los estrados y tertulias y diario universal de las bagatelas, que ofrece al público don Antonio Ruiz y Minondo* (Madrid, 1764).
[54] *Gazetilla Granadina* . . . ("Curious Little Gazette or Grenadine Weekly: Well-informed and useful for the common good") (Granada, 1764).
[55] *Semanario Económico* . . . ("Economic Weekly, made up of practical news of all the sciences, arts, and trades") (Madrid, 1765–67, 1777–78).
[56] *El Bufón de la Corte* ("The Court Jester") (Madrid, 1767).
[57] *El Bufón de Ballecas* ("The Jester of Vallecas") (Madrid, 1767).
[58] *Guía de Litigantes* . . . ("Guide to Litigants and Office Seekers") (Madrid, 1767–1806).

King's name, to "the Secretaries of the Offices and Councils to expose to the said Nipho the lists and information which he lacks and asks for. . . ." [59] Despite the royal directive, the publication of each *Guía* was preceded by a thorough censorship and followed by a series of complaints because of omissions, errors, or inopportune inclusions. Nipho continued the *Guía* until his death in 1803, when it was taken over by his son, Manuel Deogracias Nipho.

In 1768, Nipho put out *El Erudito Investigador*,[60] a one-volume work drawing on the periodicals that had preceded it. It was probably in the same year that Nipho published five issues of a short-lived weekly, *El Filósofo Aprisionado*,[61] which was designed to repeat and expand in periodical form the content of *El Erudito Investigador*.

The following year, still chasing the financial success that had so far eluded him, Nipho began planning a new weekly. Early in the year, he obtained, from the Royal Board of Commerce, permission to "set up [in print], print, and sell all news concerning commerce, arts, and manufacturing, etc. . . ." [62] On June 28, he applied to the Royal Council for permission to print the weekly *Correo General de España* [63] which, he explained in his petition, would be of "utility to the public . . . ," of "no less utility than that produced in other cultured kingdoms of Europe by other works of this type." [64] The Royal Council named as censor of the

---

[59] Quoted by Enciso Recio, *Nipho*, p. 305.

[60] *El Erudito Investigador o historia universal del origen, establicimiento y progresos de las leyes, artes, oficios mecánicos, ciencias, comercio y navegación, arte militar, usos y costumbres de todos los pueblos antiguos del mundo, desde el diluvio universal hasta la elevación de Ciro al trono de los persas, y desde aquella remota edad hasta nuestros días* ("The Erudite Investigator or universal history of the origin, establishment, and progress of the laws, arts, occupations, machinery, sciences, commerce and navigation, military art, habits, and customs of all the ancient peoples of the world, from the universal deluge to the elevation of Cyrus to the throne of the Persians, and from that remote age until our days") (Madrid, undated).

[61] *El Filósofo Aprisionado* ("The Imprisoned Philosopher") (Madrid, undated).

[62] Enciso Recio, *Nipho*, p. 260.

[63] *Correo General de España y noticias importantes de agricultura, artes, comercio, fábricas, manufacturas, industria y ciencias* ("General Mail from Spain and important news about agriculture, arts, commerce, factories, manufacturing, industry, and science") (Madrid, 1770–71). Hartzenbusch, *Apuntes para un Catálogo de periodicos madrileños desde el año 1661 al 1870* (Madrid, 1894), p. 11, indicates that the work first appeared in late 1769, but Enciso Recio, whose study of Nipho is modern and more detailed, gives Feb. 2, 1770, as the date of the first issue. See *Nipho*, p. 266.

[64] Enciso Recio, *Nipho*, p. 262.

paper the Marqués de Regalía, who accepted the appointment "despite the many demands on my time and the slight opportunity I have had to judge the material. . . ." [65] Nipho submitted the introduction and outline of the first issues to Regalía on December 12. Three days later, the Marqués approved the material which he deemed "very useful for the encouragement of commerce and the advancement of the arts." [66]

The first issue of the *Correo General de España* appeared on Friday, February 2, 1770. One of its essential and continuing features, according to Nipho's plans, was a series of detailed reports on the agricultural, commercial, and industrial capabilities and potential of all regions of Spain. The Royal Board of Commerce agreed to supervise the collection of the information, so Nipho prepared a questionnaire which, in 171 specific questions, was supposed to elicit information about local agricultural, industrial, and artistic resources; the sciences; police and government organization; the church; each area's "natural history" and public health. Regional authorities complained about the work involved, especially that of copying the sample questionnaires which had been sent them. In order to silence the complaints, Nipho promised to print the 20,000 copies of the questionnaire "which are judged necessary for as many distinct villages as are included on the Peninsula." [67] But his personal financial resources were not adequate to cover the cost of paper and printing, so, on April 3, 1771, he applied to the Royal Council for aid. Six days later, the Council granted him a subsidy of twenty-five *doblones*. The grant was confirmed by the Royal Council in a decree of May 4. Despite the official backing, most of the results of Nipho's ambitious project never reached the reading public. By late 1771, the *Correo General de España* was in serious trouble. The subscription rate was only sixty *reales* (fifteen *pesetas*) a year, yet Nipho was forced to inform his readers that he would have to reduce the price because "until now only the seventy or eighty persons who have taken every issue of the work have tolerated it. . . ." [68] However, a cut in the subscription rate was no cure, and before the end of the year the paper stopped publishing.

---

[65] Document No. 5.531–32, National Historical Archives, section of Consejos, Impresiones.
[66] Marqués de Regalía, letter of Dec. 15, 1769, National Historical Archives, section of Consejos, Impresiones.
[67] Nipho, undated letter, in *ibid.*
[68] *Correo General de España* (Madrid), 1771, no. 99, p. 377.

Its place in the history of the Spanish press was assured. It was the first paper to receive a government subsidy and the first to conceive and attempt to carry out a large-scale research project. Had it survived, it could have played an important role in Spain's economic development. In less than two years of existence, it "came to fill an important gap in aid of Spain's economic recuperation. Its program was very broad: the encouragement of the arts, the extension of commerce, stimulation of industry, the progress and happiness of agriculture and the vigor of the sciences."[69] Periodicals that came after the *Correo General de España* tended to follow its areas of interest and continue its probe of the Spanish economy.

Press historian Pedro Gómez Aparicio attributes the demise, in 1771, of the *Correo General de España* to the "scanty capacity for distributing periodicals of the era and the lack of interest in reading." [70] However, in that year, the *Gaceta de Madrid*, begun the century past by Fabro Bremundan and since under the direction of a series of editors, had shown a sizable profit. It had only 135 subscribers, plus a commitment for 500 copies which were sent by ship, via the port of Coruña, to the Americas. From a press run varying between 8,750 and 9,000 copies, it realized a profit of more than 40,000 *pesetas*.[71]

The failure of the *Correo General de España* did not leave Nipho completely unemployed. He still had the *Guía de Ligtigantes* and, in December of 1769, he had been appointed a censor. This official position may have had some bearing on the cooperation he received from the government during the planning and publication of the *Correo General de España*, especially the speed with which his plea for financial aid was answered. At least one work which he censored is known, the *Pliegos de motes para la diversión de las damas y galanes la vispera de Año Nuevo y los Santos Reyes*. Nipho approved most of the work, but he found some of the *motes* ("mottoes") "inopportune, insulting, and far-removed from the nobility of our language," [72] and ordered their expurgation.

There was little new journalistic activity in Spain during the

---

[69] Enciso Recio, *Nipho*, p. 271.
[70] "Apuntes para una historia del periodismo Español," *Gaceta de la Prensa Española*, Nov. 15, 1963, p. 35.
[71] These figures compiled by Enciso Recio (*Nipho*, p. 269) are among the very few available to the student of the Spanish press. Even today, only rough, contradictory press run and profit statistics are made public.
[72] Quoted by Enciso Recio, *Nipho*, p. 22.

balance of the decade which had begun in 1770. It was a period of comparative quiet in Europe, dating from 1763 when the Treaty of Paris ended the Seven Years' War. The rivalry of Spain and Great Britain continued very much alive in America, though the arena was remote for most Spaniards. It was not a period conducive to the development of the press if one accepts the thesis, presented by Eulogio Varela Hervías, that "there is a very clear relation between periods of political tension and the beginning or development of national presses." [73]

On March 3, 1779, the Balearic Islands' first newspaper, the *Semanario Económico, Instructivo y Comercial, que publica la Real Sociedad de Mallorca*,[74] appeared in Palma. In the same year, Nipho revised and expanded the *Caxón de Sastre*, dating from 1760-61, and published it in six volumes.

The year 1781 saw two new periodicals born in Madrid: *El Correo Literario de la Europa*[75] and *El Censor*.[76] The *Correo Literario*, supposedly the work of a "Spaniard resident in Paris," attempted to cover, as its title suggests, literary, scientific, cultural, and commercial news from most of Europe. It is less noteworthy for the detail of its news coverage and criticism than for the copiousness of its bibliography of new books, including those published in Spain. Its authorship is in doubt. Some experts attribute it to Nipho, but the most recent work on the subject, that of Luis Miguel Enciso Recio, credits Francisco Antonio Escartín, Nipho's son-in-law, with its conception and operation.[77]

Of far more interest and historic importance is *El Censor*, begun in the same year by Luis Cañuelo, a lawyer for the Royal Council. Cañuelo was a student of the writings of Voltaire, Rousseau, and Montesquieu; a Francophile; and a member of the Masons—con-

---

[73] *Gazeta Nueva: 1661-1663* (Madrid, 1960), p. xxviii.
[74] *Semanario Económico* . . . ("Economic, Instructive, and Commercial Weekly, published by the Royal Society of Mallorca") (Palma, 1779).
[75] *El Correo Literario de la Europa, en el que se da noticia de los libros nuevos, de las inversiones y adelantamientos hechos en Francia y otros reinos extranjeros pertenecientes a las ciencias, agricultura, comercio, artes y oficios, publicados en París desde el mes de noviembre de 1780* ("The Literary Mail from Europe, in which is given news of new books, of the reverses and advances made in France and other foreign kingdoms pertaining to the sciences, agriculture, commerce, arts and trades, published in Paris from the month of November of 1780") (Madrid, 1781-82 and 1787).
[76] *El Censor* ("The Censor") (Madrid, 1781-85).
[77] *Nipho*, p. 328.

sidered by the Spanish to be a French, anticlerical, extremist organization—and his views permeated the pages of *El Censor*. Writing of the periodical, historian Marcelino Menéndez y Pelayo says:

Its pages boasted of scorning and censuring everything about Spain under the pretext of removing its illusions, complaining in a loud voice that "a certain theology, a certain morality, a certain jurisprudence, and a certain political system keep us ignorant and poor," and repeating triumphantly questions from the *Encyclopedia*: What does Spain owe itself? What have the Spaniards done? They reached the point of directly attributing our "descent, ignominy, weakness, and misery" to a belief in the immortality of the soul since, absorbed in the hope of a future life and conceiving of no true or substantial happiness beyond that, we neglected the corporeal and earthly.[78]

Despite Cañuelo's official connection with the Royal Council, the weekly *Censor* was repeatedly denounced and, on occasion, its editor was forced to retract publicly what he had said in its pages. Finally, after four tempestuous years, *El Censor* was silenced by a Royal Order issued on November 29, 1785. It had been the first manifestation of Spain's "polemic press."

In 1786, Nipho returned to his first love, journalism, perhaps again in search of financial success or perhaps because, as he had written a decade and more before in the *Estafeta de Londres*, "the true task of the journalist is . . . [meeting] his moral and educative responsibilities." He joined with Manuel Casal, a medical doctor who wrote poetry under the pen name Lucas Alemán, in publishing the *Correo de Madrid o de los Ciegos*.[79] The work was semiweekly; its first issue appeared on Tuesday, October 10, and it continued on Tuesdays and Fridays until April of the following year, when it switched to a Wednesday-Saturday schedule. Its title, "Post of Madrid or of the Blind," owed itself to the new circulation technique innovated in Spain by Nipho—street sales, which were entrusted to the sightless. In addition to that bid for circulation, the publishers set up subscription offices in printing plants in all major centers of population. Despite the nationwide search for subscribers, the subscription lists never exceeded 315 and, at one point, dropped

---

[78] *Historia de las ideas estéticas*, quoted by Pedro Gómez Aparicio, "Historia del periodismo," *GPE*, Nov. 15, 1963, p. 37.
[79] *Correo de Madrid o de los Ciegos: Obra periódica en que se publica rasgos de varia literatura, noticias y los escritos de toda especia que se dirigen al editor* ("The Post of Madrid or of the Blind: a periodical work in which are published extracts from varied literatures, news, and writings of all kinds which are sent to the editor") (Madrid, 1786–91).

to ninty-seven. The paper continued in operation until February 24, 1791, when it fell victim to a Royal Order suppressing all newspapers except the *Diario de Madrid*.[80]

In 1787, a Mexican from Los Angeles, in Mexico's state of California, one José Mariano Beristain, began a newspaper in Valladolid, the ancient capital of Spain. Beristain's *Diario Pinciano, histórico, literario, legal, político y económico* [81] appeared weekly, justifying the "daily" in its title with a record of the happenings of each twenty-four-hour period between the dates of publication. Beristain's struggle to survive reflects the problems facing many periodicals of the period. In his eleventh month as editor, he informed his readers: "My resources are infinitely smaller than my eager and patriotic thoughts, and paper mills, presses, and laborers work only for money. Therefore, it is necessary that I cease with my good ideas or propose to the public another subscription plan which will finance the continuation of the *Diario* without exposing me another time to the losses I have suffered in the past year." [82] His attempts to shore up the newspaper's finances were unsuccessful and, in June, he bade his readers goodbye with these words: "My sincere good will, my honest desires and intentions are infinite, but the external aid necessary to carry them out is limited." [83]

Meanwhile, imitators of the suppressed *El Censor* appeared in Madrid and spewed forth invective. By late 1788, the government's patience was exhausted, and the authorities clamped down.[84] On October 2, Charles III, already in the twilight of his reign—he was to die on December 14—reversed the stand he had taken in November of 1762, liberalizing controls on the print media, and decreed into existence the nation's first systematical legislation designed to control "periodical papers." The new Press Rules (*Reglamento de Imprentas*) stated:

---

[80] The *Diario Noticioso Universal*, Spain's first daily, had been renamed *Diario de Madrid* in 1788.
[81] *Diario Pinciano* . . . ("Pincian Daily, historic, literary, legal, political, and economic") (Valladolid, 1787–88).
[82] *Diario Pinciano* (Valladolid), Jan. 19, 1788.
[83] *Ibid.*, June 25, 1788.
[84] *El Apologista Universal* ("The Universal Apologist") (Madrid, 1786–87); *El Corresponsal del Censor* ("The Correspondent of the Censor") (Madrid, 1787); and *El Teniente del Apologista Universal* ("The Lieutenant of the Universal Apologist") (Madrid, 1788) were among the newspapers whose editorial policies led to the crackdown.

Censors as much as authors and translators will take care that the papers and writings [entrusted to them] shall include neither lewd nor slippery expressions and no satires of any type, not even in political matters, nor things which discredit persons, the theater and national instruction: much less those things which may blacken the honor and esteem of communities and persons of all classes or stations, dignitaries and employees. [They shall] abstain from all words which might be interpreted as having or have direct allusion against the Government or its Magistrates, for which offenses the penalties established by the laws will be imposed or demanded.[85]

The order, coupled with the growing unrest in France which presented a potential danger to Spain, apparently spurred the censors to more conscientious performances. However, there is evidence to suggest that the editors and publishers were not cooperating, either consciously harassing the censors or unwittingly, through carelessness, making their work more difficult. Whatever the reason, the results were obvious, and during the summer of 1789 the nation's Printing Judge ordered that "an author or the authors [of a periodical manuscript] should present a clean manuscript, written in a clear hand, and enough ahead of time to allow it to be perused without haste." [86] The Judge also suggested that manuscripts be reduced to the same number of pages intended for the printed product and ordered his censors to sign each page, rather than just one of those included in the manuscript.

Meanwhile, in France the tide of liberalism was rolling in. Early in 1789, the States-General was summoned for the first time since 1614 and, on May 25, assembled at Versailles. On June 17, the Third Estate, whose members were drawn from the non-noble, nonclerical classes, declared itself the National Assembly and, three days later, took a mass oath not to dissolve until a constitution had been drawn up. At the beginning of July, the King, Louis XVI, ousted a liberal minister, Necker, and massed troops in Paris. On July 14, the people responded by storming the Bastille. The French Revolution had started.

The events in Paris caused shock to all Europe's absolutist governments. In Madrid, the Royal Council grew increasingly aware of the danger that the revolutionary contagion might cross the French frontier and spread through Spain. In June, 1790, a Frenchman tried to assassinate the Conde de Floridablanca, Charles IV's

---

[85] *Real Orden del 2 de octubre de 1788, Articulo 3.*
[86] Quoted by Rumeu de Armas, *Historia de la censura*, p. 95.

chief minister and a zealous advocate of regalism. Floridablanca, frightened by the attempt, imposed a strict censorship on books and pamphlets imported from the other side of the Pyrenees. By early the following year, the sense of looming danger had increased to the point that the Spanish press was seen as a channel for the spread of the "liberal disease" from France. On February 24, 1791, Charles IV acted to quarantine the Spanish people, lest they be infected. On that date, the King promulgated a decree which suppressed all the nation's major newspapers except the official *Gazeta de Madrid* and the *Diario de Madrid*, which was specifically prohibited from printing "verses or other political ideas of any kind." [87] With few exceptions, the nation's newspapers shut down. The editors of the *Diario de Madrid*, working under the direct surveillance of the government, struggled along, printing the limited news permissible. In July, the *Diario's* staff appealed for permission to broaden the scope of its offerings, an appeal that was denied until August 3, 1791, when the restrictions were relaxed slightly. However, three weeks later, Charles ordered that all copy be submitted to censorship six days before publication or "however long the President of the Council may order," [88] a rule that made operation almost impossible for a daily.

Despite drastic reduction in the number of newspapers in Spain and the rigid controls imposed on the two that remained, Spanish government fears mounted. On June 25, 1792, the border with France was closed to printed matter. In a decree a few days later, Charles IV ordered customs officials to send all papers, "either printed or handwritten, which come from France, to the Ministry of State." [89] During most of the year, the Royal Council turned down all requests for permission to begin new periodicals in Madrid, including one submitted by two such unlikely subverters of the regime as Ignacio García Malo, chief of the palace library, and Pedro Estala, librarian of the Church of San Isidro el Real. However, the ban on new publications was not adhered to as rigorously in the provinces, a reflection of a marked tendency that still exists to consider the provincial press less important than that of Madrid, the capital.

On February 22, 1790, Charles IV had granted the *privilegio real*

---

[87] *Real Orden del 24 de febrero de 1791.*
[88] *Real Orden del 25 de agosto de 1791.*
[89] *Real Orden del 15 de julio de 1792.*

to the *Diario de Valencia,*[90] which began publication on Thursday, July 1, 1790. The *Diario de Valencia* boasted 440 subscribers for the initial issue, a financial backstop which contributed to its forty-five-year life. The decree of February, 1791, closing newspapers, caused at most a short interruption in its publication schedule.

On January 1, 1792, a soldier turned priest, Luis Santiago Vado, began a daily in Murcia, a southern provincial capital; called the *Diario de Murcia,*[91] it lasted until the end of August. On August 1, the Baron de la Bruère, a French nobleman who had fled from the Revolution and was therefore presumably not suspect politically, began Seville's first daily, the *Diario Histórico y Político de Sevilla.*[92] Bruère's newspaper lasted only ten months and is noteworthy mainly because of a news-gathering device initiated by the Baron, who spotted letter boxes around the city and invited readers to drop into them news items or literary works of local interest.

By far the most important newspaper to emerge in 1792 was the *Diario de Barcelona,*[93] Catalonia's first daily and the oldest privately owned paper still published in Spain. It was founded by Pedro Pablo Hussón de Lapezaran, a Neopolitan who had been brought to Spain in 1759, when he was five years old, as a member of the retinue of Charles III. Before applying for permission for the Barcelona *Diario,* Hussón had learned the trade as an employee of the *Diario de Madrid.* On April 6, 1792, Charles IV granted him the *privilegio* to publish a daily newspaper. In the *privilegio,* Charles referred to the request made by the editors of the *Diario de Madrid* to print additional news and the permission he had granted them, which, he said, included reporting on "news items that are interesting to know . . . births, marriages, and deaths of conspicuous persons, many of the appointments and employments approved by me in the Tribunals and Offices, changes in living quarters of persons listed in the directories of strangers and office seekers, the entry and departures of strangers and office seekers, the entry and departures of regiments, the arrival and absence of important personages, and other notices of the same type. . . ." He added that on August 23,

---

[90] *Diario de Valencia* ("Valencia Daily") (Valencia, 1790–1835).
[91] *Diario de Murcia* ("Murcia Daily") (Murcia, 1792).
[92] *Diario Histórico* . . . ("The Historical and Political Daily of Seville") (Seville, 1792–93).
[93] *Diario de Barcelona, de avisos y noticias* ("Barcelona Daily: announcements and news") (Barcelona, 1792–in operation).

1791, he had ordered that all material destined for the *Diario de Madrid* be submitted to the censors six days before publication. In the *privilegio* given to Hussón, Charles stated:

I grant the above-cited Pedro Pablo Ussón [94] the Privilege which he requested to establish a Daily in the City of Barcelona with the proviso that, in its operation, he adheres precisely to the limits within which that [the *Diario de Madrid*] of my Court is published and to the provisions which are contained in my cited Royal order of August 25, 1791, inserting in the said Daily, as I wish them to be inserted, the public news and announcements of ships and their cargoes, and other things conducive to commerce and industry, and ecclesiastic news within the limits of the *Diario de Valencia* of November 22, 1790, to the extent that it can contribute to the development of the commerce and factories of the said City of Barcelona, and aid the export of the manufactured goods of the country. I charge the Regent of the city . . . to take very particular care that the editor of the Daily adheres scrupulously to the limits set forth in the concession of this privilege, insuring that the said editor present, with the anticipation deemed convenient, the articles which he would print, in order that they should be examined by him and by a censor who satisfied him, so that the printing never takes place without his license.[95]

The *Diario de Barcelona* appeared on Monday, October 1, 1792, subscribers paying two pesetas a month in Barcelona and three outside the city. As one might guess from the privilege, the contents were limited to "banal news items: announcements, offers and requests for work, lost objects, the arrival of ships . . . and as the *pièce de résistance*, articles about the natural sciences, arts, trades and similar matters, submitted, surely, to the Regent of the Audiencia, with as much anticipation as he believed convenient to demand." [96]

Meanwhile, the ban on periodicals had been somewhat relaxed in the capital. On the day that the *Diario de Barcelona* first appeared, a new semiweekly was born in Madrid—the nonpolitical, financial *Correo Mercantil de España y sus Indias*.[97] The *Correo Mercantil* was published on Mondays and Thursdays, then rushed to the

---

[94] The spelling "Hussón" is favored, appearing more often in legal documents and correspondence. The pronunciation would be the same in either case.
[95] *Privilegio otorgado por el Rey Carlos IV el 6 de abril de 1792*, quoted by Esteban Molist Pol in *El "Diario de Barcelona": 1792–1963* (Madrid, 1964), pp. 10–11.
[96] Molist Pol, *"Diario de Barcelona"*, p. 28.
[97] *Correo Mercantil* . . . ("Mercantile Post of Spain and its Indies") (Madrid, 1792–1808).

Spanish ports where shipping to South and Central America originated. It was sold in the ports themselves and sent overseas to subscribers, especially in Mexico City and Lima, Peru. According to experts on the Spanish-American press,

> The temper of the periodical, as its name indicates, was purely mercantile and it published the prices of different articles of trade between Spain and its colonies; exchange rates in different European business centers, especially London, Amsterdam, Genoa, and in Spain, Barcelona, Cádiz, and Madrid; the displacement of ships made by the various nations; the great losses of various internationally famous [banking] houses of that century; royal orders; types of insurances specifying the way in which insuring operations were carried out in Veracruz, etc.[98]

During the final years of the eighteenth century, at least four new periodicals were founded in Madrid.[99] Only one, the *Semanario de Agricultura y Artes dirigido a los Párrocos*, published by naturalist Juan Antonio Melón and intended for distribution by parish priests to the country's farmers, is considered of importance. Its content was devoted to up-to-date information on agricultural techniques. In 1808, soon after the French occupation of Madrid, the *Semanario de Agricultura* was closed, and Melón, turning his attention to the state of his nation, became one of the publishers of Spain's first anti-French periodicals.

The period between the introduction of printing into Spain and 1800 had seen the birth of communication by print in the form of *relaciones* which recorded events of unusual interest or importance in context that was isolated, both historically and physically. By the middle of the seventeenth century, there had been sporadic attempts to systemize the dissemination of information in a periodical—attempts that bore fruit in the *Gazeta* of Fabro Bremundan, whose output was often dedicated to the furtherance of his own career or to aiding the policies of his patron, Juan José of Austria.

---

[98] José A. Fernández de Castro and Andrés Henestrosa, *Periodismo y periodistas en Hispano-américa* (Mexico City, 1947). Quoted by Gómez Aparicio, "Historia del periodismo," *GPE*, Dec. 15, 1963, p. 31.
[99] *Semanario de Agricultura y Artes dirigido a los Párrocos* ("Weekly of Agriculture and the Arts, directed to the Parish Priests") (Madrid, 1797-1808; *Gaceta de los Niños* ("Children's Gazette") (Madrid, 1798-1800); *Anales de Historia Natural* ("Natural History Annals") (Madrid, 1799-1800); *Miscelánea instructiva, curiosa y agradable, o anales de literatura, ciencias y artes* ("Instructive, curious and agreeable mixture, or annals of literature, sciences and arts") (Madrid, 1797-1800).

During the eighteenth century, the influence of French periodicals on the Spanish press became marked, especially in the proliferation of papers dealing with literature, the arts, and the sciences. The nation's first dailies were founded and the financial press, dedicated to the improvement of the nation's economy, became a part of the fabric of commercial life. Concurrent with the growth of the press had been an increasing official alertness to the press's potential as a channel for, or originator of, ideas hostile to the ruling powers. Printing and books had been welcomed into Spain because of their usefulness in transmitting information. It was not long, though, before they became suspect as fear of alien ideas and external influences permeated the government. As the numbr of printing presses increased and their products multiplied, so did the complexity of controls regulating them. In the sixteenth century, seven decrees, spaced over a hundred years, were deemed sufficient. Six were introduced during the seventeenth century. However, during the eighteenth century, when the periodical press's form and direction—and its importance—became more sharply defined, the government reacted with sixty-five decrees.[100] Many periodicals had been started, but few survived beyond infancy; their lives were cut short by lack of financial success or summary death sentences imposed by the monarch. One newspaper, the *Gaceta de Madrid*, had assumed a more or less official character, reflecting the official value attached to mass communications, and another, the *Correo General de España*, had profited from an official subsidy. Yet it was a period in which the common man was, at best, apathetic toward printed matter, or, at worst, illiterate. Toward the end of the eighteenth century, a small-scale polemic press, forerunner of that which was to emerge from, and contribute to, the turmoil of the nineteenth century, was born and suppressed by the government.

---

[100] José Eugenio de Eguizábal, *Apuntes para una historia de la legislación española sobre la imprenta desde el año 1480 al presente* (Madrid, 1879), pp. 61–62.

CHAPTER SIX

Liberalism and Reaction

The nineteenth century was barely out of the cradle when the armies of Napoleon swept across the Pyrenees into Spain. The French occupation forces, harassed by Spanish *guerrilleros*, held out for more than five years before being driven back across the border by troops under the Duke of Wellington. Another invasion, that of liberalism, was not so successfully repulsed. In fact, it was welcomed—if not understood—by a part of the Spanish people and was able to put down weak roots in somewhat hostile soil. It was Spain, a land with no liberal tradition, which added the word "liberalism" (*liberalismo*) to the world's political vocabulary, applying it to a political philosophy imported from England and France. And it is to liberalism that many of Spain's orthodox contemporary historians attribute the problems of that century and this.

Elsewhere in Europe, liberalism had permeated the climate of opinion slowly, modifying man's outlook in subtle stages, and only gradually being incorporated into the fabric of political and social life. It arrived in Spain, in a sense, in full bloom, to be accepted as a modern solution for modern problems or rejected as an alien influence.

Nothing in Spain's history or its sociopolitical traditions had prepared it for the arrival of the liberal philosophy. The opposite is true: the Spanish tradition paved the way for the rejection of liberal modes of thought. The rule of absolutism had been com-

plete. The Church was entangled with the State. To the eighteenth-
and nineteenth-century Spaniard, conditioned to the iron rule of
kings and the omnipresence of the Church, liberalism was of English
or French origin, foreign and hence to be distrusted. Those who
did embrace it saw it primarily as an extension of laissez faire economic ideology to government, an extension which would result
in freedom from restraint and a declaration of independence of the
State from the Church—a theme prominent, sometimes to the exclusion of much else, in the liberal press of the nineteenth century.[1]
There is much evidence to justify the Spanish liberal's preoccupation with the temporal power of the Church. Over the centuries,
the Church had more and more "ceased to trouble about its pastoral
duties, ceased to be interested in the people, and instead became
even more interested in the struggle for privileges, very largely
economic privileges."[2]

The liberal preoccupation with the separation of church and
state was so pronounced, and voiced so repeatedly and vehemently,
that anticlericalism and liberalism became mutually identified to
the degree that even after the Church had been stripped of much
power and influence, the liberals still considered it their main enemy.

Liberalism, it has been said, had its beginnings in the Renaissance,
the Reformation, and the scientific revolution.[3] Those were the
forces which jolted much of the Western World out of medieval
patterns. What happened to them in Spain? In general terms, they
failed to penetrate Spain and the Spanish mentality, leaving alive
many of the institutions and assumptions of medievalism.

In much of Europe, the Renaissance meant an opening of frontiers
to the movement of ideas and people. For a time, Spain followed
the current, opening itself to humanist influences. But with the
ascent of Philip II to power, the trend toward integration into the
course of European development was reversed, and, according to
historian J. H. Elliott, Spain "was effectively transformed into the

---

[1] And still the definition of *liberalismo* approved by the Royal Spanish Academy. See the *Diccionario Manual e Ilustrada de la Lengua Española*, 2nd ed.
(Madrid, 1958), which defines *liberalismo* as a "system which proclaims the
absolute independence of the state, in its organization and functions, from all
positive religions."
[2] Franz Borkenau, *The Spanish Cockpit*, Ann Arbor Paperbacks ed. (Ann
Arbor, Mich., 1963), p. 9.
[3] J. Salwyn Schapiro, *Liberalism: Its Meaning and History* (Princeton, N.J.,
1958), p. 16.

semi-closed Spain of the Counter Reformation." [4] In 1558, Philip's regent banned the import of foreign books and ordered that books printed in Spain be licensed. The following year, Spanish students were forbidden to study abroad, and the Inquisition published a new Spanish Index, which it enforced with a methodical search of both public and private libraries for prohibited works. In general, the Renaissance "proved merely a short interlude in Spain where the Middle Ages lingered much longer than in almost any other European country." [5]

The Reformation, in some places, led to a growth of national spirit and the transfer of "theoretical power" from the Pope to the national monarchs.[6] Had it reached Spain, where seven centuries of Moorish invasion and domination had just ended, it would have had the opposite effect. Under the banner of a Catholic crusade against the forces of Islam, Spain's rulers had molded the semblance of a nation from a cluster of separate kingdoms; the Reformation could have shattered the unstable unity held together by religious conviction.[7] Spain did not merely recoil protectively from the Reformation: it met the new ideas with active resistance and, under Philip II, "more than anyone else . . . the leader of the Counter Reformation," [8] fought to stamp out Protestantism and restore the universal authority of the Catholic church. It was a period in which the Inquisition gained great power and helped a reactionary court "stifle any sound economic and social reforms. . . ." [9] Philip himself developed a mania for overseeing every administrative act within his kingdoms which created delays and inefficiencies in decision-making and contributed to the decline in the nation's fortunes which followed his death.

In essence, Spain isolated itself behind the Pyrenees and rejected the ideas sweeping Europe. To the Spanish, "the humanism of the Renaissance had seemed weakness, the rebellion of the Reformation had seemed impiety. . . . They fought to preserve, and for a long

---

[4] *Imperial Spain: 1469–1716* (New York, 1963), p. 217.
[5] Axel Heyst, "The Changing Face of Spain," *Contemporary Review*, Jan., 1962, p. 12.
[6] J. H. Randall, Jr., *The Making of the Modern Mind* (Boston and New York, 1940), p. 179.
[7] Jean Descola, *A History of Spain*, trans., Elaine P. Halperin (New York, 1963), p. 227.
[8] Richard Pattee, *This Is Spain* (Milwaukee, 1951), p. 33.
[9] Max Horkheimer, *Eclipse of Reason* (New York, 1947), p. 88.

LIBERALISM AND REACTION (119

time successfully preserved, the spirit of the Middle Ages. It was their triumph, their distinction, and their tragedy." [10] At a time when other nations were developing modern economic systems based on commerce and production, Spain was engaged in a non-creative exploitation of the riches of the New World. Spain's "main efforts were directed overseas: the huge riches taken from those countries—Spain failed to develop them economically—were used in Europe to foster sterile projects and policies." [11] Despite the wealth stripped from its colonies, Spain continued to be a poor country, one of the poorest in Europe. Its economy was plagued by inflation and disorder. Its national vision, turned toward the past, rejected economic modernization, and the individual Spaniard showed "scorn for commercial activities."[12]

Elsewhere in Europe, the Reformation and Renaissance were producing questioning minds—minds that struggled to answer all manner of philosophical and scientific questions. But the environment in Spain was such that it produced few if any scientists of note and very few philosophers in the mold of those of the rest of the continent.[13]

Spain had developed its own national character and in doing so, had not made the transition from feudalism to a modern state. Old patterns of behavior and thought, elsewhere discarded as outmoded, were still very much alive in Spain as the nineteenth century dawned.

The new century was marked not only by the Napoleonic invasion but also by internal strife so great that one historian has called it the century of "fratricidal introspection." [14] To press historian Pedro Gómez Aparicio, president of the National Federation of Spain's Press Associations, the beginning years of the century spelled an end to the "traditional" press and saw the birth of the "revolutionary" press. At the same time, according to Gómez Aparicio, Spain entered a period of "permanent revolution" which

---

[10] V. S. Pritchett, *The Spanish Temper* (London, 1954), p. 54.
[11] Heyst, "The Changing Face," p. 23.
[12] Américo Castro, *The Structure of Spanish History*, trans., Edward L. King (Princeton, N.J., 1954), p. 10.
[13] Crane Brinton in *The Shaping of Modern Thought* (Englewood Cliffs, N.J., 1963), p. 85, notes Spain's failure to produce scientists and suggests it was a by-product of the nation's poverty and lack of economic development.
[14] Eduardo Aunós Pérez, *Itinerario histórico de la España contemporánea, 1808-1936* (Barcelona, 1940), p. 160.

terminated only with the ending of the Civil War in 1939.[15] During that time, the press "fluctuated between anarchy and censorship, between the unleashing of liberty which, in practice, lacked moral and juridical limitations and the rigor of a Power which avoided setting norms." [16] The press became intimately bound up in the politics of the period, not as an observer and recorder of events, but as a partisan instrument of opinion formation and as a starting point for careers in the political arena. "Throughout the nineteenth century," it has been said, "journalism, for Spanish journalists, had only two exits: either to high administrative posts or to the anteroom of misery, because throughout the nineteenth century and a part of the twentieth, one can count on one's fingers the political figures who did not start out from an unrecognized and disdained mass of journalists, which they themselves later also disdained." [17] There was little sense of social responsibility shown by the press during the century, at least in the view of those students who represent the orthodoxy of the present regime. "In general," according to Juan Beneyto, former Director-General of the Press, "the Spanish press of the nineteenth century served group ideologies and appetites, but not [national] interests, except when the objective was seen to be the benefit of the newspaper." [18] The press was primarily a channel for private or political interests, a perversion of the social function it might have performed.

As noted earlier, Spain's ruler, Charles IV, had dealt severely with the Spanish press early in the last decade of the eighteenth century, summarily closing the bulk of the nation's periodicals. However, toward the end of the century, especially after 1796 when Spain signed the military Treaty of San Ildefonso with the French Directory, there was an easing of controls, and new papers were founded.[19]

---

[15] Ideas expressed in discussions with the author of this work.
[16] "El Consejo de Prensa Cumple un Año; un editorial," *Gaceta de la Prensa Española*, Dec. 15, 1963, p. 3.
[17] "Un Congreso de Historia del Periodismo" (editorial), *Gaceta de la Prensa Española*, Nov. 15, 1963, p. 3.
[18] *Historia social de España y de Hispanoamérica* (Madrid, 1961), p. 404.
[19] Among the first to appear in the nineteenth century were: *El Regañon General, o Tribunal Catoniano de literatura, educación y costumbres* ("The General Grumbler, or Cato's Tribunal of literature, education, and customs") (Madrid, 1803–04); *El Anti-Regañon General* ("The Anti-General Grumbler") (Madrid, 1803); and *Minerva, o el Revisor General* ("Minerva, or the General Inspector") (Madrid, 1805–08, 1817–18).

In France, there had been a growing comprehension of the value of the periodical press as a propaganda instrument. In 1792, the Commune had confiscated all printing equipment in Paris, charging that it had been used to "poison public opinion," and turned it over to "patriot" control.[20] Later in the same year, the liberal Girondist faction in the National Assembly proposed the establishment of a Bureau d'Esprit to form public opinion and direct the dissemination of information. Acting on the proposal, the Assembly created a propaganda section within the Ministry of the Interior.

Newspapers had proliferated during the Revolution, but not all followed the line laid down by France's new rulers. On August 29, 1799, the Directory deported the owners or editors of thirty-five periodicals and, on September 3, imprisoned the editors or printers of another eleven. On November 9, 1799, Napoleon Bonaparte, just returned from Egypt, carried out a successful coup d'état, overthrowing the Directory and setting up a provisional government, which he himself headed. One of the government's first acts was the closing of thirteen newspapers for the "duration of the war."

In 1801, the 1796 entente between France and Spain was reinforced by three new treaties. One ceded Louisiana to France in return for the establishment as a Spanish dependency of the newly created kingdom of Etruria, which was ruled over by a son-in-law of Charles IV. The other two treaties provided for the formation of Franco-Spanish squadrons and committed Spain to declaring war on Portugal if her Iberian neighbor did not renounce an alliance with England. The Portuguese refused to accept a Franco-Spanish ultimatum, and joint forces, under the command of Manuel Godoy, invaded Portugal. The invasion was successful, and the Portuguese quickly sued for peace.

The following year, the Treaty of Amiens brought about a general, but short-lived, pacification of Europe. In 1803, when war was renewed between England and France, Spain tried to remain neutral by paying its ally a monthly subsidy and granting it trade concessions, an arrangement which the British interpreted as hostile and used as an excuse to attack four Spanish frigates carrying bullion from the Americas to Europe. One Spanish ship was sunk, in an

---

[20] Juan Beneyto, *Ordenamiento Jurídico de la Información* (Madrid, 1961), p. 16.

engagement off Cádiz, and the other three were captured and taken to England. Spain reacted by declaring war.

With the nation once again involved in international strife, Charles tightened his personal grip on the print media. On April 11, 1805, he promulgated a *Reglamento Real de Imprentas* ("Royal Printing Regulation"), which, among other things, created the nation's first court devoted entirely to printing and publishing. But some powers were withheld from the new legal body. Article 17 specified:

This Print Tribunal shall not be able to grant licenses for the publication of new periodical papers. I reserve for myself that power for just motives. The Judge of Printing will name censors for the periodicals which are at present permitted or which will be permitted in the future, assigning to each periodical [a tax] of two hundred ducats to be paid annually by its respective editors on a quarterly basis. In case it is not paid, the license shall be suspended.[21]

In the following year, Napoleon, with whose fortunes those of Spain were now entangled, began the Continental Blockade, his attempt to defeat England by means of economic pressure. Portugal refused to close its ports to British shipping, and, on October 27, 1807, Spain and France signed the Treaty of Fontainebleau in which they agreed once again to send combined armies into Portugal. By the end of the year, Portugal had fallen before the French forces, and the Portuguese royal family was in flight to Brazil.

Meanwhile, the Spanish court in Madrid was torn by strife, a three-way struggle for power by Charles, his son Ferdinand, and Godoy, the Queen's favorite. Both Charles and Ferdinand appealed to Napoleon to arbitrate. The Corsican, using the appeals as an excuse, sent troops into Spain. On February 13, 1808, French forces entered Barcelona. On March 19, as troops under the command of Marshal Joachim Murat moved toward Madrid, Charles IV abdicated in favor of his son, who became Ferdinand VII. Four days later, the new monarch returned to Spain to be hailed as a hero and to discover that, on the day before, Murat had occupied Madrid. Napoleon refused to accept the abdication and summoned Charles to Bayonne, where he arrived in late April. On May 2, the people of Madrid rose against the French, and Spain's War of Independence had begun. The occasion of the uprising, which was immortalized in a canvas by Goya, was celebrated by the publication of a special newspaper which proclaimed in its title that the day had been "un-

---

[21] *Real decreto del 11 de abril de 1805.*

lucky for the French and a happy holiday for the Spanish. . . ." It added that the uprising marked the beginning of the "first year of liberty and independence and of misfortune for Napoleon, of defeat for France and the salvation of Europe, and the last [year] of Napoleonic tyranny." [22] The paper, which copied the format of the *Diario de Madrid*, reflected the elation of the people of Madrid at the momentary success of their slap at the invader. However, joy was to be short-lived and the downfall of Napoleon well in the future. On May 10, Ferdinand was forced to renounce his rights to the Spanish throne, and Charles was ordered to name Murat his "Lieutenant-General in Spain."

One of the first acts of the French was the subjugation of the press of occupied Spain to the needs of the occupiers, bringing about a radical change in the Spanish concept of the utility and goals of periodicals. The press was soon seen to be an indispensable vehicle of propaganda, a concept that long outlived the Napoleonic invasion. The French, versed in press manipulation, requisitioned major newspapers, entrusting them to French directors or Spaniards known to be sympathetic to the French cause. In Barcelona, the *Diario* was left in Spanish hands but published nothing but official communiqués issued by the French authorities. Even that was not enough for the French who "slowly assumed direction of the newspaper, adjusting it to official and extra-official needs and causing in it all kinds of transformations." [23] By mid-1808, the paper completely reflected the French position though it was published in either Castilian and French or, as a concession to regional sensitivities, in Catalan and French.

Meanwhile, in Madrid, Murat was shaping the local press to his needs. Even before Ferdinand renounced his rights to the Spanish throne, Murat had prepared a public proclamation announcing the event. He ordered one Eusebio Fernando to print the proclamation. When Fernando refused, the Marshal set up a printing plant in his own residence and began turning out a stream of propaganda, including the abdication proclamation. Other presses were at work

---

[22] *Diario napoleónico de hoy martes, aciago para los franceses, y domingo feliz para los españoles: primer año de la libertad, independencia y desgracia de Bonaparte, del abatimiento de la Francia y salvación de la Europa, y último de la tiranía napoleónica* (Madrid), May 4, 1808, p. 1.
[23] Esteban Molist Pol, *El "Diario de Barcelona": 1792–1963* (Madrid, 1964), p. 39.

in the capital, clandestine printing operations that flooded the city with anti-French propaganda and probably helped trigger the May 2 uprising. To stop the flow of invective against his forces, Murat resorted to stern measures, decreeing that "the authors, distributors or sellers of libelous printed matter or manuscripts, which provoke sedition, will be considered agents of England and shot." [24] By mid-May, both the *Gaceta de Madrid* and the *Diario de Madrid* had become instruments of the French, while other periodicals in the capital had been closed. When Ferdinand renounced the throne, Napoleon ordered the convening of a Spanish Cortes in Bayonne, a move apparently designed to cloak in an aura of legality his conferral, early in June, of the Spanish throne on his brother, Joseph Bonaparte. The *Gaceta* of May 25 carried the order, which specified that the Spanish deputation "be composed of one hundred and fifty persons, drawn from the Clergy, Nobility, and the general State, who must be in Bayonne on the 15th of the next month, to deal with the happiness of all Spain, presenting the evils caused by the former system [of government] and [proposing] the most convenient reforms and remedies for destroying them in all the nation and in particular in each province." [25]

The Spanish delegation, made up of ninety-one Francophiles, arrived on schedule and was greeted by Napoleon, who handed it a completed constitution on the French model. On July 6, after only twelve short sessions, the Spanish approved without modification all 146 articles of the constitution, which, among other things, proclaimed, for the first time in Spain, freedom of printing, a proclamation from which the periodical press was pointedly excluded. There was no immediacy attached to printing freedom, which, according to Article 145, would be established "two years after this Constitution becomes fully effective." Article 45 empowered the Senate to "name a committee of five Senators which will be charged with watching over the liberty of printing," adding, "Periodical papers will not be included in these dispositions," but would be submitted at a later date to special regulations.[26] Napoleon's sincerity in including freedom of printing in his long-range plans for Spain might well be measured by his statement to his own Council

---

[24] *Orden del día, Artículo VII. Diario de Madrid*, May 4, 1808.
[25] *Gaceta de Madrid*, May 25, 1808.
[26] Pedro Gómez Aparicio, "Apuntes para una historia del periodismo Español," *Gaceta de la Prensa Española*, Jan. 15, 1964, p. 45.

of State on August 2, 1809, when he explained that "printing is an arsenal which cannot be put into the hands of just anyone." [27]

The Spanish deputation to the Bayonne Constitutional Assembly also witnessed Joseph Bonaparte's oath of allegiance to Spain and his solemn promise to uphold the new constitution. On July 21, Joseph arrived in Madrid and, on the 25th, was crowned in the ancient capital of Toledo.

Meanwhile, the uprising of May 2 in Madrid had touched off resistance throughout the country. Murat, suffering from an unspecified "illness," retired from Spain. A *junta* formed in Oviedo declared war on Napoleon and dispatched a delegation to England to beg for help. A similar movement was begun in Valencia, where the people attacked the French in the streets. In Seville, a group of provincial nobility and local clergy led an uprising. On July 20, while Joseph Bonaparte was en route to Madrid, a Spanish army under the command of General Castaños, aided by English forces from Gibraltar, forced the French general, Dupont, to surrender at Bailén. Between 18,000 and 20,000 French were taken prisoner—less than a thousand Spaniards were killed or wounded—in the worst defeat suffered by the French since the Revolution.

With most of southern Spain held by insurgents, Joseph retired behind the Ebro River, and Madrid was returned, for a few months, to Spanish hands. Taking advantage of the withdrawal of the French, poet Manuel José Quintana called together a group of young liberals, including Juan Antonio Melón, publisher until recently of the *Semanario de Agricultura y Artes*, and proposed that they begin a newspaper devoted to propagating the liberal doctrine and opposed to the French. The paper, the *Semanario Patriótico*,[28] appeared on Thursday, September 1, 1808, and continued weekly publication until December 1, three days before French armies, led by Napoleon himself, reoccupied the capital. The first issue of the *Semanario Patriótico* proclaimed its editors' conviction that "well-directed periodical papers must be torches for illuminating the countryside, not firebrands for igniting disorder or discord, nor even less vile agitators destined to trick the people or cause them to become infatuated with the idols of fortune." [29]

---

[27] Beneyto, *Ordenamiento Jurídico*, p. 17.
[28] *Semanario Patriótico* ("Patriotic Weekly") (Madrid, 1808. Seville, 1809. Cádiz, 1810–12).
[29] *Semanario Patriótico* (Madrid), Sept. 1, 1808.

126) THE SPANISH PRESS

In mid-November, another newspaper joined the *Semanario Patriótico* in attacking the French; the *Efemérides del ciudadano español*,[30] as it was called, published just three issues before the French recaptured the city.

On December 4, Napoleon himself entered Madrid, and the editors of the *Semanario Patriótico* fled to Seville, headquarters of the Central Junta then directing military operations against the French. On May 4, 1809, after a silence of five months, the *Semanario Patriótico* reappeared, bringing its message of "liberalism" to the people of Seville. Its resurrection was short-lived, for, on August 31, it informed its readers that "insuperable problems" forced it to suspend operations. The real cause of the suspension, however, has been attributed not to the unspecified "obstacles" but rather to the "growing hostility of the readers" to its political views.[31] One of its editors, José María Blanco-White, a half-Spanish, half-Irish writer who had left the priesthood after his ordination, moved to England in a fit of pique and there published a monthly review, *El Español*, in which he attacked Spain and Spanish leaders. The other editors remained quiet for fifteen months, then again, this time in Cádiz, raised the *Semanario Patriótico*'s clamor for a constitutional government modeled after that of the French Revolution. Meanwhile, though, an official newspaper, the *Gazeta del Gobierno*,[32] published by the Central Junta, and *El Espectador Sevillano*,[33] continued to supply news and, in the case of the *Espectador*, liberal propaganda to the city. The daily *Espectador*, published by the poet Alberto Lista, was far more moderate than the *Semanario Patriótico* and far better received by the public. However, both it and the official *Gazeta* were forced, by the arrival in Seville of French troops under the command of Marshal Soult, to close down in late January of 1810. Lista, whose operation had been subsidized by the Spanish authorities, remained behind when his colleagues fled south and switched his allegiance to the invaders, publishing the *Gazeta de Sevilla* for Soult and, according to historian Manuel Gómez Imaz, "printing

---

[30] *Efemérides del ciudadano español* ("Almanac of the Spanish citizen") (Madrid, 1808).
[31] Gómez Aparicio, "Historia del periodismo," *GPE*, Jan. 15, 1964, p. 53.
[32] *Gazeta del Gobierno* ("Government Gazette") (Seville, 1809–10).
[33] *El Espectador Sevillano* ("The Sevillian Spectator") (Seville, 1809–10).

the greatest affronts against Spain and the most insulting and unjust judgments of the good patriots who shed their blood to defend it against the usurper." [34]

The French had already had a domestic defender in Madrid—Father Pedro Estala, publisher of El Imparcial.[35] Between March 21 and August 4, 1809, Estala's Imparcial had worked staunchly to swing public opinion behind Joseph Bonaparte,[36] but with no success.

The French approach to public information had been formulated at the beginning of the invasion by Maximilian Lamarque, the military chief of the Catalan region, who advised his fellow countrymen that newspapers in occupied areas should devote themselves to three areas of coverage:

1. Foreign news taken from French dailies.

2. Resumes of military operations, provided by French military authorities.

3. A brief, pointed report on the administrative works carried out by the Napoleonic forces, designed to impress the occupied areas with "the advantages of a well-run, just, and paternal Government." [37]

As noted earlier, the French authorities had shaped the content of the Diario de Barcelona almost from the moment of their occupation of Catalonia. During 1810, they completed the transformation of the newspaper by changing its name in March to the Diari del Gobern de Cataluña y Barcelona [38] and, in September, replacing the crest of the city of Barcelona on its masthead with the shield of the French Empire. At the same time, Hussón, the paper's founder, was relieved of his editorial responsibilities, despite his collaboration with the French, and replaced by one Pedro Barrera,

---

[34] Los Periódicos durante la Guerra de la Independencia: 1808–1814 (Madrid, 1910), p. 73.

[35] El Imparcial ("The Impartial") (Madrid, 1809).

[36] Estala's editorial posture might well be considered in the light of a modern appraisal of Bonaparte as "superior to Ferdinand both as a man and as a monarch," the opinion of Louis Bertrand and Sir Charles Petrie, The History of Spain, 2nd ed. (London, 1952), p. 305.

[37] Molist Pol, "Diario de Barcelona," p. 42.

[38] Diari del Gobern . . . ("Daily of the Government of Catalonia and Barcelona") (Barcelona, 1810–14).

whose antecedents are obscure, and Manuel Andrés Ygual, a poet who had praised Napoleon in an "Ode to the All-Powerful Hero of Europe." [39]

With the French in control of the *Diario de Barcelona*, the Spanish forces in Catalonia were without an organ of public information, so, in the summer of 1808, they authorized Antonio Brusi Mirabent, the son of a Barcelona stocking maker and himself a book dealer, to publish a newspaper in Tarragona, then still in Spanish hands. On August 23, Brusi began the *Gazeta Militar y Política del Principado de Cataluña*.[40] For more than four years, the *Gazeta Militar* followed the Supreme Junta as it moved from town to town ahead of following French forces. Brusi transported his rather rudimentary printing equipment on carts pulled by mules or oxen as did the ambulatory printers of the fifteenth and sixteenth centuries. On October 18, 1809, the Supreme Junta rewarded Brusi for his continuing service to the cause of Spanish independence by granting him a *privilegio* to publish the *Diario de Barcelona* once that city was freed from the French. In 1811, Brusi sent his wife, Eulalia Ferrer de Brusi, to Mallorca where, between September 6, 1811, and October 31, 1813, she published the bitterly anti-French *Diario de Palma*. At the end of 1813, the Supreme Junta settled in Vich, where Brusi changed his newspaper to the *Gazeta de Cataluña*, the name it bore until Spain reoccupied Barcelona. On June 6, 1814, Ferdinand VII ratified the *privilegio* granted by the Supreme Junta, and on the same day Brusi began publishing the *Diario de Barcelona*.

Meanwhile, the General Junta had moved from Seville, in the line of French encroachment, to Cádiz. In January, 1810, it appointed a five-man regency to arrange a meeting of the Cortes. Among the articles regulating the activities of the regency was one providing that "the Regency will . . . propose to the Cortes the question pending about the protection and assurance of freedom of the press and meanwhile will protect, according to the laws, this freedom as one of the most convenient means not only of disseminating information but also of conserving the civil and political

---

[39] In 1814, after the expulsion of the French from Spain, Hussón was tried by a Spanish court and found guilty of collaborating with the enemy. His sentence was remitted, by a general amnesty, to exile from Barcelona and exclusion from the Court at Madrid.

[40] *Gazeta Militar y Política* . . . ("Military and Political Gazette of the Principality of Catalonia") (Various, 1808–13).

liberty of the citizens."[41] By the time the regents summoned the Cortes into session, September 24, 1810, political dissension had already fragmented the legislative body. Three factions struggled for dominance. One, led by the Conde de Floridablanca until his death, clamored for the restoration of Ferdinand VII. Another, led by Melchor Jovellanos, a moderate liberal, opted for the establishment of a constitutional government modeled after that of England. The third group, headed by Manuel José Quintana, one of the founders of the *Semanario Patriótico*, favored a liberalism growing from the precepts of the French Revolution and controlled the biggest bloc of votes in the Cortes. Its strength was drawn from Spain's seaports, which were much more open to foreign influence than the inland areas and were therefore the breeding ground of new ideas. And, because of the disposition of the French forces, the coastal areas were able to send more representatives to Cádiz, thus dominating the Cortes.

While plans were being drawn up for the meeting, partisans of a constitution modeled on that of France founded a newspaper to air their views—the liberal *El Conciso*,[42] run by Gaspar María de Ogirando, a onetime translator of French liberal and revolutionary literature. The newspaper appeared every other day from August 24, 1810, to December 24, 1813, and had a press run of about 2,000 copies, the largest of any in Cádiz in that period.[43] *El Conciso*'s coverage of the war and the debates in the Cortes was accurate and succinct, but it ridiculed and satirized the Church, which it characterized as a mixture of "sordid interests, ominous egoism and crafty hypocrisy."[44]

The Cortes began work as scheduled on September 24, 1810.[45] High on the parliamentary agenda was a new press law. On October 8, Agustín de Argüelles, a deputy from Asturias who favored

---

[41] *Artículo 13* of the Regulations of January 29, 1810, under which the regency was constituted, quoted by Fernando Diaz-Plaja, *La Historia de España en sus Documentos* (Madrid, 1954), I, 89.

[42] *El Conciso* ("The Brief") (Cádiz, 1810–13).

[43] Ramón Solis, *El Cádiz de las Cortes* (Madrid, 1958), pp. 463–464.

[44] *El Conciso* (Cádiz), Sept. 28, 1810, p. 2.

[45] By the time the Cortes met, there were three official publications in Cádiz: the *Diario de las Sesiones de Cortes* ("The Daily of the Sessions of the Cortes") (Cádiz, 1810–13); *Gaceta de la Regencia* ("Gazette of the Regency") (Cádiz, 1810–13); and *Periódico Militar del Estado Mayor General* ("The Military Periodical of the General Army Staff") (Cádiz, 1810–13).

the French mode of constitutional government, presented the draft of the law to the assembled deputies. Argüelles, a gifted speaker whose oratorical abilities earned him the nickname "The Divine," told his audience that events in France illustrated the need for a free press. Freedom of the press during the Revolution, he said, "caused the chains, which had enslaved it, to fall from the hands of the French nation. However, a cruel group began to exploit the great medium [of communication] and the French nation, or, better said, its Government began to work in opposition to the principles which it had proclaimed. Despotism was the fruit that resulted." [46] On October 19, after eleven days of discussion, the Cortes approved the *Ley de Libertad de Imprenta* ("Law of Freedom of Printing") by a vote of sixty-eight to thirty-two.

The new law, according to its preamble, made freedom of printing absolute so that Spanish citizens could freely "publish their political thoughts and ideas, not only as a brake on the arbitrariness of those who govern, but also as a means of enlightening the nation in general and as the only means of arriving at knowledge of true public opinion." Article I specified that "all groups or particular persons, regardless of condition or state, [shall] have the freedom to write, print and publish their political ideas without the need for licensing, review, or any approval prior to publication." The second article abolished "all extant printing Courts and the censorship of political works prior to their printing." Subsequent provisions, however, made publication of writings about religious matters contingent on the approval of Church authorities, who had the right of previous censorship,[47] and established a Supreme Censorial Commission to "insure freedom of printing and keep abuses in check." [48]

The approval of the new printing law and its promulgation on November 10 touched off a flurry of newspaper ventures. During the time the Cortes sat in Cádiz, a period just slightly less than three years, more than fifty newspapers were started. At the height of the publishing fever, there were eighteen appearing on the streets. So great was the rush to publish that, in early 1811, an anonymous writer put out a pamphlet entitled "Diarrhea of the Presses. An account of the epidemic of this name which reigns now in Cádiz,

---

[46] Quoted by Gómez Aparicio, "Historia del periodismo," *GPE*, Jan. 15, 1964, p. 56.
[47] *Ley de Libertad de Imprenta de 19 de octubre de 1810, Artículo VI.*
[48] *Ibid., Artículo XIII.*

describing its origin, symptoms, its pernicious disposition, its termination, and its cure." [49]

With the increase in the number of newspapers, competition for readers increased, leading to editorial excesses. The liberal press was particularly aggressive, lashing out against anyone who defended the national traditions or that favorite target for invective, the Church. Among the newspapers of the period of the Cádiz Cortes were:

1. *La Triple Alianza*,[50] a weekly published by José Megía Lequerica, a deputy born in Ecuador, who used the periodical as a platform for his anti-colonialism. In the first issue, he set the tone of the paper by urging that the Cortes insure that "the rigid colonial system that has oppressed them [the American colonies] during three centuries be at least softened. . . ." [51]

2. *El Redactor General*,[52] founded by Pedro Daza Guzmán, among the first newspaper owners in Spain to consider a periodical a business operation. Guzmán, reacting against newspapers which bore the imprint of one man and reflected only his opinions, gathered together an editorial staff of top writers, including five deputies, who lent the liberal cause, as espoused in *El Redactor*, an air of dispassionate logic.

3. *Diario Mercantil de Cádiz*,[53] which dated from 1802 and, in its first years, was purely commercial in orientation. In 1808, it took its first political stand, a traditionalist, conservative position. However, with the rise of the liberal spirit in Cádiz, the *Diario Mercantil* changed direction and became an important liberal organ, vying with *El Conciso* in attacks on the Church and traditional values.

4. *El Robespierre Español, Amigo de las Leyes*,[54] published by Pedro Pascasio Fernández Sardino, a military medical officer. *El Robespierre* served as a voice for Fernández Sardino's political ideology, which was based on the most radical ideas of the French Revolution, and carried little news. Fernández Sardino had the distinction of being the sole newspaper proprietor punished by the

---

[49] Cited by Gómez Aparicio, "Historia del periodismo," *GPE*, Feb. 15, 1964, p. 24.
[50] *La Triple Alianza* ("The Triple Alliance") (Cádiz, 1811–13).
[51] *La Triple Alianza* (Cádiz), Jan. 22, 1811, p. 1.
[52] *El Redactor General* ("The General Editor") (Cádiz, 1811–13).
[53] *Diario Mercantil de Cádiz* ("Mercantile Daily of Cádiz") (Cádiz, 1802–13).
[54] *El Robespierre Español* . . . ("The Spanish Robespierre, Friend of the Laws") (Cádiz, 1811–13).

government during the meeting of the Cortes in Cádiz, being placed under arrest for a short time because of his criticism of the conduct of Spanish officers during the battle for Badajoz.

5. *El Duende de los Cafés*,[55] published by three liberals during an eight-month period in late 1813 and early 1814. Its attacks on the traditionalists were such that, with the restoration of Ferdinand VII, one of its editors was imprisoned and the other two were forced to flee from Spain.

In favor of traditional absolutism were eight newspapers, three of which merit mention:

1. *El Sol de Cádiz*,[56] which published, at irregular intervals, nineteen numbers devoted to defending the monarchy and, among other things, "exposing" the work of Masons in Spain.

2. *El Procurador General de la Nación y del Rey*,[57] the mouthpiece of Ferdinand. The King's Council underwrote its expenses with a monthly subsidy of 1,000 *pesetas*. In March, 1813, the existence of the subsidy was discovered by a liberal deputy who, on March 24, denounced the newspaper to the Cortes as a seditious, subversive publication. Its editors fled from Spain to avoid trial and almost certain imprisonment.

3. *Diario de la Tarde*,[58] an organ opposed to any reform, which was often in trouble with the authorities because of its attacks on the Cortes and the constitution. This was a newspaper which fought against freedom of the press by abusing that freedom—a phenomenon not uncommon in Spain.[59]

Meanwhile, the Constitution of Cádiz, as it has come to be known, was approved by the Cortes on March 19, 1812. It provided that Spain was to be governed by a moderate, hereditary monarch. The law-making power was to be vested in the crown and in one chamber of deputies, which would be elected by the vote of all males over twenty-five years of age. Article 371 spelled out the right to freedom of printing as detailed in the *Ley de Libertad de Imprenta* of 1810. On April 29, the Cortes published a decree which added one restriction to the *Ley*: it prohibited the reproduction of the constitution without government license.

---

[55] *El Duende de los Cafés* ("The Spirit of the Cafés") (Cádiz, 1813–14).
[56] *El Sol de Cádiz* ("The Sun of Cádiz") (Cádiz, 1812–13).
[57] *El Procurador General* . . . ("The Attorney General of the Nation and of the King") (Cádiz, 1812–13. Madrid, 1814).
[58] *Diario de la Tarde* ("The Evening Daily") (Cádiz, 1811–13).
[59] Solis, *El Cádiz de las Cortes*, p. 473.

On May 28, 1813, Spanish forces liberated Madrid from the French, who left behind a hungry, distressed city. On August 31, an outbreak of yellow fever in Cádiz forced the Cortes to retire from that port. On December 11, the representatives of Ferdinand VII and Napoleon signed the Treaty of Valençay in which Napoleon agreed to withdraw his troops from Spain. Early in 1814, the Cortes moved to Madrid and, in a session on February 2, drew up and dispatched to Ferdinand an ultimatum which ordered him to swear obedience to the constitution.

On February 23, Ferdinand crossed the frontier into Spain. His welcome was enthusiastic; his journey through Catalonia was triumphant. By the time he had made his way down the coast to Valencia, he realized the strength of his position and his popularity. On May 4, while in Valencia, Ferdinand issued a *Manifesto Real* ("Royal Manifesto") in which he declared null and void the constitution and the decrees issued by the Cortes and "restored the old order in its entirety." [60] The same day he published a decree which stated:

His Majesty has resolved that no poster may be put up, no announcement distributed, no daily [newspaper] nor anything written may be printed without its prior presentation to the person who is in charge of the government, who will grant or deny permission for printing or publication [after] having heard the opinion of a learned person or learned persons who are impartial and who neither served the invaders nor manifested seditious opinions.[61]

The press had moved back into Madrid with the Cortes, and, in the months preceding Ferdinand's decree, about twenty newspapers had been started in the capital.[62] Those of liberal coloration disappeared in May and were replaced by absolute organs, acrid in their defense of the monarchy and vindictive in their treatment of liberals and the liberal press. They were no less irresponsible than their stepbrethren in Cádiz and their invective finally disgusted the Court. On May 2, 1815, Ferdinand decreed:

[I have seen], to my displeasure, the diminishing of the prudent use which ought to be made of the press. [I have seen] that in place of em-

---

[60] Bertrand and Petrie, *The History of Spain*, p. 310.
[61] *Decreto del 4 de mayo de 1814*, quoted by Gómez Aparicio, "Historia del periodismo," *GPE*, Mar. 15, 1964, p. 32.
[62] Hartzenbusch lists twenty-three in existence at some time during 1814. See Eugenio Hartzenbusch é Hiríart, *Apuntes para un Catálogo de periódicos madrileños desde el año 1661 al 1870* (Madrid, 1894), p. 309.

ploying it in ways that serve the healthy enlightenment of the public, or entertain it honestly, it is used for impudence and personal exchanges which not only offend the persons against whom they are directed, but also offend the dignity and decorum of a prudent nation which is agitated by reading them. . . . [I am] well convinced by my own observation that the writings which particularly suffer from this vice are the newspapers and some tracts provoked by them. Therefore I have come to the point of prohibiting all those that were begun within or away from the Court; and it is my wish that only the *Gaceta* and *Diario de Madrid* be published.[63]

Ferdinand's decree for the second time—the first was during the reign of Charles IV—reduced the Madrid press to two newspapers. For the next five years, the press in Spain was "a poor, dull, colorless institution, not at all popular." [64]

Not only did Ferdinand temporarily reduce the press to unimportance, he also killed liberalism's chance for ultimate success in the country. During the French invasion, liberal politicians and army officers had used Masonic lodges as their meeting places. Ferdinand's persecution of the liberals, which extended to the Masons, tended to identify the two in Spanish minds, with the result that "liberalism was transformed from a movement into a secret sect and it never gained the support of the masses." [65]

With the exception of the *Mercurio de España*, no newspapers were authorized for nearly two years after the May, 1815, decree. The *Mercurio* hardly qualified as a new newspaper, being, in effect, the continuation of the *Mercurio histórico y político*, which had been begun by Salvador José Mañer in 1738 and discontinued when the French occupied Madrid in 1808. The ban continued through 1816 and into early 1817, when, in March, Francisco de Equía, Captain General of New Castille, gave permission to José Joaquín de Mora to begin a newspaper. Mora was a liberal whose political credentials had been somewhat refurbished in official eyes by detention in a French prison during the occupation and his subsequent escape to London where he published a Spanish-language periodical. On April 1, 1817, Mora began the *Crónica científica y*

---

[63] *Real decreto del 3 de mayo de 1815.*
[64] Gómez Aparicio, "Historia del periodismo," *GPE*, Mar. 15, 1964, p. 33.
[65] José M. Sánchez, *Reform and Reaction: The Politico-Religious Background of the Spanish Civil War* (Chapel Hill, N.C., 1964), pp. 18–19.

literaria,[66] a nonpolitical semiweekly which he converted into the liberal *El Constitucional* [67] on March 13, 1820, just four days after Ferdinand VII was forced to swear to uphold the constitution, thus ushering in a new period of press freedom. On July 3, 1817, Pedro María de Olive was permitted to resume publication of the *Minerva, o El Revisor General*, which he had begun in 1805 and which had been closed by the French in 1808. In 1818, Francisco Javier de Burgos, a poet and orator who rose to the rank of minister during the 1833-40 regency of María Cristina of Bourbon, was granted permission to put out the *Continuación del almacén de frutos literarios o semanario de obras inéditas*,[68] the resumption of a weekly that had appeared briefly in 1804. Toward the end of 1819, Captain General Equía authorized Javier de Burgos to begin the thrice-weekly *Miscelánea de comercio, artes y literatura*,[69] which first appeared on November 1, and which, converted to a daily shortly after the restoration of constitutional rule in 1820, became the *Miscelánea de comercio, política y literatura*.[70] The substitution of "politics" for "arts" in its title was reflected in its content: literary and artistic subjects were subordinated to the political. The paper maintained a moderate liberal posture until it ceased publication in September, 1821, when Javier de Burgos launched a new periodical.

The temporary demise of Ferdinand's absolute powers and the return to constitutionalism had begun in 1819, when the King resolved to strike down revolts in Spain's American colonies and massed an army of more than 30,000 men on the island of León, near Cádiz. Command of the task force was entrusted to the Conde de la Bisbal, an early Spanish convert to Masonry and, as such, an opponent of Ferdinand's restoration of the clergy to positions of temporal power. No transportation was immediately available and the troops were forced to wait for ships that had been promised by

---

[66] *Crónica científica y literaria* ("Scientific and literary chronicle") (Madrid, 1817–20).
[67] *El Constitucional* ("The Constitutional") (Madrid, 1820).
[68] *Continuación del almacén* . . . ("Continuation of the store of literary fruits or weekly of unpublished works") (Madrid, 1818–19).
[69] *Miscelánea de comercio, artes y literatura* ("Miscellany of commerce, arts and literature") (Madrid, 1819–20).
[70] *Miscelánea de comercio, política y literatura* ("Miscellany of commerce, politics, and literature") (Madrid, 1820–21).

the Czar of Russia. The prolonged delay in embarcation gave agents of the liberal movement ample time to distribute revolutionary propaganda among the idle soldiers. On New Year's Day, 1820, an Asturian officer, Ráfael Riego, led a revolt. The uprising, at first, appeared doomed to failure, but, as news of the attempt reached the rest of Spain, towns across the land rose. When the Conde de la Bisbal, who had been ordered to suppress the rebellion, switched to the rebel side, Ferdinand realized that further opposition was hopeless. On March 6, he approved a decree convoking the Cortes and, on the following day, published a second order in which he said: "In order to avoid the delays which might occur in the execution of my decree of yesterday because of doubts in the Council, and because it is the general will of the people, I have decided to swear allegiance to the Constitution promulgated by the general and extraordinary Corteses of the year 1812." [71]

---

[71] *Decreto real del 7 de marzo de 1820*, quoted by Gómez Aparicio, "Historia del periodismo," *GPE*, Apr. 15, 1964, p. 16.

CHAPTER SEVEN

ℭhe Periodical Proliferates

On March 9, 1820, Ferdinand swore to uphold the constitution. With the country once again under constitutional rule, newspapers proliferated. On March 10, Javier de Burgos led the return of the press to the political arena by substituting *política* ("politics") for *artes* ("arts") in the title of his newspaper, making it the *Miscelánea de comercio, política y literatura*. Three days later, José Mora converted the *Crónica científica y literaria* into *El Constitucional*, a liberal political organ. By the end of the first year of renewed constitutional rule, Madrid had seen sixty-five periodicals published as compared to the six permitted by the absolutist government. Some lasted for only one or two issues; others survived until October, 1823, when Ferdinand regained power and once again declared the constitution "null and void." In 1821, there were, at one time or another, forty periodicals in Madrid. In 1822, the number climbed to forty-five, only to drop to twenty in 1823 and plummet to four in 1824, the first full year of renewed absolutism. The life span of most was short. Three dailies[1] survived for two years or more, while the rest lasted an average of thirteen weeks. Monthlies staggered along for an average of six issues, and weeklies, with the exception of *El Censor* which published 100 issues, an average of seven weeks. Lack of mass interest and financial backing, added to the number of publications attempting to pick up readers,

---

[1] *El Universal Observador Español* (Madrid, 1820–23); *El Espectador* (Madrid, 1820–23); and the *Nuevo Diario de Madrid* (Madrid, 1821–23).

was responsible. Eugenio Hartzenbusch é Hiríart, in his compilation of publishing ventures in Madrid for the period between March, 1820, and October, 1823, lists 112 new periodicals,[2] a total which has prompted historian Pedro Gómez Aparicio to declare that "all those who wanted to say something, even though they had nothing to say, inevitably founded a newspaper." [3]

Among the founders of newspapers were the so-called *sociedades patrióticas* ("patriotic societies"), political groups stemming from the nucleus of informal discussion groups in Madrid cafés. The first and most important of these was the Sociedad Patriótica de los Amigos de la Libertad (Patriotic Society of the Friends of Liberty), formed by a group of young intellectuals who met in a mid-Madrid café to while away the dull days of Lent, which was being observed at the time of the restoration of the constitution. The habitues of the café began by writing and reciting poems dedicated to constitutionalism and liberty. Within a few days, the informal gatherings over coffee and cognac were transformed into an organization which, on March 27, began publishing the daily *El Conservador*.[4] The four-page paper, written and edited on the marble-topped tables of the café and printed in the nearby plant of Vega and Company, began as a politically moderate organ, as its title indicates. However, its editors rapidly transformed it into a vehicle for heady, radical ideas, more appropriate to coffee-shop banter than print. Eventually, it began attacking the liberal government to which the country had been entrusted. On September 30, 1820, having appeared 188 times, it was closed down by order of Agustín Argüelles, the constitutional government's Minister of the Interior and the spearhead in Cádiz of the freedom-of-the-press movement.

Of more importance than the patriotic societies was the secret organization named the Comuneros or Hijos de Padilla after an abortive revolt against Charles V in 1520—a revolt led by the Spanish nobleman Juan de Padilla. The organization was founded in late 1820 to further political and social revolution by any means, however extreme, that might prove efficacious. The Church was one of its prime targets. It grew quickly and claimed 40,000 adherents

---

[2] *Apuntes para un Catálogo de periódicos madrileños desde el año 1661 al 1870* (Madrid, 1894), p. 309.
[3] Pedro Gómez Aparicio, "Apuntes para una historia del periodismo Español," *Gaceta de la Prensa Española*, Apr. 15, 1964, p. 20.
[4] *El Conservador* ("The Conservative") (Madrid, 1820).

in 1821, when it began an incursion into the publishing business. Between August 1 and December 31, 1821, the Hijos de Padilla put out *El Eco de Padilla*,[5] a daily. During January, February, and most of March of the following year, the society published *El Independiente* [6] and, later in the year, *El Indicador*.[7] Two members of the society, Félix Mejía and Benigno Morales, meanwhile, published the inflammatory *El Zurriago*,[8] which was so violent, according to Hartzenbusch, that it made "the thinking public aware of the abuse that a free press could commit." [9] In its first issue it attacked Ferdinand VII as a "mandarin whose name we are unable to recall. . . ," and in later issues printed a blanket indictment of the editors of other more moderate newspapers as "traitors to the profession." [10] Despite the fact that *El Zurriago* appeared only at irregular intervals—ninety-two issues were published in the two and a half years of its existence—it claimed a circulation of 10,000 copies. It was typical of the extremist press of the period which, according to Pedro Gómez Aparicio, "launched itself on a path of unrestrained irresponsibility and filled its pages with articles, news stories, allegories, and caricatures, with the most immoderate attacks being against the clergy, the person of the monarch and the institutions of the State." [11]

Not all attacks were made on the Church and the monarchy. The liberal government and constitution were also targets, as the last lines of a widely repeated verse indicate.

> To give audience to the Liberal
> Is to tyrannize the Royalist,
> Open the door to the Sophist,
> And enchain the Truth.
> To give audience to the Liberal
> Is to humble Majesty and
> Make use of Treason, which,
> Concealed by confusion,
> Desires the death of our Ferdinand,

---

[5] *El Eco de Padilla* ("The Echo of Padilla") (Madrid, 1821).
[6] *El Independiente* ("The Independent") (Madrid, 1822).
[7] *El Indicador* ("The Indicator"), a newspaper which does not appear in Hartzenbusch's catalogue, but which is mentioned by Gómez Aparicio in the "Historia del periodismo," *GPE*, May 15, 1964, p. 22.
[8] *El Zurriago* ("The Whiplashing") (Madrid, 1821–23).
[9] *Periódicos madrileños*, p. 31.
[10] Quoted by Gómez Aparicio, "Historia del periodismo," *GPE*, May 15, 1964, p. 23.
[11] *Ibid.*, p. 25.

And control of the reins of rule.
Such is the Constitution.[12]

But the press was far from entirely extremist. There were moderate, responsible papers, run by intelligent, capable men of all political and religious beliefs who recognized and respected the potential power of their vehicles of communication. While the extremists believed—and published their beliefs—that there was no possibility of reconciliation among the various liberal groups, each convinced that only his brand of liberalism could be the salvation and foundation of the nation, the moderates advocated the unification of the liberal movement.

It was during this period that the trend toward using the press as a stepping-stone to a political career began to emerge. As already noted, Javier de Burgos was to use a series of newspapers, starting with the *Miscelánea de comercio, política y literatura,* as a means of entrance into the government of María Cristina, Queen-Regent from 1833 to 1840. On May 12, 1820, Father Juan González Caborreluz and Manuel Narganes began *El Universal Observador Español,*[13] a daily which lasted until April 23, 1823. González Caborreluz became religious preceptor to Isabel II, a position of considerable influence, and Narganes was named editor of the official *Gaceta de Madrid* when the constitutional period ended in 1823. In April, 1821, Evaristo San Miguel, a liberal who had attained the rank of colonel in the revolt against Ferdinand's absolutist rule, began *El Espectador,*[14] a daily modeled on the famed English *Spectator* and which introduced "letters to the editor" to the Spanish press. San Miguel became president of the cabinet on August 5, 1822. Another journalist of the period who became a power in government was Gabriel García who produced the *Cartas del compadre del Zurriago á un amigo suyo residente en Cartagena,*[15] an informal paper which appeared at irregular intervals at the end of 1822 and beginning of 1823. García climbed to the post of Undersecretary of State in 1836. The movement of journalists into positions of official power, which began in some numbers at this time, reached the point that a student of the press could write in 1923, "There is to-

---

[12] Quoted by Fernando Diaz-Plaja, *La Historia de España en sus Documentos* (Madrid, 1954), I, 89.
[13] *El Universal Observador Español* ("The Universal Spanish Observer") (Madrid, 1820–23).
[14] *El Espectador* ("The Spectator") (Madrid, 1821–23).
[15] *Cartas del compadre . . .* ("Letters of a comrade of the *Zurriago* to a friend living in Cartegena") (Madrid, 1822–23).

day almost no political figure of importance who does not claim to have been a journalist or who really was one." [16]

Meanwhile, as early as October of 1820, seven months after the beginning of the new constitutional period, the government had taken steps to control newspaper extremism. A group of ministers, led by Agustín Argüelles—who, during the Cortes of Cádiz ten years earlier, had led the fight for legislation guaranteeing press freedom—began to demand that the liberal Cortes pass some kind of directive, if not restrictive, measure. Eugenio de Tapia, a former editor of the *Semanario Patriótico* and spokesman for the group, outlined the group's position. He told the deputies:

The facility of communicating thoughts by means of the press is an uncontestable right of citizens and as such is sanctioned by the Constitution. In order to avoid the degeneration of this facility into license, with a notable damage to Society, it is indispensable that it should be restrained with healthy laws just as corresponding penalties for assassination and robbery have been established by the individuals of the State to insure the life and property of all.[17]

On October 22, the Cortes, fearful of being labeled reactionary, passed a timid press law which differed little from that of October 19, 1810, and did nothing to correct the ills of the press. Complete freedom to publish at will was reaffirmed, except for "writings which treat the sacred scriptures or the dogmas of our holy religion which . . . may not be printed without license from local authorities." A Junta de Protección de la Libertad de Prensa (Committee for Protection of Freedom of the Press) was set up and its seven members were ordered to meet every two years to "remove obstacles" to the proper functioning of the press and to "remedy abuses." The new law also listed five offenses of which the press could be guilty and set up punishment for them. They were:

1. "Subversion," which could be punished by two to six years in prison and loss of job and official honors.

2. "Inciting to rebellion," punishable in the same way as subversion.

3. "Inciting to disobedience to the law or authorities," for which the penalty was one month to one year in jail and a fine of fifty ducats.

---

[16] "El periodismo en España," *Enciclopedia Universal Ilustrada* (Barcelona, 1923), XXI, 1481.
[17] Quoted by Gómez Aparicio, "Historia del periodismo," *GPE*, Apr. 15, 1964, p. 24.

4. "Moral offenses," a fine equivalent to the cost of 1,500 copies of the periodical.

5. "Injuries to a particular person," one to three months in jail and a fine of 500 to 1,000 *reales*. The penalty for any second offense was twice that prescribed for the first infringement of the law.[18]

The law was ineffectual in dealing with press excesses. It did not mention graphic arts, then making an appearance in the press, caricatures, or satires, and it failed to define what actions constituted the crimes of which the press might be guilty. Those shortcomings became more and more apparent, and in November of the following year the Cortes began a series of discussions aimed at strengthening press laws. The deliberations and debates lasted until February 12, 1822, when the deputies approved an "Additional Law" to that of 1820, which defined the crimes of which the press could be guilty. Subversive writings were those which "injure the sacred and inviolable person of the King or propose rules or doctrines which are assumed subject to his responsibility. . . ." Seditious writings were those which "spread rules or doctrines or which refer to acts dedicated to exciting to rebellion or disturbing the public peace, even though they may be disguised as allegories of imaginary persons or countries or of past times, or as dreams or fictions, or anything similar." Inciting to disobedience was produced "by satires or invectives, even though the authority against which it is directed or the place where it is employed is disguised with allusions or allegories." Injuries to a particular person was redesignated as "libel" and defined as writings which "made vulnerable the reputation of individuals, even though they are not named, or indicated by anagrams, allegories or in any other form." [19]

At about the same time, the Cortes finished work on a broad administrative reform, dividing the nation into fifty-two provinces. The bill was hailed as a victory for the liberals, but it was a mere paper victory, for already in many parts of the nation, especially in Catalonia and Navarre, the people were rising in favor of the King. That grass-roots sentiment convinced the royal advisors that the moment for restoration of absolute rule was near. They counseled the King to counter the liberal press propaganda with a newspaper of his own. Acting on their suggestion, Ferdinand com-

---

[18] *Ley de 22 de octubre de 1820.*
[19] *Ley adicional á la de 22 de octubre de 1820 sobre libertad política de la imprenta.*

missioned one Luis de la Torre to begin a newspaper, which appeared on May 22, 1822, as *El Procurador general del Rey*.[20] The tone of the periodical, which appeared only five times and at irregular intervals, was set by its subtitle which read, in part, "written at the beginning of the third year of the second captivity of Señor Don Ferdinand VII, legitimate sovereign of Spain, and during the fatal crisis of the frightful persecution of Altar and Throne. . . ." [21] Shortly after the founding of *El Procurador general*, the first of three papers which the King subsidized with the expenditure of more than 30,000 *reales*, the unrest in the nation spread to Madrid. On June 30, the Royal Guards used gunfire to break up a demonstration between constitutionalists and absolutists. At least one person was killed—a Guards lieutenant of liberal leanings shot by his own troops as he urged them to be moderate in their treatment of the demonstrators. As a result of their brutal handling of the citizens of Madrid, the Guards, six battalions strong, were confined to quarters until the morning of July 7 when, led by General Luis Fernández de Cordova, they attempted to overthrow the constitutional government and reestablish the absolute powers of the King. The revolt against the liberal authorities ended with the rout of the Guards by loyal army and militia units after a bloody exchange in Madrid's Plaza Mayor.

However, the abortive attempt at a coup led to repercussions within the press. Extremist elements among the liberals blamed the bloodshed on their more moderate fellows, whose policies, they charged, had thwarted an earlier suppression of the absolutists. Using the event as an excuse, the extremists began reprisals against the moderates, the first victim being Javier de Burgos, whose newspaper *El Imparcial*,[22] founded in late 1821, was immediately forced to close down, despite the fact that the constitution provided for no such arbitrary action. Six days later, on July 13, the extremists also closed *El Censor*, the weekly founded in August, 1820, by the moderate liberal León Amarita. *El Censor* bowed out with a note to subscribers on its final Saturday, explaining that the editors, "considering that in times of political agitation and when spirits are exasperated, criticism offends and irritates, but does not correct,

---

[20] *El Procurador general del Rey* ("The General Agent of the King") (Madrid, 1822–23).
[21] *El Procurador general del Rey* (Madrid), May 22, 1822.
[22] *El Imparcial* ("The Impartial") (Madrid, 1821–22).

have agreed to terminate their work with the present issue." [23]

The closing of the two newspapers and the attempt at a coup d'état which led to it were merely small parts of an overall picture of confusion—confusion so great that at least one modern history says of the Spain of the second liberal period: " . . . anarchy prevailed all over the land in every branch of the administration." [24] But regardless of the situation within the country, the liberal ideals espoused by its government represented a threat to other regimes on the continent. In October of 1822, representatives of the Holy Alliance—Austria, Prussia, Russia, and France—met in Verona to discuss the course of events in Spain. The other three nations gave France a commitment of moral backing, though no material aid, if it would intervene in Spain with the aim of restoring an absolutist monarchy. With that promise in hand, Louis XVIII announced the following January that he had withdrawn his ambassador from Madrid and that 100,000 French soldiers were prepared to march on Spain. In March, faced by the imminence of invasion, the Cortes withdrew from Madrid to Seville, forcing Ferdinand to accompany it, despite his plea that an attack of gout made travel impossible. On April 7, the French army—the "Hundred Thousand Sons of Saint Louis"—crossed the frontier; two days later, in Urgel, a six-member Council of Regency was set up; and, in late May, the French forces reached Madrid. On May 23, the second of the periodicals subsidized by Ferdinand, the *Diario Realista de Madrid*,[25] began publication in the capital. On July 1, shortly after the Cortes had moved from Seville to Cádiz, the third of Ferdinand's subsidized newspapers appeared; called *El Restaurador*,[26] it was run by Father Manuel Martínez, whose services to the King were eventually rewarded by promotion to Bishop of Málaga. *El Restaurador* promised its readers that "with the aid given by good Spaniards and the authentic news items which the Spaniards may obtain from their provincial correspondents, we will outline hereafter the tragic history of the assassinations, fires, robberies, sackings, violences, injustices, and confusions of the revolutionaries, because nothing is more important than that the people know completely the atrocities

---

[23] *El Censor* (Madrid), July 13, 1822.
[24] Louis Bertrand and Sir Charles Petrie, *The History of Spain*, 2nd ed. (London, 1952), p. 313.
[25] *Diario Realista de Madrid* ("Royalist Daily of Madrid") (Madrid, 1823).
[26] *El Restaurador* ("The Restorer") (Madrid, 1823-24).

of the revolution and the deeds of the principal leaders so that they may profit by the lesson and detest them." [27]

By August, the French had occupied southern Spain and were besieging Cádiz. On September 30, the constitutionalists, convinced that further resistance was futile, extracted from the King a promise to "forget the past, without any exception, in order . . . to re-establish among all Spaniards the peace, trust and union so necessary for the common good and which my heart longs for." [28] Having so promised, the King was released. On the following day, safe with the French forces in El Puerto de Santa María, across the bay from Cádiz, Ferdinand "avenged himself on the liberals, suppressing, among other things, the freedom of the press provided for in the 1812 Constitution." [29] In a proclamation on that day, October 1, Ferdinand declared: "All the acts (of whatever class or type they may be) of the so-called constitutional government, which has dominated my people from March 7, 1820, to October 1, 1823, are null and void. I declare that during all this period I lacked liberty, being obliged to ratify the laws and carry out the orders, decrees and regulations which, against my will, were thought up and officially issued by that government." [30]

Freedom of the press was officially dead, for a time, in Spain, but the direct consequences of Ferdinand's proclamation were not felt immediately. The press escaped the first violence of the King's reprisals, which were directed against the leaders of the 1820 revolt and were so rigorous that the Duke of Angoulême, commander of the French armies, expressed his protest by refusing the Spanish decorations offered him.

The royalist press, feeling secure in the King's favor, attacked, as it had in 1814, the liberals and all vestiges of liberalism. When Ráfael Riego, who had been the general heading the liberal revolt of early 1820, was brought into Madrid in chains, El Restaurador crowed:

> He enters Madrid, chief of shameless rogues.
> He enters, a thief, coward and assassin.

---

[27] Manuel Martínez, Prospecto para El Restaurador (Madrid, undated), p. 1.
[28] Quoted by Gómez Aparicio, "Historia del periodismo," GPE, July 15, 1964, pp. 15–16.
[29] Joseph A. Brandt, Toward the New Spain (Chicago, 1933), pp. 21–22.
[30] Decreto real del 1 de octubre de 1823, quoted by Diaz-Plaja, España en sus Documentos, I, p. 170.

> He enters, the emperor presumptive of rascals,
> The chief of madmen, and patron of impiety.
> He enters to the consternation of his lovers,
> As a traitor Catiline: and let your destiny,
> Your horrors, your infamy and your torment
> Serve forever as an example.[31]

The attacks of the royalist press did not stop with liberal targets and, by the end of the year, the King's policies came under fire. On December 7, *El Restaurador*, turning on its original backer, urged the people to disobey various of Ferdinand's laws. The Monarch's first reaction was to confide rather resignedly, "they [the journalists] are the same dogs with different collars." [32] However, his patience soon wore thin and, on January 30, 1824, he published an order which stated: "His Majesty has resolved that in the future there will be published no papers other than the *Gaceta* and the so-called *Diario de Madrid* and the commercial and fine arts newspapers which are at present published in the Court or in the provinces or which may be published in the future with the required licenses." [33] The order left Madrid with only four newspapers—the *Gaceta*, *Diario*, *Mercurio*, and a rather subdued *El Restaurador*, which faded from the scene before the end of the year. The *Diario de Barcelona* continued as the major provincial newspaper but was subjected to sporadic harassment by the authorities. Pablo Soler Mestres, who had taken over as editor from Antonio Brusi in 1821, reporting on his dealings with the provincial captain general in 1827-28, wrote that "it seems that this particular man had taken me as a target for his shots . . . not letting me live in peace while he was captain general of this Principality, and there were few weeks when he did not complain and few months when he did not have me arrested." [34]

No new periodicals were authorized in 1824, the government presumably being determined to keep the number of newspapers at a level that would permit easy regulation of the press. Only one newspaper was given the royal green light in 1825—the *Diario literario-mercantil*,[35] which lasted from early April until July 10.

---

[31] *El Restaurador* (Madrid), Oct. 1, 1823, quoted by Hartzenbusch in *Periódicos madrileños*, p. 39.
[32] Gómez Aparicio, "Historia del periodismo," *GPE*, July 15, 1964, p. 18.
[33] *Real Orden del 30 de enero de 1824.*
[34] Esteban Molist Pol, *El "Diario de Barcelona": 1792–1963* (Madrid, 1964), pp. 82–83.
[35] *Diario literario-mercantil* ("Literary-mercantile Daily") (Madrid, 1825).

THE PERIODICAL PROLIFERATES (147

On April 1, the government arbitrarily changed the ownership and name of the *Diario de Madrid*. The name, at Ferdinand's command, was expanded to the *Diario de Avisos de Madrid*,[36] and the question of the newspaper's ownership, pending since the 1815 suppression of press liberty, was resolved by the Fiscal of the Royal Council, who "considered it his personal privilege" [37] to dispose of the rights, which he sold to Pedro Jiménez, a printer who bid 166,000 *reales* for the *privilegio*. One claimant, ignored by the official decision, was the widow of Santiago Thebín, son and namesake of a Frenchman who had brought the newspaper in 1784. Two unsuccessful candidates for ownership of the nation's oldest daily, Nicolás de Hugalde y Mollinedo and Reinaldo Mackinnon, had offered, as part of their payment for the *Diario*, to pension Thebín's widow for life. She received nothing from Jiménez.

With the exception of the founding of the short-lived *Diario literario-mercantil* and the transfer of the ownership of the *Diario de Madrid*, the year and those that followed were quiet for the press and the nation. Ferdinand's personal popularity was high. His court was not extravagant, and, owing to the skill of his Minister of Finance, Luis López Ballesteros, the damage caused by a generation of unrest was slowly repaired. The King spent the winter of 1827- 28 in Catalonia, which had been the scene of a short revolt in August, and capped that sojourn away from his court with a long tour through the country. His progress was acclaimed everywhere. The situation was deemed propitious for the withdrawal of the French troops and, early in 1828, they left Spain, ending five years in the country. No new periodical had been authorized since April of 1825, but the situation was so settled by mid-1828 that the government gave the go-ahead to three newspapers, the most important and enduring being the *Correo literario y mercantil*,[38] which lasted for five years, starting as a thrice-weekly and ending with four issues a week. One of the founders of the *Correo literario* was José María Carnerero, a skilled political chameleon who used the press, with an ability seldom matched, as a lever for his own survival and advancement, and yet managed to introduce into the Spanish press

---

[36] *Diario de Avisos de Madrid* ("Daily of Announcements of Madrid").
[37] Luis Miguel Enciso Recio, *Nipho y el periodismo español del siglo XVIII* (Valladolid, 1956), p. 164.
[38] *Correo literario y mercantil* ("Literary and mercantile Mail") (Madrid, 1828– 33).

certain literary and artistic elements that it had previously sought and failed to find.

Carnerero had begun his career under the protection of Manuel Godoy, chief minister to Charles IV and favorite of his Queen, María Luisa of Parma. Godoy sent Carnerero to Turkey as a member of the Spanish diplomatic mission. When the forces of Napoleon invaded Spain, Carnerero joined the party of Joseph Bonaparte and was rewarded with the post of literary editor of the *Gaceta de Madrid*. With the ouster of the French, he was exiled to Paris where he charmed his way into high circles. Upon his return to Spain, at the beginning of the 1820-23 constitutional period, he joined the extremist faction of the liberal movement, working first as an editor of the radical *El Eco de Padilla* and later as a director of the equally radical *El Indicador*. When the French forces of Louis XVIII marched into Spain, Carnerero ignored the liberal flight to Seville and Cádiz, choosing to stay in Madrid, where he met and made friends with the Duke of Angoulême, the French commander-in-chief. Through Angoulême, he met Ferdinand's Minister of Finance, Luis López Ballesteros, who, in turn, introduced him to Ferdinand whose favor he won by serving as public spokesman for the monarchy. In 1831, the grateful King granted him a *privilegio* to publish the *Cartas españolas*,[39] a weekly which reported on cultural matters with an elegance hitherto missing from the Spanish press. It was the first periodical in the nation to use engravings with regularity, and is cited by Hartzenbusch as "notable for its time, both literarily and typographically." [40] In November, 1832, Carnerero substituted *La Revista española* [41] for the *Cartas españolas*. The new periodical, which started as a semiweekly and converted to a daily in April, 1834, sallied into the world of politics as its predecessor had never done. It appeared just as María Cristina, Ferdinand's fourth wife, took over the reins of government from her dying husband, and it adapted its political posture to the varying views which were represented by the groups in control during her regency. On September 29, 1833, Ferdinand VII died. For ten days, *La Revista española* draped its pages in exaggerated mourn-

---

[39] *Cartas españolas, o sea revista histórica, científica, teatral, crítica y literaria* ("Spanish letters, or historic, scientific, theatrical, critical, and literary review") (Madrid, 1831-32).
[40] Hartzenbusch, *Periódicos madrileños*, p. 41.
[41] *La Revista española* ("The Spanish Review") (Madrid, 1832-36).

ing. Its grief for the dead advocate and figurehead of absolutism was replaced in the next two years by a succession of positions, reflecting, in turn, the enlightened despotism of Francisco Cea Bermúdez and the moderate position of Francisco Javier de Istúriz and attacking, for reasons of personal politics, the liberalism of Juan Álvarez Mendizábal.

On March 1, 1835, the *Revista* was merged with the *Mensajero de las Cortes*,[42] founded the previous year by Evaristo San Miguel, a former minister in the liberal government. Carnerero and San Miguel used the new periodical to further the latter's political ambitions by attacking Mendizábal when he became Prime Minister in September of 1835—attacks which culminated in his fall from power eight months later. The following year, Mendizábal was named Minister of Finance in a new cabinet and, within days of his appointment, had his revenge, forcing the merged newspaper, the *Revista española–Mensajero de las Cortes*,[43] to close down. Its final issue, that of August 27, 1836, noted only that difficulties with the printer made it impossible to publish the following day. On that ambiguous note it left the scene, the final victim of its own political activities.

The concluding years of Ferdinand's reign had seen a slight resumption of the growth of the press, particularly of specialized publications. There were two medical journals founded between 1827 and 1833,[44] a daily which reported on stock market activities,[45] and at least one woman's weekly.[46] In 1829, Madrid had five periodicals. In 1830 and 1831, there were six. In 1832, the number jumped to eleven and, in 1833, to fifteen. The year after Ferdinand's death, 1834, which saw liberals returned to key positions in the government, the number rose to thirty-six.

Only one regulation governing the press dates from that period.

---

[42] *Mensajero de las Cortes* ("The Parliamentary Messenger") (Madrid, 1834–35).
[43] *Revista española* . . . ("The Spanish Review–Parliamentary Messenger") (Madrid, 1835–36).
[44] *Décadas médico-quirúricas* ("Medical-surgical notes") (Madrid, 1821–24, 1827–28) and the *Repertorio médico-extranjero* ("Foreign medical repertoire") (Madrid, 1832–34). The latter was founded by Dr. José Lletot Castroverde and designed to bring news of medical developments to Spain from abroad.
[45] *Cotización de la Bolsa de Madrid* ("Madrid Stock Market Quotations") (Madrid, 1830–70).
[46] *Correo de las Damas* ("Women's Mail") (Madrid, 1833–36).

On May 17, 1831, Ferdinand acted to halt the pilfering of news from the *Gaceta de Madrid* by papers elsewhere in Spain. He ordered a ban on political news in any publication other than the *Gaceta*.

In Barcelona, the *Diario* was joined by *El Vapor: Periódico mercantil, político y literario de Cataluña*,[47] founded under the auspices of the provincial captain general and designed, as its name suggests, to help develop the industrial potential of the area by use of the steam engine.

Before his death, Ferdinand had attempted to insure a peaceful transfer of the crown to his daughter Isabel, born in November, 1830. He did so by issuing a proclamation abrogating the Salic law and noting that Charles IV had done the same in 1789. The traditionalists, desirous of seeing power pass to Ferdinand's younger brother, Carlos María Isidro de Borbón, argued that they knew nothing of the original abrogation, which had never been published. In addition, they insisted that the accession of the Bourbon dynasty to the Spanish throne had implanted the French system of male succession and not even two royal acts were sufficient to change a tradition so fundamental. In 1832, after the beginning of what was to be Ferdinand's terminal illness, the Council of Ministers decided that, in the event of the Monarch's death, Isabel should be named Queen, María Cristina appointed Regent, and Prince Carlos invited to take part in the regency. However, Carlos denounced the proposal and protested strongly against the June 20, 1833, appointment of Isabel as Princess of Asturias, the traditional title granted to an heir presumptive. Any chances he may have had of taking over the throne peacefully were ruined by two factors: his own refusal to maneuver toward that goal before his brother's death and his absence in Portugal when Ferdinand finally died. One of María Cristina's first acts as Regent was to outlaw her brother-in-law and confiscate his lands, a virtual declaration of war, for Carlos replied by calling on his followers to take up arms in his behalf. On October 3, four days after Ferdinand's death, a provincial postmaster in Talavera de la Reina declared for Carlos. Carlist sentiment flared across the nation, especially in the Basque provinces, where there was fear that the regency might lead to withdrawal of special rights which made the Basques semiautonomous. The call to

---

[47] *El Vapor* . . . ("The Steamship: The mercantile, political, and literary periodical of Catalonia") (Barcelona, 1833–36).

arms, which was to flame into civil war, deprived the Queen-Regent of much of the monarchist-oriented support on which she would have relied normally. To bolster her position, she sought aid from the liberals, whose centralist, commercial, anticlerical beliefs were in diametric opposition to the ruralist, clerical, agrarian, separatist, and almost feudal concepts of the Carlists. Francisco Cea Bermúdez became Prime Minister and sought to build a solid base for his government by effecting a profound and lasting reconciliation between the liberals and the Isabelist monarchists, granting a series of administrative reforms to please the liberals and maintaining royal institutions to attract the monarchists.

Among the reforms undertaken by Cea Bermúdez was that of establishing a set of norms to govern the behavior of the press and thus prevent repetition of the excesses which it had at times committed. On October 26, 1833, he named a special commission to study press controls. On January 4, 1834, the results of the committee's deliberations were published, as a Royal Decree, in the *Gaceta de Madrid*. The new press law, the *Reglamento que ha de observarse para la censura de los periódicos* ("Rules that must be observed for the censorship of periodicals"), began by stating the proposition that "The absolute and unlimited freedom of the press, the publication and circulation of books and papers, cannot exist without offense to our Catholic religion and detriment to the general welfare." It resurrected the three centuries' old practice of the Royal license, ordering that "no periodical which is not technical or which does not deal uniquely with the arts, natural sciences or literature, may be published without an express Royal license issued by the Foreign Ministry." [48] Article 4 charged the civil governor of each province with the control of the press and empowered him to collect from each periodical within his jurisdiction a deposit to insure payment of any fines that might be imposed. The deposit was set at 20,000 *reales* for Madrid papers and 10,000 *reales* for the provincial press if it were made in cash. If the deposit were in the form of credit, it was doubled. The new rules also initiated the policy of "enforced publication." Newspapers were ordered to "insert in their entirety, without the alteration of even one word of their content the day following their receipt, articles submitted to their editors . . . by the Authorities whose conduct may have been

---

[48] *Reglamento de imprenta de 4 de enero de 1834, Artículo 1.*

criticized by the said periodicals."[49] The *Reglamento* also ordered that any material withheld by the censors had to be replaced in the periodical, no newspaper being allowed to publish with "any part of its columns left blank."[50] It banned, as had its forerunners, publication of attacks on religion, the monarchy, the nation's fundamental laws, or foreign sovereigns or governments. In addition, it outlawed the formation of associations by censors "lest they pervert their judgments." Finally, it stated that "any censor who approves a work containing things contrary to our Holy Faith, good customs, rights of the Crown or any infamous libel against any group or individual will, in addition to losing his job, suffer the same penalties imposed by the law on the perpetrators of these crimes."[51]

On June 1, a regulation was introduced establishing the number of censors in the country. Madrid was to have four and each provincial capital, at least one. Salaries for the capital censors were set at 20,000 *reales* a year, far more than a newspaperman could hope to earn, if he earned at all. Provincial censors were to receive 12,000 *reales*.[52]

The immediate effect of the January 4 law was felt by two daily newspapers founded the year before. Both *La Estrella*,[53] started in October, and *La Aurora de España*,[54] begun the following month, were unable either to pay the deposit or to arrange the necessary credit. As a result, the newspapers which had loyally supported the Infanta Isabel and opposed Carlos were forced out of business, *La Estrella* closing down on February 26 and *La Aurora*, on January 5. A third newspaper which backed the monarchy, *El Tiempo*,[55] was shut down by a government order on May 19.

On January 15, Cea Bermúdez was replaced as Prime Minister by the liberal Francisco Martínez de la Rosa, who began his tenure in office by drafting a Royal Statute (*Estatuto Real*), which was

[49] *Ibid., Artículo 14.*
[50] *Ibid., Artículo 19.*
[51] José Eugenio de Eguizábal, *Apuntes para una historia de la legislación española sobre la imprenta desde el año 1480 al presente* (Madrid, 1879), pp. 174–175.
[52] *Ibid.*, pp. 178–179.
[53] *La Estrella: Periódico de política, literatura é industria* ("The Star: Political, literary, and industrial periodical") (Madrid, 1833–34).
[54] *La Aurora de España: Diario dedicado á la Reina Nuestra Señora Doña Isabel II* ("The Dawn of Spain: A Daily dedicated to the Queen, Our Lady Isabel II") (Madrid, 1833–34).
[55] *El Tiempo* ("The Times") (Madrid, 1833–34).

modeled after the French *charte* and approved on April 10, 1834. Though the statute made no mention of freedom of the press, the government under Martínez de la Rosa was tolerant of the media of mass communications, and a new political press began to bud. On May 1, a businessman-financier, Ángel Iznardi, founded the progressive *El Eco de Comercio* [56] and named the liberal Manuel Francisco Mendialdúa editor of the thrice-weekly paper. Among those who made up the editorial staff of the paper were at least three men destined to play major political roles in Spain: Fermín Caballero, Joaquín María López and Félix de Bona. On June 1, as noted earlier, the politician-journalist Evaristo San Miguel began *El Mensajero de las Cortes.* On June 10, Joaquín Francisco Pacheco started *La Abeja,* [57] a politically moderate daily, and on July 15, a group of extreme liberals, who were beginning to call themselves "progressives" and included in their number Antonio Alcalá Galiana, began *El Observador.* [58] The newspaper described itself as dedicated to the "promptest obedience to the law and to the dissemination and defense of the most liberal principles. . . ." [59]

Meanwhile, the Carlists were beginning their own press. The first rebel newspaper was founded in March in Oñate, site of the Carlist court. [60] It served as an organ for the publication of Carlist orders and proclamations and reported in detail on the fighting between the two Spanish factions. In addition, the Carlists published a series of one-page news sheets for distribution to the soldiers at the front. A second formal newspaper was started in 1836 by the Carlist General Ramón Cabrera and appeared twice each week until sometime in 1838. [61]

The Carlist press received its news from the military command. The Isabelist press, especially that of Madrid, received some news from correspondents attached to headquarters but relied primarily on "handouts," official communiqués.

Carlos returned to Spain from England, where he had spent

---

[56] *El Eco de Comercio* ("The Echo of Commerce") (Madrid, 1834–39).
[57] *La Abeja* ("The Bee") (Madrid, 1834–36).
[58] *El Observador* ("The Observer") (Madrid, 1834–35).
[59] Quoted by Hartzenbusch, *Periódicos madrileños,* p. 46.
[60] *Gaceta del Real de Oñate* ("Gazette of the Army Camp of Oñate") (Oñate, 1834–39).
[61] *Boletín del Ejército Real de Aragón, Valencia y Murcia* ("Bulletin of the Royal Army of Aragon, Valencia, and Murcia") (Cantavieja, 1836–38. Morella, 1838).

some months, in July of 1834, after having crossed the Pyrenees on foot, guided by a French mountaineer. His arrival preceded by only days the convocation in Madrid of the loyalist Cortes. The parliamentary meeting, which began on July 24, had been heralded by serious disorders in the capital. Early in the month, rioting in Madrid had led to the killing of the provincial captain-general, shot while meeting with the rioters. On July 15, an outbreak of cholera touched off rumors that monks had poisoned the city's wells. The rumors, at first whispered across the city, soon built up to a roar of hate, and, on July 17, a mob, dotted with uniformed militiamen, marched on the headquarters of the Jesuit Fathers in midtown Toledo Street. The mob killed any monks they encountered en route, then raided the monastery. The bloodbath spread to other religious orders in the city, and before the day ended as many as 100 members of religious orders had been murdered.

Such was the backdrop for the opening of the Cortes. Despite the fact that the Royal Statute banned from parliamentary discussion any matter not introduced by Royal Decree, a group of liberal deputies, including Fermín Caballero and Joaquín María López, both members of the editorial staff of *El Eco de Comercio*, presented to the government a *tabla de derechos* ("list" or "bill of rights"), which included a demand for freedom of the press as well as other individual liberties, such as equality before the law and the inviolability of home and property. The petition was brought before the Cortes which, after some minor but hotly debated changes, approved it. While it did not supersede the press laws of January 4, it did water down the effectiveness of the controls they imposed.

By early in the next year, the press found its opportunity to take advantage of the relaxed regulations. In April, 1835, the Duke of Wellington, hero of the Peninsular War against Napoleon, sent a mediator to Spain to negotiate an agreement aimed at eliminating the savagery that marked the conflict. On April 25, the Elliot Agreement, named after its British negotiator, was signed by both sides. The agreement did result in the introduction of some moderation in the war, especially in the treatment of prisoners and citizens of occupied areas, but it also touched off a rash of attacks on the government. The anti-government blasts charged that the agreement gave legal recognition to the Carlist rebellion and its claims. The liberals and the liberal press were in the forefront of the attack, for they equated Carlism with absolutism and feared that any agreement might lead to some accord between the two forces and the eventual restoration of despotic rule. The primary target of the liberals was Martínez de la Rosa, the Prime Minister. Finally, on June 8, 1836, the Queen-Regent asked for his resignation and appointed the Minister of Finance, the Conde de Toreno, to succeed him. On July 4, acting to gain the favor of those opposed to the traditional power and influence of the Church, Toreno suppressed the Society of Jesus in Spain and, on July 25, ordered the closing of all religious orders with less than twelve members. The dual decrees did not achieve the desired end of quieting anti-Church sentiment, but rather had the opposite effect, touching off nation-wide attacks on monasteries and convents, reminiscent of those in Madrid during the preceding year. Various local governments, noting the government's inability to control the areas under its influence, declared themselves under the rule of local *juntas* and in opposition to the government and the Royal Statute. By early September, Toreno's rule was judged a failure, and he was replaced by Juan Álverez Mendizábal, the liberal Jewish financial expert from Cádiz.

The major problem facing Mendizábal was that of financing the war, and he saw in the Church a source of income for that purpose. Enjoying for the moment the favor of the Cortes, Mendizábal decreed on February 19, 1836, that all monasteries and convents which had escaped Toreno's decree because of their size should be closed, and the ranks of monks and nuns be reduced to the minimal number needed for education and the care of the sick. On March 8, a second decree confiscated and put up for public sale all Church property. The appropriation and sale had been designed not only as a means of raising money for the war against the Carlists, but also as a step toward the establishment of a landowning middle class. However, it was badly mismanaged and, as a critic charged in the Cortes, "it made the rich richer and the poor poorer," [62] for those already wealthy were able to outbid all others.

Mendizábel had promised a quick end to the war, but instead of terminating it in victory for the government, his acts against the Church only intensified it. The closing of the religious orders and the confiscation of Church property sent thousands of devout Catholics swarming to the Carlist banners, ready to fight against

---

[62] Quoted by Gómez Aparicio, "Historia del periodismo," *GPE*, Sept. 15, 1964, p. 27.

the despoilers of their religion. The unexpected backlash, plus Mendizábal's general lack of political skill, wiped out his popularity, and the liberal press, led by the *Revista española–Mensajero de las Cortes*, then under the guidance of Alcalá Galiana, made him the target of its editorial attacks. On May 14, the Queen-Regent relieved Mendizábal of his duties and, the following day, named Francisco Javier de Istúriz the nation's new Prime Minister.

Among the journalists who had joined Alcalá Galiana in attacking Mendizábal had been Andrés Borrego Moreno, a newcomer to the Madrid press who was destined to earn recognition as one of the more conscientious and farsighted newspapermen of the country.

Borrego Moreno was born in Málaga in 1802 and, orphaned at an early age, was educated by a relative whose French sympathies forced him, when Ferdinand VII returned to Spain in 1814, to take his youthful charge and seek haven in Paris. In 1820, at the beginning of the three-year period of liberal rule, Borrego, brought up as a liberal, returned to Spain and founded a weekly newspaper in the city of his birth. The restoration of Ferdinand's absolute rule sent Borrego scurrying to Argentina, where he tried to found and nurture a newspaper, but without success. In 1828, he returned to Paris, where he helped found *Les Temps*, a liberal, internationally oriented newspaper, and then, in turn, served as columnist for two major Parisian newspapers, an inspector of national monuments, and correspondent for the London *Morning Herald*. Soon after Ferdinand's death, Borrego returned to Madrid with two ideas in mind. He would modernize the Spanish press, and he would bring some order from the political chaos of the land. Borrego's political goal was "to liberalize the moderates and slow down the progressives." [63] His professional goal was the institutionalization of the national press. He asked:

What is the newspaper, if not the instantaneous, multiplied, rapid, untiring, continuing, passing but yet always renewed and alive, symbol of the ideas, acts, accidents, and necessities of the life of the people: a social collective life, intelligent and varied, whose image cannot possibly be reproduced without embracing within the same frame, the uses, customs, tasks, pastimes, and meetings of the popular masses? Serving the common progress of the different agents of modern civilization, the newspaper will cease to be the organ of a party or the standard of a

---

[63] Juan Beneyto, *Historia social de España y de Hispanoamérica* (Madrid, 1961), p. 403.

sect, and will become the guide, the manual, the pointer, and the companion which at all hours offers man, considered in the infinite variety of his occupations, fast news, useful information, numerous data and facts equally interesting to the employee, the capitalist, the landowner, the businessman, the farmer, the clergyman, the woman, the student, the day workers, [in fact, to all] persons having individual and collective relations with the rest of the human beings who surround them and with whom they are destined to form an intelligent and harmonious organism.[64]

Borrego brought with him, on his return to Spain, some sound business abilities as well as a vision. He was able to raise four million *reales* (one million *pesetas*), in those times an unheard-of amount for a press operation and more than sufficient to begin a newspaper. With that capital, he put together a skilled editorial staff and imported from England the latest in printing equipment. On November 1, 1835, he began *El Español: Diario de las doctrinas y de los intereses sociales.*[65] Despite *El Español*'s self-proclaimed political and social emphasis, Borrego did not fail to cultivate its business side. In early 1836, he wrote, in an editorial:

We desire to comply with all the conditions of our prospectus and insure that *El Español*, in addition to being an organ of principles, should also be a guide and indicator, useful to all classes of society. We have learned, from experience, of the benefits that industry, commerce and the interests of the other classes can frequently receive from publicity. [Advertising] presents continually to the eyes of all those whom each [advertiser] wishes to reach, announcements which make known to them that which each [advertiser] wishes to make known and establishes a network of widespread and frequent communication between the mutual and multiple needs of all members of society. [With that in mind], we have determined to set aside a part of our periodical for the insertion of the announcements which the authorities, businesses or particular individuals wish to send us.[66]

And, to insure that no one misinterpreted the newspaper's intentions, Borrego went on to outline the prices to be charged for advertising—twelve *reales* (three *pesetas*) for eight lines of commercial ads, plus one *peseta* per additional line.

El Español began by backing Mendizábal, of whom Borrego wrote, "His program, copying the liberal ideas of the English

---

[64] Andrés Borrego Moreno, *Prospecto para El Correo Nacional* (Madrid, undated), p. 1. *El Correo Nacional* was founded Feb. 16, 1838.
[65] *El Español* . . . ("The Spaniard: A Daily of doctrines and social interests") (Madrid, 1835–37, 1845–48).
[66] *El Español* (Madrid), Jan. 2, 1836.

school, inspires in all the same confidence it gives me." But before long, Borrego switched his editorial orientation and joined the growing chorus of invective against the Prime Minister. Borrego's criticism of Mendizábal culminated in a public charge that the political leader had attempted to buy the allegiance of *El Español* by offering Gaspar Remisa, one of Borrego's major and most generous financial backers, a fourteen million *real* tax remission.[67]

Istúriz's occupancy of the post of Prime Minister was short-lived. The Cortes, led by Mendizábal, quickly passed a vote of no confidence which confronted Istúriz with two alternatives: resign or dissolve parliament. He took the second course, touching off violent demonstrations on the part of the progressives and renewed agitation for the restoration of the 1812 Constitution. A new Cortes was summoned for August 20, but on the 12th a group of army sergeants invaded the palace at La Granja, where the royal family was passing the summer, and demanded that María Cristina bring back the constitution, which she did. Istúriz was ousted and replaced by José María Calatrava, who included in his cabinet at least two journalists, Joaquín María López, a former editor of *El Eco de Comercio,* and Gabriel García, publisher of a liberal paper in 1824-25. Mendizábal was named Minister of Finance and celebrated his return to a position of power by cracking down on the press, especially those newspapers that had opposed him as Prime Minister. On August 14, the stockholders of *El Español* speedily decided on a change in editorial policy conciliatory to Mendizábal and accepted Andrés Borrego's resignation. Two days later, Mendizábal closed the political-satirical daily, *El Jorobado,*[68] which had been founded on March 1, 1836, with the express purpose of needling the then Prime Minister. On August 27, he vented his wrath on Evaristo San Miguel and José María Carnerero by shutting down the *Revista española–Mensajero de las Cortes.*

On October 24, 1836, Calatrava opened the Cortes, which was charged with drawing up a new constitution which was to be more acceptable than that of 1812. The press, protected by the freedoms guaranteed in the original and again effective document, "turned furiously against the government: mixing insults with crafty silences and publicly charging the administration with unconstitutional be-

---

[67] Gómez Aparicio, "Historia del periodismo," *GPE*, Sept. 15, 1964, p. 31.
[68] *El Jorobado* ("The Hunchback") (Madrid, 1836).

havior, ineptitude and with treason to the liberal cause." [69] The excesses of the press remained unchecked until early the following year, when its treatment of public figures became so violent that Calatrava asked the Cortes to interrupt its constitutional delibera- tions to pass a law "reconciling the liberty of the Press with the security of the State." The Cortes, on March 22, 1837, approved a press law which, among other things, fixed responsibility for a peri- odical's content on the person signing an article or, in the case of unsigned articles, on the editor, whose name "must be printed at the bottom of each number. . . ." The new law also increased the amount of legal deposits required by the 1834 law. In Madrid, the deposit was boosted to 40,000 *reales*. It was set at 30,000 *reales* for newspapers in Barcelona, Cádiz, Seville, and Valencia and at 20,000 for those in Granada and Saragossa. It remained at 10,000 *reales* for the rest of the provincial press.[70] On June 8, the Cortes approved the new constitution, and, on June 18, María Cristina swore to up- hold it. Article 2 of the constitution guaranteed that "All Spaniards may print and freely publish their ideas without previous censor- ship but with submission to the laws," and reserved "judgment of press crimes exclusively to juries." [71]

The constitution also guaranteed Spanish Catholics the right to freedom of worship and proclaimed the State's obligation to sup- port the Catholic cult and its ministers. The new recognition of the Church, though a far cry from its reestablishment as a state religion, drew protests from moderates, including a clique of officers in the government army.

The replacement of the Constitution of 1812 by that of 1837 co- incided with an advance on Madrid by two Carlist armies. The forces loyal to Isabel stopped cold the Carlist advance not far from Madrid, but a group of Royal Guard officers demanded Calatrava's resignation as a condition for pressing the attack against the retreat- ing adherents of Carlos. The Prime Minister ordered the army com- mander, General Baldomero Espartero, to discipline the upstart officers. Espartero did nothing, and Calatrava, finding his authority undermined, resigned. He was replaced on August 18 by the pro- gressive liberal (Progresista) Eusebio Bardají.

---

[69] Gómez Aparicio, "Historia del periodismo," *GPE*, Oct. 15, 1964, p. 11.
[70] Eguizábal, *Legislación española*, pp. 261–264.
[71] *Constitución de 1837, Artículo 2.*

The new Prime Minister found himself caught in a struggle between the Progresistas and the Jovellanistas, members of a reactionary, semi-secret organization made up of an odd mixture of Isabelist absolutists, backers of the Royal Statutes, and various liberals, disillusioned by the confusion that now seemed the only permanent factor in a nation in flux. Bardají tried to placate both sides, but without success and, on October 17, in an attempt to insure some order during elections called for early December, promulgated a new press law designed to strengthen official controls.

The October 17, 1837, law firmly fixed responsibility for all editorial content on a periodical's editor, thus plugging one loophole left by the March law, which had made writers responsible for the signed articles and thus encouraged them to disappear when threatened with legal action, leaving the newspaper itself free from possible prosecution. The new law also ordered that the "responsible editor" must contribute a certain quota of material to the periodical, ending the practice of naming as "responsible editor" a deputy or government figure whose official status carried with it penal immunity. In addition, it defined as "subversive publications" all "periodicals or printed matter which directly attack or discredit the Cortes or any of the co-legislative bodies." It ordered that a copy of each publication be submitted to the authorities before being put on sale and stipulated an automatic fine of 500 reales whenever publishers failed to comply. And finally, it reaffirmed the "right of rectification," ordering that anyone offended in print, "or the nearest relative of a dead person," be permitted to publish in the same periodical a reply to the offensive charges. The reply, the law ordered, would be printed without alteration and without charge, unless it was more than twice as long as the original article.[72]

The elections were held in late autumn and resulted in a victory for the moderates. The Conde de Ofalia, a diplomat and minister under Ferdinand VII, was named Prime Minister and, on December 16, formed a new government. Ofalia used the funds collected by the earlier sequestering of Church property to build up a new army which was held in reserve in southern Spain under the command of General Ramón María de Narváez, later leader of the mod-

---

[72] Decreto del 17 de octubre de 1837. The same "right of rectification" is part of the Spanish press code today; this author, in 1962, used it to answer charges of professional bias made by the newspaper Pueblo, which ended the exchange with a charming and apparently sincere apology.

erates and eventually dictator. The existence of Narváez's army aroused the jealousy of Espartero who gravitated into the progressive political camp.

Ofalia's measures produced no decided break in the war, and sentiment favoring a negotiated peace began to permeate the ranks of the moderates; this solution was flatly rejected by the progressives, who called for total victory and soon began to conspire openly against the moderate government. So blatant did the Progresista conspiracy become—and so dangerous to the precarious equilibrium of the country—that the self-proclaimed "progressive" daily, *El Mundo*,[73] published a warning about the party's plans. The government should know, *El Mundo* said, "that in the [Progressive] Clubs plots are hatched against life and assassination of the true friends of the throne is planned and arranged." [74]

In February, 1838, Andrés Borrego resumed his journalistic career, interrupted since his resignation from *El Español*, by founding *El Correo Nacional*.[75] The new newspaper followed the constitutional-monarchist line of *El Español*, which had folded on December 31 of the previous year. Borrego outlined the paper's position in an editorial which said, "The publication of this periodical is not a new venture insofar as the spirit which dominates the editorial staff and the principles which it is destined to serve are concerned. Written under the inspiration of the philosophical and social doctrines proclaimed in the old *Español*, its mission will be to continue the propagation of theories already known to and favored by the enfranchised public." [76] With that as his goal, Borrego set out to effect a reconciliation of the various political parties, a miracle beyond the powers of one voice.

In the meantime, the number of newspapers in the country had grown rapidly in the past five years, a period during which the Madrid press had more than tripled in size. In 1833, there had been fifteen papers in the capital—seven founded during the year, four dating from the year before, and four from 1831 or earlier. In 1834,

---

[73] *El Mundo: diario del pueblo* ("The World, a people's daily") (Madrid, 1836–40).
[74] Quoted by Gómez Aparicio, "Historia del periodismo," *GPE*, Oct. 15, 1964, p. 17.
[75] *El Correo Nacional* ("The National Post") (Madrid, 1838–42). During 1838, Borrego also published the *Revista Peninsular*, a political-literary magazine ("Peninsular Review") (Madrid, 1838).
[76] *El Correo Nacional* (Madrid), Feb. 16, 1838.

the first year after Ferdinand's death and a time of revived liberalism, that number jumped to thirty-six, of which twenty-six were new—four dating from the previous year and six from the period before that. In 1835, the capital city newspaper population dropped to twenty-five, with only nine new ventures launched, the casual founding of newspapers presumably discouraged by the enforcement of the 1834 law which required publishers to make cash deposits guaranteeing their business solvency and good faith. The law had caused twenty newspapers to close during the year of its enactment, four times the number that had folded in 1833. In 1836, however, twenty-nine new periodicals appeared, swelling the roster of the Madrid press to forty-three, despite Mendizábal's reprisals against the periodicals which had opposed his prime ministry. In 1837, the number dropped to forty, with twenty new papers founded and twenty continuing from the previous year, the largest carry-over until that time. The following year, there were forty-seven periodicals, twenty-three surviving from previous years. In 1839, the Madrid press passed the half-hundred mark, reaching fifty-one at a time when the city's population was less than half a million. In 1834, when the number of papers in Madrid reached thirty-six, only nine dated from previous years. In 1839, there were fifty-one, of which twenty-six were survivors from other years. The continuing increase in the total number of periodicals did not so much reflect a trend toward beginning new ventures as it did a growing ability to make a newspaper last more than a few months, an indication of a newly found financial security, stemming perhaps to some degree from an increase in circulation and allied income, despite widespread illiteracy which especially hampered the growth of the provincial press,[77] but largely due to subsidization by political figures or groups. It was a period in which Andrés Borrego could raise four million *reales* capital for *El Español* and when the *Diario de Madrid*, a public enterprise, could turn over to beneficent organizations a one-year profit, in 1835, of 35,000 *pesetas*.[78]

---

[77] Beneyto, *Historia social*, p. 402, estimates that only one of every four Spaniards was literate in 1860 and notes that in some provinces the illiteracy rate ran as high as 88 per cent. In 1840, Jaime Balmes, a journalist, wrote in his *Consideraciones políticas sobre la situación de España* that immense numbers of citizens either could not or did not take an interest in public affairs. "While this indifference lasts," Balmes concluded, "there is no hope of happiness in this unfortunate nation."

[78] Gascón de Gotor, "Orígenes y desarrollo del periodismo," *Revista Contemporánea*, XXX (1904), 425.

In 1837, by order of the Minister of the Interior, the *Gaceta de Madrid* had become the official gazette, publishing all "Laws, Decrees, Royal Orders and other dispositions of the Government," and reporting "in the greatest possible detail" on the sessions of the Cortes.[79] In 1838, it was further ordered that "all Royal Decrees, Orders or Government Instruments which are published in the *Gaceta de Madrid* . . . will, from the moment of publication, become law for all classes of persons on the Peninsula and adjacent Islands and the authorities and officials of all kinds must hasten to comply with them wherever applicable."[80] The public welcomed the *Gaceta*'s new role with some reservations, questioning its veracity and soon the expression "to lie more than the *Gaceta*" (*mentir más que la Gaceta*) became a popular means of comparison.[81]

---

[79] *Real Orden del 2 de junio de 1837.*
[80] *Real Orden del Ministerio de la Gobernación del 22 de septiembre de 1838.*
[81] Beneyto, *Historia social*, p. 403.

CHAPTER EIGHT

Political Fragmentation

By mid-1838, it was apparent that the rivalry between two generals, Baldomero Espartero and Ramón Narváez, was the pivot upon which the political reality of the moment turned. It was "clear that the control of Spain would go to the general who could end the war. . . ." [1] In 1836, Espartero had been the hero of Bilbao, preventing its capture by the Carlists. The following year, he had led the defense of Madrid and then contributed to the fall of the Calatrava government by refusing to discipline army officers demanding the Prime Minister's resignation. Narváez had won his spurs by driving back a Carlist penetration of central Spain in 1836 and then forming a well-trained army which wiped out Carlist resistance in La Mancha.

Espartero had been named Conde de Luchana as a reward for his services. Narváez's creation of the army in La Mancha won him the rank of field marshal. The promotion caused Espartero's jealousy to flare, and during a summer campaign, he ignored orders to transfer some of his troops to Narváez's command, thus precipitating a Carlist victory. The victory, the capture of Morello, touched off protests, not against Espartero but directed at the regime—protests which Espartero used to bring down the government of the Conde de Ofalia early in September. On September 6, the Duque de Frias, a onetime journalist,[2] was named Prime Minister. His tenure in of-

---

[1] Harold Livermore, *A History of Spain* (New York, 1960), p. 374.
[2] Frias had served as an editor of the Madrid semiweekly *El Siglo*.

fice was marked by a return to the military savagery of the period before the Elliot Agreement and a renewal of moderate demands for a negotiated termination of the war, a solution unacceptable to the Progresistas. In December, he was replaced by Evaristo Pérez de Castro, who found himself under fire from *El Guirigay*,[3] a daily dedicated to opposing negotiations with the Carlists, which was begun on January 1, 1839, by three young Progresista journalists. Its three founders—one of whom, Luis González Bravo, did a political about-face and twice headed governments during the reign of Isabel II—soon revealed themselves as "demagogues incapable of moderating their feverish aggression, not even showing the minimal respect due personal intimacies."[4] The life of *El Guirigay* was short, but during the six months of its existence, González Bravo, using the nom de plume Ibrahim Clarete, managed to compare favorably the assassination of a minister of the government to the lifesaving act of stanching the flow of blood from a wound,[5] and to label the ministers as "six useless, heterogenic men, who are cowards, absolutists, and who . . . command against the wishes of the nation."[6] He even, at one point, called the Queen-Regent an "illustrious prostitute."[7]

On March 8, convinced that peace could not be achieved while his policies were subjected to attacks within the Cortes, Pérez de Castro suspended its session. On June 5, still under fire from the press, he ordered restrictions imposed on newspaper activities. "Article Two of the Constitution," his order said, "grants all Spaniards the right to print and publish freely their ideas without previous censorship," but, "to our disgrace, this practice has degenerated into a wantonness so unfortunate and pitiful that it injures or kills that freedom and such that no one within the sphere of its imputations, least of all the Government, can look at it with tepid indifference."[8] The new controls, in effect, ordered officials to enforce existing laws, especially that which required submission of a copy of any periodical to local authorities two hours before the sale. Those charged with enforcing the law were authorized to sus-

---

[3] *El Guirigay* ("The Hullabaloo") (Madrid, 1839).
[4] Pedro Gómez Aparicio, "Apuntes para una historia del periodismo Español," *Gaceta de la Prensa Española*, Nov. 15, 1964, p. 30.
[5] *El Guirigay* (Madrid), Mar. 13, 1839.
[6] *Ibid.*, Apr. 27, 1839.
[7] Antonio Espina, *El Cuarto Poder* (Madrid, 1960), p. 16.
[8] *Real Orden del 5 de junio de 1839, Preámbulo.*

pend circulation of any issue "if in it are found articles which jeopardize the public peace, attack religion, or offend morality, customs or modesty." [9]

On July 7, acting under authority presumably granted by the new law, the Ministry of the Interior ordered *El Guirigay* to stop publication for an indefinite period.

On August 31, 1839, the policies of Pérez de Castro and the machinations of his Minister of Finance, Pío Pita Pizarro, bore fruit in the Convention of Vergara, which ended the war. Espartero, who had negotiated for the government, sealed the peace agreement by embracing his old friend and Carlist counterpart, General Rafael Maroto. Carlist officers were offered posts in the government army with no loss of rank or seniority, and Prince Carlos was allowed to retire to France. However, one Carlist officer, General Ramón Cabrera, continued the fight in the east of Spain.

One concession granted by Espartero to Maroto during the peace negotiations had been the promise that the Basque *Fueros* ("Privileges"), which established and maintained a state of semiautonomy in the northeastern provinces, would be respected. The Progresistas, clinging to the liberal centralist doctrine, opposed a bill which confirmed the Basque privileges. Their opposition shattered any chance of concord, so that Pérez de Castro was forced to dissolve the Cortes and reshuffle his ministry, bringing in Narváez as Minister of War. Espartero was ordered to the Spanish Levant to deal with General Cabrera. On February 18, 1840, elections, called the previous December, returned a moderate majority to the Cortes. A month later, on March 21, the government introduced a bill calling for the reform of municipal governments, reserving to the Crown the right to appoint mayors in provincial capitals and allowing provincial authorities to name those in smaller cities. While the measure was challenged by the Progresistas on the grounds that it violated the 1837 Constitution which granted municipal electorates the right to choose their own mayors, Espartero saw it as a personal rebuff— a challenge to his prestige as leader of the Progresistas and defender of the constitution.

On May 1, Patricio Olavarría, a close friend of the former Prime Minister, Álvarez Mendizábal, founded a radical daily, *La Revolución*,[10] which began with such a burst of printed violence against

---

[9] *Real Orden del 5 de junio de 1839.*
[10] *La Revolución* ("The Revolution") (Madrid, 1840).

existing institutions that its closing was ordered six days later on the grounds that "the scandal created [by the paper] has reached the point where there is no recourse owing to existing legislation governing the press." [11] On June 10, defying further enforcement of the law, Olavarría brought out El Huracán [12]—La Revolución with a new name—and thus continued in the business of blitzing the government.

In June, 1840, with the municipal reform bill still being debated in the Cortes, the Queen-Regent and her two daughters journeyed to Saragossa to review Espartero's troops, recent vanquishers of General Cabrera. From there, they set out for Barcelona, where María Cristina planned to bathe in the sea at the recommendation of her doctors. En route, she offered Espartero, recently named "Duke of Victory," leadership of a new government. Espartero agreed to accept the appointment if she, in turn, would agree to oppose the municipal reform bill. María Cristina refused, and, on July 14, the Cortes passed the measure. Espartero resigned, returning his emblems of rank and decorations to María Cristina. On July 18, demonstrations calling for the resignation of the government and acclaiming Espartero erupted in Barcelona. Members of her suite fled, leaving María Cristina at the mercy of Espartero, who "suggested" that she name Antonio González, a Progresista, to head a new government. On September 1, rioting broke out in Madrid and from there spread across the country. Popular juntas were formed in several provinces. María Cristina ordered Espartero to put down the movement, which amounted to open rebellion against the government, but the General refused to move his troops against the people. The Queen-Regent, fearing another civil war, resigned the regency and, on October 12, left the country. The Progresistas swept into power and named Espartero provisional Regent, an arrangement that was formalized by the Cortes the following May. The same Cortes abolished the municipal reform law and placed Queen Isabel, then ten years old, under the tutelage of Agustín Argüelles, the leader of the advocates of freedom of the press during the meeting of the Cortes in Cádiz, three decades before.

The means Espartero had used to gain power contributed to a decline in his popularity. The hearts of the Spanish people went

---

[11] Real Orden del Ministerio de la Gobernación del 6 de mayo de 1840.
[12] El Huracán ("The Hurricane") (Madrid, 1840-43).

out to the Queen, deprived of the care of her mother, and to María Cristina, separated from her children. In late 1840, José María Anduez, a former exile in Cuba where he had edited the *Diario de Gobierno*, returned to Spain expressly to start a newspaper backing the exiled Queen Mother. The paper, *El Trueno*,[13] appeared on December 1 and from then until its career ended on March 27, 1841, attacked Espartero. By midyear, *El Correo Nacional* of Andrés Borrego had joined in criticizing the new Regent. Other newspapers followed suit, including *El Corresponsal*,[14] founded in 1839 and dedicated to the principles of a constitutional monarchy; *El Cangrejo*,[15] begun on April 1 as an instrument for the return of the Queen and her sister to the care of María Cristina; and *El Hablador patriota*,[16] whose masthead proclaimed it was for the "Constitution of 1837," "Isabel II," and "National Independence."

By midsummer, fed up with the press campaigns challenging his policies, Espartero decided to counter with his own newspaper and entrusted its foundation to his friend and colleague, Evaristo San Miguel, then Captain General of Madrid and soon to be named Minister of War. On August 1, San Miguel began *El Espectador*,[17] resurrecting the name he had used for his first newspaper twenty years before. Among his editors was Ángel Fernández de los Ríos, beginning a long and constructive journalistic career, interlaced with political and diplomatic service. Years later, after a distinguished career as a deputy, Fernández de los Ríos was named Ambassador to Portugal, one of the nation's top diplomatic posts. Asked through what apprenticeships he had passed to achieve such a post, he answered, as could have many of his contemporaries, "By the route of the newspaper, nothing more." [18]

However, the voice of *El Espectador*, the sole organ supporting Espartero, was not enough to change the press tide, and, in September, Espartero ordered the officers of his government to crack down. Press privileges were limited.[19] The government, Espartero's order said, "respects the liberty of citizens to voice freely their ideas by means of the Press . . . but it has at the same time the obli-

---

[13] *El Trueno* ("The Thunder") (Madrid, 1840–41).
[14] *El Corresponsal* ("The Correspondent") (Madrid, 1839–44).
[15] *El Cangrejo* ("The Crab") (Madrid, 1841).
[16] *El Hablador patriota* ("The Patriotic Speaker") (Madrid, 1841).
[17] *El Espectador* ("The Spectator") (Madrid, 1841–48).
[18] Espina, *Cuarto Poder*, pp. 108–109.
[19] Joseph A. Brandt, *Toward the New Spain* (Chicago, 1933), p. 34.

POLITICAL FRAGMENTATION (169

gation to make those who are charged with carrying out the law comply with its observance."[20] With the issuance of the order, the press laws of March 22 and October 17, 1837, were rigorously enforced, and "hardly a day passed when some periodical was not withdrawn [from circulation] and denounced."[21]

On the night of October 7, a group of moderate army officers attempted a counter-coup, forcing their way into the palace to seize Isabel. The attempt failed and led to the uncovering of a widespread plot to oust Espartero. The Regent's reprisals included the execution of three of the plot's leaders and extended to the press. *El Cangrejo* was ordered to cease publication at once. On December 22, Espartero decreed: ". . . in view of the scandalous abuses to which a part of the periodical press has abandoned itself, the circulation of newspapers, circulars or writings in which the Constitution or policies of the Monarchy are attacked or which incite to the installation of any other system of Government is suspended in accordance with Article 14 of the Law of October 17, 1837, and action will be taken with equal precision against all which persist along such lines."[22]

Meanwhile, with the end of the Carlist war in 1839, the first in a series of Carlist newspapers had been founded. The newspaper, *El Católico*,[23] begun March 1, 1840, proclaimed itself "apolitical," but soon began a modest campaign in behalf of the Carlist claims. By April of 1843, it had been joined by at least two other newspapers of similar leanings, but more politically outspoken.[24]

Early in May, 1842, the Cortes reconvened. Espartero's popularity continued to wane, and even some Progresistas were showing signs of disillusionment. On May 28, five Progresista deputies, four of whom had been or still were newspapermen, presented to the government a statement condemning the government for "lacking prestige and the necessary moral force to serve the country." The statement, which took the form of a parliamentary proposition, was approved, and the same night Antonio González, Espartero's Prime

---

[20] *Orden del Regente del 9 de septiembre de 1841.*
[21] Gómez Aparicio, "Historia del periodismo," *GPE*, Dec. 15, 1964, p. 13.
[22] *Real Orden del 22 de diciembre de 1841.*
[23] *El Católico, periódico religioso y social, científico y literario, dedicado á todos los españoles y con especialidad al Clero, amantes de la religión de sus mayores y de su patria* ("The Catholic, a religious, social, scientific, and literary periodical, dedicated to all Spaniards, and especially to the Clergy, lovers of the religion of their ancestors and of their fatherland") (Madrid, 1840–57).
[24] *La Cruz* ("The Cross") (Madrid, 1842) and *La Restauración* ("The Restoration") (Valencia, 1843).

Minister, resigned. On June 15, Andrés Borrego's *El Correo Na-cional* expired with a tired sigh, its farewell leaving forever unclear the reasons for its demise. Though there were some sixty newspapers in Madrid at the time, its passing would have left the cause of moderation without an inspired voice had not its political torch been picked up by *El Heraldo*,[25] which began publication the evening of the following day. *El Heraldo* was directed by Luis José Sartorius, who, in 1847, at the age of thirty, became Minister of the Interior and, in 1853, as the Conde de San Luis, was named President of the Council of Ministers, a post equivalent to that of Prime Minister.

Two major issues caused difficulties for Espartero in mid-1842: his free trade policy and the question of Isabel's majority.

The free trade policy instituted shortly after his accession to the regency had culminated in a trade agreement with Great Britain which brought English fabrics into the country to compete with those produced domestically. Resistance to the agreement ran high in Catalonia, center of Spain's weaving industry, and, in some provinces, revolutionary *juntas* were set up. At the same time, it was rumored that the Regent had decided to sidestep provisions of the 1837 Constitution in order to prolong his stay in power. The 1837 document provided that a sovereign would become of age at fourteen. The rumors said Espartero planned to revert, in this one instance, to the Constitution of 1812, which set the age at eighteen, thus postponing for four years the moment when Isabel would begin to rule. The Catalan press, in particular, was indignant with Espartero. The Barcelona daily, *El Constitucional*,[26] warned that "if General Espartero and his followers try to resist and prolong for even one day the Regency, they will be delinquents, transgressors of the Constitution and rebels." [27] *El Imparcial*,[28] also of Barcelona, linked the question of Isabel's coming of age with Espartero's trade policies and accused the Regent of using commercial concessions to buy "in foreign Kingdoms the aid which he perhaps lacks domestically. . . ." [29]

---

[25] *El Heraldo* ("The Herald") (Madrid, 1842–54).
[26] *El Constitucional* ("The Constitutional") (Barcelona, 1837–43).
[27] Quoted by Gómez Aparicio, "Historia del periodismo," *GPE*, Jan. 15, 1964, p. 12.
[28] *El Imparcial* ("The Impartial") (Barcelona, 1840–?).
[29] Quoted by Gómez Aparicio, "Historia del periodismo," *GPE*, Jan. 15, 1964, p. 13.

Faced by hostility on the part of a national press whose editorial voice had not been moderated by his previous crackdowns, Espartero, on October 2, named a commission to draw up new and stricter laws. On October 24, *El Eco de Comercio* called for a meeting of newspaper editors to discuss the commission's work and its possible "sad consequences" to the press in general. The suggestion was picked up by Sartorius' *El Heraldo* and editorially "seconded." [30] On October 31, the editors of eleven top Madrid newspapers signed a four-point agreement which concerted their efforts to preserve press freedom. The document stated:

First. We declare that, from today on, we shall form a uniting Association which has as its object the defense of the freedom of the press within the legal limits now extant and which conform to the Constitution and the law.

Second. We declare that the Association, defender of the press, will carry out its objective by all means which conform to the Constitution and the laws and as willingly resist . . . governmental pressure . . . as well as those coming from other sources.

Third. We declare that this Association will likewise defend, in the same way, the guarantees of individual security and liberty established by the Constitution and the laws and [which are] violated and infringed in a large part of the Monarchy by the military and political agents of the government.

Fourth. We declare that this Association will defend and support in the proper manner [the fight against] . . . the postponement of the majority of the Queen.[31]

In December, his patience worn thin, Espartero journeyed to Barcelona where protests against his trade agreement with England verged on rebellion. When protestors ignored his order to lay down their arms, he commanded artillery units at the Montjuich fortress to bombard the city. The press reacted quickly. On January 2, 1843, the newspaper association, which had added three new members since its founding,[32] made a collective attack on the government,

---

[30] *El Heraldo* (Madrid), Oct. 24, 1842.
[31] The signers include: *El Eco de Comercio*, *El Heraldo*, *El Peninsular* (Madrid, 1842–43), *El Castellano* (Madrid, 1836–46), *La Posdata* (Madrid, 1842–46), *El Trono* (Madrid, 1842), *El Corresponsal*, *La Guindilla* (Madrid, 1842–43), *El Español Independiente* (Madrid, 1842), *La Revista de Madrid* (Madrid, 1838–45), and *La Revista de España y del Extranjero* (Madrid, 1842–48). In addition, *El Católico* was a party to the association, but refused, because of its Carlist leanings, to endorse all four points.
[32] *El Sol* ("The Sun") (Madrid, 1842–43); *El Reparador* ("The Observer") (Madrid, 1843); and *El Pabellon Español* ("The Spanish Pavilion") (Madrid, 1842–43).

charging that its "state of dependence" on the British government menaced the nation's industry and independence. The attack, published in all association newspapers, concluded: "The independent press protests in a most solemn and energetic manner against any commercial treaty with England which does not comply with the Constitution and which may not have been ratified by the Cortes, acting with full deliberative and decision-making freedom." [33]

The joint protest underlined for Espartero the danger to his rule from the press. On January 10, he issued an order which blasted the press for its "unchecked license" and renewed his instructions to the authorities to denounce and confiscate newspapers that "fail to respect the inviolability of the King or he who exercises royal authority. . . ." [34]

On April 3, the Cortes, dissolved by an order of January 3, was reconvened. Elections had shifted the majority from the hands of pro-Espartero liberals and had returned a respectable moderate minority. Espartero's Prime Minister, the Marqués de Rodil, did not survive long in the new legislative atmosphere, and, on May 9, Joaquín María López, a former editor of *El Eco de Comercio*, was asked to form a government. His initial proposals, which called for the ousting of several of the Regent's military appointees and an amnesty for political exiles, brought him into head-on conflict with Espartero. The Regent was still master and, on May 17, forced María López to resign. The press reacted by attacking Espartero and his closest aides. General Juan Prim y Prats, a Catalan Progresista, assumed leadership of a joint progressive-moderate movement against Espartero. The uprising spread across Spain. In the south, General Narváez, just returned from exile, took command of a strong army and marched north toward Madrid.

On July 1, the Espartero government made its last attempt to control the activities of the press. On that date, Fermín Caballero, a former editor of *El Eco de Comercio* and at the time Minister of the Interior, ordered the postal service to refuse to accept for mailing any newspaper other than the official *Gaceta de Madrid* and the pro-Espartero *El Espectador*, *El Centinela*,[35] and *El Patriota*.[36]

---

[33] Quoted by Gómez Aparicio, "Historia del periodismo," *GPE*, Jan. 15, 1965, p. 15.
[34] *Real Orden del 10 de enero de 1843.*
[35] *El Centinela* ("The Sentinel") (Madrid, 1842–?).
[36] *El Patriota* ("The Patriot") (Madrid, 1836–38, 1841–43).

By mid-July, Narváez had reached Torrejón de Ardoz, just outside of Madrid, and there defeated an army loyal to Espartero. On July 23, the news reached Espartero, who had traveled to Seville to take over command of forces there. Instead, he continued to the coast and, on July 30, embarked on a ship bound for England.

A provisional government, which included Joaquín María López and Fermín Caballero, replaced that of Espartero and began a program of reconciling the various political groups in the country. Among its reforms was the lifting of restrictive measures on the press, left over from the Espartero regime, and the declaration of Isabel's majority when she reached thirteen. On November 8, 1843, she took the royal oaths and became Queen. One of her first acts was the naming of Salustiano de Olózaga, who had served a short press apprenticeship in 1834 as editor of the *Diario de la Administración*,[37] as Prime Minister. On November 20, Olózaga formed his government. Nine days later, scandal rocked his ministry. On that day, two separate decrees signed by Isabel were published in the *Gaceta de Madrid*: one ordering Olózaga out of office and the other restoring him to office. The Cortes and the Court hummed with rumor derogatory to Isabel. On December 3, Luis González Bravo, who had called Isabel's mother an "illustrious prostitute," came to the Queen's defense, presenting to the Cortes her statement that Olózaga had coerced her into signing the decree which revoked the ouster. The government fell, and the Progresistas, weakened by the scandal, were forced to cede control to the moderates. González Bravo, whose political about-face was complete by this time, was named President of the Council of Ministers. Almost immediately he found himself the target of abuse equivalent to that which he had committed to paper in *El Guirigay*. Progresista periodicals sought party revenge for his "treason" to their principles and his overthrow of Olózaga. A provisional *junta* in Alicante called on regional liberals to unite against González Bravo, describing him as "the indecent editor of *El Guirigay*, who begs humiliating aid from the Carlist band, and—protected by ministers who rebel against the Constitution—organizes and encourages his lost cause which menaces our nation with another civil war and the horrors of death." [38]

---

[37] *Diario de la Administración* ("The Administration's Daily") (Madrid, 1834).
[38] Antonio Pirala y Criado, *Historia contemporánea: Anales desde 1843 hasta la conclusión de la actual guerra civil* (Madrid, 1876), III, 650–651.

The moderates, recalling his recent change of political camps, treated him with suspicion.

On April 9, 1844, González Bravo reacted by decreeing a reform of press legislation. The new law, while admitting that "freedom of the press is, among the rights granted by the Constitution of the Spaniards, without doubt one of the most important victories of modern civilization," put press controls on an emergency footing. "The slow transactions adopted for normal times," the decree stated, "are not good enough to reorganize nations which have arrived at the point of disintegration as a result of many revolutions, as Spain has." [39] The decree ordered that the editor who was to be responsible for all the material in a newspaper must be "an inhabitant for one year of the place in which his periodical is published." For periodicals appearing between one and seven times a week, a new schedule of deposits was set up, ranging from 120,000 *reales* in Madrid to 45,000 in the smaller cities. If the increase in deposits had not been met within three days, the original sum prescribed by the 1837 law was to be returned and the newspaper closed. The right of rectification was maintained, and the fines for press crimes were increased, but corporal penalties were discontinued. Juries were charged with determining guilt and assessing fines,[40] but it was soon discovered that the use of juries in trials backfired. Decisions were based not on the merits of each case but rather on the political posture of the paper in relationship to that of the majority of the members of a jury, giving politics precedence over justice.

On May 3, 1844, the reforms of the González Bravo government completed, the Queen turned over the reins to General Narváez, who named two newsmen to his cabinet: Juan Donoso Cortés, who had helped edit *La Abeja, El Porvenir,*[41] *El Correo Nacional,* and *El Piloto;*[42] and Alejandro Mon, who later turned from politics to writing. The new government began almost at once to pave the way for a new constitution: sale of sequestered Church property was halted; the rights promised to the Basque provinces were arranged; and relations with the Vatican, broken off by Espartero, were reestablished. On July 4, Narváez summoned a new Cortes into ses-

---

[39] *Decreto reformando la legislación de imprentas del 9 de abril de 1844, Exposición.*
[40] *Ibid., Artículos 20-30.*
[41] *El Porvenir* ("The Future") (Madrid, 1839-40).
[42] *El Piloto* ("The Pilot") (Madrid, 1839-40).

sion, a Cortes to which was entrusted basic reform of the constitution.

While the Cortes debated the provisions of a new constitution, the Spanish press continued its growth. During the year, fifty new periodicals were founded in Madrid,[43] fourteen more than the previous year. For the first time, the capital city's press census breached the ninety mark, reaching ninety-four.[44]

The political alignment of the press of the period was clear cut. The Progresistas were represented by *El Eco de Comercio, El Espectador*,[45] and *El Clamor Público*,[46] which joined in attacking plans for a new constitution. Sartorius' *El Heraldo* was the sole editorial defender of Narváez. Typical of the opposition to Narváez was that appearing in *El Clamor Público*, which described "the conduct of our adversaries who are in power and in the opposition" as marked by "a political immorality which can be no less than dangerous and unpopular." [47]

On May 23, 1845, a year and three weeks after work on it was begun, a new constitution was promulgated. It did away with "national sovereignty," giving the Queen power to appoint members of the upper house and to decide on her own marriage. It was midway between the constitutions of 1812 and 1837 on the question of religion, raising Catholicism to the position of "the religion of the Spanish nation," but providing for the existence of other creeds. Its sole reference to the press was its second article which reaffirmed the Spaniards' right to print and publish "freely their ideas without previous censorship, but subject to the laws," but which omitted the phrase putting press crimes within the jurisdiction of juries.[48]

---

[43] Eugenio Hartzenbusch é Hiríart, *Apuntes para un Catálogo de periódicos madrileños desde el año 1661 al 1870* (Madrid, 1894), pp. 87–93.

[44] *Ibid.*, pp. 318–319.

[45] *El Espectador* had ceased publication with the fall of Espartero, but resumed, as a pro-Narváez organ, on May 4, 1844, the day after González Bravo was replaced by Narváez.

[46] *El Clamor Público* ("The Public Clamor") (Madrid, 1844–64), a daily founded by Fernando Corradí, a deputy, and which carried the Progresista banner for two decades.

[47] Quoted by Gómez Aparicio, "Historia del periodismo," *GPE*, Feb. 15, 1965, p. 51. A recent judgment of a later Narváez government notes that it was common knowledge "that the financier Salamanca had grown rich through fraud, that the minister Sartorius was guilty of extortion. Narváez's personnel was either mediocre or corrupt." Jean Descola, *A History of Spain*, trans., Elaine P. Halperin (New York, 1963), pp. 374–375.

[48] *Constitución de 1845, Artículo 2.*

The government was not long in taking advantage of the omission and, on July 6, issued a decree setting up special six-man tribunals for trying press crimes and defining in detail "subversion" and "sedition." [49] The decree was signed by the Minister of the Interior, Pedro José Pidal, a former newsman whose ties to his profession were secondary to his political loyalties, as so often was the case.[50]

The press quickly defended its rights by lashing out against the government—striking out, as in the past, in all directions. But there was a new note in the attacks, a dispassionate, logical analysis which centered on the key question. Its author was Jaime Balmes, one of the century's profoundest social observers and top contemporary historians, who had founded the weekly *El Pensamiento de la Nación* [51] on February 6, 1844. "The twelfth article of the Constitution says that the power to make laws resides in the Cortes. . . ," Balmes wrote. "With what right, then, do Ministers publish the new Print Law without the agreement of the Cortes?" [52] The reasoned, calm questioning of legality rather than personal attacks or appeals to emotion was typical of Balmes, who believed that the press "is not the property of a political institution and, therefore, should not be subject to the inconsistencies which are part of politics." [53]

Moreover, the approach reflected Balmes' concern with what he considered the major problem of his time, the need to achieve the harmonious interaction of individuals within the framework of society by seeking a constructive unity on all levels rather than by attempting to sway public opinion by demagoguery.[54]

---

[49] *Decreto Real del 6 de julio de 1845.* Subversive periodicals were defined as those which worked "against the principle and form of government established by the Constitution or State with the object of inciting to the destruction or change in the form of government. . . ." Seditious publications were those which "praised or defended acts punishable according to the laws" or "which in any way incited to the commission of such acts."

[50] Pidal had helped edit the original *Espectador* between 1821 and 1823 and, in 1838, had founded the *Revista de Madrid*.

[51] *El Pensamiento de la Nación* ("The Mind of the Nation") (Madrid, 1844-46).

[52] *El Pensamiento de la Nación* (Madrid), Aug. 13, 1845.

[53] Manuel Jiménez Quílez, *Vigencia del pensamiento periodístico de Balmes en la era de la información espacial* (Madrid, 1964), p. 15.

[54] At the age of thirty-one, Balmes had written with more idealism than realism in *La Civilización* (Barcelona, 1841-43), his first periodical: "For these, civilization is order; for those, it is freedom; for some, the splendor of the sciences and fine arts occupies first place; for others, it is prosperity in agriculture, the development of industry, the extension and activity of commerce. But there is

Despite the opposition of the press and its own dubious legality, the law remained in effect until the following year. In the meantime, Spain's political attention focused on the vexing problem of finding a husband for Isabel. There were urgent reasons for at least arranging the fourteen-year-old Queen's betrothal. In addition to those dictated by matters of policy, there was that created by the Queen Mother, who had returned to Spain after Espartero's flight into exile. Her influence with her daughter was so great that it "made the life of the ministers more difficult than ever." [55] Marriage, it was felt, would free the Queen from motherly control. The front-runner for the role of prince-consort was the son of Prince Carlos, the Conde de Montemolín, but hopes of such a union were dashed by the Prince who insisted that his son should be king. For a brief period both France and England supported candidates, but agreed in September, at Eu, to withdraw from Spain's royal marital sweepstakes. Agreement was finally reached on the Duque de Cádiz, the Queen's cousin. At the same time, Isabel's sister, Luisa Fernanda, was betrothed to the Duke of Montpensier, the fifth son of Louis Philippe of France. The intrigue leading up to the dual betrothal resulted in three changes of government in early 1846. Narváez was forced to resign and was replaced, on February 12, by the ultraconservative Marqués de Miraflores. His attempts to form a government were frustrated by Narváez's friends and, on March 16, Miraflores resigned. Narváez replaced him, and though his government lasted only eighteen days, he did manage to promulgate, in the Queen's name, a defiant new press law, which stated:

Invectives or contumelies which are printed in periodicals against my Royal person or family, or against foreign Sovereigns or the Princes of their houses, or against the Constitution and the laws of the State, or against the free exercise of my constitutional prerogatives, or against the present Decree until it has reached the point of being judged by the Cortes, will be punished from now on by the immediate and definitive suppression of the periodical.[56]

---

one idea about civilization which unites all—the idea of the perfection of society." (*La Civilización*, Aug. 1, 1841.) In early 1843, Balmes discontinued *La Civilización* and began *La Sociedad* (Barcelona, 1843–44), which he closed down in May, 1844, for a combination of reasons. The law, put into effect the previous month, which raised the amount of deposit required for a periodical, stretched his financial resources. Added to that was his conviction that his ideas would be much more influential if expressed in Madrid rather than in a provincial capital.
[55] Livermore, *History of Spain*, p. 378.
[56] *Real decreto del 18 de marzo de 1846, Artículo 1.*

The law also provided for temporary closure of any periodical that attacked a public office,[57] and ordered that the "responsible editor" of a newspaper that had been either suspended or shut down could not head another publication until his case had been heard by the Cortes.[58] The same day, Andrés Borrego, who had resumed publication of *El Español* on July 1, 1845, closed down his newspaper in protest. "Having ceased, by virtue of the . . . Decree, the conditions with which the Constitution of the Monarchy treats and regulates the periodical Press," he told his readers, "we deem it necessary to suspend our work on *El Español* and in our *Revista Literaria* as a protest against force . . . and to reserve for ourselves the right of making use of our rights when the rule of law is reestablished in Spain."[59] Borrego's periodicals, as good as their word, did not appear during the eighteen days that Narváez remained in power. On April 4, the General was replaced by Francisco Javier de Istúriz, whose first act was to order his predecessor out of Madrid. On May 3, the new government repealed the March 18 Press Law.

On October 10, 1846, the joint wedding of Isabel to the Duque de Cádiz and of her sister to the Duke of Montpensier was celebrated in Madrid. The marriage took place despite the misgivings of many of Spain's farsighted students of politics, who had seen a union between Carlos' son and the Queen as the only means of resolving the nation's problems. Jaime Balmes had written long before: "Neither the absolutism of Ferdinand VII, which might be brought about by Don Carlos, nor the constitutionalism presided over by the Queen, is of any use. But if the son of Don Carlos weds Doña Isabel, of necessity there will have to be a compromise between the two political systems as a dowry brought to the marriage by both bride and groom."[60]

At the end of the year, Balmes retired from journalism, disillusioned and convinced that the future held no peace for his country. He had possessed, in his time, some glimmerings of the problems that would be created by the growth of population and the increasing complexities of life. In his opinion, as he stood apart from politics unlike most of his professional contemporaries, the solution to

[57] *Ibid., Artículo 2.*
[58] *Ibid., Artículo 4.*
[59] *El Español* (Madrid), Mar. 18, 1846.
[60] Quoted by Gómez Aparicio, "Historia del periodismo," *GPE,* Mar. 15, 1965, p. 24.

Spain's problems lay in the middle road between an absolute monarchy and freewheeling liberalism, in a constitutionalism checked by well-defined royal prerogatives. In July, 1848, he died.

The last year of his professional life and the two years of retirement preceding his death had been marked by some changes in the structure and content of Spanish newspapers. Borrego's *El Español*, attempting to meet an increased demand for "hard news," had encouraged correspondents to send reports from other major European capitals. In addition, *El Español* had pioneered in the publication of the serial story (*folletín*), primarily works translated from the French. Many of the works came to reflect the anticlerical stand of liberalism or the widespread literary preoccupation with realism.[61]

In January, 1847, the government, formed the previous April by Francisco Javier de Istúriz, fell. Its demise was, in part, caused by the maneuvering of General Francisco Serrano, partisan of the revival of Church influence and a favorite of the Queen. Istúriz was replaced by the Duque de Sotomayor, who exiled Serrano to Granada. Sotomayor's tenure was short. In March, he was replaced by the journalist Joaquín Francisco Pacheco,[62] who had to contend with both a Progresista press that favored Serrano and public awareness that the Queen's marriage had not been a union made in heaven. The liberal and anti-monarchical press offered the public, with obvious delight and no self-restraint, complete coverage of the affairs of the royal family, one of the "most embarrassing spectacles in the history of Spain." [63] As had his predecessors, Pacheco felt obliged to curb somehow the activities of his erstwhile professional col-

---

[61] Their general tone was such that Balmes, who appears to have recognized the social impact of the mass media while his contemporaries considered them solely as political tools, noted that a foreign reader of the Spanish press "would be forced to the conclusion that the most complete indifference to religion is rooted in our country." Quoted by Gómez Aparicio, "Historia del periodismo," *GPE*, Feb. 15, 1965, p. 50.

[62] Pacheco had served for a short time as editor of the *Diario de la Administración* and *El Siglo*. He switched to *La Abeja* and served as an editor of *Anales administrativos* (Madrid, 1834-35). Later he joined Andrés Borrego in the direction of *El Español* and was one of the first editors of *La España* (Madrid, 1837-39). He contributed to *El Correo Nacional*, founded the monthly *Crónica jurídica* (Madrid, 1839), and worked on another *El Español* (Madrid, 1841-42), a weekly review of politics, the sciences, and literature. After his entry into politics, he founded the daily *La Patria* (Madrid, 1849-51) and helped edit *El Belén* (Madrid, 1857).

[63] Gómez Aparicio, "Historia del periodismo," *GPE*, May 15, 1965, p. 23.

leagues. However, he was forced to resign in September, and the new press regulations, calling for a restoration of trial by special tribunal, a practice nullified by Istúriz, never became law. Pacheco was followed by the Marqués de Salamanca, who remained in power for only thirty-eight days, but put into effect a new press law aimed directly at the excesses of the moment. The law prohibited the "printing and publication of all writings which deal with the private life of Her Majesty, our lady the Queen, or her marriage or the august Royal Consort." It provided that "the periodical which violates that which is here decreed . . . will be suppressed and lose the deposit necessary for its publication. If a pamphlet contravenes that which is here decreed, it shall be withdrawn from circulation and its editor or printer will be fined 70,000 *reales*." [64]

On October 4, Salamanca handed over power to Narváez, once again called upon to form a government. He included Luis Sartorius, director of the moderate *El Heraldo* and recently named Conde de San Luis, in his cabinet, along with Juan Bravo Murillo, a former editor of *La Abeja* and a co-founder of *El Porvenir*, and Manuel Bertrán de Lis, also from the staff of *El Heraldo*.

Narváez was destined to remain in power for more than three years, preventing revolution in Spain at a time when elsewhere in Europe regimes tumbled. He succeeded in averting war in the Basque provinces and Catalonia, where General Cabrera, the holdout from the Peace of Vergara, tried to rekindle Carlist warfare. In France, Louis Philippe was thrown out and Louis Napoleon elected President. A government upheaval in Italy forced Pius IX to leave Rome, and Narváez, responding to Papal appeals, sent 8,000 Spanish troops to Gaeta to protect the Pontif. At home, he assumed dictatorial powers to suppress uprisings in Barcelona and other provincial capitals as well as two in Madrid. In October, 1849, he successfully survived a thirty-six-hour coup directed by the Royal Consort.

When Narváez resumed the reins, he inherited from his two predecessors a large backlog of press cases, periodicals that had been denounced and whose judgments were pending. On October 14, Narváez ordered such cases thrown out and assured the press that the government would "follow a course of complete legality, which

---

[64] *Ibid.*, p. 24.

ought to allow it to hope that individuals and Parties [with news-papers] would accommodate their public conduct to these prin-ciples. . . ." [65] Despite the assurances of official cooperation and tolerance if the press were to moderate its tone, Narváez's Minister of the Interior, the Conde de San Luis, troubled by crises through-out Europe, drew up an extremely restrictive press law which was presented to the Cortes on February 7 of the next year. However, Spain escaped the brunt of European trouble, and the project never became law.

The period of Narváez's ministry was one of growth for the press. During 1846, the number of periodicals appearing in Madrid reached ninety-six. However, in 1847, the number dropped to eighty-five, only to climb back to ninety-two in 1848, stimulated, perhaps, by Narváez's mildness. In 1849, it reached ninety-five and, in 1850, soared to 120.

In 1847, Spain's first labor newspaper appeared: *La Atracción* [66] was a weekly devoted to the introduction into Spain of the ideas of the French Socialist, François Fourier. In the same year, Diego Coello y Quesada began the moderate daily *El Faro,*[67] which in-cluded among its editors one former Prime Minister, Luis González Bravo, and two former cabinet members, Alejandro Mon and Pedro José Pidal. Despite its top-level staff, *El Faro*'s life-span was short. Almost the moment it spread its wings, *El Heraldo*'s director, the Conde de San Luis, determined that his newspaper should be the sole voice of the moderates, began sniping at the new competition. It took more than a year, but finally San Luis's perseverance paid off, and, on April 30, 1848, fifty-four weeks after it first went on sale, *El Faro* folded. On April 18 of the following year, one Pedro de Egaña, who was cut from somewhat the same professional mold as Jaime Balmes, began *La España,*[68] which was to last more than

---

[65] *Real Orden del 14 de octubre de 1847.*
[66] *La Atracción* ("The Attraction") (Madrid, 1847).
[67] *El Faro* ("The Lighthouse") (Madrid, 1847-48).
[68] *La España* ("Spain") (Madrid, 1848-68). Also worthy of note are such periodicals as *El Tío Camorra* ("The Quarrelsome Uncle") (Madrid, 1847-48), dedicated to the dissemination of democratic principles; *La Campana* ("The Bell") (Madrid, 1848), a liberal publication which lasted only one month; *El Siglo* ("The Century") (Madrid, 1848), a progressive organ; *El Observador* ("The Observer") (Madrid, 1848-53), liberal in orientation; *El Pueblo* ("The People") (Madrid, 1848); *La Guardia Nacional* ("The National Guard") (Madrid, 1848); and *La Ley* ("The Law") (Madrid, 1848).

twenty years by adhering to its self-proclaimed principle that *"La España* is a periodical of government, but not of the government. That is to say, *La España* is a periodical that defends the principles of order, conserves society, is jealous of national independence, and is monarchical and liberal in the purest and most honorable sense of the word." [69]

On June 1 of that year appeared one of the most influential papers of the century, the *Carta Autógrafa*,[70] the product of the work and dreams of one man, Manuel María Santa Ana. Santa Ana, who had served his apprenticeship on newspapers in Seville, his birthplace, and Madrid, personally covered his news beats, which included the various ministries; wrote and edited his own stories; and printed them lithographically. His professional philosophy was simple and radical for the Spain of the mid-nineteenth century: a newspaper should be strictly informative. Santa Ana's political affiliations were never manifest in his paper; his style was dry and impartial, a mere recording of events. In 1851, Santa Ana changed the newspaper's name to *La Correspondencia Autógrafa Confidencial*,[71] and, in 1858, settled on the title *La Correspondencia de España*,[72] which was one of the most widely read dailies in Spain. Among Santa Ana's innovations, in addition to the use of "hard news" reportage, was the introduction of crime, accident, and human interest stories to his columns, which led to the birth of the news specialist [73] and the creation of an embryo news service, the forerunner in Spain of the modern news agencies.

Despite the *Carta Autógrafa* and the continuing birth of political newspapers, the period was marked more strongly by the growth of the specialized press. In 1847, for example, at least four medical journals [74] were founded, as well as two periodicals devoted to the

---

[69] *La España* (Madrid), Jan. 9, 1849, quoted by Hartzenbusch, *Periódicos madrileños*, p. 113.
[70] *Carta Autógrafa* ("The Handwritten Letter") (Madrid, 1848-51).
[71] *La Correspondencia Autógrafa Confidencial* ("The Handwritten Confidential Correspondence") (Madrid, 1851-58).
[72] *La Correspondencia de España* ("The Correspondence of Spain") (Madrid, 1858-1924).
[73] *La Correspondencia*, for example, was the first Spanish newspaper to have a police reporter (*redactor del crimen*); a regular foreign correspondent, Peris Mencheta; and political reporters, one of whom reportedly hid under a conference table to cover a meeting of the Spanish cabinet.
[74] *El Regenerador* ("The Regenerator") (Madrid, 1847); *Gaceta homeopática* ("Homeopathic Gazette") (Madrid, 1847-48); *La Verdad* ("The Truth") (Madrid, 1847-48); and *La Union* ("The Union") (Madrid, 1847-53), which was published by the Madrid Academy of Surgery.

legal profession,[75] two that emphasized the arts,[76] three devoted to science and literature,[77] one strictly to religion,[78] one theatrical publication,[79] and a children's magazine.[80]

On March 1, 1849, the Conde de San Luis began *El País*,[81] a political sister to *El Heraldo*, in violation of a promise to Diego Coello of *El Faro* that he would start no other moderate publications. On April 1, Coello countered by beginning *La Época*,[82] which started as a moderate organ and eventually became the mouthpiece of the Unión Liberal. Under Coello's direction, editorial duties, hitherto customarily performed by any member of a newspaper's staff, were compartmentalized, special editors being appointed for political and economic news, foreign news, and for literary and social news. The function of the foreign editor was, at this time, of much more importance than ever before. In 1846, Spain's telegraphic system had been linked with that of France. In 1848, lines had been opened between Madrid and Barcelona and Madrid and Seville. The modern communications system brought more news into Madrid, Barcelona, and Seville, broadening the horizons of newspapers and enhancing the importance of editors of foreign and national news.

Years later, Fernando Cos-Gayón, one of the early editors of *El Heraldo*, was to describe the nation's communications system before the introduction of the electric telegraph:

A newspaper then was a very distinct thing from what you know today . . . especially in respect to foreign and provincial news. . . . There were neither electric telegraph facilities nor the iron roads [of the railways]. There was no communication with other countries except by means of mail carried by stagecoach, which during most of the days of the year arrived two hours, or four, or ten, or twenty hours late, rather than on time. The efforts of the public administration could not stop the rains or snows of winter and the storms of summer from delaying the trips of those coaches: delays to which the deterioration of the roads and other causes [also contributed].[83]

---

[75] *Revista jurídica* ("Legal review") (Madrid, 1847) and *El Derecho Moderno* ("The Modern Law") (Madrid, 1847-57).
[76] *El Artista* ("The Artist") (Madrid, 1847) and *El Eco de las Artes* ("The Echo of the Arts") (Madrid, 1847).
[77] *El Postillón* ("The Postilion") (Madrid, 1847); *El Seudónimo* ("The Pseudonym") (Madrid, 1847); and the *Revista científica y literaria* ("Scientific and literary review") (Madrid, 1847).
[78] *La Iglesia* ("The Church") (Madrid, 1847).
[79] *El Teatro* ("The Theater") (Madrid, 1847).
[80] *Museo de los niños* ("Children's museum") (Madrid, 1847-50).
[81] *El País* ("The Nation") (Madrid, 1849-50).
[82] *La Época* ("The Epoch") (Madrid, 1849-1936).
[83] Letter written in January, 1898, to the newspaper *La Época* at the beginning

The midpoint in the nineteenth century marked a transition for the Spanish press—a transition, foreshadowed by the *Carta Autógrafa* and *La Época*, to the professionalization of the press. Despite its tremendous growth—in Madrid alone, the number of periodicals increased from six in 1830 to 147 in 1850 [84]—the press had remained in amateur hands, a political adjunct of the interparty struggle for power. "Newspapers were a means of gaining power, of maintaining the organizations of each party. There were no professional journalists. . . ." Editors and writers were seldom, if ever, paid. "When their party attained power, they jumped [from editorial offices] to high posts in the Administration. . . . The papers were small in size, their budgets scarcely exceeding the expense of printing materials and the reams of paper they consumed. The editors collected only in political patronage when their party reached power." [85] The truth of that is borne out by Spanish history, its pages dotted by the names of men who rose to policy-making levels by following the path of journalism. In one decade, six former journalists—Luis Sartorius, Joaquín Francisco Pacheco, Joaquín María López, Salustiano de Olózaga, the Duque de Frias, and Luis González Bravo—had headed the government. One more, Juan Bravo Murillo, was soon to be named President of the Council of Ministers. At least seven others had held cabinet posts. The number of writers and editors who filled minor posts was legion. Many earned their living as bureaucrats at the same time that they earned their leaders' future gratitude as unpaid writers or editors for party organs.[86]

It was a period in which freedom had alternated with controls. During intervals of relaxation of government direction, freedom of the press was either misunderstood or warped to suit individual needs. Even under regimes which represented the most advanced ideas "and which were most dedicated to the principle of freedom of expression of thought, freedom of the press was inequitably granted." [87]

of its 50th year, quoted by Gómez Aparicio, "Historia del periodismo," *GPE*, May 15, 1965, p. 35.
[84] Hartzenbusch, *Periódicos madrileños*, pp. 312, 324–325.
[85] "El periodismo en España," *Enciclopedia Universal Ilustrada* (Barcelona, 1923), XXI, 1485.
[86] Espina, *Cuarto Poder*, p. 18.
[87] José Eugenio de Eguizábal, *Apuntes para una historia de la legislación española sobre la imprenta desde el año de 1480 al presente* (Madrid, 1879), p. 65.

CHAPTER NINE

Reaction and Revolution

Narváez's amnesty for newsmen charged with press crimes, granted in 1847, and his promise to respect constitutional guarantees of press liberty resulted in what was, for the time, nearly editorial "kid-glove" handling of him and his regime in the nation's periodicals. However, by early 1849, that moderation had worn off. The continued dominance of Narváez, and the soldiers with whom he surrounded himself, irked the public as did his policies, which more and more reflected his unflattering assumptions about the type of rule required by the Spanish nation and people. He was an authoritarian who thus summed up his diagnosis of Spain's ills and his remedy for them: "Spain is a country where there are many rascals; it needs a head to think for it and an arm to keep it in order." [1] But Narváez's personal unpopularity was not the sole fact responsible for the regime's "bad press." The nation's economy lagged far behind the pace of development elsewhere in Europe. The country was deeply in debt. The Queen's domestic life and general behavior in court lacked dignity, even morality, and served as the target for caustic press attacks. As public criticism of the government increased, Narváez became more and more stern in his dealings with newspapers. By the end of 1849, his treatment of the press could be described as "a fierce repression." [2] Official denunciations of

---

[1] Ángel Fernández de los Ríos, *Estudio histórico de las Luchas políticas en la España del Siglo XIX*, 2nd ed. (Madrid, 1880), II, 101.
[2] Julio Merino González, "Biografía de un periódico de 1870," *Gaceta de la*

newspapers were a daily occurrence and ran into the hundreds. On one day alone, March 26, 1850, five major newspapers—*La Patria*,[3] *El Clamor Público, La Nación*,[4] *La Esperanza*,[5] and *El Observador* —were forbidden to circulate and charged with violation of press statutes.[6] "There have been months," *La Patria* complained, "when the government has confiscated twenty-one of our twenty-six issues."[7]

In July, no longer content to act against individual periodicals, Narváez initiated new press regulations which asserted that "the interest of Society is above that of particular individuals when those interests are illegitimate offspring."[8] The regulations ordered provincial governors to "watch over, prevent the distribution of, and denounce" periodicals which "may work toward the destruction of the social organization and the principle and form of government set up in the Constitution of State, even though they deal only in abstractions or considerations of foreign nations."[9] The authorities were instructed also to act against printers and publishers who "initiate discussions about the Royal Person of Her Majesty the Queen, His Majesty the King, or any other individual of the Royal Family and against the free exercise of the royal prerogatives."[10] In addition, those papers were to be considered culpable which "deal with the private acts of the history of any person or family without the consent of the interested parties or, in their absence, relatives of the fourth grade."[11] And, finally, the law was extended to all publications which "might contain doctrines aimed at relaxing social ties, attacking propriety in order to weaken the Religion of the State, or offending good customs, whether they be the pages of newspapers, pamphlets or books."[12]

The effects of the midyear decree were not felt immediately by

---

Prensa Española, June 15, 1964, p. 90.

[3] *La Patria* ("The Fatherland") (Madrid, 1849-51), founded by the former President of the Council of Ministers, Joaquín Francisco Pacheco. It was the periodical which introduced Antonio Cánovas de Castillo, one of the major political figures of the last half of the century, to the semipolitical world of the press.

[4] *La Nación* ("The Nation") (Madrid, 1849-56).

[5] *La Esperanza* ("The Hope") (Madrid, 1844-74).

[6] Merino González, "Biografía," p. 90.

[7] *La Patria* (Madrid), Jan. 16, 1851.

[8] *Real Orden del 15 de julio de 1850*.

[9] *Ibid., Artículo 1.*

[10] *Ibid., Artículo 2.*

[11] *Ibid., Artículo 3.*

[12] *Ibid., Artículo 4.*

the press. In 1850, Madrid's periodical population rose to 147, but the following year the repercussions set in and the number of Madrid papers dropped to 121. The most notable newspaper appearing on the scene in 1850 was the daily *Las Novedades*,[13] which hit the streets on December 14 and rapidly topped the circulation of all other capital city papers. It was founded by the twenty-nine-year-old Progresista, Ángel Fernández de los Ríos, who became, in turn, a revolutionary, a deputy, a man of wealth, an ambassador, and an exile. By the time *Las Novedades* celebrated its third birthday, its circulation had risen to 13,000, according to its publisher, and, by 1854, had topped the 16,000 mark, "figures almost unknown in those times. . . ."[14]

For the first months of its existence, *Las Novedades* stood aside from political battles, but when Juan Bravo Murillo[15] was asked, on January 14, 1851, to form a Conservative government, Fernández de los Ríos aligned himself with the Progresistas and joined in the editorial warfare against the new chief minister.

Murillo had ridden into power on the strength of promised economic reforms. Shortly before taking over from Narváez, he had published, for the first time in Spain's history, the national accounts. His emphasis on the economic aspects of government reflected a general preoccupation with finance. Spain was on the threshold of a period of growth and expansion. Between 1848 and 1864, its commerce would triple,[16] public works would spring up in major population centers, the telegraph would be introduced and work pushed forward on the national rail system. But there was a seamy side. Fortunes were made by government officials who administered the public works and railroad expansion programs. Even the Queen Mother and her husband were involved in land speculation and gambled on the Bourse.

Though Bravo Murillo had started his political career as a constitutionalist, his regime quickly became more reactionary than that of Narváez. A Concordat was signed with the Vatican without prior submission to the Cortes. The agreement confirmed Catholicism as

---

[13] *Las Novedades* ("The Latest News") (Madrid, 1850-72).
[14] Pedro Gómez Aparicio, "Apuntes para una historia del periodismo Español," *Gaceta de la Prensa Española*, May, 15, 1965, p. 35.
[15] Bravo Murillo had been an editor of *La Abeja*, worked on the conservative *El Porvenir*, and helped publish *El Correo Nacional*.
[16] Louis Bertrand and Sir Charles Petrie, *The History of Spain*, 2nd ed. (London, 1952), p. 329.

the nation's exclusive religion, restored the Church's right to hold property, and reestablished its right of censorship. The drift to reaction was given impulse by Louis Napoleon's coup d'état, which converted the French Republic into an empire,[17] thus setting a precedent for the move away from constitutional rule. Bravo Murillo dissolved the Cortes and began governing by decree. On April 2, 1852, he acted to still a crescendo of press criticism of his government. A decree of that date reaffirmed the principle of the "responsible editor," specifying that he could represent no more than one periodical,[18] but once again made the writer responsible for signed articles.[19] The decree also raised the amount of deposit required of a full-sized newspaper: to 120,000 *reales* in Madrid, 80,000 in provinces of "the second class," and 40,000 in provinces of "the third class." The deposits for tabloids were even larger: 160,000, 120,000, and 60,000 *reales*.[20] In addition, the decree called for prison sentences of one to six years and fines of 20,000 to 60,000 *reales* for violation of the ban on criticism of the monarch, royal family, or government, and made attacks on "society, Religion, or that which is moral" punishable by two years imprisonment and fines of 5,000 to 20,000 *reales*.[21]

The opposition protested strongly against the new regulations. Fernández de los Ríos, publisher of *Las Novedades*, claimed to be doubly abused: not only was his freedom curtailed by the regulations, but his newspaper had been singled out for discriminatory treatment. The larger deposit required of tabloids, Fernández de los Ríos argued, was aimed at *Las Novedades* and constituted a reprisal for its opposition to Bravo Murillo.

On December 14, 1852, Bravo Murillo resigned "after almost two years of the sharpest repression of liberty." [22] He was followed by two short-lived governments, which lasted only until mid-September. Alejandro Llorente, a former newspaperman who served as Minister of the Interior in the first of those governments, relaxed press controls by reaffirming the provisions of laws antedating

---

[17] William C. Atkinson, *A History of Spain and Portugal* (London, 1960), p. 285.
[18] *Real decreto del 2 de abril de 1852, Artículo 23.*
[19] *Ibid., Artículo 13.*
[20] *Ibid., Artículo 19.*
[21] *Ibid., Artículo 24.*
[22] Joseph A. Brandt, *Toward the New Spain* (Chicago, 1933), p. 45.

Bravo Murillo and reestablishing print tribunals.[23] Within six weeks, however, he was faced with the problem of a careless, if not a hostile, press. Llorente, instead of turning to the traditional solution of controls, chose to try cooperation as a means of correcting what he considered to be errors of the press. On February 19, he set up a system of "handouts," ordering heads of the legislative bodies to furnish copies of proceedings to newspapers in the hope that such aid would end "the adulteration of the extracts of the sessions [of the Cortes] which the periodicals publish." [24]

On September 19, the Conde de San Luis, onetime director of *El Heraldo*, formed a government which was marked by a succession of financial scandals, many stemming from the shady operations of the Marqués de Salamanca. The press, in general, was quick to air the scandals, but the most vituperative attacks appeared in the clandestine newspaper *El Murciélago*,[25] which dedicated much of its space to calling attention to what it termed the debasement in economic life. It regularly published fictitious but pointed advertisements suggesting corruption within the government. "Any person desiring an office call at the Office of Public Works, where Don Juan Pérez Galvo will attend him," one read, adding, "The money must be paid beforehand." Another said, "War Department—Employment, grades, crosses, honors. Apply to Don Saturnino Parra, Commissioner of the Sub-Secretary of War, to treat of their price." [26]

Early in his period of office, San Luis moved to consolidate his position by exiling or deporting potential competitors for the royal favor, thus limiting the number of those upon whom Isabel could call in an emergency. Among those sent away from the court were the former minister, González Bravo; General Serrano; and General Leopoldo O'Donnell, the founder of the Unión Liberal and author, in 1843, of a *pronunciamiento* against Espartero. San Luis's exercise of arbitrary powers was extended to all areas of the government and included the press. His repressions were hateful to many Spaniards and, in February of 1854, led to scattered revolts. By early summer the whole country was in a state of unrest. On June 28, a group of army officers, led by O'Donnell, sent the Queen a letter in which

---

[23] *Ley de 2 de enero de 1853.*
[24] *Decreto del 19 de febrero de 1853.*
[25] *El Murciélago* ("The Bat") (Madrid, 1853-54).
[26] Quoted by Brandt, *New Spain*, p. 45.

they called for governmental reform, charging that the conduct of the government was contrary to the dictates "of morality and the spirit of justice. . . ." Among the specific areas of reform dealt with in the letter was that of government-press relations. The press, the letter said, is "the institution charged with discussing administrative acts and spreading enlightenment among all classes, yet it is now enchained and . . . must be liberated." [27] On July 7, O'Donnell issued a manifesto which outlined the aims set down in the letter to the Queen. The manifesto was the spark needed to ignite public feeling. The Progresistas rallied to O'Donnell's banner. Mobs formed in the streets of Madrid, chanting against the government, setting fires in key government buildings, breaking into the homes of San Luis and Salamanca, and wrecking María Cristina's palace. The Queen Mother went into exile and, on July 18, San Luis resigned. The same day the Duque de Rivas was named to head a government. His Minister of the Interior, Antonio de los Ríos y Rosas, a former newspaperman,[28] immediately acted to restrain the press, issuing a proclamation reestablishing the law of July 6, 1845. However, the life of the Rivas government was short, measured almost in hours. When he resigned, Isabel once again called on Espartero.

Espartero's government relaxed press restrictions by restoring the freedom granted under the Constitution of 1837. On August 18, Espartero's Minister of the Interior, Francisco Santa Cruz, ordered the remission of all fines imposed by Bravo Murillo's government, except those stemming from the crimes of calumny and personal injury. The reforms stimulated the growth of the press. Eighty-two periodicals were founded in Madrid during the year, nearly seventy after Espartero's return to the position of President of the Council of Ministers. One newspaper even called itself after him—El Esparterista,[29] which failed to last out the year. At one point, there was a daily or weekly for every 4,200 inhabitants of Madrid, while in the provinces the ratio was one paper per 260,000 Spaniards. The major newspaper founded during the year was the Progresista daily

---

[27] Fernando Díaz-Plaja, La Historia de España en sus Documentos (Madrid, 1954), I, 289–290.
[28] Ríos y Rosas had begun his career as an editor of La Abeja in 1835, worked on El Correo Nacional until 1842 when he shifted to El Español, then founded El Sol, which he ran until April of 1843, when he joined the staff of El Heraldo.
[29] El Esparterista (Madrid, 1854).

La Iberia, diario liberal,[30] destined to be, until the end of the century, one of the more influential publications in Spain. Among its early directors was Práxedes Mateo Sagasta, who later held a series of major government posts, including the presidency of the Cortes and of the Council of Ministers.

On September 5, Santa Cruz sent an order to provincial governors explaining the official view of the proper relationship between government and press.

The freedom to print and publish ideas, guaranteed to all Spaniards by the State's Constitution, must not be interpreted in such a way that some consider themselves authorized to ignore the laws which govern them; laws which try not only to avoid having the Press abuse its sacred role, converting liberty to license, but also to prevent those who govern from unfavorably interpreting principles in the case of the absence of regulatory dispositions and placing unjust obstacles in the path of citizens who want to exercise such an important right. The laws, therefore, constitute a reciprocal guarantee for the Press in its dealings with those in Power, and for those in Power in their dealings with the Press, to the end that both act within the spheres of their respective rights.[31]

On November 8, 1854, the Cortes met to begin consideration of a new constitution—one designed to permit the existence of religions other than the Catholic, abolish the death penalty, restore freedom of the press, and curb the power of the government to levy taxes not specified by law. However, the document and the deputies drawing it up were too modern and too liberal for the traditional monarchists and the moderates. In June, 1856, nevertheless, the Cortes finally approved the constitution. Almost at once, Espartero was maneuvered out of power by O'Donnell, who was asked to form a government. Despite its leader's early involvement with liberalism, O'Donnell's government was reactionary. In September, he threw out the new constitution and reestablished that of 1845 in slightly modified form, thus undoing the work his revolution had begun. On October 12, O'Donnell, in turn, was maneuvered out of office and Narváez recalled to the prime ministerial post.

Among the men Narváez appointed to his Council of Ministers was Cándido Nocedal, an ultra-reactionary named to the post of Minister of the Interior. Within three weeks, Nocedal acted against the press, reestablishing the laws of July 6, 1845, and April 9, 1844,

---

[30] *La Iberia* . . . ("Iberia, a liberal daily") (Madrid, 1854-98).
[31] *Circular de Ministro de la Gobernación de 5 de septiembre de 1854*, quoted by Gómez Aparicio, "Historia del periodismo," *GPE*, Sept. 15, 1965, p. 15.

both of which restricted its freedom.[32] On November 8, he ordered provincial governments to exercise the "greatest vigilance in the enforcing and observing of the laws." [33] However, the results of those measures did not satisfy the new Minister of the Interior who told newsmen that it would be "necessary to tighten even more the screws of the law." [34] He did so the following year in a short, clear, and expressive law which, among other things, gave provincial or local authorities the right "to suspend of their own volition or at the petition of the print judge, the sale and distribution of all printed matter which attacks religion or existing institutions." Two courses were left open to the editor of a suspended newspaper, neither very palatable. He had forty-eight hours in which to decide whether to accept without protest the suspension or appeal against it and face a trial for print crimes.[35] The law also raised the amount of the deposit to 300,000 *reales* in Madrid and 200,000 elsewhere and ordered that every newspaper have a director as well as a responsible editor.

The result was satisfactory from Nocedal's viewpoint. It became "practically impossible for the press to print any political commentary or even news that might be considered slightly tendentious." [36] Perhaps, in a sense, it was just as well. A newspaperman of the period describes the mass of the Spanish people as "indifferent to the question of which party ruled the country . . . ," but concerned about the future direction of the nation.[37] Nocedal's repressive measures stimulated discussion along those lines. The virtual ban on the press's political activity forced individual energies into different channels: the political journalists substituted discussion of party policy and philosophy for the traditional attacks on the government.[38] This was especially true of the liberal journals, where for nine years the two main democratic groups debated their differences in print or criticized the ideas of the Progresistas and

---

[32] *Decreto del Ministerio de Gobernación del 2 de noviembre de 1856.*
[33] José Eugenio de Eguizábal, *Apuntes para una historia de la legislación española sobre la imprenta desde el año de 1480 al presente* (Madrid, 1879), p. 212.
[34] *Ibid.,* p. 213.
[35] *Ley de 13 de julio de 1857, Artículo 4.*
[36] Antonio Espina, *El Cuarto Poder* (Madrid, 1960), p. 43.
[37] Juan Mañé y Flaquer, *Diario de Barcelona: Apuntes históricos,* quoted by Esteban Molist Pol, *El "Diario de Barcelona": 1792-1963* (Madrid, 1964), pp. 123-124.
[38] C. A. M. Hennessy, *The Federal Republic in Spain: Pí y Margall and the Federal Republican Movement, 1868-1874* (Oxford, 1962), p. 15.

moderates. The most influential organ was La Discusión,[39] founded in 1856 by Nicolás María Rivero, a deputy and disaffected Progresista, who had founded the Democratic party in 1849. Among his editors were Emilio Castelar, a history professor and the outstanding political orator of Spain, who was to become head of the government in 1873, and Francisco Pí y Margall, later to be the nation's first socialist premier. Pí y Margall's career on La Discusión did not start auspiciously. Within a few months of joining the staff as assistant editor, he published an article attacking the Progresista demands for further disentailing Church property which, it was claimed, would stem the growing pauperization of the country. Pí y Margall argued that disentailment had led to concentration of property in the hands of a rentier class which exploited workers. He called for a redistribution of large estates.[40] As a result of the article, La Discusión was fined 10,000 reales for "advocating a new agrarian law." [41] Despite the fine and a widening schism with Rivero caused by diverging views, Pí y Margall continued on the staff of La Discusión and, after Rivero's death, was named its director.

Meanwhile, Castelar, who had worked briefly on El Eco universitario [42] before joining La Discusión, published his La Fórmula del Progreso ("The Formula for Progress"), the credo of Spanish republicanism and a detailed theory of the rights and duties entailed by citizenship. Among the twenty propositions set down in La Fórmula is that of "freedom of the press," a cornerstone, in theory though not always in practice, of Spanish republicanism. Eventually, the democratic philosophies of Castelar and Pí y Margall became so distinct—Pí y Margall moving more and more toward socialism— that Castelar left La Discusión and founded his own newspaper, La Democracia,[43] which he used as a forum for a series of sharp, bitter debates with Pí y Margall. Castelar defined the goals of his periodical in its prospectus as opposition to both the dynasty and socialism.

Not all debates, however, were confined to the columns of a newspaper; some ended on the field of honor. During the regency of María Cristina, Luis González Bravo, editor of El Guirigay, and Andrés Borrego, director of El Español, had sought to settle a pro-

---

[39] La Discusión ("The Discussion") (Madrid, 1856-66, 1868-74, 1879-81).
[40] La Discusión (Madrid), July 21, 1857.
[41] Ibid., Aug. 21, 1857.
[42] El Eco universitario ("The Echo of the university") (Madrid, 1851).
[43] La Democracia ("Democracy") (Madrid, 1864-66).

fessional disagreement with pistols. Their duel was called off and honor deemed satisfied when it was discovered that their weapons would not discharge. By 1859, the practice of settling professional disputes with swords or pistols had become so widespread that Madrid newspapermen banded together to create a Tribunal of the Press which was to be a forum for the airing of grievances. For a short time, the Tribunal appeared successful in its attempts to settle "affairs of honor" without bloodshed. However, it ceased to function when two of its members—Felipe Picón, an editor of *El Clamor Público*, and Cipriano de Mazo, director of *El Occidente* [44]—retired from the bench to the field of honor to seek agreement on a case.

Meanwhile, in 1858, Narváez was eased out of the government and O'Donnell once again called upon to form a cabinet. He named José Posada Herrera to the Ministry of the Interior, and though the new Minister made no changes in Nocedal's laws, he did permit some relaxation in the controls exercised over the press.

The straitjacketing regulations between 1856 and the end of the decade had not only muzzled newspapers but also forced some out of business and discouraged the founding of new ones. In 1855, the year in which Espartero had taken over the reins of the government and revoked San Luis's regulations, the number of periodicals in Madrid rose to 151. However, during the regimes of Narváez and O'Donnell it dropped—to 135 in 1856, 128 in 1857, 126 in 1858, and 125 in 1859. The quality of the news coverage suffered also, discouraged by the danger of government sanctions inherent in the publication of anything resembling political news. The repercussions were less strong in the provinces, especially in and around Barcelona. There, "hard news" coverage improved. The introduction of the telegraph, which reached Barcelona before it was extended to Madrid, made possible more detailed reporting of international events. The province's location, on the sea and near the French border, contributed to more emphasis on foreign news and less on political activity. The newspapers were remote from Madrid and, therefore, less subject to strict enforcement of regulations emanating from the capital.[45]

The decade between 1860 and 1870 was marked by the development of a peculiarly Spanish journalistic medium—the periodical

[44] *El Occidente* ("The Occident") (Madrid, 1855-60).
[45] Espina, *Cuarto Poder*, pp. 83-85.

devoted mainly to the bullfight. The first taurine publication, *El Enano*,[46] had been founded in 1851 as a literary weekly, but gradually its emphasis shifted to bullfighting and reports on local and national lotteries. In 1858, it changed its name to the *Boletín de Loterías y de Toros* and, as such, continued until late in the century. In 1861, *Látigo, revista taurómaco*,[47] the first periodical devoted exclusively to the "national fiesta," appeared. It was followed by at least four other similar publications during the next eight years.

O'Donnell's ministry lasted until 1863. In 1859, determined to end Moorish aggression against Spain's African provinces, he personally led a force from Ceuta to Tetuán. The campaign, which cost 7,000 Spanish lives, resulted in no major victory and was cut short by the outbreak of a brief Carlist rebellion on the mainland. O'Donnell's success in damping the Carlist menace, coupled with the drama of his march into Africa, made his popularity soar at home. In 1861, nourishing the hope of restoring Spanish rule in Mexico, he joined France and England in operations aimed at forcing the government of Benito Pablo Juárez to live up to its international financial obligations.[48] General Juan Prim y Prats, against his will, was named commander of the Spanish forces. When Louis Napoleon made clear his determination to flout the Monroe Doctrine and establish Maximilian of Austria on a Mexican throne, Prim withdrew his forces without consulting Madrid. O'Donnell raged. The press had a field day. Typical of the reaction was that of the newspaper *El Contemporáneo* [49] which suggested that Prim was guilty of either "Rebellion," "Insubordination," "Desertion," "Treason," or, perhaps, of all four crimes, and called for imposition of the maximum penalties "under at least two of the existing codes: that of honor and that of military justice." [50] However, by the time Prim returned to Madrid, months later, opinion had done an about-face, and he was hailed as a hero.

Meanwhile, O'Donnell's popularity at home was fading. Ferocious suppression of an agrarian revolt in southern Spain and one-party politics had wiped away any aura of liberalism that might have surrounded him. In early 1863, he named a civilian to the Ministry

---

[46] *El Enano* ("The Dwarf") (Madrid, 1851-58).
[47] *Látigo* ... ("The Whip, a taurine review") (Madrid, 1861).
[48] Atkinson, *A History of Spain and Portugal*, pp. 288–289.
[49] *El Contemporáneo* ("The Contemporary") (Madrid, 1861-65).
[50] Quoted by Espina, *Cuarto Poder*, p. 36.

of the Navy, causing a revolt among naval officers. That act was the final blow, and he was forced to resign. The Marqués de Miraflores, who had begun his public career as an editor of the liberal *Redactor general de España*,[51] succeeded him. Miraflores' ministry lasted from March 3, 1863, to January 17, 1864. Two short-lived governments followed him—that of Federico Arrazola, which survived barely six weeks, and one led by the moderate, Alejandro Mon, like many of his predecessors, a newspaperman.[52] During Mon's tenure, the press controls were relaxed. On June 22, a new law was passed. Its first article specified that the 1857 law be modified to permit political reporting and writing.[53] The law also reduced by two-thirds the amount of deposit required of newspapers. But it did one disservice to the cause of press freedom. Article 54 of the law specified that authors of "writings which tend to relax the faithfulness or discipline of the armed forces" should be tried by military tribunals. That was interpreted to mean any writer, military or civilian.[54] However, José Eugenio de Eguizábal, a nineteenth-century expert on press law, suggests that it was intended to apply only to military personnel who wrote as a sideline.[55]

The relaxation of controls had the expected effects: the press resumed its political activity and increased in number. In 1860, the Madrid newspaper census had grown to 153. During the next two years, that rose to 156. But, in 1863, with the ousting of O'Donnell from power, the number soared to 189. In 1864, the year that Mon gave the press new, liberalized regulations, Madrid claimed 198 periodicals.

On September 16, Narváez was appointed to succeed Mon. Five days after he formed a cabinet, the government issued a proclama-

---

[51] *Redactor general de España* ("Editor-general of Spain") (Madrid, 1813-14 and 1821).
[52] Mon had helped edit the moderate *El Faro* in 1847 and 1848, and had worked on *La Estrella*, also moderate, between 1854 and 1857.
[53] *Artículo 4* of the *Ley de 13 de julio de 1857* had provided that "provincial or local authorities shall suspend of their own volition, or at the petition of the print judge, the sale and distribution of all printed matter which attacks religion or existing institutions." *Artículo 1* of the new law, *Ley de 22 de junio de 1864*, stated, "To the 4th Article of the Law of July 13, 1857, shall be added, 'One cannot apply the disposition of this article to the political press.'"
[54] It was still so interpreted in 1965. See Chapter III for a report on the trial of a civilian editor by a military tribunal.
[55] *Historia de la legislación*, p. 223.

tion granting amnesty to all newsmen being punished at the time for print crimes.[56] It was, according to Eguizábal, a move engineered by Narváez "to attract the sympathy of the press." [57]

Regardless of the effect of the amnesty on the press in general, it failed to sway Castelar from his unabating militancy in the cause of democracy. On September 29, Spain observed the thirty-first anniversary of the death of Queen Isabel's father, Ferdinand VII. Hardly had the solemn observances ended when Castelar's *La Democracia* appeared with an editorial which stated: "Thirty-one years ago, an evil king died, a king who has stained our history and debased our politics. All these years, servile adulation has never ceased. The places, where one should hear only the voice of justice, overflow with flowers to his depraved memory, as if the incense of adulation could destroy the stench which his loathsome tyranny always exhales." [58] The government was reluctant to take action, and Castelar continued his attacks on the dead monarch in a series of articles on various fallen dynasties, articles which contained veiled references to the future fate of the Bourbons.

Meanwhile, the government, faced with a multimillion *peseta* deficit for the coming fiscal year, was searching intently for means of increasing the national income. Narváez conceived the idea of having the Queen turn over 25 per cent of the vast royal estates to the government for public sale. The gift, Narváez argued, would help the country economically and, at the same time, constitute a public relations coup, restoring popularity to the royal family. The announcement of the gift, on February 20, 1865, was welcomed by spontaneous demonstrations, the people dancing and singing in the streets. The Cortes voted its gratitude. González Bravo, Minister of the Interior, telegraphed the "happy news" to provincial capitals. The regime's joy was to be short-lived. The following day, Castelar examined the "gift" in the columns of *La Democracia*. "We cannot understand," he wrote, "how it can be said at this moment that the Queen so generously gives to the country its own birthright. That is not so. The Royal house returns to the country property which belongs to the country and which it claims only because of the dis-

---

[56] *Real decreto del 21 de septiembre de 1864.*
[57] *Historia de la legislación*, p. 225.
[58] *La Democracia* (Madrid), Sept. 29, 1864, quoted by Brandt, *New Spain*, p. 77.

orders of these times and the negligence of the Governments and the Cortes." [59]

Four days later—on Saturday, February 25—Castelar again attacked Isabel's "gift." With an article entitled "El Rasgo" ("The Magnanimous Gesture"), Castelar "completely destroyed the good effect of the Queen's action and left the position of the throne more critical than before." [60] In it, Castelar summed up the Queen's gesture as "no more than an act of insolence against the laws." [61] He went on to argue that the gesture's warm reception had been based on a deliberate obfuscation of the fact—the suggestion that the sale of crown property would obviate special taxes, which in reality would still be necessary to make up the budgetary deficit.

The government could no longer remain silent. The issue of *La Democracia* containing "El Rasgo" was denounced in court and withdrawn from circulation. Government officials stormed through the office, and, according to the newspaper's own account, "all copies in the office or intended for delivery in the provinces were seized, destroyed or thrown about so that no whole column was left nor any section that had not been handled by our enemies." [62]

In spite of the protests of the authorities of the University of Madrid, Castelar was suspended from his post as professor of history. The University's Rector, Manuel Montalván, who had refused to take action against Castelar, was ousted from his job. Early in April, a new rector was appointed, and students requested permission to serenade Montalván, a traditional salute to retiring university officials. The request was granted, then withdrawn. On April 8, groups of students expressed their dissatisfaction by insulting Civil Guards stationed near the university. On April 10, the day the new rector took office, the student demonstration turned into a mutiny. Narváez ordered extra police units into the downtown area, attracting large crowds of curious *Madrileños*. As evening came, a group of workers began stoning the mounted police, who countered with their weapons. Before the crowd was dispersed and order restored, eight persons had been killed.

---

[59] *La Democracia* (Madrid), Feb. 21, 1865, quoted by José Montero Alonso, " 'El Rasgo' de Emilio Castelar," *Gaceta de la Prensa Española*, Nov. 15, 1964, p. 15.
[60] Brandt, *New Spain*, p. 80.
[61] "El Rasgo," *La Democracia* (Madrid), Feb. 25, 1865.
[62] *La Democracia* (Madrid), Feb. 26, 1865.

The following day, the cabinet met in extraordinary session and confirmed Castelar's dismissal. During the meeting, Antonio Alcalá Galiano, the Minister of National Development who had begun his public career as an editor of the liberal *Redactor general de España* in 1821, collapsed and died.

Castelar's dismissal did the government no good. "El Rasgo" had established its author as a national hero, and his dismissal helped undermine Narváez's government, which fell on June 21. Narváez turned over the reins to O'Donnell, but not before decreeing one final law aimed at limiting the influence of the press—a law prohibiting members of the military establishment from subscribing to and reading newspapers.[63]

Within days of taking office, O'Donnell acted to placate the opposition. On July 21, he stole a page from Narváez's book and decreed an amnesty for all persons convicted of press crimes. He also restored both Castelar and Montalván to their university posts. Castelar may have been grateful, but he was not at all subdued. In November, the Democrats held a party meeting in Madrid at which Castelar, one of the speakers, went into great detail to blame the repression of liberty in Spain on the monarchy. The next month, when the Queen returned to Madrid after an extended absence from the capital, she was greeted with silence, a complete absence of the acclaim customary in such cases. Castelar's *La Democracia* noted the lack of welcome and concluded by quoting Mirabeau: "The silence of the people is a great lesson for kings." [64] The paper was denounced, found guilty, and suspended from January 13, 1866, until March 18 of the same year. During the suspension, the government issued a new press law which prohibited a responsible editor from continuing in that capacity "from the moment he is sentenced for any crime against Religion, the Monarchs, or the Royal Family." [65]

Early in May, O'Donnell moved to muzzle criticism of his government by signing a law which made it a crime "to injure in print" any member of the legislative corps. The maximum punishment was to be a short prison sentence and a fine of no more than 1,000 *pesetas*.[66] A second, more serious crime, was the "grave injury" or

[63] Eguizábal, *Historia de la legislación*, p. 233.
[64] Brandt, *New Spain*, p. 83.
[65] *Ley de 6 de marzo de 1866, Artículo 1.*
[66] *Ley de 6 de mayo de 1866, Artículo 2.*

"calumny" of a senator or deputy, which was punishable under the provisions of the regular penal code and therefore subjected those found guilty to a much longer prison term.[67]

Meanwhile, a coalition of Progresistas and Democrats had lent their support to an uprising planned by General Prim, who, in early 1866, made a series of unsuccessful pronunciamentos. On June 22, army noncommissioned officers, recruited to the cause of rebellion by the progressives, revolted in Madrid. The uprising failed because of indecision and the internal rivalry so characteristic of Spanish conspiracies. Sixty-eight of its leaders were executed and nearly 2,000 of its top supporters fled into exile, among them Castelar, Pí y Margall, and Sagasta. On July 10, the Queen recalled Narváez from his army post and asked him to form a government. He did so, naming González Bravo to a key position within his cabinet. The two then proceeded to govern by decree until early the following year when they summoned the Cortes into session. The opposition group in the parliament was so weakened by the absence of its key leaders, still in exile, that Narváez's program met little resistance. Among the measures introduced and passed were reforms in administration and finance and a new press law, which revised and consolidated controls.

The new law reaffirmed the principle of previous censorship, ordering that two copies of any newspaper had to be submitted to the proper authorities in Madrid and to provincial governors and town mayors elsewhere two hours before distribution was begun. The governor or mayor had the right to prohibit the sale of any publication which contained "ideas, doctrines, accounts of events, or news offensive to the Catholic Religion, the Monarch, the Constitution, members of the Royal Family, the Senate, the Chamber of Deputies, Foreign Sovereigns—if in their respective countries they agree to reciprocate—and to the Authorities; also anything which tends to relax the discipline of the army, alter the public order, or which may be contrary to that which is moral and decent." [68] The law also provided that any newspaper denounced in court and found guilty of press crimes three times would be "definitively suppressed." [69] Not all the provisions were repressive, however. Both Narváez and González Bravo recognized the need

---

[67] *Ibid., Artículo 3.*
[68] *Ley de 7 de marzo de 1867, Artículo 7.*
[69] *Ibid., Artículo 30.*

for reform to still criticism of the government. Thus, one article stated that "decorous and non-calumnious writings which censure the official conduct of public figures are not crimes. Nor is it a crime to reveal in print information about a conspiracy against the security of the State or any plot against public order." [70]

On March 16, nine days after the promulgation of the new press laws, Eduardo Gasset y Artime began publishing *El Imparcial*,[71] one of the best newspapers in the history of the Spanish press. Gasset y Artime aimed at making his new daily a blend of political organ, devoted to the service of all liberals, and straight newspaper —and he succeeded.

Toward the end of that year, O'Donnell, one of the props of Isabel's regime, died. On April 23, 1868, Narváez, the other major prop, also died. González Bravo was named President of the Ministry. His appointment intensified the mood of dissatisfaction and unrest that pervaded the nation. Press censorship became stricter, increasing the restive feeling. In July, the Progresista daily, *La Iberia*, which had changed its name on January 2, 1868, to *La Nueva Iberia, diario liberal*,[72] defied the censors and called on the Unión Liberal to join in a revolution. "In the face of reactionary forces," the paper said, "the liberal army must be able to form itself without excluding anyone, without rancor and with the noble goal of making greatest efforts and sacrifices for the fatherland." [73]

While the Progresista newspapers in Spain cast themselves in the role of editorial shock troops, exiled liberal leaders were hammering out interparty agreement on the form of the new regime toward which the country was heading. In August, they met in Ostend and decided on the ground rules that would regulate the conduct of the republic they were determined to establish. Early in September, Prim stole back into Spain and, on the eighteenth, made his presence known with a revolutionary manifesto, issued aboard the flagship of the Spanish navy, anchored in the harbor at Cádiz.

The revolution spread rapidly. On September 30, the *Gaceta de Madrid* published a proclamation directed "To the Revolutionary Juntas of all the capital cities," which said, "The people of Madrid

---

[70] *Ibid., Artículo 27.*
[71] *El Imparcial* ("The Impartial") (Madrid, 1867–1933).
[72] *La Nueva Iberia* . . . ("The New Iberia, a liberal daily") (Madrid, 1854–98).
[73] *La Nueva Iberia* (Madrid), July 3, 1868.

have just given the holy cry of 'Liberty and Down with the Bourbons.' The army is unanimously with the people."[74] Queen Isabel received word of Madrid's pronunciamento in favor of the revolution in San Sebastián, and she crossed over into France. On October 3, General Serrano entered Madrid; Prim followed in four days; a provisional government was set up. The monarchy had been succeeded by a hierarchy of generals and newsmen.

---

[74] *Gaceta de Madrid*, Sept. 30, 1868.

CHAPTER TEN

The Federal Republic and Restoration

The events of September and October, 1868, constitute a turning point in the history of Spain and of its press. They offered to the men responsible for them a fresh start, the chance to build a political-social edifice free from the traditions imposed by the presence of hereditary monarchs. They also suggest a natural pause for a brief backward glance over the turbulent years leading up to them.

In 1810, even before a constitution had been drawn up for the nation, the press was granted complete freedom, a condition compatible with the liberal beliefs of the men to whom the Napoleonic invasion and occupation had given an opportunity to rechannel the national political tradition. That freedom was short-lived. In 1814, Ferdinand repudiated the constitutional form of government and restored his own absolute rule. The transition was violent, an abrupt reversal of the position of the press. Almost overnight, the press pendulum had swung from unrestricted freedom to rigorous control. During the next fifty years, similar swings followed every change of government, liberal administrations permitting the press to operate freely, authoritarian regimes imposing controls. As has been suggested, the periods of freedom gave birth to gross irresponsibility in at least a segment of the press—the most vocal, controversial, and tendentious segment, which was the political press. Quantitatively, it was not the largest group of newspapers—there were more literary, artistic, economic, and scientific periodicals than political newspapers—but it was the segment which attracted the attention of those in power or those who aspired to power. The political press made the most "noise," and the noise it made was the raucous roar of irresponsibility.

Irresponsibility was not inherent in the Spanish press. It was propagated by the very men who made the press free, men who saw in press liberty a tool to be used in political infighting. Almost from its beginnings, the free press was associated with partisan politics, not only by the politicians who used it as an instrument, but also by the authoritarians who saw in it a concrete manifestation of the evils of liberty. The press became more than a collection of vehicles for transmitting messages about conflicting political philosophies: it became a symbol of that conflict itself, and as a symbol associated with liberalism it did disservice to the liberal cause.

During its first fifty years of intermittent freedom, the Spanish press had not achieved an existence independent of the political establishment, even though a few journalists attempted to define its role in terms of service to society, to the nation, to itself—so far as the profession's economic structure was concerned—as well as to the political establishment. It began as a political "house organ" and continued to perform that function.

Nowhere was the close relationship of the press and political system more apparent than in the composition of the provisional government set up by Serrano on October 7, 1868. As has been noted already, two paths led to the top levels of government in the nineteenth century—a military career or a journalistic one. The provisional government was headed by Serrano, a soldier. General Prim was made Minister of War and Admiral Juan Topete, Minister of the Navy. Four of the six civilians in the government had been closely identified with the practice of journalism: Sagasta, who was made Minister of the Interior; Antonio Romero Ortiz,[1] Minister of Justice; Adelardo López de Ayala,[2] Overseas Minister; and Juan Álvarez de Lorenzana,[3] Foreign Minister. Press historian

---

[1] Romero Ortiz had served as editor of La Nación between 1849 and 1856, the year in which he helped found La Peninsula, a political daily which appeared between December, 1856, and October, 1857.

[2] López de Ayala was a contributor to El Mosaico, which appeared for a few months in 1850, and served as an editor of El Padre Cobo from 1854 to 1856.

[3] Álvarez de Lorenzana worked as an editor of El Diario español between its founding in 1852 and the September Revolution.

Antonio Espina suggests that the other two men in the cabinet—Manuel Ruiz Zorilla, the Minister of Public Works; and Laureano Figuerola y Ballester, Minister of Finance—had some connection with journalism, though they were not strongly identified with the profession.[4] Nicolás María Rivero, founder of *La Discusión*, refused a cabinet post and instead was named Mayor of Madrid and head of the Madrid Revolutionary Supreme Council. He also revived his newspaper, which had ceased publication in mid-1866.

Within three weeks of its formation, the provisional government defined the position of the press. An official manifesto stated: " . . . the revolution has . . . proclaimed the freedom of the press, without which our conquests would be no more than illusory and vain formulas. The press is the lasting voice of intelligence, a voice that is never extinguished and which vibrates across time and distance. To try to enslave it is to desire the mutilation of thought and the wrenching out of the tongue of human reason." [5]

The success of the revolution and the restoration of freedom to the press caused new newspapers to appear at the fastest clip in Spanish history. Between October 1 and the end of December, 1868, ninety new periodicals were founded in Madrid alone, one a day. An additional 245 periodicals appeared in the next two years.[6] Not all survived—in fact, many failed after a month or two—but enough managed to achieve a precarious existence so that, during 1870, Madrid had 302 newspapers and magazines.[7] The national total topped 500 in that year and by 1875 had reached 596.[8]

On February 11, 1869, a constituent Cortes assembled in Madrid. After four months of debate, a new constitution was promulgated—a constitution which provided for freedom of religion and press liberty. "No Spaniard," the document stated, "can be deprived of the right to utter freely his ideas and opinions, both in speech and in writing, making use of printing or other similar processes." [9] The assembly also declared for a monarchial form of government, in which the ruler's powers would be limited to the selection of a prime minister and the right of veto.

---

[4] *El Cuarto Poder* (Madrid, 1960), p. 103.
[5] *Gaceta de Madrid*, Oct. 26, 1868.
[6] Julio Merino González, "Biografía de un periódico de 1870," *Gaceta de la Prensa Española*, June 15, 1964, p. 90.
[7] Eugenio Hartzenbusch é Hiríart, *Apuntes para un Catálogo de periódicos madrileños desde el año 1661 al 1870* (Madrid, 1894), pp. 359–362.
[8] Espina, *Cuarto Poder*, p. 130.
[9] *Constitución de 1869, Artículo 17.*

Though there was a majority agreement on the form of government, there was none on the question of who should be made king. The Unión Liberal favored the Duke of Montpensier, the brother-in-law of Isabel. The Progresistas, on the other hand, demanded a ruling family completely free from attachments to the Bourbons. Despite the opposition, Montpensier surveyed the situation and decided that his chances were good. He turned to the press as a means of attracting support and of countering Progresista objections. During the period of his candidature, the Duke either founded or subsidized fourteen dailies and six weeklies in Madrid, all of which vociferously defended his claim to the throne. But Montpensier was to have no chance to measure the success of his campaign of press propaganda. He challenged a political opponent, the Duque de Sevilla, to a duel and killed him. Montpensier was punished by banishment. Spain continued its search for a king, General Prim noting that "finding a democratic king in Europe is like looking for an atheist in Heaven." [10] Finally, Prim offered the crown to General Espartero, hero of the Carlist wars and frequent Prime Minister. Obviously moved, Espartero considered the offer, then refused because "my age and poor health would not permit me to do a good job." [11] The next candidate to be considered was Luis, King of Portugal, who refused, at least partly as a result of a British hint that a fusion of the two crowns would be frowned upon. Feelers went out to Luis's father, Ferdinand, who expressed interest, then withdrew under pressure from the Portuguese people who saw in the situation a potential threat to their independence. The throne was next offered to the most acceptable of the German possibilities, Leopold of Hohenzollern-Sigmaringen. The consequences were disastrous, for Leopold's readiness to accept touched off the Franco-Prussian War.

The search for a ruler ended at long last with Amadeo of Savoy, second son of Victor Emmanuel and brother of the Queen of Portugal. When Amadeo indicated his willingness to accept, a vote of approval was scheduled in the Cortes. On November 9, 1870, four days before the vote was to be taken, the Republican newspaper *El Combate*,[12] which had been founded on November 1,

---

[10] William C. Atkinson, *A History of Spain and Portugal* (London, 1960), p. 300.
[11] Fernando Diaz-Plaja, *La Historia de España en sus Documentos* (Madrid, 1954), I, 352.
[12] *El Combate* ("Combat") (Madrid, 1870).

charged that the Cortes was usurping the right of the Spanish people to participate directly in the selection of their own ruler or rulers. Despite that objection, only one in a crescendo of protests, the Cortes met on November 13, and Amadeo's candidacy received 191 votes from a total of 311. The following day, *El Combate*'s editor, José Paúl y Angulo, promised that force would be used to meet force [13] and turned his editorial guns on Prim, a traitor to the Republican cause in the editor's opinion. Early the following month, *El Combate* declared that "history reserves a horrible and shameful page for General Prim," and charged that the 191 deputies who voted for Amadeo were traitors. On December 16, its pages resounded with the call, "Down with Prim y Prats and his blackguard."[14] On December 23, Paúl y Angulo wrote *El Combate* out of business. "When violence and force are the sole arms of a usurping government," his lead editorial said, "the defenders of the rights of men and of the basic liberties must exchange the pen for the gun. . . . To Combat! Down with everything! Long live the national sovereignty! Long live the revolution!" [15] The government acted, closing down the paper. On December 27, as Prim was leaving the *Cortes*, three men shoved guns through the windows of his carriage and shot him in the chest and shoulders. On December 30, two days before the scheduled arrival of Amadeo, Prim died. Public opinion immediately linked Paúl y Angulo with the crime, though according to the majority of contemporary accounts there was little or no evidence to incriminate the editor of *El Combate*.[16] However, his editorials may well have influenced the assassins. Paúl y Angulo went into hiding, then fled from Spain. After wandering across North and South America, he returned to Europe and died in Paris in 1892.

---

[13] *El Combate* (Madrid), Nov. 14, 1870.
[14] Quoted by Joseph A. Brandt, *Toward the New Spain* (Chicago, 1933), p. 148.
[15] Quoted by Hartzenbusch, *Periódicos madrileños*, p. 297.
[16] Historians Juan Valera, Andrés Borrego, and Antonio Pirala, writing not long after the event, sum up the question of Paúl y Angulo's guilt by stating, "We cannot be sure." See Modesto Lafuente y Zamolloa, *Historia general de España* (Barcelona, 1890), XXIV, 70. Harold Livermore notes in *A History of Spain* (New York, 1960), p. 389, that "no one was clearly incriminated, although a dossier of 18,000 pages, a monument of Spanish encylopaedism, was compiled." Espina writes that "there were many and terrible suggestions of guilt: his fierce hatred of the general, his threats, his campaigns in *El Combate*. . . . But his guilt is not certain. He hid, but the police did not look for him." See *El Cuarto Poder*, p. 152.

On January 1, 1871, Amadeo landed in Spain. His reign lasted just two years. It might have endured longer had Prim lived; his death removed a staunch support upon which the new King might have leaned. Few newspapers in Spain supported the Italian who had been elected King. Only one major daily, *El Imparcial*, backed Amadeo. Yet, despite its reflection of a minority opinion, *El Imparcial*'s moderation in editorials, accuracy in reporting, and perception in commentary made it extremely popular in Madrid. During Amadeo's reign, its circulation mounted to 20,000 per day, the largest of any Spanish daily.

Though Amadeo believed firmly in the idea of a constitutional monarchy and was dedicated to serving his adopted country to the best of his ability, he was unable to reconcile the divergent political views traditional to the nation. The effort, added to the disdain and even open hostility with which he was received, eventually disillusioned him, and, on February 11, 1873, he renounced the throne. "I am convinced," he wrote, "that my efforts are sterile and my ambitions [for Spain] cannot be realized." [17] His abdication message was read to the National Congress which listened attentively, passed a resolution thanking Amadeo for his unselfishness, and then declared itself a National Assembly and proclaimed the nation a Republic. The newspaperman Nicolás María Rivero was named President, but he refused the honor and the post was turned over to another newsman, Estanislao Figueras y Moragas,[18] head of a Republican minority group.

The new government moved quickly to reform many national institutions. The nobility was abolished, as was conscription. Child labor laws were passed. On March 7, with many major reforms already committed to paper, the Assembly authorized the extension of the telegraph system. In order to stimulate the speedy growth of telegraphic facilities, the Ministry of the Interior decreed that corporations, or individuals, could build telegraph stations in communities without such facilities. In return, the builder would be allowed to use all incoming material and originate his own messages for a minimal fee. The rights were to last for a determined period, after which the stations would be turned over to the government

---

[17] Diaz-Plaja, *España en sus Documentos*, p. 363.
[18] Figueras y Moragas worked on *La Asociación*, a daily, during part of 1856, then joined the staff of Rivero's *La Discusión*. In 1868, he was named one of the directors of *La Igualidad*, a democratic Republican daily.

for incorporation into the national system. It was a boon to the press, stimulating, as it did, the use of foreign news. Among the first to recognize the possibilities inherent in the situation was Nilo María Fabra, a newspaperman from Valencia who had just formed his own agency, Agencia Fabra, which was designed to supply provincial newspapers with news from Madrid. Moving with speed and secrecy, Fabra built a telegraph station in a village near Madrid and installed a correspondent in Irún, on the French border. Each day, his correspondent would collect news arriving from abroad and telegraph it to Fabra, who, in turn, peddled it to Madrid newspapers and distributed it to his provincial clients.

Meanwhile, the specter of civil disturbances and rebellion confronted the new government. The Republic had been born in the fusion of the two chambers, which was unconstitutional. The proclamation of the Republic, therefore, was a revolutionary act, its critics argued.[19] In many areas, provincial *juntas* were organized, *juntas* which acted on their own to abolish taxation and the right of the individual to own property. The *juntas* pointedly ignored orders from Pí y Margall, Minister of the Interior, to disband and return authority to municipal councils and provincial governments. The Carlists, who in 1872 had resorted to armed revolt in an attempt to replace Amadeo with their own claimant to the throne, continued to wage war in the north. In May, 1873, a Constituent Assembly was elected, and it officially adopted the federal form of government. Its proclamation gave impetus to the administrative disintegration of the country. Figueras stepped down as President of the Executive Power, naming Pí y Margall to follow him. Pí y Margall lasted one month, and was replaced by Nicolás Salmeron y Alonso who, in turn, was replaced by Castelar. By the year's end, the situation had so deteriorated that Castelar was forced to assume dictatorial powers. The nation was under martial law. Censorship had been imposed on the press, and Eleuterio Maisonnave, Castelar's Minister of the Interior, ordered the suppression of newspapers which supported the Carlists and what he termed "elements of disorder."

The Federal Republic, beset by insurmountable policy differ-

---

[19] For discussions of the illegality of the First Republic, see Brandt, *Toward the New Spain*, pp. 181-182, and C. A. M. Hennessy, *The Federal Republic in Spain: Pí y Margall and the Federal Republican Movement, 1868-1874* (Oxford, 1962), pp. 171-172.

ences within its government and the target of regional ambitions and Carlist aspirations, ended the morning of January 3, 1874, when troops under the command of General Manuel Pavía cleared the deputies from the assembly building. Pavía substituted a National Republic for the Federal Republic, and, since the army was the only effective institution left in Spain, General Serrano was named President. Meanwhile, the Bourbon monarchists waited for an opening. On December 1, Alfonso, heir to the Spanish throne and a cadet at Sandhurst, issued a proclamation in which he reaffirmed the tradition of hereditary monarchy and declared that he was both a liberal and a devout Catholic. On December 29, General Arsenio Martínez Campos, Captain General of Catalonia, pronounced for Alfonso. The following day, the government turned over its powers to General Fernando Primo de Rivera, Captain General of Madrid. The *Gaceta de Madrid* of the following morning, the last day of 1874, incorporated the coat of arms of the monarchy into its masthead in place of the emblem of the Republic. On January 3, Alfonso, who had been vacationing in Paris, set out for Spain. His ship—he had sailed from Marseilles—reached Barcelona late in the day. Only one newspaper reported its arrival, the *Diario de Barcelona*, which had, that day, joined the Agencia Fabra in employing messenger pigeons to carry news dispatches. The *Diario* and the Fabra Agency chartered a small boat to meet the royal frigate, and the news was flown back.[20]

A month after Alfonso's return, Spain's armies overran the Carlist capital of Estella, forcing the Carlist claimant, Don Carlos, to flee. The country settled into a period of relative calm. Alfonso found a strong aid and wise counselor in Antonio Cánovas del Castillo, a former newspaperman [21] and conservative politician, who formed the first cabinet of the Restoration. For the next twenty years, Cánovas was to alternate in power with Sagasta, who shaped the Republicans into a constructive opposition operating under the banner of liberalism.

In 1876, the last constituent Cortes of the century met to draw up the fundamental laws for the new regime. The constitution was

---

[20] Esteban Molist Pol, *El "Diario de Barcelona": 1792–1963* (Madrid, 1964), p. 110.
[21] Cánovas de Castillo had begun his public career as an editor of *La Patria*, and subsequently contributed to *El Oriente* (Madrid, 1851) and *El Murciélago* (Madrid, 1853–54).

conservative, yet conciliatory. Among other things, it provided for the right of all Spaniards "to express freely their ideas and opinions, both orally and in writing, using the press or other similar methods of dissemination without being subject to previous censorship." [22] In theory, the press was free and would remain so until the pronunciamento of Miguel Primo de Rivera in 1923. Cánovas, the dominant figure in structuring the politics of the ensuing five decades, favored a free press, at least a press that was legally defined as free. He also publicly advocated democratic political institutions, even though the constitution, at his behest, incorporated property qualifications which disenfranchised the lower classes. And, operating outside the constitution, Cánovas worked deliberately to insure that the middle classes could neither express their political opinions nor choose their candidates at elections. Underlying Cánovas' policies were two principles: exclude the military from politics and allow government by an elite. As a result, one has the anomalous situation of a "free" press, political by tradition and unfettered by legal definition, operating within a so-called democratic electoral framework so structured that there was "not a single honest or genuine election to the Cortes . . . until the disappearance of the Monarchy in 1931." [23]

The two, a free press and rigged political system, could not exist simultaneously for any length of time. Thus, despite the constitutional guarantee of free speech, government controls were imposed on the nation's periodicals. Within months of the ratification of the constitution, a Madrid newspaper reported, "In this editorial office we have not yet received a visit from a court official, but the signs are mortal. The issues of this newspaper destined for the provinces have been confiscated in the post office and those which remained in the printer's or in the hands of the vendors suffered the same fate." [24] Another newspaper, El País,[25] which had been created in 1870 as an organ for the aspirations of the Duke of Montpensier, founded a Sunday edition in Paris as an outlet for the articles which the censors would not permit to be published in Spain.

In 1883, the government reviewed existing print legislation and drew up a new "Print Law," which was to form the basis of similar

---

[22] Constitución de la Monarquía, Artículo 13.
[23] Gerald Brenan, The Spanish Labyrinth (Cambridge, 1950), p. 3.
[24] Quoted by Merino González, "Biografía," p. 90.
[25] El País ("The Nation") (Madrid, 1870–?).

legislation for the following three-quarters of a century. The law recognized the existence of graphics and included as printed matter "Drawings, lithographs, photographs, engravings, prints, vignettes, or any other reproduction of this type, when they appear alone and not in the body of another work." [26] Periodicals were defined as "all materials printed in a series and which appear under a fixed title one or more times a day, or at regular or irregular intervals not exceeding thirty days." [27] The law ordered the founders of new periodicals to present to the "highest governmental official of the locality in which they are to publish," a document which gave the name and address of the publisher; attested to his noninvolvement, past or present, in any legal proceeding which stemmed from infractions of existing print laws; and presented a detailed account of the projected periodical.[28] Anyone whose "civil or political rights" had been withdrawn or suspended because of legal proceedings, even those pending or in progress, was considered "unfit either to publish or direct a periodical." [29] The policy of having one person legally responsible for the content and orientation of a periodical was continued.[30] The director of each newspaper, the law stated, had to present three copies of each issue to the authorities as soon as it was published,[31] and publications were defined as the printing of six or more copies.[32]

The law did not provide for legal action against a periodical, only against its "responsible editor or director." In cases where the responsible person was involved in legal proceedings, the newspaper was required to replace him within four days or cease publication.[33] Such proceedings could be instituted by the authorities or by individuals to whom a newspaper denied the right of rectification, which was spelled out in the same terms as in earlier laws.[34]

In general, the period was one of apathy. The impetus that had raised Spain to the rank of a world power four centuries before had long since sputtered out. The continued clash of political ideas had failed to crystallize into reform. The nation was tired, and the press reflected the fatigue. Two decades before, the fusion of two

---

[26] Ley de Imprenta de 26 de junio de 1883, Artículo 2.
[27] Ibid., Artículo 3.   [28] Ibid., Artículo 8.
[29] Ibid., Artículo 10.   [30] Ibid., Artículo 9.
[31] Ibid., Artículo 11.   [32] Ibid., Artículo 4.
[33] Ibid., Artículo 13.   [34] Ibid., Artículos 14 and 15.

liberal splinter groups would, depending on a newspaper's affiliation, have been hailed as a giant stride forward or condemned in the blackest of terms. In the late 1870's, when the Centralistas and the Constitucionalistas announced their union, *El Diario Español*[35] summed up the event: "The marriage is, in effect, a fact, but it was carried out without any kind of ceremonies. In any case, we wish the newlyweds all kinds of happiness, but it will not matter much if they are divorced in a few days."[36]

The growth in the number of newspapers also leveled off, perhaps partly because of the general apathy, but also because of economic realities. Politics, not circulation, had supported at least a large segment of the press. A decline in interest in the activity of the political beast caused a corresponding sluggishness in the political press. There had been about 500 newspapers in the country in 1870 and there would be roughly the same number at the end of the century. They printed, in all, about one million copies, an average of 2,000 per paper.[37] Costs were increasing, but there was no concomitant increase in readership. As a result, there was a gradual shift to emphasis on the quality of the newspaper. The concepts of professionalism and of economic independence emerged.

In the period following the Restoration, Sagasta, who had fallen heir to *La Iberia* at the death of its founder, Pedro Calvo Asencio, sold out to Manuel Martínez Aguiar, a Spaniard who had lived for some years in Cuba and the United States. Martínez Aguiar, a man of wealth, set out to remodel *La Iberia* after the newspapers of the more advanced areas of the New World. He built new, luxurious offices; created congressional, senatorial, court, municipal, and bullfight reporters; set up a system of mounted couriers to speed their dispatches to the central editorial offices; and gathered together experts to report on art, literature, and politics. But his efforts failed to pay off. The public was not interested, and *La Iberia* found itself caught between increased costs resulting from Martínez Aguiar's improvements and innovations and static circulation. In 1881, the Marqués de Riscal founded *El Día*,[38] and introduced into Spain

---

[35] *El Diario Español* ("The Spanish Daily") (Madrid, 1852–1933).
[36] Quoted by Lafuente, *Historia general*, XXV, 88.
[37] Juan Beneyto, *Historia social de España y de Hispanoamérica* (Madrid, 1961), p. 404.
[38] *El Día* ("The Day") (Madrid, 1881–1919).

214) THE SPANISH PRESS

the rotary press, which he soon discovered could supply circulation appetites far larger than those of the paper's limited public. In 1885, the brothers Suárez, Agusto and Adolfo, founded *El Resumen,*[39] which attempted to gain readership by the liberal use of graphic arts, especially drawings which reproduced more clearly than the unreliable photographs of the time. *El Resumen* was welcomed with public interest while still a novelty, but gradually circulation dropped until the newspaper reached the point of bare survival.

In Barcelona, a resurgence of enthusiasm for Catalan independence or autonomy helped the press. In 1880, Valentín Almirall founded the first all Catalan-language daily, the *Diarí Catalá,*[40] and, in 1881, the Godó family started *La Vanguardia,*[41] which was begun as a small, partisan organ, favoring the policies of Sagasta. However, under the direction of Ramón Godó Lallana, who took charge in 1897 after the death of his father, the newspaper's founder, *La Vanguardia* grew into a national newspaper, a role it fills today, and pioneered in granting fringe benefits to newspaper employees— paid vacations, sickness pay, and pensions.

In 1888, Francisco Peris Mencheta began *El Noticiero Universal,*[42] the first attempt in the nation's history to achieve a broad-based mass circulation by reducing subscription rates to a minimum and making it possible for low income groups to subscribe on a fortnightly basis rather than by the month.

But it was neither innovations in printing and editorial organization nor the broadening of the financial base of the periodicals that was to save the Spanish press from the economic disaster toward which it appeared, with few exceptions, to be headed. It was a series of basically inconsequential accidents—news stories which gripped the national imagination and sent circulations soaring, as well as giving impetus to professional, nonpolitical news coverage.

In 1887, a lieutenant in the Spanish Navy, Isaac Peral, completed the designs for a submarine. The government arranged to have one constructed and tested, eventually, in the waters off Cádiz. The tests were a success, but the nation's naval authorities could not decide whether to order more or junk the project. The ship itself

---

[39] *El Resumen* ("The Resume") (Madrid, 1885–1900).
[40] *Diarí Catalá* ("The Catalan Daily") (Barcelona, 1880–?).
[41] *La Vanguardia* ("The Vanguard") (Barcelona, 1881–in operation).
[42] *El Noticiero Universal* ("The Universal News Bulletin") (Barcelona, 1888– in operation).

as well as the problems of its designer and the vacillation of the government captured the interest of many Spaniards. Newspapers, in general, favored the project and gave long, detailed coverage to it. Circulation inched upward. On July 1, 1888, there occurred what has become known as "The Crime of Fuencarral Street." It was the simple murder of an upper class housewife by her maid. However, during the trial, names of the famous were mentioned, woven into the testimony by the fertile imagination of the defendent, Higinia Balaguer. Though the persons named were never linked to the crime or its principals outside of Higinia's testimony, public curiosity was excited. In addition, the government moved slowly in preparing and presenting its case and attempted to shroud various aspects of the affair in secrecy. The testimony, combined with the government's blundering approach, enveloped "The Crime of Fuencarral Street" in an aura of suspense. Newspapers followed every step of the investigation and reported in detail on the trial. Circulations soared: that of El Imparcial reached 80,000, only slightly more than those of La Correspondencia de España and El Liberal.[43]

Even after Peral's submarine and the Fuencarral Street crime faded into history, circulations continued high. By the time they showed signs of serious decline, Spain was involved in desert warfare, North African units of its army defending the Moroccan city of Melilla against Rif attacks. That kept news interest high and circulations up. During 1895, trouble festered in Cuba. The challenge by Cuban nationalists to Spain's already diminished power also attracted readers and thus strengthened the press. The pattern of newspaper operation changed. Sensation, rather than political subsidies, supported the press, keeping it alive—and healthy. During the Cuban crisis, which reached its climax in 1898 with war against the United States, El Imparcial's circulation rose to 120,000. Other newspapers benefited similarly.

With the increase in circulations of major newspapers, resulting in a degree of economic stability and security hitherto unknown, the internal structure of the press changed. A new system groped for dominance; a new managerial class, businessmen rather than politicians, began assuming control of the fortunes of the larger newspapers.

Under the old management, the newsman was without pay or re-

---

[43] El Liberal ("The Liberal") (Madrid, 1879–1936).

ceived only intermittent pay. He took certain paths to secure additional compensation. From the moment he joined an editorial staff, he was able to count on a government position which provided him an income for little or no work. The prestige of his press card insured him of passes for the theaters, street cars, and even seats at the jai alai courts. He enjoyed the freedom of ballyhooing his friends and striking at his enemies in his newspaper, which made him respected and feared. He could do publicity on his own, dining in any restaurant or eating house in exchange for a short note in his newspaper.[44]

For those journalists who did not have a job in the giant bureaucracy or who possessed no private means, the news profession offered a precarious existence at best. At the turn of the century, Antonio Asenjo, a newsman and author, was entrusted with the establishment of Madrid's Hemeroteca Municipal (Municipal Archives). He recruited his help from the press, hiring newsmen whenever possible. Because of the exigencies of a rigidly structured budget, Asenjo's aides were paid from the funds earmarked for street cleaning and on the same scale as street cleaners.

Pay scales were low, if they existed at all, and newsmen were expected to work exhausting hours. An editor of La Correspondencia de España reported that he was on the job, as a rule, from ten A.M. to five A.M. the next day, wearing outdoor clothes in winter because the editorial offices were poorly heated.[45] The standard pay for an editor, in those publications which paid at all, was 150 pesetas ($37.50) a month. However, that was to change. In 1903, Torcuata Luca de Tena, publisher of the magazine Blanco y Negro,[46] founded the newspaper ABC, which he converted from a weekly to a daily during 1904 and 1905. Luca de Tena paid his editors 250 pesetas a month but, in turn, demanded that they devote their full professional attention to ABC and have no other employment.

Meanwhile, the period of political apathy had passed. The end of the short war in Cuba against the United States and the loss of the Philippines had stripped illusions from thinking Spaniards and stimulated a sharp social-political-economic appraisal of Spain and its international role. It was a period of painful national introspection, of dynamic thrust in the field of letters, and of a revival of the polemic press.

---

[44] Rafael Cansinos-Assens, "Periodismo madrileño de principios de siglo," Gaceta de la Prensa Española, Feb. 15, 1964, p. 43.
[45] Juan M. Mata, " 'La Correspondencia de España' y su tiempo," Gaceta de la Prensa Española, Apr. 15, 1964, p. 33.
[46] Blanco y Negro ("White and Black") (Madrid, 1891–in operation).

There were stern warnings of the dangers that lay ahead. Writing in *El Tiempo*,[47] Francisco Silvela, a newsman and critic who was to become premier for a short time in 1900, said:

The inevitable effect of the depreciation of a country's respect of its central power is the same as in all living bodies, producing anemia and decay in its vital force. . . . If the course of affairs is not drastically changed very soon, the risks will become increasingly great. If we delay treatment too long, the problems become more serious and remedy becomes impossible, and there is danger of a total destruction of the national ties, and our death knell as a European people tolled by ourselves.[48]

However, despite such warnings, the country was in a ferment. The liberals and conservatives continued their guerrilla warfare in the Cortes and in the press. But new voices of dissent had been raised. Socialism and anarchism had come to Spain and found followings, especially in Catalonia. Basque nationalism was making itself felt in the provinces of the north and east. Catalan nationalists still fulminated.

Liberalism had not changed. The liberals continued to attack the Church—to such a degree that the religiously oriented Spaniard viewed the press as "almost completely sectarian and anticlerical." [49] But if the liberal press appeared extreme to some, it may have seemed mild to the newspaper readers in and around Barcelona. "The virulence and animosity with which the extremist press in that area attacked everything—from the monarch, the flag, the national institutions, down to the most insignificant ministry—was unbelievable. There was no restraint, no moderation, no sense of the proprieties." [50] The chief voice of Catalan nationalism was *La Veu de Catalunya*,[51] founded in 1901 as the organ of the Lliga Regionalista (Regionalist League), a union of right-wing parties which favored regional autonomy.

Meanwhile, to counter the anti-Catholic stand common in the press, seven men [52] in the northern industrial city of Bilbao banded

---

[47] *El Tiempo* ("The Times") (Madrid, 1897–99).
[48] "Sin Pulso," *El Tiempo* (Madrid), Aug. 16, 1898.
[49] María Teresa González, "Biografía abreviada de 'La Gaceta del Norte,'" *Gaceta de la Prensa Española*, Feb. 15, 1964, p. 18.
[50] Richard Pattee, *This Is Spain* (Milwaukee, 1951), p. 56.
[51] *La Veu de Catalunya* ("The Voice of Catalonia") (Barcelona, 1901–?).
[52] José Ramón Moronati, Luis de Lezama Leguizamón, Wenceslao Anderich, José María Basterra, Miguel González de Careaga, Pedro Chalbaud, and José Ortiz Muriel.

together to found *La Gaceta del Norte*,[53] a Catholic daily independent of any political affiliation. Each contributed 25,000 *pesetas* to set up the plant and buy a secondhand rotary press. Such was the success of *La Gaceta del Norte* that ten years later it was able to buy the Madrid daily *El Debate*[54] and turn it over to the Asociación Católica Nacional de Propagandistas which used it as the foundation for a network of Catholic organs, La Editorial Católica.[55]

In 1904, led by the founders of *La Gaceta del Norte*, a group of Church-oriented newspaper proprietors met in Seville. Each was dedicated to the proposition that periodicals, as molders of public opinion, possessed a moral and spiritual responsibility. They discussed ways and means of improving the national press but disbanded without taking any positive action. Four years later, they met in Saragossa. The Spanish press, as they saw it, was "impious and irreligious. [A press] which on all levels and in all forms increases its sly and brazen attacks on the Church of Jesus Christ, incessantly vomiting forth an infinitude of dailies and magazines, broadsides and pamphlets which reach even the most peaceful and remote homes, shooting down the old, redeeming beliefs, or, at best, leaving the poisonous dart of doubt or of immortality in their hearts. . . ."[56] To counter impiety and irreligion, they formed the Prensa Asociada, which was to supply news to 212 newspapers represented at the meeting, and which still performs that function.

In the meantime, Spain had lived under a regency since 1885, the year in which Alfonso XII died of tuberculosis. His wife, María Cristina of Austria, who gave birth to a son six months after his death, ruled as Regent until May of 1902 when that son, Alfonso XIII, came of age. Cánovas, who had brought some political and administrative order to Spain, had been assassinated in 1897 in revenge for repressive measures he had brought to bear on anarchists in Barcelona. After his death, radicalism spread in Barcelona as a fiery, violent journalist, Alejandro Lerroux, assumed command of left-wing Republicans. Lerroux preached violence, calling upon the

---

[53] *La Gaceta del Norte* ("The Gazette of the North") (Bilbao, 1901–in operation).
[54] *El Debate* ("The Debate") (Madrid, 1911–36).
[55] By 1965, Editorial Católica had grown to include five dailies—*Ya* of Madrid, *El Ideal Gallego* of La Coruña, *Ideal* of Granada, *La Verdad* of Murcia, *Hoy* of Badajoz; a magazine, *Digame*; and the news agency, Agencia Logos.
[56] Quoted by Alejandro Fernández Pombo, "La Agencia Prensa Asociada fué fundada en 1909," *Gaceta de la Prensa Española*, Nov. 15, 1964, p. 60.

people to kill priests, burn churches, and overthrow the rich: [57]

Young barbarians of today, enter and sack the decadent civilization of this unhappy country; destroy the temples, finish off its gods, tear the veil from the novices and raise them up to be mothers to civilize the species. Break into the records of property and make bonfires of the papers so that fire may purify the infamous social organizations. Enter its humble hearths and raise the legions of the proletarians so that the world may tremble before their awakened judges. Be stopped by neither altars nor tombs. . . . Fight, kill, die![58]

In 1905, Alfonso himself barely escaped death at the hands of an anarchist. The same year, a group of army officers, fed up with attacks on the military in the Barcelona press, raided and burned the offices of two newspapers which had published cartoons discrediting the army. As a result, the liberal government was forced to pass a "Law of Jurisdiction," which provided that any activity directed against the army, police, or the nation should be tried by military tribunals. For the press, it meant an extension of the law of July 13, 1857, which had been interpreted as giving the military such rights over newspapers.

The period was one of political instability, to which the press contributed, too often for selfish reasons. In one eighteen-month period, there were six changes of cabinet. At least one fairly stable government was brought down by the "trust," a group of three major Madrid newspapers which had been formed in 1905 in the hope that it would constitute the vanguard of a nationwide network of newspapers working together for common goals. The three newspapers of the "trust" or, officially, the Sociedad Editorial de España (Spanish Editorial Society), were *El Heraldo*, *El Liberal*, and *El Imparcial*. In 1909, the strength of the Madrid Press showed itself. Antonio Maura, a conservative Jew of incorruptible public morals, had been named to head the government in 1907. One of his first acts was to order the Ministry of the Interior to put an end to a "slush fund" which it had used to bribe newsmen. Deprived of a source of income and struggling to live on low salaries, the newsmen of the "trust" newspapers attacked Maura at all turns and, in 1909, finally forced him to resign. However, the goal of creating a nationwide union of newspapers was never reached and, with the founding of *La Tribuna*[59] by Tomás Borrás in 1912, the power

---

[57] Brenan, *Spanish Labyrinth*, p. 30.
[58] *La Rebeldia* (Barcelona), Sept. 1, 1906.
[59] *La Tribuna* ("The Tribune") (Madrid, 1912-26).

of the "trust" faded. Borrás numbered some of the top writers and thinkers of the period among his contributors, including Miguel de Unamuno, José Ortega y Gasset, and Azorin. The quality of the contributors, plus a skilled professional staff, a combative tone, and political independence made *La Tribuna*'s circulation soar. It soon reached 80,000, enough to undermine the "trust's" monopoly on mass readership, and the "trust's" strength was broken. "We destroyed the so-called 'trust,' " Borrás was to write later.[60]

---

[60] Tomás Borrás, " 'La Tribuna,' Diario de Lucha," *Gaceta de la Prensa Española*, Mar. 15, 1964, p. 57.

CHAPTER ELEVEN

ℭhe Cynical Years

In 1914, war erupted in Europe. Spain was divided. The army, Church, and conservatives inclined toward Germany, seeing in a German victory the chance to recover Gibraltar and, perhaps, take over Portugal. The liberals, together with the Catalan and Basque regionalists, favored the Allies. Faced with such internal tensions, the government declared its neutrality on July 30, 1914. On August 19, the liberal *Diario Universal*[1] attacked the official position in a front-page editorial. "Spain," it said, "cannot be neutral because the moment will come when it will have to take sides . . . neutrality is a convention which convinces its backers with words, not with realities; it is imperative that we have the courage to make known to England and France that we are with them, that we will consider their victory as ours and their defeat as our own."[2] The owner of the newspaper, the Conde de Romanones, presumably the author of the editorial, was called to the palace to explain his position. There was no official reaction beyond that, but "the majority of the people appeared irritated with the position proclaimed by the article . . . and other newspapers and political groups protested, while shouts against the Count were heard in the streets. The opposition was violent in its attacks against Romanones."[3]

---

[1] *Diario Universal* ("The Universal Daily") (Madrid, 1903–34).
[2] *Diario Universal* (Madrid), Aug. 19, 1914.
[3] José Montero Alonso, " 'Neutralidades que Matan' del Conde de Romanones," *Gaceta de la Prensa Española*, Apr. 15, 1964, p. 12.

The three newspapers of the "trust"—*El Liberal, El Imparcial,* and *El Heraldo*—backed the stand of the *Diario Universal,* ready to cast Spain's lot with that of the Allies. So did *El Radical,*[4] a daily founded in 1910 by Alejandro Lerroux, the Catalan firebrand who had enlarged his arena to include all Spain. *La Tribuna* led the opposition. Though it frankly favored the German cause, it advocated strict neutrality as the best policy for Spain. Feelings ran high. Tomás Borrás, publisher of *La Tribuna,* took offense at the "select vocabulary" used by *El Radical* in its espousal of the Allied cause and challenged one of its editors, Domingo Blanco, to a fight.[5] Both men were injured.

At least nine newspapers sent war correspondents to Allied or German headquarters, some switching their men from the camp of one side to that of the other. The role of the neutral was profitable. Spain took over the Latin-American market from the belligerents and was able to liquidate the national debt and nearly quadruple its gold reserves. However, in 1917, a German maritime blockade coupled with incessant propaganda brought about the fall of the liberal government of Eduardo Dato. Wartime profiteering began to make itself felt in higher prices at home. These factors, combined with what historian Richard Pattee calls "faint echoes" of the Russian Revolution of 1917,[6] produced the most serious labor disturbances in the history of the nation up to that time. Workers' organizations, led by the socialist Unión General de Trabajadores (UGT) and the anarchist-syndicalist Confederación Nacional de Trabajadores (CNT), called a general strike and demanded a "socialist democratic republic."[7] The strike lasted only three days but paved the way for more dramatic demonstrations of worker power. In February, 1919, laborers in a Catalan electrical company struck to protest the discharge of seven workers. The anarchist-syndicalists used the strike as an excuse for a nationwide propaganda campaign, in which they skillfully exploited the allegiance of printers and typographers, many of whom were traditionally

---

[4] *El Radical* ("The Radical") (Madrid, 1910–?).
[5] Tomás Borrás, "La Movilización periodística en la guerra de 1914," *Gaceta de la Prensa Española,* Dec. 15, 1964, p. 41.
[6] *This Is Spain* (Milwaukee, 1951), p. 63.
[7] Harold Livermore, *A History of Spain* (New York, 1960), p. 416.

socialist or syndicalist.[8] As part of the propaganda campaign, the unions instituted a system of censorship to counter that of the government. Newspapers were threatened with a walkout if they published anti-worker manifestos or government communiqués. In Barcelona, the *Diario de Barcelona* paid the unions a fine of 1,000 *pesetas* for publishing an official proclamation from the Captain General of Catalonia. *El Progreso* paid 2,500 *pesetas* for a similar "offense," rather than face a strike.[9] The success of the "printers' censorship" was such that, in December, when delegates representing nearly 500,000 CNT members met in Madrid to map the organization's future activities, provisions for similar unofficial censorship were incorporated into its plans. The same year, editorial workers in Madrid, inspired by the laborers' dedication to the principle of social and political reform, struck for higher wages, demanding a guaranteed minimum monthly wage of between 150 and 200 *pesetas*.

The following year, 1920, saw disorder and violence spread and grow in intensity. There were 1,316 strikes reported in Spain during the year, and, in Barcelona alone, 394 citizens were killed in the streets.[10] The death toll reached its peak in mid-January, 1921, when twenty-two persons were killed during a twenty-four-hour period in Barcelona. Employers, faced with repeated strikes, formed a Federación Patronal (Employers' Federation), which sought to counter the spirit of violence abroad. After a succession of weak, vacillating governments, Eduardo Dato was asked to take over again. However, he was felled by an assassin, and Antonio Maura was called in. The opposition parties combined to make Maura's life miserable, just as the writers and editors of the "trust" had a decade earlier.

Maura had included in his cabinet Juan Vazques de Mella, the

---

[8] In 1881, 300 members of the Madrid printers' and typographers' union struck against several newspapers which had failed to live up to their commitments as employers. The press, both liberal and conservative, denounced the socialists, with whom the union was allied. The government intervened in favor of the proprietors, who thereafter refused to hire known advocates of socialism. The typographers were forced to leave Madrid and seek employment in the provinces, thus contributing to the spread of socialist doctrines throughout Spain.
[9] Gerald Brenan, *The Spanish Labyrinth* (Cambridge, 1950), p. 199.
[10] Pattee, *This Is Spain*, p. 63.

first Carlist to be included in a constitutional government and an indication of the path Maura's thinking followed. To Maura the country appeared to be headed for a dictatorship of the proletariat, unless the drift in that direction could be countered. The only answer, he argued, was a military dictatorship, an opinion that foreshadowed the seven-year rule of General Miguel Primo de Rivera.

While the country wandered through disorder toward dictatorship, some of the men who were to shape the next republican epoch were sharpening their talents in journalism. The intellectual parents of the Republic worked on or contributed to periodicals. The daily, *El Sol*, founded in 1916 by Nicolás María de Urgoiti, numbered among its editors or contributors José Ortega y Gasset, Miguel de Unamuno, Salvador de Madariaga, Juan Ramón Jiménez, Américo Castro, and Dr. Gregorio Marañón. During two decades of existence, it came to be regarded as "one of the best newspapers of Europe and the best ever in Spain. . . ." [11] It was directed by Manuel Aznar, as this was written, Spain's Ambassador to the United Nations.

Manuel Azaña, who was to become President of Spain a decade later, helped publish a monthly literary journal, *La Pluma*,[12] until 1923, when he switched to *España*,[13] another literary periodical which had been founded by Ortega y Gasset in 1915 and numbered among its contributors Unamuno, Jiménez, and Madariaga. Azaña had launched himself on a writing career in 1915 when, at the age of twenty-five, he helped found and edit a satirical weekly, *La Avispa*.[14] José María Gil Robles, leader of the Confederación Electoral de Derechas Autonomes (a confederation of groups of the Right) and Minister of War during the Republic, was named assistant editor of *El Debate* in 1923 and converted the daily to his personal political organ, just as its editor, Ángel Herrera Oria, later a cardinal, made it an organ of the clergy.[15]

Morocco added one more crisis to the increasing agglomeration of difficulties facing Spain. In 1921, impatient with the slow prog-

---

[11] Antonio Espina, *El Cuarto Poder* (Madrid, 1960), p. 283.

[12] *La Pluma* ("The Pen") (Madrid, 1920–23).

[13] *España* (Madrid, 1915–24).

[14] *La Avispa* ("The Wasp") (Alcalá de Henares, 1905). For a detailed study of Azaña's journalistic background see Frank Sedwick, *The Tragedy of Manuel Azaña and the Fate of the Spanish Republic* (Columbus, Ohio, 1963), pp. 7–35.

[15] Harry Gannes and Theodore Repard, *Spain in Revolt*, 2nd ed. (New York, 1937), p. 41.

ress made in pacifying Spain's Moroccan protectorate, Alfonso XIII went over the heads of his ministers and advisers to order a spectacular operation. A Spanish column of 20,000 men, commanded by General Manuel Fernández Silvestre, advanced on Annual, but was ambushed by Rif tribesmen under the command of the redoubtable Abd-el-Krim. The Spanish force, though superior in numbers, was routed: 10,000 soldiers were killed, and 4,000 were taken prisoner. Silvestre, whose incompetence had led to the debacle, committed suicide, and there was a nationwide demand, led by elements of the press, for a complete investigation. A commission of enquiry was appointed, and it reported that the military operation had been undertaken without proper preparation. The King's role, however, was not made public. Popular pressure mounted, and a second commission was appointed. Its report was due in late September, 1923, and it was common knowledge that it would place responsibility on Alfonso. On September 13, a week before publication of the report, General Miguel Primo de Rivera, Captain General of Catalonia and nephew of the man who proclaimed the Restoration of 1874, made his pronouncement and, with the King's support, replaced parliamentary government with a military dictatorship. It was the forty-third *pronunciamiento* since 1814 and the eleventh to succeed. No more was heard of the Annual report.

The new dictator dissolved the Cortes and imposed stringent press censorship. Primo de Rivera ordered that no political news be published in Spanish newspapers except that authorized by himself, members of his government, or the official in charge of giving information to the press. The measure, the government said, was designed "to prevent the spread of alarm through false reports." [16] Primo de Rivera then named José Calvo Sotelo, a onetime provincial correspondent for Prensa Asociada, the Catholic news agency, to the post of Minister of Finance. The economy boomed, a reflection of worldwide growth, despite Calvo Sotelo's economic incompetence.

The press declined, however, not only in power but also in size. In 1920, according to a survey made by the national Instituto Geográfico y Estadístico, the nation had 290 dailies, forty-one of which were in Madrid and twenty-two in Barcelona.[17] By the time the dictatorship had ended, the total had dropped: Madrid,

---

[16] *The New York Times*, Sept. 27, 1923, p. 6, col. 5.
[17] Quoted in "El periodismo en España," *Enciclopedia Universal Ilustrada* (Barcelona, 1923), XXI, 1490.

for example, had only sixteen papers.[18] There was, during the dictatorship, also a shift in content emphasis. Many newspapers replaced the political news and commentary deleted by the censors with reports on science and technology, areas of development then attracting the attention of Spaniards.[19] Some periodicals resisted. Typical of those that did was *España*, then under the directorship of Ortega y Gasset and Azaña. *España* countered the censors by publishing censored material with dots indicating official deletions, and sometimes confusing its readers in the process, since censors paid no heed to logical consistency in their barren search for the specter of political comment or criticism. *España* let the deletions speak for themselves, but took some pains to underline its own fruitless opposition to the regime by carrying, in each issue, one or more firearms advertisements, strange fare for a literary magazine.[20] In February, 1924, the government incurred the wrath of the nation's intellectuals by ordering Miguel de Unamuno into exile. The February 16 issue of *España* set the announcement of his exile in black, funereal type, usually reserved for obituaries. The message was clear. Once again the death knell had sounded for intellectual freedom. However, the mourning was premature. Intellectual freedom did not perish, though *España* did. Its baiting of the censors had gone too far, and it was forced to close after the issue of March 29. The torch was passed, not to the censored periodicals, but to the universities. During nearly seven years of dictatorship, intellectuals sniped at Primo de Rivera to the extent that he was repeatedly forced to close universities, including one eighteen-day suspension of activities at the University of Madrid.

By 1929 it was apparent that Primo de Rivera had lost the support of the army. In that year, he was forced to contend with a small-scale unsuccessful revolt, led by units of the nation's artillery. The national expansion, which had been happily heralded five years before, was slowing down in the wake of mounting deficits, and the resulting depression wrote "finis" to the dictator's economic programs. In January, 1930, Calvo Sotelo resigned. Primo de Rivera made one final attempt to rally the support of the nation; then, on

---

[18] Henry Buckley, manager of the Madrid bureau of Reuters and a correspondent in Spain during the Republic, an interview on Apr. 16, 1965.
[19] Eléna de la Souchère, *An Explanation of Spain*, trans., Eleanor Ross Levieux (New York, 1965), p. 116.
[20] Sedwick, *The Tragedy of Manuel Azaña*, p. 26.

January 28, he too quit. Due to the aggressiveness of one Spanish correspondent, Emilio Herrero, the world knew of the fall of the dictatorship, via the services of international news agencies, hours before reports began circulating in Spain. When the news did reach the Spanish people, reactions were mixed. The intellectuals and politicians of the left were delighted. However, many Spaniards were confused and frightened, fearful that the change in government would result in disruption of the national order. To insure some stability, the King named General Dámaso Berenguer, chief of the military household, to head the government. Berenguer named to his cabinet several well-known liberals, who had been bitter in their opposition to Primo de Rivera, including José Estrada, who had needled the dictator in the columns of a clandestine newspaper, called *El Murciélago* after a similar underground sheet of 1854.[21] Berenguer then issued an amnesty for all political prisoners, suggested that reforms in education would be forthcoming, and hinted at elections. He also announced an end to censorship. However, freedom from censorship was not forthcoming. Domestic censorship remained in effect, and by mid-February foreign correspondents were beginning to note that the government was exerting pressure on them.[22]

The new government deliberated and promised but did not act. The ending of the dictator's repressions was marked by a wave of strikes calling for labor reforms. By later in the year, it appeared that little or no progress was being made toward the goals desired by the liberals. On November 15, 1930, philosopher Ortega y Gasset struck at Berenguer and the monarchy in the columns of his newspaper, *El Sol*. The Berenguer regime, Ortega y Gasset wrote, was unprepared to restore to the country the political institutions of freedom. Berenguer, at the behest of the King, struggled to perpetuate the fiction that no fundamental changes had taken place in the country and thus the government could "use normal means to return to normalcy," according to Ortega y Gasset, who wrote,

He [Berenguer] wants to restore the status quo once more as if twenty million Spaniards existed for the status quo. He looks for some one to spread that fiction, some one to carry out policies based on the assumption that "nothing has happened here." So far, he has offered no more than a general amnesty.

---

[21] José Montero Alonso, " 'El Error Berenguer' de José Ortega y Gasset," *Gaceta de la Prensa Española*, June 15, 1964, p. 34.
[22] *The New York Times*, Feb. 17, 1930, p. 4, col. 2.

This is the error of Berenguer of which history will speak.

And since it is an irremediable error, we ourselves, and not the regime; we ourselves, the people of the streets, have to say to our fellow citizens: Spaniards, your Spain does not exist. Rebuild it!

The monarchy is destroyed![23]

Among those who read—and heeded—the philosopher's call to action were members of an army garrison at Jaca in eastern Spain. On December 12, 800 soldiers, led by Captain Fermín Galán, who had been imprisoned during the dictatorship for attempted revolt, declared the nation a Republic. They arrested the civil governor; cut communications with Madrid; hoisted the red, yellow, and purple flag of the Republic over the townhall; and published a proclamation threatening with summary execution those who opposed them, whether by force or "in speech and writing." [24] Then they marched toward Saragossa, the first leg of the journey to Madrid. At Saragossa, loyal troops intercepted and defeated them. Fermín Galán and his second-in-command, Ángel García Hernández, were executed. On December 15, revolutionaries staged another uprising at a military airport near Madrid. It too was put down, but to calm the country the government was obliged to impose martial law and stiffen censorship. Such measures were not enough to still the crescendo of leftist criticism or to dull the demands for elections. Finally, Berenguer yielded, announcing that he would summon a Cortes into session, but under the provisions of the old constitution. There was a great wave of protest, and, on February 14, 1931, he resigned. He was replaced by the Conde de Romanones, owner of the *Diario Universal*, who reimposed the censorship which had lapsed two weeks before Berenguer's resignation. Censorship, Romanones argued, merely reflected the general confusion of the moment and was not a fixture of his regime. "It would be futile," he told newsmen, "to deny that affairs are upset here and the internal press censorship indicates that things are not normal." He did, however, end censorship of the foreign press corps.[25]

In order to silence the criticism which had caused Berenguer's resignation, Romanones suggested a compromise, that of holding constituent elections to consider specified amendments to the Constitution of 1876. This proposal failed to win popular support, how-

---

[23] José Ortega y Gasset, "El Error Berenguer," *El Sol* (Madrid), Nov. 15, 1930.
[24] Edgar Allison Peers, *The Spanish Tragedy, 1930–1936: Dictatorship, Republic, Chaos* (New York, 1936), p. 14.
[25] *The New York Times*, Mar. 5, 1931, p. 20, col. 7.

ever, and a new government was formed by Admiral J. B. Aznar, who called municipal elections for April 12. When early returns from urban areas showed large Republican majorities, the Republicans took over, without waiting for all the votes from rural areas to be counted.

It is not possible here to write in any detail of the tangled web of politics, frustrations, maneuvers, and counter-maneuvers that marked the rise and decline of the Second Republic. It is too complex. Within the framework of a history of the Spanish press, one can leap only from peak to peak, hopeful that an impression of a five-year period will emerge.[26]

On April 14, with the votes in, Alfonso XIII was driven to Cartagena, where a Spanish naval vessel carried him into exile. He left without formally abdicating. Republican leaders took over. At 8:50 P.M., Niceto Alcalá Zamora, provisional President, went on the radio to proclaim the Republic. Only sixty-five minutes earlier, Colonel Francisco Macía had broadcast from Barcelona a greeting from the Generalidad of Catalonia to its sister republics in Spain. Thus, even before the Republic was born, divisive factors were at work. A plebiscite affirmed the Catalan position. There were 592,-961 votes for home rule, only 3,276 against.[27] Even before the proclamation of the Republic, another divisive ideology was raising its head. In March, Ramiro Ledesma Ramos, a fanatical admirer of Hitler and German Nazism, began publishing *La Conquista del Estado*[28] in which he proclaimed his policy. He was joined by Onésimo Redondo, a former law student who had taught Spanish at the University of Mannheim, where he too learned to admire the Nazis, and together they formed the Juntas de Ofensiva Nacional-Sindicalista (JONS), modeled after the Nazi party but allowing a place to the Roman Catholic religion. On July 13, Redondo founded *Libertad*,[29] a weekly devoted to the dissemination of his political ideas, which was converted to a daily in 1938 and incorporated into the chain of newspapers run by the Movimiento Nacional (National Movement or Falange).

---

[26] For detailed studies of the Republic, one could consult Brenan, *The Spanish Labyrinth*; Peers, *The Spanish Tragedy*; or Henry Buckley, *Life and Death of the Spanish Republic* (London, 1940).
[27] Hugh Thomas, *The Spanish Civil War* (New York, 1961), p. 53.
[28] *La Conquista del Estado* ("The Conquest of the State") (Madrid, 1931).
[29] *Libertad* ("Liberty") (Valladolid, 1931–in operation).

Meanwhile, popular feeling against the monarchy had not sub-sided despite the proclamation of the Republic. On Sunday, May 10, just four weeks after the election that had led to Alfonso's self-exile, a demonstration flared outside a monarchist club in downtown Madrid, where a phonograph was blaring the royal anthem. The crowd, defying government attempts to restore calm, turned its attention from the club, cordoned by police, and marched on the offices of *ABC*, the monarchist daily, a few blocks away. They stoned the windows of *ABC*'s offices and threw gasoline against its walls. Finally, Civil Guardsmen fired into the air, and the crowd sullenly backed away. However, feelings did not subside until late that night when the Minister of the Interior announced that the newspaper had been suspended, its offices searched, and its editor imprisoned. It was the first of repeated suspensions for *ABC* during the Republic. The following day, convents and churches were burned all across the nation, as tempers continued to flare, fed by "orgies of extremist propaganda." [30] On June 2, the workers' news-paper *El Socialista* [31] spoke up for the radical spirit of the times: "The real people must prevent by any means the return of the class of lepers whose sores we buried from sight on April 14." [32] During June, elections were held and deputies named to a constituent Cortes. By the next month, the attacks had become more specific. *Solidaridad Obrera*, [33] another workers' newspaper, called for the ouster of two conservative cabinet members: "The hour has come to kick out the Alcalá [Zamora]–[Miguel] Maura combination. They are pure Bourbons in blood. Down with the enemies of the Revolution and with the hangmen." [34] The same month, the Cortes assembled and began drawing up a new constitution.

In August, Miguel de Unamuno, author, philosopher, visionary, and, until the end of the dictatorship, political exile, looked at the nation through the eyes of an old man and saw the dangers of fragmentation. Unamuno, who had contributed his first article to a newspaper fifty-one years before, turned to the press to call upon the peoples of Spain to unite, work together for the national good, and sacrifice individual or party interests to the State. "We observe,"

---

[30] Pattee, *This Is Spain*, p. 146.
[31] *El Socialista* ("The Socialist") (Madrid, 1931–34).
[32] *El Socialista* (Madrid), June 2, 1931.
[33] *Solidaridad Obrera* ("Worker Solidarity") (Barcelona, 1931–32).
[34] *Solidaridad Obrera* (Madrid), July 2, 1931.

he wrote, "that there is a tendency, the offspring of a revolutionary mental laziness, to believe that mottoes can solve everything. Those who back the republic and those who favor revolution, and others of the same type, have acquired already a mythical and almost magical feeling. . . . It is enough for them to suggest that something is of monarchical origin for them to consider that everything has been said. Such saintly simplicity and blessed laziness." The solutions to problems would not be found in condemning the monarchy or the traditions vested in it, but rather in constructive, united labors for the nation's future, he suggested.[35]

For a period, as the government hammered out the proposed constitution, the nation appeared to heed Unamuno's call for unity and the sacrifice of petty interests. "The government did its utmost to sink differences for the common good, and it must be added that the press showed remarkable restraint in its treatment of the most difficult situations." [36]

However, that was to change, to such a degree that before the end of the Republic, Unamuno wrote editorials in *Ahora* [37] attacking everything including, at least once, the Republican Constitution,[38] which he himself had helped frame.

On October 20, largely at the instigation of Azaña, a *Ley de Defensa de la República* ("Law for the Defense of the Republic") was presented to the Cortes. It gave the government the right to nullify the constitutional guarantees whenever it felt itself subject to aggressive attacks. One section dealt specifically with the press. One of the acts of "aggression against the Republic" was the dissemination of news which could "weaken [national] credit or disturb peace or public order." [39] Although the nature of the news that might result in such effects was not defined, thus allowing much latitude in the application of the law, the penalties were spelled out—imprisonment or exile, which could last as long as the law remained effective; and fines of up to 10,000 *pesetas*.[40] The law was passed on October 22, two days after its introduction. During the life of the Republic, it was "used frequently and sometimes indis-

---

[35] "España, España, España!" *El Sol* (Madrid), Aug. 21, 1931.
[36] Peers, *The Spanish Tragedy*, p. 68.
[37] *Ahora, diario gráfico* ("Now, graphic daily") (Madrid, 1931–36).
[38] *Ahora* (Madrid), June 5, 1936.
[39] *Ley de la Defensa de la República, Artículo 1, sección 3.*
[40] *Ibid., Artículo 2.*

creetly, and became a frightful weapon for silencing newspapers, breaking up meetings, and hauling malcontents off to jail." [41] After the Civil War, its existence and repeated application during the Republic became part of the justification for the press controls of the Franco regime.[42]

In November, anti-monarchical sentiment flared up. Alfonso XIII was tried in absentia and condemned to perpetual banishment. The Cortes sat most of the night of November 19 before it handed down the sentence, which was passed by acclamation at four A.M. the following day. In the issue of the following day, *ABC* called the proceedings a "rancorous and needless act of persecution." [43] The *Ley de Defensa* was put into use and the newspaper was fined 1,000 *pesetas* and suspended for three days.

On December 9, after five months of bitter debate, the Cortes produced a left-leaning constitution, one that has been described as "perhaps excessively liberal, progressive, and democratic for a nation not used to shouldering collective social responsibilities. . . ." [44] Article 17 guaranteed freedom of speech. "All persons," it said, "have the right to express freely their ideas and opinions, availing themselves of any medium of diffusion, without being subjected to previous censorship, the exercise of the right remaining subject to the norms of communal legislation." [45] But there was the usual kicker: Article 25 added, "The rights and guarantees stated in the corresponding articles can be totally or partially suspended in all or part of the national territory, by decree of the government, when it is imperative to the security of the state in cases of apparent or immediate gravity." [46]

The year 1932 began with scattered violence across the country. On January 17, 10,000 Catholics assembled for a meeting in Bilbao. A mob of socialists, opposed to the show of religious solidarity, fired on the meeting, killing three persons. After that, the mob, still unsated, burned the offices of the Catholic-oriented *Gaceta del*

---

[41] Sedwick, *The Tragedy of Manuel Azaña*, p. 103.
[42] For an example, see Gabriel Eloriaga, "Los Principios sobre la Libertad de la Información en la España actual," *Working Paper No. 9, United Nations Conference on the Freedom of Information* (Rome, 1964), p. 10.
[43] Quoted in Peers, *The Spanish Tragedy*, p. 77.
[44] Sedwick, *The Tragedy of Manuel Azaña*, p. 84.
[45] Arturo Mori, *Crónica de las Cortes Constituyentes de la Segunda República Española* (Madrid, 1932–33), I, 144.
[46] *Ibid.*, p. 145.

Norte, destroyed a convent, and sacked the offices of the Catholic Action party. The government imposed a 1,000-*peseta* fine on the convent, charging that the nuns had fired at the mob from the building's roof.

When reports of the events in Bilbao reached Madrid, *El Debate* charged that the disturbances were due to "propaganda countenanced by the authorities and carried out with the cooperation of the government." [47] The government invoked the *Ley de Defensa* and ordered the newspaper to close down operations. Then, in quick succession, it suspended the Communist organ, *Mundo Obrero* of Madrid, and the Barcelona workers' daily, *Solidaridad Obrero*. The suspensions touched off an acrimonious argument in the Cortes, where Antonio Royo Villanova, a newspaperman and deputy, attacked the government's position and powers, and called for the formulation of a print law. Azaña, the Prime Minister, defended the government. Excerpts from the exchange, which took place on April 10, merit inclusion here.

Azaña: The rule to which the press is now subject is that of absolute freedom: the parliamentary rule of which Señor [Royo Villanova] speaks is one of absolute freedom, but also of responsibility. Señor Royo Villanova, where did you get the idea that any parliamentary regime or any Print Law which has been invented is going to establish absolute freedom, without responsibility, for those who write?

Royo Villanova: Responsibility, yes; repression and inquisition, no!

Azaña: Responsibility, Señor Royo Villanova, means that the writer or journalist who commits any of the acts which the law for the Defense of the Republic describes as punishable, suffers the consequences. . . . Does previous censorship appear better to Señor Royo Villanova?

Royo Villanova: I said nothing about that. Who's talking about previous censorship?

Azaña: Good for you that you didn't. I am so happy, but now I am going to shock you once more. If there is any journalistic company— and I believe that there isn't—which would prefer previous censorship, I could arrange it, even though it might involve much work. The company would quickly regret it. The present regime, I repeat, is that of absolute freedom.

Royo Villanova: Oh, brother! (*¡Vamos, hombre!*)

Azaña: Anyone can say what he wishes, providing he does not attack the Republic in the ways defined by the law.

An unidentified deputy: That's a joke in bad taste.

Azaña: It may be in bad taste, but it is not a joke. (Grumbles from the deputies.) It is absolutely serious. What Señor Royo Villanova has

---

[47] *The New York Times*, Jan. 20, 1932, p. 1, col. 5.

said is a joke. What I say is not. It is absolutely serious, even if it doesn't please you.[48]

After that exchange, the Cortes turned its attention to the subject of divorce and, in succeeding months, discussed agrarian reform, the position of the Church and clergy, education, and such questions as Catalan autonomy. By mid-1932, many more moderate Republicans had become disenchanted with the regime. On August 10, a revolt, organized by monarchists and retired army officers, broke out in Madrid. After street fighting, loyal troops, aided by the police and some civilians, won the day. At the same time, General José Sanjurjo, the Chief of the Civil Guard and a hero of the desert warfare of the preceding decade, led a rising in Seville. It too was promptly put down, but leftist elements took advantage of the fighting to burn three monarchist clubs, some aristocrats' mansions, the Seville offices of *ABC*,[49] and the building which housed the monarchist-oriented daily, *La Unión*.

The government responded to the revolts with a wave of newspaper suspensions. On August 10, the day of the uprising in Madrid, *ABC* and *Informaciones*, both of Madrid, were ordered to stop publishing. Their suspensions lasted for five months. *El Correo de Andalucía*, a Sevillian daily founded in 1899 by Cardinal Barcelo de Espinola y Maestre, was suspended indefinitely. In all, 128 newspapers were either ordered to suspend publication or closed down.[50] According to Pedro Gómez Aparicio, writing in 1962, "Never had the press of any country suffered, at the hands of a system which called itself 'democratic,' such an extensive and ferocious attack, not only against its freedom, but against its very existence." [51] To counter government repression, a League for the Defense of Freedom of the Press was formed in Madrid, but was dissolved in October "because of lack of attendance at its meetings." [52]

ABC and *Informaciones* resumed publication in early 1933 but were forced to shut down in March because of a wave of strikes in the printing trades. The labor demonstrations were touched off by

---

[48] Mori, *Crónica*, V, 383–384.
[49] A Seville edition of Madrid's *ABC* had been founded in October, 1929.
[50] Manuel Fraga Iribarne, *Horizonte Español* (Madrid, 1965), p. 245.
[51] "La libertad de Prensa en la República," *Ya* (Madrid), Sept. 21–23, 1962, quoted by Fraga Iribarne, *Horizonte Español*, p. 245.
[52] *The New York Times*, Oct. 12, 1932, p. 7, col. 2.

a dispute between the printers' union and *ABC* over the hiring of nonunion workmen. *ABC*, which had paid its employees full wages during the five months of its suspension, refused to submit the quarrel to negotiation. The dispute flared into a strike which left Madrid with no newspapers for several days, except for those run by nonunion labor—*Época* and *El Debate*—and they managed to circulate only because the government provided armed guards for street vendors of periodicals.

On February 16, the *Gaceta del Norte* was fined 10,000 *pesetas*, then equal to about $800, for publishing a photograph showing police clubbing crowds protesting the destruction of a religious monument in Bilbao.

During the summer, the Civil Governor of Mallorca ordered that an English-language daily in that island's capital, Palma, be censored because it had criticized the U.S. Consul-General in Barcelona. Attacks "on any authority," the Governor said, "are contrary to the law of Spain and subject to prosecution." [53] In November, a *New York Times* correspondent reported from Barcelona that "although the existence of censorship in Spain is officially denied, it has never ceased. In Barcelona, it has recently been applied with extra severity under orders issued by the Governor General." [54]

During 1933, José Antonio Primo de Rivera, the son of the former dictator who had died in exile, founded the Falange Española, which was to become, after the Civil War, Spain's only legal political organization and, in the mid-1950's, was transformed from an elitist, militaristic company into a framework for the more nebulous, all-embracing Movimiento Nacional. He also ventured into journalism, publishing one issue of a party newspaper called *El Fascio,*[55] in which he outlined his basic political philosophy: "The country is a historic totality . . . superior to each of us and to our groups. The State is founded on two principles—service to the united nation and the co-operation of classes." [56] During the years before his death in November, 1936, at the hands of a Republican firing squad, he defined and redefined the role of the state and the people in the political structure he envisaged, but nowhere did he mention or

---

[53] *Ibid.,* July 25, 1933, p. 22, col. 3.
[54] *Ibid.,* Nov. 3, 1933, p. 11, col. 2.
[55] *El Fascio* ("The Fasces") (Madrid, 1933).
[56] Quoted by Thomas, *Civil War,* p. 70.

even indicate awareness of the importance of the mass media.[57] Two themes permeate his political pronouncements: the organic state and the "fallacy that is liberalism." The latter theme has recurred in the Spain of the post–Civil War period in an elaboration of José Antonio's views, which themselves were not new to Spain. A few excerpts will clarify his reaction to liberalism or, more precisely, classical liberalism.

Liberalism is the mockery of the unfortunate. It proclaims marvelous rights: freedom of thought, freedom to propagate ideas, freedom to work. . . . But these rights are mere luxuries for the favored ones of fortune. The poor, in a liberal regime, may not be bludgeoned into working; but they are starved out.

The liberal State believes in nothing, not even in itself. It stands by with folded arms before experiments, including even those aimed at the destruction of the State itself. It is satisfied if everything develops in accordance with certain regulation forms of procedure. For example: by the liberal criterion, it is legitimate to preach immorality, antipatriotism, rebellion, and so forth. The State does not interfere because it is bound to admit that quite possibly those who preach those things are right. But what the liberal State will not tolerate is that a political meeting should be held without giving notice so many hours in advance, or that someone shall fail to send in three copies of a set of regulations to be stamped at a given office.

As the liberal State followed this teaching [*The Social Contract* of Rousseau] faithfully, it ceased to be the resolute executor of the country's destinies and turned into a mere spectator of electoral struggles. The only things that mattered to the liberal State were that a certain number of gentlemen should be seated at the voting tables, and that the ballot boxes should not be broken—whereas to be broken is the noblest fate that can befall a ballot box.

While Liberalism was writing marvelous Declarations of Rights on a piece of paper which practically no one read—among other reasons, because the people were not even taught to read—it was making us spectators of the most inhuman sight ever witnessed: in the greatest cities of Europe, in capitals of States with the finest liberal institutions, human beings, brothers of ours, were being huddled together in formless, horrifying black or red houses, shackled by want and by the tuberculosis and anemia of hungry children, and enduring every so often the sarcasm of being told that they were free and sovereign to boot.[58]

---

[57] The most accessible collection of his writings and speeches is in *Textos de José Antonio Primo de Rivera*, ed., Agustín del Río Cisneros (Madrid, 1959).
[58] *The Spanish Answer: Passages from the spoken and written message of José Antonio Primo de Rivera*, trans., Juan Macnab Calder (Madrid, 1964), pp. 120–121, 122, 44, 131.

It was thus that the founder of the Falange viewed classical liberalism. His analysis and appraisal was not unique to him, nor, in fact, was it unusual. It was, and in fact is, shared by many others of diverse political opinion and background in many lands. But it was the analysis of José Antonio Primo de Rivera that structured the ideology of the Falange and moved from there into the rationale of the regime that followed the Civil War and, finally, into the columns of the national press, especially the Prensa de Movimiento, which is, in simple terms, the Falange press and which, in 1964, numbered forty-one dailies in its chain.[59]

In November of 1933, national elections were held. It was a victory for the right. Azaña's party, Acción Republicana, won only eight seats in place of the thirty given it two years before. In all, the parties which had supported the leftist government gained only ninety-nine seats, 192 less than it had held until then, while the parties of the center, led by the radicals, won 167 seats, and the right won 207.

The new government failed to restore order to the country. Discontent continued in Catalonia. The Basque provinces seethed under the treatment they were receiving from Madrid, and Andalusia chafed over the dimmed prospects for agrarian reform. Censorship continued unabated. As a result of an article in *Informaciones* calling for higher pay for Civil Guards and customs officials, the Minister of War, Diego Hidalgo, banned all political newspapers from military barracks, forbade military clubs to subscribe to such periodicals, and ordered all officers, even those on the retired list, to refrain from public writing. In April, Lawrence Fernsworth, an American correspondent, looked back over the years since the dictatorship of Primo de Rivera and decided, "The dictatorship has passed, but the confiscations, suspensions, and finings continue. Newspapers regularly go to the censor before publication." [60] He cited the suspensions, within the previous weeks, of two weekly newspapers and two dailies in Barcelona, plus the jailing of two editors, and the fining of the Barcelona daily, *La Veu de Vespre*, for carrying a news story which the provincial authorities charged

---

[59] Instituto de la Opinión Pública, *Estudio sobre los Medios de Comunicación de Masas en España* (Madrid, 1964), I, 31. The Prensa de Movimiento also operates fifty-eight radio stations. *Ibid.*, II, 606.
[60] *The New York Times*, Apr. 15, 1934, Sec. IV, p. 2, col. 5.

238) THE SPANISH PRESS

was "inexact and of an alarmist nature." The same story was later printed by Madrid newspapers and proved to be true.

On October 1, the Cortes convened, as the law provided. Right-wing leaders, led by Gil Robles, the assistant editor of *El Debate*, demanded power. The government resigned, and President Alcalá Zamora called upon Alejandro Lerroux, the onetime radical Catalan newspaperman, to form a government. His rise to power was followed by two rebellions, one in Asturias, the other in Catalonia, where regional leaders proclaimed an independent Catalan state as part of a "Federal Spanish Republic." In Asturias, a true revolution broke out. Army units battled against an estimated 6,000 miners armed with machine guns and tanks. An estimated 1,400 lives were lost, and about 3,000 participants were wounded. By the end of the month, Spain's prisons were full, and the screws of censorship had been turned as tight as official power could make them. The press was forbidden to report even on the proceedings of parliament. On November 4, reacting against the parliamentary censorship, deputies belonging to the Socialist and Union Republican parties decided, in separate meetings, to boycott the Cortes until censorship was lifted.[61]

Among those in jail was Manuel Azaña, the former Prime Minister, who had been arrested while in Barcelona to attend the funeral of a friend. The authorities apparently assumed that he was implicated in the attempt to declare Catalan independence, though there appears to have been no evidence; nor, for that matter, was there any formal charge. In mid-November, some of the top leaders of the Republic, including Américo Castro, Federico García Lorca, Juan Ramón Jiménez, and Gregorio Marañón, drew up a document attesting to Azaña's integrity and condemning his arrest. They presented the document to Madrid newspapers, but the government refused to permit its publication.

In early December, five newspapers were suspended in Barcelona, and *La Vanguardia* was fined 1,000 *pesetas* for printing a picture of two Catalan rebels who had fled into France. *Vanguardia* protested in print the following day against the fine and noted that Madrid newspapers had been permitted to use the picture. It was fined 2,000 *pesetas* for taking that editorial liberty.

On January 15, 1935, the newspaper *Ya*, now one of Madrid's

[61] *Ibid.*, Nov. 5, 1934, p. 2, col. 5.

more successful dailies, was founded by a group of Catholics. The lineup of newspapers in Madrid at that time included three which still operate today: *Ya, ABC,* and *Informaciones. Informaciones* was then owned by Juan March, a onetime smuggler who had become Spain's richest man and who was to help finance the Nationalist armies during the Civil War. March operated *Informaciones* as a monarchist organ but kept a foot in the liberal camp by also running *La Libertad,* a morning newspaper. *El Sol,* Ortega y Gasset's newspaper, limped along, receiving its major financial support from *La Voz,* its evening counterpart. *El Siglo Futuro* [62] served as the voice of the Carlists. The Communists operated *Mundo Obrero* and the Socialists, *El Socialista.* The press picture was rounded out by the forty-five-year-old *Heraldo de Madrid; Ahora; Época; La Tierra,* the shadiest of the papers; and *El Liberal,* which achieved a wide circulation among young males who read with interest its columns of advertising devoted to "masseuses" and other covers for prostitutes.

On March 21, José Antonio Primo de Rivera began publication of *Arriba,* a Falangist weekly, which was closed down by the Republican government on March 5, 1936, and reappeared as a daily on March 29, 1939.

Confusion and disorder continued in Spain throughout the year. By the end of 1935, the Republic had seen the rise and fall of twenty-five governments, and there was much talk of the need for a revision of the constitution. New elections were called for February, 1936; elections which were won by the Popular Front, an assemblage of Republicans, Communists, Socialists, Anarchists, and Syndicalists. Behind the facade of government, the extremists in the Popular Front worked toward the disintegration of bourgeois society. In June, José Calvo Sotelo, a conservative deputy who had been Minister of Finance during the dictatorship, reported to the Cortes that in four months of Popular Front rule there had been 269 murders; 170 churches, ten newspaper offices, and sixty-nine political clubs burned; and 113 general strikes as well as 228 partial work stoppages.

On July 12, a group of Socialists, disguised as Assault Guards, took Calvo Sotelo from his home and murdered him in revenge for the death of one of their colleagues a few days earlier at the hands

[62] *El Siglo Futuro* ("The Future Century") (Madrid, 1875–1936).

of the Falangists. At his funeral, some of his followers attempted
to riot, and two were killed by police. In their coverage of the
events, *Época* and *Ya* attacked the national authorities and were
suspended briefly by the government.

Calvo Sotelo's death triggered a military revolt which had been
in preparation for months. On July 16, army units in Morocco rebelled and occupied the cities of Ceuta and Melilla. On July 18, a
British pilot, flying a chartered plane, ferried General Francisco
Franco from Las Palmas in the Canary Islands to the Spanish mainland. The Civil War had begun. A vital period in Spain, and for
the Spanish press, had ended. "The outbreak of the war in 1936,"
it has been said, "wrote finish to the richest and most turbulent
period of Spanish journalism. We can say that between 1900 and
1936 the Spanish press grew up and reached a level equal to that
of the most developed nations of the world. Offsetting this during
the period was a somewhat chaotic, extremist note, rich in audacity
and limited in prudence." [63]

It is not the purpose of this work to trace the course of the war,
which led to victory for the Nationalist forces of Franco, nor is it
feasible to record in detail the sequesterings of newspapers, their
deaths, and the changes wrought in individual periodicals. A few
examples will suffice to indicate what occurred.

In Madrid, which remained under Republican control until the
end of the war, extremist elements took over *ABC* and ran it until
early 1939. In July of 1936, at the outbreak of the war, a group of
Socialists attacked the offices of *Informaciones*, putting it out of
business. Its building was destroyed during the subsequent fighting.
With the exception of *Ya*, all the other newspapers in the city were
shut down either by the Republicans or, at war's end, by the Nationalists. In Barcelona, the *Diario de Barcelona* appeared for the
last time under its owners' management on July 19, 1936. On the
following day, it was taken over by a regional political organization, which had cast its lot with the Republicans, and appeared on
July 22 as *Estat Català*,[64] which was distributed without charge.
The following day, at the order of provincial authorities, it was
rechristened *Diario de Barcelona*. In midsummer, 1937, it was
turned over to a committee of its employees, which was to serve

[63] J. M. R., "Periodismo," *Enciclopedia Universal Ilustrada: Suplemento Anual,
1959-1960* (Madrid, 1961), p. 1647.
[64] *Estat Català* ("The Catalan State") (Barcelona, 1936).

as a publishing board. However, the committee managed to publish only two numbers—those of August 1 and October 31. It did not appear again until November 24, 1940.

Elsewhere, organs to carry the messages of the Nationalists were quickly set up. In Navarre, traditionally Catholic and monarchist, the Church and Carlist sentiment rallied behind the forces led by Franco. On August 1, two weeks after the outbreak of hostilities, the Falange founded the daily *Arriba-España* [65] in Pamplona. On August 11, party members began *Amanecer* [66] in Saragossa.

In Lérida, typical of those centers of population which were occupied, in turn, by units of both armies, the course of the press was troubled. Its two prewar dailies, *El Correo* and *La Tribuna*, were closed. The editor of the conservative, Nationalist-leaning *Correo*, Mosen Sole, was killed by local extremists. Until 1938, Republican forces occupied the city and produced three newspapers: the syndicalist *Combate*, the anarchist *Acracia*, and the communist *U.H.P.* On April 3, 1938, Nationalist forces moved into Lérida. The local Falangist leader, Javier Bañeres, began a party propaganda sheet called *Ruta*,[67] which appeared only until the military leaders took over its plant to publish the *Hoja Informativa del Quinto Cuerpo de Ejército de Aragón*,[68] devoted primarily to battle news. At the end of 1938, when the fighting moved toward Barcelona, which was to fall the following January, the printing plant was turned back to the Falange, which, on December 20, began publishing *La Mañana*,[69] today Lérida's sole daily.[70]

Meanwhile, the Nationalist forces began to look forward to victory. The military government, headed by Franco, met in Burgos to outline the shape of the "new Spain"—the nation which would emerge from the ashes and blood of the civil strife. Out of that series of meetings came the Press Law of April 22, 1938, which, as we have seen, was to regulate the nation's periodicals for another year of war and nearly twenty-seven years of peace. It was a law

---

[65] *Arriba-España* ("Hurrah Spain") (Pamplona, 1936–in operation).
[66] *Amanecer* ("Dawn") (Saragossa, 1936–in operation).
[67] *Ruta* ("The Way") (Lérida, 1938).
[68] *Hoja Informativa* . . . ("The Informative Sheet of the Fifth Corps of the Army of Aragon") (Lérida, 1938).
[69] *La Mañana* ("The Morning") (Lérida, 1938–in operation).
[70] Valentín Domínguez Isla, " 'La Mañana' de Lérida cumple un cuarto de siglo," *Gaceta de la Prensa Española*, Apr. 15, 1964, p. 50.

grounded in a long tradition of controls and in years of distrust of the press. As repellent as it may have been to foreign observers— Herbert L. Matthews, a correspondent for the *New York Times*, called the press it produced "one of the greatest insults to the intelligence of the Western World" [71]—it represented nothing new in Spain's history of government-press relations. The pendulum had merely swung to the extreme of controls in theory as well as in practice, and the apologists for the reversion to open authoritarianism could claim justification for their position in the practices of the Republic. Those who had shaped the law could argue, and did eventually, that in Spain a free press seemed always to be associated with instability. They might have argued also that, insofar as they were products of a culture grounded in the past, they were conditioned to react with fear to a free press, as well as to political freedom, and to seek authoritarian answers to political and social questions.

---

[71] *The Yoke and the Arrows: A Report on Spain* (New York, 1957), p. 101.

CHAPTER TWELVE

Toward the Future

On the morning of July 21, 1966, as Madrid subways began disgorging crowds of shop and office workers, dingy gray police cars sped through the city's streets. The drivers braked at each newspaper stand, and out piled officers who gathered up all copies of *ABC*, the monarchist morning newspaper.[1] By order of the government, the entire issue was being confiscated. The offense which touched off the confiscation was the publication of an editorial arguing that Don Juan, Conde de Barcelona and Pretender to the Spanish throne, should become King in the shift to monarchy which, the writer assumed, would follow the death or retirement of Franco.[2]

It was the first such action directed at a major publication under the provisions of the *Ley de Prensa e Imprenta*, which had been approved on April 9, 1966, little more than three months before. As such, it symbolized the persistence of the traditional modes of thought and operation—a tradition grounded in the years immediately following the introduction of printing into Spain and reinforced over the centuries by the alternate swings between excesses of freedom and strict controls. The confiscation was reminiscent

---

[1] Unlike the United States, where metropolitan morning newspapers usually appear on the eve of the date of publication, Spanish "morningers" do not go on sale before about eight A.M.

[2] Technically, according to a National Referendum held in 1947, Spain is a monarchy with the throne temporarily unoccupied. Franco is cast in the role of regent.

of the high-handed manner in which Arias Salgado, as Minister of Information and Tourism, had directed the fate of the Spanish press until mid-1962. Yet, the very publication of such an editorial would have been unthinkable in the days of Arias Salgado's prepublication censorship. Its existence, despite its confiscation, reflected the "liberalization" of Fraga Iribarne.

The editorial which had offended official sensibilities was written by Luis María Anson. Entitled "Everybody's Monarchy," it argued that Don Juan had the support of a wide segment of Spain's many-hued spectrum of political groups, including socialists and Christian Democrats as well as monarchists; and even suggested that it was Franco's "clearly evident desire" that Don Juan should some day become "king of all Spaniards." It may be that the identity of the editorial's author was as much a cause of the confiscation as were its contents. Anson, in charge of information in Don Juan's advisory council, was, in a sense, Fraga's opposite number in the monarchist camp. Foreign newsmen in Spain suggest that at least part of the reason for the confiscation was Fraga Iribarne's desire to "slap down" Anson.[3]

Whatever the reasons, government spokesmen refused to specify their objections to the editorial. The day following the confiscation, a Ministry of Information and Tourism spokesman told newsmen, "It is correct to say that the government retained copies of *ABC* under the provision of Article 64 [4] of the Press Law because of an article published in that newspaper and entitled 'Everyone's Monarchy'"—that and nothing more.

The same day, *ABC* announced that it was "presenting a statement to the competent authorities expressing its respectful but energetic protest against the seizure."[5] The protest ended in an appeal to a lower court requesting the release of the confiscated issue.

---

[3] Richard Scott Mowrer, correspondent for the Chicago *Daily News* and the *Christian Science Monitor*, a letter of July 23, 1966. A similar view was expressed by Harry Debelius of the American Broadcasting Company in a letter of Aug. 11, 1966.
[4] The article gives the government the right to confiscate "printed matter or a publication . . . wherever they may be found as well as the matrices in order to prevent their distribution" when government officials "have knowledge of an act which may constitute a crime committed by the press or printing business. . . ." *Ley de Prensa e Imprenta, Artículo 64.*
[5] *ABC* (Madrid), July 2, 1966, p. 1.

The court ruled in favor of *ABC*, and the government, in turn, appealed to a higher court, the Public Order Tribunal, which, in September, finally voided the confiscation—a victory for *ABC* and for press liberalization.[6]

The press had begun exercising its new freedom within days after Franco signed into law the Press and Print Bill. The men who put out the nation's newspapers—the editors, reporters, columnists, correspondents, and editorial writers, who are the blood and sinews of that communications phenomenon we call the "press"—had for years chafed under restrictions, and moved quickly to breathe deeply of the new air of freedom. They soon discovered, if a reading of the press law had not so persuaded them, that press freedom was limited.

In April, 1966, when the new law went into effect, the port and commercial city of Barcelona, the most European of Spain's provincial capitals, was torn by disturbances: university students were engaging in their almost annual springtime protest against government-controlled university unions. On April 19, police were twice ordered to the University of Barcelona campus—once to break up a protest meeting for which university authorities had refused to grant permission, and once to put a stop to student abuse of a professor, the target of rotten eggs, insults, and shoving and pushing. On April 20, Spanish newspapers, which a month before would presumably have "played down" the events, gave extended coverage to them and even commented on the students' position in editorials. *Ya*, Madrid's Catholic morning newspaper, noted that while firmness was necessary in dealing with students, "the recent events show firmness is not enough." [7] The comment suggested, according to *New York Times* correspondent Tad Szulc, that the "regime should recognize reality" as well as employ firmness.[8]

There were other symptoms of relaxation. The press engaged in an "unprecedented debate" on the kind of regime that should follow that of Franco.[9] A ban on periodical publications in any language indigenous to Spain other than "Spanish," or more precisely

---

[6] "Spaniards Await Ruling on Regime," *The New York Times*, Sept. 25, 1933, p. 3, col. 1.
[7] *Ya* (Madrid), Apr. 20, 1966, p. 1, quoted by Tad Szulc, "Press Reporting Unrest in Spain," *The New York Times*, Apr. 21, 1966, p. 11, col. 1.
[8] *Ibid.*
[9] Mowrer, letter of July 23, 1966.

Castilian, was lifted, and a weekly newspaper published in Catalan appeared in Barcelona.[10] But there was a debit side to the press ledger—cases similar to the confiscation of *ABC* on July 21. Issues of five other publications—limited circulation magazines—had been confiscated. They were mainly Catholic publications which had commented on police clubbings of priests demonstrating in Barcelona during the month of May.[11] Before the new law, government reprisals against Church publications would have been unusual, for they were exempt from state censorship. Under the new law, they became subject to the same regulations as any non-Church periodical. Another magazine, *Semana*, appeared on the streets with four pages ripped from one edition. The missing material was an article on Prince Carlos Hugo, the Carlist claimant to the throne, which had been torn out by members of the weekly's editorial staff after a warning from Ministry of Information and Tourism officials that it would not be acceptable for general circulation. There are reports that on other occasions officials had threatened periodicals with law suits if offensive material were published. The threats were made informally, either in private conversation or by telephone, never in official communications.

It is still too early, at the end of 1966, to make a final judgment of the new press law. There is no perspective from which to judge, not enough evidence. One can say only that "all the votes are not yet in," for only time can give positive answers. The new press law does not mean "instant freedom." History, distrust, and traditional modes of response are not easily erased. As Fraga Iribarne saw it, liberalization meant slow, deliberate, directed progress toward a goal—a series of steps "where every movement must be calculated with precision." The new law, he made clear, was not the final goal. It was no more than "a major step . . ." toward a future goal.[12]

Three months after the law went into effect, the government appraised its first results and decided, "As a result, Spain has been enabled to get to know herself better, fold by fold, inch by inch. And, certainly, to be better known by others. And, too, the process

---

[10] *Tele-Estel* ("Tele-Star") (Barcelona, 1966).
[11] Included were *Juventud Obrera* ("Working Youth") (Madrid, 1965–in operation), a Catholic Action weekly; *Signo* ("Sign") (Madrid, 1936–in operation), another Catholic Action weekly; and *La Voz del Trabajo* ("The Voice of Labor") (Saragossa, 1956–in operation), a Franciscan monthly.
[12] "Press and Printing Bill Passed by Cortes," *ES: The Week in Spain* (Madrid), Mar. 28, 1966, p. 2.

of maturing in matters political, religious, social and simply human, has speeded up splendidly. . . . What is more, Spaniards have gained greater human and social awareness, taking on the responsibility for their obligations and also awareness of their rights." [13] That would be a vast, breathtaking success for a law little more than three months old; perhaps that statement tended more to reflect optimism over future potential than to mirror current reality.

A more realistic position was taken by Emilio Romero of the labor daily *Pueblo*, one of the men who had helped maneuver the law into being. The new law, he said, was "not the best law but it . . . [was] opportune and instrumental. . . . [It is] good for the members of the profession because they are going to have freedom and responsibility. It is good for the regime, because it injects life into politics and furnishes control over politicians. It is neither advanced nor behind the times; it is exactly what is called for by the present moment." [14] In other words, it is a Spanish law, reflecting the good and the bad in Spanish history and traditions, and designed by Spaniards for the Spanish press—not perfect, not even satisfactory, but not without hope.

---

[13] "Spain on the Move: Dispassionate Examination of an Epoch," *ES: The Week in Spain* (Madrid), July 18, 1966, p. 3.
[14] Quoted by Harry Debelius in a letter of Aug. 11, 1966.

Bibliography

BOOKS AND PAMPHLETS

Alonso, Martín. *Ciencia de lenguaje y arte del estilo.* Madrid: Aguilar, 1953.

Atkinson, William C. *A History of Spain and Portugal.* London: Penguin Books, 1960.

Aunós Pérez, Eduardo. *Itinerario histórico de la España contemporánea, 1808-1936.* Barcelona: Bosch, 1940.

Bataillon, Marcel. *Erasmo y España: Estudios sobre la historia espiritual del siglo XVI.* Translated by Antonio Alatorre. Mexico City: Fondo de Cultura Económica, 1950.

Beneyto, Juan. *Historia social de España y de Hispanoamérica.* Madrid: Aguilar, 1961.

——. *Ordenamiento Jurídico de la Información.* Madrid: Instituto de Estudios Políticos, 1961.

Bertrand, Louis, and Sir Charles Petrie. *The History of Spain.* 2nd ed. London: Eyre and Spottiswoode, 1952.

Borkenau, Franz. *The Spanish Cockpit.* Ann Arbor Paperbacks ed. Ann Arbor: University of Michigan, 1963.

Borrego Moreno, Andrés. *Prospecto para El Correo Nacional.* Madrid: Compañía Tipografía, undated.

Brandt, Joseph A. *Toward the New Spain.* Chicago: University of Chicago, 1933.

Brenan, Gerald. *The Spanish Labyrinth: An Account of the Social and Political Background of the Civil War.* 2nd ed. Cambridge: Oxford University Press, 1950.

Brinton, Crane. *The Shaping of Modern Thought.* Englewood Cliffs, N.J.: Prentice-Hall, 1963.

Buckley, Henry. *Life and Death of the Spanish Republic*. London: Hamish Hamilton, 1940.

Bugeda, José. *Una Sociología del Periódico*. Madrid: Ministerio de Información y Turismo, 1963.

Calvo Serer, Rafael. *La Literatura universal sobre la Guerra de España*. Madrid: Editora Nacional, 1962.

Castro, Américo. *The Structure of Spanish History*. Translated by Edward L. King. Princeton, N.J.: Princeton University, 1954.

Chapman, Charles E. *A History of Spain Founded on the Historia de España y de la Civilización española of Rafael Altamira*. New York: Macmillan Co., 1922.

Chaves, Manuel. *Historia y Bibliografía de la Prensa sevillana con un prólogo del sr. d. Joaquín Guichot y Parody, cronista oficial de la ciudad*. Seville: E. Rasco, 1896.

Cleugh, James. *Spain in the Modern World*. New York: Knopf, 1953.

Delegación Nacional de Prensa. *Anuario de la Prensa Española*. Vol. I (1943-44). Madrid: Delegación Nacional de la Prensa, 1944.

Delegación Nacional de Prensa, Propaganda y Radio del Movimiento. *Nuevo Horizonte de la Información*. Madrid: Ediciones del Movimiento, 1962.

Descola, Jean. *A History of Spain*. Translated by Elaine P. Halperin. New York: Knopf, 1963.

Diaz-Plaja, Fernando. *La Historia de España en sus Documentos*. 4 vols. Madrid: Instituto de Estudios Políticos, 1954.

Dirección General de Prensa. *Anuario de la Prensa Española: 1965*. Madrid: Dirección General de Prensa, 1965.

Eguizábal, José Eugenio de. *Apuntes para una historia de la legislación española sobre la imprenta desde el año de 1480 al presente*. Madrid: Imprenta de la Revista de Legislación, 1879.

Elliott, J. H. *Imperial Spain: 1469-1716*. New York: St. Martin's Press, 1963.

Eloriaga, Gabriel. *Información y Política*. Madrid: Editora Nacional, 1964.

―――. "Los Principios sobre la Libertad de la Información en la España actual." *Working Paper No. 9, United Nations Conference on the Freedom of Information*. Rome: United Nations, 1964.

Enciso Recio, Luis Miguel. *Nipho y el periodismo español del siglo XVIII*. Valladolid: Universidad de Valladolid, 1956.

Espina, Antonio. *El Cuarto Poder*. Madrid: Aguilar, 1960.

Fernández de Castro, José A., and Andrés Henestrosa. *Periodismo y periodistas en Hispano-américa*. Mexico City: Secretaria de Educación Pública, 1947.

Fernández de los Ríos, Ángel. *Estudio histórico de las Luchas políticas en la España del Siglo XIX.* 2 vols. 2nd ed. Madrid: González Rojas, 1880.

Foltz, Charles, Jr. *The Masquerade in Spain.* Boston: Houghton Mifflin, 1948.

Fraga Iribarne, Manuel. *Discurso de Excmo. Sr. Ministro del Departamento en el Acto de Clausura de la II Asamblea del Consejo Nacional de "Festivales de España."* Madrid: Ministerio de Información y Turismo, 1964.

———. *Horizonte Español.* Madrid: Editora Nacional, 1965.

———. *A resume of the speech given by the Minister of Information and Tourism before the National Council of the Movement, April 8, 1964.* Madrid: Ministerio de Información y Turismo, 1964.

Franco, Francisco. "Mensaje al Pueblo Español," in *Pensamiento Político de Franco.* Madrid: Servicio Informativo Español, 1964.

Gannes, Harry, and Theodore Repard. *Spain in Revolt.* 2nd ed. New York: Knopf, 1937.

Gerth, Hans, and C. Wright Mills. *Character and Social Structure.* New York: Harcourt Brace, 1953.

Gómez Imaz, Manuel. *Los Periódicos durante la Guerra de la Independencia: 1808-1814.* Madrid: Tipografía de la Rev. de arch., bibl. y museos, 1910.

Harris, Robert E. G. *A Report from Spain—The Press in an Authoritarian State.* Los Angeles: University of California, 1964.

Hartzenbusch é Hiríart, Eugenio. *Apuntes para un Catálogo de periódicos madrileños desde el año 1661 al 1870.* Madrid: Sucesores de Rivadeneyra, 1894.

———. *Unos cuantos seudónimos de escritores españoles con sus correspondientes nombres verdaderos.* Madrid: Sucesores de Rivadeneyra, 1904.

Hennessy, C. A. M. *The Federal Republic in Spain: Pí y Margall and the Federal Republican Movement, 1868-1874.* Oxford: Oxford University, 1962.

Horkheimer, Max. *Eclipse of Reason.* New York: Oxford University Press, 1947.

"La imprenta en España." *Enciclopedia Universal Ilustrada.* Barcelona: Hijos de J. Espasa, 1923. XXI. 1488-94.

Instituto de la Opinión Pública. *Estudio sobre los Medios de Comunicación de Masas en España.* 2 vols. Madrid: Instituto de la Opinión Pública, 1964.

International Commission of Jurists. *Spain and the Rule of the Law.* Geneva: International Commission of Jurists, 1962.

International Press Institute. *Government Pressures on the Press.* I.P.I. Survey No. IV. Zurich: International Press Institute, 1955.

————. *The Press in Authoritarian Countries*. Zurich: International Press Institute, 1959.

Jiménez Quílez, Manuel. *Vigencia del pensamiento periodístico de Balmes en la era de la información espacial*. Madrid: Magerit, 1964.

J. M. R. "Periodismo." *Enciclopedia Universal Ilustrada: Suplemento Anual, 1959-1960*. Madrid: Espasa Calpe, 1961.

Kayser, Jacques. *One Week's News. Comparative Study of 17 Major Dailies for a Seven-Day Period*. Paris: UNESCO, 1953.

Lafuente y Zamolloa, Modesto. *Historia general de España*. 25 vols. Barcelona: Montañer y Simon, 1890.

La Souchère, Eléna de. *An Explanation of Spain*. Translated by Eleanor Ross Levieux. New York: Vintage Books, 1965.

Lea, Henry Charles. *A History of the Inquisition of Spain*. 4 vols. New York: Macmillan, 1922.

Livermore, Harold. *A History of Spain*. New York: Grove Press, 1960.

Madariaga, Salvador de. *Spain: A Modern History*. New York: Praeger, 1958.

Martínez, Manuel. *Prospecto para El Restaurador*. Madrid: P. Martínez, undated.

Martínez de Salinas y Mendoza, Eduardo. *Textos Legales: Prensa*. Madrid: Ministerio de Información y Turismo, 1958.

Matthews, Herbert L. *The Yoke and the Arrows: A Report on Spain*. New York: George Braziller, 1957.

Maura y Gamazo, Gabriel. *Carlos II y su Corte*. 3 vols. Madrid: F. Beltran, 1911-15.

Menéndez y Pelayo, Marcelino. *Historia de las ideas estéticas en España*. 3rd ed. 9 vols. Madrid: Viuda de Tello, 1909-12; also vols. 1-5, *Edición nacional de las obras completas de Menéndez Pelayo, con un prólogo del Excmo. Sr. D. José Ibáñez Martín, dirigida por Miguel Artigas*, 43 vols. Santander: Consejo Superior de Investigaciones Científicas, 1940.

Merriman, Roger Bigelow. *The Rise of the Spanish Empire in the Old World and in the New*. 4 vols. New York: Macmillan, 1934.

Ministerio de Información y Turismo. *Anteproyecto de Ley de Prensa e Imprenta*. Madrid: Ministerio de Información y Turismo, undated.

————. *España Hoy*. Madrid: Ministerio de Información y Turismo, 1964.

————. *1965 Guía del Ministerio de Información y Turismo*. Madrid: Ministerio de Información y Turismo, 1965.

Molist Pol, Esteban. *El "Diario de Barcelona": 1792-1963*. Madrid: Editora Nacional, 1964.

Mori, Arturo. *Crónica de las Cortes Constituyentes de la Segunda República Española*. 13 vols. Madrid: Aguilar, 1932-33.

Nipho y Cagigal, Francisco Sebastián Manuel Mariano. *Prospecto para el Diario Noticioso, curioso-erudito y comercial, público y económico*. Madrid: Imprenta de A. Marin, 1757.

Palau y Dulcet, Antonio. *De los origenes de la imprenta y su introducción en España*. Barcelona: Librería Palau, 1952.

Pattee, Richard. *This Is Spain*. Milwaukee: Bruce, 1951.

Peers, Edgar Allison. *The Spanish Tragedy, 1930-1936: Dictatorship, Republic, Chaos*. New York: Oxford University Press, 1936.

Pérez de Guzmán y Gallo, Juan. *Bosquejo histórico-documental de la Gaceta de Madrid*. Madrid: Sucesora de M. Minuesa de los Ríos, 1902.

"El periodismo en España." *Enciclopedia Universal Ilustrada*. Barcelona: Hijos de J. Espasa, 1923. XXI. 1481-88.

Pirala y Criado, Antonio. *Historia contemporánea: Anales desde 1843 hasta la conclusión de la actual guerra civil*. 6 vols. Madrid: Manuel Tello, 1875-79.

Primo de Rivera, José Antonio. *The Spanish Answer: Passages from the spoken and written message of José Antonio Primo de Rivera*. Translated by Juan Macnab Calder. Madrid: Almena, 1964.

———. *Textos de José Antonio Primo de Rivera*. Edited by Agustín del Río Cisneros. Madrid: FET-JONS, 1959.

Pritchett, V. S. *The Spanish Temper*. London: Chatto and Windus, 1954.

Randall, J. H., Jr. *The Making of the Modern Mind*. Boston and New York: Houghton Mifflin, 1940.

Real Academia Española. *Diccionario Manual e Ilustrada de la Lengua Española*. 2nd ed. Madrid: Espasa Calpe, 1958.

Robbins, Frank H. *The Columbus Letter of 1493: A Facsimile of the Copy in the William L. Clements Library with a New Translation into English*. Ann Arbor: Clements Library, 1952.

Rumeu de Armas, Antonio. *Historia de la censura literaria gubernativa en España*. Madrid: Aguilar, 1940.

Sánchez, José M. *Reform and Reaction: The Politico-Religious Background of the Spanish Civil War*. Chapel Hill, N.C.: University of North Carolina, 1964.

Schapiro, J. Salwyn. *Liberalism: Its Meaning and History*. Princeton, N.J.: Van Nostrand, 1958.

Sedwick, Frank. *The Tragedy of Manuel Azaña and the Fate of the Spanish Republic*. Columbus, Ohio: Ohio State University Press, 1963.

Siebert, Frederick S. *Freedom of the Press in England, 1476-1776: The Rise and Decline of Government Controls*. Urbana, Ill.: University of Illinois Press, 1952.

Solis, Ramón. *El Cádiz de las Cortes*. Madrid: Instituto de Estudios Políticos, 1958.

Spanish Information Service. *Pensamiento Político de Franco*. Madrid: Servicio Informativo Español, 1964.

Thomas, Hugh. *The Spanish Civil War*. New York: Harper & Brothers, 1961.

United Nations Educational, Scientific and Cultural Organization, Department of Mass Communications. *World Communications*. Paris: UNESCO, 1956.

Varela Hervías, Eulogio. *Gazeta Nueva: 1661-1663*. Madrid: Privately printed, 1960.

Whitaker, Arthur P. *Spain and the Defense of the West*. New York: Praeger, 1961.

Zamora Lucas, Florentino, and María Casada Jorge. *Publicaciones periódicas existentes en la Biblioteca Nacional*. Madrid: Ministerio de Educación Nacional, 1952.

PERIODICALS

ABC (Madrid), 1956-66.

A.F.L. "The Press in Spain: Complete Government Control," *Winnipeg Free Press*, Sept. 5, 1960, p. 8.

Ahora, diario grafico (Madrid), June 5, 1936.

Alisky, Marvin. "Spain's Press and Broadcasting: Conformity and Censorship," *Journalism Quarterly*, XXXIX, no. 1 (Winter, 1962), 63-69.

Arriba (Madrid), 1956-66.

Avisos ordinarios de las cosas del Norte (Saragossa), Jan. 7 and July 7, 1676.

Barkocy, Michael A. "Censorship Against *Time* and *Life* International Editions," *Journalism Quarterly*, XL, no. 4 (Autumn, 1963), 517-524.

Benito, Ángel. "The Training of Journalists," *L'Enseignement du Journalisme*, XIII (Spring, 1962), 87-92.

Borrás, Tomás. "La Movilización periodística en la guerra de 1914," *Gaceta de la Prensa Española*, no. 162 (Dec. 15, 1964), pp. 39-42.

———. " 'La Tribuna,' Diario de Lucha," *Gaceta de la Prensa Española*, no. 153 (Mar. 15, 1964), pp. 57-60.

Cansinos-Assens, Rafael. "Periodismo madrileños de principios de siglo," *Gaceta de la Prensa Española*, no. 152 (Feb. 15, 1964), pp. 43-45.

"El Caso Novais," *El Español* (Madrid), no. 127 (Mar. 20, 1965), pp. 6-8.

Castelar, Emilio. "El Rasgo," *La Democracia* (Madrid), Feb. 25, 1865.

Cáxon de Sastre (Madrid), 1761.

El Censor (Madrid), July 13, 1822.

Cianfarra, Camille M. "Spain Punishes Monarchist Paper by Reducing Its Newsprint Quota," *The New York Times*, Dec. 18, 1954, p. 4.

————. "Tight Press Curb Mapped by Spain," *The New York Times*, Dec. 16, 1954, p. 18.

La Civilización (Barcelona), Aug. 1, 1841.

El Combate (Madrid), Nov. 14, 1870.

El Conciso (Cádiz), Sept. 28, 1810.

"Un Congreso de Historia del Periodismo" (editorial), *Gaceta de la Prensa Española*, no. 149 (Nov. 15, 1963), pp. 3-4.

"El Consejo de Prensa Cumple un Año; un editorial," *Gaceta de la Prensa Española*, no. 150 (Dec. 15, 1963), pp. 3-4.

Correo General, histórico, literario y económico de la Europa (Madrid), 1763.

El Correo Nacional (Madrid), Feb. 16, 1838.

Dabney, Virginius. "A Report on the Press in Spain and Portugal," *Saturday Review*, July 9, 1966, p. 50.

La Democracia (Madrid), 1864-65.

Diario de los literatos de España (Madrid), 1737.

Diario de Madrid, May 4, 1808.

Diario Noticioso, curioso-erudito y comercial, público y económico (Madrid), Feb. 1 and 2, 1758.

Diario Noticioso Universal (Madrid), May 29, 1759.

Diario Pinciano, histórico, literario, legal, político y económico (Valladolid), Jan. 19 and June 25, 1788.

Diario Universal (Madrid), Aug. 19, 1914.

Discursos eruditos de varios ingenios españoles (Madrid), 1764.

La Discusión (Madrid), July 21 and Aug. 21, 1857.

Domínguez Isla, Valentín. " 'La Mañana' de Lérida cumple un cuarto de siglo," *Gaceta de la Prensa Española*, no. 154 (Apr. 15, 1964), pp. 49-52.

El Duende de Madrid, Dec. 8, 1735.

Entrerio, Fernando (pseudonym). "The Peculiarities of Censorship Under the Franco Regime," *Iberica: For a Free Spain*, X, no. 5 (May 15, 1962), 5-7.

La España (Madrid), Jan. 9, 1849.

El Español (Madrid), Jan. 2, 1836, and Mar. 18, 1846.

Estafeta de Londres (Madrid), 1762.

Fernández Areal, Manuel. "Un proyecto realista," *Diario Regional* (Valladolid), Nov. 6, 1964, p. 1.

Fernández Pombo, Alejandro. "La Agencia Prensa Asociada fué fundada en 1909," *Gaceta de la Prensa Española*, no. 161 (Nov. 15, 1964), pp. 59-63.

Fraga Iribarne, Manuel. "Declaraciones del Ministro de Información a un periódico danés," *Ya* (Madrid), Mar. 14, 1965, p. 9.

Gaceta de Madrid, May 25, 1808, Oct. 26, 1866, and Sept. 30, 1868.

Gazeta de Zaragoza (Saragossa), May 11, 1697, and May 6, 1688.

Gazeta Ordinaria de Madrid, July 4 and 28, 1677, and Apr. 2, 1680.

Gómez Aparicio, Pedro. "Apuntes para una historia del periodismo Español," *Gaceta de la Prensa Española*, no. 149–to date (Nov. 15, 1963–in progress).

———. "La libertad de Prensa en la República," *Ya* (Madrid), Sept. 21-23, 1962.

González, María Teresa. "Biografía abreviada de 'La Gaceta del Norte,' " *Gaceta de la Prensa Española*, no. 152 (Feb. 15, 1964), pp. 16-21.

González Bravo, Luis. "Cenerrada," *El Guirigay* (Madrid), Mar. 13 and Apr. 27, 1839.

Gotor, Gascón de. "Origenes y desarrollo del periodismo," *Revista Contemporánea*, XXX (1904), 37-42.

El Guirigay (Madrid), 1839.

El Heraldo (Madrid), Oct. 24, 1842.

Heyst, Axel. "The Changing Face of Spain," *Contemporary Review* (no volume number), Jan., 1962, pp. 12-16.

"Hipócritas," *ABC* (Madrid), Jan. 19, 1962, p. 6.

Informaciones (Madrid), 1956-62 and 1965.

Mañé y Flaquer, Juan. "Diario de Barcelona: Apuntes históricos," *Diario de Barcelona*, Oct. 16-30, 1872.

Martínez de Banos, Angela. "The Organization of the Profession," *L'Enseignement du Journalisme*, XIII (Spring, 1962), 92-96.

Mata, Juan M. " 'La Correspondencia de España' y su tiempo," *Gaceta de la Prensa Española*, no. 154 (Apr. 15, 1964), pp. 33-37.

Merino González, Julio. "Biografía de un periódico de 1870," *Gaceta de la Prensa Española*, no. 156 (June 15, 1964), pp. 87-91.

Montero Alonso, José. " 'El Error Berenguer' de José Ortega y Gasset," *Gaceta de la Prensa Española*, no. 156 (June 15, 1964), pp. 32-42.

———. " 'Neutralidades que Matan' del Conde de Romanones," *Gaceta de la Prensa Española*, no. 154 (Apr. 15, 1964), pp. 6-14.

———. " 'El Rasgo' de Emilio Castelar," *Gaceta de la Prensa Española*, no. 161 (Nov. 15, 1964), pp. 10-21.

The New York Times, 1920-66.

Noticias Principales y Verdaderas (San Sebastian), Jan. 19 and Mar. 10, 1688.

La Nueva Iberia (Madrid), July 3, 1868.

Ortega y Gasset, José. "El Error Berenguer," *El Sol* (Madrid), Nov. 15, 1930.

La Patria (Madrid), Jan. 16, 1851.

El Pensamiento de la Nación (Madrid), Aug. 13, 1845.

Presidencia del Gobierno, *Boletín Oficial del Estado*, CCV, no. 57 (Mar. 8, 1965), 3557.

"Press and Printing Bill Passed by Cortes," *ES: The Week in Spain* (Madrid), Mar. 28, 1966, p. 2.

"Press Law in Spain," *America: National Catholic Weekly Review*, CV. no. 2 (Apr. 8, 1961), 47-48.

Prittie, Terrance. "Franco's Finesse," *The Guardian* (Manchester ed.), June 5, 1964, p. 6.

El Procurador general del Rey (Madrid), May 22, 1822.

La Rebeldia (Barcelona), Sept. 1, 1906.

Relación o Gazeta de Algunos Casos particulares, assi Politicos, como Militares, sucedidos en la mayor parte del Mundo, hasta fin de Diziembre de 1660 (Madrid), 1661-62.

El Restaurador (Madrid), Oct. 1, 1823.

Ridruejo, Dionysio. "Spain's Restless Voices," *Catholic World*, no. 197 (May, 1963), pp. 88-94.

Semanario Patriótico (Madrid), Sept. 1, 1808.

Silvela, Francisco. "Sin Pulso," *El Tiempo* (Madrid), Aug. 16, 1898, p. 6.

El Socialista (Madrid), June 2, 1931.

El Sol (Madrid), 1930-31.

Solidaridad Obrera (Madrid), July 2, 1931.

"Spain on the Move: Dispassionate Examination of an Epoch," *ES: The Week in Spain* (Madrid), July 18, 1966, p. 3.

"The Spanish Scene," *Guidepost: Spain's American Weekly* (Madrid), Aug. 20, 1965, pp. 10-11.

La Triple Alianza (Cádiz), Jan. 22, 1811.

Unamuno, Miguel de. "España, España, España," *El Sol* (Madrid), Aug. 21, 1931.

"Uncensored" (a report from an anonymous correspondent), *Iberica: For a Free Spain*, X, nos. 7-8 (July-August, 1962), 13.

United Press International. *Madrid Dispatches*, 1956-65.

———. *Stockholm Dispatch No. 10*, Apr. 29, 1965.

Varios discursos (Madrid), 1755, no. I.

Welles, Benjamin. "U.S. Disturbed by Spain's Press," *The New York Times*, Jan. 21, 1962, p. 16.

Ya (Madrid), 1956-62 and 1965-66.

OFFICIAL DOCUMENTS

Constitutions, 1812-1932.

Decrees of the Ministerio de Information y Turismo, 1952-66.

Decreto del Ministro de Gobernación de 2 de noviembre de 1856.

Fuero de los Españoles.

Ley de la Defensa de la República, 1931.

Ley de Libertad de Imprenta de 19 de octubre de 1810.

National Historical Archives. Consejos, Impresiones. Document, 5.531-32.

Normas reglamentarias de los Tribunales de honor en la profesión periodística, Ministerio de Información y Turismo, 1955.

Novísima Recopilación, Libro VIII, Titulos XV and XVI.
Press and Print Laws, 1866-1941.
Royal Decrees, 1749-1853.
Royal Orders, 1815-56.

INTERVIEWS

Beneyto, Juan. President of the Consejo Nacional de la Prensa. Feb. 18, 1965.

Brisard, Pierre. Madrid correspondent for Agence France Presse. Apr. 20, 1965.

Buckley, Henry. Manager, Reuters, Madrid office. Apr. 16, 1965.

Cañadas Nouvilas, Gabriel. Secretario-General Técnico del Ministerio de Información y Turismo. Feb. 12, 1965.

Cebrian, José Luis. Editor of *El Alcázar.* Feb. 27, 1965.

Gómez Aparicio, Pedro. President of the Asociación de la Prensa. Mar. 23, 1965.

Jiménez Quílez, Manuel. Director-General de la Prensa. Apr. 7, 1965.

Mendo, Carlos. Director of the Agencia EFE. Mar. 19, 1965.

Milks, Harold. Manager, Associated Press, Madrid office. Apr. 13, 1965.

Royo Masia, Vicente. Editor of *Confidencial.* Apr. 15, 1965.

Seara, Luis G. Director of the Instituto de la Opinión Pública. Feb. 25, 1965.

Index